Stella Riley was b
before taking up
first novel was pu

Though she now lives in Shropshire, she lived for some time in Banbury and in Knaresborough. Both settings feature in *Garland of Straw* and in *The Black Madonna*, which is also available from Headline.

C000260547

Garland of Straw

Stella Riley

HEADLINE

First published in Great Britain in 1993
by HEADLINE BOOK PUBLISHING PLC

First published in paperback in 1994
by HEADLINE BOOK PUBLISHING PLC

ISBN 0 7472 4183 X

Printed and bound in Great Britain by
HarperCollins Manufacturing, Glasgow

HEADLINE BOOK PUBLISHING PLC
Headline House
79 Great Titchfield Street
London W1P 7FN

For Rupert
who helped in his own, very special way

Northamptonshire
June 4th, 1647

'*Abundance of the common troopers and many of the officers, I found to be honest, sober, orthodox men . . . but a few proud, self-conceited, hot-headed sectaries had got into the highest places and were Cromwell's chief favourites.*

I perceived that they took the King for a tyrant and an enemy and really intended absolutely to master him or to ruin him.'

Richard Baxter, Army chaplain.

Prologue

On the day he was about to leave his thumbprint on the page of history, George Joyce stood outside Holdenby House looking his sovereign in the eye and trying to quell the faint queasiness in his stomach.

It wasn't that he was a nervous man. Far from it. He was an Agitator; one of that resolute body of men, recently elected by their various regiments to represent them. He had zeal, determination and the stirring ideas of other, more original minds, to inspire him. But when your fellow Agitators had singled you out for a mission of such massive importance that it would either make or break both your military career and your reputation in the ranks, it really wasn't surprising that your palms started to sweat.

It had all seemed so simple when Edward Sexby had first proposed it and even simpler, that evening in Drury Lane, when they'd put it to the Lieutenant-General. George was to stop the Parliament denuding the Army of artillery (and thus hastening its disbandment) by securing the Oxford magazine; and then, with a troop of volunteers at his back, he was to proceed to Northamptonshire and prevent a second civil war by making sure that neither the Scots Commissioners nor their Presbyterian allies in the Commons put an ace up their collective sleeve by carrying off the King. Bold, radical and gloriously straightforward – or so George had thought.

The Oxford magazine had been no problem. The stout lads in charge of it wouldn't surrender their guns to St Peter himself without something tangible in the way of back-pay. No. The problems had begun here at Holdenby when – out of all the sixty-strong garrison guarding the King – just one loyal Presbyterian had slipped the net and escaped.

One man – only one. It ought not to matter; but if that man was going to re-appear at the head of a royal rescue party, it most assuredly did. And therein lay George's quandary. Old Noll had only agreed to the securing of the King's person. Neither he nor Ned Sexby had said anything about *removing* him. But the difficulty, as things stood, was in doing one without the other.

George had scoured his memory for a directive and eventually found it in the Book of Solomon as quoted in Free-Born John's last pamphlet. *'Take the wicked away from the King and his throne shall be established in righteousness.'* It was enough. More, it was like being spoken to by the master himself from his lonely cell in the Tower.

So, George had wasted no more time. He'd made his decision and obtained the King's agreement to it – with the result that here they all were, at six o'clock on a June morning, outside the strangely convoluted turrets of Holdenby House. Charles Stuart, flanked by General Browne and his fellows; and himself, backed by the neat ranks of his five hundred volunteers. And still things weren't going according to plan.

George didn't know whether the night had brought the King fresh counsel or whether the man just liked playing games. But whereas last night his Majesty had seemed quite happy to quit Holdenby, he was now standing his ground and demanding to know who had issued this order. The whole enterprise once more looked doomed to crumble at a touch . . . and George could feel all his muscles going into spasm.

'W-well?' prompted the King with arid composure. 'I ask you again, what authority you have to take me away?'

'The soldiery of the Army,' replied George uneasily. 'We only wish to avoid further needless bloodshed.'

'We all wish that, Mr Joyce. But have you nothing in writing from Sir Thomas Fairfax, your General, to do what you do?'

George could see the ground being cut from beneath his feet. He couldn't very well say that Fairfax knew nothing about it – any more than he could admit that Cromwell *did*. And he certainly couldn't mention the Council of Agitators.

4

So, as sharply as he dared, he said, 'Your Majesty must cease these questions. I've already given a good enough answer.'

The royal brows rose.

'I am afraid that I can't agree. Come now, Mr Joyce – deal ingenuously with me and tell me what commission you have.'

There was a brief, tricky silence, broken only by the jingling of harness and the shuffling of hooves. Then, with flat desperation, '*Here* is my commission,' said George, gesturing to his troopers. 'Behind me.'

The dark Stuart eyes looked them over with something that might have been wry humour. 'It is as fair a commission and as well-written as any I have seen in my life. But I hope you will not force me to go with you – for you ought not to lay violent hands upon your King.'

'And we will not. But we do humbly entreat your Majesty to go with us.'

For a moment, it seemed that Charles was going to refuse point-blank and George waited, his pulse beating uncomfortably fast. But then, with an almost imperceptible sigh, the King allowed one of his servants to help him into the saddle and said, 'Very well. But I would know where it is you intend to take me.'

George expelled a breath he didn't know he had been holding. 'I had thought Oxford . . . or perhaps Cambridge.'

The King considered it.

'I like neither,' he announced at length. 'I would prefer, I believe, to go to Newmarket.'

A rush of heat seared George's neck. Newmarket was where the Army was even now making a general rendezvous. If the King did go there . . . why, *that* would fix those thrice-damned Presbyterians in Parliament who thought they could make peace without bothering to consult the lads who'd won the war for them – or even paying them, come to that!

Exultation burst along his veins like bubbles in wine and bells were still chiming inside his head long after his cavalcade had swung into motion. He'd done it. He'd actually done it! For once the King was in their hands, the future of every man in the Army would be brighter . . . And it was Cornet George Joyce they'd have to thank for it!

Not bad for a one-time apprentice-tailor, he thought

dizzily. Not bad at all. And it only went to show, not just how much the war had changed things, but how much more a properly managed peace might change them yet.

'*You cannot do without me,*' the King told the Army officers. '*You fall to ruin if I do not sustain you.*'

'*Sir, you have an intention to be the arbitrator between the Parliament and us,*' replied Commissary-General Ireton, '*and we mean to be it between your Majesty and Parliament.*'

Said the King, '*I shall play my game as well as I can.*'

'*If your Majesty has a game to play,*' returned Ireton, '*you must give us leave to play ours.*'

A Reversal of Fortunes

July to December, 1647

Tell me not of a face that's fair
  Nor lip and cheek that's red,
Nor of the tresses of her hair,
  Nor curls in order laid,
Nor of a rare seraphic voice
  That like an angel sings;
Though if I were to take my choice
  I would have all these things.
But if that thou wilt have me love
  And it must be a she
The only argument can move
  Is that she will love me.

Alexander Brome

One

In the County of Yorkshire, roughly mid-way between Knaresborough and Boroughbridge, lay the tiny village of Stavely. And overlooking the village, from a slight rise in the ground some two miles away, stood the imposing structure of Brandon Lacey.

It had not always been imposing. In 1377, when it had fallen into the gift of John of Gaunt, Duke of Lancaster, it had merely been solid, unpretentious Lacey Manor. But then, for reasons of his own, John had bestowed it on Hugh Brandon; and from that day, its metamorphosis had begun.

By the time Sir Robert Brandon inherited it in 1625, it had become a sprawling, inconvenient pile in which numerous conflicting styles battled for supremacy. Then, thanks to the Civil War, Sir Robert had re-built the gatehouse, reinforced walls and turrets, and added sentry-walks and cannon – all of which gave it the appearance, less of a home than a fortress. Now, however, with the war over more than a year, the walkways were deserted, the sakers and culverin lay gently rusting and doves nested again in the ugly stone dovecote in the court. A hatchment hung on the huge, iron-studded door to the house, the stone-flagged hall was draped with black and a pall of silence lay over every dark, winding corridor.

Sir Robert was dead.

Inside the oak-panelled parlour, Lawyer Crisp re-assembled his papers with an air that was partly fussy, partly nervous, and covertly observed the persons gathered before him. By reason of their station, three of these sat at a discreetly respectful distance from the rest and looked scarcely more at ease than he was himself. Of the remaining five, four were clad in funereal black and bore expressions

9

ranging from vacuity to intense impatience; the fifth, looking singularly out of place and at the same time supremely oblivious of the fact, wore the buff coat and tawny silk sash of the New Model Army.

The lawyer heaved a morose sigh. There was going to be trouble; he had always known it and had told Sir Robert so – but to no avail. It was, of course, an unworthy thought, but he couldn't help wondering if Sir Robert had not counted on the sure knowledge of being safely in his grave before his bombshell burst upon the world in all its sinister glory. For bombshell it undoubtedly was. Let those who would call it a Will, Mr Crisp knew better. And the explosion, when it came, would emanate not from Sir Robert's sister nor his trio of faithful retainers, nor even probably from the soldier at the hearth – but from that piece of razor-tongued wilfulness with misleading pansy eyes.

The girl upon whom these dire forebodings were centred sat impeccably straight in her chair and continued to stare disparagingly at the man standing by the empty fireplace. He remained impervious to her regard and, realising it, her mouth compressed into a contemptuous line. Since entering the house, he had spoken to none of them – not even to Mistress Sophia, Robert Brandon's sister – and, indeed, seemed scarcely aware of their presence. He had simply arrived late at the graveside and then, after exchanging a mere two words with Lawyer Crisp, followed them back to the house for the reading of the Will. He leaned carelessly against the ornate stone mantel, his arms folded above that offensive orange sash, and surveyed the richly appointed parlour of Brandon Lacey as though he owned it. A stranger, an interloper and – to her, at least, thought the girl bitterly – an enemy.

It was all very well for Mother to complain that such thoughts were unsuitable in a lady, or for Uncle James to say that the war had been over for more than a year and was therefore best put behind them. It was not over for her and never would be until the King occupied his rightful place again. And since the war had cost the lives of her father and eldest brother and kept her from the man whose wife she should have been these last five years, she had no more intention of forgetting it than she had of being civil to a Roundhead upstart who – if he had the sensitivity of a rat would have had the grace to make himself less obvious.

Animosity ran flickering through her veins and she began to tap an impatient tattoo with one foot. Ellis should be here, she thought with an anguish that bordered, as it all too often did these days, on irritation. With Sir Robert's death, Brandon Lacey was now his and he would soon have dealt with that mannerless oaf on the hearth. Of course, it was useless to expect Sophia to assert herself for, despite being the only Brandon present, she existed largely in a world of her own. And Uncle James – once a bishop but now, thanks to Parliament's persecution of the episcopacy, prematurely retired – was bent on preserving his peace by assiduously avoiding her eye.

Switching her attention from the despised Parliamentarian sash, she turned fathomless violet eyes on Mr Crisp and said, 'Surely you must be ready by now, sir? Or are my mother, my uncle and myself to resign ourselves to spending the night here?'

'Not at all, Mistress Clifford,' came the repressive reply. 'Not at all. Indeed, if everyone is ready, I will begin directly.'

'Please do,' she invited acidly. 'For if we're given much more time in which to prepare ourselves, I fear we shall all be asleep.' She watched the little lawyer flush with annoyance, aware of a saturnine gaze from the hearth turning on her for the first time. 'Well?'

Mr Crisp nodded curtly and then looked inquiringly at the deceased's sister. 'With your permission, Mistress Brandon?'

Draped in innumerable scarves and beset with three tabby kittens, Sophia Brandon gave her sweet, myopic smile and said, 'I hope it won't take long. Trixie is whelping, you know.'

This caused Ellen, Lady Clifford to frown delicately. Much of an age with Sophia, but infinitely better preserved, she did everything delicately and thus did not allow her frown to deepen when her daughter said, 'Really, Sophy? If the pups were sired by Dante, I'd like one.'

'Of course, dear.' Sophia gently disentangled a kitten from

11

her hair. 'Come over in a couple of weeks or so and take your pick. They're as likely to be pure-bred as not, I suppose.'

Accustomed to Sophia's haphazard and ever-increasing menagerie, the girl accepted this with perfect calm. 'I'll come then. But it's a wolfhound I want – so I hope Trixie hasn't been consorting with one of your stray mongrels. And now, Mr Crisp,' she looked once more at the lawyer, 'you were about to begin, I think?'

He cast her a glance of acute dislike, cleared his throat and embarked, with understandable reluctance, upon his duty.

'This is the last Will and Testament, duly attested and signed, of Robert William Brandon, Knight; master of the estates known as Brandon Lacey in the County of Yorkshire, Steeple Park in the County of Oxfordshire and Ford Edge Manor in the—'

'I *beg* your pardon?' demanded Mistress Clifford indignantly. 'You know as well as I do that Ford Edge has no place in Sir Robert's Will. It's Clifford land.'

Mr Crisp opened his mouth, closed it again and then directed a glance of resentful appeal at the girl's maternal uncle. James Bancroft stared carefully into the middle distance and said nothing. But Ellen Clifford murmured, '*Do* be still dearest. You know how things were arranged.'

'Only too well,' responded her daughter tartly. And with complete disregard for both soldier and servants, added, 'My father made over Ford Edge to Sir Robert to prevent it being purloined by those rogues in Westminster who call themselves a Parliament. But it was only on paper – a mere ploy, devised because Sir Robert's reputation as a Parliament-man enabled him to protect the Manor from sequestration. It had no meaning beyond that – as Sir Robert would have been the first one to admit!'

'Unfortunately,' began the lawyer cautiously, 'the fact remains that—'

'The fact remains that Sir Robert was no more than *keeper* of Ford Edge – and that document should say so!'

Small measures of Mr Crisp's patience and nervousness deserted him in equal parts. 'With respect, Mistress, it *cannot* say so for it is not legally true. Your father entered into this agreement with Sir Robert in 1644 on my advice. At that time it was the only means of saving Ford Edge from the Sequestration Committee. Such arrangements were not entirely uncommon, but they were useless if not protected by the full weight of the law.' He paused to mop his brow and glance furtively at the Parliamentarian officer before whom he was being forced to make these disclosures. 'Both Sir Charles and Sir Robert understood this and acted accordingly.'

There was a brief silence before the girl said flatly, 'You're saying that, because both my father and Sir Robert died without either terminating or re-structuring their agreement, Ford Edge is as much Brandon property as is this house?'

'Yes,' said the lawyer. 'It is.'

'I see.' She sat back in her chair with an air of dangerous calm. 'Then I can only assume that Sir Robert's Will makes whatever provision is necessary to rectify the situation.'

An unpleasant chill travelled the length of Mr Crisp's spine and a tiny tremor afflicted his left eye. 'J-just so.'

'Then you had better enlighten us. Fond as I was of Sir Robert personally, and despite his – his near-kinship to us, I never liked the arrangement and will be glad to see the end of it.' She directed a brief, distasteful glance at the man in the orange sash. 'Ford Edge is a loyal household and I dislike both the subterfuge and the appearance of having colluded with rebels.'

Mr Crisp bit his tongue and repressed the observation that she would have disliked the loss of her home still more. And, with feeble reproof, Lady Clifford said, 'Venetia, dear – *please!*'

'I'm sorry, Mother – but these things have to be said.'

'Quite possibly,' remarked a deep, rich, and slightly sardonic voice. 'But not now.'

With one accord, eight pairs of eyes riveted themselves upon the tall, dark-haired speaker and, in the faintly stunned silence that followed, no one seemed even to breathe. Then the girl said glacially, 'You are no doubt entitled to your opinion, Captain—'

'Colonel,' he corrected, indifferently.

'*Colonel.* You are not, however, entitled to voice them. This is a family matter.'

13

'It's a Will-reading. Or would be if you could hold your tongue for a time.'

A faint flush touched the girl's cheeks and, raising derisive brows, she said, 'You are in a hurry, Colonel? No doubt you have a mutiny to quell, or yet another petition to write, or a church to wreck? Or perhaps a King to kidnap?'

Lady Clifford moaned and even James Bancroft was alarmed enough to focus his eyes on the Colonel's face. Critical references to the Army's recent seizure of the King's person were risky in any company, particularly in that of one who might conceivably have had a hand in the plot. But the Colonel's expression did not change and he merely said, 'Nothing so dramatic, I'm afraid. Now, may we proceed?'

'By all means. No one here has any wish to detain you.'

He did not trouble to answer and Lawyer Crisp took advantage of the resulting lull to resume. The sooner it was done now, he told himself stoically, the better.

He began with the minor bequests to Goodwife Fox the housekeeper, Mr Lane the steward and Dick Carter the bailiff: all involved small sums of money, an appropriate personal gift and the promise of continued employment at Brandon Lacey, none provoked any comment. Next came a set of three miniatures to Lady Clifford and two dozen bottles of wine for James Bancroft. The erstwhile bishop's eyes brightened and her ladyship sniffed elegantly into her handkerchief.

Mistress Sophia came next in the lists, receiving three hundred pounds a year, a small but pleasant house in nearby Knaresborough and the firm assurance that Brandon Lacey was to continue her home for as long as she wished to remain there. Sophia accepted all three with her habitual air of abstraction and Venetia wondered if she was even listening. Certainly, with the best will in the world, her own attention was beginning to flag beneath the ponderous legal phrases.

Two minutes later, her ears sharpened again when Mr Crisp said, 'And to the only child of my marriage, Ellis William Brandon, I hereby give and bequeath without entail and for his use absolutely, my estate of Steeple Park in the County of Oxfordshire. I appoint my man of law, Mr Isaiah Crisp, executor of this bequest and entrust to him the

14

prosperity of the said estate during my son's absence from England and, when circumstances permit, to discharge from it such sums as may reasonably be required by my son for his subsistence.'

The lawyer paused, as if waiting for interruption. None came. A slight frown creased Mistress Clifford's brow but she said nothing. Mr Crisp resumed, his speech noticeably more rapid.

'To Venetia Anne Clifford, whom I have long hoped to welcome as a daughter, I leave Ford Edge Manor for her to maintain or dispose of within her family as she sees fit, on the following condition; that she regard her contract of betrothal with my son Ellis William as null and void and espouse instead my natural son, Gabriel Robert Brandon, to whom I bequeath my estate of Brandon Lacey and all other monies and properties not hitherto named in this document and of which I die possessed.'

Lawyer Crisp drew a long gulp of air and wondered why he had tried to lose the word 'natural'. It was both stupid and pointless. Ineffective too, if the stifling atmosphere in the room was anything to go by.

Venetia Anne Clifford came slowly to her feet, her face as white as paper.

'Is this some sort of macabre joke?' she asked in a voice like splintering ice. And then, when Mr Crisp continued to stare silently at his papers, 'I'm to forget my betrothal to Ellis and marry a – a *bastard* I never knew existed till today?'

'In order to gain outright possession of Ford Edge – yes,' said Mr Crisp. 'In view of the equivocal nature of Sir Ellis's position at the present time—'

'Don't be coy! You mean because Ellis has never shared his father's politics and prefers to remain in exile rather than capitulate to his King's enemies.'

Wordlessly, Mr Crisp inclined his head.

'The latter being equally true of my brother, Harry – to whom Ford Edge rightfully belongs?'

'Yes. In view of these and other factors, I believe Sir Robert felt that some practical alternative was called for.'

'Whatever else this is, Mr Crisp,' said Venetia unsteadily, 'I can assure you that it is not practical.'

There was another unpleasant silence, during which Lady Clifford glanced with anxious confusion at her brother and Dick Carter, the bailiff, permitted himself a grin of secret enjoyment.

Then, his expression even more enigmatic and his tone drier than ever, the Colonel said, 'And if the condition is not met, what then?'

Venetia's calm broke and she whirled on him with glittering eyes. 'That is hardly any concern of yours! I don't know who you are, but—'

'Then you're remarkably slow.' A strange smile touched his mouth and he said coolly, 'I'm the bastard, of course.'

She stared at him, transfixed, dimly aware that someone behind her – Dick Carter, probably – was trying to turn a snigger into a cough. Then Mistress Brandon stunned them all further by saying gently, '*You're* young Gabriel?'

The Colonel detached himself from the mantelpiece and bowed. 'Gabriel, certainly – but not so young, I'm afraid.'

She smiled. 'I met you when you were five.'

'I remember. You gave me a white mouse.'

'Sophia?' Lady Ellen's voice was weak with shock. 'You knew that Robert had a . . . had a . . .'

'Another son,' supplied James, forced into speech by fear of mass carnage.

'Oh yes,' agreed Sophia placidly. 'He was so proud, you see. He had to tell someone.'

'And Margaret – Robert's wife? Did *she* know?'

'I shouldn't think so. Does it matter? She's been dead for years, after all.' Sophia soothed the kittens in her lap and allowed her gaze to drift back to her illegitimate nephew. 'Robert was right. You don't favour the Brandons. He spoke well of you though, these past few years.'

'I'm flattered,' came the astringently unhelpful reply.

'Did you know about this?' asked Venetia abruptly.

He looked at her. 'The Will? Hardly!'

'Then you're unbelievably cool for a man who's just acquired a fortune!'

'Thank you. Self-control is a useful thing.'

'So is six thousand acres!' she snapped, stung by the

discreet barb. 'One can't help but wonder what you did to deserve it.'

'As far as I'm aware, absolutely nothing.'

'Nothing? Come now, I'm sure you're too modest. It seems to me that a man would need a very good reason indeed before disinheriting his rightful son in favour of a by-blow.'

'Venetia!' expostulated Lady Clifford. 'I understand how you feel – I'm sure we all do – but there's no need to be vulgar.'

Gabriel Brandon gave a brief, derisive laugh and the girl snapped, 'I'm sorry I can't remember my company manners, Mother. But the situation *is* vulgar – monstrously so. Brandon Lacey belongs to Ellis. And, as for me, I'd sooner starve in a ditch than comply with this insanity.'

'Before you allow yourself to be carried away by grandiose gestures,' remarked the Colonel, 'it might be wise to discover what the consequences are likely to be.'

'I don't make gestures of any kind. I mean what I say!'

'Oh? Then, if you intend to go on saying it, perhaps we might continue this in private.'

She stared at him. 'Why?'

Dark grey eyes travelled to the silent trio in the corner and then returned to her face. 'I'd have thought the answer to that was perfectly obvious . . . unless you habitually discuss your personal affairs in front of servants?'

He was right, but she had no intention of giving him the satisfaction of admitting it. Her brows arched scornfully and she said, 'If you had been reared in a gentleman's establishment, you would know better. These people are almost family and it's their right to be present. And if you plan to set yourself up as a country squire, you'd do well to accustom yourself to the fact.'

'If and when I set myself up as anything, I'll manage my affairs as I see fit. But we are straying from the point again. Mr Crisp, I, at least, would like to know how matters are to be left if we refuse.'

'It – it is a complex situation, sir.'

'Then let's simplify it,' suggested the Colonel briskly. 'Suppose you begin with Brandon Lacey. Is it mine to do with as I wish?'

17

'*God in heaven!*' exploded Venetia, almost choking with wrath. 'You'd sell the place before Sir Robert is even cold?'

'Let us first establish whether or not I can,' he responded, his gaze still on the lawyer. 'Well?'

'N-no, sir,' admitted Mr Crisp reluctantly. 'Sir Robert insisted on a rather unusual form of entail which effectively prevents you from disposing of the property – either by sale or by deed of gift – during your lifetime.'

'And what happens if I die?'

'It goes to the – to the legitimate heirs of your body.'

Venetia gave a short, unamused laugh. The irony was not lost on the Colonel either but he had no time for it. He merely said, 'If you're talking about my children, I'd be obliged if you'd say so. But supposing I have none? What then?'

'In the event of your dying without issue,' came the obstinately prim reply, 'the estate descends to Sir Ellis' heirs.'

'Legitimate ones, I hope?' remarked Venetia acidly.

'Naturally.'

A frown had entered the Colonel's eyes.

'What you are saying, I take it, is that my half-brother has no personal claim.'

'None.'

'Not even if he could obtain indemnity from the Parliament for his part in the late war?'

'No, sir.'

There was a small, indefinable silence and then Gabriel said dryly, 'I see. Sir Robert appears to have thought of everything.'

'Quite,' said Venetia. 'That makes it nice for you, doesn't it?'

'You would naturally think so,' he replied absently. And to the lawyer, 'What about Ford Edge?'

Mr Crisp sighed.

'In the event of the marriage failing to take place within the next six months, Sir Robert instructs that you are to replace him, as keeper of Ford Edge Manor, taking full responsibility for the running of the property and making all necessary decisions on behalf of Lady Clifford and her family.'

'*What?*' Venetia's face was a mask of incredulity. 'But that's more than Sir Robert ever did himself! *I've* run Ford Edge these last three years. He can't seriously have supposed I'd give it all up to a—'

'Bastard,' supplied the Colonel, coldly. 'I think you've made that point more than adequately. And I'm rather more interested to know how I can be forced to manage your manor as well as this one if I choose not to do so. Mr Crisp?'

'From the time of Sir Robert's death, Ford Edge became assigned to you in the High Court,' came the unhappy reply. 'You are responsible for its taxes and its tenants. Failing your presence, I am to handle all matters concerning the estate – but no legal or financial transaction will be complete without your signature.' He paused and then, drawing a long breath, added, 'And there is one thing more. No contract of betrothal can be entered into nor any marriage portion be fixed for Mistress Clifford or her sisters without your approval.'

A strangled sound escaped Venetia and all traces of the Colonel's former indifference evaporated as he stared grimly at the lawyer.

'Brilliant! And how long is this farce to last?'

Mr Crisp quailed visibly.

'It may only be terminated on Sir Henry Clifford's taking of the Negative Oath or the pardoning, by Parliament, of all proscribed persons. Or b-by your marriage to Mistress Clifford.'

The suddenly harsh gaze swept back to Venetia.

'Well? Would your brother be willing to swear loyalty to the Parliament?'

She tilted her chin and, controlling her voice as best she could, said, 'As willing, I imagine, as the Parliament will be to issue a mass pardon.'

The Colonel said nothing. Since she was right, there was little point in telling her that Henry Ireton's *Declaration of the Army* had proposed just such an Act of Oblivion but that the Presbyterian brood at Westminster had refused to consider it. So finally he said, coolly, 'Do you know where your brother is?'

'Not precisely. And I wouldn't tell you if I did.'

'Don't be childish. I'm trying to find a way out of this mess

19

and it would help if I had your co-operation. Now, can you get a message to him?'

She shrugged. 'Perhaps.'

'Then I suggest you do it. Unless you can think of some ingenious alternative?'

The violet eyes were sharp with suspicion.

'Why should you care? As far as I can see, you've nothing to lose – since, in any event, you appear to keep Brandon Lacey. I should have thought you would have been delighted with the prospect of getting your hands on Ford Edge as well.'

'Would you? But then, you don't know me, do you? Whereas Sir Robert, it appears, knew me a good deal better than I'd supposed.' And then, less cryptically, he said to Mr Crisp, 'Is there anything else we should know?'

'Not from me, sir. But there are letters for you and Mistress Clifford which I am instructed to request you to read privately.'

The Colonel gave an exasperated sigh.

'Then you may give me mine now and I'll take it with me.'

'You mean you're leaving?' demanded Venetia. 'Just like that and with nothing settled?'

'What did you expect – that I'd stay and argue all night? I've told you what to do; contact your brother. And in the meantime, my place is with my regiment.'

'Wonderful! And exactly how do you propose the two estates are to be administered?'

'In the same way as before,' he responded with laborious patience. 'By their respective stewards and bailiffs – presumably with a little help from Mistress Brandon and yourself. How else? Since the Will allows us six months grace, I suggest that we take advantage of it.'

'In the hope, you would have us believe, that my brother will return and take the oath?'

'Precisely.'

'He won't do it.'

'So you say. It's possible, however, that you're mistaken. He wouldn't be the first to pocket his principles.'

'He'd be the first Clifford to do so,' retorted Venetia. 'Not everyone can be bought, you know.'

20

'I do know. I feel sure, however, that I can depend on you to persuade him.'

She faced him stubbornly. 'And if I don't?'

'Then no doubt all of us will live to regret it.'

'Don't try to be clever. That's not what I meant and you know it! I want to know if you . . . if you're considering carrying out Sir Robert's wishes.'

'My dear girl!' The grey eyes mocked her. 'Is this a proposal?'

Venetia clenched her hands on the folds of her skirt to prevent herself from slapping his face. Then, in a voice shaking with temper, she said, 'No, you insolent oaf – it is not! And in case you haven't grasped the fact, I wouldn't marry you if my life depended on it!'

Entirely without haste, he surveyed her from head to foot before saying deliberately, 'How fortunate, then, that it doesn't. For after witnessing your ill-conditioned behaviour this afternoon, it will be a cold day in hell before I ask you!'

And, with a slight bow for Mistress Brandon, he twitched his letter from the lawyer's nerveless fingers and walked calmly out of the house.

Two

'So that,' concluded Venetia, 'is it. I'm required to forget the man I've been betrothed to for nearly six years in order to marry a base-born Roundhead usurper. And neither Mother nor Uncle James appear to realise how impossible it is.'

It was the following afternoon and, having been unable to cope with her sisters' curiosity immediately on her return from Brandon Lacey, she now faced them with a sang-froid she was far from feeling. In a single hour, her life had been turned inside out and something within her was still quivering with a sickening mixture of rage, fear and disbelief . . . and worse than all of them, the gnawing suspicion of being caught in a trap.

Elizabeth's eyes filled with easy, sympathetic tears.

'It's hard to believe that Mother could be so unfeeling.'

'She isn't.' Iron discipline kept Venetia's tone cool and light, with only the minimum of sarcasm. 'She feels for me deeply, she says – and it would be much the best thing for all of us if Harry were to come home. On the other hand, I was both thoughtless and just the tiniest bit selfish to risk offending our new lord and master.'

Seventeen-year-old Phoebe supported her chin in both palms and regarded her eldest sister with bright-eyed interest. 'And did you offend him?'

'Oh yes,' replied Venetia with grim satisfaction. And related her final catastrophic exchange with the Colonel.

Phoebe groaned. 'Do you think he meant it?'

'I certainly hope so.'

'And you don't think you might have been a bit hasty?'

'No.' Venetia glanced from Phoebe to Elizabeth and then back again. 'What do you expect me to do? Bow my head meekly and give myself to a misbegotten bumpkin in an orange sash?'

'No . . . not exactly. But I don't suppose he likes the situation any better than you do. And it's hardly his fault, after all.'

'That,' pronounced Venetia darkly, 'is a matter of opinion. Oh, the marriage clause undoubtedly came as a surprise to him. But I'd wager my best pearl necklet that he's put a lot of time and effort into getting Brandon Lacey.' She smiled savagely. 'It would serve him right if I *did* marry him.'

There was a pause and then Phoebe said mildly, 'Is he nice?'

'Don't be stupid! He's a Roundhead.'

'So? They can't all be monsters, can they?'

'I neither know nor care. Anyway, this one is also illegitimate.'

'Yes. Well, that is a problem, I suppose. But what's he like as a person?'

'Rude and callous and arrogant.'

'Oh dear! But he was in rather an awkward position, wasn't he? And I don't suppose you were at your best yourself.' This said with a glint of mischief. 'Perhaps we should give him the benefit of the doubt?'

Her sister's gaze was icy.

'I haven't the remotest intention of giving him anything. And if you're about to observe that he might improve on acquaintance – I can only say that so, probably, do toads, snakes and weevils. But that doesn't necessarily mean that I should grow to like them.'

'Oh . . .' Phoebe thought for a moment. 'So he's really impossible?'

'Utterly.'

'And even if his birth and politics weren't what they are,' offered Elizabeth earnestly, 'Venetia loves Ellis.'

'Does she?' asked Phoebe. And, to Venetia, 'Do you?'

'Well, of course I do! I should have thought it was obvious.'

'Not to me it isn't. You may have been betrothed to Ellis for six years but you can't have laid eyes on him more than a handful of times in the last three. And I always did think it silly to let your betrothal drag on so.'

'What choice did we have? In the beginning, none of us expected the war to last beyond the first big battle – and by the time everyone realised it wouldn't be settled so easily, Ellis was dashing all over the country with George Goring.'

'I accept that. But you must have seen a fair amount of him while you were in Oxford with the Queen in '44, so why didn't you get married then?' demanded Phoebe with relentless logic. 'It's what *I* would have done. And I can't imagine Tom Knightley waiting six years for Elizabeth. Six *months* is too long for him!'

A hint of colour stained Venetia's cheekbones. Fortunately, however, Elizabeth held Phoebe's attention by bending her head in maidenly modesty and murmuring something incomprehensible.

'Come on, Bess – you know it's true. And it's the same for you, isn't it?'

'I – why – it's really not—'

'Oh, stop behaving like Mother and be honest,' said Phoebe severely. 'You know you can't wait for next Spring – and that's as it should be. I only wish it were me. Still, perhaps I'll stand more chance when you and Venetia are married. It's not easy being the plain one of the family.'

Elizabeth stretched out a comforting hand.

'You're *not* plain, dearest.'

'No,' agreed the cynic on the windowseat. 'But everything's relative, isn't it? And I haven't exactly noticed a trail of eligible suitors beating a path to the door on my account. Not once they've seen you and Venetia anyway.'

An impartial observer might have conceded that Phoebe had a point, for the Fates which had given Venetia eyes of ever-changing amethyst and Elizabeth ones of deep, translucent blue had decreed that her own be an unremarkable grey; and while Venetia's hair was silver-fair and Elizabeth's guinea-gold, Phoebe's unruly curls were that shade of honey-brown commonly referred to as mouse. Seen without her sisters, she would be considered a pretty girl; seen with them, she appeared ordinary.

Smiling a little, Venetia said, 'Hence your enthusiasm for Colonel Brandon, I suppose?'

'No!' said Phoebe indignantly. And then, with a gurgle of laughter, 'Well, perhaps. But can you blame me? You're four-and-twenty, after all – and if you don't marry soon, you never will. And then I'll spend the rest of my life being known as Venetia Clifford's sister.'

'A fate worse than death!'

'Well, it is.' Phoebe eyed her sister thoughtfully and entirely without rancour for a moment and then said, 'So what does this Colonel look like?'

Venetia's smile faded. 'Oh heavens – *I* don't know!'

'You must do! You spent over an hour in his company yesterday and all you've said so far is that he wore an orange sash. You must have noticed more than that. Is he tall?'

'Yes. I think so. And dark. But before you get carried away with some notion of a handsome hero, allow me to tell you that he must be at least thirty-five and – as far as I'm concerned – distinctly unmemorable.'

Phoebe was not discouraged.

'Well, at least that proves he can't be horribly ugly.'

Venetia came abruptly to her feet.

'It seems to me that *you'd* better marry him.'

'I can't. There's no point to it. You're the one who's been offered Ford Edge as a bride-price.'

'A fact of which I am thoroughly aware.'

'But if he doesn't ask you – or you refuse him and Harry doesn't come back either,' said Elizabeth slowly, 'what will happen?'

'We'll all be dependent on his goodwill,' admitted Venetia reluctantly. 'As much as if we were his tenants.'

'Oh.' The blue eyes grew anxious. 'I don't think Tom's father will like that.'

'Do you suppose that any of us will?' snapped Venetia.

'N-no.' Tears gathered on Elizabeth's lashes. 'But I shan't be able to bear it if I'm not allowed to marry Tom after all.'

Venetia stared at her, a sensation of sick helplessness welling up inside her. Finally she said tonelessly, 'Don't cry. Your contract of betrothal's already drawn up and the dowry agreed. I shouldn't think the bastard can alter that. It will be all right, I promise. And I . . . I'll see what can be done about contacting Harry.'

'How?' asked Phoebe. 'We don't know where he is. And even if we did, it wouldn't do any good. He won't take the Oath. Not after Kit.'

The name of their dead brother hung on the air, paralysing them all. Then Venetia drew a long breath and said, 'We'll see. It's stupid to worry ourselves yet. Harry may come . . . or the Parliament may yet grant him a pardon.'

'Or the horse may talk,' muttered the eternal optimist in the window. 'And you and the Colonel may come to like each other.'

This, however, was too much for Venetia and, crossing to the door, she said distantly, 'Don't count on it. You'll excuse me if I leave you – but one more word on this subject and I'm likely to throw a fit. I'm going for a walk.'

Venetia did not go straight outside but retired first to her bedchamber where, after wasting a good deal of paper, she finally wrote two short and rather brusque letters. Then she pushed both them and Sir Robert's unhelpful, posthumous epistle up her sleeve and slipped quietly out into the garden.

The sky was overcast and the air hot and heavy, as though a storm was brewing. Venetia frowned anxiously and hoped that it was not. A small but promising harvest stood out in the fields and, after the disastrous one of last year, they could ill-afford to lose it. Ford Edge had problems enough – broken fences, leaking roofs, war-crippled workers, widows and orphans – without facing a winter of near starvation. And things were little better at Brandon Lacey; indeed, she doubted they were better anywhere in England. The only advantages some families had were uncomplicated owner-ship of their home and lands and the presence of their menfolk.

Without conscious thought, her feet carried her across the paddock to the vine-tangled spinney which lay between Ford Edge and the tiny village of Brearton. It was gloomy beneath the trees but, well-accustomed to this particular path and dwelling once more on the aggravating matter of Ellis's prolonged absence, she did not notice it.

It was over a year since Ellis had paid his last fleeting visit – when, following the fall of Oxford in June of '46, he had come with Harry to announce their joint departure for France. Since then, Venetia had received only one letter from her betrothed and none at all from her brother. She did not even know precisely where they were. Yet somehow – unless they made a swift, miraculous appearance – she was going to have to fight for their respective inheritances against the lunacy of Sir Robert's Will. And though she loved them both and would do it willingly, she could not help wishing that the burden wasn't hers alone.

She sat down on a fallen log and tried to assess the situation logically but her only clear thought was the depressing knowledge that, if there was a way out, it would be up to her to find it. Mother was hopelessly impractical and Elizabeth, sweetly helpless; Uncle James inevitably withdrew at the first sign of unpleasantness and Phoebe was little more than a child. All of them needed looking after and there was only Venetia herself to do it.

The last years had changed her. She knew that – and saw it daily reflected in other people's eyes. Somewhere between Kit's death and Father's, and the fight to keep Ford Edge solvent, the bright, carefree girl who had danced at Whitehall had grown hard and bitter and a little too sharp. It was only a shell, of course – she knew that if others did not. But now, with this new and terrifying obstacle to face, there was little chance of her ever shedding it.

Harry, of course, would not come back – or, if he did, it would not be to take the oath. They all knew it; even Mother, though she preferred not to believe it. When Kit's life had been snuffed out by a Roundhead bullet at Lichfield, something in Harry had died too. For Kit had been his twin – the laughing, extrovert side of his own more sombre nature. And Harry had never been the same since.

Venetia pulled out Sir Robert's letter and scanned it anew until the phrases burned into her brain.

'*I know well that, as you read this, you will be angry . . . I ask not for forgiveness but for an open mind. War alters us all and*

28

Ellis is no longer a fit mate for you. He will lean on your strength rather than learn from it. I do not exclude him for his politics but for that irresponsibility in his nature which I had hoped to see him shed.' And then, towards the end, *'Gabriel will find this no easier than you and he will need your help. Teach him how best to tend the land, work with him . . . I believe you have much to offer each other. Do not waste what remains of your youth. You know I have always loved you as a daughter.'*

A bitter smile touched her mouth and she crumpled the letter in her hand. His daughter? Yes, she too had wanted to be that – but not by wedding his rebel bastard and thus making herself a laughing-stock through the county. It was unthinkable . . . impossible . . . and for reasons that she could explain to nobody.

Phoebe had referred, in all innocence, to the summer of 1644 – but Venetia had not needed her little sister to remind her. It had been the summer that the Queen fled abroad and the last one she herself had spent in Oxford before returning to Ford Edge. And for a single, cataclysmic week, Ellis had been there too.

Most people would have called what followed a foregone conclusion and certainly, in an Oxford gripped by war-fever, it wasn't at all unusual. Perhaps if Venetia's circle had been composed of the older, soberer kind . . . but her friends had been Kate d'Aubigny, tragically widowed at Edgehill and recklessly engaged in plotting, and Margot Deveril, a young matron with a small son and a whole string of lovers – both of whom had learned to live only for the moment. And so, since she had already been betrothed to Ellis for two years, it had not seemed so wrong during that one bitter-sweet week in June, to anticipate their marriage.

Venetia's throat tightened painfully. She couldn't marry Gabriel Brandon – not after that. But what was the alternative? That her family become virtual tenants in their own home and Harry lose his inheritance? That Philip Knightley cancel his son's betrothal contract with Elizabeth and Phoebe be forced to look for a husband amongst the ranks of the New Model Army? And for them all an endlessly uncertain future, waiting for a day that might never come? For it had to be admitted that his Majesty's prospects of regaining his throne looked far from promising. Since the Parliament had paid the Scots for possession of his person and brought him south, King Charles had been held in honourable captivity at Holdenby – until last month when the Army had seized him. And if France or Ireland or the Netherlands *were* planning to help him, they were being remarkably slow about it.

Deep in thought, she missed the tell-tale crack of a twig behind her. Then her breath stopped as a large hand clamped itself firmly over her mouth and a low voice growled, 'Well, well my pretty pigeon. And what might you be doing here all alone?'

Venetia sat absolutely still and waited for the hand to be removed. Then, without turning her head, she said, 'Try that again, Captain Peverell, and I'll bite your impudent fingers off.'

Grinning unrepentantly, Ashley Peverell strolled around the log and dropped carelessly down beside her. 'Keep awake, then. If you'd been paying attention, I wouldn't have got so close.'

'That is hardly the point.'

'Yes it is. For all you know, this place could be crawling with poke-noses. And I, for one, have no wish to decorate a rope's end on account of your carelessness.'

She flushed a little and met his eyes for the first time. 'You're right, of course. I'm sorry.'

'I forgive you.' The bright, silver-green gaze inspected her shrewdly. 'Problems, my child?'

'Of a sort.'

'Thought so. Like to tell your Uncle Ash all about it?'

Venetia smiled wryly. Lean, tanned, outrageously good-looking and every inch the adventurer, Ashley Peverell was more likely to steal a girl's heart than cherish her secrets. She said, 'I hope you never meet my little sister. You're just the kind of rogue to appeal to her.'

'Suit yourself,' he shrugged, accepting the rebuff with unimpaired good-humour. 'Let's get down to business, then. Have you any messages for me?'

'Yes – two. Rob Hart's fallen under suspicion at home and thinks it best to miss the next meeting in case he's followed.

And Geoffrey Carnforth's back. He escaped from the Gatehouse a month ago and is lying low at Scotton. He didn't trust me enough to write a letter.'

'Are you surprised? The poor devil's been caught that way before when his mistress filched some papers of his and sold 'em to the local Committee. Can't trust anyone these days.' He rose and straightened his sash. 'I'll go and see him. I've got to go to Scotland and from there I'll be taking ship for France. Carnforth had better come with me. He can't skulk round here for long without being picked up again.'

'Scotland and France?' Venetia came slowly to her feet. 'Does that mean that something is happening at last?'

'Soon, I hope – while Parliament and the Army are still too busy squabbling amongst themselves to bother watching us. I suppose you heard that the Army has driven eleven Presbyterian members, Denzil Holles and William Waller among them, out of the House with a charge of starting another war by inviting the Scots back?'

'Yes. And I couldn't help wondering, since it was reputedly the work of Cromwell's son-in-law, if it didn't have more to do with the rumours that Holles was hoping to have Cromwell arrested. After all, I doubt Henry Ireton's the man to sit by while his wife's father goes to the Tower. And there's been bad blood between himself and Holles ever since that silly business of the duel.'

Captain Peverell lifted one amused brow.

'I heard something of that but, being abroad at the time, missed the details. What happened?'

'It was just after the Agitators had presented their petition for arrears of pay and the like,' said Venetia. 'Ireton attempted to justify it in the face of the Commons's condemnation and – according to the news-sheets – Holles challenged him across the floor of the House. Ireton pointed out that he wasn't wearing a sword and said that duelling was against his principles. Holles replied with the suggestion that all Independents were deadly cowards; and the pair of them had to be forcibly separated by Sir William Waller. But not, so rumour has it, before Mr Holles pulled Commissary-General Ireton's nose.'

'And these are our great and illustrious leaders,' grinned

Captain Peverell. Then, 'Of course, what Henry Ireton would *really* like is a whole fresh House of Commons – presumably one that will pay him instead of trying to put him out of a job; but, in the meantime, getting rid of the leading Presbyterians so as to leave himself and his fellow Independents with a majority is a smart move.' He shrugged. 'Encouragingly for us, the whole thing is fast turning into a "sink them before they sink us" situation.'

'So I've gathered,' said Venetia. 'But what are our plans for taking advantage of it?'

'Ah! Well, as to that, it's best you don't know.'

'Thank you,' she said frostily. 'I'm constantly amazed that you let me help you at all.'

'No, you're not. You know very well that you fill the role of liaison officer in these parts to perfection.' He draped a casual arm about her waist. 'And speaking for myself, sweetheart, I couldn't manage without you.'

She moved easily away from him.

'I should save your blandishments for those likely to appreciate them. Are you going to Paris?'

'I might. Why? Want me to bring you back a silk petticoat?'

'I wouldn't say no,' Venetia retorted, knowing that he couldn't afford it. 'But what I really want is for you to take a letter to Harry.'

He removed his hat and bowed with a flourish.

'Anything to accommodate a lady.'

The violet eyes narrowed. 'Does that mean you know where he is?'

'Not exactly. But I imagine he's still debating theology in some seminary or other. Someone will know.'

'Well, I hope so. It's important.' She produced the letters from her sleeve and added negligently, 'And so is the letter to Ellis . . . if you can find him.'

The mobile face assumed an expression of profound gloom.

'Can't you settle for the petticoat? It'd be a damned sight easier. Finding Harry is one thing . . . finding Ellis is quite another. He's never still.'

'So I've gathered,' said Venetia, her voice becoming

suddenly brittle. 'But the simple fact is that he is now *Sir* Ellis, and if he wants to add "of Brandon Lacey" he'd better come home and do something about the Roundhead bastard that Sir Robert has named as his heir!'

Three days later, after a long, gruelling ride and with only hours to spare before rejoining his regiment at Reading, the Roundhead bastard sat in the house in Shoreditch where he had grown up and watched his foster-brother methodically polishing a sword.

'Well, Jack?' he asked, after a silence of infinite proportions.

Jack Morrell's hand stilled from its work and he looked up, his pleasant, ugly face marked with faint perplexity.

'What do you want me to say? That I congratulate you on your good-fortune? I do, of course. It's the chance of a lifetime . . . in its way.'

'That is certainly one way of looking at it.'

'It's just . . . I suppose it's just that I can't quite picture you as the lord of the manor. I thought all your ambitions lay with the Army.'

'They do.' Gabriel frowned absently into his tankard of ale and then set it abruptly down on the hearthstone. 'I ought to be delirious with joy – but I'm not. Quite frankly, I feel like a bloody pawn on a chess-board.'

Jack eyed him thoughtfully. 'You didn't know, then? The old man gave you no reason to expect it?'

'None. Perhaps if I'd visited him in May when he asked me . . . but I couldn't, so it's useless to speculate. And the devil of it is that he's sewn me up so neatly, I don't see how I'm to get out of it.'

'It's only proper that he should have done something for you, though.'

'Maybe. But not this.'

'Perhaps not. But it wasn't right to leave you neither fish nor fowl by insisting you bear his name and yet be brought up as one of us. And as for never telling you who your mother was – unless the letter he left you has finally rectified that omission?'

'No,' came the brief, quelling reply.

33

'Oh.' Recognising that he'd trespassed too far, Jack resumed his work and sought for another topic. 'How's the rightful heir going to take it?'

'Ellis? God knows. Our paths have crossed only once and it was scarcely a fortuitous meeting. My impression then was that he didn't know of my existence and I saw no reason to enlighten him. Perhaps I should have done.' A gleam of humour appeared in the storm-grey eyes. 'If he was planning to marry the Clifford girl from choice, there must be more to him than I'd imagined.'

Jack laughed. 'What's she like?'

'Beautiful – or would be if she'd been carved from marble. As it is, she's got the tongue of a shrew, an expression that gives you frostbite and no manners at all. Which, if Sir Robert's letter is to believed, doesn't say much for me. He seems to have nurtured the notion that she was destined to be my soul-mate.' Gabriel gave a short, bitter laugh. 'It's ironic, isn't it? He knew me no better than to suppose I'd be bowled over by a pretty face but well enough to guess that a double indictment for theft would be more than I could stomach.'

'Theft? Who put that idea into your head?'

'Guess . . . And I can't entirely blame her. I've no real claim to either estate. But very few people are likely to believe that I don't want one.'

Jack scratched his head and thought about it. 'What baffles me is why Sir Robert would suggest such a crazy scheme. I didn't know him well – but he never struck me as eccentric. So to try and tie you to a wench you never saw before last week—'

'Quite. He paints her in such glowing colours that it makes one wonder why he didn't marry her himself,' remarked Gabriel acidly. 'He could have done, too – for she's not exactly fresh out of the nursery. She must be five-and twenty if she's a day and should have been married off long since. Come to think of it, that's probably what ails her.'

Jack could not help laughing.

'You really did take a dislike to her, didn't you?'

'I'm glad you're amused. Were it not for the prospect of spending the rest of my days with that patronising vixen, I'd probably laugh my boots off with you.'

Suddenly sobered, Jack said, 'You're surely not going to do it?'

'Not if I can help it.' Gabriel rose and, walking to the window, stared unseeingly into the narrow, cobbled lane. 'But the burning question is – can I?'

'Well, of course. The brother is bound to come back, isn't he? It stands to reason.'

'So I'd have thought – but the exquisite Mistress Clifford says not.' Gabriel turned, his expression suddenly grim. 'I want no part of it, Jack. My knowledge of estate-management could be written on a pinhead and my interest in learning is smaller still. Besides which, I already have the only career I ever wanted and it suits me. I don't want to give it up and I don't like being used to deprive two men of their birthrights. But I'm in a cage. Brandon Lacey is mine whether I like it or not; and if I don't also steal Ellis's fiancée from him, I get life-long responsibility for the Clifford lands as well.'

'It's a problem,' agreed Jack, sighing. 'But I wouldn't let it rush you into marriage.'

'I don't intend to.' The grimness dissolved into a sudden, unexpectedly attractive smile. 'And couldn't even if I wanted to, for the antipathy was wholly mutual. I don't know which revolted the lady most – my illegitimacy, or this.' He gestured lightly to his tawny sash.

'There's your answer, then. If all else fails, propose and let her refuse you.'

'I would – except that it's only half a solution. What I need is a loop-hole big enough to crawl through. But heaven knows how I'm to find the time to look for it because my duties on the Army Council alone are enough to prevent me being granted any more leave. We're already knee-deep in manifestoes of one sort or another. And, even as we speak, Ireton and Lambert are busy drawing up a list of propositions which we hope will form a sound basis for agreement with the King. All that aside, there's the daily business of persuading the men to remain patient in the face of Parliament's everlasting procrastination over pay.'

Jack's expression hardened.

'Well, you'd better keep trying. You can't go on bending the Commons to your will by marching on London. And don't fool yourself with the idea that the City will back the Army against Westminster because it won't. It was less than thrilled when the Eleven were driven out; and all that the merchants and tradesmen want is a chance to rescue the economy before it collapses, not a set of newfangled notions from your Independent friends or the Army in its midst, creating havoc.'

'We're aware of that,' responded Gabriel. 'But the New Model is more than just an army, Jack. It's a powerful voice demanding to be heard. And it's a damned sight more representative of this nation than Denzil Holles and his colleagues.'

'So you say. But if what I hear is true, it's also on the brink of mutiny.'

'There *is* unrest – but that's hardly surprising, is it? If you make a sword for someone and they don't pay, you can take them to law. The rank and file of the Army doesn't have that option. The infantry regiments are owed roughly six months' wages and the cavalry, almost a year – but even though arrears have finally been promised, we've yet to see the money. And as for Parliament's plan to disband the bulk of the Army and send the rest to Ireland . . . the ordinary trooper is worried that, if he's ignored here in England, he'll be totally forgotten once he's crossed the Irish sea. Can you honestly wonder that he refuses to budge till he's been justly treated?'

'I suppose not,' came the grudging response. 'But disbandment's a necessity, Gabriel. The country can't afford a massive fighting force now the war's over.'

'No one's disputing that. And the Army will disband once it's been paid. I don't consider that unreasonable . . . particularly in light of the fact that, although the Parliament apparently can't find the money to pay *us*, they've found it fast enough for the bands of reformadoes that have been pouring into London; those fellows who were disbanded when the New Model was first formed. Christ, Jack – they've even offered full arrears to any of our boys who'll desert! And, if all else fails, they'll happily invite the Prince of Wales over at the head of a Scottish invasion. Is that what you want?'

'Hardly,' said Jack shortly. He had no need to ask if it was true. With a goodly portion of the Army Council also sitting in the Commons, Gabriel was very unlikely to be mis-informed.

For a moment, neither of them spoke; and then, in a more moderate tone, Gabriel said, 'I'm no Independent idealist, Jack. You know that. But I do demand justice for my men . . . and we really did try all the usual channels. But when our petitions were burned by the public hangman as sedition, tempers naturally became a bit frayed. And the result, as you're aware, is that the regiments elected agents to speak on their behalf.'

'A collection of radical agitators out to cause trouble,' nodded Jack. 'As I understand it, every man-jack of them is a disciple of John Lilburne.'

'Very likely. And we've got green ribbons sprouting like weeds, as a result,' agreed Gabriel tersely. 'I'll even admit to being vaguely in sympathy with them myself on some issues. But as far as the men are concerned, it's simply a matter of one grievance breeding others, and most of the more extreme notions would wither fast enough at the prospect of some back-pay.'

Jack grunted and, laying down the sword, reached for his untouched mug of ale. 'Well, I hope to God something gets settled soon. The war's been over a year or more and – speaking as a common fellow who hasn't been inspired by the Army's lofty notions – I just want to live a normal life again.'

'With the King back on his throne, no doubt – wings suitably clipped?'

'Yes. And I'm not the only one who thinks that way. But I'd also like some assurance that this country hasn't gone through a civil war only to end up with something that, however well it's cloaked, amounts to nothing more than martial law. If the Army comes marching into London in pursuit of its demands, martial law is what it will be seen as. Because Parliament's already promised you everything you've asked for – hasn't it?'

'Oh yes,' came the sardonic reply. 'It's *promised*. The only trouble is that the reformadoes are still in London, men are still enlisting in the Militia and our fellows are still without pay. In short, the only thing we've asked for which has actually been given to us is indemnity against acts committed during the war. It's all pie-crust, Jack – and I'm as heartily sick of my situation as you are of yours. I fought in Europe for ten years without a tithe of these complications; and, if it weren't for the support I owe my men, I'd probably have left England six months ago to find work abroad. Now, of course, it's too late. I'm bound hand and foot by this bloody Will.'

Jack looked him in the eye.

'Tell me something. Do you know who concocted this plot to seize the King?'

'I might hazard a tolerably accurate guess.'

'I thought as much. Cromwell?'

'He probably knew of it – but, if pressed, I'd put my money on Edward Sexby,' shrugged the Colonel. Then, 'And now I'd like to ask *you* something. Why are you so damned edgy?'

Jack drained half his tankard in one jerky movement and then, after a brief hesitation, said baldly, 'Annis is pregnant again.'

'Ah.' A faint frown touched the grey eyes. 'I see.'

'She seems quite well so far and I've managed to get Peter Chamberlen to attend her. Only—'

'Chamberlen?' queried Gabriel. 'Isn't he the fellow who used to physic the King but now writes political tracts along the lines of Free-born John?'

'That's him. He's full of peculiar ideas on midwifery and says that if Annis spends most of her time in bed – which is where she is now, by the way – all will be well. But she's miscarried four times in the last three years and she was so ill last time that—' Jack broke off and ran his hand through his hair. 'I tell you, Gabriel, I'm scared to death for her. And if she comes through this – baby or no baby – I'll make bloody sure it never happens again.'

'Allowing for Annis's feelings in the matter, I should imagine that's easier said than done,' began Gabriel. And then stopped as the door was flung wide and his foster-brother's niece erupted into the room.

'Why, Gabriel!' she cried. 'How is it that you always come when I'm out?'

'Or conversely,' he replied, moving lazily towards her, 'why are you always out when I come?'

Bryony Morrell tucked a recalcitrant marigold curl back into her cap and fixed him with an intense brown stare. She was just sixteen and had lived with her Uncle Jack and Aunt Annis since her parents had been carried off by the plague in the second year of the war. And though Gabriel – like everybody else – thought she was still a child and expected her to regard him as just another uncle, Bryony knew that he was no relation at all and that she had been passionately in love with him for a whole year. The only difficulty, since he came so rarely, was how to make him aware of her developing charms. And so, seizing her opportunity with both hands, she said artlessly, 'You will stay to supper, won't you?'

'I'm afraid not, sweetheart. If I don't rejoin my men tonight, I'm likely to be shot for desertion,' replied Gabriel. And, with a slanting grin at Jack, 'either that or be offered Denzil Holles' hand and my back-pay.'

Bryony tugged his attention back to her.

'Oh please stay! We haven't seen you for so long and I'm sure you could stay if you really wanted to.'

'You malign me. I really am remarkably busy right now. But cheer up. Your Uncle Jack – wise in all things – is convinced I may be working closer to home in the not-too-distant future. And, if that's so, I'll be less of a stranger.'

She appropriated his arm and smiled up at him with what she fondly hoped was subtle allure, thinking how tall and lean and tanned he was – and how broad his shoulders were. Of course, she recognised that thirty-four was perhaps a *little* old, but somehow, in Gabriel's case, it only added to his glamour. Even the elusive hint of silver in his thick, dark hair was attractive – and there was no doubt that he looked incredibly elegant in his uniform. It was this last thought that made Bryony say dreamily, 'If the Army comes to London, will you drill your troops for me?'

'No. But if an exhibition muster is arranged, I'll send word to Jack so that he can bring you along. Will that do?'

Bryony pouted but, before she could speak, her uncle said

flatly, 'You'll not catch me gawking at a military display. I've better uses for my time.'

Gabriel smiled blandly. 'Business good, is it?'

'Moderately.'

'We've taken on three more apprentices,' offered Bryony.

'Three more? Well, well. But with the Morrell name recognised as one of Europe's foremost armourers, I can't say I'm surprised. Even Cromwell has one of your blades.'

'So has the King – though I doubt he's allowed to carry it,' retorted Jack. 'My father crafted it shortly before he died.'

'I remember. It has to be said, however, that Old Noll has made better use of his.'

'Better for whom?'

'All of us, I hope.' Gabriel switched his gaze to Bryony and flicked her cheek with a careless finger. 'If you're a good girl and take especial care of your aunt, I'll take you to have your fortune told when I come again. But meanwhile, duty calls . . . though I could find the time to swallow some bread and cheese if anybody cared to offer it.'

Bryony gave him a beaming smile and sped off towards the kitchen. Gabriel waited until she was out of earshot and then said, 'With regard to the business we discussed earlier . . . I take it I can count on your discretion?'

Jack blinked. 'Of course. If that's what you want.'

'It is. Discuss it with Annis, if you wish – but no one else. I may or may not be forced into marriage with Venetia Clifford, but until I know which it's to be, the less people who know of the situation, the better.'

'As you like. Though I can't help wondering whose reputation you're protecting.'

'Mine, of course,' retorted Gabriel blandly. 'From what I've been privileged to see of the lady, she wouldn't give a tinker's curse if our problems were shouted from every steeple. I, on the other hand, value my privacy.'

'Shy as a maiden aunt,' agreed his foster-brother with a grin. 'But if you can't find your loop-hole, you're going to have to grow out of it. Fast.'

Three

After an absence of twelve tiring and tiresome days, Colonel Brandon arrived back in Reading late that evening to find the streets still busy with boisterous groups of off-duty troopers. He smiled wryly to himself. Soldiers were soldiers the world over. And though the New Model might consider itself an Army of Saints, this didn't make the alehouses and brothels any less busy – a fact for which, under present circumstances, he and his fellow-officers ought to be duly grateful.

Gabriel turned his horse into the stableyard of the tavern which served him as a billet and was confronted with the sight of his servant and companion, Walter Larkin, sitting astride a mounting-block, systematically whittling at a piece of wood.

Mr Larkin, a small and wiry person of some fifty summers and possessed of a face closely resembling a walnut, rose slowly.

'You're back then,' he said laconically.

'As you see. Have you been here all the time?' Gabriel dropped from the saddle and set about unlatching his bags.

'Don't flatter yourself. Maybe I've just been enjoying the rest.' There was a watchful gleam in the narrowed eyes. 'How was the funeral?'

'Much the same as any other.'

'And the Will?'

'Unique.' Gabriel swung round and deposited the bags in Mr Larkin's arms. 'Do you mind if we leave the gory details until I've got inside? My throat's full of dust and I'm devilish hungry.'

'Aye. You would be. It's just a shame your supper's going to have to wait a bit.'

'Why? Has something happened?'

'In a manner of speaking. You'd best go into the taproom and see for yourself. I *was* going to leave well alone. But seeing as you're here . . .' A cryptic smile touched the seamed face. 'In the meantime I'll go and order you some food. If you cut the sympathy and just pull rank, it shouldn't get too cold.' Upon which he disappeared in through the back door.

Swallowing his irritation, the Colonel strode round to the taproom. Small, ill-lit and reeking of beer and onions, it was deserted save for his Major – sitting alone in a corner and drinking his way, silently and with dedication, through a bottle of brandy. Patience fled before a gust of pure exasperation and Gabriel said bitingly, 'I hope you're not on duty. Because if you are, I'll take great pleasure in personally putting your head under the pump.'

Eden Maxwell set down his glass and leaned back in his chair. Despite the amount he had drunk, the hazel eyes were still clear and his voice quite unslurred as he said coolly, 'You ought to know by now that I don't let these little lapses affect my work. Neither – despite my best endeavours – do they ever result in blissful crapulence. Ned Moulton is duty-officer for tonight.'

Gabriel walked across the room and tossed his gloves down on the greasy table. It was perfectly true that Major Maxwell's mercifully rare departures from temperance were always carefully timed and that he had, in any case, an uncanny ability to drink without apparently getting drunk. But if, after three years, he still couldn't face his personal life without diving headfirst into a bottle, his Army career would inevitably end on the dung-heap. And, since he was rather good at his job, that would be a pity.

Gabriel hooked a stool forward with one foot and sat down, fixing Eden with a quelling stare. 'This has got to stop, you know. What is it this time? Another letter from home?'

'What else?' The tone was faintly jeering but the face, with its scarred left cheek, remained empty of expression. 'A long-winded, maternalistic eulogy from my youngest sister, cataloguing the lives of both my son and my so-called daughter over the last year. Every quaint remark, every small attainment, every spot and sneeze. Felicity's given me a list of the lot. And in the hope that all this will have softened me up, she ends with a heart-wrenching appeal for me to realise that even if Viola isn't my child, it's by no fault of her own – and that I should therefore put it behind me and go home before my son forgets who I am.'

Gabriel sighed and, without any real hope of being attended to, said, 'Well, she's right, isn't she?'

'Right?' Eden gave a harsh laugh and slopped more brandy into his glass. 'Of course she's bloody right! The trouble is that I can't do it. I forced myself to visit Thorne Ash last year while we were waiting for Oxford to fall – mainly in order to tell the family of Tom Tripp's death – and I didn't last twenty-four hours. Viola is already the image of her mother and she's only two. Every time I looked at her, all I could see was Celia. Celia dancing in the garden with my sister, Amy; Celia smiling at me on our wedding-day; Celia in bed with Hugo Verney at the exact hour my father's body was being brought home on a bier. Perhaps you could live with that – but I can't. And the sooner Felicity and my mother accept it, the better.'

'And your son – Jude, is it? Is he supposed to accept it as well?' asked Gabriel deliberately.

The brandy went down in one swallow and the glass hit the table with unnecessary violence. 'You think it's easy? It isn't. But how many choices do you think I have?'

'The same one I've been advocating for some time now. Pull yourself together. After all, quite apart from the matter of your son, you must be needed at home from time to time for other reasons.'

'Not especially. Oh – it's true that Kate's settled in Genoa with her money-lending husband and that Felix has followed them there to complete his education as a goldsmith. But there's always Amy and brother-in-law Geoffrey in London. And meanwhile my mother has Felicity to help her – and Ralph Cochrane.'

'And if Ralph doesn't stay? There's no reason why he should, after all. He merely went – as your friend – to help out for a time because you didn't feel up to going yourself. What if he decides he wants to resume his career as a soldier?'

'He won't. Soldiering was never Ralph's first choice and

43

Basing House sickened him. He'd much rather be a farmer and, at Thorne Ash, he can be,' said Eden. 'Also – in due course and unless I'm much mistaken – he'll probably marry Felicity. No. I don't really think I'm needed at home.'

'Then why do your mother and sister persist in asking you to go back?'

'Who knows? Family feeling, perhaps.' As always happened at these times, Eden found himself suddenly regretting his outburst. Gabriel Brandon knew all about his chaotic affairs, of course the only one outside the family and Ralph Cochrane who did. But it still, on the whole, was something that Eden preferred not to talk about. It cut too near the bone.

His customary reserve settling back over him like a mantle, Eden said lightly, 'And, speaking of family feeling, you went away to attend a funeral, didn't you? Was it someone close?'

'That depends on your point of view,' replied Gabriel. He might know what Eden's problems were but he had no intention of discussing his own. He rose from the table saying, 'With any luck, Wat should have managed to find me some food. But, before I go, perhaps you'd better tell me if anything important has happened in my absence.'

'Nothing cataclysmic. Fairfax has sent for Sir John Berkeley to mediate between us and the King; the Agitators have been demanding an immediate march on London, but have been successfully stalled by Cromwell; and there was a meeting of the Council today for the purpose of discussing these proposals Ireton and Lambert have been drawing up. Nothing that you won't find out about tomorrow from better-informed persons than myself – and nothing that need keep you from your supper.'

'Thank God for that.'

The Colonel turned to go and then stopped as Eden said wryly, 'Ah . . . and Gabriel?'

'Yes?'

'My thanks.'

Gabriel's brows rose.

'Don't mention it. If it means you won't drink any more, it was my pleasure. Does it?'

'Yes,' said Eden. 'I believe it does.' And then, his mouth twisting in a bitter smile, 'Until the next time, anyway.'

Wat Larkin, who had begun life in the stews of Alsatia and spent the majority of his early years evading the law, was singularly unimpressed by the news that Colonel Brandon had become a man of property and still less enamoured with the possibility of his approaching nuptials.

'Unsuitable,' he said dourly. 'Highly unsuitable. Not for us at all, it isn't. It'd stifle you in a month. No. You'd better get out of it.'

People sometimes remarked on Gabriel Brandon's relationship with Wat. Mere acquaintances tended to wonder which was the master and which the man – and close friends simply asked how on earth Gabriel put up with such a disrespectful old devil. To the first, Gabriel returned no answer whatsoever, and, to the second, only that fifteen years companionship was bound to breed a certain licence. To no one at all did he see the need to explain that, since the age of nineteen, Wat had followed him all over Europe, through good fortune and bad, mending his boots, tending his wounds, nurturing his career; and that, more than the man he had just seen buried in Yorkshire or even the foster-brother he'd left behind in Shoreditch, Wat Larkin was the closest thing he had to a family . . . and the only person in the world to whom he would confidently entrust his life.

Not that the two men always agreed. Far from it. But, right now, Wat's reading of the situation accorded completely with his own so Gabriel said merely 'I'm aware of that – but it's easier said than done. I'm saddled with Brandon Lacey no matter what I do; and, as for the other matter, my best hope lies in the girl's brother.'

'Not if I can help it,' sniffed Mr Larkin. 'But I suppose we'd better try and find him, for all that. And it's no good relying on some finicky wench either. She's bound to mess it up. And I haven't spent the best years of my life turning you into something like a soldier to have it all come to nothing. No. There's nothing else for it. I'll have to go to France myself. If Clifford's there, I'll find him.'

Gabriel eyed his henchman thoughtfully. Amongst his other dubious talents, Wat had the nose of a bloodhound and the instincts of a ferret . . . and, since he could also lie like a trooper, he would presumably have no difficulty in mingling with the exiled Royalists.

'It's worth a try,' he said, at length. 'In fact I was rather hoping you'd offer. But, in all fairness, I ought to warn you that even if you find him it may be a wasted journey. The girl says his principles won't let him take the Oath.'

'With his birthright at stake? I doubt it.' Wat spat hard and accurately through the open window. 'But if the worst comes to the worst, we'll just have to leave the country. That wouldn't be such a bad thing anyway. Quality professionals are always in short supply. And at least you get paid.'

'True. And you have no idea how much I wish I could do it,' came the wry reply. 'However, I'll set about getting a travelling pass for you – and I'd also better find out what Ireton and Lambert have put in this latest set of proposals concerning proscribed persons.' A faint, sardonic gleam touched the grey eyes. 'You never know. There may be something that will tempt Sir Harry Clifford home on the next boat.'

Major-General John Lambert listened to Colonel Brandon's request that, as a member of the Army Council, he be permitted to read the *Heads of the Proposals* and then said, 'I'm afraid I can't oblige you. Henry Ireton has one copy and the other is with the committee that was appointed to lick it into shape. But I can give you the main points, if you like – or you could ask Henry.'

Reflecting on Ireton's passion for protracted debate, Gabriel said, 'I think I'll settle for hearing it from you. I've a meeting with my Captains at four.'

Lambert's heavy-lidded gaze acquired a touch of amusement and he waved the Colonel into a chair. 'Then I'll be brief. What we have done may be divided into four main sections. On the religious side, bishops would remain but be deprived of their judicial powers; neither the Book of Common Prayer nor the Covenant would be enforced; and

46

there would be toleration to all but Papists. With regard to Parliament, we've proposed limiting the power of the Lords – and both Houses are required to set a date for their own dissolution, after which there would be biennial parliaments, each lasting no less than four and no more than eight months. We've also suggested electoral reform to give more constitutional power to highly populated areas. In short, representation would be in proportion to taxation.' He paused. 'You don't like the idea?'

'On the contrary. I was just wondering how it's all going to go down at Westminster.'

'With a good grace, we hope.

'Next, a Council of State would be set up – and this would control the Militia for ten years. After that, the King is permitted to make his own appointments – subject to Parliamentary approval. And, working along the same lines, we've proposed that domestic government be carried on much as it's always been but that, for the next decade, officials will be chosen by Parliament – after which his Majesty may select them from a list of names supplied by the House.'

'Strong stuff,' commented Gabriel. 'And I don't imagine that the King will exactly be panting to agree to it.'

'No,' admitted Lambert coolly. 'He isn't. Yet.'

The dark grey gaze sharpened.

'He's already seen the *Proposals*? Before they went to the Council?'

'Yes – and certain alterations were made as a result.'

'Such as what, for example?'

'Such as the reinstatement of the royal veto.'

'Ah. You don't think,' suggested Gabriel, 'that this may perhaps cause the men to feel a trifle betrayed? That they may wonder just how far their officers are prepared to go in placating the King?'

The Major-General sighed. 'Yes. I do think it. But if it provides a settlement, they'll soon forgive us. And where's the alternative? We've got to come up with something that the King will consent to – because, without that, we have nothing and the chaos will continue.'

Since this was palpably true, Gabriel saw the wisdom of

letting the matter drop in favour of pursuing his original errand. He said lightly, 'So what other inducements have you found to tempt his Majesty?'

'Further leniency towards his supporters,' replied Lambert. 'No Royalist would hold office during the next five years or be eligible to sit in either House before the end of the second Parliament. But only five men would be named subject to Parliamentary judgement. Any who will join with us in preventing a new war are permitted to compound for five percent of their estates.'

It was as much as any Cavalier could reasonably expect and Gabriel experienced mild stirrings of optimism. Sir Harry Clifford's name could not be on the list of five. He wasn't important enough. And so there was no reason why he shouldn't come home . . . only a battery of excellent reasons why he should.

Smiling genuinely for the first time in several days, Gabriel congratulated both the Major-General and the absent Ireton on the soundness of their proposals and expressed his heartfelt hope that the King would give them his blessing. Then, leaving Lambert to speculate on Colonel Brandon's sudden change of mood, he walked back to his quarters whistling.

Three days later, Wat left for Dover with an overseas pass in one pocket and a letter from Colonel Brandon to Sir Henry Clifford in the other. Gabriel saw him off and then turned his attention to the task of preventing four hundred men with time on their hands from becoming either slipshod or restless.

Within twenty-four hours this was made somewhat easier when the Lord General decided to move the Army a little further from London while Parliament considered the four final demands placed before it by the Army Council. Since Fairfax had recently been given command of all Parliamentary forces and the deserters had been officially disbanded, this was a reasonable move. It also, Gabriel observed caustically to Major Maxwell as they prepared to transfer the regiment from Reading to Bedford, gave the men a few more mundane matters with which to occupy their minds.

This was true when he said it. Unfortunately, almost before the Army had settled into its new quarters or finished installing the King amidst the splendours of Woburn, several things happened in rapid succession.

It began with Presbyterian gangs of apprentices, reformadoes and watermen converging on the Skinners Hall to sign an engagement in favour of maintaining the Covenant. This upset the Army, to whom liberty of conscience was almost as important as arrears of pay, and also earned condemnation from the now equally Independent-spirited benches of Westminster. But all might have been well had not the Parliament – with the disastrous lack of timing which was fast becoming its trade-mark – decided to placate the Army at the expense of the City by taking control of the Militia back into its own hands.

The results, though cataclysmic, were not without an element of farce. In the wake of a respectable, petition-bearing party of Aldermen, the Skinners Hall Engagers swarmed into both Houses of Parliament and, taking the nation's representatives prisoner, refused to let them out until they repealed the Militia Ordinance.

Since there were only nine peers in attendance that day, the Lords capitulated almost immediately. The Commons, on the other hand, held out until it became plain that continued resistance would only result in them missing tomorrow's breakfast as well as tonight's supper. With sullen abruptness, they did all that was asked of them and then adjourned themselves; after which both Speakers, all nine peers and fifty-eight Independent MPs prudently removed themselves from the City and sent an urgent appeal for help to the Lord General. London, they said, was in uproar; the Eleven were returning and the City was organising its own defence. The Army, they said, would have to Do Something.

Fairfax considered it. He would have preferred to keep the Army out of civil government but that left Parliament at the mercy of mob-rule. More important still, it left the way open for Denzil Holles and the Presbyterians to make an approach to the King at the very moment the *Heads of the Proposals* were being formally presented to him; and that, given his

Majesty's talent for playing both ends against the middle, could put any possibility of settlement as far away as it had ever been.

Sir Thomas conferred with Lieutenant-General Cromwell and then reluctantly did what the Agitators had been demanding in solo and chorus for the last two months. He ordered the New Model to strike camp and commence a slow march on the capital.

Gabriel Brandon received the order from one of the Lieutenant-General's staff without batting an eyelid. When the fellow had gone, however, he communed silently with the ceiling for a while before murmuring softly, 'Dear me . . . dear me. What *is* Brother Jack going to say?'

On Saturday August 7th, Bryony Morrell hung precariously from a railing outside the Fishmongers Hall and craned her neck for a first glimpse of the procession. It must be very near now and about to swing into view round the corner from Canning Street. Already she could hear the tuck of drum and tramp of feet over the decidedly feeble encouragement of the crowd. And soon, therefore, soon she would see Gabriel.

A line of disapproval momentarily marked her brow. Why weren't more people cheering? It was all very well for Uncle Jack to say that the Army had no right interfering in City or Parliament business, but people had been getting pretty sick of having to protect their property from roving bands of drunken *ex*-soldiers; and surely *someone* had to restore order?

Bryony had only a hazy grasp of politics. Not so long ago, the world had been split into Roundheads and Cavaliers. Now it seemed to be largely made up of Presbyterians and Independents. The first, so far as she could make out, were divided in their views on the Covenant, but united to a man in wanting everything put back exactly as it had been before the war. The second wanted an end to the miseries of the Covenant and a fresh start based on a whole battery of new ideas. The City was largely Presbyterian, the Army almost totally Independent and the Parliament (when present all in one piece) somewhere in the region of half-and-half. The result, it seemed to Bryony, was complete confusion.

She peered up Fish Street Hill, her eagerness sharpening

with every second. Thanks to Aunt Annis – who had taken her visiting some decrepit old relative in Rotherhithe – she had missed yesterday's triumphal progress to Westminster, when the MPs who'd fled had been escorted back in style by soldiers with laurel leaves in their hats. But today the bulk of the Army was marching through the City and out across London Bridge towards Croydon – and Bryony had made very sure she wouldn't miss that too. She'd waited until Uncle Jack was occupied with a customer and Aunt Annis resting in her room and then, scrambling hastily into her best amber taffeta, she'd slipped out through the scullery and taken to her heels.

The crowd eddied around her and she experienced a moment of concern for her gown – the only one she possessed that was neither wool nor plain cloth; and then all was forgotten as the head of the procession finally came into sight.

Bright silk flags heralded the first regiment of cavalry and the lone, solidly-built rider at the head of it. Byrony frowned. This man was not – could not be – Sir Thomas Fairfax, who everyone said was quite young and romantic-looking and always rode a white horse. No. The middle-aged fellow on the long-tailed roan must be Lieutenant-General Cromwell, about whom there was nothing even remotely romantic and whose nose was every bit as big as people said.

The crowd continued to hover between a few ragged cheers and a good deal of low-voiced muttering. Ignoring them, Bryony clung to her plinth with one hand and enthusiastically waved her scarf with the other as the first divisions of admirably disciplined troopers rode by.

'Typical,' said a voice dryly.

Bryony swivelled her head and looked down into the vivid, mobile face of a shabby young man standing just in front of her. 'I beg your pardon?'

'Typical,' he repeated obligingly. And then, in response to her blank stare, 'It's just like a girl to care more for the excitement of seeing a few brawny fellows in uniform than the significance of what's actually happening here. However, I suppose there's still time for you to grow out of it. Can you read?'

'Of course! Better than you, I daresay.'

51

'Good.' A vagrant smile lit the night-dark eyes. 'Then have a leaflet.'

Bryony looked down at the broadsheet he had folded tenderly into her hand. ENGLISHMEN AWAKE! ran the caption in bold, black letters. She snorted. Englishmen. Not a word, as usual, about English*women*.

'No thanks,' she said, shoving the pamphlet unceremoniously back at him. 'I'd sooner read Gerard's *Herbal*. And right now I'd like to watch the procession.'

'I'm not stopping you. I just thought you might be glad of some company, that's all. You don't look old enough to be out on your own on a day like this.'

'Now *look!*' she began furiously. Then, drawing a long, steadying breath, she gave him her most withering look and said, freezingly, 'I can take care of myself and the only person annoying me is you. So go and get on with peddling your stupid bits of paper before I start screaming.'

For a brief moment violent brown eyes met gently satiric black ones and then the young man shrugged.

'Suit yourself,' he said. And elbowed his way off into the crowd.

Feeling rather pleased with herself, Bryony restored her attention to the marching ranks of the New Model and the important business of searching for Gabriel's banner. It was green. Green for good hope, he said – but she preferred to think of it as the colour of true love. Either way, its mission today was to warn her of his coming so that she might be ready with her best smile.

For the first hour she was kept happily engrossed by sheer spectacle . . . The dull gleam of helmets and breastplates, orange sashes glowing against soft buff leather, well-polished sword-hilts and pikes reflecting the light – the constant stream of fine-looking young men who marched or rode through the City like heroes. But even this novelty eventually wore off and, by the time the procession was drawing towards its close, Bryony's only feeling was one of resentful depression.

She had seen cavalry, infantry and dragoons, flags of every hue save one, and a grand total, had she but known it, of eighteen thousand men. But there had been no Gabriel. Her feet were hot, her back ached with standing, her head was beginning to throb; and, as if things weren't quite bad enough, the sky had turned unpleasantly overcast and was threatening an imminent downpour.

Heaving a morose sigh, Bryony stepped down from her perch and prepared to embark on the weary walk home. The crowds were dispersing a little but, even so, she would be lucky to reach Shoreditch before the rain came. There was no doubt about it, she decided gloomily. Today had been an utter disaster.

It was about to get worse. Barely had she set foot up Fish Street Hill when, without quite knowing how it came about, she found herself passing through a battle zone. Two rival groups of apprentices, who had begun by hurling insults at each other across the road, suddenly progressed to more tangible missiles picked up from the gutters. A fish-head whistled past Bryony's nose and a rotting tomato hit her squarely on the shoulder. Howling with fury, she swung round in the direction from which it had come and received a handful of filthy cabbage leaves full in the face.

A voice with no hint of apology in it yelled at her to get out of the way. Spitting cabbage and regretfully postponing a fierce impulse to kill, Bryony picked up her skirts and scampered out of range. It was just unfortunate that, at the exact moment she judged it safe to stop running, her foot slipped on a half-eaten mutton pie and she went down like a sack of meal on the cobbles.

Winded by the fall and gasping for breath, she heaved herself painfully on to her knees and stared first at her grazed palms and then at her ruined taffeta. A great tide of misery welled up inside her and heavy spots of rain began to land on her head. It was too much. She burst into angry tears.

'If this is what you call looking after yourself, I'd say you could definitely do with a bit more practice.'

Bryony opened her eyes on the rather blurred vision of a pair of painstakingly cared-for but well-worn boots.

'Go away!' she wailed. 'Just – just *go away*!'

'And leave you sitting in the road, crying your eyes out? Don't be stupid!' The young man of the pamphlets hunted through his pockets and eventually produced a frayed but reasonably clean handkerchief. 'Here – wipe some of that stuff off your face and get up. If you sit there much longer, you'll be soaked to the skin.'

'I'll be s-soaked anyway,' sobbed Bryony, ignoring the handkerchief and clambering to her feet. 'I l-live in Shoreditch and I c-can't afford a chair.'

'One thing at a time,' he said. And, grasping her wrist, towed her briskly into the shelter of a shop doorway.

It was then that she became aware of two things. First she noticed how badly her rescuer limped, and second that he wore a knot of bright green ribbon thrust jauntily through one of his buttonholes.

'Now,' he said, once more proffering the handkerchief. 'Stop crying and do what you can to clean yourself up. Then we'll see about getting you home. And don't tell me to go to the devil again. I may not be a gentleman but, fortunately for you, I'm no Pharisee either.'

Bryony wiped her face and hands and then set about scrubbing ineffectively at the hopelessly stained taffeta.

'Oh God!' she muttered despairingly. 'Look at it! It's my only silk dress and Uncle Jack will probably say that it was all my own fault and refuse to let me have another one for years.'

The young man tactfully refrained from observing that her uncle probably had a point – or even that there were worse things to do without. He didn't want to start the girl crying again. And so, not realising his mistake, he said cheerfully, 'Oh well . . . look on the bright side. At least none of this happened before the Army marched by – so your soldier-boy saw you at your best.'

'He didn't. He wasn't even there,' came the tearful reply. 'It's all been for nothing.'

Her reluctant hero cast his eyes heavenwards and murmured something under his breath. Then, with careful patience, he said, 'Perhaps we'd better see about getting you home. You say you've no money – sadly, neither have I. But I suppose you could always take a chair and have your uncle pay for it.'

She thought about it and came to the rather muddled conclusion that things were already quite bad enough without her adding to them. Peering uncertainly up at the sky, she said, 'I think, on the whole, that I'd rather walk. And the rain's easing off a bit, isn't it?'

It was – but any fool could see that it wouldn't last. Sighing, the young man said so.

'Well, if I don't mind, I don't see why you should!' snapped Bryony. 'I'm perfectly capable of going on my own, after all.'

'I've heard that one before,' he retorted. 'Come on. Let's go before it starts throwing it down again.'

She scurried after him, determined and faintly conscience-stricken. 'I can manage, I tell you. And, unless you're going that way yourself, you can't possibly walk all the way to Shoreditch just to escort me.'

'Can't I?' His tone was silky-smooth and he did not stop to face her. 'Why not?'

'Well . . . because you've hurt your foot, haven't you?'

'Not recently. And it isn't likely to get any better. But if you'd rather not be seen with a cripple, you only have to say.'

Not unnaturally, it took Bryony some time to recover from this attack. But finally, as they were crossing into Gracious Street, she said cautiously, 'Why do you wear that ribbon on your coat? Is it for some feast-day?'

He shot her a surprised glance.

'No. It's a political token.'

'Oh.' Her heart sank and she realised that, after the leaflets, she ought to have expected it.

Laughter warmed the intelligent face.

'Don't worry. I'm not about to deliver a lecture. If you want to hear me speak, you'll have to come to the Whalebone one evening. And I can't even offer you another pamphlet.' He paused and then added casually, 'You had a point there, by the way. It's time we stopped dividing the nation. And – despite what we're taught – I've a sneaking suspicion that women are equal to men in God's sight.'

It was social blasphemy and Bryony's jaw dropped. Then she said weakly, 'My goodness! If that's what all you green-ribbon people think, I'm not surprised your ideas haven't caught on.'

'And what makes you think they haven't?' he grinned. 'As a matter of fact, we're collecting quite a following – both in the Army and outside it. All we lack, you might say, is a name.' The grin widened and he lifted one brow. 'Then again, since we're led by Free-born John, perhaps we don't really need one.'

Bryony stopped dead. She knew everything about John Lilburne except what he actually stood for. Uncle Jack muttered quite a lot about outlandish notions to do with tithes, the excise, freedom of speech and the like, but she usually did her best not to listen. Frowning a little, she said, 'I don't see how Mr Lilburne can lead anything when he's always in prison.'

'Don't exaggerate. He's only been there twice before.'

'Oh. But he's there now, isn't he?'

'Sadly, yes. Sent to the Tower by the House of Lords for sticking his fingers in his ears and denying their jurisdiction. However, it'll take more than a little thing like that to silence Free-Born John. He's still able to continue with his writings, you see – and there are plenty of people like myself to get them printed and circulated.'

Bryony started to walk on slowly. There was no doubt that, although the day had been catastrophic in most respects, it had not been without adventure. And despite his limp and shabby clothes, her companion was somehow profoundly likable. On a sudden impulse, she held out her hand and said, 'I'm Bryony Morrell. And you?'

'Samuel Radford,' he replied, making a brief but polite bow over her fingers. 'Once of Banbury but, for the last year or so, of Cooper's Lane in Blackfriars. Delighted to make your acquaintance.'

Bryony dimpled and then withdrew her hand to pick up her skirts as they crossed Cornhill. Not that there was much point in it. The taffeta was smothered in a variety of unpleasant stains and damp from the incessant drizzle. And with her hair beginning to snake its way wetly down her back, it wasn't surprising that people were staring at her. She must look quite a sight.

Two thoughts became one and she said diffidently, 'I'm sorry I was so rude to you – and I'm truly grateful to you for coming with me. But I think it might be better if you didn't come quite *all* the way to my door.'

Mr Radford homed effortlessly in on the core of the matter. 'Uncle a Presbyterian, is he? Well, don't worry. He won't offend me – nor I him, hopefully. Unless he's some kind of petty tyrant?'

'Oh no – not at all! It's just that I went off without telling anybody. And now, coming home in such a mess and with you holding the kind of views Uncle Jack doesn't approve of . . .'

'An explosion is likely?'

'Well, yes. He always thinks he knows best, you see. Come to think of it, when you're sixteen *everyone* thinks they know best.'

'And the sad truth is that they generally do,' he responded dryly. 'But not always. So let's just say I've my own reasons for coming in to help you explain your appearance – and then save our breath for walking. Here comes the rain again.'

Twenty minutes later, and thoroughly drenched, they walked into the Morrells' simple but cosy parlour to be confronted not just by Jack and Annis but by the very last person Bryony had expected to see.

'My God!' said Gabriel, on a faint but unmistakable quiver of laughter. 'I suppose I always suspected that you hadn't enough sense to come in out of the rain – but I did think you'd given up playing mud pies.'

A tide of hot colour stained the girl's skin but, before she could speak, Annis Morrell said anxiously, 'Where on earth have you been? We've been worried sick.'

'It's perfectly obvious where she's been,' cut in Jack. 'Though, even allowing for the rain, I don't quite see how watching today's display of military might has resulted in her coming home in this condition.' He paused, irritably surveying his niece. 'Well?'

Bryony pushed her hair back with both hands and continued to stare at the Colonel while, all around her, drips started to form little puddles on the stone floor.

'What are you doing here?' she demanded unsteadily. 'You were supposed to be marching to Croydon with the Army.'

Sam's brows registered surprise but he had the sense to keep his mouth shut. After all, it was no business of his if Mistress Bryony was hankering after a fellow nearly old enough to be her father – and one, moreover, who hadn't the wit to realise that now wasn't the time to make fun of her.

'Not me, I'm afraid,' responded Gabriel negligently. 'My regiment is one of the four left to protect the Parliament and the Tower from any further unpleasantness.' He stopped and then, regarding her with mild foreboding, said, 'Oh dear. Never say you only went to watch the march-past in the hope of seeing me there?'

Bryony's flush deepened. Fortunately, before she was forced to answer him, Jack said, 'Never mind all this. I'm still waiting for an explanation and an introduction.'

'All right. *All right!*' Bryony drew a long, bitter breath. 'I got in the way of an apprentice fight and then fell over. And this is Mr Radford. I never met him before today but he walked home with me so I wouldn't get into any more trouble. And now – if you're satisfied – I'm going to get out of these clothes.' And she flounced soggily from the room, leaving a trail of wet footprints behind her.

Jack gazed silently at the ceiling and then looked across at Samuel. 'If she hasn't expressed her gratitude, allow me to do it for her. You've been more than good – particularly in view of the weather.'

Sam shrugged. 'I won't melt. And I daresay anyone with a grain of sense would have done as much.'

'I doubt it,' said Annis warmly. 'And since you've had a soaking for your pains, you must let us find you some other clothes and stay to supper while we dry your own.'

He started to protest and then was stopped by an unexpected discovery. Neat as wax in her blue gown and with her soft, brown hair covered by a demure cap, Annis Morrell was a small, no more than ordinarily attractive woman in her mid-twenties. But she had a smile that completely transformed her face, and for a sharp, fleeting instant, she reminded him of his favourite sister.

The illusion lingered as she drew him towards the hearth without even appearing to notice his limp and told him to throw his coat over the settle. Then, turning to her husband, she said, 'And now – if you'll get Mr Radford some dry clothing, I'll go up and help Bryony out of that dress.'

'Why?' asked Jack. 'If she could get into it unaided, she can take it off the same way.' And then, meeting his wife's gaze, 'Oh – very well. But I won't have you running round after her. She doesn't deserve it and you're supposed to be staying off your feet.'

'Twenty-four hours a day?' twinkled Annis. And, reaching up to plant a kiss on his cheek, she drew him firmly through the door.

Sam was left to the realisation that he was being thoroughly inspected by a pair of sardonic grey eyes.

'A word of advice,' said Gabriel at length. 'If you're staying to supper, it might be as well if you pocketed that green ribbon. Being less familiar with it than I am myself, Mr Morrell has yet to recognise its significance and, under the present circumstances, it might be better if he didn't.'

Holding his sodden coat between his hands, Sam said warily, 'You're talking about his niece's escapade?'

'I am talking,' came the arid response, 'about the renewed flight of the Eleven, the Army's presence in London and the fact that the King appears more likely to accept the *Heads of the Proposals* than the terms currently on offer from Parliament. In her usual fashion, Bryony has only added fuel to the fire. And I'm simply suggesting that you refrain from piling on any more.'

Sam decided that there was a lot of sense in this and, though deception went against the grain, it was hardly likely to matter. Shrugging slightly, he pulled the now rather bedraggled ribbon from his buttonhole and thrust it deep into his pocket.

'Anything to oblige,' he said.

'You misunderstand.' Gabriel rose and reached for his hat. 'It's your digestion that's at stake, not mine. I'm leaving.'

'You're what?' said Jack, walking back into the room clutching an armful of clothes. 'I thought you were eating with us this evening.'

'Ah. Didn't I say?' the Colonel's smile was deliberately provocative. 'I've an assignation with a rather merry little widow in Cornhill.'

'No. You didn't say.' Mr Morrell eyed him blandly. 'I suppose I should have expected it, though. Making hay while the sun shines, are you?'

'Something like that. And even if I wasn't . . . I rather think that you and I have argued enough for one day. Don't you?'

Four

While Wat Larkin rattled round Paris like a pea in a colander looking for Harry Clifford, and Bryony Morrell pursued her acquaintance with Sam Radford in the frail hope of making Colonel Brandon jealous, Venetia Clifford counted the days since the departure of Captain Peverell and clung grimly to her sanity.

It wasn't that she didn't have a myriad of other things to think of. There was the harvest to be prepared for, the household accounts to be seen to and the usual discreet business of collecting and passing on Royalist messages. Then, of course, there was the news from London.

Mercurius Aulicus had disappeared with the war but other papers had taken its place and Venetia paid a fat fee to a Smithfield carrier for the privilege of receiving John Dillingham's *Moderate Intelligencer*, Samuel Pecke's *Perfect Diurnall* and Marchamont Nedham's strongly Royalist, and therefore unlicensed, *Mercurius Pragmaticus* within a week of their publication. Normally she devoured these as soon as they arrived. At any other time, an account of Oliver Cromwell forcing the Commons to nullify all votes taken during the absence of the Independent members, or the news that his Majesty was demanding amnesty for every one of his supporters, might possibly have bred a spark of interest. Now, however, even the startling reasonableness of the *Heads of the Proposals* paled into insignificance beside her personal concerns . . . and the waiting began to seem interminable.

The worst thing was having no course of action open to her, being almost powerless to control her own destiny. The second worst thing was the continual, gentle nagging of her mother.

Lady Clifford never insisted or demanded or allowed her voice to grow shrill. She simply maintained a perpetual flow of plaintive remarks, wistful looks and melancholy sighs. And the effect, as Venetia well knew, was one of water dripping on a stone.

It had started immediately after the reading of the Will: qualified sympathy coupled with gentle criticism. Then came, 'Of course, it's a pity that you and Ellis weren't married years ago, dearest. But now, even if he were here, there's no denying that he's no longer quite the match he once was, is there?'

And finally, 'This dreadful Colonel holds us all in the palm of his hand, doesn't he? Do you think that – if you refuse to marry him – he has the power to evict us? Of course, I care nothing for myself. Though I can't help remembering all the happy years I've spent in this house since your father first brought me here as a bride . . . But there! Were it not for my girls, I'm sure I should be perfectly content in the meanest cottage.'

There was, as Venetia was well aware, only one aim in all this; that of delicately pressing her into the ultimate sacrifice. Marriage to a Roundhead bastard for the good of the family. And if Ashley Peverell didn't return soon with some good news, there was a growing possibility that she would actually have to do it.

There was pressure too – of different, unintentional kinds – from Elizabeth and Phoebe. Elizabeth merely wandered about looking lachrymose and Phoebe observed that, since Venetia couldn't marry Ellis and wouldn't marry the Colonel, she was likely to end her days a spinster. The only one who never said a word on the subject was Uncle James. But then, Uncle James could rarely be parted from his books long enough to say anything.

On the day before they were due to begin harvesting, Venetia donned her second-best habit and set off, as she did every Wednesday, on her routine trip into Knaresborough. It was, as always, market day and though this sometimes made it difficult for Venetia to get into town alone, the extra bustle was extremely useful for cloaking her activities once she was there.

Colourful booths selling everything from rushlights to canaries surrounded the Market Cross and lapped against the neat, irregularly-gabled shopfronts. Venetia left her horse in the stables of the Golden Anchor and then sauntered casually between the stalls, pausing every now and then to feign interest in the items on display. All around her was a hubbub of voices – some crying their wares, some indulging in cheerful barter and others merely gossiping; and the smells – cheese, leather, animal dung and human sweat, to name but a few – changed at every step. Venetia ignored them all and continued drifting systematically towards the seamstress's establishment opposite the Toll Booth.

The Widow Jessop, who ran a small haberdashery business from her front parlour, looked up from the tray of embroidery silks that she was showing to the corn-chandler's tediously indecisive wife and immediately went into action.

'Good day, Mistress Clifford. You'll have come for your fitting, of course – and I have everything ready. Mistress Horner – I'm sure you won't mind if I leave Polly to wait on you while you make up your mind?'

'Oh no,' came the huffy reply. 'Not at all.'

'Very good of you, I'm sure,' said the Widow with a small smile. 'And now, Mistress Clifford – if you'd like to step up to my workroom?'

They climbed the narrow staircase in silence and, not until the door was firmly closed behind them, did Venetia say quietly, 'Something's wrong, isn't it?'

'Yes.' Mary Jessop looked tensely back at her. 'I've a young man hidden in the cellar. He's been there two nights already and a party of soldiers were in town yesterday asking questions about a man of his description – so I need help to get him away before he's discovered.'

'Who is he?'

'I don't know. When somebody comes to me like this through the network – and thankfully it doesn't happen often – I make sure I never learn their names. It's safer that way, and if something goes wrong for them afterwards I'm not upset by hearing about it.'

In certain respects, it sounded eminently sensible; in

others, Venetia wasn't so sure. She said, 'So what *do* you know about him?'

'He put into Bridlington Bay two weeks ago carrying letters from France to various loyal gentlemen in York, Newark, Oxford and London. Unfortunately, he was recognised in York and had to make his way here cross-country as best he could.' The Widow paused and spread her hands in a gesture of helpless anxiety. 'You know how it is. I can count on my son, but I've two servants and that girl Polly in the house and I don't know how far I dare trust them.'

Venetia nodded.

'Very well. I'll see what can be done. But first, if you consider it safe, I think I'd better meet him.'

There was a moment's hesitation. Then, 'Very well. The cellar entrance lies beneath the floor of my storeroom – and since Joan's out doing the marketing and the scullery-maid's abed with the toothache, it should be safe enough, so long as you're reasonably quick. Just give me a moment to make sure Polly's busy in the shop and I'll take you down.'

Five minutes later, Venetia stood in the stockroom and watched as the Widow unlocked a small door in the corner. Then she was descending a narrow, stone stairway into the gloom below.

The fact that it was no conventional cellar but actually a cave, hollowed out of the massive cliff above the River Nidd on which both town and Castle were built, came as no surprise to Venetia. Many of the houses on the market-place were built above similar caverns – hewn from the rock centuries before by calloused hands and now simply converted into cellars. She had seen one before, many years ago when she and Ellis were children. And it was that recollection that brought the first glimmerings of an idea.

The glow of a lantern illuminated one corner and revealed a man sprawling, book in hand, upon a pallet. As Venetia rounded the stair, he jerked himself upright and she had an impression of long dark hair, a face that had not seen a razor for several days and crumpled dusty clothing. Then, in familiar, lightly-drawling tones, he said, 'My God! The delectable Venetia . . . or I'm hallucinating.'

'Perish the thought,' she said. And, on a shaken laugh, 'I don't believe it. *Francis?*'

'The very same.' Francis Langley came swiftly to his feet. 'Though, in my present sorry condition, it's scarcely flattering of you to identify me quite so easily.'

'Don't worry. It wasn't the outside I recognised,' she retorted. And moved across the uneven floor to give and receive an embrace.

Francis Langley was a friend from her Whitehall days; one of the stylish, poet-courtiers from that other, civilised life they had all lived before the war – who, like Lovelace and Davenant and the rest, had left his lace-trimmed elegance behind in order to fight for his King in the field. And he was right, she reflected sadly, as they sat down side by side on the lumpy pallet. There was nothing of the old Francis in this unkempt vagabond with the muddy boots; only the echo of sophistication in his occasionally theatrical manner and a slim volume of verse lying carelessly at his feet.

She said, 'I don't understand how you come to be here. Someone told me you'd been captured at Naseby and agreed to take service in France rather than rot in a Roundhead gaol.'

'I did.' A faintly crooked smile touched his mouth. 'But you couldn't honestly expect me to continue expending my energy on foreign fields when there is unfinished business here at home – now could you?'

The violet gaze widened.

'You're saying you deserted? From the French army?'

'Quite. But there's always the Netherlands or Italy if I need to flee abroad again,' he responded negligently. 'As far as I'm aware, I haven't committed any cardinal sin in either of those places. Not that flight has any part in my plans. Despite recent misfortunes, you'd be quite surprised at the new skills I've acquired.'

'Yes,' said Venetia tartly. 'I daresay I would. But that still doesn't explain how someone could conceivably have thought you a suitable choice for the sort of mission you appear to have been entrusted with.'

Francis Langley's sapphire eyes achieved an expression of utter innocence. 'And what mission is that, dear heart?'

She subjected him to a long, critical regard and then laughed. 'Not bad. Not bad at all. But you don't have to waste your talents on me, you know.'

'I don't? How very disappointing.'

'No, it isn't. It ought to cheer you up no end,' she remarked, not without a certain degree of satisfaction. 'I don't know why you think Widow Jessop let me in here. But rather than put you to the trouble of asking, I think it's high time I informed you that I'm the one with the inestimable honour of arranging the next leg of your journey.'

Captain Langley's brows rose a little but he evinced no signs of alarm and merely observed that he could think of no one in whose hands he would rather place himself.

'I'm glad to hear it. And I rather think our first step ought to be to remove you from here to a house on the other side of the square. Tonight, if possible,'

Francis abandoned court-gallantry in favour of a more business-like tone. 'Why?'

'Because it's not Mistress Jessop's function to provide sanctuary for more than a night or two – and if you're found here, she'll be in as much trouble as you. There are already soldiers out looking for you.'

'So I believe. And this other house will be safer?'

'It certainly should be.' Venetia thoughtfully traced an outline on the floor with the toe of her shoe. 'Also, if this goes where I think it does, we can transfer you there without you even having to step outside.'

For a moment, Francis stared blankly down at her feet and then he met her eyes with an expression of awed fascination. 'My dear girl – can you be talking about *tunnels*?'

'What else?' She smiled at him. 'Several houses on the market-place have connecting cellars, you know; and there are at least two underground sallyports from the Castle – which were very useful when Cromwell had it under siege back in '44. But all that's beside the point. First I have to make sure that Sophy's house is empty – and then the Widow's son will have to do a little discreet house-breaking to unbar the trap for you.'

The Captain's gaze held traces of faint hilarity.

'And who, may one ask, is Sophy?'

'Sophia Brandon – Ellis's aunt,' replied Venetia tersely. And then, as if no longer able to help herself, 'I expect it's a silly question, but you don't happen to have seen Ellis at all?'

'I'm afraid not. Why? Are you worried about him?'

'In a manner of speaking,' Venetia began – before breaking off as the Widow's voice drifted anxiously down from the top of the stairs, asking her to hurry. Knowing better than to ignore the warning, Venetia rose from the pallet and shook out the dark blue folds of her skirt. 'I'll have to go. If someone sees me emerging from the stockroom, it's going to take a bit of explaining – beside which, there's a good deal to be done if we're to get you out of here tonight. And there'll be other chances to talk, I'm sure.'

'Of course,' agreed Francis. 'But, just in case there aren't, may I ask if you've heard anything of Kate?'

Venetia's face stiffened. 'Kate?'

'Kate Maxwell.'

There was a short, chilly silence. Then, 'Nothing that I imagine you will be glad to hear,' she said forbiddingly. 'I believe that she was at Basing House when it fell – along, it seems, with her husband, Luciano del Santi.'

Francis drew a sharp, faintly rasping breath and, beneath the stubble, his face lost some of its colour.

'Christ,' he said quietly but with a rarely-heard ring of feeling. 'They sacked Basing and then burned it to the ground. Did she – do you know if she survived it?'

'No,' she said, 'I don't. And after the way she treated Kit, you can't really wonder that I've never troubled to find out.'

Upstairs in the parlour with the Widow Jessop, Venetia dealt with the problems of Captain Langley's immediate future efficiently enough. Mistress Brandon's house, said the Widow, had been empty for a year or more – ever since the retired cleric to whom Sir Robert had let it had died the previous Spring. As for breaking in to it, well, it wasn't what she liked to ask of him, but doubtless her son, Matthew, would be able to accomplish the task without anyone being the wiser. Then, if Mistress Clifford wished it, the anonymous gentleman downstairs could be transferred through the cellar tunnel with as much food, wine and other comforts as he and Matthew could carry.

Mistress Clifford agreed that this was precisely what she wished and promised to take care of the gentleman herself once the transfer had been completed. Then, collecting her mare from the inn, she rode home in a dark mood that – just for once – had nothing to do with Colonel Brandon.

What she had said to Francis during those last moments in the cellar had been true. She hadn't made any attempt to discover if Kate Maxwell was still alive because thinking of Kate conjured up images better left undisturbed. For Kate had not only been her own friend, but also Kit's affianced wife. Until, that was, he had found her nestling in the arms of an Italian goldsmith, and had gone back to the war filled with the new, wild recklessness that had killed him.

Venetia gave herself a mental shake. Such thoughts did no good and she had more pressing concerns – such as how, at the exact time they were due to start harvesting, she was going to get Francis Langley safely away from Knaresborough without her movements arousing suspicion in the bosom of her family. If they knew what she was about, her mother and Elizabeth would be aghast; less at the risk she herself was running than the one facing the family as a whole if she were caught. And as for Phoebe . . . well, Phoebe was still young enough to want to join in just for the fun of it. Concealment, therefore, had always been a prime consideration, and, in the past, had not proved especially difficult. But then, she hadn't previously had to do much more than pass a few messages to and fro. She certainly hadn't held a man's life in her hands. And, for this reason if for no other, Venetia was perfectly well aware that she needed help.

There was, fortunately, someone she could turn to. Sym Potter had been Kit's groom and faithful shadow and was thus entirely to be trusted. He was also in charge of Ford Edge's stables, and when one had, somehow, to provide Francis Langley with a horse, this fact was likely to be more useful than anything else.

Venetia rode slowly into the stableyard and allowed Sym to help her from the saddle. Then, making sure they could not be overheard, she began telling him what she wanted.

The following morning dawned overcast but dry and the harvesting began with a will. Knowing that every pair of hands counted, Venetia and Phoebe donned their oldest gowns and set off to lend their aid with the lighter tasks. Phoebe, of course, was bubbling with her usual enthusiasm; Venetia was only there because she considered it her duty – and knew that neither Mother nor Elizabeth were likely to show their faces until they could be gracious and charming at the harvest supper.

It was a long day and, by the end of it, Venetia's hands were covered in scratches, her nails chipped and ragged and her back stiff as a board – all of which made it difficult to look forward to repeating the whole process on the morrow. Phoebe, on the other hand, went off to bed with a song on her lips and an offer to wake Venetia at five. Venetia thanked her politely and reflected that there were times when Phoebe's unflagging cheerfulness made one want to strangle her.

The next day seemed even longer. Venetia gritted her teeth, dispatched Sym Potter, via the Widow Jessop, to take Francis a suit of Kit's clothes and laboured grimly on. Heaps of neatly-bound sheaves started to rise in the fields and Sym returned with the message that the Captain was tired of lurking in the heather and eager to be off. Venetia gave him a series of hurried instructions, set a date for the following night and then tumbled wearily into bed, wondering how she would find the energy to carry these plans through after another day like the last two.

As it turned out, the following morning brought other worries entirely. Venetia awoke in the ghostly pre-dawn light to find Phoebe leaning over her – for once, without the vestige of a smile; and when she allowed herself to be dragged to the window, it was perfectly clear why. Rain was lashing down like grapeshot.

'It will all be ruined,' said Phoebe miserably. 'What are we going to do?'

'I don't know.' Venetia turned away from the window, a lead weight growing in her chest. 'We could try bringing in what's already been cut, but if we can't dry it, it will go on growing in the barn. And as for the rest – it's quite likely that this rain and wind will flatten it. Until the weather improves again, we won't know.'

'But what can we do in the meantime?' asked Phoebe, unable to accept defeat. 'There must be something!'

'There is,' came the flat reply. 'Pray!'

The deluge continued all day, thundering down on the roof of the house and beating against the windows. Sick with rage and anxiety, Venetia shut herself off from the rest of the household and tried to work out whether or not she could pay the next quarter's taxes. It wasn't a particularly pleasant task, but it was better than having to put up with her mother's unending flow of uninformed advice and remarks which all began with the words 'If only . . .'

By the time the rain finally eased off, Venetia was fairly and depressingly sure that there would be little left in the fields worth saving, but that this wasn't the time to think about it. Whether she liked it or not, her first responsibility tonight was to Francis Langley.

She waited until just before eleven, when it was fully dark and the house asleep, then slipped quietly out to the spinney where Mr Potter was ready with three horses. An hour later, she was gliding wraithlike through the back door of the house on the market-place.

Francis was waiting for her in the narrow passageway, shaved, dressed and looking rather more like his old self than when she had seen him last. His tone, however, had not varied by so much as a hairsbreadth.

'Don't think I'm ungrateful, beloved . . . but I shall be extremely glad to move on. That tunnel of yours was full of rats, spiders and God knows what else, and though in years to come my passage through it will doubtless make amusing telling, just now I'm barely past shuddering. Also, I'm exceedingly tired of groping about here by the light of one paltry candle and living off cheese and cold pies.'

'I daresay you are, but it's better than prison,' responded Venetia bracingly. 'And you'll get more substantial fare at your next billet. Meg Shaw keeps a good table, I believe.'

'I rejoice to hear it. Are we going now?'

'In a moment. Sym's meeting us at the bottom of Briggate with the horses, so we've only to get that far unnoticed. But first I wanted to ask you about these letters you're carrying. Can you tell me who they're for and what they're supposed to achieve?'

'Under the circumstances, it would be rather churlish of me not to, wouldn't it?' he shrugged. And went on to list some half-dozen prominent Royalists whose homes lay as far apart as Newark and Kent. Then he said, 'And as for their purpose, her Majesty is on the same road she trod five years ago, busily distinguishing between those she can rely on and those she can't. The only trouble is that, between composition fines and fear for their families, even the most well-intentioned of gentlemen are unlikely to be in a position to offer anything very positive in the way of aid.' He paused and then said, 'Is the King still at Oatlands?'

'No. After cutting the City Presbyterians down to size, the Army moved its Headquarters to Putney and installed his Majesty at Hampton Court,' replied Venetia acidly. 'I gather that Cromwell is still trying to persuade him to sanction the *Heads of the Proposals* while the Parliament is simultaneously offering a rehashed version of the same scheme they put forward eight months ago at Newcastle. Ah yes – and there is a rumour that his Majesty is also entertaining the Scots, which, if it's true, means that he now has a third string to his bow.'

A faint frown entered the dark blue eyes.

'And you consider that a good thing?'

'Don't you?'

'Not necessarily. The more options the King feels he has, the more he's inclined to vacillate. That, in my opinion, is what lost us the war.'

'But if he can obtain concessions by pitting one faction against the other—'

'*If* he can,' said Francis. 'But do you honestly think they'll go on letting him? And, that being so, it seems to me he'd be better off settling for the suitor offering the best terms. In short, the one willing and able to put the crown back on his head.'

Venetia surveyed him coolly.

'You've changed your tune, haven't you? I don't recall you being quite so ready to compromise five years ago.'

71

'No. But defeat soon teaches you that it's better to save something than lose all. And I,' he finished blandly, 'am now a realist of epic proportions. Shall we go?'

Outside the night was black as sin. Cautioning Francis to remain silent and keeping close to the wall, Venetia led the way out of the market-place and into Castlegate. Lights still showed at the windows of the Green Dragon and an inebriate chorus of 'Cuckolds All In A Row' drifted raggedly into the street from the open doorway. Venetia quickened her pace and nearly lost her presence of mind along with her balance when a cat shot, yowling, under her feet.

'Very good,' murmured Captain Langley in her ear. 'Given the circumstances, most women would have screamed.'

'Not to mention quite a few men,' she hissed back. 'Come on – before someone sees us.'

The brooding bulk of the Castle's east gate loomed to their right and Francis peered curiously up at it. Then, since it was too dark to see very much, he turned his back on it and dutifully followed Venetia. They rounded the corner into Gracious Street and descended the hill to the point where the road traversed the town ditch; there Venetia swung off to the right and came to an abrupt stop.

Francis cannoned unwarily into the back of her and opened his mouth to apologise. A vicious jab from her elbow changed his mind and a horse whinnied from somewhere near at hand.

'Sym?' whispered Venetia.

'Here, Mistress.' The groom's face rose up, a faint pale blur in the blackness. 'We'll need to think on, though. There's soldiers on bridge.'

She drew a sharp breath. 'How many?'

'Hard to say. I've only seen three but like as not there'll be others in t'ale-house.'

'Damn!' Venetia thought fast and then said, 'All right. We'll have to bluff our way through. Fetch me that flask of brandy we packed in the Captain's saddlebag, will you?'

'Brandy?' inquired Francis hopefully.

'Yes. We don't want them to get a good look at you, so it will be best if you're drunk.'

'Willingly, my loved one.' Laughter rippled through his voice. 'I'll even sing, if you like.'

'"Cuckolds All In A Row"? I think not. In fact,' said Venetia, taking the flask from Sym and anointing Francis with its contents, 'I'd feel better if you were unconscious.'

'Then you'll have to bob me on the noll, dear heart.'

'Don't be too sure I won't!'

Five minutes later, after a hurried consultation, they rode slowly down to the bridge over the Nidd and its three burly guardians. With Venetia bringing up the rear and Sym beside him holding his reins, Francis lay slumped over his horse's neck, alternately warbling and detonating into its mane.

> *Hail good fellow, I drink to thee*
> *Pardonay* Hic! *je vooz ompree;*
> *To all good fellows wherever they* Hic!
> *With never a penny of money.*

'No – and never likely to have so long as there's brandy to be had,' scolded Venetia shrilly with more than a trace of local accent. 'But I'll put a stop to your little games, my lad. It's written that the way of transgressors shall be hard. And if the Lord won't see to it, I'll do it myself!'

'Halt!' One of the troopers moved forward with a lantern while his colleagues levelled their muskets. 'Stand and identify yourselves.'

Sym cast an apparently nervous glance at Venetia and then said woodenly, 'Nathaniel Benson and his lady-wife returning to Wetherby with their servant.'

'At this hour?' The tone was suspicious. 'How come?'

'Because my husband's been in this den of iniquity too long already!' Her hood pulled tight around her face so that not a vestige of hair showed, Venetia rode into the light and gestured scathingly to Francis. 'Look at state of him! He should've been home from York three days since – not loitering here, squandering money on horrible vices while his business goes to the dogs.'

The soldier scratched his head and thought about it. 'Ah. Been on a bit of a binge, has he?'

'No. Steeping himself in wickedness and vile corruption –

that's what *he's* been doing. Those who aren't strong in Lord are prey to devil's lures. And no matter how hard I try to put fear of God into him, he's still weak as water.'

As long as you've got any ink in your pen
With never a penny of money, sang Francis.

'Be quiet, you drunken sot!' Reaching out, Venetia cuffed him hard about the head. 'You stay away wi'out so much as a word, so I have to leave our children and come looking for you – and what do I find? You're not just sodden with drink – as if that wasn't bad enough – oh no! You're cavorting shamelessly with lewd, half-naked women. Whores of Babylon! And I'd just like to know how much of our hard-earned brass *that* cost?'

Francis made an oddly strangled sound and began to slide gently from the saddle while Venetia continued to rant. Grinning, one of the troopers laid down his musket and obligingly helped Sym to heave him upright, murmuring, 'Do this often, does he?'

'Often enough,' muttered Sym. And, with a jerk of his head, 'She drives him to it, nagging bitch.'

'What's that?' snapped Venetia.

'I was just saying you've a heavy cross to bear, Mistress,' offered the trooper, stepping back and eyeing her with a sort of cautious admiration. 'But it'll do you no good talking to the gentleman now. I reckon he's a bit too far gone to hear you.'

'Very likely,' she agreed darkly. 'But he'll be sober soon enough – and sorry too, if I have anything to do wi' it. Now . . . are you going to let us pass – or have you nowt better to do than annoy honest folk?'

'Just doing our duty, Mistress.' The fellow with the lantern stepped back and gestured to his comrades to do the same. 'There's Malignant fugitives abroad hereabouts.'

'Then you'd best get back to looking for them, hadn't you?' sniffed Venetia. And, setting her horse in motion, led her little party away across the bridge to the open road beyond.

They rode up the hill, round the bend and down again in a

silence broken only by a series of gentle hiccups. Then, when Sym pulled up at a point where a track led off to their right through the forest, Francis finally sat up and gave way to the mirth which had been consuming him.

'S-such talent, my loved one. I don't know which was better . . . the script or the performance.'

The moon peered fitfully from behind a cloud, giving Venetia a glimpse of a bright, laughter-flushed face.

'I'm glad you enjoyed it.'

'Didn't you?'

'Of course. But I'm afraid we haven't time to dwell on it because this is where I must leave you. Sym will guide you from here.'

The amusement evaporated instantly.

'While you ride home alone in the dark? I think not.'

'Then you'd better revise your ideas,' she responded coolly. 'For reasons you may possibly be able to work out, I need to be home before dawn, and if I come with you I won't be. Also, without Sym you'll have to take the main roads, and I don't want to have gone through all this for nothing. Consequently, I am riding back alone and you are following Sym to Wetherby. And that is final.'

Francis eyed her thoughtfully. Even plainly dressed and white with fatigue, she was as beautiful as ever; but he was beginning to realise that, in other ways, she had changed dramatically. He said slowly, 'Venetia, what's wrong?'

A bright, brittle smile invested her face. It was the first time, he realised, that she had smiled at all.

'Everything,' she said. 'Absolutely everything. But since there's nothing either you or anyone else can do to help, you'll have to forgive me if I don't elaborate. And besides, it will give you and Sym something to talk about on your ride, won't it?' The quality of her smile altered fractionally. 'Good luck, Francis – and God keep you.'

And without waiting for his reply, she turned her horse's head towards the forest and set off on the lonely ride home.

Five

Though not quite as bad as she had feared, the results of the harvest were poor enough to give Venetia a number of sleepless nights. And the discovery that the country as a whole had fared little better was no comfort. There was, moreover, still no word from either Harry or Ellis – or even Ashley Peverell; and by the middle of September, with Lady Clifford becoming daily more fractious and Elizabeth impersonating an Early Christian Martyr, Venetia could feel herself slowly sinking beneath the weight of her responsibilities.

For a long time she tried hard to keep her feelings to herself – mainly because she did not expect airing them to do much good. But then, on the evening of a day when little had gone quite right, Lady Clifford unwisely piled on the last straw.

'I've been thinking that we might perhaps ask Lawyer Crisp to call,' she said, setting a stitch in the piece of embroidery which she picked up each evening but somehow never succeeded in finishing. 'After all, it is two months since the Will was read and he may now have more information for us.'

Venetia looked up from her ledgers and kept her gaze carefully blank. 'About what, exactly?'

'Well, about Colonel Brandon's intentions.'

The music that Elizabeth and Phoebe had been making on lute and virginals trickled to a stop and there was a brief, telling silence. Venetia laid down her quill. 'Yes. I daresay he may. But I wasn't aware that you were particularly interested in whether the Colonel plans to resign from the Army and settle at Brandon Lacey.'

'Don't be difficult, dearest.' Lady Clifford set another

stitch and gave a plaintive smile. 'I was referring to the Colonel's intentions with regard to yourself.'

'Ah . . . I see. You're thinking that, if he's decided to honour me with a proposal of marriage, he may have communicated the fact to Mr Crisp.'

'Well, one can't help wondering.'

'No, Mother.' Venetia came rather abruptly to her feet. '*You* can't help wondering. I, on the other hand, would rather not think of it until I absolutely have to – and that, thank God, is not yet.'

'But the uncertainty! Surely—'

'You think I like it any better than you? I don't. I just find it preferable to betrothing myself to that man.' She drew a deep, unsteady breath. 'Have you any idea at all what it is you're asking of me?'

'My dear child!' Her ladyship's face became a picture of hurt affront. 'I have taken the greatest care not to ask *anything* of you.'

'No. But you've dropped enough hints!' returned Venetia bitterly. 'So why not come straight out and say what you mean for once? For the sake of everyone's future security and to preserve both Harry's inheritance and Elizabeth's betrothal, you want me to forget Ellis and marry a man who, until eight short weeks ago, you wouldn't have allowed through the front door. Isn't that so?'

'Not at all!' Some of Lady Clifford's wistful sweetness deserted her and the tambour-frame fell unheeded into her lap. 'I simply want what's best for you.'

'And an illegitimate rebel soldier will be better for me than the loyal, well-born gentleman I've been betrothed to for five years?'

'No. Yes. Oh – how you do *twist* things!'

'You can think of another way of putting it?' asked Venetia sardonically. And then, 'But of course you can. It's the land that matters, isn't it? And, so long as we get it back, you wouldn't care if Gabriel Brandon had two heads.'

'But he hasn't,' muttered Phoebe. 'And at least he's likely to be physically present.'

Venetia swung round to face her.

'That is a singularly stupid remark!'

78

'No it isn't. If Ellis had come home after the war, you'd be married by now and none of this would have happened. So it seems to me that Sir Robert may have had a fair point in doing what he did.'

This time the silence crackled with tension.

'I see,' remarked Venetia. The smouldering gaze travelled to Elizabeth. 'And what do you think?'

Elizabeth quailed visibly.

'You – you *know* what I think. I c-can't bear you to be made so unhappy and I wish with all my heart that you could marry Ellis.'

'Even if it means kissing goodbye to Tom Knightley?'

The soft blue eyes filled with swift, easy tears and it was left to Phoebe to say flatly, 'That's not fair and you know it.'

'*Not fair?*' echoed Venetia gratingly. 'My God! Is it fair that I'm being asked to sacrifice myself for the common good? Or don't I count?'

'Dearest, of course you do!' said Lady Clifford soothingly. 'It's just that, if Harry won't come back and take the Oath, there doesn't seem to be any other alternative. Unless you want to be left a mere tenant in your own home.'

'Instead of which,' responded Venetia acidly, 'I can be irrevocably tied to a complete stranger whose beliefs I utterly despise, share his bed and board, minister to his wants and bear his children. A delightful prospect, isn't it?' Her glance swept mockingly over them all. 'What, nothing to say? Not even that I'm making too much of it and that it won't be nearly as bad as I think? Dear me! Can I have made an impression at last?'

'What are you saying?' asked her mother, at length. 'That you won't even consider it?'

'No. I'm saying that I'm not prepared to make any promises. And that I'd be grateful if, just for once, you could all make some small attempt to see this from my point of view. Upon which calm and entirely reasonable note,' finished Venetia coolly, 'I'll bid you good night.'

On the following morning, Venetia decided to ride to Brandon Lacey. This was not purely in order to escape her family. She was also guiltily conscious of not having visited

Sophia since she had briefly called to inspect Trixie's new pups. These, unfortunately, had proved to be lamentably cross-bred bundles of multi-coloured fur that bore little resemblance to their elegant mother. Venetia, who'd had her heart set on a wolfhound, had refused to take one. Now, however, it occurred to her that since the last of the aged spaniels had gone to its rest Ford Edge seemed somehow bereft . . . and Phoebe would enjoy having a pup even if it *didn't* grow into anything anyone could recognise.

All these were perfectly valid reasons for going to Brandon Lacey and, deep down at the back of her mind, Venetia had an even better one. She had refused point-blank to see Lawyer Crisp, but she was not averse to making a few private inquiries of her own, and, in certain respects, Sophia was the best place to start. At any rate, there was no harm in trying.

Venetia found Mistress Brandon in that portion of the stable-block where the animals were kept when she remembered to stop them following her into the house. Three ferrets occupied a large cage in one corner and an indeterminate number of rabbits resided in another. A red squirrel shared a beam with an injured jackdaw and, below them, five long-legged Jacob's-coat puppies gambolled around Sophia and the understandably ruffled tabby cat in her arms.

'Why – Venetia, dear,' said Sophia vaguely but with genuine pleasure. 'How nice. Have you come to see how the pups are doing?'

'In a manner of speaking, yes.' Venetia kissed the older woman's cheek and smiled at her. 'I really came to see you. But I've also decided that – if your offer is still open – I'd like to change my mind and take one of Trixie's offspring after all.'

'But of course.' Sophia beamed. 'Pick whichever one you like. They may not be precisely beautiful but they have very affectionate natures.'

This was so like Sophy that Venetia could not help laughing, and twenty minutes later she was sitting in the winter parlour with a bright-eyed little dog on her knee, wondering what had possessed her. The brown and black markings on its face gave it a lopsided appearance which was intensified by the fact that one ear was up and the other down; it had a pointed nose, four worryingly large paws and a tail like a brush. Venetia grinned at it and let it lick her chin. Mother was going to have a fit.

Sophia placed a glass of raspberry cordial on the table at Venetia's elbow and drifted into a chair on the other side of the empty hearth.

'What will you call him?' she asked.

Gypsy, thought Venetia immediately. But a remnant of sense remained and she said carelessly, 'I've no idea. Phoebe can decide.' She paused for a moment to sip her cordial and consider how best to approach the subject she had really come to discuss. Then, deciding that subtlety was a waste of time with someone as perpetually abstracted as Sophia was, she said, 'Have you heard anything from Colonel Brandon?'

'Colonel . . . ? Oh, Gabriel. No. Should I have done?'

'Probably not. I just thought that, if he was planning to move in here, he might have advised you of the fact.'

'Ah,' said Sophia. 'Yes. I suppose so.'

Venetia sighed and tried again.

'Sophy . . . what do you know about him? It's not that I'm being vulgarly curious. I just think that, under the circumstances, I've a right to know. And I can't very well ask Lawyer Crisp or the Colonel himself, can I?'

'No, dear. I suppose not.' Sophia tugged ineffectively at the fringed silk shawl that was threatening to slide off her shoulders. 'I'm just not sure how far I can help you. I really don't know very much at all.'

'Then let's start at the beginning. You said you met him when he was five. Was that the first you knew of his existence?'

'Yes. As far as I recall, it was the year before Ellis was born. Margaret was eager to see me married, so she and Robert took me to London to find a husband.' A faint, mischievous smile touched the plump face. 'As you can see, nothing came of it.'

'But while you were there, Robert presented his – his baseborn son to you,' persisted Venetia, absently allowing the puppy to chew the finger of her riding glove. 'How did that come about?'

'He just took me to visit him one morning, while Margaret was out shopping.'

'Where?'

'Where? I'm not sure. The Exchange, I suppose.'

Venetia had to put a severe curb on her impatience.

'No, Sophy. I meant – where did you visit Robert's son?'

'Oh. At an armourer's house in Shoreditch. Their name was Morton or Morris or some such.'

'And that's where the Colonel was brought up?'

'As far as I know. He seemed very happy and I remember thinking what a nice little boy he was.'

'You'll have noticed a difference in him then,' muttered Venetia. And aloud, 'No doubt his mother was there too. The armourer's daughter, perhaps?'

'Oh no. I don't think so. In fact, I don't recall him having a daughter. Just two boys a little older than Gabriel. No, dear. I think they were a sort of foster-family. Robert was probably paying them.'

'I see.' Venetia thought about it. 'In which case, who *was* his mother?'

'Presumably some unfortunate girl who couldn't look after him herself.'

'Yes. I can imagine. A dairymaid or laundress or yeoman's daughter.'

Sophia shrugged slightly. 'I'm afraid that's something you'll have to ask Gabriel himself.'

Venetia stared moodily into her glass.

'I'm hoping that won't be necessary. To be frank, I shan't care *who* his mother was so long as I don't have to marry him.' She looked up. 'And I imagine that you can't exactly be relishing the prospect of seeing him become master of Brandon Lacey either.'

The myopic gaze seemed to focus slightly. 'Why not?'

Venetia choked on her wine.

'*Why not?* Because of Ellis, of course!'

'Ah, yes. Ellis.' There was a short meditative pause. 'But then, you know, I doubt Ellis would ever have settled to country life. He's a charming young man, but not one to apply himself to anything for very long. Too fond of excitement, perhaps.'

'What are you saying?' asked Venetia stiffly.

'Only that it's possible that Robert knew what he was doing,' came the placid reply. 'And that we ought, therefore, to give Gabriel the benefit of the doubt.'

'Including me?'

'Well yes, dear. In view of the circumstances – particularly you,' said Sophia.

Venetia rode home with Gypsy in her lap and a dark tide of foreboding in her heart. As she had expected, her mother pronounced the puppy totally unsuited to a gentleman's establishment and ordered it to be kept out of the parlour. Phoebe, on the other hand, loved it.

While Venetia waited for a message from France, Charles Stuart was busy tying another knot in the affairs of the nation. He persuaded Cromwell and Ireton to support his desire for a personal treaty with the Parliament by telling them that he much preferred their *Heads of the Proposals* to the old Newcastle Propositions; and then he told the Scots that if they would declare in his favour, he'd soon stem the rising power of the Independents.

The first ploy worked best, for, when those Independent members wanting to see the monarchy abolished proposed that no further negotiations be carried on with his Majesty, Cromwell personally saw to it that the motion was defeated. But its ramifications did not end there. Amongst the ranks of the Army (still unpaid despite Fairfax's attempts to raise £50,000 from the City) was born a suspicion that the Lieutenant-General's goodwill towards the King boded less well for the Army than it did for the Lieutenant-General himself. And, coinciding as this did with Parliament's rejection of the *Heads of the Proposals* and John Lilburne's cries that Cromwell was actually prepared to let him rot in the Tower rather than help him to get out of it, the Lieutenant-General immediately found himself less than popular.

Amidst the resulting deluge of hostile news-sheets and pamphlets, two other events slid by with scarcely a ripple. The Presbyterian Lord Mayor of London was impeached for raising forces against the Army and quickly replaced by an Independent; and the Commons passed an ordinance forbidding any Royalist to hold municipal office or vote in elections.

September moved inexorably towards October and Venetia began to wonder if the remaining three months were any more likely to provide a solution than the last three had done. Then, just when she had almost given up expecting it, Ashley Peverell came back and frightened her silly.

It wasn't his reappearance that paralysed her nervous system. It was the manner of it. She returned one afternoon, from visiting a tenant whose child was sick, to find the Captain comfortably ensconced in the parlour with her mother and sisters.

It was fortunate that, just for a moment, she was too shocked to speak for it gave him a chance to hand her her cue.

'Ah,' he said, rising easily to his feet and executing an unnecessarily extravagant bow. 'Mistress Clifford, I presume? I was hoping I might have the pleasure of meeting you, and now, of course, I can only bless my good fortune.' The audacious grey-green gaze swung back to Lady Clifford. 'But I forget my manners, Madam, and must crave your forgiveness. My only excuse is that being faced with four such exquisite ladies has made me a trifle light-headed.'

It was exactly the kind of gallant flummery that her ladyship liked and, smiling benevolently, she said, 'I fear you flatter us, sir. But allow me to present you to my eldest daughter. Venetia, dear, this is Mr Peverell. He is a friend of Harry's, newly-arrived from France.'

Venetia, who was no mean conspirator, achieved an expression of surprised pleasure. 'Oh? And have you seen my brother recently, sir?'

'Less than two weeks ago. In fact – as I was just on the point of telling your lady mother – he entrusted me with a letter to you all.' He pulled a sealed packet from his pocket and handed it to Lady Clifford. 'I gather it contains news of some urgency. Since I'm sure you'll wish to read it in private, I'll relieve you of my presence.'

Her ladyship blinked and Phoebe, unwilling to lose the fair-haired stranger so quickly, said, 'There's no need for that. And, after your kindness in calling on us, I'm sure we'd all be very pleased if you would stay for supper.'

Ashley Peverell gave her a smile of dazzling charm.

'I only wish I could, for there's nothing I'd like better. Unfortunately, however, I'm already overdue for an appointment in York and so I'm afraid I have no choice but to leave immediately.'

Lady Clifford rose and extended her hand.

'Then we will not detain you, Mr Peverell. But if you are ever passing Knaresborough again, I hope you will find the time to call.'

He kissed her fingers and bowed to each of her daughters in turn. 'Nothing,' he vowed, 'shall prevent me.' And he lifted one impudent eyebrow at Venetia.

Allowing none of her very natural feelings to show in her face, Venetia followed the only sensible course and offered to show him out. Then, when they were safely out of earshot, she said in a furious undervoice, 'Have you completely lost your mind? After all your lectures on taking every precaution, what on earth possessed you to come here so openly?'

He grinned. 'Scared you, did I?'

'You nearly gave me an apoplexy!'

'Yes. I thought I might. But it wasn't so much of a risk, you know. I'll take care that your family never clap eyes on me again – even though it's something of a sacrifice. Why didn't you ever tell me what a beauty your sister Elizabeth is?'

'Because she's betrothed,' snapped Venetia. And then, drawing a steadying breath, 'That letter from Harry: since you've seen him, you presumably know what he says. Is he coming back?'

He had hoped she wouldn't ask. 'No.'

Venetia's insides turned very cold. No. A monosyllabic death-knell. The breath snared in her throat and she said, raggedly, 'Not ever?'

'I doubt it,' replied the Captain uncomfortably. 'Look, as far as I know, he's explained everything in his letter so I think you should just read it for yourself. Besides, we don't have much time.'

They had just entered the stableyard where his horse stood waiting and Venetia regarded him stonily. 'I see.

Then, if there's more, you'd best tell me quickly.'

Something darkened the normally carefree expression and Ashley Peverell said baldly, 'I found Ellis, too.'

'And?'

'And when he'd read your letter, he got remarkably drunk. Then, after he'd sobered up, he became rather more philosophical and said that the bastard was welcome to enjoy Brandon Lacey while he could because he won't hold it long once the King occupies his rightful place again.'

'I hope he's right,' said Venetia remotely. 'But, while we wait for that to happen, is Ellis coming home?'

It was the moment Ashley had dreaded and he had to force himself to look Venetia squarely in the eye to preserve himself from any suspicion of subterfuge. It really wasn't his fault if the majority of Ellis bloody Brandon's reasons for staying in France weren't fit for the ears of Ellis bloody Brandon's affianced wife.

'No,' he said, at length. 'He isn't. He said that his presence here won't solve anything and that, if there was a way to foil his father's wishes, he was sure you'd find it.'

'Did he?' Her skin was perfectly bloodless. 'I'm flattered. Is that all?'

'Except that this would be a – a particularly bad moment for him to leave France, yes,' he replied neutrally. 'He intended to write you a letter. But when I went back next morning to collect it, he appeared to have rushed off on some mission or other and no one knew when to expect him back.' He paused and then said awkwardly, 'I'm really sorry. It's not what you were hoping for, is it?'

'No. No, it isn't.' The violet eyes met his with carefully detached composure. 'But that's not your fault, And at least you tried.'

Back in the parlour were three bewildered and tearful faces. They hadn't waited for her before reading the letter. Harry, it appeared, had taken great pains to explain that he was unlikely ever to return to Ford Edge except secretly, as a visitor, and for a very good reason. He had made his conversion to Catholicism and was even now studying to become a Jesuit priest.

Venetia accepted the annihilation of all her hopes with the same glacial control she had shown Ashley Peverell. Then, when the anxious incoherence of her mother and sisters finally dwindled into silence, she did the only thing left to her. She promised to go and see Lawyer Crisp.

Isaiah Crisp received Mistress Clifford in his rather cramped Finkle Street office with a marked degree of reserve which still didn't prevent him from remarking that it might have been more suitable for him to have called on her at home.

'I daresay. But at Ford Edge I wouldn't have been able to talk to you in private.' She met his eyes with a complete absence of expression. 'This isn't easy for me.'

The lawyer seated himself behind his desk and surveyed her warily over his latticed fingers. 'We are talking, I take it, about the situation created by Sir Robert's Will?'

'What else?' She was silent for a moment and then, with an effort that could be seen, said clinically, 'I have received word from my brother and, for reasons into which we needn't go, he has decided he can't possibly return to England at this time. Or quite possibly ever.'

'I see.' The dry lips pursed thoughtfully. 'That is somewhat unfortunate.'

'Quite.'

'Have you thought what you will do?'

'I've thought of little else. But unless Colonel Brandon is obliging enough to drop dead between now and Christmas, I don't seem to have too many alternatives. And that, of course, brings me to what I wanted to ask you. Has he been in touch with you at all?'

Mr Crisp strove to disregard what he personally considered to be Mistress Clifford's ungenteel turn of phrase and merely said. 'No. He has not.'

'Oh.' She swallowed and kept her hands clasped tightly together. 'So you've no idea what his intentions are with regard to – to myself?'

'None.' The girl's imperfectly veiled discomfiture repaid Isaiah in some small part for the way she had spoken to him at the Will-reading.

'But I should have thought that – on such a delicate matter – the Colonel would naturally be courteous enough to inform you of his decision first-hand.'

'If the Colonel was a gentleman, I'd agree with you. Since he undoubtedly isn't, I suspect it will not cross his mind,' remarked Venetia. And then, 'He doesn't seem very eager to claim his windfall, does he? But perhaps that's because I'm tied up with it.'

Mr Crisp thought that this was all too likely. Venetia Clifford was an undeniably beautiful woman, but no one's idea of a comfortable wife. He said tactfully, 'Doubtless he has affairs of his own to wind up.'

'Yes. I can imagine what sort, too. But since we're all aware that resigning from the Army is unlikely to be his problem – and men of his sort don't commonly let their mistresses stand in their way – I can't quite see why he's so slow to take possession of his fortune.'

'Fortune?' echoed the lawyer. And then, 'Ah.'

'What's wrong? Have I offended your sense of decorum again? Or no.' The amethyst gaze sharpened. 'It's something else, isn't it? Something you're not telling me.'

Looking faintly stricken, Mr Crisp tried to retrieve his error. 'You are mistaken.'

'I think not.' For a long, unpleasant moment she continued to gaze at him without speaking. Then, leaning back in her chair, she said gently, 'Well? You can hardly tell me it's none of my affair, can you? The rest of my life is at stake here – not to mention the security of my family. And, in case you've forgotten, you were as much my father's man-of-law as you were Sir Robert's.'

Mr Crisp thought about it and came to the reluctant conclusion that since what he now knew might well influence the situation, she probably had a point. 'Very well. I will tell you what I have already told Mistress Brandon. There is, in fact, very little money.'

'What?' Venetia sat up again rather sharply. 'But that can't be right. Sir Robert was a rich man!'

'Yes, Mistress Clifford. He *was* a rich man. Unfortunately, however, over the last two years very few of his investments have prospered. And the cost of fortifying and garrisoning

Brandon Lacey throughout the war was by no means small. Then there were the sums he occasionally paid to Lord Fairfax for the maintenance of the northern army, and, of course, the rather substantial debts incurred by Mr Ellis before he left England. The result is that, by the time his affairs were settled, Sir Robert's capital amounted to little more than five hundred pounds.'

Venetia stopped wasting time trying to believe it. It sounded all too likely. Instead, she set her mind to grasping the implications and, at last, said abruptly, 'Does Colonel Brandon know?'

'Not yet. Having had no communication from him, I am unsure of precisely where he is to be found.'

Putney, she thought instantly. But had the sense not to say it. 'You realise what this means, don't you?'

'I believe so. It is possible that, when the Colonel discovers the precise nature of his inheritance, he may feel it wise to keep hold of Ford Edge. In short, he may decide that marriage with you is not in his best interests.'

Venetia stood up and found that she felt rather sick. 'It's worse than that, isn't it? The quickest way of improving his finances is by selling land. And, unless I'm married to him, he'll be fully entitled to sell ours.' She drew a long, painful breath and stared down at Mr Crisp out of eyes that were no longer discreetly blank. 'I can't let him do that.'

The lawyer looked back and made three interesting discoveries. A long-delayed inkling of what all this really meant to her; a subterranean feeling of pity; and the knowledge that, here in his dingy little office, he was witnessing Mistress Clifford's decision.

He said, 'You are saying you'll marry him?'

'If he asks me, I'll have to,' came the bleak reply. 'What else can I do?' And all the time her mind was saying, *I am in a cage. And I am afraid*. Then, breaking free of the treadmill, she said, stiffly, 'I don't like to ask . . . but I will need your help. If the Colonel knows there is no money, he almost certainly won't contemplate marriage. And so I – I'd be grateful if you'd delay telling him.'

Mr Crisp considered this. Then he said primly, 'I have my duty to perform. If Colonel Brandon asks how matters stand,

I must, of course, tell him.' A small, dry smile touched his mouth. 'But then again, he may not ask.'

It was cold comfort. It was also all she was likely to get. Venetia thanked him and left.

Six

Blissfully unaware of Venetia's discoveries, Gabriel Brandon was indeed at Putney and grappling with several problems at once. The arrival of two more Scottish gentlemen to talk with the King at Hampton Court had provoked a clutch of rumours that a Scots invasion was imminent, and a corresponding surge of activity amongst the green-ribboned followers of John Lilburne – who now, thanks to a remark of Cromwell's, were known to all and sundry as Levellers. But more immediately worrying than either of these incidents was the darkening cloud hanging over the Lieutenant-General.

The simple truth was that, after bending over backwards to please the King, both Cromwell and Ireton had been left high and dry by Parliament's refusal to accept the *Heads of the Proposals*. They couldn't re-instate themselves in the jaundiced eyes of the Army by making good their promises of a swift and speedy settlement . . . and nor could they suddenly abandon their much-publicised support for the King without appearing totally unstable. And therein lay the cause of all their present troubles.

To Gabriel's certain knowledge, Cromwell had suspended his own visits to Hampton Court – along with those of his wife and daughter. He was also reputedly shifting his quarters every third or fourth day because he feared assassination. But with Harry Marten and the Republicans telling the Commons that Honest Noll had the King's promise to make him Earl of Essex and also demanding his impeachment for continuing to speak against the abolition of the monarchy, things were showing scant sign of settling down. And the resulting uncertainty, as Gabriel observed acidly to his Major, was lying throughout the Army like an unlit fuse.

Eden Maxwell looked up from the pistol he was servicing. 'They won't touch Cromwell. They daren't. Our boys may call him a Grandee and misdoubt his motives once in a while – but, if the Scots invade, who else do you think they'll want leading them? Then again, with the radicals screaming that no one should have more than two thousand pounds a year, every landowner in the country is going to be scared witless about what will happen if they allow the King to be disposed of. And what price Republicanism then?'

Gabriel prowled to the window and stared through it. He was in an uncharacteristically edgy mood and had been for the last week – the reason being that it was now nearly the end of October and there was still no sign of Wat.

'I know – I know. But it's what's happening now that concerns me. Tomorrow morning, the Army Council is going to sit down and spend countless bloody hours discussing this latest Leveller document – when what we really *ought* to be doing is putting our heads together with Parliament and the King to find some kind of mutually acceptable compromise. And universally desirable though a good many of Lilburne's notions may be, they're too far-reaching to be even remotely practical at this stage. So I really don't see *The Agreement of the People* providing a solution.'

'My God.' Eden grinned. 'If the rest of the Council feels as you do, it's going to be a merry meeting.'

'I don't know how they feel. Since I'm likely to find out in excruciating detail over the next few days, I haven't troubled to—' He broke off on a sharp breath. 'Hell's teeth! If that's who I think it is, I'll drop him down the nearest well.' And was off through the door without stopping to explain himself.

Eden watched him go, faintly startled amusement marking his brows. Then, laying his pistol gently down on the table, he rose unhurriedly and followed him outside.

A group of some dozen or so troopers stood huddled at the end of the street in the biting wind that blew round the corner. And in the midst of them, his face vivid as ever and his arms full of pamphlets, Samuel Radford was holding forth with apparently eloquent conviction.

Colonel Brandon bore down like a tidal wave causing the men on the fringes of the group to melt discreetly away. The rest remained glued nervously to the spot while a pair of stormy, intensely irritable grey eyes swept comprehensively over them.

'I regret that we've neglected to provide you with suitable employment, gentlemen,' said Gabriel at length. 'I'd be sorry to see you fall victim to any kind of infectious malady through standing idle on such a cold day.'

The troopers shifted uneasily and stared down at their feet. They knew exactly what he meant, of course. A man was entitled to his opinions so long as he never permitted them to interfere with his duty. Listening to impassioned speeches about how Cromwell was about to betray the common soldier in the same way he'd already betrayed John Lilburne, was another matter entirely.

Sam Radford surveyed the Colonel with unimpaired composure. 'You can't keep the truth from them indefinitely, you know. They're bound to hear it sooner or later.'

'I'll deal with you presently,' came the curt reply. 'Major Maxwell . . . you can find a use for these men?'

'I could find several.' Eden paused and then, looking at Sam, 'Don't I know you?'

'You've certainly *seen* me,' agreed Sam. 'At the sign of the Ragged Staff in Banbury some years ago. That whey-faced tutor of yours used to be a regular visitor.'

The hazel eyes widened.

'My God! You're Jonas Radford's brother!'

'The very same.'

Eden's grin held a hint of malice. 'Your views on liberty of conscience must be like a hair-shirt to him. Unless he's no longer the archetypal Puritan he once was?'

'I neither know nor care,' shrugged Sam. 'But I doubt if he's changed. Granite doesn't.'

Gabriel marked this exchange and made a mental note to find out what else the Major knew. But, when he was finally left alone with Samuel, he merely said crisply, 'I thought I'd made it plain that – though I'm not, in principle, utterly opposed to your views – I don't welcome attempts to inflame my men to mutiny.'

93

Sam sighed. They had met three times now at the Morrells' house in Shoreditch, but while Jack remained happily unaware that he was harbouring a Leveller, the Colonel had somehow found the opportunity to lecture Sam on staying away from the Army and being careful what ideas he planted in Mistress Bryony's hitherto empty little head.

'You did,' he said. 'But the present situation—'

'I know precisely what the present situation is. Lilburne hoped Cromwell would get him out of the Tower by persuading the Commons to question the Lords' right to have put him there in the first place – but Cromwell has declined to set both Houses at each other's throats in order to oblige him. So now Lilburne has decided to force his hand with an appeal to what I believe he has called "the hob-nailed and clouted shoes" of the Army.' Gabriel smiled grimly. 'I, however, am here to inform you that now is not a good time for you to be here assisting him in it.'

Considering black eyes met implacable grey ones.

'Are you sure,' asked Sam, 'that you have the right to make me leave?'

'No. But I'm damned sure I have the means.'

'*There is now no power executed in England but a power of force?*' Knowing perfectly well that Cromwell had recently disciplined an officer for saying something very similar, Sam quoted provocatively from Free-born John. 'Ah well. Since you say you have the means to remove me, you'd better use them hadn't you?'

And he sat calmly down upon the cobbles.

It took two troopers to carry Mr Radford away and Gabriel was left with a feeling of having been made to look rather foolish. On the following morning, therefore, he entered the church of St Mary the Virgin for the opening of the Putney Debates in entirely the wrong frame of mind for a meeting whose aim was that of reconciliation.

He wasn't the only one.

Edward Sexby – who, together with civilian John Wildman, had drafted *The Agreement of the People* – launched the first quarrel of the day.

'We sought,' he said, 'to satisfy all men, but, in going to it,

94

we have *dis*satisfied all men. We have laboured to please the King, but I think, unless we all go and cut our throats, we shall not please him; and we have supported a House which consists of a company of rotten members.' He paused. 'The Lieutenant-General and Commissary-General Ireton have attempted to settle the Kingdom on the foundations of King and Parliament – but I hope they will do no more in that direction. I hope that, henceforth, any settlement that is made will rely on the Army.'

This, it appeared, was more than Henry Ireton was prepared to stomach. Surging to his feet, he said flatly, 'I have neither purpose nor desire to set up the King – and I think I have demonstrated this. But I do not seek and *would* not seek the destruction of either Parliament or King. Neither will I concur with those who will not attempt to preserve both, and make good use of both, for the Kingdom.'

Gabriel sighed, stared up at the timber-trussed roof and waited to hear precise details of the document they were supposed to be discussing.

These, as it turned out, were contained in four surprisingly brief articles – three of which bore certain similarities to the *Heads of the Proposals*. But the last clause maintained that the '*power of this and all future Representatives of this nation is inferior only to theirs who choose them*' and that the people's consent was the only foundation of just government.

A jumble of dissenting voices filled the church and Colonel Brandon sank down in his pew, chin on chest. He could not help feeling that the Leveller programme had a certain amount of right on its side. Unfortunately, however, he couldn't see it being anything more than a charming pipe-dream during his lifetime, or, quite possibly, for a long time after it. And if anyone tried to implement it now, it was also likely to prove a sure road to chaos.

Cromwell apparently thought so, too, but was minded to be diplomatic. 'This paper contains in it very great alterations to the government of the Kingdom,' he said carefully. 'And what the consequences of such an alteration as this would be, wise and godly men ought to consider. If we could leap out of one condition into another, I suppose there would not be much dispute. But what if – whilst we are disputing these things – another company of men shall gather together and put out a paper as plausible as this? Would not the result of that be confusion? So give me leave to say this. There will be very great mountains in the way of this . . . and it is not enough to propose things that are good in the end. It is our duty as Christians and men to consider the consequences.'

Despite this well-reasoned appeal, the afternoon wore on in heated argument. Ireton wanted nothing to do with the *Agreement* – and pointed out that, having vowed its adherence to the *Heads of the Proposals*, the Army could not change tack just because the said *Proposals* no longer pleased them. Cromwell continued trying to achieve some degree of unity between the opposing factions before debate began in earnest. And Wildman and his fellow-Levellers wanted a quick decision before Parliament put the King in such a position that he could simply choose who to hang first.

The result was that they eventually agreed to begin the following day's agenda with a prayer meeting. Gabriel left the church convinced that, thus far, the proceedings has been a waste of time – and was therefore not disposed to be tactful when Hugh Peter blocked his path to remark that his lack of spiritual ardour was setting a poor example to his regiment.

Gabriel did not like Hugh Peter. Neither was he prepared to be told how to do his job by a rabble-rousing preacher who dabbled in espionage and politics. Raising openly derisive brows, he said so.

Peter flushed angrily. 'You are arrogant, sir!'

'And you're not, I suppose?'

'I am merely tending the souls in my care and establishing the rule of the Saints for the greater glory of God!'

'Are you?' said Gabriel. 'My mistake, then. I thought it was for the greater glory of Hugh Peter.' And strode away without waiting for a reply.

It was fortunate for the state of Colonel Brandon's temper that, once the prayers were over, the second day of the debate opened with a constructive decision to consider each Article of the *Agreement* separately. For one short, exhilarating moment, Gabriel had visions of them making some progress. But as soon as Article One was read out with its requirement that constituencies be proportioned according to the number of inhabitants, Henry Ireton immediately rose up and asked whether this implied that there was to be universal suffrage.

He was answered by Thomas Rainsborough – the only senior officer wholly and openly in sympathy with the Leveller cause. 'I hope so. For the poorest man in England has a life to live as well as the greatest – and so everyone who has to live under a government ought first to consent to it.'

Gabriel silently conceded that Rainsborough had a point. Ireton didn't. He merely fixed him with a saturnine dark gaze and said, 'Your argument relies on natural rights but denies all civil ones. For my part, I think that no person has a right to a share in choosing what laws we are ruled by unless he has a permanent, fixed interest in the Kingdom – either in land or in one of the trading corporations.'

'Nothing can convince me why any man born in England should not have his voice in elections,' snapped Rainsborough hotly. 'All Englishmen are subject to English laws – and the foundation of all law lies in the people. Where does it say "I am a poor man – therefore I shall be oppressed"? And I would know what we have fought for, if not for our laws and liberties!'

A number of people tried to speak at once and the debate started to strain in several different, impassioned directions before Edward Sexby adroitly moved the argument on to a different level.

'There are thousands of soldiers as poor as myself who have ventured their lives for their birthright and their privileges as Englishmen,' he said. 'Yet now it seems that unless a man has a fixed estate, he *has* no birthright – and that if he were granted one it would be to the destruction of the kingdom. Well – if that's so, I should like to point out that I consider myself to have as much birthright as any here – and I will surrender it to no man!'

'Rather than disturb the good constitution of a Kingdom where I may live in godliness, honesty and peace,' returned Ireton caustically, 'I will part with a great deal of both my birthright and my property.'

For the first time in several days, Gabriel found himself grinning wryly. You had to hand it to Henry. He was an absolute master of the lofty principle. And if one hadn't already known how devoted he was to the rights of property-owners, one might almost have believed he meant it.

Someone tried once more to insist that such radical changes to the existing franchise would never be accepted.

'Then what has the soldier fought for all this while?' mocked Rainsborough. 'Has he fought to enslave himself, to give power to men of riches – to make himself a perpetual slave? I think not. If we are afraid of change – why did we fight the late war? Why, indeed, are we here now?'

There was, of course, no answer to this and, pressing his temporary advantage, Rainsborough proposed that the question of suffrage be referred to the Army as a whole. He received insufficient support, however, and had to accept, with a good grace, the passing of a counter-proposal that this and other matters be referred instead to a committee.

Rejoicing at not hearing himself named to serve on this, Colonel Brandon walked back to his quarters intending to spend the evening with Eden Maxwell over a bottle – only to change his mind as soon as he entered his room.

Wat was back.

'My God,' said Gabriel by way of greeting. 'You took your time. I'd begun to think you'd found yourself a nice little widow and settled down with her.'

'That'll be the day,' grunted Mr Larkin. And then, coming straight to the point, 'Do you want the full story?'

'Traveller's tales and a blow-by-blow catalogue of events? I don't think so. Just the gist will do.'

'All right, then. I found him but he's not coming back – and it wouldn't be much good if he did.'

A frown touched the grey gaze. 'Why not?'

'Because the bloody fool's done the one thing that'll never be forgiven him,' said Wat bitterly. 'He hasn't just turned Papist, he's actually enrolled himself in a Jesuit seminary off the Rue St Antoine and is training for the priesthood.'

There was a long, catastrophic silence. Then Gabriel said, 'Did you speak to him?'

'Eventually. He said he knew all about Sir Robert's Will from his sister and he could only give you the same answer he's given her. God has called him to a new life.'

'That's nice.' The crisp voice was suddenly infused with a blast of rare temper. 'And does he take no thought for what's left of the old one?'

Wat spat into the fire. 'Not so as you'd notice. Oh – he shed a few tears for the worry it must all be causing his mother, but at the end of the day he said that his sister will have to do what she thinks best because he'll never come back to England again unless the Order sends him.'

'So he's washing his hands of it and letting the rest of us bear the consequences? Wonderful. What kind of man *is* he, for Christ's sake?'

'The kind who prefers visions to nasty reality.'

'As if we haven't enough of those here,' muttered the Colonel. And then, running a weary hand through his hair, 'If his sister knows all this, she must be fit to be tied.'

'Very likely,' agreed Wat sourly. 'But not to you. So you'd better go and have a quiet chat with the Lieutenant-General and then leave for the continent with his letter of recommendation in your pocket.'

'I wish it were that simple.' Gabriel laid his hands lightly on the back of a settle and stared sombrely down at them. 'Running away isn't going to solve anything . . . and, if I once start, I'll be doing it for the rest of my life. And do you really think Cromwell is going to help me escape what he'll see as a moral duty? He won't. He'll be too glad to know of another northern stronghold safely in the hands of one of his own officers.' He paused and then, an ironic smile twisting his mouth, said 'No, Wat. I wish I could just cut and run and not care what kind of mess I leave behind me, but I can't. I wouldn't be able to live with myself afterwards.'

Wat looked at him with profound disgust. Then, 'Sod it,' he said pungently. 'I thought as much. You're going to marry the blasted wench, aren't you?'

It was a long time before Gabriel spoke and, when he did, his voice was as dry as dust. 'It's beginning to look as if I'll have to.'

It was perhaps fortunate that, during the following week, the Colonel was too busy keeping abreast of other developments to devote much time to his personal concerns. While the

Army Council discussed the authority of the King and the increasingly thorny question of Army discipline, the Council Committee continued trying to form an acceptable amalgamation of *The Agreement of the People* and the *Heads of the Proposals*. The Levellers, who were by no means happy at the alterations being made in committee, managed to offend Ireton so successfully that he stormed out saying he would not attend another meeting. And the Lord General reluctantly set a date for a general rendezvous.

By Sunday November 7th, Putney was crackling with tension and, fearing an outbreak of Leveller-inspired mutiny, Cromwell used the next day's Council Meeting to order all officers and Agitators back to their regiments. Gabriel heaved a sigh of relief and hoped for a period of quiet in which to calm his men down.

Thanks to the Brothers Lilburne, he didn't get it. On November 9th, the Commons released John Lilburne on bail. On the 11th, warned, so rumour said, by Henry Lilburne of possible threats to his life, the King achieved the impossible and caused a blaze of wild speculation when he slipped quietly away from Hampton Court. And on the 15th, at the rendezvous on Corkbush Field, Colonel Robert Lilburne almost succeeded in making the long-feared mutiny a fact.

The rendezvous to which Gabriel's regiment was bidden was far more orderly than that held at Corkbush Field. However, it wasn't until Fairfax had restored order by promising to support the dissolution of Parliament and the King was known to be safe on the Isle of Wight that Gabriel was finally able to snatch a few hours in which to visit his foster-family. And when he did, it was to find that Annis had gone into premature labour.

Alone in the parlour while servants, midwife and doctor all ministered to his wife, Jack Morrell paced up and down with a face as white as paper and his hair all on end.

'They won't let me see her,' he announced by way of greeting. 'They just keep telling me be patient. But how *can* I be patient? That's my Annis up there!'

Over the rumble of voices above and hurried feet on the stairs, Gabriel heard the unmistakable sounds of Annis's travail and knew a craven desire to be elsewhere. Since, however, he obviously couldn't leave, he said uncomfortably, 'Yes. But I'm sure she's being well looked after. And you'd only be in the way, you know.'

Jack ignored this and took another turn round the parlour. 'Why is it taking so damned long? Dr Chamberlen told me that premature babies often come quicker. But this has been going on for hours! What if something's going wrong and they haven't told me?'

Gabriel tried remarking, somewhat unconvincingly, on the number of seven-month infants who grew into perfectly healthy children. Jack eyed him witheringly and, without breaking stride, asked what the devil he knew about it? Not without relief, Gabriel gave up attempting to offer intelligent comfort and ransacked a cupboard in search of the brandy bottle instead.

The afternoon wore by on leaden feet. Gabriel drank rather more of the brandy than Jack but retained sufficient sense to keep quiet about his own affairs – even though the whole purpose of his visit had been to discuss them. And then, at a little after four o'clock the air was pierced with a thin, reedy wail and Jack stopped dead in the midst of his perambulations.

'Did you hear that?' he whispered. 'It sounded . . . it sounded like a baby.'

'Amazing,' grinned Gabriel, hazily. 'Especially as that's precisely what we've spent the last four hours waiting for.'

Jack didn't stop to listen. He hurled himself at the door and took the stairs three at a time. He had to wait a little longer, of course, before they let him in – but by then he didn't mind for they'd told him the only thing he wanted to know. Annis was weak from exhaustion but no longer in any danger. The baby, which though small seemed healthy enough, was a boy.

Inwardly shuddering, Gabriel listened to Dr Chamberlen's enthusiastic dissertation on the use of short forceps – invented, so he said, by his grandfather – and, with rather more interest, to his theory that simple hygiene could prevent the spread of infection. Then, when the doctor had finally left, he dutifully admired his foster-brother's son and heir and agreed that he was beautiful, even though all babies looked the same to him and this one was redder and more wrinkled than most. After that, he left Jack sitting with a grin a mile wide beside his wife's bed and returned to the parlour in time to catch Bryony returning from unwilling banishment in a neighbour's house.

'What is it?' she asked breathlessly. 'Is Annis all right? Will they let me go up?'

'It's a boy and your aunt is sound asleep. And yes, I'm sure you'll be able to see them both. But not, if you don't mind, before you've told me whether or not you're still associating with Samuel Radford.'

The brown eyes widened but she did not look especially guilty – only impatient to be off. 'From time to time. Why?'

'Because he's under arrest for his part in the recent Corkbush Field fiasco.'

'*Under arrest?*' she cried indignantly. 'But that's monstrous!'

'No it isn't. If he insists on mixing with people whose main aim is to murder Cromwell in his bed, it's his own fault.' He paused. 'Are you in love with him?'

For a moment, because the question was so ridiculous, she couldn't believe he had asked it. Then she said shortly, 'No. Of course I'm not.'

'Good. Because I wanted to point out that it behoves you to watch your step. In fact, I'd like your promise that you will. Otherwise, I'll have no alternative but to discuss the matter with Jack.'

Bryony opened her mouth on a hasty retort and then thought better of it. After all, the fact that he cared was undoubtedly a step in the right direction . . . and might be turned to even better account. An odd gleam entered her eyes and she said mildly, 'All right, I'll promise to be as careful as you like. But only on condition you do what you can to get Sam out of gaol. How's that?' And, without waiting for an answer, she turned and ran lightly upstairs.

Minutes later, Jack joined Gabriel with the amused observation that, between mother and cousin, his son wasn't going to lack cosseting.

'He'll thrive. They'll see to it,' nodded Gabriel. And then,

'Jack . . . I know this isn't really the time but I may not find another. Within the next few weeks, I'm going to have to go back to Yorkshire. And unless Venetia Clifford meant what she said about refusing me, it's becoming more and more likely that I'll have to marry her.'

Jack stared at him, the smile evaporating from his face. 'That's a bit drastic, isn't it? Are you sure?'

'Unfortunately, yes.' And, in as few words as possible, he related the tale of Wat's discoveries, before adding dryly, 'So you see, I can't just vanish and leave everyone else to pick up the pieces. It wouldn't be fair.'

'Why not? It's what Sir Harry Clifford is doing, isn't it? And he's the one who ought to be worrying about his family – not you.'

'I know. But he won't. And if I follow his example, what does that make me? I don't even have the excuse of a divine vocation . . . just a life I'd have preferred to keep.'

'And a woman you don't want to marry?'

'Ah.' A crooked smile twisted the hard mouth. 'Yes. That too. But perhaps closer acquaintance will alter that.'

'And if it doesn't?'

'I'll just have to make the best of a bad job and find an accommodating mistress,' returned the Colonel flippantly. Then, differently, 'I don't have a choice, Jack. If I did, I'd take it – believe me. But with things as they are . . . well, I just wanted to prepare you for the possibility of having to receive Venetia Clifford as my wife.'

'*Your wife?*' echoed a shocked voice from the doorway.

Gabriel and Jack swung round to find Bryony gazing across at them, the blood slowly draining from her face.

'Your wife?' she said again uncertainly. 'You – you're getting married?'

'Oh lord,' muttered Jack.

'Yes,' replied Gabriel expressionlessly. 'If the lady accepts me, I'm afraid I am.'

Bryony stared at him with all the intense, suffocating emotion of one barely past her seventeenth birthday and for a moment there was utter silence. Then the floodgates opened.

Colonel Brandon waited until the inevitable chaos of moving

the Army's Headquarters to Windsor was over before seeking an interview with the Lieutenant-General and, when he got it, stated his dilemma with the least possible fuss.

Oliver Cromwell – thickset, wart-faced and potentially the most powerful man in England – listened in silence and then said simply, 'No one rises as high as he, who knows not where he's going. I take it you have sought God's counsel over this?'

Gabriel hadn't but he knew better than to say so. One of several things he disliked about Cromwell was that gentleman's tendency to cloud everything with religion. Neatly sidestepping the question, he said, 'Over the last few weeks, my duty in the matter has become increasingly clear.'

'Mm.' There was a pause and then the Lieutenant-General said abruptly, 'Lambert's been keen for some time now to see you promoted. I suppose you knew that?'

'No.' Behind his serviceable buff leather was a feeling of sick disappointment for what might have been. 'No, sir – I didn't know. And naturally that makes me even more reluctant to resign my commission.'

The thick brows rose.

'Resign? Why on earth do you think you need to resign? It's quite possible to be both a landowner and an officer, you know. I'm one myself – as is the Lord General and a score or so others I could name.'

'Yes, sir,' came the wry response. 'But, if you'll excuse me saying so, all of you were bred to it. I wasn't.'

'Then you'll have to learn quickly, won't you?' Cromwell regarded the younger man consideringly for a moment. 'You've a promising future, Colonel, and, because it would be a pity to waste what the Lord has given, I'll see you get leave of absence from the beginning of December. But, if you can't sort out your affairs in Yorkshire and be back at your post before Easter, I'm afraid that it *will* be wasted. Do I make myself quite clear?'

A hint of rare colour stained Gabriel's cheekbones. It was the reprieve he hadn't dared hope for and, if only he could take advantage of it, the future might not be so bleak after all.

'Quite clear, sir,' he said formally. 'And I'm more than grateful.'

'Good.' Nodding curtly, Cromwell got to his feet and then

frowned as the door burst open on his son-in-law. 'Well, Henry? Hounds of hell chasing you, are they?'

'No.' Thirty-six years old and perpetually immaculate, Henry Ireton's enigmatic dark eyes dwelled briefly on Gabriel and then returned to the Lieutenant-General. 'I just came to inform you that the messenger we've been waiting for will be passing through Holborn tonight. But perhaps I'd better come back later when you're less busy?'

'No . . . wait a moment.' There was a long, meditative silence and then the Lieutenant-General said slowly, 'Colonel Brandon . . . I'm told you're a man who knows how to keep his own counsel. Is that true?'

'I certainly hope it is, sir,' replied Gabriel warily. He owed Cromwell a debt and one which he hoped to repay, but not, if he could help it, through complicity in one of the Lieutenant-General's little schemes.

Fortunately – though for entirely different reasons – Ireton was equally unenthusiastic. 'I don't doubt the Colonel's discretion – but he'll want to know what we're doing and why. I, on the other hand, can find you an honest trooper who'll simply do as he's told.'

'And let it all out in his cups afterwards,' replied Cromwell briskly. 'No. I think I'd rather put my trust in Colonel Brandon.'

Ireton shrugged and sat down.

'I hope it's not misplaced.'

'It won't be.' The Lieutenant-General collected Gabriel's deliberately wooden gaze and said, 'With the Lord's help, Henry and I hope to intercept a particularly important letter. All we want from you are the services of an alert sentry. Would you be prepared to help us in this way?'

Gabriel didn't feel he had much option. It was becoming a depressingly familiar sensation. 'Naturally, sir. You have only to ask.'

And that was how, several hours later, Gabriel found himself standing in the pouring rain at the wicket-gate of the Blue Boar Tavern, in a black mood liberally laced with incredulity, waiting for a man with a saddle on his head.

The letter – supposedly a reply from the King to one previously intercepted from the Queen – was expected to say whether or not his Majesty intended to throw in his lot with the Scots and encourage them to invade England on his behalf. This much, since it was logical to assume that Cromwell had a spy in his Majesty's household, Gabriel was prepared to accept. But that the missive was travelling from Carisbrooke to France via Holborn was rather harder to believe, and that it would arrive at around ten o'clock and in such an obvious manner, downright preposterous.

Gabriel pulled the brim of his hat down against the driving rain and sought what shelter he could between gate and wall. It was fairly obvious what Cromwell hoped to do. If he could catch the King kissing the Scots, he'd be able to end his own embarrassing courtship of the crown with a display of outraged virtue – and hope that the Army would like him better in the role of innocent dupe than that of Charles Stuart's boot-licker.

The sound of approaching footsteps recalled him to his duty and he straightened, peering through the wet darkness towards the wicket. A large, bulky shape loomed and insinuated itself, with difficulty, through the gate. Gabriel remained perfectly still and, against all expectation, found himself stifling a laugh. Dead on cue and exactly as had been foretold, it was indeed a man with a saddle on his head, though, in view of the weather, he looked marginally less ridiculous than he might have done otherwise. It was enough, thought Gabriel, detaching himself silently from the wall, to make you wonder if the rain hadn't been organised in advance as well.

Inside the taproom, Lieutenant-General Cromwell and Commissary-General Ireton were swilling ale like common troopers and Colonel Brandon allowed himself a brief moment in which to enjoy the spectacle. Despite the borrowed, ill-fitting uniform, Old Noll managed to appear fairly convincing. Henry, on the other hand, looked about as comfortable as a nun in a brothel. Suppressing a grin and careless of who he dripped on, Gabriel picked his way across the room and said simply, 'He's in the stables, saddling a horse.'

Cromwell surged to his feet, upsetting his tankard and sending a tide of beer into his son-in-law's lap. It could have been an accident, but catching the glint in the Lieutenant-General's eye and knowing his peculiar fondness for horseplay, Gabriel didn't think it was.

Ireton didn't think so either. His face like thunder, he shoved back his stool and stalked wordlessly to the door.

Outside in the yard, the man with the message was already leading his horse back towards the gate. Ireton advanced on him with a drawn sword and ordered him to stop.

'Stop?' asked the messenger, surprised but not noticeably alarmed by the challenge. 'What for?'

'Because we've to search everyone going in or out.'

'We have – we have,' agreed Cromwell cheerily. 'But you look like an honest fellow . . . doesn't he look like an honest fellow, Hal? I think so. I do indeed. And therefore it will probably suffice just to look through that saddle. What do you say, Hal? Wouldn't that be enough?'

'Yes.' Ireton already had the saddle half-unfastened and was plainly not inclined to waste time acting. 'Quite enough. But I think we'll take it into the stable out of this infernal rain.'

The bemused messenger was left looking helplessly at the Colonel. 'What the devil's going on here tonight?'

'Don't ask me,' shrugged Gabriel. 'It's orders. That's all I know.'

Some ten minutes later, Cromwell returned to heave the fellow's saddle back on to his long-suffering horse and send him on his way. Gabriel waited for a moment and then, with what he personally felt was forgivable curiosity, said, 'Did you find what you were looking for, sir?'

All the apparent geniality of the past hour fell from the Lieutenant-General like a discarded cloak and his face was suddenly very grim indeed.

'What I was looking for – yes; what I hoped for – no,' he replied flatly. 'I've spent half the last year trying to tempt the King into an accommodation that would preserve the best of our heritage and form a sound basis for the future. Tonight I have finally been forced to recognise that I'll never achieve it – that Charles Stuart will never allow *anybody* to achieve it. In short, he's in league with the Scots and prepared to countenance an invasion.'

In the last few days before he left Windsor, Gabriel put his apprehensions concerning the King to the back of his mind and concentrated on his forthcoming departure. He had told Cromwell the complete truth about his changed circumstances and was aware that, being a Yorkshireman, his immediate superior John Lambert would probably also discover it in due course – but that was where he hoped it would end. The only difficulty, therefore, was in excusing his prolonged absence to the only person likely to question it.

Major Maxwell held his tongue as long as was humanly possible and then, on the Colonel's last night at headquarters, said resignedly, 'All right. I give up. How the devil have you managed to get permission for four months out of the coop when I can't even get four days? Is it a secret mission . . . or compassionate leave? Or does Old Noll just like the colour of your eyes.'

'None of those, although the middle one was probably closest.' Gabriel smiled faintly and reached for his wine-cup. 'In fact I've inherited some land in Yorkshire which will require my attention for a while.'

'Have you? My congratulations.' Eden raised his glass. And then, 'But my God . . . *another* Grandee in our midst!'

'I'm afraid so. Though I don't see why you should mind. You're one yourself, after all.'

Reserve settled over the scarred face like a mask.

'Quite. But only in theory.'

Gabriel resisted the temptation to remark that, if it was possible to own land only in theory, he would be glad to learn the secret of it – and, instead, said mildly, 'Very well. By all means let's change the subject. You may or may not be glad to know that I've a small job for you during my absence. It concerns your friend, Samuel Radford.'

Eden's brows soared.

'He's no friend of mine. I scarcely know him.'

'No. But you know a damned sight more about him than I do,' responded Gabriel. Then, with the ghost of a rueful smile, 'The situation is this; he was arrested at Corkbush Field and I've half-promised a certain young lady that I'll at least try to secure his release. The only trouble is that I haven't time to do it.'

'And that's where I come in, I suppose.' The Major looked back at him with a species of resigned amusement. 'Pardon me for asking, but are you sure he really *ought* to be released?'

'More or less. He's an extremely tiresome young man with a whole host of wonderful, impractical notions – but I don't for a moment think he'd be party to an assassination. And the worst of it is – you can't help liking him.'

'A dangerous combination if ever I heard one,' observed Eden calmly. Then, 'Ah well. If it's going to uphold your devastating reputation with the fair sex, I suppose I'd better do it. But I hope you know what you're letting loose. Because your likable Mr Radford's brother is the most fanatical hell-fire Puritan you're ever likely to meet; and, if my information is correct, his sister ran off with one of the Cavaliers who helped hold Banbury throughout the war.'

'Dear me.' Gabriel leaned back and regarded his friend over folded arms. 'They sound quite a family. And as for you . . . you're better than an almanac.'

Seven

Exactly one week later, Gabriel left Mr Larkin at the Red Bear in Knaresborough and set off, grim-faced and alone, to do his endeavour.

He found the village of Brearton without difficulty and, directed at some length by a loquacious blacksmith, eventually turned his horse's head into the beech-canopied track that led to the gates of Ford Edge Manor. Then, since they stood open, he rode on up the gently rising ground and was rewarded with his first sight of the house . . . a pleasant residence of pale, ivy-clad stone with large mullioned windows, a row of gabled attics piercing the sky and a substantial, square-fronted gatehouse.

The courtyard within was deserted and the location of the stables not immediately apparent. Dismounting without haste, Gabriel stood for a moment, one hand resting lightly on the saddle, and contemplated the great oak door. Then, with a faint sigh of resignation, he tethered his horse to a crumbling stone urn and pulled the bell.

A sound rather like the clatter of cooking pots rent the air. Gabriel winced and waited. No one came and the door remained securely shut. Reluctant to try the bell again, he debated the possibilities and lingered wistfully on the notion of retreat. Then he turned his back on the door and strode resolutely round to the side of the house in the hope of at least finding the stables.

He found a small walled garden instead . . . once presumably filled with flowers and shrubs until someone had conceived the notion of growing vegetables there. And, on the far side of it, where the few remaining rose bushes still bordered a path, was a long sapphire cloak topped by a bright, gold head.

Gabriel checked briefly and then bore noiselessly down on his quarry until he was able to say gently, 'Good morning, Mistress Clifford.'

The girl gasped and wheeled to face him – and he found himself gazing into a pair of startled and completely unfamiliar blue eyes. He frowned.

'Ah. My mistake, it seems. I took you for the lady who, I suspect, is probably your sister.'

Elizabeth swallowed and clutched her cloak more securely about her. 'M-my sister?' she echoed blankly.

Gabriel smothered a sigh. 'Mistress Venetia?'

'Oh. Yes, I see.' She eyed him with palpable confusion, absently absorbing both his buff coat and tawny sash. And then, like a bolt from the blue, understanding finally dawned. '*Oh*!'

'Precisely,' he agreed sardonically. If the girl had looked nervous before, she now appeared positively petrified. 'I am the unfortunate fellow you're doubtless used to hearing referred to as the Roundhead bastard.'

A tide of crimson flooded Elizabeth's face and – muttering something that might have been a suggestion for him to follow her but was in fact wholly incomprehensible – set off back towards the house as if the devil was at her heels.

Gabriel wasted several seconds swearing irritably up at the empty sky and then strode after her. It was plainly going to be one of those days . . . but then, what else had he expected?

Entering the house through a side door and lured wraithlike through stone-vaulted passageways, Gabriel eventually arrived at the foot of what he assumed was the main staircase. Another, younger girl was in the act of descending it and, seeing her, his acquaintance from the garden said breathlessly, 'Oh Phoebe – thank God! You talk to him. I don't know what to say.' Then she rushed up the stairs and vanished.

For a moment there was a sort of stunned hush, broken only by sounds of unusual domestic activity from above. Then the brown-haired girl looked down on him with a severity belied by the faint quiver of her mouth and said, 'My goodness. Whatever have you done to poor Bess?'

'Nothing intentional – or even particularly unusual.' He

moved deliberately into the light and waited for her reaction. 'I merely introduced myself.'

Phoebe's hand tightened involuntarily on the banister. Then she said obscurely, 'Heavens! You're him, aren't you?'

Gabriel's sense of humour started to re-assert itself.

'Probably – but without clarification I can't be sure.'

She gave a gurgle of laughter, skimmed down the last few steps and subjected him to a long, critical appraisal. 'I must say, you're not a bit what I expected.'

'And what was that, precisely?'

'I'm not sure,' replied Phoebe. And she wasn't. Venetia had said that he was tall, dark and somewhere in his middle thirties – and that much was true. What she *hadn't* troubled to say was that he was lightly tanned and built like a Greek athlete . . . or that the long, wavy hair framed a face which, though too severely-sculpted to be called handsome, was certainly attractive enough to make most girls remember it. 'I suppose I thought you would look older and more . . . more like a Roundhead.'

She realised as soon as it was out that she ought to have phrased it differently. Far from appearing offended, however, the Colonel merely raised his brows and said, 'Oh? Well, I don't know how many of us you've met – but if you were expecting fangs, horns and cloven hooves, I can only say that your experience has been unfortunate.'

Phoebe grinned and then, in response to a loud thump from above, said, 'You'd better come into the parlour.'

'Willingly. If I can first stable my horse?'

'I'll send someone out to see to it,' came the quick reply. 'Please go in. I won't be long.'

The parlour was a pleasant room with large windows and an ornately plastered ceiling but its elegance was overlaid with an air of faint dilapidation. Gabriel surveyed it thoughtfully until Phoebe re-appeared talking rapidly.

'I'm sorry. I suppose no one answered the door to you? Mother has set all the servants to re-arranging the bedchambers, you see. But, if she hasn't already retired with a headache, and Bess has been able to tell her you're here, she should be down in an hour or so. Sooner if she's satisfied with the dress she already has on. And, in the meantime, I can at least offer you a glass of wine. I've no idea what it is – but I expect it's quite good. Uncle James is very particular. He used to be a bishop, you know.'

His eyes alight with amusement, Gabriel accepted the glass from her and said, 'Uncle James, I believe I have met . . . and also Mother and Bess. But who are you?'

'Oh – didn't I say? I'm Phoebe. There's Venetia, then Elizabeth and then me. Of course, Harry is the eldest of us now . . . but I suppose I'd better leave Venetia to tell you about him.' She paused, frowning a little. 'And that reminds me. I'm afraid I don't know precisely where Venetia is. She had an argument with Mother – over the bedchambers, you know – and went off in a temper.'

'An argument over the *bedchambers?*' he asked. And thought, *Oh Christ. What am I letting myself in for?*

'Yes. I know it sounds ridiculous – but Venetia did have a point. After all, it wasn't really very tactful of Mother to start preparing the house for a wedding before . . . well, before we know there's actually going to be one.' Phoebe flushed a little but kept her gaze fixed stubbornly to his face from which all traces of amusement had now vanished. 'I know I shouldn't ask – but have you decided whether or not you're going to . . . to . . .'

'Ask your sister to marry me?' supplied Gabriel aridly. 'Yes. I have. And you're right. You shouldn't have asked. Unless, of course, you're in a position to tell me whether or not Mistress Venetia will accept if I do – in which case we could leave her out of it altogether and settle the business between us.'

The flush deepened. 'I suppose I asked for that.'

His brief flash of annoyance evaporated instantly and a vagrant smile touched his mouth. 'Yes. I, on the other hand, needn't have made my point with a mallet.'

'No. And if it wasn't for the prospect of having to see Venetia again, I daresay you wouldn't have done.'

Gabriel narrowly avoided choking over his wine.

'Oh it's all right,' Phoebe assured him. 'I know what she can be like. But she has good points too, you know – and she never used to be so sharp. It's because of the war and having to—'

'Colonel Brandon,' said a sad, faded voice from the doorway. 'How nice. I hope my little one has been looking after you?'

Setting down his glass, Gabriel turned to face Lady Clifford and bowed. 'Very well indeed. But I understand that I've called at an inopportune moment – so perhaps it would be better if I—'

'No, no. Not at all.' Her ladyship drifted across the room in a cloud of patchouli and sat down. She did not, the Colonel noticed, invite him to join her. 'It is more than time we settled this unfortunate business, don't you think?'

'With respect, Madam, Mistress Venetia's absence makes that rather difficult.'

'Of course. But I'm sure she will return quite soon . . . and, in the meantime, there are a number of things which you and I might profitably discuss.'

'Are there?'

'I believe so.' She turned to her daughter. 'Dearest, the Colonel and I would like to speak privately.'

Having little alternative but to take the hint, Phoebe moved reluctantly to the door. One look at the Colonel's face, however, was enough to inform her that Mother was unlikely to emerge from the encounter much wiser. She left the room grinning mildly – and walked straight into her eldest sister.

'Oh lord! Where have you *been?*' she hissed.

'Taking Gypsy for a walk,' responded Venetia, briskly stripping off her gloves. 'Why? Has something happened?'

'Not yet – but I'm sure it's just about to.' Phoebe took a long, fortifying breath. 'Colonel Brandon is here.'

Venetia froze. 'Where?'

'In the parlour being interrogated by Mother. But don't worry. I doubt she'll get much out of him so you've plenty of time to change.'

'Change? Why should I wish to do that?'

'I should have thought that was obvious,' replied Phoebe, critically surveying her sister's serviceable winter cloak and the plain woollen gown she wore beneath it. 'Your hair's in a tangle and your hem is all muddy. You don't want the Colonel to see you looking like that, do you?'

Venetia took off her cloak and laid it across Phoebe's arms. 'Since his opinion is a matter of supreme indifference to me, I don't see why not.'

'But you *can't!*'

'Watch me,' she invited grimly. And stalking up to the parlour door, she opened it and went in.

Ellen Clifford's latest attempt at delicate persuasion died on her lips and a small shudder passed over her. Gabriel merely turned slowly and, keeping his expression utterly blank, inclined his head in token acknowledgement.

'Mistress Clifford.'

'Colonel Brandon,' returned Venetia, mockingly. 'How kind of you to honour us with a visit.'

'Kindness, so far as I'm aware, has little to do with it. Or perhaps you don't feel we have anything to say to each other?'

The violet gaze travelled briefly to Lady Clifford and then back again. 'On the contrary. I would, however, prefer to hold our conversation in private.'

After her behaviour at Brandon Lacey, Gabriel was unable to resist raising faintly malicious brows. 'Really? You surprise me.'

Venetia's hands clenched savagely on the limp folds of her gown but before she could speak, her mother said peevishly, 'Don't be silly, dearest. That would be quite improper.'

'In which case, it should accord perfectly with the situation as a whole, shouldn't it?' responded Venetia tartly. 'I'm sorry, Mother – but etiquette is a little out of place here and, if you won't leave this room, then we must. Colonel?' And, so saying, she opened the door and swept through it.

With an almost imperceptible shrug, Gabriel bowed once more to Lady Clifford and then strolled unhurriedly in Venetia's wake. He found her awaiting him on the other side of the passage in a small, cluttered room that was plainly used as some kind of office. As soon as he appeared, she said, 'Shut the door, for God's sake – or we'll have half the household standing around listening.'

'Not unless they've finished re-arranging the bedchambers,' he murmured, doing as she asked. Then, turning to face her, 'Very well. Do you want to start or shall I?'

Venetia was cold with apprehension and her nerves vibrated like plucked wires. 'I think perhaps you should.'

'Then I'll be brief. I am aware – as I presume you are – that your brother has decided not to return. This—'

'*How do you know that?*'

Gabriel watched the blood drain slowly from her skin and realised that he ought to have expected some such reaction.

'Since you failed to assure me that you could reach him, I sent someone to Paris to find him.'

'I see.' Venetia willed her voice to remain steady. 'In which case, you must also know *why* he won't come back.'

'Yes. But you needn't worry. I'm not in the business of religious persecution.'

She surveyed him with weary derision.

'Do you expect me to believe that?'

'It's immaterial to me what you believe.'

'Naturally! And, of course, so long as Harry holds by his decision, you don't *have* to persecute him, do you?'

'Meaning what?'

'Only that I doubt his chosen vocation came as a big disappointment to you.'

Gabriel put a severe curb on his tongue.

'This would be a lot easier if you refrained from making assumptions,' he returned coldly. 'In fact, I find his attitude totally incomprehensible and can only marvel at your stoic acceptance of it. But then, having already told me he wouldn't come back, you were presumably expecting something of the sort.'

There was a short, tense silence.

'No.' Venetia swung abruptly away towards the window. 'No. I wasn't. Oh – Harry's been flirting with Catholicism for years but I never thought he'd carry it this far. I just thought he'd refuse to take the Oath because of Kit.'

'Kit?'

'Harry's twin. He died at Lichfield.'

'Ah.' A frown entered the dark grey eyes. 'I see.'

'Do you? I doubt it.' She turned back to him, her expression once more under control and bitterly hostile. 'However, none of this is of any consequence to you, is it? If it were, you wouldn't have come here wearing that damned uniform. So – since we both know that you hold all the cards – you may as well get on with whatever it was you came here to say.'

Gabriel saw no reason to tell her that his only other suit of clothes was still in Wat's hands undergoing much-needed restoration. He merely wished that she didn't have such an unfailing knack of making his hackles rise. And that he could walk out of the house, never to return.

Fixing her with his most shuttered gaze, he punished her with a long, excoriating silence. Then, as impassively as he was able, he said, 'When last we met, you told me that nothing would induce you to marry me – and, if that's still true, you have only to say so. If, on the other hand, you've decided that circumstances alter cases, I'm here to give you the chance to change your mind.'

It was precisely what she had needed to hear, but still something shifted unpleasantly behind Venetia's ribs.

'What are you saying?' she asked faintly.

'How much plainer do I have to make it?' came the irritable response. 'With no pleasure and a good deal of natural reluctance, I am signifying my willingness to marry you. Do you want me to go down on one knee?'

Very slowly, she lowered herself into the nearest chair and continued to stare at him with acute suspicion. 'Why? Why are you doing this?'

Gabriel drew a breath of pure impatience.

'Since you won't believe me if I tell you, that question seems rather pointless.' He paused. 'Well? After almost six months, it can hardly require much consideration.'

Venetia started forcing her frozen brain to work. He obviously hadn't spoken to Lawyer Crisp yet – but there were no guarantees as to how long that would last. And so, if she was going to save Ford Edge, it had to be done now.

'Are you serious?' she asked remotely.

'Would I be running such a stupid risk if I wasn't?'

'I – I don't know.'

'Well that's a step in the right direction, at all events. I thought you could forecast my every move,' returned Gabriel caustically. And then, 'All right. Let's see if we can find a motive that will appeal to you. I don't want your family's ruin

118

on my conscience; I need a well-bred wife to give me standing within the county; I want to remain in the Army and can't see myself running this place as well as Brandon Lacey; I want to spite my half-brother so badly that I can't resist taking his woman as well as his home. Take your pick. The truth – or something very like it – is in there somewhere.'

Venetia believed him and was convinced she knew what it was. Every line of her face expressing contempt, she said cuttingly, 'I'm sure of it. I'm only surprised it's taken you so long to admit it.'

'My fastidious nature,' excused Gabriel, shutting his anger behind an impersonal smile. 'But now that I've revealed myself – do you suppose I might have an answer?'

Her hands were shaking and, when she came to her feet, she discovered that her knees were too. She felt sick and very, very cold – as if she had been suddenly stricken with an ague. But there was no further reason to delay. It was time to step from her precipice and go hurtling down into the abyss; time to give the rebel bastard in front of her the satisfaction of hearing her eat her words.

Concentrating on keeping her voice level, she said, 'Why not? It would be a shame to keep Mother in unnecessary suspense, wouldn't it? And, as you say, I've already had long enough in which to think about it.'

'Quite.' As tense as she, Gabriel remained utterly motionless. 'So?'

'So I'll marry you,' came the bald, ungracious reply. 'For the sake of my family, I can't do anything else – and you know it. There is, however, one condition.'

A lead weight was settling in Gabriel's chest.

'And that is?'

'That you never, ever expect me to betray my friends, or forsake my cause in favour of yours. I may be forced to marry you, but I despise both the Parliament and the Army in equal measure. And it would be stupid of you to try and change that.'

Gabriel eyed her thoughtfully for a moment and reflected that, if stipulations were to be made, he could think of one or two more useful ones. He said, 'I am unlikely to waste my energy trying to change anything about you, Mistress, and I think it's true to say that I have no expectations of you whatsoever. But there is one thing I demand; and that is some small show of civility in front of others. I trust I make myself quite clear?'

Her lip curled scornfully. 'Perfectly.'

'I'm glad. Because if you forget it, I am very much afraid that you may not care for the consequences.' He smiled blandly. 'And no, I am not threatening to beat you. I'm merely dropping a word of warning in your shell-like ear.'

For the first time, Venetia found the look in his eye slightly worrying. She had never previously doubted her ability to keep this baseborn upstart in his place; now, however, she had a sudden nasty feeling that it might not be quite as easy as she'd thought.

Pushing her misgivings to a distant corner of her mind and smiling back with acidulous kindness, she said, 'Don't worry. After spending four years in the Queen's household, I think I can safely promise that it won't be *my* manners that show you up.'

Gabriel ignored the temptation to remark that – since he, too, knew better than to scratch, spit or break wind in public – it wouldn't be his either: 'Good. And now that we understand one another so well, perhaps we'd better set a date for our wedding. Will the last Monday in the month suit you? At least that avoids the necessity of us having to spend Christmas together.'

'According to your friends at Westminster, Christmas no longer exists,' came the bitter reply. 'But yes. I suppose that day is as good as any other. Here in our own chapel – and as quietly as possible.'

'Naturally.' It was the Colonel's turn to look satirical. 'I'll speak to the local clergyman, inform Sir Robert's lawyer and leave the rest to you. That way we need not meet again until the day itself.' He picked up his hat. 'And now I'll relieve you of my presence.'

Mention of Lawyer Crisp sent alarm feathering down Venetia's neck but she hid it and said, 'Not yet, you won't. First you have to go and make my mother's day by formally asking for my hand.'

His brows rose. 'You want me to realise that your mother

considers me rather lower down the social scale than her cook? Don't bother. I already know it.'

'You misunderstand.' Smiling grimly, Venetia crossed back towards both him and the door. 'As long as Ford Edge is returned to us and she doesn't actually have to have you living in the house, you could be a hunchback from the gutter. So go and tell her that all her cares are over. *I* am going to get changed.'

Back in the parlour, Gabriel found that her ladyship had used the intervening time to surround herself with her entire family. Elizabeth occupied the windowseat, Phoebe prowled restlessly about the hearth and the erstwhile bishop sat near his sister with his nose in a book. All of them impaled him with their eyes as soon as he entered the room and each female face expressed differing degrees of anxiety.

No one spoke. And because Gabriel had not expected to have to do this at all – let alone in front of an audience – he simply fixed Lady Clifford with an austere grey gaze and said curtly, 'Your daughter and I have agreed to be married on the 27th of this month. I trust that meets with your approval.'

Her ladyship gave an involuntary gasp of relief, her brother nodded vaguely before returning to his book and Elizabeth's beautiful blue eyes filled with sudden tears. Alone of them all, only Phoebe looked directly at him in that all-important moment. Crossing to his side, she stood on tiptoe to kiss his cheek.

'It will be all right,' she murmured comfortingly. 'Once it's done, Venetia will get back to being her old self. You'll see. And though I can't do much to make things better, I can at least be your friend. If you'll let me.'

Back at the inn, Gabriel found Mr Larkin staring gloomily into the bottom of an ale-pot.

'I'm glad you've been enjoying yourself,' remarked Gabriel in a close approximation of his usual tone. 'But is that the best entertainment this town can offer?'

'It'll do me,' replied Wat. And then, looking up, 'She accepted you, then.' It was not a question.

'Yes.' Gabriel pulled off his gloves and stood frowning down at them. 'But not graciously.'

'What else did you expect?' As always, abrasiveness covered deep concern. 'So what are you going to do now?'

Lightless grey eyes rose to meet his and the lean mouth twisted in something not quite a smile.

'Get drunk?' suggested the Colonel.

On the following morning, with his temples still pounding, Gabriel sallied forth to inform Mr Crisp of his impending marriage. The little lawyer received him with a caution which eventually became circumspect pleasure; and because Gabriel had scant interest in money beyond having enough of it to meet his basic needs, he did not ask the one question that might have substantially altered the tenor of their meeting. Mr Crisp saw him out with suitable politeness and satisfaction, and Gabriel set off through the first flakes of snow to visit his Aunt Sophia at Brandon Lacey.

Surrounded by Trixie, Trixie's three remaining offspring and no less than five cats, Sophia welcomed him into the parlour with her usual sweet smile and not a trace of surprise. Then, when she had settled him into a chair with a glass of wine, she said, 'I'm glad you've come. Perhaps you know if turnips are a good thing or not.'

'I beg your pardon?'

'Turnips,' she repeated. 'Dick Carter is a good man but he will persist in consulting me – and I've no idea at all about what crops would be best planted where or when.'

'Neither have I,' he returned dryly.

'Oh dear – haven't you?' For a moment she appeared nonplussed. Then, brightening, 'But I daresay you'll soon learn. And, in the meantime, I'm sure you'll manage to *appear* knowledgeable. It's what men do, isn't it?'

He laughed.

'Some men, perhaps. But in my profession, the fellow who makes decisions without really knowing what he's doing doesn't tend to live long.' He paused for a moment; then, with a trace of awkwardness, said, 'I have a number of things to tell you but, before I do, I would like to make it clear that I regard this house as your home – not mine. And, during the brief occasions when I'm forced to reside here, I shall take every care not to intrude upon you.'

For several seconds, Sophia's short-sighted brown eyes stared at a point just in front of his face. Then she said pensively, 'Well, that's highly commendable, of course . . . but it all sounds very disagreeable. Unless you're just not fond of animals? I do try to keep them out of the house – but since Robert died there hasn't been much incentive.'

The Colonel looked back at her somewhat uncertainly.

'It's nothing to do with the animals, Mistress Brandon. I was merely attempting to reassure you.'

'I know – and you need not,' she smiled. 'But I do wish you'd call me Sophy. After all, you can't go on addressing me formally . . . and "aunt" would sound rather silly.'

Since she was probably no more than a dozen years his senior, he thought it would sound extremely silly. And because her uncritical acceptance of him was as warming as it was unexpected, he smiled reluctantly back and said, 'Sophy, then. And thank you.'

She shook her head and attempted to recapture the rose silk shawl that was sliding from one elbow. 'You're very unhappy, aren't you? Why don't you pour us both some more wine and tell me about it.'

This time she succeeded in startling him and Gabriel took the time to wonder if her apparent vagueness was really all it seemed. Then, because she was right and he had the feeling that she might actually understand, he found himself doing exactly what she had suggested.

He told her everything. His desire to stay in the Army, his unwillingness to accept Brandon Lacey, his determination to shed responsibility for Ford Edge; and finally, in a few short, telling sentences, he described the previous day's meeting with Venetia. Sophia stroked the cat in her lap and said slowly, 'I wonder . . . I wonder if Venetia has seen Lawyer Crisp at all.'

'I've no idea. If she has, neither of them mentioned it to me. Does it matter?'

'Oh yes. It would explain why she agreed to marry you.'

Gabriel frowned slightly. 'Surely we already know that.'

'Perhaps. But if she also knows about the money, it would have been the last straw. Don't you see?'

'No,' he said. 'I don't see. What *about* the money?'

'The fact that there isn't any,' replied Sophia simply. 'Didn't Mr Crisp tell you?'

'Not a word.' The frown deepened. 'Sophy . . . in plain terms and as briefly as possible – what are you saying?'

'Oh dear!' She sighed and fidgeted with her shawls. 'I don't know what you were expecting your inheritance to be – but the simple truth is that you've got Brandon Lacey and very little else. About five hundred pounds, to be precise. I'm sorry.'

Gabriel's expression cleared and a hint of laughter warmed his eyes. 'Sorry? Why? When you've never had much more than twenty pounds at a time, five hundred sounds like a fortune.'

'Oh. Yes, I daresay it would. But it's not, you know. Not when you have to pay taxes on an estate of this size – and with the poor harvest we've just had.'

'But enough, wouldn't you say, on which to manage until we can begin to do better?'

She nodded.

'Then there's no problem, is there?' He shrugged. 'I don't yearn for riches and my requirements are very simple.'

'Yes,' agreed Sophia unhappily. 'But Venetia wouldn't know that. In fact, she's quite likely to assume the opposite. And, if Lawyer Crisp told her how things stand here, she may have worried that you'd want to fill your coffers at the expense of Ford Edge.'

The Colonel leaned back in his chair, staring thoughtfully into his wine. 'And do you think it likely that he has told her?'

'It's possible. You see, Mr Crisp acted for Sir Charles Clifford as well as for Robert.'

'So he may have felt some responsibility towards her? Yes. I see.' A small, sardonic smile curled his mouth. 'And, if he did, dear Venetia must have been a good deal more eager for our marriage than she would have me know. What a pity it didn't make her a bit more courteous.'

Sophia bent her head over the cat and examined a battle-scar on one of its ears. 'So you'll still marry her?'

'Since the reasons for doing so haven't changed, yes. But the likelihood of her having colluded with the lawyer to pull the wool over my eyes doesn't make me like it any better.'

'No. I suppose not. But she is more to be pitied than blamed, you know. She never used to be hard. Only with Kit dying and then her father – and Ellis going abroad the way he did, life hasn't been very easy for her.'

'It hasn't been easy for a lot of people,' came the flat response. 'Fortunately, however, most of them have managed to retain some basic shreds of civility. And if you're suggesting I should make allowances – I can only say that I'd be happy to do so if only her manner didn't make it impossible.'

Sophia sighed and then changed tack with her usual lack of warning. 'When are you going to move in?'

'Here? I rather think that's for you to say.'

'Tomorrow, then.'

Humour returned and, raising one brow, he said, 'So I can talk to Mr Carter about the turnips?'

'Turnips?' echoed Sophia blankly. 'Oh – yes. But I was really thinking that it would be a good idea if you started establishing yourself amongst our people, and learning a little about how the estate is run, before the wedding.'

'So that Venetia won't have yet another stick to beat me with?' inquired Gabriel blandly. 'It's a kind thought. Unfortunately, however, I doubt it will make much difference. And her armoury is already more than adequately stocked.'

Eight

While Gabriel, accompanied by a still extremely taciturn Mr
Larkin, installed himself at Brandon Lacey and began
attempting to acquaint himself with tenants, rents and
acreages under the initially wary eye of his bailiff, Venetia
fought a ceaseless campaign against her mother's desire to
invite half the county to her wedding and refused point-blank
to order a new gown for the occasion.

'But you must!' wailed Lady Clifford. 'Apart from
mourning clothes, you've had nothing new for three years.
What will people *think*?'

'They won't think anything – for the very simple reason
that they won't be there to see,' came the stubborn response.
'I've told you. I won't have the Ingilbys, the Slingsbys,
second-cousin Anne from Skipton – or any of the other
people you've mentioned – summoned here to see me marry
an illegitimate rebel soldier. And that is final.'

'But it will look so *odd*, dearest, so hole-and-corner.
Sordid, even.'

'So? Better that than to have them all sniggering behind
their hands while I'm standing at the altar. And as for what
I'll wear, it seems to me that black would be eminently
suitable – especially as your future son-in-law will doubtless
turn up in his uniform.' Venetia paused, eyeing her mother
bitterly. 'Oh – very well. If it will make you happy I'll wear
my violet silk. But any more talk of new clothes and wedding
guests and I won't get married at all!'

It did not, in fact, make her ladyship happy – for she had
been looking forward to a shopping spree in York on her own
account. But her daughter's last words made her see the
wisdom of saying no more on the subject . . . and the result
was that Christmas approached and passed on an air of

uneasy truce. Then, two days later, everyone dressed themselves with care but little real enthusiasm for the wedding.

Dismissing her maid at the first opportunity, Venetia sat, stony-faced, before the mirror. The gown looked well enough with its wide, sweeping neckline and falls of silver lace and her hair, drawn up at the back, formed a torrent of gleaming ringlets over her ears. On the surface, she looked exactly like the girl she had been five years ago at Whitehall. Underneath, she felt empty and tired and old.

'You look beautiful,' offered Elizabeth timidly from behind her. 'But perhaps just a touch of rouge . . . ?'

'No.'

'Oh. Well, no doubt you're right. And you can always pinch your cheeks a little before you—'

'I said no! Allow me some pride, at least.'

Elizabeth flushed and, unable to think of an answer, turned away. Then the door opened and Phoebe arrived on a tide of pink taffeta.

'He's here,' she said baldly. 'He arrived just now with Sophy and a funny little man in grey. Mother's taken them straight into the chapel. And Uncle James is waiting downstairs for you.'

Venetia's insides jerked themselves into a knot. For a moment she stared blindly at her sisters through the mirror and then, using every effort of will she possessed, drew herself slowly to her feet.

'Very well,' she said distantly. 'I'm ready.'

It was more than Phoebe could bear. Grasping the frozen hands in her own, she said, 'Don't! Don't look like that. I know this isn't what you wanted – but it won't be nearly as bad as you think.'

'Won't it?'

'No. He's really quite nice, you know. I liked him.'

'Yes. I daresay you did.' Venetia gently withdrew her hands and turned towards the door. 'But then, you like everyone – so it's hardly a recommendation, is it?'

Downstairs in the hall, James Bancroft offered her his arm and a small spray of Christmas roses along with an uneasy smile. He said, 'Chin up, my dear. Sacrifices such as yours do not go unrewarded. And for now, remember what the psalms tell us. *"Who is going through the vale of misery, use it for a well".'*

'Yes, Uncle. Unfortunately, just at the moment I'm more inclined to remember *"I myself have seen the ungodly in great power; and flourishing like a green bay-tree."* Shall we go? The sooner today is over, the better.'

Having been added to the house around the time of the Reformation, the interior of Ford Edge's small chapel was adorned only by the elegance of its pendant vaulting and a pair of marble effigied tombs. It was also wickedly cold . . . its stones gripped by the same severe frost that whitened the trees outside. And while Elizabeth slipped into place beside their mother, Venetia stood in the shadows of a pilaster, watching the meagre congregation surreptitiously shuffling in their seats or rubbing their hands together in a vain effort to combat the chill. She herself was already too numb to care.

To the left of the aisle behind her mother and sister, sat the Knightleys . . . the only local family Venetia had not been able to veto since they were soon to take Elizabeth to their bosoms . . . and much further back in the rear pews were a handful of Ford Edge's most loyal servants and tenants. To the right of it were only the groom himself, at whom Venetia dared not look, a small man with thinning hair and – unbelievably – Sophia. Venetia's fingers tightened on the fragile stems of her posy. She had heard, of course, along with everyone else in the district, that the Colonel had taken up residence at Brandon Lacey; what she had not expected was that Sophy would use the occasion to cloak him in respectability by choosing to sit directly behind him.

'My dear?' Her uncle's soft voice drifted anxiously through the icy cocoon around her. 'It's time.'

She started and drew a tiny, ragged breath. Then, laying her hand on his arm, she embarked on the shortest and most terrible journey of her life.

There was no music, no flowers, only the flickering pinpoints of a few candles. Venetia kept her gaze fixed firmly on the carved crucifix over the altar and tried not to see the dark-haired man waiting in front of it. He was a stranger and an enemy; and if she caught sight of that despised uniform now, she was afraid she might turn and run.

She arrived at the altar-rail and was dimly aware of Uncle James stepping back from her side. Then it began.

The familiar opening words of the service spun round her like a whirlpool. '*To join together this man and this woman . . . holy matrimony . . . an honourable estate.*' Yes, she thought desolately; they would be joined together – but in a travesty that was neither holy nor honourable. '*If any of you know cause or just impediment . . .*' Yes, cried a voice in her head. I know one – but no one cares.

The service wore on. The adversary at her side made his responses in crisp, expressionless tones and when her turn came, Venetia was relieved that her own voice was also cool and steady. Only her hand, when she held it blindly out to receive the ring, shook a little; then it was taken briefly in a cool, light clasp and the narrow gold band slid over her knuckle, heavy as an iron fetter.

Far, far away in the distant recesses of her mind, she heard Reverend Williams pronounce them man and wife and knew that the moment when she must turn her head to receive the bridal kiss was upon her. The moment in which she could no longer avoid looking at her new husband and would have to come face to face with what she had done.

Stiff and aching in every sinew, she shifted her position and received a confused impression of bleak, storm-grey eyes, and dark hair lying against a wide, lace collar. Instead of buff leather, her fingers encountered claret broadcloth and the dreaded orange sash had been replaced by one of pale grey silk. A wave of weakening relief swept over her and made her eyes sting with rare, unaccustomed tears. Then his mouth brushed hers in the most fleeting of kisses and the fragile protective shell which had sustained her throughout the last few hours shattered into a thousand pieces.

It was done. They were married.

Gabriel offered his arm and she laid her fingertips on it. Had Venetia but known it, he felt every bit as trapped as she, and with as good a cause. But of course she did not know; and wouldn't have cared if she had. Only Sophia cared . . . and to some extent, Phoebe; and Wat Larkin, marching grimly out of the chapel in Gabriel's wake, his eyes like knives in Venetia's back.

Back in the hall, tables were already prepared for the wedding-feast and servants bustled about offering wine. Venetia stood, as if carved from marble, amidst somewhat timid kisses and noticeably awkward good wishes. Gabriel returned Sophia's hug and then remained marooned, with Wat glowering belligerently at his shoulder, until Phoebe arrived at the head of a rescue party.

'Gabriel? I may call you that, may I not, now that you're my brother?' Smiling sunnily up at him, she slipped her hand through his arm and lifted up her face to be kissed. 'This is Frances Knightley and her brother Tom. Tom is to marry Bess in the spring.'

Gabriel bowed to Mistress Frances and received a frigid little curtsy in reply. But the stocky, unremarkable young man who seemed an unlikely match for the fair Elizabeth, held out his hand and said cheerfully, 'Pleased to meet you, Colonel. How do you find Yorkshire?'

'A trifle cold,' responded Gabriel, accepting the hand in a firm grasp. 'But I daresay that's only to be expected.'

Tom grinned and did not pretend to misunderstand.

'Barring unforeseen developments, it'll warm up in a few months or so – and meanwhile your best defence is a thick skin. But I suppose you've already discovered that.'

'You might say so.' The grey eyes surveyed Mr Knightley with faintly cynical humour. 'And now you can tell me whether you came over to greet the pariah of your own volition, or whether a certain young lady twisted your arm.'

'*Oh!*' said Phoebe indignantly. 'As if I would!'

'It's no good. Your measure's been taken,' sighed Tom, shaking his head. And then, to Gabriel, 'A bit of both, actually. I don't share your views myself, of course . . . but a couple of my best friends do. And I've always found that makes it a bit difficult to tar everyone with the same brush.' He shrugged. 'I suppose what I'm saying is that – contrary to what my father thinks – I believe there's good and bad on both sides.'

'My own view entirely,' agreed Gabriel. 'But then – being a professional soldier – I would think that, wouldn't I?' And, for the first time that day, he smiled.

A few minutes later, having waited until her betrothed left the Colonel's side, Elizabeth pulled him into a corner and said, 'How brave you are, Tom!'

'Brave? Why? As a matter of fact, I thought him quite a pleasant fellow. And so would you if you stopped letting Venetia colour your mind and gave him a chance.'

Bewilderment filled the blue eyes.

'But he's a Roundhead and – and—'

'And illegitimate. Yes, I know – and I agree that's unfortunate. But it's hardly his fault, after all. And, as for him being on the wrong side . . . well, plenty of other good men are on it with him. John Lambert, for one.' He smiled at her and squeezed her hand. 'Above all, Bess, you ought to remember that he didn't *have* to marry Venetia. He could have just let things go on as they were and kept hold of Ford Edge. But he didn't.'

On the far side of the room, trapped by her mother and Tom's parents, Venetia watched the Colonel talking first to Tom himself and then to Phoebe. Then she met the severely critical regard of the little man at Gabriel's elbow and, for some reason she could not identify, found herself forced to look away.

'Mother – who *is* that person?' she said abruptly, unaware that she had cut across something Philip Knightley had been saying. 'He looks like a stablehand.'

Lady Clifford sighed and cast a glance of helpless appeal at Tom's father. Then, 'I really don't know, dear – but I wouldn't be surprised. Colonel Brandon simply introduced him as Mr Larkin and said he would be acting as groomsman.'

Venetia sniffed. 'Well, it's a pity he couldn't find someone a bit more presentable. But I suppose, under the circumstances, that would be asking too much.'

Philip and Ruth Knightley exchanged significant glances and her ladyship murmured despairingly, 'Venetia – please! Not today.'

'Heavens, Ellen – you mustn't worry about us,' said Ruth, her face alight with shocked enjoyment. Then, laying a sympathetic hand on Venetia's arm, 'My dear, I think your conduct through this sordid business has been truly heroic. And I want you to know that—'

'Wait a moment,' frowned Venetia. 'Am I to understand that you know why I've made this marriage?'

'Well, yes. Once everything was settled – and with Tom's wedding to dear Elizabeth so close – your mother naturally explained it all to us.'

Lady Clifford quailed before her daughter's basilisk stare and Venetia thought, *Oh God. How could she be so stupid? If Ruth Knightley knows the truth, it'll be half-way round the county by now.*

Totally oblivious to the undercurrents, Mistress Knightley sailed blithely on. 'But I want you to know that, despite the stain of your husband's birth, no one will ever think the worse of *you*. We're all far, far too sorry for you to do that.'

Venetia's nails dug into her palms.

'Why thank you, Ruth. You've no idea what a comfort that is. Instead of worrying about being regarded as the bastard's wife, I can simply enjoy being the object of everyone's sympathy, can't I?'

Lady Clifford shuddered and said rapidly, 'I think it's time we all sat down to eat, don't you? Venetia, dear – perhaps you'd go and ask your uncle to announce it?'

'By all means,' came the mocking reply. 'Having put Cook to so much trouble, it would be a pity not to see the charade through to its bitter end, wouldn't it?'

Whilst maintaining a light conversation with Phoebe and Sophia, Gabriel conducted a discreet and ruthless appraisal of his bride. If looks were all, he thought judicially, he would have nothing to complain of. The mass of silver-gilt hair above that long, slender neck; the alabaster skin and the perfect oval of her face, set with its incredible ever-changing eyes, all these combined to give Venetia the kind of beauty one rarely saw. But, unfortunately looks were *not* all; and he had never at any time seen her actually smile. Nor, to be truthful, did he expect to.

Collecting Phoebe's gaze and speaking in a tone any man in his regiment would have recognised, he said, 'Tell me something. How long has your sister known that Sir Robert didn't die a rich man.'

Startled and not a little discomfited, Phoebe flushed. 'I – I

133

don't know. Several weeks, perhaps. But she only told us last night.'

'And did she also mention hoping that I'd remain ignorant long enough for today's fiasco to take place? Or no. Why should she? She just waited until she was sure before telling you anything at all.'

Phoebe cast a glance of agonised appeal at Sophia only to find her busily engaged in removing a brooch from the silk fringe of her shawl. Sighing, she said, 'It's very bad, I know. But you mustn't blame her too much. She—'

'I don't,' said Gabriel blandly. 'I do, however, worry about Lawyer Crisp's evident conflict of loyalties and feel that both he and I would be happier knowing he can't be placed in this situation again.'

Sophia's fingers stilled on the hopelessly tangled fringe and her gaze rose to his face. Before she could speak, however, Phoebe said baldly, 'Isn't there *any* money?'

'Very little. Why?'

'Oh – I don't know. I just thought that you and Venetia have problems enough already . . .' She paused and then, as her uncle arrived at her elbow, said hopefully, 'Of course, it would be even better if you could think of some way of making a fortune yourself.'

The well-meaning naïveté of it made Gabriel smile.

'Depending on one's point of view, I daresay it would. But I'm unlikely to do it in the Army.'

'The Garland,' murmured James Bancroft dreamily. 'You could look for the Lacey Garland.'

Phoebe and the Colonel eyed him blankly. Sophia, on the other hand, smiled vaguely and said, 'Why not? Everyone else has.'

'You don't believe in it?' James asked.

She shrugged. 'As a child, I did. Like every generation before us, Robert and I all but took the house apart. But when – despite consistent searching – something remains hidden for two-and-a-half centuries, it's probably because it doesn't exist.'

'*What* doesn't exist?' asked Phoebe, her face alight with interest. 'What are you talking about?'

'The Lacey Garland,' said her uncle, as though this

explained everything. 'But as Mistress Sophia says, it's probably no more than a charming legend. And now I think we had all better take our places at table. Your mother is beginning to look a trifle fraught.'

With carefully concealed reluctance, Gabriel occupied the seat beside his bride. Since exchanging their vows, they had tacitly avoided speaking to each other. Now however, Venetia hissed irritably, '*Must* that dreadful little man of yours scowl so? Or is that his natural expression?'

'With Wat, it's rather hard to tell. Why? Does it unnerve you?'

'Hardly.'

'Good. In that case, all you need do is get used to it – and try remembering that his name is Walter Larkin.' He met her eyes with pleasant finality. 'I ought perhaps to point out that, after fifteen years, my relationship with him isn't going to change now.'

Venetia opened her mouth on a suitably pithy retort and then, without quite knowing why, thought better of it.

'Very sensible,' remarked Gabriel. 'Have some fish.'

Gritting her teeth, she did as he suggested. The mere thought of food sickened her, never mind the smell of it, but being so closely under Ruth Knightley's inquisitive stare it was necessary to keep up appearances.

On the other side of the table, Phoebe was busy interrogating Mistress Brandon. 'But what *is* this Garland – and who hid it – and why?'

Sophia gazed at her venison pasty for a moment and then regretfully laid down her knife. 'I don't know, dear. All we're sure of is that Lacey Manor was granted to Hugh Brandon by John of Gaunt in 1378. According to the story, the Duke made the gift as a mark of his – his admiration for Hugh's wife, Philippa; and he is also supposed to have given her a personal token to remember him by.'

'The Garland,' breathed Phoebe. 'And Hugh hid it away because he was jealous.'

'Very likely,' agreed Sophia, returning to her plate with a faint smile.

The youthful face took on a faraway look.

'Pearls beyond price . . . rubies from India . . . a portrait of

135

himself, framed in gold. I wonder what he gave her?' And then, meeting her eldest sister's eye, 'Did *you* know about all this?'

'The Garland legend? Yes. I believe El—' Venetia stopped and then went on defiantly, 'I believe Ellis did once mention it. But I don't think it's worth getting too excited. After all, if you don't know what you're looking for – how are you to know when you've found it?'

'*I'd* know,' said Phoebe firmly. 'I'm sure I would.'

Gabriel regarded her with lazy amusement over the rim of his glass. 'Then, if Sophy and your sister don't object, I suggest you come to Brandon Lacey and look for it.'

Pink with pleasure, she said eagerly, 'May I really?' And, to Sophia, 'You wouldn't mind?'

'Not at all,' came the tranquil reply. 'If your mother can spare you for a few days, you could come to stay.'

A little later, when Phoebe was concentrating on fishing pieces of candied fruit out of her syllabub, Venetia directed a moody sideways gaze at the Colonel and said, 'Did you have to encourage her in this nonsense?'

'Is there any harm in it?'

'Not harm, precisely. But you don't know what she's like. She'll turn the place inside out and then, when she doesn't find what she's looking for, she'll start all over again. Phoebe,' concluded Venetia bitterly, 'is one of nature's most persistent optimists.'

Gabriel looked back at her with detached irony.

'She is also entitled to her dreams,' he replied. 'And just because you and I know they won't last . . . is that any reason to disillusion her?'

Effectively silenced, Venetia sought refuge in her glass and left him to field a series of tactless queries from Philip Knightley concerning Parliament's condemnation of *The Agreement of the People* and the various terms currently being offered to the King. Gabriel responded with cool urbanity but refused to be drawn. The meal started to seem interminable and, outside the windows, the sky grew dark.

Finally, however, the party transferred itself to the parlour while the congealing remains of the feast were cleared away. The atmosphere of determined conviviality began to grow somewhat strained but, because Lady Clifford had insisted on everyone staying the night, it was necessary to at least try and maintain it. Tom Knightley worked hard at keeping the gentlemen's glasses filled and persuaded Elizabeth and Phoebe to lead the company in a few songs.

James Bancroft joined in the singing – along with Tom's father and sister and Sophia Brandon. But, under the differing gazes of Wat, Lady Clifford and Ruth Knightley, Gabriel merely watched the proceedings over folded arms from the mantelpiece and Venetia sat, silent and aloof, by the window. Tom groaned to himself and hoped no one would be crass enough to try bedding the newlyweds in the traditional way.

No one did. As early as was possible without appearing rude, people began stifling yawns or remarking on the lateness of the hour and slipping gratefully away to their rooms. And therefore, still in complete silence and much sooner than she had hoped, Venetia found herself guiding Colonel Brandon up the stairs to the chamber which, for this one night, she had no alternative but to share with him.

It was a large, panelled corner-room with windows on two aspects and a huge carved bed. It was also decidedly cold – and draughty enough to make the fire smoke. Gabriel glanced around him and then, turning to Venetia, unlocked his jaws.

'Yours?' he said.

'No.' She was still standing, candle in hand, just inside the door. 'It's the one Queen Henrietta Maria once slept in. You're supposed to be suitably impressed.'

'I'm more inclined to hope her Majesty came in the summer,' he replied, picking up a pair of tongs and setting about expertly re-banking the fire. Then, without turning his head, 'Aren't you staying?'

The fact that he didn't sound as if he cared either way added to, rather than diminished, the curious sense of unreality that had been creeping over Venetia. She said, 'Don't be stupid. Ruth Knightley's already having enough fun at my expense. Do you really think I'm about to risk giving her yet more by creeping about the house at the dead of night or sneaking into my own bed beside her daughter?'

Gabriel rose from his task, dusting his hands.

'A simple "yes" would have been enough,' he remarked.

'But if it was the smoke that was keeping you at a safe distance, you will observe that I appear to have corrected the problem.'

It was nothing to do with the smoke and he knew it perfectly well, thought Venetia edgily. She just didn't want to sleep with him but wasn't sure it could be avoided. Looking back, she realised she should have made it a stipulation on the day he'd proposed – but she hadn't dared do so in case it made a difference; and, even if she had, there was no guarantee he would have honoured his promise . . . not now they were shut in the same room together for the whole of the night.

Eyeing him warily, she took a couple of steps away from the door to set the candle down on a small table beside the bed. She felt chilled to the marrow and not nearly as controlled as she would have liked to appear. She said abruptly, 'There is wine, if you want it.'

'Not particularly. Do you?'

She shook her head and once more the silence yawned dangerously about them. He did not *look* as if he was waiting to pounce – and she knew he actively disliked her. But neither of these was any safeguard because he was a common soldier – with, presumably, a common soldier's habits; and though Venetia was not in the least vain, she could not help knowing that men generally considered her desirable.

Gabriel sighed and, recognising the futility of all the innocuous, tactful approaches he might have made, said, 'I think we can agree that our situation is unfortunate. But at some point we're going to have to start making the best of it – and now would probably be as good a time as any.'

'What did you have in mind?' she asked.

'Well, to begin with, let us stop staring at each other like two cats defending their territory,' came the crisp reply. 'And since we've plainly nothing to say to one another, I suggest we bring this day to a summary end by going to bed.'

A visible tremor passed over her. 'And then?'

'We sleep. What else?' Then, with weary irascibility, 'Oh my God! You don't seriously suppose that – after the hellish day we've had and considering how we feel about each other – I'm likely to be devoured by lust, do you?'

She flushed. 'I sincerely hope not.'

'Good. Because, hard though it may be for you to accept,

I'm not inclined towards rape and have an undoubtedly plebeian preference for more than just a body between the sheets. Even, I'm afraid, when the goods on offer are as decorative as you.'

'There's no need to be offensive,' snapped Venetia. 'I've no way of knowing *what* your preferences are. And I don't particularly want to find out.'

'No one's asking you to.' Gabriel ran a hand through his hair and strove for a lighter tone. 'All right. Now we've cleared the ground, let's see if we can progress. I promise not to molest your body if you don't molest mine. And, though that bed could comfortably accommodate a family of six, we can always lay the bolster down the middle in time-honoured fashion if you've any doubts as to my intentions. Well?'

Venetia knew that what he said made sense. The trouble was that she was too stubborn to admit it – and neither could she bring herself to undress while there was any chance of him watching her.

'Do what you like,' she said carelessly. 'I'm going to sit by the fire for a while.'

Just for a moment, Gabriel continued to stare meditatively at her and then an unholy glint entered his eye.

'Suit yourself,' he shrugged. And began calmly discarding his clothes.

Being careful not to hurry, Venetia stalked to the hearth and sat down with her back to him. She heard the sound of him unbuckling his sword, of his coat being laid across the chest, of his boots hitting the floor; and finally, releasing a breath she did not know she had been holding, she heard the bed creak as he got into it.

She did not know how long she sat there, getting steadily colder as the fire burned low and the candles guttered in their sockets. But eventually common sense prevailed and, rising stiffly, she looked across the room to see if the Colonel was asleep. He lay on his side breathing evenly, one well-muscled arm relaxed against the pillow. As quietly as she was able, Venetia picked up her night-rail from the foot of the bed and retired with it into the farthest corner of the chamber. It was only then that she realised she had a problem.

After ten minutes of writhing and twisting to reach the laces of her gown, she had succeeded only in manipulating them into a beautiful knot and wearing herself out. It was the last, treacherous straw and she could have screamed with vexation. Then, as she contorted herself for one final effort, a maddeningly bland voice from the bed said, 'Would you like some help?'

Venetia froze and peered at him through descending coils of hair. Far from being decently asleep, the Colonel was propped up on one elbow, watching her struggle.

'It's entirely up to you, of course,' he continued smoothly. 'But unless you're prepared to sit up all night or come to bed as you are, I just thought a little assistance might not come amiss.'

Feeling every bit as foolish as he no doubt thought her, and not trusting herself to speak, Venetia marched over to the bed and wordlessly presented him with her back. If he said anything clever or dared to laugh at her, she would hit him.

Strong, deft fingers busied themselves with the knot and for a while there was silence. Then the lace was tugged free of its eyelet holes and Gabriel said, 'There – it's done. Anything else?'

'No.' Venetia retreated smartly to her corner. 'I can manage the rest. Thank you.'

'Don't mention it.' His brows rose over eyes filled with mocking amusement. 'And don't worry. You haven't aroused my animal passions – or even come close to it.'

'Then you won't mind turning away while I undress,' she responded in a voice that was no longer quite steady.

'My dear girl, I'll do better than that,' said Gabriel. And, reaching over to the table beside him, he snuffed out the last remaining candle to leave his new bride modest and unsullied in the dark.

Wildfire

January to August, 1648

Fight on brave soldiers for the Cause
Fear not the Cavaliers.
Their threatenings are as senseless as
Our jealousies and fears.
'Tis you must perfect this great work
And all Malignants slay
You must bring back the King again
The Clean Contrary Way.

When Charles we have made bankrupt
The power and crown bereft him
And all his loyal subjects slain
And none but Rebels left him,
When we have beggared all the land
Sent our trunks away
We'll make him then a glorious Prince
The Clean Contrary Way.

Satirical Royalist ballad

One

By the time Samuel Radford got out of Newgate, he'd had more than enough of the place. It was his first imprisonment – which, considering what he'd been up to in the last couple of years, was pretty remarkable; and it had only lasted a little over six weeks which was luckier still. But neither of these facts lessened the stink or the noise, nor made up for the lack of anything approaching proper daylight. And though Sam tried to follow Lilburne's example by expounding his ideas to his fellow-inmates, he didn't find it helped much.

After his arrest, he had been hauled before the Committee of Examinations, refused to take the oath on the grounds that he didn't know what he was being charged with and been returned smartly to his cell. This much, according to everyone he knew who'd been in a similar position, was strictly routine. The next step was to prepare a defence that admitted nothing and hope for a chance to use it. Sam, with time on his hands, had prepared at least three. By the end of December, he was wondering how long he should wait before petitioning for a second hearing – and then he found himself suddenly free.

This was unexpected enough. More surprising still was the fact that he found Eden Maxwell waiting laconically at the prison gates to inform him that he owed his release to Colonel Brandon. Sam stared at him blankly for a moment and then, working it out, silently blessed Bryony. He said, 'I see. Well, I hope the Colonel doesn't expect this to make me change my ways – because, if so, he'll be disappointed.'

Eden's brows rose. 'I'm glad you're grateful. It makes everything so worthwhile.'

'Oh, I'm grateful all right – just not fundamentally altered.

But there's no need for you to put yourself out any further. I'll explain it all to him myself when I see him.'

'That's nice. Unfortunately, you may have to wait a while. He's got leave of absence until April.'

'Then I'll just have to possess my soul in patience, won't I?' grinned Sam. 'Unless, of course, you'd like to give me his address?'

Back at his meagre lodgings, Samuel discovered that his belongings had been turned upside down by the Stationer's Company on the pretext of searching for illicit pamphlets but that his rent had apparently been paid by the City Levellers. The Lord gives and the Lord takes away, thought Sam philosophically . . . and set about unearthing his only other suit of clothes from the chaos. It was even more threadbare than the one he was wearing but at least it didn't reek of Newgate. Then, before bothering to put the room to rights, he went down into the yard and risked inflammation of the lung by sluicing himself long and hard under the icy water of the pump.

Two hours later, Annis Morrell ushered him into her parlour with an expression of kindly concern and pressed him down in the settle beside the fire.

'You look dreadful,' she said. 'What on earth have you been doing these past few weeks?'

Sam hesitated and then, because he couldn't go on covering his tracks forever, said, 'If you really want to know, I've been in Newgate.'

Annis took a small step back and cast a nervous glance across at baby John, sleeping peacefully in his cot on the far side of the hearth.

'It's all right.' He rose quickly. 'I haven't got gaol fever as far as I know – and I washed and changed before I came. But you're quite right. I ought to have thought of it. I'm sorry.'

She took a good, long, look at him. He was extremely pale and had lost weight but he didn't look at all feverish. She said slowly, 'I forgive you. But before you sit down again, you'd better tell me *why* you were in prison.'

'I was arrested for distributing so-called inflammatory

pamphlets amongst the soldiers at Corkbush Field last month. In short, I'm what you'd call a Leveller.'

Annis eyed him calmly. 'But I knew that.'

'You – you did? How?'

'Because of the green ribbon you had in your lapel when you first walked in with Bryony. I suppose it was Gabriel's idea to remove it?'

'Yes. Yes, it was.' He hesitated. 'Excuse me for asking – but did your husband notice it too?'

'No. But I think it's time you put that right,' said Annis placidly. And then, 'Tell me . . . does Bryony know about your stay in Newgate?'

'Of course I know,' said a flat voice from the doorway. 'I may even have played a part in getting him out again.'

Sam turned swiftly and then felt his smile freeze as he absorbed the utter despondency on Bryony's face. Annis, however, being quite used to her niece's recent dejection, merely said, 'What do you mean by that?'

'What I say.' Bryony closed the door and crossed the room towards them. 'If you must know, I asked Gabriel to see to it. But that was before he went rushing off to Yorkshire – so he probably forgot.'

'He didn't,' said Sam quietly. 'Why else do you think I hurried here? As soon as I learned who'd arranged my release, I knew it was you I had to thank for it.'

'Yes. Well. I just wish he'd got you out for Christmas. Not that it makes much difference now we're no longer supposed to celebrate it.' Her expression, which had become marginally brighter, turned into a frown as she looked at her aunt. 'He's told you everything, hasn't he? Are you going to tell Uncle Jack?'

'No. Mr Radford will do that himself.'

'But he *can't!*'

'On the contrary. If you and he want to remain friends now his activities have started landing him in gaol, there's no question but that he *must*.' Annis smiled faintly. 'And you may find Jack less unsympathetic than you think. At any rate, you're going to have to find out.'

Sam drew a long breath. 'He's in the workshop?'

'Yes.'

'Then I'll go now and get it over with.'

'I'm coming with you,' announced Bryony dourly. 'We might as well share a joint lecture. And afterwards, if nobody minds, you can take me for a walk.'

Jack looked up from the work he was supervising with one of his apprentices and then, telling the lad to go and oil the grinding-wheel, strolled forward to meet his visitors.

'Well, well,' he said. 'The wanderer returns. I was beginning to think we'd offended you.'

'No. It's I who am about to offend you,' said Sam. And, for the second time in an hour, made his confession.

When he had finished, Jack surveyed him in brooding silence. Then he said, 'It's a little late to applaud your honesty. But it certainly explains a few things.'

'Very likely,' said Bryony. 'But now that you know – are you going to tell Sam to stay away?'

'If his coming here is going to put us all under suspicion and result in the house being taken apart by agents of the Committee of Examinations, I'd be mad if I didn't,' returned Jack irritably. And to Sam, '*You* must know what I'm talking about – so explain it to her. And, in the meantime, try to convince me I'm not going to wake up one morning to find her being hauled off by a couple of pursuivants.'

A sudden grin lit Sam's mobile face. 'Do you need convincing?' he asked. 'Her interest in national affairs registers at several points below zero.'

For an instant it looked as if Mr Morrell was going to smile back and Bryony held her breath. Had she but known it, however, Jack was in something of a quandary. The trouble was not just that he liked Sam – but that, ever since the day Peter Chamberlen had delivered Annis safely of their son, his hostility towards the good doctor's Leveller friends had somehow dwindled. He had even, though he'd have bled to death sooner than admit it, come to the reluctant conclusion that they had one or two good ideas. The result was that he fixed Mr Radford with an austere eye and said, 'All right. I take your point. But I want your word that you'll never involve her in anything even remotely illegal.'

146

'I won't,' said Sam simply. 'Anything else?'

'Yes. I'd like to observe that if either one of you has anything in mind beyond mere friendship, you can forget it right now. I don't think I'm an unreasonable man; but it will be a cold day in hell before I let my niece marry a fellow with only part-time employment as a cloth-cutter – and one, moreover, who's likely to spend half his life in gaol. Clear?'

'Clear,' agreed Sam unsteadily.

'Clear,' echoed Bryony. Then, with the ghost of a smile, 'Don't worry. I like Sam – but I wouldn't marry him if I was at my last prayers.'

'And I'd as soon wed a well-brought-up Puritan,' remarked Sam cheerfully. 'But I suppose it takes all sorts, doesn't it?'

Once out in the crisp air of the street, Bryony relapsed immediately into depression and stalked silently in the general direction of Bunhill Fields. Sam thrust his hands deep into his pockets and followed her, his limp slightly more pronounced than usual after six weeks enforced inactivity.

'What was it like in Newgate?' asked Bryony abruptly.

Having been under the impression that she had demanded this walk in order to tell him her own troubles, this wasn't the opening Sam had expected. He shrugged slightly and said, 'The first week was the worst. They put me in the common gaol with all the cut-throats and pickpockets and so forth. It's filthy and overcrowded and you daren't sleep in case somebody steals your boots. Fortunately, my friends found out where I was and brought me enough money to pay for a cell with a bed – which, though small and rather damp, seemed like luxury.' He paused and then added dryly, 'It's robbery, of course. Eleven shillings a week, excluding food and linen. But then, they're selling to a captive market. You might call it a monopoly.'

She looked at him. 'Politics, Sam?'

'Yes. You should know by now that I can't help it. But I'm quite amenable to changing the subject.' He raised one dark brow. 'Well? Are you going to tell me what's wrong?'

Her mouth drooped again and she stared down at her feet.

'It's Gabriel. He – he's gone off to marry some horrible woman in Yorkshire . . . and I can't *bear* it. It wouldn't be so bad if he loved her – but he doesn't. He's only doing it because of her stupid land.'

Sam frowned. He wasn't especially well-acquainted with the Colonel and they clashed on certain vital issues, but he nevertheless said, 'Are you sure? I wouldn't have thought he was the type to marry for money.'

'He isn't! He's being honourable and sacrificing himself. *She's* the mercenary one. And, as if that wasn't quite bad enough, Uncle Jack says she's a Royalist.' She paused and heaved a morose sigh. 'I suppose I'd better explain it all from the beginning.'

Sam thought so too but, at the end of it, wasn't sure he was much the wiser – except on one point.

'Bryony . . . I know you have a fancy for the Colonel. But, quite apart from being almost your uncle, have you never thought that he's perhaps a little old for you?'

She cast him a glance of acute disfavour.

'You sound just like Annis.'

'I'm sorry. I don't mean to. But I can't help thinking that he must be old enough to be your father.'

'He's not! He's thirty-four and I love him!'

'And what about when he's approaching fifty and you're just turned thirty? Oh – all right, all right. You're not a child and you know what you're doing. But all this doom and gloom is pretty futile, don't you think? After all, if he's married there's not a lot you can do; and if he's not, you've been upsetting yourself for nothing.'

'*Nothing?* You don't know what it's like!' she replied tearfully. 'I've loved him for ages – at least a year. And he would have noticed me in time. I know he would.'

'At the risk of having you hit me, I'd have to say that I sincerely doubt that. You may not regard him as an uncle – but I'll wager my last groat he looks on you as his niece. And a fellow with any scruples at all doesn't let himself fall in love with a seventeen-year-old relative.'

Bryony scowled. 'Do you *have* to be so depressing?'

'Yes. It's my fatal flaw. Yours, of course, is being naturally crabby.'

'I'm not!'

'Yes, you are.' He grinned companiably. 'I suppose it might be mended, though. You just need the right diversion – only I don't have time to find it right now. I really ought to go and spread word of my release to those whom it will interest. And of course I want to talk to John.'

'Mr Lilburne?' An odd gleam entered Bryony's eye. 'The Commons have let him out on bail.'

'My goodness! It's not like you to be so well-informed,' he teased. 'But yes. They have. And it was just my damned luck to be clapped up at more or less exactly the same time – which is why I'm eager to see him.'

'Will you take me with you?'

Sam stopped dead. 'What?'

'I asked you to take me with you. I didn't mean now, today – but sometime. Will you?'

There was a brief, incredulous silence and then he said, 'Are you mad? Your Uncle Jack would have my head!'

'Not if he doesn't know about it.' Bryony smiled, winsomely. 'Go on. Say you'll take me.'

Sam hunched his shoulders and stared at her narrowly.

'Why? Why should you want to meet Free-born John?'

'Well, he's famous, isn't he? And popular. Oh – people may disagree with him but they don't seem to actually dislike him. Unless I've got it wrong?'

'No. You haven't got it wrong. So what are you saying? That you'd like to witness this phenomenon for yourself? Even if it means enduring a political lesson in order to do so?'

'Well, yes.' Bryony surveyed him innocently and played her trump card. 'I may be ignorant – but I'm not stupid. And if Free-born John is everything you say, he won't have any trouble educating me, will he?'

'No,' said Sam shortly. 'He won't. And that's precisely what I'm afraid of.'

During the first week of January a tremor of shock passed over London when it was learned that his Majesty had rejected Parliament's latest peace terms in favour of signing an Engagement with the Scots. People muttered darkly about a potential invasion; apprentice disturbances assumed a suddenly Royalist flavour; and the Commons immediately took the dual precautions of disbanding the Committee of Both Kingdoms and voting that no more negotiations be carried on with the King. But no one, so far as Jack Morrell could see, was doing anything about rising prices and continually falling trade.

It took Bryony several days to persuade Sam to introduce her to his hero and, by then, what had begun as no more than an idle suggestion had become a mild obsession. Not unnaturally, Sam put this down to her usual habit of wanting things she couldn't have and never dreamed that he himself was partly responsible. But the truth was that Bryony, in pursuing her campaign through a series of questions, found herself increasingly intrigued by the answers. She learned how Sam had first met Lieutenant-Colonel Lilburne at the siege of Banbury in 1644 – how he'd talked through the night with him and been inspired with a sense of purpose that had stayed with him ever since. And it made her think. Sam had been eighteen then, only a year older than she was now; but she could not imagine any man – no matter how charismatic he might be – having such an effect on her. She did not, of course, realise that Sam was already doing so.

The small house in Halfmoon Alley to which Sam eventually took her lay close to the Gate House at Westminster and presented an appearance of neatness struggling against chaos. A baby in the crook of her arm and two toddlers clutching at her skirts, Elizabeth Lilburne attempted to make room amidst books and papers for the bread she had just taken from the oven; and her husband sat on the other side of the table, clutching a sheaf of closely-written notes to his chest. Both of them were laughing. They turned with one accord to welcome their guests.

Afterwards, Bryony could never remember precisely what she had expected John Lilburne to be. Like Sam and a lot of other people both before and since, she only knew that he was none of the things she had imagined. Her first impression was of a well-dressed man in his early thirties, with short dark hair, a moustache and a face mildly disfigured by scars from the accident which had all but blinded one eye; her second was that he looked rather ill. But these were only superficial things. The attributes that made Free-born John what he was came from inside, passion tempered with humour, integrity with warmth, zeal with charm. And something else less easy to identify . . . but which Bryony eventually recognised as a simple ability to care.

She sat quietly while he and Sam discussed committee reports from the Army, from towns outside London and from a tavern called the Whalebone. Then they moved rapidly on to the latest progress of something called the Long Petition.

'And this time, men must be prepared to support it with action, knowing that they're fighting for their liberties and privileges – otherwise I wouldn't give three pence for ten thousand hands,' concluded Lilburne crisply. 'But enough of that now.' He sat back in his chair and eyed Bryony with a faint gleam of mischief. 'Sam tells me you wanted to meet me because I'm famous. Is that true?'

She cast Sam a glance of burning resentment and blushed. 'Partly. I daresay he also told you I haven't two opinions to rub together?'

'I don't think he put it quite like that. In fact, I distinctly recall him describing you as curious.'

Bryony put an arm round two-year-old Bess and absently lifted her on to her knee. 'Does that make a difference?'

'Oh yes. Curiosity is the sign of an open mind – not an empty one. And if you don't ask questions, how are you to draw conclusions?'

This was a view which had never before occurred to Bryony and she found it encouraging. She looked at Sam again, half-expecting him to deflate her with some teasing remark but he merely folded his arms and grinned. So, turning back to the man who'd been called everything from England's Physician to the Seducer of the Army, she said diffidently, 'Is that what you did – in the beginning, I mean?'

'Me? No. I was taken to visit Dr Bastwick in prison. He'd been gaoled along with Prynne and Burton for writing pamphlets against the bishops and that struck me as unfair. I felt – as indeed I still do and with much greater cause – that a man should be able to express his views freely, without fear of arrest. So I volunteered to get Bastwick's *Litany* printed in the Low Countries and to distribute it here.' He paused briefly and shrugged. 'I was caught, of course. And that was when it really began.'

'I don't understand,' said Bryony, puzzled. 'Hadn't it begun already?'

'No.' Elizabeth looked up from the pie she was preparing. 'Up till then, he'd just been one more young fellow dealing in illicit pamphlets. But when he refused the Star Chamber oath, he managed to become the people's champion.'

'Whose story is this?' complained her husband. And then, to Bryony, 'It wasn't so much that I refused the oath. Others had done that before me. The difference was that I rejected it on the grounds of its illegality – and as a free-born Englishman.' He smiled again. 'That was exactly ten years ago. And, as you'll appreciate, it was a turn of phrase I've never been allowed to forget.'

Bryony smiled back at him – mainly because it didn't seem possible to do anything else. 'And then?'

'He was whipped at the cart's tail and put in the pillory,' said Sam, unable to stay silent any longer, 'And when they gagged him to stop him speaking, he produced handfuls of pamphlets from his pockets and threw them to the crowd.'

'After which he was locked up in the Fleet for two years,' added Elizabeth with an odd mixture of fondness and irritation.

Free-born John looked from his wife to his friend and back to Bryony, his eyes full of laughter.

'You see? No one allows me to speak.'

'No one that I know of can stop you.' Elizabeth placed a small lump of pastry in her son's grubby fist and set about rolling out the rest. 'If they could, you might be at home more often.'

'I'd only get under your feet.'

'I could accustom myself to it,' she said. And then, noticing Bryony's uncertainty, 'Don't worry, my dear. It's true I hate him being in prison, but I wouldn't have him ignore injustice in order to sit at home in his slippers. And this latest sentence is a disgrace. All John did was to give evidence in a case of army corruption – and with Noll Cromwell's approval too!'

'Is that why the House of Lords sent you to the Tower?' asked Bryony, faintly shocked.

'Not entirely,' replied Lilburne. 'I'm there because, in accordance with Magna Carta, I denied their lordships' right to judge either myself or any other commoner of England in a criminal matter.'

'M-Magna Carta?' she echoed. And then, feebly, 'Oh. Yes, of course.'

There was a small silence and an expression of amused severity crossed the fine-boned face. 'Never pretend, my child. If you don't know – ask.'

'I – I will,' promised Bryony, fervently. 'I'll ask Sam on the way home. But first there's something I'd like to ask you – if I may?'

'And what might that be?'

She hesitated briefly, drew a deep breath and said simply, 'Please may I come again?'

It was the first visit of many and the beginning of Bryony's metamorphosis. Sometimes she talked to Free-born John herself and sometimes she merely listened to him talking to others while she helped Elizabeth with the baking, the ironing or the children. And gradually, almost without realising it, she started to absorb the full, complex scope of the Leveller programme.

From John himself, she learned that law was the surest sanctuary of the weak. 'But laws must be openly declared in English for every free man to read – for where there is no law declared, there can be no transgression. Then again, when a law *does* stand, it is – or should be – as binding upon a Duke as on a cottager. Or where's the use of it?'

She heard and was stirred by his arguments in favour of religious toleration and freedom of speech and the press. She shed tears over his descriptions of the brutality of gaols like Newgate and the shocking living conditions of the poor, then applauded his ideas on prison reform and his assertion that schools, hospitals and the opportunity to work ought to be provided for the destitute. And, eventually, she asked a series of tentative questions about the right to vote.

153

'As things stand,' he told her, 'only men who own land worth more than forty shillings a year can vote. Our aim is to extend the franchise to all except servants and beggars.'

'And women?' asked Bryony, daringly.

Lilburne's bright dark gaze held a glint of something that might have been approval. He said, 'I'm often accused of wanting to change the world in a day. But even *I* can see that getting women the vote may take a night as well.'

'Why?'

'Because, though many have minds of their own, many more are under the sway of their husbands. As the law says they should be.'

'Then why not change the law?'

Elizabeth looked up from feeding the baby and smiled. 'That sounds like a fair question.'

He smiled back. 'It is. And, though very few people agree with me, I personally think that one day it will happen. But not, I suspect, in my lifetime.'

'And meanwhile women go on being classed as servants or beggars,' remarked Bryony disgustedly. 'I don't think much of that.'

'Nor I,' agreed Elizabeth. 'Unfortunately, however, it's the way of the world. And as John has said, even *he* can't change everything.'

'No. I suppose not. But it would be nice to know he'd at least *thought* of it.' Bryony stared into space for a moment and then, turning back to Free-born John, said, 'All right. Tell me instead exactly what Sam means when he talks about the sovereignty of the people. The way he explains it, you'd think the Parliament was only there to do our bidding. But that can't be right, can it?'

'It is precisely right,' came the concise reply. 'When Parliament took up arms against the King, it did so on the grounds of *salus populi suprema lex:* the welfare of the people is the supreme law. Now, if that statement is true – and it is – the Parliament is as accountable to you or I as any ambassador to his prince and can only expect our support so long as it acts in our interest.' He paused and, holding the girl's gaze with his own, added, 'It's very simple. Despite four years of civil war, we are still labouring under the same destructive grievances we had before. And if tyranny can be resisted in a King, then it can equally well be resisted in a Parliament.'

After such conversations as this, Bryony found it more and more difficult to go home and keep her counsel – particularly when, as often happened, her uncle grumbled about the apparent inability of the nation's representatives to solve their current problems. But it was another, quite different comment that nearly proved her undoing; for when Jack said he'd trust the Levellers a damned sight more if he didn't suspect them of trying to make everybody equal, she immediately informed him that the only parity Mr Lilburne wanted was in the eyes of the law.

'I beg your pardon?' asked Jack, staring at her. 'Did you use the word *parity*?'

Bryony coloured a little, cursed her own stupidity and set about trying to retrieve her mistake. 'Have I got it wrong? It's what Sam says. At least, I *think* it is.'

'Ah. I see. For a moment you had me worried. But do go on. What else does Sam say?'

'J-just that, really,' she shrugged. And then, 'Oh yes. He says the Levellers won't endure oppression from Cromwell and Ireton any more than they'd endure it from the King and his Cavaliers. But that none of them want to destroy property or set up any sort of universal community.'

Jack continued to survey her thoughtfully.

'You appear to have acquired a remarkably good memory all of a sudden. Friend Sam must be pleased with himself. But I hope – so far as you are concerned – he's confining himself to mere talk?'

'Of course he is.'

'Good! Because, little though I relish the thought of being constantly regaled with pearls of wisdom fresh from the mouth of John Lilburne, I'd be even less happy if I found out you'd been relaying them elsewhere. And that,' finished Jack flatly. 'is something you would be well-advised to remember.'

Bryony nodded and smiled . . . and decided that what Uncle Jack didn't know wouldn't hurt him.

As soon as she learned of the Wapping meeting, Bryony

was consumed with a desire to attend it. Not surprisingly, however, she met with a wall of resistance.

'No,' said Sam.

'But why not?'

'Because it's one thing to visit John in private and quite another to risk being seen at a public meeting. Also, I gave your uncle a promise I intend to keep.'

'You're saying the meeting is illegal?'

'Not in itself, no.' Sam ran a hand through his hair and stared at her exasperatedly. 'You know perfectly well it's being held to convince the waverers about the petition. But you don't need to be convinced, do you? Despite everything I said about the likelihood of it being condemned as sedition, you've already signed it.'

'And why shouldn't I?' sniffed Bryony. '*You* have. And you're busy enough persuading other people to do so. I should have thought you'd have been pleased.'

'And so I would be if you were free to do as you wish. But you're not – and I gave my word to keep you out of trouble.' He paused briefly. 'Why are you so set on going, anyway? John won't say anything you haven't already heard.'

She shrugged. 'It isn't so much what he'll say as the way he'll say it. You've said yourself he uses different skills before a crowd.'

'That'll teach me to keep my mouth shut,' breathed Sam to himself. Then, 'That's as maybe. But I'm afraid this is not the occasion for you to witness them. I'm not taking you, Bryony. And that is quite, quite final.'

She seethed for a moment; then, veiling her expression thought, *We'll see about that.*

Getting away from Shoreditch at around four o'clock on the afternoon of January 17th was made easy by the fact that Annis was visiting her sister and Jack had a customer. Getting back at goodness knows what time would be a different matter, but Bryony refused to let it worry her. She simply wrapped herself well against the biting cold and set off on foot in the direction of Aldgate.

Dusk was falling by the time she got to East Smithfield and finding Well Yard amongst the plethora of narrow alleyways was more difficult than she had expected. She consequently arrived at the house of Mr Williams the gardener a little later than she had anticipated and found it crammed with people. Bryony drew a deep breath, freed her elbows from her cloak and fought her way to a place in the corner from which she could just see Free-born John. He appeared to be deep in discussion with a young man she'd seen once in Halfmoon Alley and who, according to Sam, was the co-author of the *Agreement of the People*. Bryony racked her brain for his name and eventually came up with it: John Wildman.

Eventually Lilburne called the meeting to order and began with an account of the petition's progress.

'As you know, we are now in touch with towns all over the kingdom through our agents and committees. Apart from London and Southwark, our greatest achievements so far lie in Kent; but I have hopes that our friends in Hertfordshire and Buckinghamshire may soon rival that. On a practical note, we are ordering a further three thousand copies of the Petition to be printed and sending a thousand of them for distribution amongst the Army. At the moment, we have something like forty thousand signatures.' A sudden smile lit his face. 'You won't be alone, my friends. And if every man who cares for his posterity will stand up now and be counted, he'll find himself one of a *hundred* thousand.'

A mumble of talk filled the room. Lilburne let it run its course; then, collecting every eye, said, 'And now to the Petition itself. It contains no intended treason towards the Commons. Quite the reverse. We state only that, since the Commons is the supreme representative of the nation, it should assume supreme authority. We want it to cease acknowledging the legislative power of the Lords; to stop toying with the notion of restoring, not just the King, but also his veto; to prevent courts and committees holding capricious authority over us, the people.' He paused again. 'As I say. No treason – only a raising of its stature.'

'What about reform?' someone asked.

'The Petition respectfully suggests those we would like undertaken. Reform of the law, of prisons, of the electoral system – and of the House itself by the ejection of lawyers; freedom of conscience and speech, the abolition of monopolies . . . and measures to end the too long continued shame of this nation that we know as poverty.' Lilburne's voice suddenly rang like a clarion call. 'These things need no introduction. You would not be here if they were not as dear to your hearts as they are to mine. No. The reason you are here, gentlemen, is to decide whether or not you wish to *do* something about them.'

Bryony cheered and then, clapping a hand over her mouth, tried to disappear inside her cloak. It was a waste of time. Two minutes later, Sam materialised beside her.

'You bloody little fool!' he hissed furiously. 'Haven't you *any* sense?'

'It's all right,' she whispered, rather more confidently than she felt. 'There won't be anybody here who knows me.'

'Oh, won't there? What about that fellow over there? The one with the fat face. His name's Masterson – and he says he's a Presbyterian minister from Shoreditch. Just the sort, I'd have thought, to be Uncle Jack's bosom friend.'

Bryony's heart sank. George Masterson might not be precisely intimate with her uncle but they did know each other – and that was more than enough. She raised frightened eyes to Sam's face and said, 'What shall I do?'

'Pull your hood round your face, keep behind me and pray he hasn't already noticed you. Though why I bother giving advice, when you never take it, is completely beyond me.'

The meeting wore on in a series of questions and answers. How could they petition at all when they had no licence to do so? Wasn't petitioning the Commons in itself a recognition of a corrupt authority? And finally: weren't the Levellers merely spitting into the wind when they tried to free a people who, for the most part, were perfectly content to remain enslaved?

Free-born John's eyes gathered new brilliance and he took his time about answering so that, by the time he spoke, no one even seemed to be breathing. Then, with matchless sincerity, he said, 'It is true that some are unwilling to save themselves; but we are in this world to do the best we can – not only for our own generation, but for all those which will follow. And posterity will doubtless reap the benefit of our endeavours . . . whatever shall become of us.'

The echo of his words seemed to lap the edges of the room

for a moment before the silence disintegrated into a jumble of voices. Bryony found that her eyes were wet and reached instinctively for Sam's hand. He accepted it in a too-firm grasp and said, 'That's it. Let's go.'

'Now?' she asked. 'But it's not over.'

'It is for you – unless you want to go and discuss tonight's work with the minister!' he snapped. And, without giving her time to argue, dragged her briskly to the door.

He lectured her most of the way home on the error of her ways and, when she got sick of it and answered back, they quarrelled. Sam informed her that she was the silliest brat it had ever been his misfortune to meet and Bryony retorted that since he was so damned clever, how come he'd managed to end up in Newgate?

Ten yards from the Morrells' door, Sam stopped dead and said, 'I hope you've got some good excuses ready because I've no intention of coming in to help you.'

'Nobody asked you to. In fact, if you really want to know, I wouldn't care if I never saw you again!'

'Good! Because if that fellow Masterson comes calling, you'll be locked in the attic for a month.'

'Don't be stupid,' she sniffed, turning towards home. 'Uncle Jack isn't a – a despot, you know.'

'Pity,' said Sam tersely. And set off homewards.

He was half-way down the street when Bryony finally realised that he wasn't going to turn round and make it up with her. For an instant she hesitated, torn between pride and the lead weight settling in her chest. Then, because she knew perfectly well that the fault was hers, she jettisoned her ill-temper and called softly to him. 'Sam?'

He stopped and turned to look at her. 'Well?'

'I – I didn't mean those things I said.'

'No?'

'No. And I'm sorry.'

There was a short pause. Then, 'I should bloody well think so,' grinned Sam, and without bothering to say goodnight he limped off away across the cobbles.

They were right to worry about George Masterson – but not for the reasons they thought. The following morning found him before the House of Lords, recounting Lilburne's words faster than he could actually remember them. And since some of these, after the summary departure of Sam and Bryony, had concerned Lieutenant-General Oliver Cromwell, the result of his betrayal was never in doubt.

The Commons instantly withdrew Lilburne's bail and sentenced Wildman to the Fleet. Free-born John's brief moment of liberty was over.

Two

'I reckon I'm as reluctant as the next man to insult anybody's hospitality,' remarked Wat sourly on the heels of a particularly massive belch. 'But if I have to eat one more bloody balm-cake or another piece of curd tart, I'm likely to throw up on the spot. And that's a fact.'

Moving easily with the motion of his horse, Gabriel turned his head and grinned. 'Don't worry. We're going to the Skilbeck's next and they don't run to such luxuries. It'll be rye bread with a lump of cheese. And if you don't think you can stomach it, you can always go home.'

Wat pulled his cloak up against the occasional flurries of snow and relapsed into silence. In the two weeks since the wedding, the Colonel had continued following the pattern set in the three weeks before it. He spent long hours closeted with his bailiff and even longer ones in the saddle, getting to know every inch of the estate and every man, woman and child who lived on it. Unfortunately, from what Mr Larkin could see, it was going to take a damned sight more than simple application to make Brandon Lacey pay for itself.

The Skilbeck farm comprised a small stone cottage with a thatch badly in need of repair, a tumbledown barn and the blackened shell of an out-building. Half a dozen scrawny hens pecked morosely around the cottage door and a goat with a nasty glint in its eye was tethered near the woodpile.

Gabriel dismounted from his horse and led it to the lee of the barn. Then, glancing shrewdly at Wat, he said, 'Rob Skilbeck fell at Marston Moor. His widow does her best but she lost last year's fleeces in a fire and her eldest boy is only fourteen. Sound familiar?'

Wat grunted. He had seen at least four other families with

similar problems and it was precisely why he felt the outlook facing Gabriel was so bleak. He said, 'Is this another one who can't pay the rent?'

'No. This is one where the rent is paid no matter what hardship it causes,' came the grim reply.

The door was thrown open as they approached it and a gangling nine-year-old clutching a bucket said anxiously, 'Best not to come in, sir. Ma's right poorly wi' fever.'

'Is she, Ned? I'm sorry to hear that.' Gabriel smiled comfortingly. 'But I doubt we'll catch it, you know, and if it won't disturb her to receive us—'

'Ned?' A freckle-faced girl of roughly Phoebe's age appeared in the doorway behind her brother. 'Whatever are you doing to keep Colonel standing about in wind? Please, sir – come in, do. It's only tertian ague ails Ma and she'll be that glad to see you.'

Inside, the cottage was spartan but scrupulously clean and a cheerful fire blazed on the hearth. To one side of it stood an empty spinning-wheel and, on the other, flushed, shivering and wrapped in blankets, sat the Widow Skilbeck.

'Colonel Brandon,' she said feebly, struggling to rise. 'It's right good of you to come out here on day like this.'

Gabriel shook his head and pressed her back into her seat. 'I'm sorry to find you so unwell, Mistress – we won't stay to plague you. I merely wondered if there is anything you need?'

'No, no. Janet's dosing me well enough, and our Joe's taking care of beasts.'

'He's taking care of ones as haven't wandered,' muttered Janet darkly. And then, 'Ned – for Lord's sake, go and feed goat and shut door before our Ma perishes.'

Ned vanished with his bucket and Gabriel looked thoughtfully at the girl. 'Fences down, Janet?'

'Aye, and fast as Joe mends one, sheep find their way through another. We've lost four to Barton this last week – and small chance of getting 'em back neither.'

'That'll do, Janet,' said the Widow. 'We're managing just fine and I'll be about myself in a day or two. Now get a couple of stools so the Colonel and his friend can sit down, and pour 'em some ale.'

'There's no need for that,' Gabriel began. And then the yard outside was filled with an ominous rumbling.

Being that much nearer, Wat was through the door before him. Then they were both hopping over the still rolling logs to the place where Ned lay, apparently unconscious, with the goat munching cabbage leaves off his chest. Grasping the broken tether, Wat hauled the animal away while Gabriel, with Janet crouching worriedly beside him, ran his hands lightly over the boy's bony frame.

'Nothing seems to be broken,' he said. 'He's just rather grazed and scratched . . . and, of course, we don't know how hard he hit his head when he fell.'

Without warning, Ned's eyes opened to peer first at the Colonel, then at his sister and finally, with acute dislike, at the goat. 'Bloody evil-tempered devil,' he said bitterly. 'Ought to be stewed afore it kills somebody!'

There was a brief moment of silence. Then, his face creasing into unaccustomed lines, Mr Larkin gave way to rare laughter.

Back in the cottage, with Janet bathing Ned's injuries before the hearth, Gabriel looked at the Widow and said, 'I know you won't ask, but would you object if I sent a couple of men over to help Joe with the fences?'

'There's no need—'

'Yes there is, Ma.' Janet looked defiantly up from her task. 'We can't even afford the Peruvian Bark for your fever, let alone to be losing more stock to Jem Barton.'

'Sounds to me as if somebody ought to drop a word in this fellow Barton's ear,' muttered Wat.

'Quite,' agreed the Colonel pleasantly. 'And, when we leave here, I'll be doing just that.'

'Ah. Well, you won't need me, will you?'

'No. But why?'

'Why do you think?' came the irritable reply. 'Young Ned can't be left to stack all those logs back by himself and somebody's got to make that blasted goat properly secure. Then again, if some of these fences were looked at today, there might be a few less beasts missing tomorrow.' As usual, Wat protected his motives with a forbidding scowl. 'Good job I haven't got anything better to do, isn't it?'

'I see,' remarked Venetia, looking up from the news-sheet in her hand, 'that the Committee of Both Kingdoms is to shed its Scottish members and resume its previous incarnation as the Derby House Committee.'

'Yes.' Gabriel's head remained bent over the litter of ledgers and papers on the table. 'But since – thanks to his Majesty – we may shortly find ourselves at war with the Scots, that's hardly surprising, is it?'

An all-too-familiar glint lit the violet eyes and Sophia groaned to herself. In the three weeks of her marriage, Venetia had settled discordantly into Brandon Lacey and achieved a certain routine. During the day while Gabriel was out, she peered into cupboards, inspected linen and ordered a relentless programme of dusting, sweeping and polishing. In the evenings, after dinner, she opened the kind of hostilities to which Gabriel was bound, in the end, to retaliate. And the result, thought Sophia with rare gloom, was an atmosphere that could be cut with a knife.

'It's not as surprising as the fact that the Army has somewhat ostentatiously surrendered its powers to the new committee,' replied Venetia sweetly. 'But now that Lieutenant-General Cromwell has apparently given up all hope of persuading the King to shower honours upon him, I suppose he feels it's time to make friends with Parliament again.'

Gabriel looked up, his expression unreadable.

'It may also have something to do with the possibility of the Scots crossing the border.'

'Yes . . . well, the Parliament only has itself to blame for that. The King wouldn't have turned to the Scots if the Commons wasn't so entrenched in its views. My God, I should think he can recite their demands to music by now. Three years of Presbyterianism and control of the Militia for twenty . . . abolition of the episcopacy and fifty-eight of his friends to be prosecuted.' She paused scornfully. 'He rejected those terms at Uxbridge and again at Newcastle, so can the Parliament seriously have thought he'd like them any better last month at Carisbrooke?'

'I don't suppose they did think it – but neither do I consider the repetitive nature of the Four Bills a sufficient excuse for sanctioning an invasion,' responded Gabriel dryly. 'Also, if all the King wanted was a new set of terms, he could have taken the *Heads of the Proposals*.'

'He probably would have done if Parliament had let him. You must be sorry they didn't. After all, it would suit you and your friends down to the ground to have his Majesty fall into your lap like a ripe plum.'

His mouth curled and, in a tone Venetia was beginning to recognise but still could not interpret, he said, 'Naturally. Why shouldn't those who won the war dictate the peace?'

'Because it's not their place to do so.'

'No? Then whose? The King's been in check for two years but has failed to recognise it. And if he doesn't concede the game soon, someone will be forced to make him.'

Since this came very close to what Francis Langley had said, Venetia was silent for a moment. Swiftly taking advantage of the temporary lull, Sophia said desperately, 'Isn't there any other news you can read to us, dear?'

'Oh yes.' Venetia dropped the sheet she was holding and reached for another from the pile in her lap. 'There were riots in Canterbury on Christmas Day when the Mayor tried to insist on shops opening as usual. It began with a game of football – forbidden, of course – and ended with cries of *"Up with King Charles and down with Parliament!"'* She paused to direct a mocking smile in Gabriel's direction. 'What else? Ah yes. The Army has pardoned its mutineers in what I can only assume to be a feeble-minded attempt to placate the Levellers; and Colonel Rainsborough is being made Vice-Admiral – presumably for the same reason, since I doubt he knows anything about Naval matters.'

Gabriel reflected that a pardon for the mutineers ought to have made it simpler for Major Maxwell to get Sam Radford out of prison. Removing Rainsborough from the Army Council was undoubtedly a smart move but *not* one likely to placate the Levellers. Then, smiling blandly back at Venetia, he said, 'Do go on. I'm riveted, I assure you.'

'Are you?' She disinterred a single broadsheet from the heap. 'Then how about a little poetry?'

You shall have a King – but whom?

Was ever King served so?
To make room for Oliver, Oh fine Oliver, Oh brave Oliver,
Oh rare Oliver, Oh gallant Oliver, Oh!
Now Oliver must be he, now Oliver must be he
For Oliver's nose is the Lancaster rose
And then comes his sovereignty . . .

She paused and then added brightly, 'Just at present, the Lieutenant-General doesn't seem terribly popular with anybody does he?'

'No. But then he never has been popular amongst the Cavaliers,' came the totally unruffled reply. 'He's defeated them too often.'

Sophia took one look at Venetia's face and rose hurriedly from her chair, spilling shawls in every direction.

'I'll ask Meg to bring some wine,' she said. And fled.

Gabriel watched her go, a faint frown marking his brow. Then, turning back to Venetia, he said flatly, 'Much as I hate to spoil your fun, this endless skirmishing has got to stop. It serves no purpose and is making life very uncomfortable for Sophy.'

An almost imperceptible hint of colour stained Venetia's cheeks and she said irritably, 'I know. But I daresay she'd find silence equally uncomfortable. The only thing we have in common is our differences, so what else do you suggest we talk about? What else *is* there?'

'Local affairs . . . domestic matters . . . the estate? Things that Sophy knows about too and that we ought to be able to discuss without quarrelling. Besides which, when I leave here in the spring, you'll be the one left here making day-to-day decisions with Dick Carter, so it's important that you know Brandon Lacey as well as you do Ford Edge.'

She stared at him, 'You really mean to stay in the Army?'

'Of course. What's the matter? Didn't you believe I would?' he asked. And then, 'But no. Of course you didn't. You thought I had ideas above my station.'

Venetia did not bother to reply and instead tried to decide whether this declaration made things better or worse. If Gabriel resigned his command, there might be some chance

166

of people eventually forgetting his unfortunate background. But if he didn't, the Army would keep him away from Yorkshire for months at a time – and she would be free not just of his unwelcome presence but to pursue her own activities.

Her face was not an especially easy one to read but Gabriel had no difficulty in following the tenor of her thoughts. He said, 'Obviously I should have made a point of reassuring you before. But now that you know, it may make it easier for us to co-exist over the next couple of months. And – who knows – if the Scots invade, you may even find yourself a widow. How's that for a cheering thought?'

'I could reconcile myself to it,' she snapped.

'I thought you could. And, having given you that to look forward to, at least I can stop worrying about you dropping something nasty in the cherry cordial.' He paused and then, rather less flippantly, said, 'Which reminds me. Does your stillroom contain any Peruvian Bark?'

'I believe so. Why?'

'Jane Skilbeck has a fever and no money to spare for an apothecary. I thought you might have some sent over to her. Or better still,' finished Gabriel gently, 'you might consider taking it yourself.'

That night, after her maid had finished preparing her for bed, Venetia sat by the fire, fathoms deep in thought. It was fast becoming clear that her initial reading of the Colonel had been an over-simplification. Indeed, the only thing she was still sure of was that his dislike of her equalled hers to him – and that, having allowed her to occupy a room half the house away from his own, he had no designs on her body. It was, of course, a relief; but at least if he'd tried to share her bed, she would have had the immeasurable satisfaction of saying no.

Sighing, she reached for the poker and idly stirred the fire. He was going back to his regiment and leaving her to care for Brandon Lacey. That, too, surprised her. She hadn't expected him to trust her . . . and wasn't sure she wanted him to. She didn't know how she was going to cope with responsibility for two estates – or whether she was even willing to try.

The papers making Ford Edge hers had been given to her on the day after the wedding and, each morning since then, she had held them in her hand and told herself that they made everything worthwhile. It wasn't entirely true, but it was important to try to believe it. What she had *not* done, however, was to decide what to do with them.

Unless she was prepared to allow the whole fiasco to begin again, it would be stupid to hold on to Ford Edge herself for the law gave a man rights of disposal over his wife's property. But to whom could she safely entrust it? Mother had no interest in estate-management; Elizabeth was soon to wed Tom Knightley; and, at not quite eighteen, Phoebe was surely too young for such a responsibility. And there was no saying who she might marry.

A familiar, blistering resentment settled over Venetia. There were times when she felt she could have murdered Harry for putting them all in this position. As for Ellis . . . all she knew was that his careless defection hurt more than all the rest put together and that her feelings towards him defied definition – except in one particular, which she preferred not to contemplate.

Rising abruptly, she moved about the room putting out candles and forced herself to think of something else. She would take the Peruvian Bark to Mistress Skilbeck, she decided. It would be as good a way as any of finding out how hard the Colonel was having to work at making his people accept him. A small, grim smile touched her mouth and then was gone. Yes. Perhaps it was time to start enlivening her days by taking an observer's interest in Brandon Lacey. It was certainly time she rode over to see how things were going at Ford Edge. As for the evenings, they could be mended equally simply. She would invite Phoebe to stay.

The fact that the whole Skilbeck family wholeheartedly sang the Colonel's praises was no especial surprise, but that they also apparently adored the Colonel's dreadful little friend *was*. Venetia gritted her teeth, pinned a smile to her face and heroically refrained from comment. Then she went off in search of less impressionable prey.

She didn't find it. After four days of random visiting, the

only dissenting voice was that of Jeremiah Barton and, since that was plainly because the Colonel had ordered him to return the Skilbeck's escaped sheep, it had to be discounted. Everyone else, it seemed, had formed a very favourable impression and – in their typically laconic way – did not mind saying so.

'Colonel's got a good head on his shoulders,' said one.

'No flummery about him,' said another. 'Knows he's got a lot to learn and isn't too proud to ask.'

And so it went on. Venetia progressed from astonishment, through mild resentment, to a sort of grim respect. In a far shorter time than she would have considered possible, Gabriel Brandon had somehow managed to overcome both the disadvantage of his birth and the natural mistrust local people had of strangers. The question now was whether he would follow this up with sensible management or ruin it with a series of radical changes designed to make a quick profit. A month ago, she'd have been sure which of the two it would be. Now she wasn't, but would have bled to death sooner than let Gabriel suspect it.

She visited Ford Edge, consulted with her bailiff and bore with her mother as best she could, but she put off visiting Lawyer Crisp. Then, at the beginning of February and just before the snow began to fall in earnest, Phoebe arrived at Brandon Lacey full of her usual zest and bubbling with plans for finding the Lacey Garland. Sophia greeted her with thankful pleasure, Gabriel with amused affection and Venetia (who had hoped her sister might have lost her enthusiasm for dismantling the house) with carefully concealed resignation.

'I can't decide where to begin,' confessed Phoebe over a dish of pigeon with braised livers. 'Should I start with obvious places like the attics and cellars – or should I hunt for priest's holes and secret places in the panelling?'

'I hate to dampen your ardour,' remarked Venetia, 'but I doubt there's even one priest's hole – the Brandon's have been Protestant to a man ever since Lieutenant-General Cromwell's unpleasant great-great-uncle dissolved the monasteries. And the wainscot can't have been put in much above seventy years ago. Sophy?'

'Quite true, I'm afraid.' Sophia absently handed a tidbit to Trixie who, despite all Venetia's attempts to keep her out, always managed to join them at meal times.

Phoebe looked slightly daunted for a moment before the solution occurred to her. 'All right. Perhaps the panelling *is* too new to hold the actual hiding place . . . but we don't know what's behind it, do we?'

There was an instant of acute silence during which Gabriel hid in his wine-glass and even Sophia looked a trifle stunned. Then Venetia said calmly, 'No. And we're not going to destroy it in order to find out.'

'Of course not. But couldn't I just—'

'*No*, Phoebe. Sophy and the Colonel said you could look – not that you could bring the house down around our ears.'

Catching a gleam of entirely new speculation in his sister-in-law's eye, Gabriel took immediate action to ward off the inevitable question.

'It seems to me that a task of this magnitude requires a certain amount of organisation,' he remarked gravely. 'So perhaps you should make a list of all the parts of the house unchanged since Hugh and Philippa's time. After all, if the Garland had been hidden in rooms that have been structurally altered in any way, it's likely that it would have been found when the work was done.'

She regarded him approvingly. 'That's a good idea.'

'I know.' The provocation of his tone was blunted by a singularly charming smile. 'Mine always are.'

Phoebe began systematically touring the house early next morning but still found time to ask her sister the question Gabriel had so adroitly prevented her voicing over supper.

'You've been married a month and you're still not calling your husband by his given name. Why?'

The violet eyes continued to frown down at a recipe for whitening lace, meticulously if semi-illegibly written in Sophia's mother's crabbed hand. 'Why do you think?'

Phoebe sighed. 'But isn't that rather silly? The way I see it, you wanted Ford Edge and he gave it to you the only way he could; he's a Parliamentarian but he doesn't ram it down our throats; and his illegitimacy doesn't appear to make him any less a gentleman than any other we know. So what's he done that's so wrong? Or are you going to spend the rest of your life blaming him because he's not Ellis?'

Venetia drew a sharp breath and her fingers clenched around the binding of the recipe-book. 'I'm not.'

'Aren't you? Then what *are* you doing?'

'Stop it, Phoebe! It's not your business.'

'I know. But no one else dares talk to you,' came the stubborn reply. Then, coaxingly, 'I'm only asking you to give him a chance. And it's not just me that likes him, you know. There's Sophy and Tom as well.'

'God in heaven!' breathed Venetia, finally wheeling round to face her persecutor. 'As far as I'm concerned the whole damned world could look upon him as a latter-day saint – but that still wouldn't necessarily make him the husband I wanted. And, in case you haven't noticed it, he feels exactly the same about me. In short, we automatically bring out the worst in each other – and there's nothing you or anyone else can do about it.'

Having made her list, Phoebe began her search in the attics and, though she got horribly dirty and didn't find anything to lead her to the Garland, she felt herself amply compensated by the discovery of chests full of outmoded finery. At the end of a week, she was enjoying herself so much she had almost forgotten what she had set out to do.

Naturally, she could not resist trying some of these monstrosities on – or, having mischievously arrayed herself as an Elizabethan youth, slipping down to try the effect on Sophia. The only trouble was that she picked the wrong time for it and came swaggering down the stairs to find herself face to face with two completely unknown Roundhead officers.

One of them – tall, dark-haired and square of face – simply stared at her as if he couldn't quite believe his eyes. The other – more compactly-built and red-headed – inspected her from head to foot and smiled.

It was a slow, tantalisingly sweet smile and it had the oddest effect on Phoebe. She blushed furiously and all of her usual cheerful nonchalance drained abruptly away into her little calf-length boots. Then the parlour door opened and

Venetia appeared. For a moment, Phoebe assumed that the change of expression on the red-haired man's face was the usual response to her sister's beauty, until he said blankly, 'My God. Venetia Clifford.'

Having already been told who her visitors were, Venetia would have responded with suitable composure had not Phoebe attracted her attention by embarking on a stealthy retreat. Eyes widening in disbelief, Venetia took in the agonised, dust-smeared face beneath the feathered, moth-eaten cap, the dingy ruff, grotesquely-padded purple doublet and all-too-revealing trunk-hose. Finally, against all expectation, she started to laugh.

Phoebe promptly gave up subtlety and took to her heels.

Hilarity still lingering in her eyes, Venetia was left looking at Major-General Lambert and Major Maxwell. She said pleasantly, 'You'll have to forgive my sister. The show was meant to be private, but her timing is lamentable.'

'Oh, I wouldn't say that,' murmured Eden.

'No. You wouldn't,' Lambert crossed to make a formal bow over Venetia's head. 'I don't know if you recall it, Mistress Clifford, but you and I have met before – under the auspices of my friend, Tom Knightley.'

The laughter evaporated from her face leaving it rather tense. 'I remember it perfectly – as, indeed, I remember Major Maxwell. But you are both labouring under a misapprehension. I am Venetia Brandon now and I rather think that you must be here to see my husband.'

Eden opened his mouth on an unwary remark and then shut it again. There was something very odd here . . . something which went far beyond Gabriel's sudden marriage but which he couldn't quite put his finger on. Therefore, since his own position was already a little awkward, it was best to stay silent and leave the talking to Lambert.

The Major-General was already making all the right, congratulatory noises. Venetia listened politely and then ushered them both into the parlour, saying coolly, 'I'm not sure where the Colonel is or how long he'll be.'

'There's no hurry.' Lambert accepted the chair she indicated and smiled. 'We were in Knaresborough inspecting the castle – and, being so close, we couldn't resist paying

Gabriel a visit. If we'd known he was but recently married, however, we might have been a little more circumspect.'

She smiled back somewhat perfunctorily, handed both men a glass of wine and said, 'Inspecting the castle?'

'Yes. I'm here to prepare for a Scots invasion we all hope won't actually happen,' came the calm reply. 'And, since Parliament ordered Knaresborough Castle to be slighted almost two years ago, it's my duty to discover why very little has actually been done – and take whatever steps are necessary to correct the situation.'

'I see,' said Venetia coldly. 'But perhaps you aren't aware that the local people have petitioned Parliament *against* the slighting?'

'Ah.' The Major-General looked slightly uncomfortable. 'I am aware of it, yes. But—'

'But the security of the North comes first,' interposed a crisp voice from the door. Then, as both Lambert and Eden swung to face him, Gabriel grinned and said simply, 'I knew it. You can't do without me.'

While she watched the three men greet each other, Venetia quietly thanked God that the Colonel had arrived before she'd been asked any awkward questions. Eden had been remarkably restrained so far – but he must know she'd previously been betrothed to another, quite different Brandon and therefore be speculating about a possible connection between Ellis and Gabriel. And if he was working up to a tactful inquiry, Venetia would much prefer not to be present.

Murmuring something about having to speak to the cook, she winnowed her way to the door and made a graceful exit. Then she leaned against the wall with her eyes shut for a moment and prayed that the Major-General wouldn't accept an invitation to sup with them.

'Venetia?' hissed Phoebe from the half-landing. And when her sister looked up, 'Who are they?'

Venetia ascended the stairs and absorbed the glories of Phoebe's best rose-coloured taffeta and becomingly arranged curls.

'Oh my God. All this for Major-General Lambert? Or no. It's more likely to be Eden Maxwell, isn't it?'

'The one with the red hair?' asked Phoebe, a becoming flush mantling her cheeks. And then, 'Maxwell? He isn't related to that girl Kit wanted to marry, is he?'

'He's her brother.'

'Oh Lord! So *that's* how you know each other.'

'It's part of it. But while I was at Whitehall, I was also fairly well-acquainted with his wife.'

'Oh.' Instant disappointment. 'Oh. I see.'

Venetia crossed her fingers in the folds of her skirt and hoped no one would be silly enough to add fuel to the fire by telling Phoebe the truth about Eden Maxwell's marriage. Then she said casually, 'I'm just hoping they don't stay long. I don't feel like raking over the past with Eden Maxwell and I'd as soon not listen to John Lambert's plans for demolishing the castle.'

Phoebe's eyes rose sharply. 'Is that what he's here for?'

'Yes. By the time Parliament has finished, there'll be scarcely a castle left intact anywhere; and they won't have been destroyed in warfare but by an army of grubby little men with mattocks and shovels,' came the bitter reply. 'And what, I wonder, will posterity make of *that?*'

Inside the parlour, Gabriel established a few basic facts and realised that he had little choice but to acquaint Lambert and Eden with his personal circumstances before Eden started coming up with a few theories of his own, or Lambert heard the tale from Tom Knightley. He therefore stated the facts in a tone calculated to discourage further questions before saying coolly, 'So there you have it. And now perhaps we can close this discussion and talk of something else. The recent Vote of No Addresses, for example. Is it true that the Lords have passed it?'

John Lambert, who was as good at hiding his thoughts as anyone Eden had ever seen, immediately embarked on a smooth explanation of how their lordships had naturally been worried that ending negotiations with the King might eventually lead – not only to abolition of the monarchy – but also to that of their own Upper House. They had, consequently, resisted the Vote until, on the excuse of riots in the City, the Commons had asked for two thousand soldiers to guard Whitehall from violence. Then, and only then, had their lordships taken the hint and given way.

Throughout this, Eden remained deep in thought. He had known Gabriel for too long and liked him too well for a little thing like illegitimacy to matter in the slightest. But there were others who wouldn't see it that way – and, reading between the lines, it rather looked as if Venetia might be one of them. As for what all this meant to Gabriel himself, Eden couldn't begin to guess. The only certain thing was that his situation wasn't one anyone would envy.

The Major-General accepted both an invitation to sup and an offer of accommodation for the night; and, when Venetia came back into the room, Eden watched her receive the news with glacial courtesy. He sighed and resigned himself to an uncomfortable evening.

Sophia greeted their unexpected guests with her usual uncritical vagueness and Phoebe decided that it was enough just to be able to watch Major Maxwell. Venetia kept her tongue firmly between her teeth and wondered how long she could put off asking about the Major's sister.

For obvious reasons, talk at the table centred largely around the possible coming of the Scots.

'Both we and the Parliament are doing everything we can to avert it, of course,' said Lambert. 'Commissioners are being sent to Edinburgh; and Oliver St John and the Lieutenant-General have opened a dialogue with the Queen, aimed at putting the Prince of Wales on the throne.'

Venetia's eyes rose. 'Does Cromwell *know* the Prince?'

'Not personally. But—'

'No.' She smiled faintly. 'I thought not.'

There was a tiny pause. Then, as if she hadn't spoken, Gabriel said, 'And what of the Scots army?'

'At the moment, its prospects don't sound very hopeful,' shrugged Lambert. 'The Duke of Hamilton is apparently having trouble persuading Covenanters to enlist alongside Catholic Royalists and both Leven and David Leslie have refused to command. Argyll, of course, is opposed to the Engagement full stop.' He paused to select a piece of chicken from the dish in front of him. 'But, as I see it, the Scots may be the least of our problems. There are too many factions for

175

my liking – too much general discontent. And that madman Lilburne is no help.'

'Free-born John?' Sophia smiled vaguely. 'Such a remarkable young man. What's he done now?'

'The usual sort of thing,' supplied Eden. 'He's called Cromwell a traitor and dug up that old rumour about him wanting the King to make him Earl of Essex.'

There was another pause and then Venetia said delicately, 'Excuse me asking, but *is* it just a rumour?'

Lambert's brows rose. 'The fact that Cromwell supported the Vote of No Addresses proves that it is.'

Venetia's expression was a masterpiece of polite disbelief and, seeing it, Phoebe said hastily. 'Have you met Mr Lilburne, Major?'

'Once or twice,' nodded Eden. Then, turning cheerfully to the Colonel, 'Which reminds me. I got Sam Radford released by vouching for him in your name, so if he does anything stupid, you'll be the first to hear of it.'

Sardonic grey eyes met mischievous hazel ones.

'Thank you,' murmured Gabriel.

'Don't mention it,' returned Eden. And smiled.

Already more than half enslaved, Phoebe drew a long, painful breath and forced herself to say brightly, 'Venetia tells me that she knows your wife, Major Maxwell – and that you have children. You must miss them very much when your duty keeps you with the Army.'

Eden's face froze into an expressionless mask and there was a sudden, catastrophic silence, which Sophia and Lambert plainly understood no better than poor Phoebe.

'I – I'm sorry,' she stammered. 'Have I said something I shouldn't?'

'Not exactly,' said Venetia smoothly. 'You've just brought the conversation on to a personal level that both the Major and I would have been happier to avoid.' Then, to Eden, 'It's no good, is it? We both know I can't let you leave here without asking about Kate.'

The scarred face relaxed fractionally.

'She's well, as far as I know. She married Luciano del Santi and lives with him in Genoa – where I believe he's taken over the running of his uncle's business empire. They have a son.'

He paused and then added stiffly, 'It's a little late to say it, but I was sorry about Kit.'

Venetia merely inclined her head. If she spoke, it would probably be to say something best left unsaid; and she'd only begun this to prevent Phoebe finding out that, though the gallant Major was married, he lacked a wife.

Had she but known it, she had wasted her time. As the party moved from the table to parlour, Phoebe grasped Gabriel's arm and said rapidly, 'You'd better tell me what I did wrong or I'm likely to do it again.'

He considered her for a moment. Then, 'You referred to a part of Eden's life which he prefers not to discuss.'

'But *why*? I don't see the harm in it. I only mentioned his—' She stopped, sudden horror darkening her eyes. 'Oh God. Has – has one of them died?'

'No. To put it bluntly, three years ago his wife left both him and their children to elope with her lover.'

Phoebe lost a little of her colour.

'That's *horrible!* How could she *do* such a thing?'

'Not being personally acquainted with her, I couldn't say. But Eden is finding it very difficult to re-adjust.'

'Well, of course.' The blue-grey eyes grew suspiciously bright. 'He must have loved her very much.'

'I believe he did,' agreed Gabriel. 'But don't approach this subject with him or even let him guess that you know. He's not the kind to appreciate sympathy. And if you show any, he'll take you apart with his tongue.'

Three

Major-General Lambert and Major Maxwell left Brandon Lacey the following morning and, as soon as they had gone, Venetia descended wrathfully upon her husband.

'Why on earth did you have to tell Phoebe about Celia Maxwell? Didn't it occur to you that, since I could have told her myself, I might just possibly have had a good reason for not doing so?'

'No, I can't say that it did. I simply wished you hadn't seen fit to mention Eden's wife at all – after which, I was more concerned with ensuring Phoebe didn't compound her mistake,' he responded coolly. 'If that has created some problem, however, you'll have to explain it.'

'Then you can't have eyes in your head,' came the tart reply. 'Didn't you *see* how she was looking at Eden? She seems to have been struck by a *coup de foudre*, so I endeavoured to nip it in the bud and hoped you'd have the sense to keep quiet. Only, of course, you didn't.'

Gabriel's brows rose.

'My mistake. I ought to have realised that your muscles would go into spasm at the mere possibility of having another Roundhead in the family. But it won't happen, you know. Eden is neither free nor ready to marry again. And even Phoebe can't fall in love in the space of one evening.'

'No? Think about it. She's seventeen years old, incurably romantic and overflowing with compassion. *He* is attractive, almost but not quite unattainable, and the victim of personal tragedy. With Phoebe, that's all it takes.'

'Then doubtless it's just as well that they're unlikely to meet again,' came the maddeningly patient reply. 'Is that all you wanted to say?'

Venetia checked her temper with an effort.

'Not quite. You might have told me that you knew him.'

'And *vice versa*. However, if you're seriously worried, we could each prepare a list of everyone we've ever met in order to compare notes . . . though, as far as I'm aware, the only other acquaintances we're likely to have in common are Luciano and Kate del Santi – whom I met briefly at Basing House in October '45.' He paused, a hard smile bracketing his mouth. 'And that, I would suggest, is where this conversation should end.'

'By all means!' she snapped contemptuously. 'After all, I don't suppose there's much point in asking if your conscience is ever troubled by the screams of those you and your friends roasted alive.'

'None at all.' He did not bother to qualify it but the expression in his eyes was wholly at odds with the butter-smooth tone. Then, without giving her time to probe further, he said, 'Dick Carter is in the bookroom, waiting to hear my suggestions for improving the estate's finances. You may join us, if you wish. It's entirely up to you.'

Venetia kept her face carefully blank.

'Why not?' she said aridly. 'If you've arranged a miracle, I'll be the first one to applaud.'

Mr Carter's heart sank when he realised that Mistress Venetia was joining the Colonel and himself for their meeting. He didn't approve of women meddling in business matters and this one was more difficult than most. However, since there wasn't much he could do about it, he greeted her respectfully and then gave all his attention to the Colonel.

'As you're aware, I've spent the last two months trying to acquire a basic working knowledge of Brandon Lacey,' began Gabriel briskly, 'and, though I realise I still have a lot to learn, the time has come to start making a few decisions. Our position is a very simple one. I've paid the last quarter's taxes and have the means to meet the next two. But by the third quarter of this year – even with a good harvest – we are likely to be in trouble.'

Dick Carter nodded gloomily. None of this was news to him and, though he had plenty of ideas for improved farming methods, they wouldn't show a profit for at least a couple of years. Venetia continued to regard her husband cynically. Since the bulk of Brandon Lacey's revenue came from rents, there was really only one solution – and she wondered why it was taking the Colonel so long to admit it.

Perched on a corner of the desk, Gabriel frowned down at the quill he had been idly twirling in his fingers. He said, 'The obvious answer is to raise the rents . . . but I'm afraid that I'm not prepared to do it. We've too many men disabled in the war, too many sons lost and too many widows; and, for the last couple of years, their harvests have been as poor as ours.' He looked up. 'In short, these people have the same problem in making ends meet that we do – but with far fewer resources. And I'm not about to fill our coffers at their expense.'

His voice, though crisp and dispassionate as ever, sounded remarkably sincere – and, had it not been for the tenor of their earlier conversation, Venetia might even have been tempted to believe him. As it was however, she told herself that only a fool would trust a Roundhead and said coldly, 'So, what *are* you going to do?'

'Something you may consider rather radical,' he replied. 'I'm proposing that we go into the cloth business.'

She stared at him impatiently.

'What are you talking about? We keep sheep – which means we're involved in the wool trade already.'

'Quite. But let's start at the beginning.' Gabriel looked at Dick Carter. 'We have roughly two hundred sheep of our own and, after shearing, we send the wool off to be spun, woven and dyed. Then we sell it in York. At the same time, virtually all our tenants are doing much the same with a much smaller quantity of fleeces – except that most of them do their own spinning and a few weave as well. Is that a fair assessment?'

Mr Carter agreed that it was.

'Very well. Then I propose that we stop paying outsiders and start using the expertise of our own people. I'd like to put wheels and looms into the empty cottages at Scar Croft, fix a daily rate for labour, and offer the job of spinning and weaving Brandon Lacey's wool to any tenant willing and able

181

to do it. I also want to try persuading the tenants to sell their wool to us instead of taking it to York. That will enable us to command a higher price because we'll no longer be in competition with each other and will be dealing in greater bulk.' He paused. 'Well? What do you think of it so far?'

'I think it's despicable!' said Venetia hotly. 'You'll employ children because they're cheaper – and take their parents' independence away at the same time!'

There was a long, reflective silence. Then, in a voice that any of his subordinates would have recognised, Gabriel said, 'I'm not sure whether you're congenitally incapable of listening or whether you just can't help thinking with your stomach. Either way, it's a fault you'd find it useful to overcome. I can't be the only person who finds continual repetition and self-justification tedious.'

Just for a moment Venetia was too stunned to reply. Then she surged to her feet, a tide of colour staining her skin. 'How *dare* you? I don't take that tone from anyone alive!'

'Then you should beware of using it yourself, shouldn't you?' He eyed her with mocking indifference. 'If you're going – go. If not, sit down and listen to the facts.'

Venetia would have given a good deal to have walked out – anything, in fact, except the satisfaction of letting him drive her to it. She sat down with a bump and stared him derisively in the eye.

'Thank you,' said Gabriel. 'And now let us be clear. I simply want to use our resources to maximum advantage . . . and in a way which will benefit our tenants as much as ourselves by keeping their rents down. Does that make sense?'

Still inwardly seething, Venetia merely shrugged.

'It makes sense, Colonel,' said Dick Carter cautiously, 'and I daresay as a good many folks'd be happy wi' arrangement. Only trouble is, you'll be setting up looms and like but not getting use out of 'em during best part o' year. Sheep are only sheared once, thou knows.'

'Quite,' agreed Gabriel, an odd gleam lighting his eyes. 'So I want to plant flax. As much of it as we can grow.'

The bailiff pursed his lips. 'You can't grow flax year in and year out. It takes too much out o' soil.'

'So I understand. But since you've been expounding the various advantages of crop-rotation to me at every opportunity, I'd have thought you'd be glad of the chance to put your theories into practice,' responded Gabriel. 'Well?'

Something that was almost a smile surfaced on the weatherbeaten face. 'I wouldn't mind giving it a go, Colonel, and that's a fact.'

'I need more than that. I'm relying on you to make it *work*. Our looms will have to be kept busy with wool through the spring and summer and with linen for the rest of the year – otherwise we're more likely to lose money than make it. So, if you don't think we can grow flax successfully, you'd better tell me now.'

'We can grow it right enough. Land's in good heart and soil's right for it hereabouts. But as to how *much* we can grow – well, I'd have to think on that'n.'

'It seems to me,' remarked Venetia to no one in particular, 'that the biggest problem would be with the retting.'

The grey eyes encompassed her immediately.

'Retting? You're talking about soaking the plants so the fibres can be removed? Why is that a problem?'

'Because as the plants rot, they taint the water and start to smell – so it's illegal to place them in running streams. And that means you'll need either a suitable pond or some kind of shallow vat.' She gave him a bright, indulgent smile. 'But I'm sure you won't let a little thing like that stand in your way.'

'Not if I can help it,' agreed Gabriel. He rose and faced his bailiff. 'How long will you need in which to come up with the necessary facts and figures regarding our flax capability?'

'Not long. Two or three days, happen.'

'Make it two. And, in the meantime, I don't want any word of this leaking out around the estate. Clear?'

'Clear, Colonel.'

'Good. Then I think that's all for now. I'll see you again the day after tomorrow and, as always, I thank you for your patience.'

He waited until Mr Carter had left the room and then, turning to Venetia, said, 'You may now speak your mind. Am I to assume that none of this has your approval?'

'Do you care either way?' she retorted.

'Not especially, though I should have thought the estate had enough problems without you and I working against each other.' He folded his arms and eyed her sardonically. 'So, what's bothering you? Is it the thought of Brandon Lacey becoming involved in trade? Or just the usual simple mistrust of my motives?'

'Both.' Even if she'd been convinced that there was no more to his plans than met the eye, nothing would have induced her to admit the flair and originality of them. Not after the way he'd spoken to her in front of Dick Carter. She said, sweetly, 'As yet, however, I don't know whether I approve or disapprove. Only time will tell. All I can say, with any certainty, is that although many gentlemen have commercial interests, they don't situate them in their own back yards. There's something rather vulgar about it. But I daresay you wouldn't understand that.'

'No,' agreed Gabriel blandly. 'So perhaps it's just as well I'm only a nasty, common soldier. For if I were a gentleman, you'd be free to wipe your boots on me without fear of reprisal, wouldn't you? And the tenants would be left to starve in genteel time-honoured fashion.'

Two days later, while the Colonel was busy with his bailiff, Venetia's maid handed her a small, sealed missive containing just six words written in a hand she did not recognise. *The old mill at Ferrensby. Noon.*

Venetia contemplated it thoughtfully and felt a faint lifting of her spirits. Captain Peverell, of course. Who else? And if he'd risked writing to her rather than wait for her to resume the weekly pilgrimage to Mary Jessop, it could only mean one thing. There was work to do.

The Ferrensby mill was almost completely derelict and had been for years. Venetia eyed it thoughtfully from the back of her mare for several minutes before slipping to the ground by means of a convenient boulder. Then, leaving Dulcie tied beneath a tree, she plodded through the melting snow to peer in at the gaping doorway. The time, so far as she was able to guess it, must be just a little past midday.

Inside the ruin, shadows jostled with patches of greenish

light and pigeons cooed softly from somewhere overhead. Venetia stepped cautiously under the lintel and said softly, 'Is anyone there?'

No reply. Not even an echo. Clutching her cloak around her, she advanced to the centre of the rubble-strewn floor. And then a voice, disembodied in the gloom, said, 'You came. How utterly delightful. *Bienvenue, ma chère.*'

Shock paralysed every nerve and muscle and for a long, eviscerating moment, Venetia was incapable of anything except simply keeping herself upright. But finally she managed to say, raggedly, 'You're a bit late.'

'Sadly, yes. But don't they say *better late than never?*'

'Some people may. I, however, am not one of them.'

Perfectly assured and exquisitely-dressed, beneath a trailing black cloak, Sir Ellis Brandon detached himself from the shadows and advanced on her, smiling. 'You're not very welcoming, sweetheart.'

'Did you expect me to fall on your neck?'

'Let us say that I hoped.'

'Then you're doomed to disappointment, aren't you? Just as I was when I hoped you'd come back,' responded Venetia stonily. Then, as numbness gave way to pain, 'I needed you here two months ago and you knew it – but you stayed away and couldn't even be bothered to send a proper message. My God! What kind of welcome do you think you deserve?'

'A smile – a kind word – a kiss?' he shrugged.

'Then you'd better seek them elsewhere.' He was close enough now for her to see the jewel winking in his ear and smell the faint, familiar perfume of his clothes. The burnished chestnut hair was the same . . . and the bold, brown gaze; but a neat replica of the King's beard had joined the moustache. Between the two, his mouth looked somehow harder than she had remembered it. 'At the moment I feel more inclined to throw something at your head.'

'So do it.'

'Don't tempt me.'

Ellis sighed and reflected that he should have known better than hope that the surprise of seeing him would make her forget to be angry. The only thing one could ever count on with Venetia was her obstinacy. He therefore gave up trying to make her smile and said, 'Very well. What do you want me to say?'

She drew a long, uneven breath. 'An apology might be a good place to start. And then, perhaps, an explanation?'

'My dear . . . Do you really need to hear me say I'm sorry? Don't you know that I've been in torment ever since Peverell brought me your letter?'

'No. Since you declined to write, how could I?'

'Ah. But that wasn't entirely my fault, you know. Her Majesty commanded my presence at a series of meetings concerning a scheme to rescue the Duke of York. Should I have put my own affairs before the safety of a boy left alone in the hands of his father's enemies?' He took her hands and held them against his chest. 'And, even if I had – what good would it have done? I couldn't overset that damnable Will or give Ford Edge back to you. I could only have made everything harder than it already was. Can't you see that?'

Venetia withdrew her hands and turned away from him.

'Just now, all I can see is that you left me to sink or swim, as if the five years of our betrothal had never been.'

'My heart, I've already explained—'

'No, you haven't. All you've done so far is give me your excuses and shower me with meaningless endearments.' She swung abruptly back to rake his face with lightless eyes. 'I'm still waiting to hear what I actually mean to you, Ellis – and whether you give a tinker's curse that I've been forced to marry your bastard brother.'

He stood very still and allowed her words to lap the edges of the mill. Then, with a faint sigh, he said, 'You think I like it any better than you?'

'If I knew that, I wouldn't be asking.'

'In that case *you're* the one who has forgotten – not just our betrothal – but the relationship we once had.' He paused. 'You're busy blaming me . . . but could not I just as easily blame you? After all, you were the one who put Ford Edge above everything else. And, in the light of my father's bloody Will, would you have acted any differently even if I had been here?'

There was an element of justice in what Ellis said. But then he was persuasive. He'd always been persuasive – even as a

186

child. He was the one who'd talked Kit and Harry both into and out of trouble; then, when something arose that neither charm nor cajolery could mend, he'd developed a habit of simply disappearing. And, so far as Venetia could see, he was still doing it.

She said remotely, 'We'll never know, will we? As it was, you and Harry left me with very little choice. *Someone* had to think of the family . . . and I had Mother constantly at my elbow.' She moved somewhat irresolutely back to the light of the doorway. 'I'm very tired of being the one who's left to cope with life's nasty realities.'

Ellis followed her and, swift to recognise the subtle shift in her mood, permitted himself a moment in which to enjoy the cameo-like purity of her profile. She had always been a beauty and she still was. It was just a pity she was also strong-willed, shrewd and alarmingly capable.

On a note of carefully-judged compassion, he said, 'Is it very bad, your marriage?'

'In itself, probably not,' she replied colourlessly. 'There's an automatic hostility between us, of course. But he – he doesn't force his presence on me or disgust me with his manners or even attempt to control my life. So in those ways, I suppose you'd say it could be worse. No. The thing that hurts is the – the *finality* of it. The knowledge that this is it – unchangeable and fixed in lead forever.'

Once more, Ellis closed the space between them.

'There's very little in life that can't be changed, sweetheart. For example, the bastard may hold Brandon Lacey – but he'll not have it for long. Similarly, now that Ford Edge is yours, there's nothing to stop you leaving him.'

He felt rather than saw the tremor that afflicted her.

'With you?' she asked remotely.

Ellis hesitated and then risked it. 'If you don't mind leaving Yorkshire to share my poverty – yes.'

Seconds ticked by in silence. But finally, rigid with strain, she said, 'And turn myself into another Celia Maxwell? I don't think so.'

A faint smile touched his mouth and then was gone.

'I take your point – but it leaves us only one option that I can see. Do you want me to kill him for you?'

This time she wheeled to face him so quickly that he barely had time to guard his expression and was faintly taken aback by the raw anguish in hers. 'Stop it! Don't you know, even now, that this isn't a game?'

'I wasn't treating it as such.'

'Yes you were! It's what you do – what you *always* do. *Dear God!*' Suddenly, without quite knowing how it had come about, she was crying. 'Why do you say things you know you don't mean? *Why?* Is ordinary comfort beyond you?'

'Of course not.' His arms closed about her. 'I just wasn't sure how it would be received if I offered it.'

A thousand memories racing back to plague her, Venetia clung to him briefly and then, brushing the tears impatiently from her face, said, 'I don't think I know the answer to that myself.'

'Then perhaps we should find out.' Ellis smiled, tracing the line of her cheek with light, confident fingers.

His intention was clear and, for a moment, the temptation was almost irresistible. But reason rushed back like an icy deluge, telling Venetia that she had made this mistake before and lived to regret it.

'No! Under the circumstances, that's probably the very last thing we should do,' she replied, removing herself from his arms and into the unrelenting drizzle outside. 'I'm sorry, Ellis. I realise there are things we should discuss and questions you'll want to ask about Brandon Lacey, but I don't think I can handle them today. Later, perhaps – but not yet. Do you mind?'

It was by no means what Ellis had hoped for but, since he couldn't say so, he merely shook his head sadly. 'Is this what it's come to? You haven't even asked how I got here or what my plans are – or even what news there is from France. Has my re-appearance really been such an unpleasant shock?'

'A shock certainly – and one I need time to come to terms with.' She continued walking steadily back towards her horse. 'You said something about trying to rescue the Duke of York. Are you leaving for London immediately?'

'Not quite. I've a few things to do here first. But since I can't have my presence in the district too widely known, I was rather hoping to engage your assistance.'

'Ah . . . I see.' Despite everything, Venetia found she was still unprepared for the wave of hurt that swept over her. 'I suppose I ought to have realised that you must have had a reason for wanting to see me.'

'My God! You really are determined to think the worst, aren't you?' Catching hold of her elbows, he jerked her to a standstill in front of him and gave her a little shake. 'What does it take to convince you? This – or this – or this?' His mouth trailed burning kisses along her jaw before descending purposefully on hers. 'Do you think I've forgotten that week in Oxford or what it meant? *Do you?*'

'No. But you should. We both should.' Shaken by half-remembered emotions, Venetia went on, 'This is exactly what I wanted to avoid. Can't you see? What h-happened between us three years ago was improper but not wrong because we expected to marry. Only now *I* am married – and not to *you*. And that makes everything different.'

There was a brief silence.

'Does he know?' asked Ellis.

'No.' A rare flush stained her skin. 'There hasn't been any occasion for him to find out.'

The brown eyes widened. 'You mean he's never—'

'No. Fortunately, he doesn't like me very much.'

Tiny sparks of mischief danced in Ellis's eyes and he laughed. 'I hate to disillusion you, sweetheart – but liking doesn't always have very much to do with it. And, in the light of your manifold charms, it does tend to make one wonder a little about his preferences.'

'They're pretty mundane, I should think.' Having spent years both at Whitehall and in France, Venetia had no need to ask what he meant, but was alarmed at quite how offensive she found the insinuation. She untied Dulcie and waited pointedly until he helped her into the saddle. Then, 'But, just now, he's rather more interested in finding ways to make Brandon Lacey pay.'

Ellis smiled invitingly up at her.

'Short of money, is he? What a shame! Will you come again tomorrow and tell me all about it?'

'I may . . . and then again, I may not.' For the first time, she smiled back at him – but not without a gleam of malice.

'I'm afraid you'll just have to wait and see. Unless, of course, you're eager to meet your brother and prepared to come knocking at his gate?'

Since Dick Carter's estimate of the amount of flax Brandon Lacey could grow was more than encouraging, Gabriel devoted the rest of the day to a detailed discussion on the quickest and most efficient means of putting his ideas into practice. Then, over supper, he explained it all to Sophia.

'It sounds promising,' she said, when at length he paused for breath. 'But won't it be expensive to set up?'

'Not especially.' With a mental shrug, Gabriel stopped contemplating his wife's unusually still face. 'The Scar Croft cottages are in a good state of repair; and, as for the spinning-wheels, looms, carding-combs, gears and hackles – Carter tells me I can probably buy most of it from a widow at Boroughbridge who's selling up to go and live with her daughter. I'll ride over to see her tomorrow and then, if all goes well, I can begin sounding out the tenants.'

'Do you think they'll agree to work for you?' asked Phoebe, transferring a collop from dish to platter.

'I sincerely hope so. Carter and I have fixed what we feel is a fair daily rate – and this whole scheme is as much for their benefit as it is ours.' He paused, his gaze returning to Venetia. 'I also intend to go over to York next week to introduce myself to the Merchant Adventurers Company. And it occurred to me that, since Mistress Elizabeth's wedding will soon be upon us, you might like to accompany me in order to visit your seamstress – or whatever it is that you deem necessary on these occasions.'

Venetia continued pushing food around her plate and gave no sign of having heard him. Then, becoming vaguely aware of the silence, she said, 'I'm sorry. You said something about going to Boroughbridge?'

'Tomorrow,' he agreed. And, in a tone of complete impassivity, repeated his invitation to York. 'I should also add that I'm not suggesting that you and I go alone. Sophy may like to come too . . . and Phoebe, if she can spare the time from her quest.'

'Well, of course I can!' Phoebe's face glowed with

pleasure. 'Heavens! We haven't been to York for ages, have we Venetia? And though you wouldn't have a new gown for your own wedding, you'll certainly need one for Bess's because mother will have half the county there.'

'Yes.' Venetia drew a long breath and strove for some semblance of interest. 'I suppose she will. But fashion has changed very little since the war and I must have at least a dozen gowns I've scarcely worn since I left Oxford.'

Phoebe opened her mouth on a furious protest and then, catching the Colonel's eye, shut it again.

As it happened, Venetia was well aware that she ought to have been more gracious but, after the vicissitudes of the day, Gabriel's unexpected consideration was just one shock too many. She relapsed into brooding silence, left the talking to Phoebe and decided that, since Boroughbridge and Ferrensby lay in opposite directions, it would be quite safe for her to meet Ellis tomorrow; if, of course, she decided she wanted to go.

In the parlour, Sophia winced as she hitched the inevitably trailing shawl back around her shoulders and remarked that the damp weather was playing havoc with her bones.

'You should go and take the waters,' advised Phoebe, with a glimmer of mischief. 'Uncle James swears by them.'

'Yes, dear. I know he does. But he's fortunate in not being possessed by an overly-acute sense of smell.'

Gabriel raised faintly amused eyes from a list of spinning and weaving equipment. 'Waters?'

'From the springs at Haregate-head,' said Phoebe. 'Haven't you heard of our Spa? It's quite famous, you know. People come for miles – and doctors have even written books about it. Wait a minute and I'll show you.'

Gabriel watched her whirl to the door and resignedly laid down his papers. Sophia smiled myopically and hoped that the work he'd been engaged on wasn't especially urgent.

Phoebe eventually re-appeared clutching not one but two publications. 'Look – I've found Dr Deane's *Spadacrene Anglica*. Isn't that lucky?'

'Thrilling,' agreed Gabriel, accepting a second volume optimistically entitled *Cures Without Care*.

Phoebe was already leafing through her book. 'Oh – listen

to what he says of the Tewit Well. "It cheereth and reviveth the spirits, strengtheneth the stomach, causeth a good and quick appetite and furthereth digestion".' She looked up, grinning. 'Not a word about rheumatic pains, Sophy – but it appears to relieve nearly everything else.'

'So I believe,' shuddered Sophia. 'But it's so bleak up there . . . just moorland with a handful of tiny cottages and nowhere to shelter from the wind.'

'Dr Stanhope,' said Gabriel on a faint quiver of laughter, 'is worried about more than the wind. "What unseemly shifts have I seen many strangers of note put to for want of a convenient place of retirement after drinking draughts of this water which is apt – with some violence – now and then to open the body".'

'It's perfectly true,' nodded Sophia. Then, in response to Phoebe's unseemly giggles, 'And not at all funny either.'

'I'm sorry,' gurgled Phoebe, hanging over Gabriel's shoulder. 'What else does he say?'

'He expounds the virtues of the Sulphur Well but says it's frequented by poor, sick people who probably "wash their sores and cleanse their besmeared clouts where others after dip their cups to drink",' came the bland reply. 'All in all, it doesn't sound like a place to revive anyone's spirits, but I suppose there's no accounting for taste.' And then, with a particularly wicked smile, 'Perhaps we should try it. After all, there must be something capable of improving Venetia's health and temper!'

Despite the fact that rain overnight had washed away the bulk of the snow, Venetia arose the following morning with no intention of going to Ferrensby. Her feelings towards Ellis were still too confused – and, in any case, it would do him no harm to wait in vain. So she watched Gabriel depart for Boroughbridge with Wat Larkin and the bailiff . . . and then, leaving Phoebe peering behind tapestries to examine the stone walls of the gallery, she sat down to the task of reviewing the household accounts.

Concentration proved even more elusive than she had expected. Ellis intruded constantly upon her thoughts; and somewhere amidst the debris of her mind was another, quite separate hurt which refused to be identified until Phoebe bounced in and unwittingly released it.

'I haven't come to argue,' she announced, standing in the doorway with her hair full of cobwebs. 'I just wanted to point something out. If Gabriel can offer to spend money we all know he can ill-afford on silk-mercers and dressmakers, the very least *you* can do is to manage a polite refusal. Or so it seems to me, anyway. Think it over.'

And was gone without waiting for an answer.

For a long time, Venetia sat staring at the space where Phoebe had been. The thing she had been unable to name was quite clear now. With everyone about her firmly committed to supporting Gabriel, she was being made to feel like an outcast – and it hurt. But worse still was the tiny seed of self-doubt which suggested that it might just possibly be her own fault.

She pressed the heels of her hands against her closed eyelids and thought about it. There was laughter and companionship in the house from which she had chosen to exclude herself because something inside her recoiled at being even remotely pleasant to a Parliamentarian. That much was true. But why couldn't Sophia and Phoebe at least respect her views instead of constantly criticising? Or was she herself so far gone in self-pity that she no longer saw anything as it really was? She didn't know. The only sure thing was that, if she didn't turn her thoughts in a less destructive direction, she would go out of her mind.

Ellis was waiting for her in the doorway of the mill and his smile told her how sure he'd been that she would come. Aggravated by it, Venetia said abruptly, 'Does Ashley Peverell know you're here?'

'Naturally.' He strolled unhurriedly across to lift her from the saddle. 'You know the good Captain. He expects to be kept informed of every leaf that falls.'

She withdrew from his grasp and avoided his kiss by turning to shake out her skirts. 'So why didn't you contact me through the proper channels? He must have told you that if you couldn't approach me directly, you should do so through Mary Jessop.'

'No. As a matter of fact, he felt that I shouldn't get in touch with you at all,' came the smooth reply. 'After all, your marriage to a Roundhead does make your position somewhat precarious, doesn't it?'

It wasn't the whole truth of course. Captain Peverell had also made it plain that, since he had chosen to linger in the arms of his French mistress rather than offer moral support to his affianced wife, the best favour he could offer Venetia now was to stay well away from her. But Ashley was unlikely to say this to Venetia herself; and, in the meantime, Ellis had his own fish to fry. He said, lightly, 'I don't know whether he's protecting you or his precious network. But though both are perfectly understandable, it seemed to me that he was asking too much. Was I wrong?'

She drew a long, faintly unsteady breath.

'No. I believe some part of me is glad to see you. At least – no matter what our personal difficulties may be – there's no doubt about our being on the same side.'

The weary bitterness in her voice finally gave Ellis the lever he had been looking for. He said, 'What's wrong, Venetia? Is the bastard making life difficult for you?'

'Difficult?' She gave a tiny, mirthless laugh. 'On present showing, he bids fair to make it downright impossible – but not in the way you'd expect.'

'How then?'

'By the ease with which he's charming everyone else,' she replied, walking slowly towards the meagre shelter of the mill and scarcely aware of his arm around her waist. 'Phoebe adores him, Dick Carter would probably walk through fire for him and the tenants hang on his every word. As for Sophy – you'd think she'd given birth to him herself.'

Ellis smiled absently and, spreading his cloak on a fallen beam, drew Venetia down to sit beside him. 'Of course. Any stray mongrel can be assured of a warm welcome from my dear aunt. But who *was* his mother? Do you know?'

She shook her head. 'I haven't asked him. I meant to, naturally, but somehow I never got round to it.'

'My dear girl! Don't you think you should? She may have given him a pack of coal-heaving brothers by now.'

'I sincerely hope not! But you're right, of course. I ought to have asked about her – and I shall.' Then, sitting suddenly upright, 'I almost forgot. Were you aware that Sophy's known about Gabriel for the last thirty years?'

The faintly satisfied gleam vanished abruptly from Ellis' eyes and he drew a sharp breath. '*Sophy* knew? No. I wasn't aware of it. But then, that's all of a piece with the rest, isn't it? The first I heard of any of this was when your letter arrived. I could come face to face with my so-called half-brother on the street and not recognise him. An enviable position, wouldn't you say?'

'No. It's damnable,' she replied quietly. Suddenly, for no reason she could name, most of her anger withered away and slipping her hand companiably through his arm, she said, 'Ask me what you want and I'll tell you.'

This was exactly what he had hoped for but he was careful not to let it show. Turning to look into her face and gripping her fingers, he said, 'Everything. I need to know everything, because one day he and I will meet.'

There was a short, airless silence.

'Then I'd better begin at the beginning, hadn't I?' said Venetia. And, as concisely as possible, her tone more often sardonic than distressed, she embarked on a detailed appraisal of Gabriel. She described his physical appearance and his manner, his background as far as she knew it and his activities at Brandon Lacey; and, since it was important for Ellis's sake not to distort the picture, she tried – for the very first time – to be objective.

Ellis listened without interruption and at the end of it all drawled, 'Well, well . . . so the master of Brandon Lacey is a rebel mercenary, reared in the house of some backstreet tradesman. He's done well for himself, hasn't he?'

'Except for the money – yes.'

'A bagatelle, my dear. I'm sure this sordid little commercial venture of his will soon fix that. And, once he's lured the tenants to work for him, he can make sure they go on doing so by raising the rents. Simple.'

The violet eyes looked starkly back at him.

'Is that what you think?'

'Don't you?'

'I – I don't know. He sounded so genuine – and he's got

195

everyone else convinced. So I can't help starting to wonder if I'm the only one marching in step – or whether I'm simply blinded by my own dislike.'

'It sounds to me as though you're the only one bright enough not to be taken in by him,' came the flat reply. Then, 'He's a Roundhead, Venetia. It was he and his kind who killed Kit and your father, who are keeping the King from his rightful place. Others might be able to forget that – but not you. And, even if you wanted to, he's going to be fighting us in the field again soon enough.'

'Yes.' She stared down at her hands, frowning a little. 'I realise that. But will the Scots really invade? And how likely are they to win if they do? As I understand it, they're having trouble raising an army – and another failure won't help his Majesty's cause in the least.'

'It won't be a failure,' Ellis assured her confidently. 'England's so discontented now that, should someone just apply the match, the whole country would go up in flames.'

'I'm not so sure about that. We've had two bad harvests and the price of food has gone up as a result. But the man who riots over the cost of bread won't necessarily take up arms to put the King back on the throne – much as he'd like to see him there.' She paused and, rising from his side, added dryly, 'It will take more than a handful of raw recruits with slingshots to defeat the New Model, Ellis. And if they beat us again, the consequences could be severe.'

He lifted one brow and surveyed her quizzically.

'Are you saying we shouldn't take the risk?'

'Not at all. I'm merely being realistic.' She shivered, pulled her cloak closer about her and said diffidently, 'We've talked of everything except your immediate plans. How soon are you leaving for London?'

He smiled ruefully. 'As soon as I can lay my hands on sufficient funds.'

'But Mr Crisp is holding your Oxfordshire lands in trust. Can't you . . . ?' She stopped and then said slowly, 'No. I suppose not. After the roasting he got for telling me how things stood at Brandon Lacey, he's not likely to risk keeping the Colonel in the dark a second time.'

'My own thoughts exactly,' agreed Ellis smoothly. It was

as good an excuse as any – and watertight so long as neither Isaiah Crisp nor Venetia mentioned his name to one another. 'Anxious as I am to confront the by-blow, I'd prefer to do it on my terms rather than his . . . which leaves me in something of a quandary as to how to pay my tavern-bill and finance my journey to London.'

'How much do you need?'

'My dear!' He dropped a brief kiss on her lips and then shook his head. 'I couldn't possibly take it from you.'

'Why not? The Duke of York has to be got out – as much for his father's sake as his own. You must know as well as I do that Parliament's been toying with the notion of deposing the King in his favour. So tell me. How much?'

'Fifty pounds might suffice.' And then, catching the look in her eye, 'I know – I know. But discretion involves bribes and a whole host of other incidental costs.'

Venetia thought rapidly, trying to work out how she could find a sum of that size in a hurry: 'I can't promise anything – but I'll see what I can do. How long can you wait?'

'Unfortunately, only until tomorrow.'

She nodded. 'All right. Tomorrow, then, but not here. Three days in succession would be too risky. I'll meet you at dusk in Stavely church . . . on one condition.'

He took her hand and placed a kiss in her palm.

'Name it and it's yours.'

'Buy yourself another suit of clothes. However elegant it may be, tawny velvet isn't exactly calculated to help you pass unnoticed. And it's enough to give any qualified plotter an apoplexy.'

Four

Gabriel returned from Boroughbridge well-pleased with the bargain he had struck, but all too aware that he had less than a week in which to complete his plans. The result was a flood of orders upon which Mr Larkin found himself dispatched on a tour of every family on the estate, and Mr Carter received the task of making the Scar Croft cottages fit for their new purpose.

The bailiff thought anxiously about all his other duties and the fact that lambing was nearly upon them.

Wat spat into the fire and said, 'You don't want much, do you? But if I'm going, I suppose you'd better tell me what to say.'

'You simply tell the head of each house that I'd be glad of their presence here on Sunday after church – and that there will be ale for those who want it,' grinned Gabriel. And, turning to Mr Carter, 'As for the cottages – I'd like the downstairs rooms knocked into one. It shouldn't be too difficult.'

'Happen it won't be. But by Wednesday?'

'No. By Tuesday,' said the Colonel. 'I want to be installing the looms on Wednesday – and there'll be a lot of cleaning to do when the workmen have finished.'

'And what,' asked Mr Larkin dourly, 'will *you* be doing?'

'Completing my costings, haggling with Warner the dyer, finding a way of retting our flax without breaking the law, and hopefully getting a licence from the Merchant Adventurers in York,' came the crisp reply. 'Nothing very arduous. But then, you know how congenitally work-shy I am.'

Wat began his Odyssey next morning armed with a list thoughtfully provided by the Colonel, and the suggestion

199

that, if he started from the top, he ought to arrive at the Skilbeck place in nice time for the noonday meal.

Mr Larkin had merely grunted. Jane Skilbeck was a good-looking woman and he'd grown fond of both her and her children. But that was as far as it went . . . and if Gabriel thought otherwise, he was wide of the mark. Wat hadn't avoided wedlock all these years only to fall victim to it now; and besides, another few weeks would see him safely back in the Army where he belonged.

The reaction of the tenants to Gabriel's summons was uniform and predictable. Wat sidestepped each family's barrage of questions with practised ease, put away two bowls of Jane's mutton broth, and went off to complete his rounds just as the intermittent drizzle became a deluge.

It was a long and increasingly tedious afternoon and Wat's mood grew steadily worse. But finally, as dusk was falling, he paid his last call and rode morosely back through the village towards Brandon Lacey.

He was just debating whether mulled wine or a hot posset would best combat the chilling effect of the rain when his eye was caught by a flurry of movement in the churchyard. Two figures, both heavily cloaked, converged from opposite directions and disappeared swiftly into the shadows of the porch. Wat snorted to himself and continued stoically on his way. It wasn't exactly the best of weather for a lover's tryst; but if they waited for a dry day in this place, like as not they'd wait for ever.

He arrived back, changed out of his wet clothes and talked one of the maids into mulling some wine for him. Then he went in search of Gabriel – which was how he happened to be crossing the passage which led to a seldom-used side-door when Venetia walked in.

Just for a second they both stood absolutely still, their eyes locked together. Then Venetia raised deliberately satiric brows and stalked wordlessly by . . . leaving Wat's arm damp from contact with her cloak and his mind awash with black suspicion.

By the time his tenants started streaming somewhat uneasily into the house on Sunday morning, Gabriel had discovered, with some surprise, that he was enjoying himself. He'd come to Brandon Lacey knowing nothing of the land or its uses, forced himself to learn out of duty and attacked its problems from necessity. But daily involvement and the satisfaction of seeing his plans take shape had changed all that. Caring for the estate's tenants wasn't so very different to caring for his regiment, and strategic planning was useful for more than taking a town. Also one always enjoyed the things one was good at.

He watched them come in, clutching their hats and looking nervously around them. Very few, he guessed, had ever been inside a house like this – and they were intimidated as much by their surroundings as by what he himself was going to say to them. But great jugs of ale stood comfortingly on the trestles and both Sophia and Phoebe were ready with welcoming smiles. It was just a pity, he thought looking at Venetia sitting straight-backed and silent by the hearth, that his wife couldn't be equally helpful.

When the time came, he spoke for ten minutes, outlining his project simply and with dispassionate clarity whilst keeping a weather eye on the faces in front of him. And, when he had finished, he let the echo of his words lap the edges of the room for a moment before saying, 'If you have any questions, I'll be happy to answer them. Alternatively, if you want a few minutes in which to digest what I've said and talk amongst yourselves, ale is ready and waiting.'

The faint air of tension dissolved into a ripple of approval and someone said jovially, 'You've given us a fair bit to think on, Colonel – and no mistake. But I reckon I can speak for rest when I say you've not gone about it so badly. You might even make a Yorkshireman yet.'

'Now I *am* worried,' retorted Gabriel with the sudden, flying grin which, as always, rendered his face younger and less formidable. 'And so, I think, should *you* be.'

This time there was a rumble of scattered laughter and then the men headed for the beer tables, talking as if their tongues had been frozen for a week. But Jane Skilbeck and a handful of other widows remained in an uncertain huddle by the wall until Venetia walked gracefully over to them with a tray of small tankards.

'Some refreshment for you, ladies. I thought spiced wine might be more welcome than ale on such a cold day.'

One by one, they bobbed a startled curtsy and carefully accepted a cup, leaving Jane to express their thanks.

'Not at all,' said Venetia. 'I just wanted the chance to say that, since you're all the equal of any man here, you're equally entitled to express your opinions.' And she encompassed them in a dazzling, faintly mischievous smile.

Gabriel stared at her. The unpretentiousness of her manner and the thought which had provided the mulled wine were unexpected enough; but that smile gave him the disorientating feeling of looking at a completely different person. Putting himself in Venetia's path as she left the women, he said slowly, 'That was uncommonly well done. I'm impressed.'

'Are you?' The amethyst eyes surveyed him witheringly. 'That's nice. I'd hate to have put myself to so much trouble for nothing.'

Gabriel's brief moment of admiration died stillborn. He said, 'My mistake. After your talented performance just now, I thought we might stand some chance of a civilised exchange for once.'

'Why bother when we both know it can't last?' she said. And walked away.

He immediately found himself surrounded by a group of men eager to ask questions and had no difficulty whatsoever in banishing Venetia from his mind. Her hostility, after all, was nothing new. And right now he had a job to do.

He did it well. Even Venetia, watching once more from the hearth, had to acknowledge that. He explained, reiterated and clarified without ever wandering from the point, often with a good deal of dry humour. And, long before the ale showed signs of running out, it was becoming plain that he'd succeeded. First the women cast their votes in favour and then, gradually, most of the men. At the end of an hour, Phoebe was already helping Dick Carter to list names and skills . . . before two had passed, the last of the stragglers left the house a good deal more jauntily than they had entered it.

Gabriel drew a long breath and let his head drop back in a moment of silent communication with the ceiling. Then he faced his helpers with a grimly satisfied smile and said, 'The day is ours. All we have to do now is make tomorrow live up to it.'

In the end, Venetia decided to go to York – but only, so far as Gabriel could see, because Phoebe had set her heart on the trip and Sophy preferred to stay at home with a sick rabbit. They therefore set off early on Monday morning on a twenty mile ride which, but for Phoebe's determination to talk non-stop, would have been accomplished largely in silence. Gabriel lent half an ear to her chatter whilst wishing he'd asked John Lambert for an introduction to the Merchant Adventurers. He also found himself wondering why Venetia and Wat were glowering at each other even more than usual, but concluded that it was better not to ask.

They entered York beneath the high, crenellated turrets of Micklegate at around eleven o'clock and made their way across the Ouse into the bustling medieval heart of the city. Carts, drays and carriages thronged the streets and rumbled noisily over the cobbles, spattering unwary passers-by with the refuse from the gutters; hawkers cried everything from hot pies to pamphlets, church bells clanged and a hundred different smells charged the air. Wat brightened. It was the best place he'd seen since leaving London.

At the top of High Ousegate, Gabriel paused to consider his direction and, seeing this, Venetia said coolly, 'I think this is where we leave you. The Merchant Adventurers Hall is over to your right, on Fossgate, and the best mercers' establishments lie the other way. So all you need do is say where and when you wish us to meet you.'

'No later than three and at some respectable inn, which I am sure you can name more easily than I.'

'The Bear on Stonegate, then.' And, without waiting for him to reply, Venetia rode away.

Phoebe cast Gabriel an expression of apologetic resignation and shrugged. Then she set off in pursuit of her sister. As soon as she'd caught up with her, she said, flatly, 'If this mood's going to last all day, we might as well have stayed at home.'

Venetia turned and eyed her remotely. The truth, of

course, was that the business of amassing Ellis's fifty pounds had left her extremely tense. She'd managed to get just over half of it from Ford Edge but the rest had come out of the household budget at Brandon Lacey. And although she tried to tell herself that she had only taken what rightfully belonged to Ellis anyway, her conscience still troubled her – and as a consequence she'd been unnecessarily shrewish with Gabriel the day before.

Phoebe was right, though; and there was no point in worrying about what couldn't be mended, so she summoned a smile and said, 'I'm sorry. I don't mean to be a killjoy. Let's stable the horses and fortify ourselves with a glass of cordial.'

'And a couple of slices of curd tart?' grinned Phoebe. 'By all means. I'm absolutely ravenous!'

By the time they entered Mr Sutcliffe's shop, hard by St Helen's church, Venetia was already fully acquainted with the indecisive nature of her sister's requirements.

'I'm not sure if I want taffeta or silk – and I can't have blue because that's what Bess will be wearing. Also, since I'm to attend her, I suppose I'd better be careful not to choose anything that will clash. But that means pink would probably be best and I really wanted something a little more sophisticated. What do you think?'

'That we've only got three hours – not three days,' replied Venetia dryly. 'Come on. Let's get started.'

While his wife and sister-in-law debated the rival merits of primrose taffeta and jade silk and turned Mr Sutcliffe's trestles into a glowing kaleidoscope of colour, Colonel Brandon sat in the majestically-timbered hall of the Merchant Adventurers and applied to the cautious gentleman on the other side of the table for a licence.

'To do what, precisely?'

'To sell Brandon Lacey's cloth here in York,' said Gabriel, 'just as Sir Robert must presumably have been doing for many years. But in slightly greater quantity.'

Alderman Cooper laid his fingertips together and thought about it. 'Our business here is largely concerned with export. I take it you have no ambitions in that direction?'

'None. We can increase our yield – but not to those levels.'

'Mm. And what quality will you be producing?'

'The best,' returned Gabriel with more assurance than he actually felt. 'Worsteds, mostly. And linen.'

A mildly interested gleam lit the Alderman's eye and he drew a sheet of paper in front of him. 'I see. Then supposing you give me some idea of the estate's capability? Number of fleeces – flax acreage and so on.'

Gabriel battened down a strong desire to remark that he didn't see how such details concerned anyone but himself and reeled off a series of extremely conservative estimates. Then he said blandly, 'And now; supposing you tell me the current market rates for wool and linen, and whether or not you're prepared to grant me a licence. After all, I've no wish to waste either your time or mine unnecessarily.'

It was almost two hours before he repaired to the nearby tavern where Mr Larkin had elected to wait for him and, when he did, the look on his face spoke for itself.

'You got it, then,' said Wat.

'Naturally. Did you think I wouldn't?'

'No. I'm just flummoxed as to why you're going to all this trouble. There must be easier ways.'

'Suggest one.'

'Well *I* don't know, do I? I'm not a bloody farmer.' Wat paused and then said abruptly, 'There's one thing I do know, though. You could do with keeping a better eye on that missus of yours.'

Gabriel draped his cloak over a corner of the settle, signalled for the pot-boy to bring more ale and then sat down. 'And what makes you think that?'

'Because she's either got one extremely *good* friend or a whole parcel of poxy Royalist ones. And I reckon it'd pay you to find out which, before something nasty comes of it.'

The Colonel took his time about answering. Then he said, expressionlessly, 'All right. You know something I don't. So tell me about it. I'm listening.'

As soon as Gabriel walked into the parlour of the Bear on Stonegate, Phoebe embarked on a rapturous description of the length of apricot silk which lay, neatly wrapped, on the bench beside her. He smiled, observed that it would no doubt suit her to perfection and then, when she paused for breath, looked impassively across at Venetia.

'And what about you? Haven't you bought anything?'

'No.' She forced herself to speak pleasantly and gave the same excuse she had given Phoebe. 'I don't really need a new gown . . . and nothing I saw was sufficiently tempting.'

'No? But then, you're remarkably hard to please, are you not?'

'She's hopeless,' said Phoebe, for once entirely oblivious to undercurrents. 'She actually refused the loveliest mauve-green watered silk I've ever seen.'

The dark grey eyes remained fixed on Venetia, their expression unreadable but faintly disquieting.

'How very strong-minded of you. Or was it native thrift? Or then again,' he suggested blandly, 'perhaps you just didn't have the right incentive?'

Along with Wat and Dick Carter, Gabriel spent the following day overseeing the final stages of preparation on the Scar Croft cottages. Encouragingly, there had been no shortage of volunteer labour so the inner walls had been swiftly demolished and made good, leaving ample time for the whole interior to be whitewashed before a small army of laughing, excited women arrived with brooms, buckets and mops. Gabriel praised, joked and dirtied his hands along with the rest. Then, at around four in the afternoon, he turned round to find Major Maxwell at his elbow.

'My God,' said Eden, looking first at the hive of industry about him and then at his commanding officer's paint-spattered smock. 'Another myth exploded!'

'Quite.' Gabriel rubbed his hands on a rag and grinned. '*Aren't* you glad you didn't simply wait at the house and let someone come down in search of me?'

'Absolutely. But the truth is that I didn't have time for that. I'm going south with reports for Fairfax – regimental strengths, the state of the northern defences and so on – and I thought I'd pay you a flying visit on the way, to ask if you've any messages for anyone.'

'You're a liar,' said Gabriel calmly. 'You just want to know whether I've fallen in love with civilian life.'

The hazel gaze was watchful. 'And have you?'

'No. Satisfied?'

Eden nodded and then, unable to leave well alone, said abruptly, 'Venetia's still strongly Royalist, isn't she?'

'Has she left the fact open to doubt?'

'No.'

'Then why ask?'

There was a tiny, strained pause.

'So that I could remind you to be careful,' said Eden.

'I see.' Gabriel stared impassively at him for a moment and then said, 'You're thinking that, since my marriage already bears certain striking resemblances to your own, I ought to beware of letting it end up the same way.'

'Something like that, yes.'

'Your concern is appreciated. Fortunately, however, you're apparently missing the one small but vital detail that makes all the difference.'

'And what might that be?'

'Isn't it obvious?' A faint, chilly smile touched the Colonel's mouth. 'You married Celia for love.'

As a result of her all-too-brief glimpse of Major Maxwell, Phoebe spent the majority of the evening in a sort of rosy glow that eventually made Venetia decide to eclipse him by revealing something that had been on her mind for some time. Waiting until they were all retiring for the night, she therefore followed Phoebe into her bedchamber and, closing the door behind her, said baldly, 'If you can forget Eden Maxwell for a minute, there's something important we need to talk about.'

Phoebe flushed a little and, waving her sister towards the room's only chair, hoisted herself on to the edge of the bed. 'What is it?'

Venetia sat down and tried to think how best to begin.

'Firstly, I think it's time you went home. Oh – don't misunderstand me. It's not that I want to be rid of you. But now that the weather's improving, there's nothing to stop you riding over from Ford Edge whenever you like if you're still determined to go on searching for the Garland. Besides, with Elizabeth's wedding no more than three weeks away, Mother is going to want your help.'

The honey-brown head nodded thoughtfully.

'I know and I had been thinking as much myself. Was that all you wanted to say?'

'No. That's only the beginning,' said Venetia wryly. 'You know that, as things now stand, Ford Edge belongs to me absolutely. What you may not have realised is that it would be very foolish of me to keep it.'

'Foolish? Why?'

'Because a husband has rights over his wife's property and I don't want to have gone through all this for nothing.'

Phoebe opened her mouth to observe that, if Gabriel had any designs on Ford Edge, he'd never have married Venetia in the first place; then, recognising the futility of it, she merely said, 'So what are you going to do about it?'

Venetia looked her straight in the eye.

'Subject to your consent, I'm going to give it to you for your eighteenth birthday.'

The colour drained from Phoebe's face and she slithered slowly to her feet. 'Is – is that a joke?'

'Quite the contrary. If you think about it, it's the only sensible solution. Quite apart from her total ignorance of estate matters, Mother is almost certain to pre-decease both of us, and Bess will soon be married to Tom.' Venetia paused and managed a touch of mordant humour. 'I know it's a huge responsibility, but look on the bright side. Once word gets round, you'll have every eligible man in Yorkshire knocking at the door.'

'And every fortune hunter, too,' retorted Phoebe with rare asperity. 'I can't believe you're serious. And it's all so unnecessary. Gabriel won't touch Ford Edge.'

'Possibly not, but I can't take the risk. I'd rather entrust it to you and know that it's safe. Unless, that is, you don't want it?'

Phoebe drew a long, unsteady breath. 'Want it? Of course I want it! It's my home. I'm just not sure I'm capable of looking after it properly.'

'I am.' Venetia stood up and smiled at her. 'If I wasn't, do you honestly think we'd be having this conversation?'

Wat arrived back from Boroughbridge at around noon on the following day in charge of two expertly laden carts, and then sat down to whittle at a piece of wood while the Colonel superintended the unloading of them. Spinning wheels, carding-combs and spare spindles disappeared smartly inside one cottage and the two looms were taken carefully away for erection in the other – along with the gears needed to modify them for weaving flax.

'What's the matter?' His inventory in one hand and a piece of mutton pie in the other, Gabriel paused at his henchman's side. 'Something wrong with your back, is there?'

'No there bloody isn't. I'm as fit as you. Fitter, probably. But I reckon I've done my share. And you seem to be having enough fun for both of us.'

'You think I should play the lord of the manor and leave the real work to the peasants?'

A reluctant grin dawned on Wat's taciturn features, 'That'll be the day.'

'Quite. So what's curdling your liver this time? The fact that I refuse to open fire on Venetia without proper ammunition – or some half-baked notion that I like what I'm doing now so much I won't want to leave it?'

'So long as it *is* half-baked,' muttered Wat, paring expertly at the rough, doll-like shape between his hands.

'Hell's teeth!' Gabriel turned away to point two fellows carrying a large trestle in the right direction and threw the crust of his pie to a dog. Then, carefully lowering his voice, he said, 'How many times must I say it? If I can't make this place pay for itself, it's going to be a millstone round my neck. And, since I can't rely on Venetia to keep things going for me, I've somehow got to create sufficient organisation and enthusiasm to survive my absence. Those are the realities, Wat, and they're not especially pleasant. So I'm damned if I'll apologise for enjoying beating them.'

'Did I ask you to?' Mr Larkin rose in a shower of woodshavings. 'Far be it from me to spoil anybody's pleasure. Live and let live, that's what I always say.'

It was, as Gabriel well knew, the closest Wat would ever get to an apology. Laughter warming his eyes, he said, 'Of course. How silly of me to think otherwise. My nerves must be shot.' And found that Wat was laughing with him.

By the time the light started to fail, both cottages were fully equipped and in pristine order. The looms stood proudly side by side, their warp threads expertly renewed by John Parker of Mole Farm; five lovingly polished spinning-wheels formed a graceful semi-circle around a log-stacked hearth; and a variety of smaller items hung from hooks on the walls. Just as Gabriel had intended, the project was a source of pride to all who'd had a hand in it – and he prayed that the feeling would last till after shearing. For the only thing missing now was the wool and, by the time that came, he fully expected to be back with his regiment.

Lambing moved into full swing and took precedence over everything else; Phoebe went home to Ford Edge, reluctantly leaving Venetia to settle matters with Lawyer Crisp before explaining them to Gabriel; and, in South Wales, one Colonel Poyer refused to hand Pembroke Castle over to the officer sent to replace him.

The Pembroke incident was a small thing in itself but Gabriel found it worrying. Recent months had seen a series of riots begin over the price of fuel and shortages of food but end as Royalist demonstrations. And every news-sheet one picked up these days spoke of plots to rescue the King and invasions from abroad. There was unrest in the City, continued resistance to disbandment within the Army and a tide of Leveller feeling running throughout both. Even Parliament was divided within itself. In such a precarious situation it would take only the smallest hint of mutiny – even across the border in Wales – to destroy the balance completely.

By the time Venetia chose to inform him that Phoebe was destined to become the new mistress of Ford Edge, Gabriel was preoccupied with preparing to plant the flax. He therefore remarked that, though Venetia doubtless knew her own business best, he'd have thought her mother might be less than happy with the arrangement.

Having already endured an affronted lecture from Lady Clifford, Venetia was well aware of this. But instead of telling Gabriel so, she took a deep breath and, taking advantage of the fact that they were alone for once, said, 'That reminds me. There's something I've been meaning to ask you.'

'Oh?' His hand travelled on across the page and the dark head remained bent.

'Yes. I have been wondering – indeed, I'm sure you can't *blame* me for wondering – who your mother was.'

There was a long, airless silence before his eyes rose, harsh and impenetrable, to meet hers, and even then he did not speak. Venetia stood it as long as she could and then said, 'Well? Under the circumstances, that's not such an unreasonable question, is it?'

'Under what circumstances?' asked Gabriel. His tone was bland as butter but none the less dangerous for that.

'Don't be coy. For better or worse, we're married—'

'Mostly for worse, I'd say.'

'Quite. But the fact remains that, after almost three months, I still don't know anything about your background.'

'So?' He rose abruptly and moved to the shadows on the far side of the hearth. 'Don't they say ignorance is bliss?'

'I don't. I say that it's generally the things you don't know about which have a habit of dropping on you from a great height. Such as Eden Maxwell, for example.'

'Oh my God! Are we back to that again?'

'No. We are advancing to the subject of your mother.'

'Correction. *You* are advancing to it. I am merely wondering why it should suddenly matter.'

'I've already explained that. After all, if your mother is still alive or you've a host of relations lurking somewhere, I think I've a right to know – before any of them take it into their heads to turn up on the doorstep.'

'And embarrass you with their vulgarity.' It was not a question. 'Of course. I should have guessed.'

A faint, betraying flush touched her skin and, irritated by it, she said defiantly, 'Think what you like. I'm only asking what anyone would ask. And, quite frankly, I can't see what you're making so much fuss about.'

Gabriel contemplated her over sardonically folded arms and wondered if that were really true or if Venetia somehow knew she had picked on the one thing he never discussed with anybody. He wouldn't put it past her. She was quite capable of looking for a weakness to exploit. And that, of course, was why it would be foolish to let her know she'd found it.

Though he didn't relish being called a bastard, his illegitimacy no longer bothered him. After all, he'd had many years in which to get used to it, and, in the world of the professional soldier, it was neither a handicap nor even particularly unusual. The question of his mother, however, was another matter entirely. He ought, by now, to be totally indifferent to the fact that he knew absolutely nothing about her – but somehow he wasn't. And he didn't really know why.

It wasn't as if he thought of it often or with any sense of pain. Those days were long gone, left behind in his childhood. Neither did he feel as if knowing might be in any sense important. At almost thirty-five, he was beyond all that. No. Inwardly, it wasn't a problem. The only trouble was that he still couldn't bring himself to discuss it. Not with Jack, not with Wat, and certainly not with Venetia; except that, if he didn't say something, she'd continue twisting the knife.

In a tone of stinging mockery, he said, 'Very well. Let's see if I can set your mind at rest. I was reared in the house of one John Morrell, an armourer of Shoreditch. Both he and his wife are now dead – as is the elder of their two sons. But my foster-brother, Jack, is very profitably engaged in the family trade and possessed of a wife, a baby son and an orphaned niece. He is also about as likely to visit Yorkshire as the Pope. How's that?'

'A start,' said Venetia. She half-wished she'd never begun this, but knew that if she didn't pursue it now the chance would be lost forever. 'And your mother?'

'Need not concern you since you will never meet her.'

His voice contained a warning that kept five hundred troopers in their place. Venetia ignored it and said, 'But she is still alive?'

'I haven't the remotest idea.'

'Oh!' There was a faintly nonplussed pause; and then, 'When did you last see her?'

'So far as I am aware – never.'

'*Never?* But surely she—'

212

'No. You find that surprising? You shouldn't.' Gabriel could feel both patience and tolerance being stretched to the limits. 'When a girl conceives a child out of wedlock, she is either cast off, forced into marriage or hidden away until she can come back looking pure and unsullied. In only one of those instances is she guaranteed to keep her child.'

'Yes. I suppose so.' Venetia stared thoughtfully at her hands for a moment and braced herself to look up at him for the final onslaught. 'So it was Sir Robert who placed you in Shoreditch?'

'Obviously.'

'Where he presumably visited you from time to time?'

'Yes.'

'Then no doubt he told you who your mother was.'

The sudden blaze of temper in Gabriel's eyes told Venetia that she had finally pushed him too far.

'*Christ!*' he said furiously. 'Are you just doing this to pass a dull evening, or are you set on drawing blood? For it must by now have occurred to you that I'm not especially fond of being interrogated.'

'Then it's a pity you didn't simply answer the question when I first asked it,' she returned unevenly. 'It's not my fault you're making it deliberately difficult. I just wanted to know if she was a – a local girl or someone Sir Robert met elsewhere.'

'No you didn't. You want to know if she was a scullery-maid or a tavern-wench or a whore. After all, since Sir Robert wasn't married at the time of my birth, she must have been some such, mustn't she? So take your pick. Which do you think?'

'Oh – this is ridiculous! How should I know?'

Seconds ticked silently by and an unpleasant chill made its way down Venetia's back. Then Gabriel said blisteringly, 'How indeed? And that, believe it or not, makes two of us.'

In the days between this unfortunate exchange and Elizabeth Clifford's wedding, Gabriel reverted to a policy of strict neutrality and saw as little of his wife as was possible. He therefore had no means of knowing that – far from wishing to renew her attack – Venetia actually regretted it. She had poked and pried into something which didn't concern her and finally, with neither tact nor good sense, forced an unpleasant and understandably painful admission. She would have felt better if she had been able to apologise. Unfortunately, however, Gabriel seemed determined not to give her the chance.

On a gusty day at the end of March, they therefore set off for Ford Edge with even less than their usual accord. In deference to Sophia's mulberry silk and Venetia's silver-green taffeta, Gabriel brought the lumbering coach out of retirement but flatly refused to condemn himself to sharing its discomfort. He therefore rode silently alongside, leaving Sophy alone with Venetia's stony profile.

They arrived to find the courtyard jammed with carriages and the house seething with the cream of the county's gentry. In the first thirty seconds, Venetia recognised the Ingrams of Temple Newsham, Sir William Ingilby of Ripley Castle and her father's formidable cousin, Lady Anne Clifford of Skipton. Then, as if what lay ahead wasn't likely to be quite bad enough, Gabriel removed his cloak to reveal a new severely-cut suit of dark grey broadcloth, and a tawny silk sash wound flamboyantly around his waist.

Her heart sank and his smile confirmed the suspicion that she was being punished.

'Merely nailing my colours to the mast,' he explained blandly. 'It's what people will be expecting, after all, and it would be a pity to disappoint them. Don't you agree?'

The ensuing half-hour told Venetia exactly what to expect of the rest of the day. Ruth Knightley asked her a series of impertinent questions in between oozing spurious sympathy; her mother, still presumably smarting over not being given Ford Edge, ostentatiously cold-shouldered her; and even those who tried to pretend nothing had changed were palpably ill-at-ease. As for Gabriel, the only people who acknowledged his existence were Phoebe, Uncle James and the prospective bridegroom. Venetia's nerves were soon stretched taut as lute-strings and she was acutely thankful when the time came to enter the chapel.

This wedding was not like her own. A consort of viols played discreetly in the background and the altar was decorated with a profusion of spring flowers. Elizabeth floated serenely down the aisle in pale blue silk embroidered with silver lilies and, when she reached Tom's side, he turned to greet her with unashamed love and pride. Venetia stole a brief, involuntary glance at the grimly forbidding mask beside her and then restored her attention to the ceremony. Life, she decided, was an unmitigated disaster.

Back in the hall, with the wedding-breakfast still to live through, she kissed Elizabeth's cheek, congratulated Tom and complimented Phoebe on the glowing apricot gown. Then, before her nerve could fail, she stalked purposefully back to Gabriel and said flatly, 'I owe you an apology. If I'd had any idea what I was meddling with, I wouldn't have done it. But the fact is that I did – and I'm sorry.'

The grey eyes looked back with cynical indifference. 'Dear me. Can this be a change of heart? And, if so, why?'

'Because I'm occasionally able to admit being in the wrong. I've also possibly been less than fair to you in the past. I imagine that you don't like our marriage any better than I do – but at least you've retained a sense of proportion. I, on the other hand, have picked up the olive-branch only to hit you over the head with it.'

An odd quiver that might have been laughter passed over the still face but when he spoke his tone had not varied by so much as a hairsbreadth. 'You have a point to make?'

'Yes. I'm trying to say that it won't happen again.'

'Ah. Forgive me for saying so, but I'll believe that when I see it. Unless, of course . . .' He paused reflectively. 'Unless of course you'd care to back it up with some small expression of goodwill?'

'Such as what for example?' asked Venetia warily.

'Don't worry.' His smile mocked her. 'I'm not going to demand your body. Since we're only waving white flags and not yet sealing a treaty, that would be carrying things a trifle too far. No. I merely thought you might keep a benevolent eye on the goings-on at Scar Croft after I leave next week.'

Her lungs malfunctioned and she wondered why. She said, 'Despite any impression I may have given to the contrary, I'd have done that anyway.'

His brows rose.

'Even before you were stricken with remorse?'

'Oh yes.' She shrugged wryly. 'The only difference is that I certainly wouldn't have let you know it.'

There was a small, almost companiable silence.

'Feminine logic,' remarked Gabriel, 'has always been beyond me. But I suppose no one's perfect.'

The wedding-breakfast was a lavish display of panoplied pheasant, Bavarian creams, dressed lobster and endless other delicacies. Having been denied the chance to hold a spectacular reception for her eldest daughter, Lady Clifford had plainly set out to make up for it with the marriage of her second. Venetia did not begrudge Elizabeth her day; she just wondered where the money was to come from to pay for it and whether Phoebe stood any chance at all of curbing their mother's natural extravagance.

The boards were drawn, drums and a shawm joined the viols and Tom led Elizabeth into an *allemande*. Gabriel made his intentions clear by calmly re-filling his glass but Venetia found herself whisked into the dance by one of Tom's cousins and a sort of determined gaiety set in. Then, as the noise was reaching its peak, the door burst open and Will Haslam of Ravensthorpe burst in with his hair all on end.

'News!' he shouted wildly. 'There's news!'

Couple by couple, the dancers froze in their tracks and the music dribbled into silence. Sir Charles Haslam bent a beetle-browed gaze on his son and barked, 'This had better be good, boy. It's bad enough that you're late.'

'I'm sorry. But I was in Leeds, you see, and when I heard the rumours, I had to stay to find out more,' replied Will rapidly. And, with a bright-eyed glance around the company at large, he went on, 'Yesterday, London celebrated his Majesty's Accession Day with bonfires. Everyone who passed by was forced to drink his health and the butchers were saying they'd like to turn his gaoler – that fellow Hammond – into collops. But that's not the best bit by any means.'

'Then get on with it, there's a good fellow,' beseeched Tom ruefully. 'I'd like to continue dancing with my wife.'

There was a tiny ripple of laughter which died instantly as Will spoke. 'There's mutiny in Wales. Rowland Laugharne's men have joined with Colonel Poyer. They've driven the Roundheads out of Pembroke, taken Tenby and declared for the King. *Now* do you forgive my interruption?'

His answer was a second's incredulous silence, followed by a huge cheer and a spattering of applause. Faces beamed, hugs were exchanged and toasts were drunk. Gabriel set his glass down on the mantelpiece and looked on in openly sardonic silence until, as if recognising him for the first time, Philip Knightley said, 'Well, Colonel? It seems your fine army is no longer as united against his Majesty as you'd doubtless like to think.'

'What I think has little to do with it,' came the prosaic reply. 'But if you're seriously interested, I'd be tempted to say that Colonel Poyer's activities probably have less to do with a sudden surge of Royalist feeling than enforced disbandment on only two months back-pay.'

A murmur of angry unease filled the room and Venetia felt alarm feather her spine. Sir William Ingilby muttered, 'The fellow sounds like a damned sectary to me.'

'Far from it.' With complete assurance, Gabriel detached himself unhurriedly from the hearth and strolled forward to confront his accusers. 'I'm afraid I'm just a common mercenary who entered the service of Parliament believing its cause was just, but who now sees it dealing less than fairly with his men. As for the King – I've no more wish to see him deposed than you. But if anyone here thinks he can be restored to the throne unconditionally, they are living in a soap-bubble.'

Several people spoke at once in a confused medley of dissent, over which Sir Charles Haslam was heard to remark that no one could dictate terms to the Lord's Anointed.

'If everyone believed *that* this country would have been spared four years of civil war,' responded the Colonel dryly. 'I'll be blunt, gentlemen. As I see it, nothing will satisfy you except putting back the clock. But the only way you can do so is by force of arms – and you have already failed in that once. Do you seriously expect to do better a second time?'

'Yes!' cried Will Haslam. 'And a third, if necessary!'

The grey gaze impaled him derisively.

'Have you ever visited the German states?'

'No. But—'

'You should. The wars there have lasted thirty years and left the country devastated. Do you want that here? And to what end? So that Charles Stuart may dispense with Parliament altogether and order the kingdom as he sees fit?'

There was a moment of perfectly appalled silence. Then the unexpected happened. Tom's sister, Frances, began to sing and, after the first few words, voice upon voice joined in with her.

> *What booker can prognosticate*
> *Concerning king's or kingdom's fate?*
> *I think myself to be as wise*
> *As he that gazeth on the skies.*
> *My skill goes beyond the depths of a pond*
> *Or rivers of the greatest rain*
> *Whereby I can tell all things will be well*
> *When the King enjoys his own again.*

Gabriel remained motionless while the chorus gathered strength about him. Only a handful of people stayed out of it. Phoebe – who, together with Sophia, looked utterly stricken; Tom Knightley – plainly uncomfortable about the whole business; and, oddly enough, Venetia. The rest, so far as he could see, were all singing fit to burst.

It ought to have been intimidating; it was certainly meant to be. The unfortunate truth, however, was that the only feeling it produced in him was a strong impulse to laugh . . . and that would probably provoke them to violence.

There was only one sensible thing to do and, deliberately avoiding Venetia's eye, Gabriel did it. He moved unhurriedly through the chorus, now embarking somewhat less confidently on the third verse, and walked out of the house, closing the door behind him with a gentle click.

> *Full forty years the royal crown*
> *Hath been his father's and his own;*
> *And is there any one but he*
> *That in the same should sharer be?*

For who better may the sceptre sway
Than he that hath such a right to reign?
Then let's hope for a peace for the wars will not cease
Till the King enjoys his own again.

Five

Venetia drove home with Sophia, gloomily wondering what she was going to say to her husband when she got there. She hadn't joined in the singing because she hadn't liked the mood which had prompted it – and was also somewhat reluctant to renew hostilities with Gabriel when she'd only just finished apologising to him. But if she said nothing at all, he was bound to see it as some sign of weakness; and that would never do – because the truth was that she was as pleased by the news as the others had been. She felt, though, that there were better ways of showing it.

When she arrived at Brandon Lacey, however, it was to discover that Gabriel had more important things on his mind than probing into hers. He had returned to find a summons awaiting him from Major-General Lambert and was wasting no time at all in obeying it.

'You're leaving *now*?' asked Venetia blankly. 'Why?'

'Why not?' Once more dressed in his uniform, Colonel Brandon finished adjusting his sash and turned to pick up his wide-brimmed hat. 'Lambert wants me to spend a couple of weeks helping to organise the two new Yorkshire regiments before I report back for duty. And the sooner I leave, the sooner I can start doing it.'

'But where are you going?'

He lifted one faintly ironic brow.

'I think I'd be ill-advised to tell you that. After all, I'd hate you to be put in a position of choosing between your wifely duty and your friends. And now I really must go. Explain matters to Dick Carter for me – and try not to miss me too much. Goodbye.'

Then, leaving Venetia unsure whether she wanted to laugh

or throw something at his head, Gabriel sketched a mocking bow and strode off into the hall, shouting cheerfully for Wat.

By the following morning, Venetia had reached the conclusion that it was only sensible to put her new-found freedom to instant use. She therefore rode purposefully into Knaresborough to consult with the Widow Jessop and then set about putting herself discreetly back in circulation.

The result was that the next two weeks flew by in a frenzy of activity. In between renewing all her former Royalist contacts and assuring them of her continued commitment to the Cause, Venetia spent hours at Ford Edge passing on every ounce of knowledge and experience she possessed to Phoebe; she conferred with Dick Carter about the shearing, went out to the fields after the flax had been sown and was present at Scar Croft when the first of the wool was scoured, dried, oiled and carded. She failed to celebrate her twenty-fifth birthday, saw almost nothing of Sophy, noticed, but stopped caring, that the house was once more full of animals, and fell into bed each night in a state of total exhaustion.

Every day brought fresh news from outside. The news-sheets said that the Independents had defeated a Republican motion to depose the King – and then that the King himself had almost succeeded in escaping from captivity on the Isle of Wight. Next came word of the four thousand apprentices who'd stormed Whitehall with cries of '*Now for King Charles!*' only to be dispersed by a vicious cavalry charge led by Cromwell. And, finally, Venetia heard that the Scots Parliament had apparently demanded that their English counterparts should disband their army of sectaries and re-open negotiations with his Majesty. It was all grist to the Royalist mill and tremendously encouraging. Venetia finally began to hope that the King really might enjoy his own again. And when Ashley Peverell sent word that he wished to see her, she was sure of it.

Their rendezvous point was the Dropping Well – a place deep in the shadowy whisperings of Knaresborough forest, where strange, petrifying waters dripped from the overhanging rock-face to form a pool. It was a peaceful spot and one which, in happier days, Venetia had been particularly fond of. Today, however, it seemed suddenly menacing and she rather wished she'd taken the precaution of being a little late.

As always, the first she knew of Captain Peverell's approach was when he spoke from behind her.

'If you've been communing with the prophetess, I hope you thought to ask whether Hamilton will cross the border this year or next.'

Venetia started and swung round to face him.

'*Must* you do that? You nearly gave me an apoplexy.'

'Guilty conscience!' he grinned. 'Unless, of course, you were half-expecting to see horrible apparitions?'

'Other than yourself, you mean?'

Ashley winced and clapped a hand over his heart.

'You really know how to wound a fellow, don't you?'

'In more ways than one. But I notice that you still live,' she retorted. And then, differently, 'Pleasant as this is, it's not what we're here for, is it?'

'No.' The laughter evaporated from the bright grey-green eyes, leaving them suddenly business-like. 'You've re-entered the network. I wanted to be sure it was safe for you to do so.'

'You think I'd have done it otherwise?' Venetia folded her cloak about her and sat down on a boulder. 'My husband is away devoting both his energies and his eternal efficiency to drilling the two new northern regiments.'

'I know that,' said the Captain calmly. 'I've even spent a bit of time watching him do it. But Skipton's not what I'd call a particularly safe distance – he could come back at any time. I take it you have thought of that?'

She shrugged and took care not to let him see that he'd told her something she didn't know. 'Naturally. But he'll only come back in order to go away again.'

'He's returning to his old command?'

'Yes. If it weren't for Lambert, he'd be there now.' She paused. 'Is this all you wanted to talk about? I was rather hoping you had something for me to do.'

'And so I might have – if the circumstances are right.' He eyed her thoughtfully for a moment and then, as if at random, said, 'I heard about the amateur theatricals at your sister's wedding.'

223

Venetia sighed. 'Who told you?'

'Who didn't? I've never come across such a collection of idiots so eager to be congratulated on their indiscretion. But no one seems able to tell me how the Colonel took it.'

'I'm not surprised. He isn't in the habit of giving out reliable clues. In the few seconds before he walked out, for example, I had the ridiculous feeling that he was trying not to laugh. But that can't be right, can it?'

'Why not? From where he was standing, the whole affair was probably better than a play. And if he's made a list of the leading characters, a lot of our friends could find themselves unable to stir a step without finding some damned poke-nose at their elbow. Some people,' stated Ashley simply, 'are congenitally unsuited to conspiracy. And that, of course, brings me to the point. Where's Ellis?'

Her breath caught. 'In France?'

He remained perfectly still, his fair head bathed in greenish light. 'No, my child. Not in France. Try again.'

For a moment, the silence was pierced only by the incessant dripping of the well while Venetia considered her options and then, seeing the expression on the Captain's face, discarded most of them.

'All right. How did you know?'

'That you'd seen him? Call it an educated guess. With Ellis, it really isn't very difficult. I suppose he touched you for money? Or no – don't answer that. Of course he did. The only interesting bit is likely to be the reason he gave for wanting it. Well?'

Not for the first time, Venetia found the speed at which Captain Peverell's mind worked mildly alarming. But, since there was little help for it, she said baldly, 'He's got a plan to rescue the Duke of York.'

'Oh my God,' groaned Ashley. 'That's all we need!'

'What do you mean? The Council of War has just voted to put James on the throne, hasn't it? So I'd have thought that getting him out of the country would be a priority.'

'It is.' He folded his arms, leaned against a tree-trunk and surveyed her with faint exasperation. 'Which is why it's not the kind of thing to be left to someone who's perpetually getting his knife caught up in his cloak.'

224

Venetia's back straightened imperceptibly and she frowned. 'What are you saying? That Ellis is inept?'

'My dear girl – he's the world's worst. He's reckless, impulsive and too fond of the bottle; his schemes inevitably go off at half-cock because he hasn't planned them properly, and he's got a nasty habit of abandoning one project in order to throw himself headfirst into another. In short, the only thing he's good at is not getting caught.'

It was a long time before Venetia spoke and when she did her voice was curiously remote. 'Is that why you tried to stop him getting in touch with me?'

'Partly.' In spite of everything he'd just said, Captain Peverell still found himself reluctant to tell her all the other things he knew about her erstwhile fiancé. 'You don't believe a word I've said, do you?'

'I . . . I think you do him an injustice.'

'Very tactful. Then try this for size. If you want to go on doing your bit for the King, despite being married to one of Cromwell's Colonels, your life is complicated enough. You don't need Ellis as well.'

'Perhaps not.' The violet eyes looked starkly back at him. 'But you're suggesting that I turn him away. And I can't do it. There's – there's too much between us.'

'I understand that. But will the Colonel?'

'He won't know anything about it.'

'For how long? This is Ellis we're talking about.' Ashley ran a distracted hand through his hair and some of the characteristic humour re-appeared in his face. 'You like living dangerously, don't you?'

'What other way is there?' She rose to face him. 'It's going to rain again. If you've a job for me, name it. If not, say so and let me go home.'

'Just like that?'

'No. Not just like that. But if you don't trust me—'

'Have I said I don't?'

'Not in so many words. But why else have we been having this conversation?'

'If you don't know that, you can't have been paying attention,' he sighed. 'It's *Ellis* I don't trust. And so long as you can assure me that your activities on each of our behalves

225

will remain quite separate, I shan't have anything to worry about.'

Venetia drew a long breath. 'Consider yourself duly assured. *Now* will you tell me what you want me to do?'

'Willingly.' Captain Peverell gave her the blithe, charming smile that frequently heralded his less welcome assignments. 'It's the usual problem. We're short of funds and I'd like you to go round with the begging-bowl.'

Asking for contributions to the Cause had never been one of Venetia's favourite occupations. It was always the same people one had to approach: families already crippled with taxes and composition fines; men under house-arrest who couldn't afford to be caught helping the King a second time; houses already stripped of their valuables and equally bereft of sons, husbands or fathers. Venetia knew the position only too well. Her own jewels, for example, had gone to the King years ago. On the other hand, as she well knew, money had to be raised somehow and there was no other way of doing it. So she put on a becoming gown, exhumed her most persuasive manner and set off in the carriage to do her best.

The results were neither better nor worse than she expected. Most families gave what they could, a handful listened politely before showing her the door and the rest could offer nothing but goodwill and promises. At the end of four far from enjoyable days, Venetia handed a little over three hundred pounds to the Widow Jessop for collection by Captain Peverell and told her to tell him that the well was running dry. Then she rode thankfully back through the blustering wind to see how things were going at Scar Croft.

Due, she had to admit, to the Colonel's passion for organisation, the whole enterprise was running like a well-oiled machine. The work was evenly distributed amongst those willing and able to do it; wages were scrupulously paid at the end of each week by Dick Carter; and the general mood was one of elation – as if each man and woman considered the success of the venture to be their own personal achievement. No matter when Venetia called at the cottages, it was always the same. And each time she left, she seemed to take a bit of their enthusiasm with her.

On this particular day, however, the sensation was destined to be short-lived. She had barely rounded the bend in the track when a horseman appeared from the clump of trees ahead and caused her heart to plummet. Ellis.

'Are you out of your mind?' she hissed, casting a nervous glance over her shoulder. 'Broad daylight – and here, of all places? *Anyone* could see you!'

'Then come share my undergrowth, sweeting,' he invited carelessly. 'But you know . . . I wish that, just for once, you could look pleased to see me.'

'And I wish *you'd* use a modicum of common-sense,' she snapped back, turning Dulcie off the road and into the meagre shelter beside it. 'What are you *doing* here? You're supposed to be in London, arranging Prince James's escape.'

'It's done – or as good as.' Ellis slid from the saddle and held his hands out to her. 'Come down and I'll tell you about it.'

'Don't be stupid! There are a dozen people less than a hundred yards away – any one of whom would recognise you. If you want to talk, do it quickly, because I'm certainly not staying.'

'You worry too much. The bastard's away, isn't he?'

'For the time being. But he'll be back and, if you're seen, he'll hear of it,' said Venetia flatly. 'Now, come to the point. Have you got James out or haven't you?'

'Not yet – but it's all arranged,' came the airy reply. 'At the moment he's getting his gaolers used to the idea of him moving freely about St James's by playing hide-and-seek with his brother and sister every evening. Then, when the time is right, he'll be smuggled out of the palace and away to Gravesend before anyone even knows he's gone. It's so exquisitely simple that it can't fail.'

'I hope you're right. But if it's still to be carried through, why have you left London?'

Ellis had no intention of explaining that the plot he'd just described owed nothing to him, or that those involved in it had suddenly and, in his view, quite inexplicably cast him from their midst. Shrugging, he said, 'Oh there's time enough. I'll be back before anything happens . . . and meanwhile, we've other irons in the fire.'

227

'Such as what, for example?'

'Need you ask? Naturally our next move will be to rescue the King himself.'

Even without Ashley Peverell's strictures ringing unpleasantly in her ears, this didn't sound especially convincing. Venetia looked forebodingly down on Ellis's windswept, chestnut head and said, 'If that's the case, shouldn't you be on the Isle of Wight? And wouldn't it be more sensible to concentrate on one thing at a time?'

He smiled indulgently back at her.

'My loved one, you don't understand how these things are done. There are a myriad of details to be taken care of and some of them involve a good deal of travelling. As for the King, we need to start planning his escape before—'

'Did you hear something?' cut in Venetia sharply.

Ellis glanced briefly about them. 'Only the wind.'

'Are you sure?' She paused, straining her ears.

'Perfectly. Don't worry. There's no one there. You're just a trifle on edge.'

'Can you wonder at it? This is sheer lunacy! I ought to have ridden straight past you and gone home.'

'But you didn't. I wonder why?' Ellis reached up to capture one of her hands. 'Perhaps it's because you're aware that taking the occasional risk is one of life's small pleasures . . . or perhaps you're more pleased to see me than you care to admit.'

'Don't count on it,' began Venetia. And then stopped, staring blindly past him through the trees . . . into the dark sardonic gaze of her husband.

Her nerves snarled into a painful tangle and shock immobilised every muscle. Ellis, meanwhile, was still totally oblivious and had succeeded in removing her glove in order to murmur mischievous endearments into her palm. Venetia experienced a strong desire to box his ears, followed by the futile wish that the ground would open and swallow them both up. Then, summoning what was left of her scattered wits, she dragged her hand free and muttered savagely, 'Turn round. And leave the talking to me.'

Startled by her tone, Ellis spun smartly on his heel and froze. The wind suddenly increased its vigour, howling around them as if it were somehow part of the drama before dying down again with equal abruptness. Then Gabriel rode slowly and inexorably towards them.

'Well, well,' he said, in the mild tone Venetia was beginning to recognise for what it was. 'I appear to have arrived at an inopportune moment.'

'Not at all,' she returned carelessly. 'This is an old friend whom I met by chance. His name is—'

'Don't,' said Gabriel.

'I beg your pardon?'

'Don't say anything you might regret.' The impassive eyes moved to encompass Ellis and there was a tiny, cataclysmic pause. Then, 'Welcome, brother. I've been wondering how long it would be before we met again.'

The breath hissed between Ellis's teeth and he lifted one contemptuous brow. 'Don't call me brother! My father may not have been fastidious in these matters – but I am. And I'll have no by-blow claiming kinship with me.'

'That is your privilege,' came the indifferent reply.

'*Again?*' said Venetia jerkily. 'You wondered how long it would be before you met *again*?'

'Yes.' A ghostly smile touched the hard mouth. 'Our paths have crossed once before – albeit briefly – at the battle of Langport in '45. Did I neglect to mention it?'

'You know you did! My God – of *course* you did!' Nervous wrath threatened to choke her voice. 'It's just another of your little snares, isn't it?'

'If it was, I'd have let you tighten the noose by lying to me.' With annoying calm, Gabriel dropped lightly from the saddle and looped his reins over a convenient branch. 'And now I suggest that you hold your tongue before your temper gets the better of you. In fact, it might be as well for all concerned if you went home.'

'I think not,' she snapped. 'Why should I?'

Ellis laughed and threw his cloak back from one shoulder to reveal his sword. 'Why do you think? He wants to fight, sweetheart. And he doesn't want you to watch.'

'You make a hell of a lot of assumptions,' observed the Colonel aridly. 'Why should I want to fight you? I'm sure your blood is much the same as anyone else's.'

229

'Since you're unlikely to see it, you'll never know,' drawled Ellis. And then, over his shoulder to Venetia, 'He's a conceited bastard, isn't he?'

'Very possibly,' replied Gabriel. 'But doesn't it take one to know one?' This time the smile was more pronounced and distinctly mocking. 'Of course, we could stand here exchanging insults till Kingdom come. Alternatively, we could put the short time which is all we will have together to better use. It's entirely up to you.'

Since the Roundhead obviously had no intention of fighting, Ellis could not resist pricking him a little – mainly for Venetia's benefit. He said, 'The only use I have for it is to spit you like a pig.'

'If you meant that, you'd have drawn your sword ten minutes ago. But don't despair. Although I've nothing against you at the moment, that could all change. And if it does, I may well be persuaded to give you the opportunity you say you want.'

'I'll look forward to it.'

'By all means do. Just remember that – like most things in life – it may not quite live up to your expectations.' The crisp voice was suddenly laced with bored impatience. 'For now, however, let us content ourselves with exposing a few basic facts. You resent my existence, my usurpation of your inheritance and my marriage to your loved one. Naturally. You would be unique if you didn't. But I would like to point out that none of these things were of my choosing.'

'Is that an excuse?' scoffed Ellis. 'Or an apology?'

'From what I've seen so far, it's probably best described as a waste of breath,' returned Gabriel blightingly. 'But let us not be hasty. I was about to state that no one can order their own birth. It might also surprise you to learn that I never wanted Brandon Lacey – and that you could have had it back with my very goodwill if only our father hadn't made it impossible. As for Venetia . . . well, I'm sure she has already explained the circumstances of our marriage more than adequately.'

Ellis managed to look derisively incredulous but appeared temporarily lost for words. Venetia had no such lack.

'Why are you saying these things?' she demanded darkly.

'Perhaps because they needed saying?' Gabriel's eyes remained fixed on his half-brother. 'Whether you believe me or not is your own affair. Mine is to have tried.'

'Tried?' flashed Ellis. 'To do what, pray? Effect some kind of tawdry reconciliation between us? *Christ!* If you honestly thought you could do that, you must be sixpence short of the shilling! But you didn't think it, did you? You're just trying to smooth things over in case I've any notion of planting a knife in your back one dark night.'

'And have you?' invited the Colonel gently.

'Of course he hasn't!' said Venetia in a desperate attempt to side-step calamity. Ellis had got bravado written all over him and was quite likely to overlook the fact that a stupid, swaggering threat to assassinate an Army officer could put him behind bars. 'What do you think he is? A common murderer?'

'That is what I'm attempting to find out.'

'Then let me set your mind at rest,' offered Ellis irrepressibly. 'I have never in my life done anything in the least common. So if I decide to terminate your existence – which, as you quite rightly say, I thoroughly resent – my method will be one of the utmost refinement.'

Venetia groaned and stared at her husband out of eyes dark with stress. His expression remained completely shuttered but, for a fleeting instant, she thought she detected a tiny, betraying tremor that might possibly have been laughter. Then he said, blandly, 'I'm relieved to hear it. I, of course, have no refinement whatsoever – so I'll conclude this fascinating encounter with a crude warning. I assume, since it's what landed us all in this mess, that you are an active Royalist. In itself, that is none of my business, but if you involve Venetia in your schemes, you will make it so. I trust I make myself clear?'

Venetia curbed the temptation to inform Gabriel that she'd damned well do as she pleased without interference from him and, instead, placed a discreet kick in Ellis's ribs. It was a waste of time. Ellis leaned negligently against Dulcie's flank and said, 'He doesn't know you very well, my sweet. If he did, he'd know that no one tells you what to do. Not even me.'

'*Certainly* not you,' she snapped. And then, to the Colonel, 'You've made your point – though it rather sounds as if *you* are now the one making assumptions. However. What you're saying is that you want Ellis to keep away from Brandon Lacey in general and me in particular. Is that it?'

'So long as he continues involving himself in Royalist conspiracies – yes,' came the cool reply. 'And that is for his own good.'

'Such concern!' said Ellis sarcastically. 'You'll be telling us next that you'd be sorry to see me arrested.'

Gabriel surveyed his half-brother dispassionately and decided that he'd had enough of him. 'I may have had some such idea to begin with. Now, however, I'm rapidly realising that any regrets I might have would be extremely short-lived. In fact, if this goes on much longer, I'm likely to lock you up myself just to break the monotony.'

'Try it!' Ellis surged forward, half-drawing his sword.

'Oh – go and set fire to yourself!' returned Gabriel. And, turning his back, prepared to re-mount his horse.

Just for a split second, Venetia thought Ellis was actually going to attack. Horrible possibilities crowded her mind and, without waiting to be sure of his intentions, she brought Dulcie round to buffet him squarely in the back. He lurched forward and went sprawling on the turf. Gabriel turned and looked thoughtfully from Ellis to Venetia and back again. Then, trying desperately not to laugh, he said, 'I'm not sure of my cue. Should I say *Pride goeth before a fall* or *He who diggeth a pit shall fall therein*? Never mind. I'm sure either is equally suitable.'

Red in the face and covered in bits of leaf and twig, Ellis struggled to his feet and turned furiously on Venetia. She scowled ferociously back and, while the Colonel was rising effortlessly into his saddle, muttered, 'I'm sorry, but you've already done enough damage for one day.'

'Say goodbye, Venetia,' Gabriel's pleasant but unmistakably magisterial tones prevented any further exchange. 'We're going.'

She would have given anything she possessed for the pleasure of refusing, but the necessity of curtailing the meeting before Ellis made things any worse outweighed all other considerations.

'Goodbye,' she said woodenly. And rode off towards the track without waiting for an answer.

Gabriel gave his half-brother one last, ironic smile.

'I suggest you try to remember what I've said, because I meant every word. And if I'm driven to remind you, my methods may become a little more . . . pointed.'

Venetia rode home at a cracking pace, leaving Gabriel to follow as he saw fit. She was in the hall, stripping off her gloves with shaking hands when he came in – and one look at his face told her that it wasn't over yet. She said unevenly, 'Well? I take it you want to lecture me about daring to associate with the man I was betrothed to for five years. And no doubt you're also going to hammer home your objections to my involving myself in Royalist matters. Of course, there's no need for either. I think we can safely say that I'm well aware of your views. But I don't suppose that's going to stop you, is it?'

Gabriel's eyes were decidedly grim but when he spoke his voice was remote as ever.

'In fact, I've only one word to say to you. Pack.'

She stared at him. 'What?'

'Pack. You're coming with me to London tomorrow.'

It was the very last thing she had been expecting and a bubble of faint hysteria formed in her chest. She shook her head and said, 'Oh no. I really don't think so.'

'Then you misunderstand me. This isn't a suggestion or even an invitation. I am simply stating a fact.'

She was suddenly very still. 'You can't make me.'

'On the contrary, I think you will find that I can.' He paused and then, reading her thought, said, 'You're wondering why? It's very simple. I'm not leaving you here to embroil yourself in any hare-brained scheme of Ellis's making. And if anything was needed to convince me that I can't trust you, it was provided by the quite remarkable docility and restraint you showed just now. For if you weren't up to your charming neck in nefarious activities, you'd have told me to go hang myself.'

This was uncomfortably close to the mark and Venetia silently damned his astuteness. Then, with a creditable assumption of amusement, she said, 'Dear me. Ellis has a lot to answer for, hasn't he? You'll be looking for plotters under the bed next.'

'Only under yours,' he responded. 'But we're wasting time. I'm leaving at first light tomorrow and you're coming with me. So, unless you want to arrive in London with just the clothes you stand up in, I suggest you go and start preparing yourself.'

She thought rapidly. He was right, of course. He could make her go with him. But perhaps a few weeks in London would be no bad thing. At least she would be at the centre of events for once. Shrugging carelessly, she said, 'Very well. But I hope you've given some thought to where I'm supposed to stay once we get there?'

'I don't need to. You'll stay in Shoreditch with my foster-brother and his wife.'

Venetia's heart sank. That really was all she needed. It was going to be appalling. It couldn't be anything else.

In a last-ditch attempt to improve the situation, she said flatly, 'All right. But I won't go unless you ask Phoebe to come, too.'

His brows rose. 'Phoebe? Why?'

'Why do you think? If I'm going to be surrounded by your family, I want someone of my own with me. And Phoebe might enjoy it. She's never been to London – nor, once her birthday comes and she inherits Ford Edge, is she likely to get another chance for a while.' She stopped, regarding him stubbornly. 'Well? It's not so much to ask, is it?'

There was a moment's silence. Then, entirely without warning, Gabriel's severity dissolved into a spectacularly disarming smile.

'Not of me. But then I'll be in quarters with the Army. It's Jack who'll have her digging up his cellar in search of buried treasure. But I'm sure he'll cope. He's nothing if not philosophical.'

Six

In the end, Venetia succeeded in augmenting the party by more than just Phoebe. She naturally insisted on taking her maid – and then added that since she and Phoebe could not be expected to go about London alone in these unsettled times, they had better take a reliable groom to escort them. Apart from asking if she also wanted to take her own cook and laundress, Gabriel made surprisingly little objection to this and so Sym Potter joined their cavalcade.

The journey was accomplished with military precision and relentless speed. Venetia, Phoebe and Jane bounced along in a coach piled high with luggage, while Gabriel, Wat and Sym rode alongside. After two days of having her bones reduced to pulp, Venetia suggested that if Gabriel was in such a hurry he had better go on ahead with Wat and leave the rest of them to travel at a less frenetic pace. Gabriel replied that there was nothing he'd like better – were it not for the increasing number of Royalist ex-soldiers now making a very good living at highway robbery. Venetia withdrew into stony silence and asked no more questions.

Phoebe, fortunately, showed no such reticence and, by the time they reached London, Venetia knew all about Jack, Annis, the baby and Mistress Bryony. It was not until the coach drew up before the Morrells' house in Shoreditch, however, that she discovered Gabriel had apparently made no attempt to warn his foster-family of their coming.

She said flatly, 'I don't believe this. You're foisting four people on them without so much as a by-your-leave?'

'Yes.' Gabriel held out his hand to help her from the carriage. 'But don't panic. I'm sure they'll cope.'

Annis and Bryony were in the parlour polishing the

furniture when the Colonel led his wife and sister-in-law in on them. Bryony gasped, then stood rooted to the spot, and Annis's initial reaction of surprised pleasure was swiftly replaced by an urgent desire to hide her dusters.

'Why – Gabriel!' she said weakly, trying not to stare at the cool, blonde beauty at his elbow. 'How nice.'

'Isn't it?' Grinning a little, he bent to kiss her cheek and dropped his hat neatly over the pot of polish on the table. 'I see I needn't ask how you are. Motherhood obviously agrees with you – and I'm sure you'll tell me that my nephew is a model baby. What did you call him, by the way?'

'John. And yes – as it happens, he *is* a good baby.'

'I'm delighted to hear it.' Gabriel's eyes travelled thoughtfully to his rigid foster-niece. 'Well, Bryony? You may not feel inclined to throw yourself on my neck, but I should have thought securing Mr Radford's release from Newgate ought to be worth a smile at least.'

'Of course,' she replied stiffly. 'And if I'd known you were so eager to be thanked, I'd have done it the instant you walked in. As it was, I thought you might prefer to introduce your – your companions first.'

'Did you? Then allow me to do so.' He drew Venetia and Phoebe smoothly forward. 'Mistress Venetia Brandon and Mistress Phoebe Clifford; my wife and sister-in-law, whom I've brought here in the hope that you'll look after them while I return to Headquarters.'

Venetia could have hit him – and one glance at Bryony told her that she wasn't the only one.

'After hearing you put it like that, I'll be amazed if they agree to stay,' observed Annis. Then, smiling at Venetia, 'But I hope you will, for you're more than welcome. And Gabriel was never in any doubt of it.'

'Which is why he's virtually holding a gun to your head?' asked Venetia. Then, 'You are more generous than he deserves. But you can't possibly want to be saddled with two complete strangers – not to mention our maid and groom.'

'Why not? There's room enough. And as for being strangers . . . well, that is easily mended.'

Few people could resist Annis in a persuasive mood. Venetia said feebly, 'But your husband—?'

'Her husband,' said a disembodied voice, 'would be more than happy to speak for himself, if only some great hulking fellow wasn't blocking the doorway.'

Venetia jumped, Gabriel spun neatly on his heel and Phoebe giggled. Jack faced them all with his pleasant, unremarkable smile and said simply, 'I've seen the luggage and spoken to Wat. But I wish someone would explain why it's taking Annis so long to get the wine out.'

'Need you ask?' Gabriel grasped his foster-brother's hand. 'We were waiting for you.'

'And pigs fly.' Jack's gaze settled confidingly on Venetia. 'No one in this house has any manners. Mistress Brandon, I presume?'

A smile hovered on the edges of her mouth. 'Yes.'

'Welcome to the family.' He turned to Phoebe. 'And you must be Mistress Clifford.'

She beamed at him. 'Yes, I'm Phoebe and I'm very happy to meet you. Gabriel's told us so much about you.'

Mr Morrell achieved an expression of profound anxiety.

'I hope,' he said, 'that you didn't believe him?'

'Only the good bits,' she assured him. Then, with a mischievous, slanting glance at the Colonel, 'And I sincerely hope you'll do as much for me when the time comes.'

After the ice had been melted over a glass of wine, a still oddly restrained Bryony took Venetia and Phoebe up to her chamber to tidy themselves while Annis had the spare rooms prepared. Jack let the parlour door close behind them and then said bluntly, 'Wat tells me you've instructed him to go straight to Windsor and find quarters for you – so I gather you're not staying.'

'No.' Gabriel smiled faintly. 'I'm sure you will all do well enough without me.'

'We'll have to, won't we?' There was a moment's hesitation. 'She isn't quite what I expected.'

'Venetia? No. She's on her best behaviour. And as long as I'm not here, it may even last.'

Jack looked at him. 'If it's that bad, why bring her?'

'Because I couldn't leave her to her own devices in Yorkshire. Didn't Wat say?'

'He muttered something about your half-brother and

237

Royalist plots. But he so obviously loathes her that I wasn't sure whether to believe him.'

'Believe,' advised Gabriel dryly. And, in as few words as possible, gave the gist of his meeting with Ellis. Then, 'I need hardly add that we didn't take to one another. Worse still, I've a nasty suspicion that my dear half-brother is an unhandy conspirator.'

'So you removed your wife from his baleful influence and brought her here to London where plots lurk round every corner? Brilliant! And who, may I ask, is supposed to keep an eye on her while you're planning another nice little war and casting dice with the Levellers for the settlement of the kingdom? Or is that a silly question?'

Gabriel re-filled his glass and pushed the wine-bottle across the table. 'Just do what you can. I wouldn't wish your business to suffer.'

'Thanks,' grunted Jack acidulously. 'But do you think I haven't enough to do keeping up with Bryony – without having to watch your wife and sister-in-law as well?'

'Phoebe needn't worry you. Venetia, of course, is another matter. As for Bryony . . . I detected a peculiar gleam in her eye earlier. Is she still passionately in love with me and likely to drop hemlock in Venetia's soup?'

'I wouldn't have thought so. Oh, she moped for about a month after she learned you were to be married, but then Samuel Radford got out of Newgate. And now she's got more important things on her mind.'

Laughter stirred in the dark grey gaze.

'Are you telling me she's become a little Leveller? No, no. It can't be true. The last time I saw Bryony she thought green ribbon was a love-token.'

'And now she quotes Free-born John by the yard, knows her rights under Magna Carta and argues a fairly sound case in favour of manhood suffrage,' came the mildly exasperated reply. 'I spend half of my time wondering where she is and the other half listening to "Sam says". I don't know which is worse. But it's my fault. I should have shown young Radford the door while I had the chance.'

'I'm amazed that you didn't.' Gabriel drained his glass and stood up. 'If you get seriously worried about Bryony, let me know. Wat is remarkably skilled in surveillance.'

'Wat is remarkably skilled at a good many things – not all of them entirely desirable,' observed Jack dryly. Then, 'You're not going already, are you?'

'I'm afraid so. I've been away a long time you know.'

'But you haven't even begun to tell me what it's like being the lord of the manor.'

'If you must know, it's bloody hard work! Now, are you going to show me your son and heir or not?'

Mr Morrell rose with unashamed alacrity.

'I thought you'd never ask.'

'Ah. Do I detect a hint of the doting parent?'

'Yes. And you needn't laugh. You'll be just the same yourself one day.'

A slow, bitter smile bracketed the Colonel's mouth.

'Don't hold your breath,' he said.

It took Venetia less than twenty-four hours to recognise that staying in Shoreditch wasn't going to be nearly as bad as she had feared. Though by no means luxurious, the Morrell's house was extremely comfortable, spotlessly clean and large enough for her not to have to share a room with Phoebe. Mr Morrell's workshop lay on the far side of the yard, his apprentices took their meals in the kitchen and, though his wife preferred to do certain household tasks herself, she also kept two maidservants and a cook. But more important than any of this was the fact that both Jack and Annis were friendly to a fault. If they knew how matters stood between herself and Gabriel, nothing they said ever showed it. The only fly in the ointment, therefore, was Bryony – who met every overture with monosyllabic frost and whose eyes frequently held a sort of baffled disapproval.

Had Venetia but known it, Bryony was utterly confused. Until Gabriel had walked into the parlour, she assumed that she still loved him as much as ever. But if that was so, she ought surely to have experienced some emotional cataclysm on being suddenly confronted with his wife – and the fact that she hadn't done so came as something of a shock. Consequently, she kept Venetia at arm's length and would have done the same with Phoebe – had not Phoebe's natural friendliness made it impossible. And the result was that Bryony eventually lowered her defences a little and grudgingly remarked that Venetia was very beautiful.

'Yes,' agreed Phoebe readily. 'She is. And some people think our sister Bess even prettier. I don't mind, of course. But I can't help being glad they're both married.'

Bryony smiled perfunctorily. 'Does Gabriel love her?'

'Heavens, no – nor she him. Far from it.'

'Then why didn't she stay in Yorkshire?'

'I've been wondering that myself – but neither of them will discuss it. In fact, most of the way here they hardly spoke to one another at all. But that's a blessing sometimes, because they disagree on just about everything.'

'Politics, you mean?'

'Mostly,' admitted Phoebe. Then, shrugging, 'You probably know that our family supports the King. My father and eldest brother died fighting for him during the war and Venetia is committed to seeing him restored to the throne.'

'With the same powers he had before?' asked Bryony.

'I suppose so. Does that make a difference?'

'Of course! It's the crux of the matter.'

'Oh. I'm afraid I don't understand these things very well – or care about them as much as I should. It all causes too many arguments. But you probably find that naive.'

'No I don't.' A sudden grin illuminated Bryony's face. 'I used to be pretty much the same myself. Only then . . . well, I met someone. His name's Sam and he's a Leveller.'

'Goodness!' Phoebe regarded her with flattering awe. 'And are you one too?'

'Yes.' Bryony hesitated and then, unable to help herself, said proudly, 'I've signed the Long Petition. But for heaven's sake don't tell Uncle Jack! He knows Sam's got me interested in freedom of speech and so on, but he'd have a fit if he knew some of the other things I've been up to. Worse still, he'd forbid Sam to come here any more.'

Phoebe eyed her consideringly.

'Are you in love with him?'

'With *Sam*? Good heavens, no!' grinned Bryony. And

then, with a tiny frown, 'At least . . . no. Of course not. Why do you ask?'

'Oh, no reason,' came the would-be careless reply. 'I just thought that if you were, you might be able to tell me what it feels like.'

While Venetia formed an unlikely friendship with Annis and Phoebe and Bryony exchanged seventeen-year-old confidences, Gabriel settled back into Army routine, attended a series of meetings with his superiors and grimly set about preparing his regiment for active service.

It was becoming increasingly plain that war could not be far off. In Ireland, Lord Inchiquin had changed sides and joined the Confederates to declare for the King; in Scotland, the Duke of Hamilton was still determined to cross the border at the head of an invasion force; and Wales was already under arms. As for England, London was flatly refusing to pay another penny towards the maintenance of the Army and, elsewhere, discontent over ruined trade and cries for an immediate treaty with the King were spreading faster than the plague.

Then, two days after Gabriel's return to duty, Eden Maxwell took a message to Cromwell in Whitehall and returned with the news that the Duke of York had escaped from St James's Palace disguised as a girl.

Colonel Brandon looked up from the litter of paperwork spread out in front of him. 'Has he? Good.'

Eden tutted reprovingly.

'What kind of attitude is that? There was going to be a call of the House tomorrow in order to depose the King in the boy's favour – thus solving all our problems.'

'Or compounding them still further.'

'Probably. But it doesn't do to say so. And, truth to tell, we've more pressing matters to worry about. I suppose you know the agitators are meeting at St Albans tomorrow?'

'After which we'll be walking on egg-shells again. Quite.' Gabriel paused. 'Old Noll didn't happen to say if he felt the City might be persuaded to pay its assessments before our fellows start wanting to march in and collect them by force?'

'No.' Eden frowned a little. 'In fact, there's talk of the chains going back up across the streets as a precaution against that very possibility.'

'Oh my God. It gets better by the minute, doesn't it? As things stand, we can either hold the City or fight the Scots – and we've got the Levellers nipping at our backsides and telling the men that Cromwell's forsaken them. The Royalists,' finished Gabriel bitterly, 'must be bloody ecstatic. And who shall blame them? We've had two years in which to settle this mess and all we've done is create an even bigger pig's ear than we had in the first place.'

Neither Gabriel nor Eden expected the St Albans meeting to do anything except aggravate the situation – and they were right. The agitators began by condemning the personal ambition of Cromwell, Ireton and the other so-called Grandees and then drew up a petition demanding the immediate adoption of the *Agreement of the People*. Gabriel did not consider this clever. And when Samuel Radford arrived at his quarters that evening, he lost no time in telling him so.

Sam listened in faintly amused silence for a while and then said, 'Until they're asked, how can you be sure the majority of the people really will refuse the *Agreement*?'

'Don't be ridiculous! Right now, the country is automatically hostile to anything even remotely connected to the Army. We haven't a shred of goodwill left to us.'

'And whose fault is that?'

'I'd say the honours are fairly equally divided between Parliament and the City. They're the ones forcing us to go on living at free quarter by their refusal to pay us – and that is naturally aggravating to honest men who are still paying war taxes. Or do you have another explanation?'

'I don't think we'd better go into that,' said Sam slowly, 'I didn't come here to quarrel.'

'No?' Gabriel's brows rose. 'What, then?'

'Can't you guess? I came to thank you for getting me out of Newgate. I realise, of course, that you didn't do it for me, but I'm grateful nevertheless.'

'But not, so Major Maxwell informs me, grateful enough to try and stay out of further trouble.'

Sam grinned apologetically. 'Did you think I would be?'

'Not having any enormous faith in miracles, no. I do, however, expect you to stop Bryony doing anything foolish.' The Colonel eyed his visitor coolly. 'I understand that you've managed to convert her to your cause, which, considering that six months ago she hadn't two sensible thoughts to rub together, says a lot for your powers of persuasion. But now you'd better rest on your laurels. Because if she gets into trouble, I'll see that they put you back in Newgate and throw away the key.'

'There's an interesting admission in there somewhere, if only we dared pause to explore it,' observed Sam blandly. 'As for your warning . . . Mr Morrell's already said much the same thing and I'm doing my best. Not that it's always easy.'

'Am I supposed to sympathise?'

'God forbid! *As ye sow, so shall ye reap* and all that.' Sam picked up his hat and turned to go. Then, looking back with a gleaming smile, he said, 'Ah yes. I almost forgot. Congratulations on your marriage. Your wife is quite a beauty.'

The Duke of York's escape naturally made Venetia wonder about a few things, but then Ellis was driven to the back of her mind by a growing awareness of Bryony's addiction to the sayings of Free-born John and a brief but telling encounter with Mr Samuel Radford. Venetia had nothing personal against the Levellers. She just didn't want her overly-susceptible sister to become one. And so, in order to minimise this danger, she spent the majority of the next few days showing Phoebe the sights.

They stared up at the walls of the Tower, crossed the narrow, shop-lined reaches of London Bridge and took a boat up the river as far as Westminster. Then they walked along King Street to Whitehall, where weeds sprouted in the courtyards and the only comings and goings were those of black-clad lawyers. Venetia, remembering it as it had been before the war, felt desperately sad and could not wait to get away. For if, as the song said, cobwebs festooned the walls inside, she did not want to see them.

On the following day they explored the City and Venetia had her first sight of the posts and chains that had originally been put up as part of London's war-defences but were now being used as riot barricades. She smiled aridly to herself . . . and then gradually ceased to smile at all. There were beggars everywhere. Young men with sightless eyes or shattered limbs, and hollow-eyed widows whose children did not even have the energy to cry. Venetia and Phoebe gave what they could, knowing all the time that it was not enough. It would never be enough . . .

Elsewhere, the streets were busy but the bustle lacked its usual cheerfulness and the only people doing a roaring trade were the pamphlet-sellers of St Paul's yard. Venetia suspected that a goodly portion of the literature on sale was probably unlicensed and when a hawker offered her a copy of *A Whip for the Present House of Lords* by Mr John Lilburne, she was sure of it. She waited until Phoebe wasn't looking and then bought one to take home to Sophia.

They spent the next day quietly in Shoreditch before sallying forth again to tour the shops. In the Exchange, shuttered premises emphasised the fact that few people these days had money to spend and poorly-stocked shelves bore witness to falling profits and iniquitous prices; and Cheapside, once and still the throbbing heart of the City, proved little different. While Phoebe chose some ribbon in a haberdasher's, Venetia gazed idly at the empty goldsmith's shop across the street that had once been the home of Luciano del Santi. Then, as she was about to return her attention to Phoebe's purchases, a man emerged from the tavern on the opposite corner of Friday Street.

Venetia's breath snared and she flew to the shop doorway in time to see the black-cloaked figure disappear into Old Change. For a moment she contemplated following, then she realised that the chances of catching up with him now were probably very small indeed – and that if she went running off down Cheapside, Phoebe and Sym would think she was mad.

It was both regrettable and annoying because she had absolutely no doubts about the identity of the man. It was Ellis.

Back in Shoreditch, Gabriel was waiting for them. It was the first time they had seen him since the day they'd arrived.

Phoebe greeted him exuberantly and then made a discreet exit; Venetia, with other things on her mind, said sardonically, 'My goodness! This *is* an unexpected honour. Are you sure you can spare the time?'

'No. But the knowledge that you've missed me makes the sacrifice more than worthwhile,' came the smooth reply. 'Or have you just missed having someone to quarrel with?'

'Neither. I merely think you've got a monumental nerve to deposit us here like unwanted baggage and then disappear for a week without so much as a word.'

His brows rose. 'Is there some problem?'

'No. But—'

'Then I fail to see why my absence should matter in the slightest. But you'll doubtless be happy to learn that you are guaranteed the pleasure of my company tomorrow evening.'

The violet eyes narrowed. 'You're dining here?'

'No. You and I – and Phoebe if she cares to come – are dining with the Lieutenant-General.'

For a moment, Venetia appeared incapable of speech. Then she said unevenly, 'I'd rather cut my throat.'

'Oh don't be so bloody silly!' Eyes and voice were suddenly stripped of both courtesy and patience. 'We won't be the only guests. And if I can put up with your friends, you ought to be able to tolerate mine.'

Venetia struggled to control her breathing.

'Would you sit down to supper with Goring or Rupert?'

'Why not? After all, I've already done so with Philip Knightley and he's a damned sight more objectionable than either of them.' Gabriel paused briefly. 'This isn't a request, Venetia. Since I inherited Brandon Lacey and married you, Cromwell has been taking a personal interest in me. In many respects, I could do without it. But I'm not prepared to sink my career by telling him so.'

She frowned. 'What are you saying?'

'I'm saying that I'll call to collect you at about five tomorrow,' came the unhelpful reply. 'And, as always, I'd be glad if you could sheathe whatever resentment you feel with at least an appearance of civility.'

'Not go?' echoed Phoebe incredulously, when Venetia

related the gist of this conversation. 'Of course I want to go! And, quite honestly, I should have thought you'd want to go, too. *Know thy enemy* and all that . . . not to mention showing that you're not in the least intimidated by them.'

A martial light entered Venetia's eye.

'Intimidated? *I?* That will be the day.'

'So we'll go?'

'Yes. And what's more, we'll give the damned Roundheads something to think about.' Venetia flung open her coffer and began throwing clothes across the bed. 'Call Jane! There's a lot to do.'

Gabriel collected his ladies at precisely the hour appointed and found them already waiting, swathed in their cloaks. It was, therefore, not until they arrived at Cromwell's house in King Street that he was privileged to see them in their full glory; and by then, of course, it was too late to do anything about it.

The sleeves of Phoebe's apricot silk had been re-trimmed with great falls of creamy lace, pearls encircled her throat and ribbons were twined cunningly through her curls. Her brows had been plucked into a delicate arch, her lashes artfully darkened and her lips subtly enhanced. She looked both older and more sophisticated than Gabriel had ever seen her and he wasn't sure he liked the effect. Compared to Venetia, however, she was a mere candle to the sun.

Leaving only a feathering of tiny curls, the silver-gilt hair had been drawn back from her brow into a luxuriant coil from which a torrent of ringlets cascaded over her ears. Like Phoebe's, the exquisite face had been skilfully enhanced with cosmetics and an ornate locket lay at the base of the slender throat. But it was the elaborate gown of dull gold silk, with its heavily embroidered underdress and daring décolletage that stopped Gabriel in his tracks; not because she looked beautiful – but because it told him everything he needed to know about her intentions.

'I see,' he remarked dryly, 'that you've come dressed to kill. But are you sure you haven't overdone it a trifle?'

'Oh no. I don't think so.' She smiled sweetly and opened her fan with an expert flick. 'I chose this gown specially. I've only worn it once before – and that was for the masque of *Philogenes and the Furies* at Whitehall. The King played the leading role himself, you know . . . and I was amongst the Chorus of Beloved People.'

'I see.' The grey eyes grew openly sardonic. 'The point being, of course, that you still are.'

'I'm so glad you understand.' She laid her fingers on his right arm and waited for Phoebe to take his left. Then, allowing her smile to gather an element of malice, she said, 'Don't worry. I won't say a word out of place unless I'm provoked. And I'm sure the great and mighty leaders of the Army will be able to cope with a mere woman.'

Although his guests that evening were colleagues either from the House or the Army, the Lieutenant-General had assumed his incarnation of bluff geniality. He began by complimenting Gabriel on acquiring such a lovely wife and then jovially commanded Venetia to tell him if 'this busy fellow' was looking after her properly.

She withdrew her hand and smiled coolly.

'Admirably, sir. And if he does not, I promise that you shall be the very first to hear of it.'

Cromwell gave his great, neighing laugh.

'Good, good. That should keep him on his toes, eh?' Then, turning to his wife, 'Ah, Betty, my dear. Come and meet Colonel Brandon's charming bride.'

Elizabeth Cromwell, a plump-faced woman in moss-coloured taffeta, welcomed Venetia with a faintly startled glance at the gold gown and stepped promptly into a pit of her own making. 'I believe,' she said, 'that, like myself, you are well-acquainted with his Majesty?'

Venetia's face froze into a polite mask.

'It's certainly true that I spent several years at Whitehall. But if you feel able to call the King your friend, I fear you must have the advantage of me.'

'Oh I wouldn't say that, my dear. But my daughters and I visited him quite regularly at one time, you know.'

'Yes. I do know. And I'm sure his Majesty was suitably grateful,' came the silken reply. Then, 'May I present my sister, Mistress Clifford?'

Well-accustomed to dispersing awkwardness, Phoebe

curtsied to her hostess and beamed at the Lieutenant-General. He patted her hand and commanded her to enjoy herself.

'Oh – I'm sure I will.'

Phoebe had already caught sight of a familiar russet head on the far side of the room and was so dizzy with anticipation that she could cheerfully have kissed the Lieutenant-General on his long, rosy nose.

'Capital! Take them away and introduce them, Colonel. I think you'll find that you know most people. And then, later – after we've eaten – I'd like you to join myself and some of the others for a brief, informal meeting.'

Gabriel inclined his head courteously but without noticeable enthusiasm and led his ladies away. Venetia said abruptly, 'Is he always like that?'

He eyed her witheringly. 'No. And I shouldn't complain if I were you. At least he didn't ask God to bless our union. Now. Who shall we choose to be civil to first?'

'How about the earthworms?' suggested Venetia, staring broodingly across the room. Then, in response to Phoebe's inquiring giggle, '"*O Cromwell! Thou art led by the nose by those covetous earthworms, Vane and St John.*" It's Mr Lilburne's view, of course. But I daresay—'

'That's enough!' Gabriel clamped his hand over hers and started heading for a group largely composed of officers and their wives. 'This is neither the time nor the place. And if you can't stomach Harry Vane, stay away from him.'

'My pleasure,' she muttered. And forced herself to smile as John Lambert turned to greet them.

Truth to tell, Venetia didn't dislike Major-General Lambert. He had an amusing air of cynicism – and, being less of a Puritan than many of his fellows, was happier discussing tulips than religion. Now she discovered that his wife, Frances, was equally easy to swallow – a vivacious, quick-witted brunette with easy manners and a good deal of style. But the biggest surprise was undoubtedly Henry Ireton. Having read the *Heads of the Proposals*, Venetia had known that he was intelligent; she hadn't, however, expected a cool, clinical logic that made him impossible to despise. Fortunately, his wife, Cromwell's daughter, Bridget, was a different matter. She had her father's nose, little conversation and the sort of piety which, in other times, would have been best suited to a convent.

From the fringes of the group, Major Maxwell watched Phoebe standing mute while her sister turned the talk away from the peace negotiations taking place in Europe aimed at finally ending the German wars after thirty long years, to the Scots' progress towards raising an army. He grinned to himself and strolled idly round to the younger girl's side.

'That's torn it,' he murmured confidingly in her ear. 'They'll be at it hammer and tongs until dinner. Come and let me find you a glass of cordial.'

Phoebe beamed and slid discreetly away from Venetia's side saying shyly, 'I'm so glad you're here. I hoped you might be.'

Eden's brows rose a little but, assuming that she was just pleased to find a familiar face, he said, 'You're in luck, then. I'm not usually summoned to these affairs.'

'Why not?'

'I'm not important enough.'

'Oh. But Gabriel is?'

'A full Colonel with estates in Yorkshire? Absolutely. The only thing he needs now is a seat in Parliament.'

Phoebe grinned. 'No he doesn't. He likes to get on with things, not sit around endlessly discussing them.'

'That,' agreed Eden, on a quiver of laughter, 'is probably a very fair assessment. You like him, don't you?'

'Very much. Don't you?'

'Of course. But then, he and I are on the same side whereas I imagine your views coincide with your sister's.'

Phoebe's breath caught. She wasn't to know that Eden was trying to establish how much Venetia resented Gabriel's politics. She thought – or rather hoped – that his words had a more personal implication; that he had sought her out because he was attracted to her. And consequently she said softly, 'I suppose they do, after a fashion. But Venetia spent years at Court. I didn't. So, she feels a personal attachment to the King . . . whereas I care more for the people I know. Whatever their allegiances may be.'

Eden smiled wryly. 'You might feel differently if you were married to a Parliamentary soldier.'

Again she misinterpreted his thoughts, this time catastrophically. 'Why don't you divorce her?' she blurted out.

The scarred face froze. 'I beg your pardon?'

Phoebe flushed. 'I'm sorry. I just thought—'

'I doubt very much if you thought at all!' snapped Eden. 'However. Since you ask – and so that you're not tempted to do so again – I won't divorce Celia because I don't want my private life sold for a penny on every street corner.'

'B-but it wouldn't be – surely?'

'Of course it would! It happened to the late Earl of Essex and the press is a hundred times more active now than it was then.' He folded his arms and looked down on her, breathing rather hard. 'And if you've some misty-eyed notion that all my ills can be cured by the love of a good woman, you are utterly mistaken. I haven't the slightest desire to marry again. Nor do I intend to do so.'

From the far side of the room, Venetia watched her little sister wilting under Eden Maxwell's gaze and came to the shrewd conclusion that the Major was putting an end to Phoebe's calf-love – and none too gently, at that. Then she flicked a cool, meaningful glance at Gabriel, excused herself with practised grace from Frances Lambert and set off to see how much damage had been done.

So intent was she on evaluating the look on Phoebe's face that she did not notice the lady purposefully approaching her until they all but collided, and even then Venetia merely murmured an absent apology and would have continued on her way if the lady hadn't suddenly addressed her.

'Venetia Clifford! I *knew* I wasn't mistaken.'

Venetia turned sharply and then stood very still as surprise invaded every muscle. The flaming red hair was instantly familiar – as were the startlingly blue eyes. But the fine-boned face that ought to have gone with them was now decidedly matronly and the once slender figure had vanished beneath layers of firm, dimpled flesh.

'Isabel?' she said weakly. 'Isabel Molyneux?'

The palimpsest vision smiled thinly. 'Lady Gillingham now. George's father died last year, you know.'

Venetia murmured a few words of banal condolence. She had known the late Earl only by sight and repute – and though she and Isabel had served the Queen together at Whitehall and then again in Oxford during the war, they had somehow never gone beyond vague day-to-day courtesies.

She said, 'The Cromwells are friends of yours?'

'Betty is,' drawled Isabel. 'She likes having a Countess to grace her parties. And as for my willingness to oblige . . . well, necessity makes strange bedfellows. But I imagine you know that. So what brings *you* here?'

There was a small, grim silence. Then, 'My husband.'

'Your husband? Ah yes. Of course. I remember now. You were betrothed to Edward Brandon weren't you?'

'Ellis Brandon,' corrected Venetia stonily. 'Yes I was. But I didn't marry him. I married his half-brother, who happens to be one of Cromwell's Colonels.'

'Dear me . . .' The vivid blue gaze widened a fraction. 'How enterprising of you. And how intriguing that Ellis should have been hiding a secret brother all these years.'

'He wasn't.' Out of the corner of her eye, Venetia could see Mistress Cromwell starting to shepherd her guests in the direction of the table and realised that if she didn't reach Phoebe now, the opportunity might be lost. She therefore said baldly, 'The simple fact – as I'm sure dear Betty will be only too eager to tell you – is that my husband is illegitimate. Excuse me. I really must find my sister.' And stalked purposefully off.

When questioned, Phoebe stonily refused to answer; and before Venetia could press the matter, Mistress Cromwell arrived to draw them in to dinner. Venetia found herself placed between the saturnine elegance of Henry Ireton and the pedantic bulk of Bulstrode Whitelocke. The first expounded the difficulties of dealing with a King who refused to accept that changes must be made; the second attended with great thoroughness to his dinner. Diagonally opposite her, Gabriel had Bridget Ireton on one hand and pretty Frances Lambert – with whom, Venetia noticed, he was enjoying an apparently amusing flirtation – on the other. On the rare occasions when their eyes met, his expression was

251

one of bland mockery; and it was that, decided Venetia, which was making her want to push his face into the apricot custard.

The meal – which had plainly been chosen on grounds of economy rather than taste – seemed interminable and, when at last it was over, most of the gentlemen disappeared in the Lieutenant-General's wake. Venetia was glad to see that Eden Maxwell was one of them but could not help wondering precisely what Gabriel was saying to account for the flash of temper she glimpsed in both their faces as they went out. Then, leaving a still stubbornly reticent Phoebe in conversation with Frances Lambert, she moved away to the window for a breath of air. Seconds later, Lady Gillingham materialised at her elbow.

'My dear, I came to apologise,' said Isabel. 'I'm so immersed in my own problems that I often forget others have them, too.'

Venetia surveyed her thoughtfully for a moment and then, with a wry smile, said, 'That's my besetting sin as well.'

'Then it seems we've a lot in common.'

'Perhaps. But at least you are here voluntarily.'

'You think so?' Her ladyship gave a small bitter laugh. 'I'm here because of money – or rather the lack of it. Our lands are under sequestration and the composition fine is set so high we can't possibly meet it. Consequently, I've little choice but to make Betty Cromwell my dearest friend in the hope of gaining her husband's influence.'

Venetia's brows rose. 'Will that help?'

'I've no idea – but I've tried everything else and George, of course, is utterly useless. However. Do tell me. How did *your* marriage come about?'

'It was . . . arranged,' admitted Venetia neutrally. 'Ellis never shared his father's politics – so Sir Robert eventually chose to disinherit him in favour of the natural son who *did*. And I became part of the bargain.'

'My dear – I'm so sorry,' said her ladyship warmly. 'It must be very difficult for you.'

'At times. But that is less to do with Gabriel's birth than the complete and utter conflict of our loyalties.'

There was a moment's silence while the cornflower eyes

gazed attentively back at her. Then, 'Gabriel?' inquired Isabel gently.

'My husband – Colonel Brandon.'

'Ah. Of course.' Another pause. 'Doubtless the red-headed gentleman I saw with your sister before dinner?'

'No. The dark gentleman who is advancing on us this very minute,' returned Venetia. And then, as Gabriel arrived beside them, 'That was quick. Have you worked out how to prevent a second war or simply how to win it?'

'Neither – but the debate continues.'

'Then I'm sure it's only a matter of time.' She smiled coolly. 'May I present an old acquaintance of mine? This is the Countess of Gillingham. Isabel – my husband.'

Colonel Brandon bowed over the plump hand and wondered precisely what his wife had said to account for her ladyship's rigid stare. Then, because he was pressed for time and didn't really care what the woman thought of him, he said crisply, 'I'm sorry to be so precipitate, Venetia, but I'm afraid I'll have to take you back to Shoreditch.'

Her brows rose. 'Already? What a shame.'

'Quite. But I'm sure you'll master your disappointment. And I, meanwhile, will attempt to console Phoebe.'

The thread of meaning in his voice told Venetia everything she needed to know about his conversation with Major Maxwell. Meanwhile, Isabel Molyneux watched him walk away and then said reflectively, 'Did he say *Shoreditch*?'

'Yes. It's a little out of the way, of course but—'

'Out of the way? My dear, it's the back of beyond! But I daresay I might find my way there – if you'll permit me to call?'

'Why, of course, if you wish,' replied Venetia, startled but not altogether displeased.

'Good. We can tell each other our troubles and talk about old times,' smiled Isabel. 'Shall we say the day after tomorrow?'

Seven

At Headquarters, Colonel Brandon burned the midnight oil over administrative details another officer might have left to chance and devoted the rest of his time to the Council of War. On the morning following Cromwell's dinner party, the agitators were hauled in to receive a stern reprimand for their activities at St Albans; and, on the day after that, senior officers and agitators alike spent far longer than Gabriel thought necessary beseeching the Lord to guide them in their deliberations and hold them fast to their duty.

It was the second such prayer meeting to be held at Windsor. At the time of the first, Gabriel had been in Yorkshire on the brink of marrying Venetia, but he'd heard that by the end of it leaders of both the Commons and the Army had drunk toasts and sworn to live and die for each other. The second, of course, was opening under rather more trying circumstances. Royalist riots, widespread calls for the restoration of the King and the temporary suspension of the Vote of No Addresses; hostile action in Wales, a Scots army lurking somewhere north of the Tweed and continued demands for the disbandment of the New Model. Conviviality therefore seemed unlikely. But if there was any possibility of Henry Ireton falling on Edward Sexby's neck, Gabriel was not averse to seeing it.

Not unnaturally, it did not happen. The day passed in an orgy of self-recrimination and exhortation and the next morning continued in much the same vein. The Lieutenant-General, wallowing in emotion and with tears in his eyes, besought everyone present to consider their actions both as an Army and as Christians, to see if any iniquity on their parts could be the cause of their present troubles. This resulted in a good deal of public soul-searching, during which Gabriel let his chin sink on to his chest. Unable to resist a good opportunity, High Peter lectured him about his blatant lack of interest and informed him that his attitude was an insult to every God-fearing man present. Gabriel raised inimical brows and retorted that he had no objection to anyone speaking as the spirit moved them, but wished they'd be a little less long-winded about it.

His wish was granted on the following morning. It was May 1st and, before the meeting had been in session an hour, news arrived that Adjutant-General Fleming – that gallant, well-liked officer, sent to replace Colonel Poyer and thus left fighting him ever since – had been slain in a surprise attack near Carmarthen. All South Wales was in revolt and, in time-honoured fashion, the Welsh had taken to the hills lock, stock and barrel, leaving the New Model without so much as a crust. Gabriel swore quietly to himself. Time, it seemed, had finally run out; and the second war they'd all been trying so hard to prevent, was now upon them.

For a while the Council looked set to dissolve into angry chaos and then, in one of his rare moments of ascendancy, the Lord-General took charge. Fairfax might be no great orator and deeply disturbed by the growing political role of his Army, but he knew how to deal with a military crisis. Without waiting to consult Parliament, he immediately ordered Cromwell into Wales with two regiments of Horse and three of Foot. Then he declared the meeting over.

Gabriel rose to leave but was detained by John Lambert.

'A word,' said the Major-General grimly. 'Since you're not destined for Wales with Oliver, you'll probably be sent North with me. In fact, I intend to make sure you are. And I'd guess that we'll get our marching orders very soon now.'

'You're asking if my boys will be ready?'

'Hardly. Knowing you, they've been ready for the last month. No. I was merely giving you prior warning – in case you've personal arrangements to make or wish to spend a few hours with your wife before we leave.'

'Ah.' His expression did not waver by so much as a hairsbreadth. 'I see. Thank you.'

'Think nothing of it,' shrugged Lambert. And then, frowning a little, 'What the devil is going on over there?'

Gabriel looked. A goodly proportion of officers and every one of the agitators were gathered together, discussing the treacherous way in which the King had brought about a new war. They were already reaching the conclusion that it was their duty, if ever the Lord brought them back in peace again, 'to call Charles Stuart, that man of blood, to an account for the blood he had shed'.

Lambert and Gabriel exchanged mutually distasteful glances. Then, with one accord and in complete understanding, they turned on their heels and left.

The Major-General was soon proved right in his prognostication. On May 2nd, while the Parliament was busy ordaining the death penalty for blasphemy and heresy, word arrived that Sir Marmaduke Langdale and a party of Royalists had taken Berwick and that Carlisle had also fallen. Within an hour, Colonel Brandon had his orders. He was to take his regiment North with Lambert in two days' time.

Leaving a plethora of small details in the capable hands of his Major and promising Wat that he would be back by midnight, Gabriel swung himself into the saddle and set off for Shoreditch. He didn't particularly want to go – and wouldn't have done except that basic courtesy demanded it. He couldn't very well leave without a word to Jack and Annis and the only thing left was to hope that Venetia would restrain her glee. If she exulted in the discovery that her King had successfully begun another war, Gabriel thought he would very probably strangle her.

An elaborate chair with a crest on its panels stood in the middle of the Morrells' yard, attended by two liveried chairman and a runner. Gabriel sighed faintly, stabled his horse and established the fact that Jack was at a guild-meeting. Then, without much enthusiasm, he went inside.

Annis sat on one side of the hearth with the baby in her lap and, in the windowseat, her flaming head bent close to Venetia's fair one, was the Countess of Gillingham. All three looked up as he entered. Only one of them smiled.

'Thank heavens!' said Annis. 'We were beginning to think you were already half-way to Wales.'

He grinned. 'Without saying goodbye? Perish the thought. No . . . my talents are being directed elsewhere.'

'And soon – which is why you're here now.' Venetia rose and faced him with a calm she did not quite feel.

'Of course.' The grey eyes were cool. 'I depart for the North the day after tomorrow.'

'Leaving Phoebe and me here, I suppose?'

'That rather depends on Jack and Annis.'

'You know you needn't ask.' Annis laid the baby back in his cot. 'But you can't go without seeing Jack and he won't be back much before seven, so you'd better stay to supper.'

'Since it may be the last decent meal I get, I'd be delighted,' came the bland reply. And with the merest hint of a bow for the Countess, 'But I've interrupted your afternoon. Forgive me.'

'There's nothing to forgive.' The bright, cornflower gaze seemed to look, not just at, but through him. 'I should be leaving anyway.'

Gabriel surveyed her with the double-edged smile that was so peculiarly his own. 'Not, I hope, on my account?'

'No, no. I only called to bring Venetia a copy of Herrick's *Hesperides* and have already stayed far longer than I meant.' Her ladyship rose in a rustle of sapphire taffeta and enveloped Venetia in a brief, scented embrace. 'Goodbye, my dear. I've so enjoyed our little talk and I'll call again in a few days to see how you liked the book.' She cast a vague, impartial smile in the direction of Gabriel and Annis. 'I'm more than happy to have met you again, Colonel. Who knows? Perhaps our next encounter will have a little more substance to it. Mistress Morrell – a thousand thanks for your hospitality and please don't trouble to show me out. I can easily find my own way and my chair is waiting in the yard. Goodbye.' And she sailed from the room on a tide of heliotrope.

For a moment after she had gone, there was a sudden, acute silence. Then the Colonel said gently, 'Can anyone tell me why that woman looks at me as if I'd got two heads?'

'She doesn't,' said Venetia defensively.

'Actually, she does,' said Annis. And then, on a tiny choke of laughter, 'But I wouldn't worry about it, Gabriel. She's probably just ensnared by your fatal fascination.'

'My what?' He tossed his hat and gloves on the table and sat down. 'The last female to succumb to my charms was Bryony. It's hardly an impressive record, is it?' He paused, ignoring Venetia's stare. 'Where is she, by the way? Roaming the City with Samuel Radford?'

'No. In Westminster with Phoebe, visiting a friend,' said Annis. And then, moving towards the kitchen, 'I'd better go and see what Joan's doing to the meat. There's wine on the dresser if you want it.'

The door closed behind her and Gabriel was left looking at Venetia. She said, 'Something's happened, hasn't it?'

'To send me North? Obviously. If you must know, your Royalist friends have taken Berwick and Carlisle.'

She drew a tiny, ragged breath. 'It's war, then?'

'Of course it's war! What else did you expect? What else did you *want*?'

'I . . . I don't know.' She paused; and then, meeting his gaze, said, 'You thought I'd be glad? So did I.'

'And aren't you?'

'Do I look it?'

Turning abruptly away, she went to the dresser and set about pouring wine. Gabriel watched her, a faint frown at the back of his eyes. Then, when she handed him the cup, he said warily, 'Your views have changed?'

'On the King's rights and the necessity of restoring him to the throne? No. Not at all,' came the flat reply. 'But you can't walk round London these days without seeing the effects of the last war . . . and there comes a point when you have to count the cost.'

It was not what he had expected but, oddly enough, he had no doubts about her sincerity. He thought for a moment and then said, 'Tell me something. Precisely what do you see in his Majesty that continues to command your loyalty?'

Her brows arched incredulously. 'You don't know?'

'No. So far I've merely made assumptions.'

259

'Then let me either confirm or dispel them for you.' She moved gracefully to the other side of the hearth and sat down facing him. 'I'm aware that the King has failings and I know what they are. But I also know how seriously he takes his responsibilities and how impossible it is for him to fail in what he sees as his duty.'

'So your loyalty is a personal one.'

'To a degree, yes. But it's also about the very nature of kingship and everything it stands for. Order and stability in church and state – protection from that useless, quarrelsome brood in Westminster. Tradition, if you like.'

Gabriel looked up from the ruby liquid in his cup, his face carefully expressionless. 'And divine right?'

Venetia gave a tiny, wry laugh. 'Like a lot of other things, it did no harm so long as it wasn't discussed. It only really became an issue when his Majesty started using it as a platform. As for the rest . . . Charles isn't a bad man or even a particularly bad king. He's made mistakes, yes – and he's often stubborn. But he never oppressed the people or wanted anything except to do his best for them, according to his lights. And the simple truth, at the end of the day, is that he's just been unlucky.'

'You make him sound tragic.'

'I didn't intend to.' The amethyst eyes grew suddenly stark. 'But it may be true. For good or ill, his conscience rules him. He only ever went against it once that I know of and that was when he let them execute Strafford.'

'As I understand it, he had little choice in that.'

'Yes. That's the whole point. Don't you see? He let Pym and the rest browbeat him into doing as they wanted. And he's never forgiven himself for it.'

There was a long silence during which, amongst other things, Gabriel reflected that this was the nearest they had ever come to having a proper conversation and wondered if she knew it too. Before he could ask, however, the door opened and Bryony and Phoebe walked in with Samuel Radford.

Phoebe greeted Gabriel with unaffected pleasure, Bryony with studied nonchalance and Sam with all his usual, half-veiled humour. Then, while Bryony plunged recklessly into a series of questions concerning the cauldron of rumours currently simmering in the City, Phoebe drew her sister away to the window and said baldly, 'I think I've seen Ellis.'

Venetia's heart lurched.

'You can't have done. He's in France.'

'Not any more. He was in Westminster an hour ago. I only saw him for a minute, of course, and the beard almost fooled me. But no one else strides along swishing his cloak quite as Ellis does. And that's what I recognised most.'

Venetia thought of and discarded a number of smart ploys. 'Have you mentioned this to Bryony or Mr Radford?'

'No – and I wasn't planning to.' Phoebe eyed her sister anxiously. 'What are you going to do?'

'Do? Nothing. I think you were mistaken. And, even if you weren't, I can hardly comb London looking for Ellis, can I?' Then, changing tack with a vengeance, 'Now,' she said, 'Tell me where you've been all afternoon and how you arrived back with Samuel Radford in tow.'

Phoebe assumed an innocent expression and returned an evasive reply. She didn't expect to get away with it, of course, but it would do until she could think of something convincing.

Jack returned from his guild-meeting at a little after seven, in full possession not just of the news about Berwick and Carlisle but also the City's reaction to it.

'There's a general feeling that both we and the Parliament are being used as a catspaw by the Royalists,' he observed once they were all sitting down to a substantial supper of beef and oyster pie, roast ham and a fricassee of eels. 'And much as most of us would like to see the King back on the throne, there are very few who'll engage in a new war in order to put him there.'

'Well, that's some comfort,' said Gabriel aridly. 'We poor soldier boys have enough to do fighting on two fronts, without the possibility of being faced with a third.' And then, with a faintly wicked gleam, 'But you can't be quite as disgruntled as you sound, surely? After all, so much fighting-talk must be good for business.'

Jack swallowed a mouthful of ham and refused the provocation. 'I could live without it. But it's an ill wind, as they say.' He paused, looking across at Mr Radford. 'And where did *you* spring from? Did you turn up here in time for supper, or were you also visiting Bryony's mysterious friend in Petty France?'

'Neither. I happened to meet the girls on their way home and merely offered to escort them,' shrugged Sam with more ease than he actually felt. He liked Phoebe but he had been aghast when he'd learned that Bryony had taken her to visit Elizabeth Lilburne. However, since all he could do now was hide his natural apprehensions, he grinned audaciously and said, 'As for supper – you couldn't seriously expect me to refuse to stay when I'd been asked, now could you?'

'Not once you smelled the pie, anyway,' remarked Bryony, pushing a dish of buttered parsnips towards him. 'And Beth isn't mysterious, Uncle Jack. She's a very nice woman with three small children. Isn't that so, Phoebe?'

Phoebe nodded vigorously and made haste to change the subject by asking Gabriel about his forthcoming journey. He answered her blandly, watched her without appearing to do so and wondered if – thanks to Bryony – his little sister-in-law wasn't learning a few devious tricks herself.

The evening sped by. Sam left just before ten and it was a full hour after that before Gabriel finally reached for his hat and said that he, too, must go.

Jack rose with him, his pleasant face becoming suddenly grave. He said, 'How long do you think it will take?'

'To beat the Scots? God knows. It will depend largely on how soon they cross the border. It might be over in a week. Or it could take months.'

Annis moved to Gabriel's side and stood on tiptoe to kiss his cheek. 'You'll take care, won't you?'

'I always do.' He hugged her, then moved on to kiss Phoebe and Bryony in turn. 'Be good, you two. I don't know why, but I've a vague idea you're up to something.'

Phoebe merely held him rather hard and buried her face in his coat. Bryony sniffed and remarked that some people had nasty, suspicious minds.

Venetia remained awkwardly to one side.

'Don't worry.' Gabriel crossed towards her, a sardonic smile touching his mouth. 'No one expects any great demonstration of emotion between us. The only thing to say, therefore, is that I'd prefer you to remain here for the time being. If, however, this unfortunate business looks as if it's going to drag on, I'll engage to send you word.'

'I'll look forward to it,' she replied ambiguously. And then, as if in reluctant response to some impulse she could not quite understand, 'Go safely.'

An arrested expression lit the dark grey eyes but he merely kissed her hand with deliberate formality and turned back to his foster-brother. 'See me off, Jack?'

Mr Morrell nodded. 'Don't I always?'

'Then we'll go now.' Gabriel awarded the ladies a smile of rare charm, swept them an extravagant bow – and was gone.

Outside, the moon peered fitfully between the clouds and there was a light drizzle. Jack said moodily, 'You'll have an unpleasant ride to Windsor.'

'That,' replied the Colonel, mounting his horse, 'is the least of my problems.'

'Quite.' He reached up and grasped Gabriel's hand. 'Watch out for yourself. You hear me?'

'I hear.'

'Good. See you remember it.' Jack released his grip and stepped back. 'God go with you,' he said.

Gabriel rode back towards the City at a pace dictated by the darkness and the state of the road. He was much later than he had meant to be, but there was little point in running the risk of laming his horse. And he rather enjoyed riding alone at night. It gave him the chance to think.

The last houses of Shoreditch fell away behind him, leaving him in a brief expanse of open country. Deciding to skirt the City, he turned right towards the windmills of Upper Moorfields. The rain filtered steadily through the trees and the moon disappeared behind a cloud.

Afterwards, Gabriel was never sure if it was the sudden darkness that made him check his pace or whether he'd heard that first, betraying scrape of metal against metal. Whichever it was, however, the result was the same. In that single fragment of silence between one hoofbeat and the next, there came a furtive but perfectly audible whisper. Then the moon came out again just as a body dropped from the tree above him and bore him to the ground.

Even as he fell, Gabriel was acutely aware of two things; the pair of shadows closing in swiftly from the road ahead and the knife approaching his throat. The first could wait, the second couldn't. With a supple, violent twist he managed to alter the moment of impact so that his assailant received the brunt of it; and before the fellow could recover his breath, he used the full force of his forearm to deflect the murderous blade. Then he brought his fist smashing back into the anonymous face.

There was a distinct sound of splintering bone and the man howled, but Gabriel did not wait to see how much damage he'd inflicted. He sprang to his feet, snatched the knife from the slackened grip and, tearing his sword from its scabbard, turned immediately to face his other attackers.

They were almost upon him – one holding a sword and the other a cudgel – and, as they advanced, they were moving gradually apart from each other. Gripping the purloined dagger firmly in his left hand, Gabriel let them arrive at a precisely calculated point in front of him and then stopped them with a swift, double-sweep of his sword. Jack's craftsmanship glinted maliciously in the light; thirty-five inches of steel with a cunningly-wrought gilt-bronze basket hilt. Anticipation sparkled through Gabriel's veins and his mouth curled in a chilly smile.

'If you want me, you'll have to come and get me,' he said. And, without warning, engaged the enemy blade in a savage assault which had just one aim.

His only chance was to disarm or disable one of his assailants while he dealt with the other. It worked, but not quite as fast as he'd hoped; and in the instant he achieved the exact position he needed to score the first man's knuckles and send his sword spinning from his hand, the billet connected sickeningly with his left shoulder.

The force of the blow sent him blundering awkwardly into the trunk of a tree and pain burned down his arm, rendering his left hand useless and causing the dagger to fall silently into the grass. Instinct warned that he now had only seconds in which to deal with the cudgel-bearer before the other man retrieved his sword. Side-stepping a second blow to his head and feeling the draught of it stir his hair, Gabriel thrust hard and accurately with his sword. The point passed cleanly through the fellow's throat and he slowly crumpled, blood pumping from his mouth.

Before he even hit the ground, Gabriel was already wheeling to meet the oncoming rush of the swordsman. The blades exploded together like bells on a Sunday, then slithered to a brief disengage before beginning again. Gabriel pressed a relentless attack which forced his assailant to give ground before him. A line of concentration marking his brow, he pursued a series of moves which eventually appeared to provide his opponent with an opening. Then, just as he was in danger of losing his arm, Gabriel made a perfectly-timed thrust past the oncoming blade and straight into its owner's heart. Surprise registered briefly on the fellow's face and he dropped like a stone.

Very slowly, Gabriel expelled a long, weary breath and sheathed his sword – for once, without bothering to clean it. Now the danger was over, his shoulder had become a mass of screaming agony and he wondered distantly whether or not he would be silly to try riding on to Windsor. Then the matter was answered for him as a knife whistled through the air to take him just above his right elbow.

He gasped and dropped to one knee, peering through the darkness at the man who'd unhorsed him and who now crouched beside a gorse-bush, blood black on his broken face.

Stupid, thought Gabriel dizzily, through waves of pain. *Stupid and careless. Another knife. You should have checked.* Then, gritting his teeth and summoning every ounce of will, he closed his teeth around the hilt of the dagger and dragged it free of his protesting flesh.

It was all the man by the bush had been waiting for. He had seen how efficiently the Colonel had dispatched his two friends and had shot his last bolt – ineptly, it seemed. Now he did the only thing left to him. He fled.

Gabriel watched him go with grim relief, spared a moment to marshal his senses and then set about trying to remove his sash so that he could use it to stem the flow of blood that was already darkening his sleeve. This, due to the grinding torment in his shoulder, took some time, but he eventually achieved it and hauled himself to his feet. The next task – that of getting back on his horse – was even more difficult and left him feeling rather sick. Then, thanking God that his Jenny was well-trained, he turned her slowly back in the direction of Shoreditch.

It was an excruciating and seemingly endless ride but he finally arrived in the Morrells' yard and was able to drop gratefully from the saddle. A soft glow of light showed at the parlour windows, suggesting that – despite the lateness of the hour – someone was still up. Praying that it was Jack, Gabriel tapped lightly on the door and waited, slumped against the architrave.

The door opened a crack and a face peered out. It wasn't Jack. It was Venetia, still wearing the simple blue gown she'd worn that afternoon but with her hair tumbling wildly down her back. Just for an instant, she stared at him incredulously; then she flung the door wide and said, 'Come in and sit down before you fall down.'

'That,' he murmured vaguely, 'sounds like a good idea.'

Once in the parlour, he lowered himself with care on to one of the settles beside the fire and Venetia followed with a branch of candles. Light spilled over him, revealing the ghastly pallor of his face and the blood-soaked sash wound inexpertly about the upper part of his right arm.

Venetia set the candles down with a bump.

'You look terrible!'

'And feel it.' He managed something close to a smile. 'In case you're wondering, Jack keeps the brandy in the corner-cupboard.'

Again, she did not hesitate but crossed the room to return with a hefty measure in a pewter mug. Then, placing the bottle beside him and briskly stripping off her cuffs, she said, 'What happened?'

Gabriel took half the brandy at one swallow and felt its warmth invading his veins. 'I was set upon by three men.'

She looked sharply at him and then continued rolling up her sleeves. 'Footpads?'

'It would be nice to think so. What are you doing?'

'What does it look like? I'm going to see to your arm.'

'Which one?' he asked wryly. Then, meeting her eyes, 'The blood probably looks worse than it is. What really hurts is my other shoulder. And, in either case, I think you should call Jack.'

'Why? Are you afraid I might faint?' She smiled grimly. 'Don't be. I'm not exactly a novice at this. How do you suppose I spent my time in Oxford during the war? Sit still while I find what I need.' And she left the room without waiting for an answer.

Gabriel drained the mug, filled it again and let his head drop back against the settle. By the time she came back with a bowl of hot water, cloths and various pots of ointment, the brandy was beginning to take effect and he was able to smile hazily and say, 'Don't tell me. You want me to take my clothes off.'

'Some of them,' she agreed calmly. 'And it's not likely to be nearly as much fun as you think.'

It wasn't. Getting out of the buff-coat brought about a resurgence of raw anguish in his shoulder and set his arm bleeding copiously again – with the result that Venetia simply took a pair of scissors to his shirt rather than try getting it off over his head. Then, seemingly unworried by his naked torso, she knelt at his side and set to work cleaning the knife-wound.

'How is it?' asked Gabriel presently.

'Deep but fairly clean. I take it that one of the men you don't think were footpads stabbed you?'

'More or less.' The grey eyes, kept carefully blank with rigid self-control, rested on her reflectively. 'Why shouldn't I think they were footpads?'

'I've no idea. It's just the impression I got.'

He sighed and then winced as she touched a particularly vulnerable spot. 'My unfortunate sense of humour again. Dare I say that hurts?'

'I'd be amazed if it didn't.' Venetia looked up briefly, recognised that he looked a trifle sick and went grimly on with her task. 'And, strange as it may seem, I'm not doing this for my own amusement.'

'Why, then?'

'Silly question. I'm here and it needs doing.'

'Ah.' He paused and kept his mouth tightly shut while she applied some thick green paste from a pot beside her. Then, drawing a careful breath, he said, 'All right. Sensible question. What are you doing still up at this hour?'

'I couldn't sleep.' She laid a pad neatly over the wound and began binding it into place. 'If you want the truth, I was thinking of the conversation we had earlier and the fact that, although I set forth my position, we never established yours.'

'With regard to what?'

Venetia pushed the shining fall of silver-gilt hair unceremoniously behind her ears and leaned forward to tear the bandage between her teeth. Then, tying the twin strips into a business-like knot, she said, 'Everything.'

Distant humour touched his expression.

'As Wat would say – you don't want much, do you?'

'Look on the bright side.' She set the bowl of reddened water on the hearth, stood up and poured him another drink. 'At least it will give you something else to think about while I inspect the rest of the damage.'

'There's sense there somewhere I suppose.' Gabriel eyed the brandy dubiously. 'You realise that if I drink this I'm likely to be totally cupshot?'

'That, believe it or not, is the general idea. Turn yourself round slightly to face the hearth.'

He did not move but instead said, 'You could do with some of this yourself, by the look of you.'

'I could indeed, but not yet. Now. Turn round.'

He did so and her breath caught. A livid bruise was spreading from well below his arm up to some point beneath the long, dark hair and the whole area was hideously misshapen. Venetia bit her lip and considered her options.

'As bad as that, is it?' asked Gabriel prosaically.

'It's not good. How much can you move your arm?'

'Without crucifying myself, scarcely at all.'

'Can I touch it?'

'If you don't mind me swearing.'

He broke into a cold sweat as she manipulated his arm but kept his tongue firmly between his teeth. Then, when it was done, he said raggedly, 'Well?'

'I think it's dislocated.'

'So do I. Do you know how to get it back in?'

She swallowed. 'I've seen it done a couple of times.'

'Well, that's probably twice more than Jack.' He drained the tankard and let it drop to the floor. Then, swivelling back so that he could read her face, 'Would you mind trying? I wouldn't ask . . . but it hurts like hell.'

She started to refuse and then the diffidence in his eyes coupled with the white shade bracketing his mouth unlocked something behind her neat, blue bodice. She said slowly, 'Are you sure? I might do more harm than good.'

'I don't think you *could*,' he said frankly. 'Please?'

And that, for some reason Venetia did not even try to fathom, settled it.

The next few minutes were singularly unpleasant for both of them. Having seen Kit's shoulder replaced after a riding accident and that of a youthful lieutenant in Oxford following some skirmish or other, Venetia knew roughly what had to be done. Doing it, however, was a different matter altogether. Her first cautious attempt ended in failure and caused Gabriel to curse under his breath. She let him rest for a moment and then, clamping her jaws firmly together, made a second, more positive approach.

Gabriel's arm slid unerringly back into its socket and he gave an involuntary, shuddering groan, allied with a word rarely used in mixed company. Then he slumped back into the settle, breathing rather hard and with perspiration glistening like rain all over his skin.

Venetia stepped back feeling rather queasy. She said unevenly, 'I think I'd better make a poultice.' And fled to the stillroom.

Grateful to be left alone, Gabriel shut his eyes and concentrated on not being sick. Although his shoulder was still on fire, the grinding torture of the past couple of hours had gone. The relief was indescribable.

Venetia finally returned bearing a steaming, malodorous concoction wrapped in muslin. Gabriel regarded it questioningly and she said flatly, 'Don't ask. Just accept that if you still hope to ride North on Thursday, this is the best chance I can offer you.'

He smiled. 'After what you've done for me so far tonight, do you think I'd start quibbling now?' He flinched as she laid the poultice carefully in place and then, meeting her eyes, said, 'I really can't thank you enough, you know.'

'Then don't try.' She picked up his discarded mug, crossed the room in search of a second cup and then reached wearily for the brandy bottle. 'Will you join me? I don't touch it as a rule and Mother would undoubtedly have a fit. But then Mother's idea of dealing with illness and injury is taking flowers to the sickroom.'

Gabriel laughed and immediately regretted it. He took the tankard from her and watched her sink down on the other side of the hearth. Then he said quietly, 'Why, Venetia? Why go to so much trouble – for me, of all people?'

'You mean I should have let you suffer in order to keep you from fighting the Scots?'

'Something like that, yes.'

'And what good would it have done?' She sipped her brandy and looked wryly at him. 'You didn't want this war. It's been forced on you. And we may all regret it before it's done. I decline to compound my mistakes.'

Respect had stirred before only to die stillborn. Now it came suddenly into full bloom – and brought with it the very first seeds of liking. Gabriel accepted and absorbed them. Then he said, 'And if the King wins?'

'*If* he does, I may feel differently. But will he?'

'As things stand, I suspect not but anything is possible. It will depend largely on the level of active support he can raise here in England and how long it takes the Lieutenant-General to subdue Wales.'

Venetia said abruptly, 'Do you like Cromwell?'

'I admire his military skill,' came the dry response. 'I don't care for his outpourings of emotion and his conviction that God is on his side. I also suspect that, without Ireton to direct his hand, he'd be revealed as a much less capable administrator than he currently appears.' Gabriel paused, staring down into his mug. 'But he still knows how to appeal to the common soldiers – and they'll follow him in the field even though, deep down, they no longer completely trust him to serve their interests in other matters.'

'I see. It's not much of a recommendation, is it?'

'Possibly not. But, for what it's worth, I think he will try to preserve the existing order as long as he can.' Gabriel shifted his position and grimaced slightly. 'I hope he does. Because if Parliament's dissolved and the King deposed, all that will be left is the Army – with nothing to balance against it. And military rule will never work. What's needed is a practical, universally acceptable compromise built on the foundations we already have.'

In some dim corner of her mind, Venetia realised that she ought to have initiated this conversation months ago . . . but that now, while he was in pain and deathly tired, was not the time to pursue it. Setting her cup to one side, she said abruptly, 'That poultice must be cooling by now. Given a bed – do you think you could sleep?'

'Only for a week or so. *Is* there a bed?'

'Yes.' She rose and faced him squarely. 'There's mine . . . if you can bear to share it.'

His brows rose and a hint of colour returned to his cheeks. 'That's generous of you. Are you sure?'

'Why not? It's not an invitation, you understand – just a practical solution. And we've done it before, after all.' A swift, genuinely amused smile dawned. 'The only difference is that this time I don't think I need worry about you being overtaken by lust.'

Wat arrived an hour after dawn, frightened the maids silly by hammering relentlessly on the door and then stormed inside to confront Mr Morrell. 'Where is he?'

'Gabriel?' asked Jack, never at his best before breakfast. 'He left here late last night to—'

'He may have left – but he came back again. His horse is in your stable, still saddled and with blood all over it.'

'*What?*' The sleepy gaze sharpened. 'No – it can't be. If he'd come back here, I'd know.'

'Excuse me, Mr Morrell, sir.' One of the maids stood timidly at his elbow. 'I reckon I ought to tell you—'

'Not now,' said Jack. And to Wat, 'Did you say *blood*?'

'Yes. And it don't belong to the mare, neither.'

'Wonderful.' Jack threw open the parlour door and strode

271

in. Then he stopped dead, staring at the litter of bloodstained rags, the empty brandy bottle and, lastly, at Gabriel's maltreated coat. Finally, he drew a bemused breath and said, 'What the devil's been going on?'

The little maid hovered in the doorway.

'It's how we found it this morning, sir.'

Wat rounded on her. 'Have *you* seen Colonel Brandon?'

'No, sir. Not a sign since he left last night.'

'Well, it's obvious somebody must have!' snapped Jack. 'And since it wasn't Annis or myself, it must have been—'

'Me,' said Venetia, walking forward as coolly as if she was in full Court dress rather than a trailing chamber-robe. 'He was injured in some sort of attack and I did what I could for him. I'm sorry about the mess.'

'So where is he now?' demanded Wat singlemindedly.

'Asleep. He has a knife-wound in his arm and an injured shoulder. But I can assure you that he'll live.'

There was a long, thoughtful silence. Then Jack said slowly, 'Since the house is full, which bed did you put him in?'

The merest hint of colour stained her skin but her expression remained perfectly impervious.

'Mine,' she said. 'But I wouldn't jump to too many conclusions. As bruised as he is, Gabriel's unlikely to be able to enjoy a good laugh for quite some time.' Then, taking advantage of the ensuing silence, she picked up the buff-coat and placed it almost symbolically in Wat's hands. 'He needs a shirt, by the way. His own is quite unwearable.'

By the time Colonel Brandon put in an appearance, the household was assembled round the breakfast-table and everyone knew where he had spent the night and why. He therefore walked into a barrage of varying speculation about his health, his adventures in Upper Moorfields and probably, although no one was tactless enough to mention it, his relationship with his wife. A glint of amusement lurking at the back of his eyes, Gabriel gave a deliberately understated account of his injuries and responded to Phoebe's and Bryony's excited questions with patient good-humour. Venetia – still in her robe and with her hair loosely confined in a ribbon – merely looked on, saying nothing. Then, as soon as the opportunity presented itself, she rose and said lightly, 'Now my room is my own again, I think I should dress.'

Phoebe and Bryony regarded her consideringly and exchanged meaningful glances when Gabriel also stood up.

'Then, since I'll be leaving very shortly, perhaps we might have a word in private now?' he said pleasantly.

'Of course – if you wish.'

'I do.' Ignoring the breathless hush around the table, he followed her purposefully out into the hall and, with the door closed behind them, said, 'The general curiosity is already at a peak, so I'll be brief. I just wanted to thank you properly for your help.'

'Think nothing of it,' shrugged Venetia, suddenly aware of a vague and inexplicable sense of constraint. 'Are you sure you feel fit enough to ride?'

'No – but it's necessary. And Wat will be with me.' He hesitated briefly. 'There's one more thing. Aside from the fact that last night has hopefully brought us to a better understanding of each other . . . I wanted you to be assured that, unlike our collective relatives, I am making no other untoward assumptions. And I won't.'

She looked back at him with mild surprise.

'I know,' she said. 'If I'd had any doubts on that score, I'd have spent the night with Phoebe.'

Before he left, Gabriel spent a few minutes alone with his foster-brother. Jack immediately said, 'It's a fine state of affairs when a fellow can't travel at night without being half-killed by footpads.'

'Ah.' The dark eyes hardened a little. 'But you see, they weren't footpads.'

Jack stared at him. '*Not?*'

'No. I distinctly heard one of them say, "This must be Brandon. Take him." And that, coupled with the fact that at no time did any one of them seem remotely interested in my purse, naturally leads me to suppose that this was a personal attack whose purpose was not robbery.'

'But – but *why?*'

'I've no idea – and unfortunately I haven't the time to find out,' said Gabriel briskly. 'I'm only telling you in case any other unpleasantness occurs during my absence. There's no need for you to mention it to Venetia.'

'Hell's teeth!' muttered Jack. Then, watching the Colonel rise somewhat stiffly to his feet, 'You're pretty cool for a man who's just escaped assassination.'

'Do you expect me to dissolve into a jelly?'

'Maybe not. But some discussion might be nice.'

'To what end?' Gabriel grinned suddenly. 'And I'm sure you've other questions you'd like to ask.'

Jack eyed him sardonically. 'Meaning you'd answer them?'

'Why not? It's actually very simple. Venetia and I shared a bed out of nothing more than simple expediency. And if you'd seen the shape I was in last night, you'd have no difficulty in believing it.'

'What's to say I don't believe it anyway?'

'My long acquaintance with your suspicious nature.'

A reluctant smile dawned. 'Yes. Well, you've never exactly lived like a monk, have you? And she's a remarkably beautiful woman. So naturally I wondered if you hadn't . . .'

'Availed myself of the obvious compensations?' finished Gabriel, helpfully. 'I'm sorry to disappoint you – but no.' And then, pausing briefly by the door, 'But you're right about one thing. She's certainly remarkable.'

Eight

Venetia watched from her window as Colonel Brandon climbed stiffly into his saddle and rode away with Wat. Then she told her maid to inform Mistress Phoebe, Mistress Annis and anyone else who was interested that she was nursing a headache and sent for Sym Potter.

When he arrived, she said baldly, 'Would you recognise Sir Ellis Brandon if you saw him?'

'Aye,' he said cautiously. 'Happen I would.'

'Good. Then I'd like you to try and find him for me.' A totally incredulous expression crept across the weather-beaten face and Venetia smiled wryly. 'I know. But it shouldn't be as difficult as it sounds. He's been seen in both Cheapside and Westminster. So if you start frequenting the Bull's Head Tavern or The Leg in King Street, you should trip over him fairly quickly.'

'And if I do?' asked Sym without noticeable optimism.

'You can tell him I want to talk to him,' came the flat reply. 'Urgently and in private.'

After Sym had gone, Venetia sat down and tried to make sense of the last twenty-four hours. This wasn't easy – for while one half of her was claiming that she had done nothing at all illogical, the other was asking what on earth had possessed her. Tending the Colonel's wounds had been one thing; under the circumstances, anyone would have done as much. But risking the status quo of her marriage by suggesting that he spend the night in her room was another matter entirely. In the cold light of day, it looked like an act of sheer folly. And were it not for the fact that she'd barely touched the stuff, Venetia would have been tempted to blame the brandy.

Not that anything had happened. Gabriel had merely

275

collapsed into restless slumber and she herself had lain staring into the darkness until shortly before Mr Larkin had come hammering on the door. It had been no more intimate or romantic than their wedding-night – just a good deal less tense. And that, of course, was the crux of the matter. Whether she liked it or not – and despite everything Gabriel had said – a change *had* occurred and it was irrevocable. For you couldn't go on being actively hostile towards someone you'd invited to sleep in your bed.

Venetia drew a long, thoughtful breath. So that was it, then. She no longer disliked him. More, she had just proved – without any particular consideration – that she trusted him. But *why*? Had it been born out of the strangeness of last night . . . or had it been growing slowly for weeks without her noticing it? She did not know – and, as yet, wasn't even convinced she wanted to. Right now, the only thing she was certain of was that life's complications were breeding faster than she could handle them.

A carriage trundled into the yard below and, looking down, she recognised it as that of Lady Gillingham. Venetia drew back from the window and hoped that someone would have the sense to present her excuses. She liked Isabel – but now was no time for trivial gossip. There were more important things to think about.

Phoebe had seen Ellis and Gabriel had implied that the attack on him might have been personal. Two apparently random facts which, however improbable it seemed, might possibly be connected. Venetia did not think Ellis would stoop to sending hired ruffians after his half-brother. He was much more likely to make some foolish, flamboyant personal gesture in front of the largest audience he could find. But it was impossible to be sure. '*Do you want me to kill him for you?*' he had said and she'd assumed he hadn't meant it. But supposing she'd been wrong – or that his encounter with Gabriel had acted as some kind of catalyst? What then?

It was too unpleasant a thought to dwell on and Venetia came abruptly to her feet, telling herself that she had absolutely no proof that Gabriel's attackers hadn't simply been footpads after all. He certainly had not said so; he'd just made an oblique statement which he'd later passed off as some sort of weak joke. Venetia didn't find it funny but she hoped that a joke was all it had been.

She waited until Isabel had left and then forced herself to go downstairs and face the inevitable speculation. It was not as bad as she'd feared. Alone in the parlour, Phoebe looked up from the letter she had been reading and said, 'It's all right. Her ladyship's gone. And Gabriel explained the situation to Mr Morrell – who explained it to Annis who passed it on to Bryony and me. So there'll be no awkward questions and no winking at each other behind your back. I won't even tease you about being better friends with Gabriel. I'll just say that I'm glad of it.'

The amethyst eyes looked ironically back. 'Pleasing you was naturally my prime motive. What did Isabel want?'

'She thought you might like to go to the Exchange with her. But I explained about last night and—'

'You did *what*?'

'It's all right,' soothed Phoebe. 'I just said that Gabriel had been set upon by footpads and you'd been up very late, tending his wounds.'

'I see. I'm sure she found that fascinating.'

'There's no need to be sarcastic. She merely asked how serious his injuries were and said she hoped the ride North wouldn't prove too much for him. Then she sent her fondest love to you and left. Satisfied?'

'Do I have a choice?' asked Venetia, irritably. And then, 'Is that a letter from Mother?'

'Yes.' Phoebe sighed and held it out. 'She's invited Aunt Margaret and Cousins Henry and Jane to come and keep her company. And we both know what *that* means.'

'Quite.' Venetia finished scanning her parent's characteristically self-centred epistle and dropped it distastefully back on the seat beside her sister. 'They'll stay for months. But it's no good worrying about it now. We'll just have to see what can be done when we get home again.'

'Why don't we go now? We might as well. Or perhaps, knowing Ellis to be in the vicinity, you've other ideas?' suggested Phoebe. And then, when no answer was forthcoming, 'I really did see him, you know.'

'So you said.' This was by no means a subject that Venetia felt prepared to discuss. 'What you *haven't* said is precisely where you went yesterday afternoon – and how involved you're becoming with Bryony and Mr Radford.'

'I'm not involved at all. I like them both very much, of course, but I'm not about to turn Leveller. I want an end to the squabbles not another means of prolonging them.'

'I'm glad. Lilburne may be a remarkable fellow . . . but as *Mercurius Melancholicus* says, he's quite likely to shed his feathers at Tyburn one of these days.' Venetia eyed her sister invitingly. 'However. I'm still waiting to hear where you went yesterday afternoon.'

'Are you?' Phoebe rose, shook out her skirts and headed for the door, smiling faintly. 'Ah well, fair exchange is no robbery, as they say. So you tell me your secrets and I'll tell you mine.'

During the days that followed, the Scots Parliament sent their English counterparts a list of peremptory demands ranging from enforcement of the Covenant and suppression of the Book of Common Prayer, to opening fresh talks with the King. Westminster, still desperately trying to prevent a full-scale invasion, tactfully replied that it would gladly maintain the said Covenant and would be honoured to join with the Scots in offering his Majesty the same Presbyterian-based terms it had presented so often before. Meanwhile, Gabriel went North with Lambert as planned, leaving Fairfax to follow with the rest of the Army in due course.

To Jack and Venetia, keeping abreast of the news and finding themselves in unexpected accord – and to Sym Potter, tramping fruitlessly from tavern to tavern in search of Sir Ellis Brandon – it was becoming obvious that the discontent which had been simmering away for months was about to boil over. Feelings in the City were running as high as they'd done in the early part of 1642 – the only difference being that this time the target was Parliament. Slogans were daubed on walls, under-employed apprentices roamed the streets in gangs and two thousand men from Essex marched into Westminster with a petition asking that the Army be disbanded and the King offered terms he could accept. A tidal wave was once more gathering and this time, as Jack grimly observed, there was nothing solid to cling to.

In the midst of all this, John Lilburne was finally summoned before the Court of the King's Bench to present his appeal for *habeas corpus*. Bryony became suddenly charged with discreet vigour and eventually bludgeoned Sam into taking her with him to see what could be seen.

By the time they arrived, the portals of the Court were already inhabited by some two dozen people and more were coming up every minute. Sam winnowed his way as near to the front as he could and, during the ensuing wait, set about peddling copies of *A Prisoner's Plea for Habeas Corpus* to those about him. Then, at long last, there was a shift in the crowd and it began to part like the Red Sea for John Lilburne and his gaolers.

He looked even less well than he had done on that fateful night in Wapping. Bryony held Sam's hand tightly. All about them, people were shouting goodwill messages which Freeborn John acknowledged with a smile and a lift of his hand. Then, just as the guards pushed him inside, his eyes found Sam and Bryony and he winked.

'He looks so *thin*,' she murmured.

'He isn't eating properly,' replied Sam bitterly. 'The Lords promised him two pounds a week subsistence during his imprisonment but they haven't paid a penny of it – any more than the Commons ever paid the compensation they awarded him for his Star Chamber sentence. And when you add the fact that he's still owed pay arrears for his services to the Army, you'll realise that, if Westminster ever kept its word about anything, he'd be very comfortably off – instead of which he hasn't got sixpence to scratch with.'

The doors of the Court started to close and the crowd immediately set up a vociferous demand for them to be left open, which resulted in several minutes of hurried consultation within. Then the doors swung slowly back on their hinges and two troopers stationed themselves uneasily in the space. The crowd tossed a few humorous remarks at them and then settled down to listen to the goings-on inside.

The hearing opened with Mr Lilburne being asked who his

counsel was. He settled his spectacles calmly on his nose and said, 'I intend to make my own plea. Indeed, I must do so – for there is not a lawyer in England who will dare say a quarter of what I wish to say for myself.'

'Very likely,' responded Justice Bacon sourly.

Free-born John knew how to hold centre-stage as well as any actor. He smiled and, suiting the action to the words, said, 'By your leave, I shall state my case holding my plea before me as lawyers do their briefs.'

'So long as *you* are brief, you may hold it howsoever you please,' came the tart reply. 'Begin.'

Like most of those about her, Bryony found the substance of Lilburne's appeal familiar. It was couched in much the same terms as *A Prisoner's Plea* and relied largely on the argument that, according to Magna Carta, the House of Lords had the power neither to try nor incarcerate him. He spoke at some length and, every time he made a particularly strong point, he paused to regard the judges over the rim of his spectacles while the crowd outside cheered.

When he finally came to the end of his statement, Justice Bacon rose unhesitatingly to deliver the court's reply.

'We have borne with your eloquence most patiently, Mr Lilburne. However, I must point out that the House of Lords is a superior court to this one . . . and I have no jurisdiction to interfere with its judgement. I therefore have no alternative but to remand you back to the Tower.'

An angry growl rumbled through the crowd and the soldiers in the doorway tensed visibly. A woman shrieked, 'If you're frightened to gainsay their lordships – why did you let John appeal at all, you great gobby lout?'

There was a murmur of general agreement. Inside the court, Free-born John threw back his head and, in a voice ringing with passion, said, 'If this is good law which you declare to me, then we are indeed all perfect slaves!'

The well-wishers surged like boiling soup. Justice Bacon, deciding that enough was enough, ordered the troopers back inside the court and had the doors slammed shut.

'What now?' shouted Bryony, over the noise around her.

'Nothing,' replied Sam tersely. 'They'll take him out another way to prevent trouble. Not that there'll be any.

Carrying him out of there by force isn't the answer – and there are regiments in the Mews, just waiting for the chance to break our heads if we should be silly enough to try.'

'But we can't just walk away!'

'Unfortunately, that's the only thing we *can* do.' He paused and then, staring down into her face, said abruptly, 'I'm taking you home. I ought never to have brought you in the first place. Trouble erupts at the least provocation these days – and what kind of protection do you think I'll be if we get caught in the midst of a riot?'

Bryony looked back into the bright, dark eyes and suddenly discovered something so breathtakingly obvious that she ought to have known it long ago. Over the strange hiatus in her chest, she said slowly, 'As much as anyone else – and more than most. But I wouldn't want you hurt for my sake. And naturally you must keep your promise to Uncle Jack.'

Sam swore under his breath. Then he said irritably, 'Do you think that's all I care about?'

'I know it isn't. But it's fairly important, just the same.' She smiled and, as if it was the most natural thing in the world, added reasonably, 'After all, if we can't manage to convince him that you can look after me, he's never going to consent to our being married, is he?'

For a long, airless moment Sam stood very still and simply stared at her. Then, drawing her briskly out of the crowd and down the steps into the drizzle outside, he said aridly, 'For the sake of brevity, I'll overlook the fact that the last time we spoke of your affections they were securely centred on Colonel Brandon. But precisely what have I done to make you think I'd any idea of marrying you?'

'Nothing.' Not at all cast down, Bryony returned his gaze with a sort of shining confidence. 'But you love me, don't you? Every bit as much as I love you.'

Sam worked hard at keeping both his eyes and his voice carefully blank. 'Have I said as much – or even hinted it?'

'No. But—'

'Then I suggest you wait until I do. And as for your sudden decision to love me . . . you'll have to forgive me if I say that I find it very hard to believe.'

She frowned a little and then her brow cleared again and she nodded. 'I can't really blame you for that. I was very silly about Gabriel, wasn't I? So it's up to me to prove that I've grown up . . . and that what I feel for you is real. For it is, you know. And one day you'll believe me.'

'Perhaps,' said Sam, steering her uncompromisingly towards the river so that he could hail a boat and take her home. 'But in the meantime, don't expect to charm any unwary declarations out of me, my girl – for I can tell you here and now that you certainly won't do it.'

While Bryony wondered how she could have come to love Sam so much without even knowing it, the New Model managed to defeat Rowland Laugharne's Welshmen at a place near St Fagan's and Londoners took to the streets shouting for the King instead of attending the thanksgiving services for their Army's victory. Riots in Bury St Edmunds over the setting up of a maypole had to be crushed by the county militia, the Surrey bank became a hotbed of discontent, and Sym Potter told Venetia that, though he'd so far been unsuccessful in finding Sir Ellis Brandon, he had met another acquaintance of hers.

'Captain *Langley*?' echoed Venetia.

'Aye. He said he'd be at The Leg on King Street tomorrow morning. But he's seen neither hide nor hair of Sir Ellis. I've already asked him.'

'Maybe not – but he'll have other news.'

'Happen he will.' Sym's gaze was dourly disapproving. 'You intend going, then?'

'Well, of course,' said Venetia. And, with a faint smile, 'But not, you will be glad to hear, on my own.'

They arrived at The Leg the next day to find Francis swathed in a shabby cloak and lounging in a corner with a pot of ale. His eyes, however, were full of all their usual languid audacity and, as Venetia slid on to the settle beside him, he drawled, 'God's greetings, my dear. You'll have to forgive me for not doing you the courtesy to bow – but I've never learned to do it clumsily and Court graces don't exactly belong in a hole such as this.'

'Modest as ever, I see,' remarked Venetia. And then, 'How

are you, Francis? And – more to the point – what have you been up to all this time?'

'Oh – this and that. I spent a few weeks on the Isle of Wight conferring with a fellow named Firebrace who's been trying to arrange the King's escape.' He sighed faintly. 'I don't envy him his task. He'd have accomplished it two months ago if his Majesty hadn't been unshakably convinced that he could get between the bars at his window without bothering to remove any of them.'

'And he couldn't?'

'No. He got stuck and the venture had to be called off. If it were not so serious, it would be comic. And, of course, the farce goes on. Firebrace hatched another plan involving disguises but the man who was to have gone in wearing it looked so peculiar that the guards wouldn't admit him. And when Firebrace decided to go back to his original scheme – but with the aid of files and *aqua fortis* – the King calmly said that he'd gone off that idea. Marvellous isn't it?'

Venetia sighed. 'But his Majesty is well?'

'Perfectly. In fact, Parliament's recent troubles have put something of a spring into his step. I only hope, for his sake, that his confidence isn't misplaced.'

'Yes.' She frowned down at her hands. 'How much real support does he have? The kind that's more than just weariness of Parliament, the Army and the excise?'

'It's hard to say. Essex is ready to rise . . . and Kent too – though I'll know more of that tomorrow when I join up with Lord Holland's force. As for what's happening further north, I know no more than you. Though the plain truth is that small pockets of rebellion will do us no good whatsoever unless we can ensure that they happen simultaneously. And that requires a miracle of organisation.'

Venetia's mouth curled. She said, without thinking, 'Gabriel could probably do it. How unfortunate that his services are already committed to the other side.'

The dark brows rose. 'Gabriel?'

'My husband,' she replied absently. Then, colouring uncomfortably, 'Ah. But you wouldn't know about that.'

'No,' agreed Francis smoothly. 'Supposing you tell me.'

She hesitated and then, in as few words as possible, did so. When she had finished, Francis eyed her in silence for a long moment before saying with rare simplicity, 'I won't waste time sympathising with you. I'm sure it's the last thing you need. But I can't help wondering why you're trying to find Ellis.'

'Let's just say that I have my reasons.' Venetia paused. 'Do you know who arranged the Duke of York's escape?'

'An intelligence officer named Bamfield. Why?'

'I just wanted to make sure of something.' She gave a small, bitter laugh and abruptly changed the subject. 'Eden Maxwell has gone North with Lambert, by the way. And Kate's in Genoa with her Italian. I thought you'd like to know.'

'You had that from Eden?' he asked sharply.

'Yes. He serves under Gabriel, so we've met a couple of times.' She stopped, struck by the rapidly escalating clamour from the street outside. 'What *is* that?'

Francis rose and peered through the window. A motley procession was marching purposefully in the direction of Westminster, surrounded by sympathisers and chanting '*For God and King Charles!*'

Francis looked down on Venetia. 'You hear? It's the Surrey men with their petition.'

'Demanding what?'

'All the usual things. Disbandment of the Army, dissolution of the Commons, re-instatement of the King and restoration of all the old, known laws. Where are you going?'

Venetia was already heading towards the door where Sym stood, clutching a tankard of ale. Over her shoulder, she said, 'Where do you think? I want to see for myself.'

Mr Potter stepped nimbly into her path.

'Best stay here and let 'em pass, mistress. There'll likely be trouble afore day's out.'

He was immediately impaled on a very direct violet gaze.

'I appreciate your concern but I won't have you control my actions,' said Venetia crisply. 'Stand aside.'

'Don't be stubborn, dear heart.' Francis had arrived at her elbow. 'Do you think that either he or I want to chance a cracked head on your account?'

'Then you'd better leave me to take care of myself, hadn't you?' she retorted. And ducked smartly under Sym's arm into the flowing tide of bodies in the street.

She was dimly aware, as the crowd swept her along, that Sym and Francis had dived in behind her and were trying desperately to catch up. It ought not to have been funny but, with exhilaration bursting through her veins, she could not help laughing. At her side, a girl in a soiled, gaudy dress laughed too and, over the din around them, shouted, 'That's right, love! We'll tell them buggers in Parliament a thing or two – and show 'em we're not frightened neither.' Venetia smiled back, kept a tight hold on her cloak and joined in with the collective cry.

Things quietened down a bit as the head of the procession reached Westminster and sent its petition in to both Houses – thus enabling Francis and Sym to finally battle their way to Venetia's side. Aside from the fact that her hair was tumbling down her back, she was quite unscathed and appeared to be enjoying a cheerful conversation with a girl in red whose occupation Francis identified at a glance.

'Are you *completely* insane?' he demanded, without a trace of his customary languor. 'You might have been killed.'

'Hardly,' sighed Venetia. 'And, anyway, I wasn't.'

The crimson-clad girl eyed Captain Langley admiringly and then winked at Venetia.

'Some people have all the luck! Your husband, is he?'

Venetia shook her head and, unable to resist the temptation, said coyly, 'Just a . . . friend.'

She was rewarded with a scream of raucous laughter and a bawdy jest. Francis winced but was not noticeably embarrassed. He said, 'Come on, Venetia. Enough is enough and it's time you got out of here and went home.'

'Not yet.' She shook his hand away. 'I'm not stirring a step until I know how the Commons have replied.'

Since it was impossible to remove her from the midst of the crowd against her will, Francis exchanged a look of mutual frustration with Sym and set about using his considerable powers of persuasion. Venetia listened politely before advising him to stop wasting his breath. And then the crowd

285

started to surge onwards again. Though the Lords had acknowledged the petition, it appeared that the Commons was refusing to do so. Somewhere ahead of Venetia, Francis and Sym, the men of Surrey had begun forcing their way into Westminster Hall.

The old chant of *'For God and King Charles!'* gradually transformed itself into a thunderous new cry of *'An old King and a new Parliament!'* Francis swore furiously and tried once more to stem Venetia's progress forward. She halted briefly, tore her arm from his grasp to an ominous accompaniment of rending stitches and resumed her stride. The girl in red swirled away ahead of her and was lost from sight.

The crowd accelerated its progress, leaving Francis and Sym with little alternative save that of simply keeping up. Then they were borne on into the vast, timbered space of Westminster Hall. The scene was one of utter confusion. Angry voices rang out ahead of them and, from behind, Francis could already hear the steady tramp of booted feet.

'Hell's teeth!' he muttered. And, seizing a handful of silver-gilt hair, hauled Venetia ruthlessly into the shelter of one of the lesser-court alcoves which lined the walls.

She howled and then forgot her pain as the first ranks of well-drilled infantry marched purposefully past her. On they came, row upon row, into the centre of the Hall where the Surrey ringleaders stood waiting to face them. Venetia held her breath while the very air seemed to shimmer with tension. And then all hell broke loose.

The petitioners, determined to avoid being evicted before they had received their answer, made a futile attempt at resistance and without anyone being quite sure how it had happened, a soldier was spitted on the end of somebody's blade. Infuriated but still remarkably disciplined, the five-hundred strong regiment immediately started clearing the Hall at push of pike as mercilessly as if they had been on a battlefield. Shouts and screams filled Venetia's ears as, crushed between Francis and Sym, she watched men being knocked unconscious and trampled beneath the feet of their friends who were now fleeing into Palace Yard.

It was over in minutes, for the petitioners had no chance at all against trained troops and they left the Hall littered with their wounded. Very slowly, as if cramp had invaded every muscle, Venetia turned from the human wreckage in front of her to look sombrely up at Captain Langley and said, 'They only came to deliver a petition, for God's sake! Why couldn't the Commons just accept and acknowledge it?'

'You know why,' returned Francis bitterly. 'It's because, having made war on the King to put an end to his so-called tyranny, Parliament has now become the tyrant his Majesty never was. But this is no place to discuss that. Let's see if we can find a boat.'

This, as it turned out, was impossible as the river had become the setting for scenes even more violent than those which had just taken place inside Westminster. Many of the petitioners had taken to the water in small boats from whence they were subjecting the troopers to a hail of coal and brickbats. Keeping Venetia well back from the centre of the disturbance, Francis looked on in silence while he pondered the safest way of getting her home. Before he could make a decision, however, the soldiers on the waterside came to the end of their patience when one of their officers was felled by a flying billet. They reached for their muskets and began to fire at will on selected targets. A man was hit in the shoulder and another went down like a stone from a bullet to the head. The mood of the day had suddenly changed into one which would result in more than a few bruises and broken bones. Suddenly people were dying.

Venetia started as the first shot rang out and then froze as her eye was caught by a familiar scarlet gown. For a moment, its owner stood arms akimbo in one of the boats, mouthing a series of shrill and probably vulgar taunts at the musketeers on the bank; then it jerked convulsively . . . and with an odd, dream-like slowness, toppled into the water to float like a bright pool of blood on the surface.

Her eyes wide and stark, Venetia took a step forward only to be stopped by Francis's hand.

'No,' he said flatly. 'There's nothing you can do for her. I'm sorry you're distressed, but I can only suggest that the next time someone gives you a piece of good advice, you take it. Now. Let's get out of here while we still can. I've an appointment in Kent that I don't want to miss.'

With Sym's help, Venetia managed to get home and into her bedchamber unseen, which, since her gown was torn and her hair in total disarray, saved a lot of unwanted explanation. It also gave her the opportunity to sob her heart out in private.

During the course of the next week or so, Parliament succeeded in conciliating the Common Council of the City by giving it more control over the Militia. Jack was pleased but Venetia considered it no epitaph at all for those who had died at Westminster and, in the event, it did nothing to stop the storm which was about to break. On May 21st, Kentish Royalists – aided, no doubt, by Captain Francis Langley – took possession of Rochester, Sittingbourne, Sandwich and Faversham; and five days later, despite the Parliament having hurriedly agreed to re-open talks with the King, Deptford and Dartford went the same way. Then, as Sir Thomas Fairfax was on the point of abandoning his intention to march northwards in favour of moving to secure Southwark, mutiny erupted in the Fleet. Six ships declared for his Majesty, refused to take Vice-Admiral Rainsborough back on board, reduced the castles of Walmer, Sandown and Deal, and finally laid siege to Dover.

While the City lay under a pall of expectancy and Venetia lived with a maelstrom of mixed emotions, the House of Commons gloomily recognised its mistake in appointing Rainsborough to the Navy where his Leveller views were universally despised. Hence they made the Earl of Warwick Lord High Admiral – effectively setting Rainsborough aside – and settled down to an uneasy night of hoping for the best.

Jack brought the news back to Shoreditch along with all the latest rumours. 'They're saying twenty thousand Kentish Royalists will rendezvous with a similar number from Essex tomorrow at Blackheath. They apparently intend throwing a bridge of boats over the Thames to ease communications between the two counties – in which they expect to be supported by the Navy.'

Annis laid down her fork and pushed her plate aside. She said tonelessly, 'It's starting all over again, isn't it? The taking of sides and being at odds with your neighbours . . .

and the killing. And for what? So the Parliament and the Army and the King can go on squabbling endlessly amongst themselves while the rest of us suffer?'

Jack laid his hand silently over hers, his expression profoundly grim. For a moment or two, no one spoke. Then Venetia asked if the City would rise.

'I doubt it. The general feeling is still that this rebellion can only depress trade even further. On the other hand, the Common Council is equally unlikely to help Parliament fight against the King because most people would be happier with him back on the throne.'

'One sees their dilemma. But it's a pity they can't decide where they stand,' she remarked dryly. And then, quoting one of the latest Royalist pamphlets, *'If Mammon be God, serve him; if the Lord be God, serve him. If Fairfax be King, serve him; if Charles be King, restore him.'*

'Quite. And if his Majesty hadn't signed this thrice-blasted Engagement with the Scots, the merchants and aldermen might have sufficient faith in his word to consider committing themselves to his cause,' returned Jack smoothly. 'As things stand, however, the balance of power lies north of the Tweed. For if Hamilton's army crosses the border while Fairfax is tied up here and Cromwell's still fighting in Wales, I doubt if Lambert has enough men to stop them marching all the way to London. And that's not a prospect which I imagine any of us wish to contemplate. Not even you.'

In the event, the Lord General prevented the Blackheath rendezvous by the simple expedient of occupying the place first. Then he sent a force to relieve Dover, left another to hold Croydon and set off with eight thousand men to reduce Rochester. Finding the opposite bank of the Medway strongly fortified against him, he pressed on to Maidstone. He took it in a hard-fought action during the night of June 1st and without being challenged by the bulk of Lord Holland's Royalist army – which was apparently lurking on nearby Pendenden Heath under the Earl of Norwich.

It wasn't until Isabel Molyneux arrived in Shoreditch, full of airy apologies for having stayed away so long, that Venetia learned the latter – and when she did, her expression became one of sheer exasperation.

'*Lord Norwich?* He must be sixty-five if he's a day and he knows about as much of warfare as I do! Less, probably.'

'My dear, I entirely agree with you. If it had been his son, now . . . well, things would be very different.'

'Not necessarily,' said Venetia. 'George Goring spent the last year of the war in a perpetual stupor. At least his father's mistakes will be made out of ignorance rather than the bottle.' She drew an impatient breath. 'My God. Norwich and Holland. What a perfectly matched pair! Francis must be tearing his hair out.'

'Francis?' Isabel yawned delicately.

'Francis Langley. I believe he may be serving under—'

'Of course! Celia's brother.' The too-vivid eyes exhibited mild interest. 'She and Hugo Verney went to Paris after the war, didn't they? I wonder if he ever married her? Or no. He couldn't, could he? His wife is still alive. And, as I recall, Celia was married to Kate Maxwell's brother. Did you ever meet him?'

Sighing, Venetia bowed to the inevitable.

'Yes. He was the man you saw with my sister, that night in King Street.'

'Really? *Not* the red-haired fellow with the scar?'

'The very same. He . . . he's my husband's Major.'

'*Is* he? Heavens – how incestuous it all sounds!'

Venetia gave way to unwilling laughter. 'And how like you to think so!'

'I know. Dreadful, isn't it?' Isabel settled into her seat with the air of one preparing to enjoy a cosy gossip. 'But do tell! How is your husband after his misadventures? I must say, under the circumstances it was extremely noble of you to salve his cuts and bruises. Then again . . . a man who knows how to please one in bed can be forgiven almost anything.'

Utterly disconcerted, Venetia said, 'I daresay. But I know nothing of Gabriel's talents in that direction.'

As soon as the words were out, she regretted them.

Isabel's brows soared. '*Really?* But how clever of you!'

Venetia stared warily back. 'Is it?'

'But of course! If the King gets his throne back and everything returns to normal, you'll be able to have your marriage dissolved on the grounds of non-consummation. It's quite, quite brilliant!' The plucked brows rose. 'Surely you must have thought of it?'

Venetia hadn't – and for one very good reason. A dissolution such as Isabel described naturally relied on medical evidence . . . evidence Venetia, of course, could not provide. But since she had no intention of revealing that she had slept with Ellis, she said lightly, 'Of course I've thought of it. Who wouldn't? But it isn't something I care to discuss.'

'Naturally. Most people would throw up their hands in horror. I, however, am beyond that.' Her ladyship paused; and then, her voice growing curiously smooth, 'We all have our secrets, my dear. Mine, for example, is that my beloved husband takes his pleasure with other men. But you may possibly have suspected that.'

Venetia's breath leaked away. 'No.'

'No? But you must have been aware that I had lovers.'

'Well – yes. I knew that, of course. But . . .'

'But you thought it was just in my nature. Quite.' For the first time, something shifted behind the empty cornflower eyes. 'I wanted a child, you know. I still do. But I need to find a man capable of giving me one.'

There was a long, airless silence. Finally, Venetia said reluctantly, 'I don't wish to pry . . . but surely George's preferences needn't stand in the way of—'

'They shouldn't – but they do. He's incapable with me. He always has been.' A hint of indefinable emotion entered the level tones. 'Can you imagine how that feels when one is seventeen and beautiful? Because I *was* beautiful, wasn't I?'

'Very,' agreed Venetia, feebly. 'You still are.'

'No. Not any more. Not since I started getting fat. I eat like a bird, you know, but still I put on weight. And men don't look at me any more.'

Venetia frowned a little. 'Have you consulted a doctor?'

'I've seen dozens – not one of whom was able to help and all of them costing a fortune. Which brings us back to George again; if he didn't squander so much money on his *bel-amis*, we might have some chance of paying our composition fines and then I wouldn't have to associate with the likes of Betty Cromwell.' Isabel shrugged, her eyes once more completely expressionless and her voice at distinct variance with her words. 'Of course, if my mother-in-law wasn't such a miser, we could secure the estate anyway. God knows she's got the money. She's just too niggardly to part with it. She hates me, you know – and always has. She blames me for not giving her a grandchild.'

'But that's monstrous!' said Venetia.

'Quite. Everything is my fault and none of it her darling George's. Sometimes I wonder how I've stood it all these years. Do you know, the old witch even spies on me and cross-questions my friends. That's why I've never suggested you should visit me in Covent Garden. I've no one left whom I can trust and I didn't want Susannah to get her claws into you as well.' The flow of words stopped abruptly and Isabel drew a sharp, unsteady breath. 'I'm talking too much. But you can't imagine the relief of being able to speak openly without fear of being judged.'

Venetia smiled bleakly. 'Oh – I think I can.'

'Really? But surely you have your sister?'

'No. Phoebe's political principles are of the flexible variety and she's too young to understand the other dilemmas brewing in my life so I've no choice but to continue keeping them to myself.'

For a moment, there was silence. Then Isabel reached out to lay her hand over Venetia's own and said simply, 'You have a choice now. And I can promise total discretion.'

Venetia kept her face expressionless while she thought it over. Silence was golden and secrecy had become a hard habit to break, but the prospect of pouring her increasingly muddled thoughts into a sympathetic ear was suddenly very tempting indeed. She said cautiously, 'Thank you. I appreciate the offer and will bear it in mind.'

'But you don't entirely trust me.'

'On the contrary.' A wry smile crept into the violet eyes. 'The trouble is that I don't know where to begin.'

Isabel sat back and folded her hands in her lap.

'The usual place is at the beginning.'

There was another small silence. 'I'm not sure where that is,' said Venetia aridly. 'But I suppose it's Ellis. Someone once described him as one complication too many . . . and they were probably right. He's back in England, you see, and I don't really know why. Worse still, I'm afraid to find out.'

Her ladyship smiled invitingly.

'Tell me,' she said.

Nine

After its first rush of successes, the Royalist cause seemed to fall into sharp decline. Lord Byron took Anglesey for the King – but Tenby and Chepstow surrendered before the end of May, leaving only Pembroke to withstand Cromwell's siege. Sir Hardress Waller defeated the Cornish Cavaliers, risings in Northamptonshire and Leicestershire were crushed with scarcely a murmur . . . and Parliament kept the loyalty of the City by announcing its intention to open new negotiations with the King – and also pardoning Denzil Holles and the other expelled Presbyterian MPs.

Consequently, by the time the remnants of the Royalist army reached Blackheath on June 3rd, Francis Langley had begun to wonder if the situation was not already beyond redemption. The truth, of course, was that the rising in Kent had begun much too soon. It had been planned to coincide with the invasion of the Scots – thus forcing Fairfax to divide his forces. Instead, it had flared up overnight in response to rumours that the County Committee intended to bring in the Army to burn and plunder – and that the Prince of Wales had landed at Sandwich. The first was mere scare-mongering gossip . . . and the second turned out to be an imposter. But by the time this was discovered, the die had already been cast.

Nevertheless, things had gone well at first. Dover, Rochester and Canterbury had fallen to their grasp and that part of the Fleet lying in the Downs had supported them. Francis and his friend, Sir William Compton, had experienced a faint stirring of optimism. And then had come Maidstone.

Since seven thousand of Lord Norwich's eleven-thousand-strong army were nothing more than an armed mob of untrained countrymen, he had elected to hold them in reserve and leave the task of fighting the Lord General to his more seasoned troops. And fight they had, reflected Francis bitterly. They'd defended each barricade and made Fairfax take every street by inches, until it was obvious that all was lost and a quarter of them lay dead or badly wounded. Then and only then had they abandoned Maidstone to the New Model and re-joined Lord Norwich – whose so-called reserves were already melting away like a handful of butter on a hot day. And then, of course, his lordship had been seized by the inexplicable conviction that, if they moved nearer to London, the City would declare for the King; which was why the three thousand men he had left were now all encamped on Blackheath in the rain – with the City gates shut fast in front of them and four troops of New Model Horse under Colonel Whalley approaching cautiously from the rear.

Then word started to filter through the assembled ranks that my lord Norwich had deserted them all and disappeared. As soon as Francis heard it, he stormed off to investigate – and collided with Major General Sir William Compton, returning from the same errand.

'Well?' he asked. 'Where the devil is he?'

'Chelmsford,' replied Will despairingly. 'He seems to have heard that thousands have risen in Essex, so he thought he'd take a ride over there and see for himself.'

'Alone and without bothering to consider how his absence would look to the men?'

'He probably didn't think anyone would miss him. Are your fellows getting nervous?'

'What do you think?'

'So are mine,' grunted Will. 'And if we're not careful, there are going to be more desertions.'

'Then I suppose it behoves you and I to see what we can do to promote confidence,' sighed Francis. 'How fortunate it is that you're a man of vast experience.'

The twenty-three year old brother of the Earl of Northampton, who had spent the first war holding Banbury for the King, grinned suddenly. 'And how fortunate that *you've* the cachet of having served under Rupert,' he retorted. 'Come on. Let's get started before there's nothing left to save.'

They did their best. They went from troop to troop explaining, cajoling and exhorting until they were hoarse but many of the men were too frightened to listen. Panic spread amongst them like wildfire and they started to desert – at first in handfuls and then in droves.

When, at length, it became plain that they must salvage something rather than lose all, Will Compton took the desperate step of proposing that they cross the river. This, he pointed out, would have the dual effect of distancing them from Whalley – who, now their numbers were so reduced, could pick them off any time he chose – and also place them on the Essex side of the Thames where they would have more freedom of movement and hopefully also be able to re-unite themselves with their errant Commander-in-Chief.

Any action being better than none, the idea found universal favour. The five hundred or so men who were left immediately set about crossing the river piecemeal in a flotilla of small boats with their horses swimming beside them. Then, once the evacuation was complete, they proceeded to surprise the districts of Stratford and Bow and establish themselves therein. By evening, Captain Langley was wet and tired and uncharacteristically short-tempered. And when Lord Norwich finally deigned to re-appear with the news that the Essex rising was but a myth, Francis had to commit the social sacrilege of shoving his hands into his pockets to keep himself from giving his lordship a severe shaking.

They took Bow Bridge – thus effectively severing communications between Essex and London; but the only support they received from the City were the sightseers who came by day and the little gaggles of watermen and apprentices who crept out by night to swell their miserably depleted ranks. Colonel Whalley, meanwhile, marched his men across London Bridge and settled at Mile End to assist Skippon's Trained Bands in blocking their advance; and in Chelmsford, the rising Lord Norwich had been unable to detect began with a bang when the local militia seized and imprisoned their County Committee for trying to stem the Royalist tide.

The first forty-eight hours at Bow were therefore naturally fraught with tension and Francis divided his time between wondering why Whalley didn't attack and trying to help Will Compton keep the men's spirits up. Then, whilst making a routine check on his sentries, he found himself face to face with Sir Ellis Brandon.

His brows soared and he said sharply, 'Where in Hades did you spring from? I wasn't aware you'd joined our small but merry band.'

'I haven't,' shrugged Ellis carelessly. 'I merely slipped along to let his lordship know that Parliament has rushed through an Indemnity Ordinance for all the Essex men – in the hope, no doubt, that it will tempt them to release the Committee members and go peacefully home again.'

'Thus leaving us without visible means of support. Wonderful. That's all we need.'

'I know. So Lord Norwich has ridden to Chelmsford—'

'Not again!'

'I beg your pardon?'

'Oh – never mind.' Francis fully understood the need to prevent the Essex rising from crumbling. He just hoped that this time his lordship had seen fit to make his intentions known – and also taken the precaution of leaving someone in command. He thought for a moment and then said abruptly, 'Your erstwhile fiancée is looking for you. Did you know?'

'Venetia?' said Ellis vaguely. 'No. Is she in London?'

'Yes. Approximately three miles from where we stand, to be precise, at the home of one Jack Morrell in Shoreditch. But it might be better if you sent a message rather than simply calling on her, for the said Mr Morrell is—'

'The bastard's foster-brother,' interposed Ellis, his eyes narrowing suddenly. 'Quite. From which I gather that dearest Venetia has made you privy to all our tribulations.'

'I wouldn't say all. Just some of them.'

'And did she also tell you why she wanted to see me?'

'Not a word,' replied Francis coolly.

'I see.' The brown gaze regained its usual, insouciant gleam. 'Ah well. No doubt all will be revealed in due course . . . and I am naturally agog to know why the bastard brought her south with him. One imagines that he wanted to keep her under his eye. But if she's managed to meet *you*, he can't have been making a very good job of it, can he?'

Francis found that Ellis's attitude grated on him. Flicking a speck of mud from his cuff, he said languidly, 'It's not a matter to which I've devoted much thought. But do tell me. If you're not staying here to pull rude faces at Colonel Whalley, what exactly *are* you planning to do?'

'Oh . . . this and that. Actually, I'm awaiting the outcome of certain private business. But I thought I might go to Scotland and join the invasion force.'

'Dear me. How very intrepid of you. And do you really think you'll be able to get that far?'

'Oh yes,' came the airy reply. 'Like most things, passing unnoticed isn't very difficult when you know how. And, having managed to get to and from the Isle of Wight without being picked up, I really don't anticipate any problem getting to the Duke of Hamilton.'

'I see. I trust his Grace will be suitably impressed,' said Francis. 'And now, I'm afraid, you must excuse me. So much time and so little to do, you know. Or should that be the other way about? No matter. Doubtless you can find your way out of our little camp without assistance . . . and if not, I'm sure any of our fellows will be delighted to point you in the direction of Shoreditch. Goodbye.' And he continued on his way, wondering what Venetia had ever seen in the fellow in the first place.

During the course of the night, Sir George Lisle, that veteran of the first war, slipped out of London with a large party of other Royalist gentlemen to join their ranks. And Lord Norwich returned from Chelmsford with the news that Sir Charles Lucas had successfully persuaded the Essex Trained Bands to continue bearing arms for the King. His lordship had also arranged that their own little force would join that of Sir Charles on the following day at Brentwood.

This, as Will Compton remarked to Francis while they prepared to decamp, was the only sensible decision the Earl had made since Maidstone. There was little they could achieve by themselves and nothing worth going back to Kent for. If rumour was to believed, Fairfax had relieved Dover and Canterbury was about to fall to Commissary-General Ireton . . . and though Deal, Walmer and Sandown still held out for the King, it was anybody's guess how long they could continue to do so because that part of the Fleet which had remained loyal to Parliament was already blockading them.

The rendezvous at Brentwood was accomplished amidst a fog of mutual relief on the 8th. Lord Norwich's motley collection of soldiers, apprentices and watermen combined with Sir Charles Lucas's army of militia and countrymen to form a total strength of some four thousand. Then the two forces set off *en masse* through the continuing showers for Chelmsford.

'It's not as bad as it looks, you know,' said Will to Francis during the course of the ride.

'Isn't it?' Captain Langley had progressed a good deal from the young man who'd gone off to the second Bishop's War with the hazy idea that the quality of an army was directly related to its size. 'Most of our fellows are raw recruits and less than half of them are armed. Or am I merely allowing myself to be unaccountably depressed by the weather?'

'Probably,' returned Will promptly. 'I never knew such a fellow for wanting to keep his coat dry and his boots clean. However. I was about to point out that – although the troops themselves aren't up to much yet – we at least have the advantage of a couple of superb officers.'

'You and I?' grinned Francis.

'In addition to you and I. George Lisle served with distinction right through the war and, as for Charles Lucas, soldiering's been his life. You know they say he was among the first to step through the breach at Breda?'

'No. I didn't know that. But so long as *he* doesn't say it, I daresay I shall like him well enough.'

Major-General Sir William Compton sighed and gave up. 'You know your trouble, don't you? You won't join the rest of us in exchanging a few bloodthirsty war stories.'

'I'm glad you've noticed that. I've been living in absolute dread of your giving me a day-by-day account of the siege of

Banbury.' A faint smile lurked behind the sapphire gaze. 'But your diagnosis was only half-right. My real trouble is that – though I've finally learned to do it adequately – fighting offers me nothing I want. In short, I'd rather be somewhere civilised with a book in my hand.'

They stayed the night at Chelmsford before departing again for Braintree – having been joined this time by my lords Loughborough and Capel. Colonel Whalley dogged them every step of the way but plainly did not feel he had enough men to risk an attack. He did not even attempt to prevent them invading Lord High Admiral Warwick's house, staying to dine and marching away in possession of two brass field pieces, three hundred muskets and pikes and a goodly supply of match, ball and powder. He simply did what he had been doing ever since Maidstone. He followed.

At Braintree they spent some time attempting to organise their army and holding a Council of War. The original intention had been to press on into Suffolk or Norfolk but Sir Charles Lucas suggested that it might be better if they marched instead to Colchester. Having been born there, he explained, it was possible that his name might bring in a substantial number of new, much-needed recruits. It was an eminently reasonable notion with which Lord Norwich and the other senior officers were pleased to agree. Consequently, on the following morning, to Colchester they went.

Or that, at least, was the general idea. Turning it into a fact proved rather more difficult – mainly because Honeywood's Trained Bands were blocking their way at Coggeshall and the ubiquitous Whalley was still pressing on in their rear. It was also rumoured that, having dealt with the bulk of resistance in Kent, Fairfax was now in hot pursuit of them as well. The result was they ended up having to go back through Braintree and make a night march by way of Halstead before finally arriving outside Colchester in the early morning of Monday June 12th.

Judging by the sixty or so armed horsemen spread across the road before the Head Gate to deny them access, their coming had been expected and was less than welcome.

'Oh dear,' murmured Francis. 'Perhaps Sir Charles isn't quite as popular hereabouts as he seems to think.'

Sir William shrugged. 'The place isn't exactly known for its Royalist sentiments – but I've heard that it's not in perfect sympathy with Fairfax either. At any rate, we'll soon know, won't we?'

Even as he spoke, a party of gentlemen left Sir Charles's side at the gallop and bore down on those standing before the turnpike. A scattering of pistol-shots tore the air and one of the Colchester men dropped where he stood, causing the rest to part like melting cheese before the onslaught.

'Hell's teeth!' muttered Francis. 'This isn't exactly the kind of beginning calculated to foster friendly relations.'

'It's no good thinking of that,' replied Will. 'We're committed now. And where else can we go?'

Veteran of both the German and the English wars, Sir Charles Lucas was not the man to be daunted by a small skirmish. Once the way was cleared, he led the army on with the kind of exquisite confidence that Francis could not help but admire and opened a dialogue with the suspicious faces peering down on him from above the gate. He pointed out that, having been born and bred not a mile distant, he needed no introduction; he spoke persuasively of the King and warned of the coming of Fairfax. But it was not until he vowed that his men would neither plunder the town nor molest its inhabitants that the gates were finally and grudgingly opened so that he and the army could make their way inside.

After that, Francis found that things started to happen very quickly. My lords Norwich and Capel very sensibly set aside their seniority of rank and handed responsibility for defence over to Sir Charles – who, like them, held a commission under the Prince of Wales but who had the inestimable advantage of being a professional soldier. And within an hour, Francis and his brother officers found themselves being subjected to a brisk but thorough briefing.

'Our scouts report that Fairfax has met up with Whalley and Honeywood at Coggeshall – and could therefore be here by tomorrow,' said Sir Charles flatly. 'That means we have very little time, gentlemen – and so must put that which we *do* have to good use. We didn't come here with the intention of withstanding a siege and I still hope it won't come to that.

But, just in case it does, I want barricades erected on all the surrounding roads and supplies brought in from the outlying district as quickly as possible. Cheese, flour, gunpowder, pitch – all the usual things. And cattle, of course. There is, however, just one small stipulation. No beasts are to be commandeered from any but those you know to be our enemies. Clear?'

There was a rumble of reluctant assent and Francis murmured wickedly to Will, 'Exactly *how* does one recognise a Roundhead sheep?'

'One doesn't,' came the soft, sardonic reply. 'One merely takes 'em all and hopes for the best.'

'And now,' continued Sir Charles, 'to the matter of the town's defences. Naturally, you will see them for yourselves as you go about your other duties – but, basically, we are protected to the north and east by the River Colne and surrounded for the most part by a wall some six to seven feet thick. Unfortunately, however, the walls follow the line laid down by the Romans and, except at one point, allow us no bastion from which we can hope to take our enemy in the flank.' He paused and then, smiling wryly, said, 'On the other hand, we can command the London Road from a battery in St Mary's churchyard; and my father's house – being situated on the higher ground just outside the town – will doubtless prove a very useful outpost. And that, gentlemen, is all I can profitably tell you. Accept your individual assignments from Major Savage – and don't expect much sleep tonight. That's all.'

Will Compton got the task of posting look-outs and arranging duty rosters. Francis, somewhat less suitably, found himself dispatched in search of provisions. He set off with half a dozen troopers and a couple of carts and resigned himself to a difficult and tiring afternoon.

In fact it was past ten in the evening before he returned – damp, hungry and bad-tempered – to the room in the tawny-stone Castle Keep where Will and a handful of other officers were snatching an hour's rest. And then, pulling off his hat to eye its bedraggled feather with acute disfavour, he said irritably, 'They say the sun shines on the righteous. Have we done something wrong?'

Sir William looked up from his lists and grinned.

'What's the matter, Francis? Had a bad day?'

'Heavens, no! I've ridden along countless muddy lanes, wasted a good deal of charm on red-faced fellows reeking of onions, missed my dinner and come back with a cartload of turnips, two sacks of flour and a few cheeses. I've had an absolutely *splendid* time.'

There was a scattering of weary laughter and, pushing a plate of bread and cold meat in the Captain's direction, Lieutenant Ross said ruefully, 'It sounds as though you did better than me, at all events. Every farmer I approached with a view to acquiring some livestock swore blind he'd been heart and soul behind the King from the first.'

'You shouldn't have asked them,' observed Will calmly.

'But Sir Charles said—'

'I know perfectly well what Sir Charles said – but what he doesn't know won't hurt him. And this is an emergency. If my fellows in Banbury had worried which were loyal cattle and which weren't, we'd have starved to death in '44.'

'As I understand it,' remarked Sir George Lisle from the hearth, 'you were down to your two last horses as it was.'

'We were. And that is precisely the point I'm trying to make,' returned Will austerely. 'When you don't know what you'll need, you take everything you can get.'

'There's a quaint family motto in there somewhere if only I could be bothered translating it.' A chunk of beef in one hand and a cup of wine in the other, Captain Langley subsided with less than his usual grace on to a settle. 'However. Let no one say I am a mere frippery fellow. What orders do we have for tomorrow?'

'You really want to know?' Tossing down his pen, the young Major-General stretched and stood up. 'Word has come in that Fairfax is a mile and a half away at Lexden with a couple of troops of Whalley's Horse. They'll presumably wait for the rest of the Army to arrive before they come any closer . . . but Sir Charles thinks we can expect to see some action in the next twenty-four hours.'

'So?' yawned Francis.

'So we're going to draw up in battle formation across the London Road and give the Lord General a warm welcome.'

304

There was a small, tense silence. Then, frowning at the slightly frayed end of his sash, Francis said gently, 'And how many men does popular rumour credit Sir Thomas with?'

'Around five thousand,' replied Will tersely.

'Ah. Is that all?' The sapphire eyes rose again, blandly smiling. 'Then – aside from the fact that they're well-trained, well-armed and every other thing that we're not – we don't have anything to worry about, do we?'

Taking Lieutenant Ross and a dozen of his own troopers with him, Francis set off at dawn on another foraging mission and this time came back with ten sheep, half a dozen cows and most of his customary sangfroid. He found the rest of the army busily deploying in full battalia – infantry in the centre, as usual, with cavalry on either wing. And pitifully small wings they were too, he decided coolly, as he rode in search of Major-General Compton and his orders.

'My scouts say Barkstead's Foot has just come up to join Fairfax, so we can expect them fairly soon I should think,' Will informed him crisply. 'Lord Norwich has put you on our right under Colonel Farr. You'll find your outer flank protected to a degree – because the land drops sharply away to the river just there. I myself will be over on the left beyond the Maldon Road with Sir George.'

'Protected by what?'

'Pikemen and musketeers in the nearby hedges,' he shrugged. 'The devil of it is that we've only about six hundred Horse altogether.'

'My own thoughts precisely.' Francis turned to go and then, looking back, drawled gently, 'Ah . . . and don't try and be a hero, Will – there's a good fellow.'

Sir Thomas Fairfax sent the usual summons to surrender and word filtered through the Royalist throng that Lord Norwich had replied that, having heard the Lord General was sick with the gout, he would shortly 'cure him of all diseases'. This inspired a certain amount of witty bravado and then everyone settled down to await the inevitable attack.

Waiting with his men, Francis employed his usual tactics of maintaining a gentle flow of eloquence. He suspected that his fellows would prefer a neck-or-nothing officer with a repertoire of bawdy jokes to one who remained perpetually calm and had a peculiar brand of humour. He didn't know that his style and elegance were a source of pride to his troops and that his deliberate coolness had a way of steadying even the most faltering nerves.

Although he took care not to let it show, Francis always hated the last hour before a battle. He did not consider himself a coward, but he found that, once everything was done, you were always left with too much time to think of what lay ahead. And the result, naturally, was that when Fairfax's regiments finally came into sight, he was extremely glad to see them.

Drums were beating and colours flying. It was clear from the first that the New Model's cavalry severely outnumbered their own, and equally clear that the Lord General hoped to enter Colchester as quickly as he had Maidstone by launching an immediate attack with his infantry. Francis tensed in the saddle and waited for Colonel Farr's signal. Then, when it came, he raised his sword high in the air and shouted, '*Now*, gentlemen. For God and King Charles!'

He'd learned the art of the successful cavalry charge from Rupert of the Rhine. At Angers, one was taught to pause half-way in order to discharge one's pistol, but the Prince had changed all that. 'Let your horse do the work,' he had said. 'Ride as fast as you can in close formation and smash into the enemy. That's the way to win.' And he was right. It *had* been the way to win . . . until Cromwell picked up the idea and taught it to his fellows as well.

Away to his left, Barkstead's infantry was being hotly repulsed by Sir Charles and Lord Norwich's raw, untried recruits. Francis experienced a moment of faint elation. Then he and his troopers met the enemy cavalry head on and the battle exploded around him.

As always happened at such times, thought was suspended in favour of pure reflex. Controlling his horse with his left hand and the pressure of his knees, Francis alternately attacked and defended himself with his sword-arm – slashing and thrusting, swivelling and lunging with a good deal of force but no finesse whatsoever. An iron-helmeted trooper swept down upon him and was disabled with a savage blow to the wrist, only to be replaced with another and another. Francis's ears were full of the sounds of steel on steel, of men screaming as they fell; and of his own voice, yelling commands and encouragement. Further away the rattle of musket-fire was being thunderously punctuated by the dull boom of artillery, and, somewhere, a lone trumpet urgently reiterated the Recall. Francis didn't know that the Royalist infantry had already repelled Barkstead's Foot once and was about to do it again. He simply blocked out everything except for a fragment of song which echoed eerily in his head while he addressed the job in hand.

> *Captains in open fields on their foes rushing*
> *Gentlemen second them with their pikes pushing.*
> *When cannons are roaring and bullets are flying*
> *He who would honour win must not fear dying.*

Well, his men *weren't* fearing it, but against such superior numbers, sheer courage was not enough and gradually they started to give ground. Suspecting that his losses were already higher than their little army could afford, but with no idea what was happening throughout the battle as a whole, Francis fought on for a while longer while they continued to be pushed further and further back on their own lines. Then, choosing to save what he could rather than allow his fellows to be massacred, he started bellowing an order to retreat. Five minutes later, he became aware that the rest of the cavalry must have suffered a similar fate, for Sir Charles Lucas was already withdrawing the infantry back inside the town walls. The battle for Colchester, it seemed, was over – at least for today.

But of course it wasn't quite over. There was still the miserable business of fighting a lengthy rear-guard action around the Head Gate while the Foot completed its withdrawal – during which they managed to capture a Parliamentary cannon but were unable to prevent the last four or five hundred men being caught or killed. After that, however, things grew marginally brighter.

Scenting an easy victory, Colonel Barkstead pressed on

through the Head Gate and fell immediately into the trap Sir Charles had thoughtfully prepared for him. A body of Horse galloped hell for leather downhill at him from the street ahead and a party of Foot nipped him in the flank. Taken by surprise and caught between the devil and the deep, the Colonel's men turned and fled. The Head Gate slammed shut behind them, its bar dropped reassuringly into place – and Lord Capel pegged it with his cane.

Amidst the chaos within, Francis slid wearily from the saddle and wiped the sweat from his eyes. It was growing dark and he was bone weary but there was still work to be done, making sure that those houses which had been fired during the fight were properly doused. And after that, as evening became night and Fairfax attempted to storm their defences, it was necessary to somehow find yet more energy in order to repel the attack.

It wasn't until the early hours of Wednesday morning that he finally came across Will Compton pacing up and down the west wall by the Balkerne Gate and, hazy with fatigue, said, 'You're still in one piece, then.'

'Barely,' came the frank reply. 'They came more or less straight through us and tried to pincer the infantry. If it hadn't been for the musketeers, they'd have done it, too.' Sir William hesitated as if marshalling his thoughts. 'You know what will happen now, don't you?'

'I imagine they'll settled down for a siege.'

'Yes. I can't say I'm looking forward to it. After Banbury, I hoped never to be in this situation again. And this time – unless the Scots move both quickly and with remarkable effect – there's no one to send help.' He paused again. 'I'm so full of my own memories, I never thought to ask. Have you ever been besieged?'

Francis nodded slowly. 'I was at Bristol when Rupert surrendered it. And I can't help but remember something he said about not being able to hold a town that doesn't want to be held.' A faint, resigned smile touched his face and then was gone. 'I just wonder how true we're likely to find that here . . . or whether instead our main problem will be coming up with a hundred different ways to cook turnips.'

* * *

While Sir Thomas Fairfax tightened his grip on Colchester, by blockading the River Colne, Samuel Radford's personal dream finally became a reality. And when he was sure that absolutely nothing could go wrong, he floated off to Shoreditch on a tide of pure elation to tell Mistress Morrell.

Not having clapped eyes on him for the last three weeks and suffering the torments of the damned as a result, Bryony stood like a stone and let his torrent of words flow past her while she tried to decide whether she wanted to throw herself on his neck or box his ears. But at length the blaze of sheer excitement in his eyes and the newspaper he was brandishing in his hand pierced her cocoon and, instead of demanding where the hell he had been all this time, she heard herself saying weakly, 'What? You've done *what*?'

'Helped found a Leveller newspaper!' shouted Sam, for the fourth time. 'Look at it – the first edition, hot from the press! And it's licensed, too!' He caught her about the waist and swung her crazily around the parlour. 'My God! I'm even being *paid*! Not vast sums, it's true, but paid nonetheless. Can you believe that?'

Hovering on the brink of laughter and faintly breathless from something other than exertion, Bryony shook her head and took the opportunity to lean a little closer. 'No. Is it really legitimate?'

'More than that. It's virtually sacrosanct,' he crowed. 'It belongs to Gilbert Mabbott, the official censor, for God's sake! It's too good to be true!'

She stared dreamily into his face. 'Yes.'

Sam looked into softly inviting brown eyes and experienced an upsurge of perfectly natural temptation. For a moment, he hesitated. Then, too full of exhilaration to resist but still with enough sense to make it appear casual, he dropped a light, fleeting kiss on her lips.

Bryony let her head fall back and reached up to put her arms around him, only to find herself embracing empty air. From two paces away, Mr Radford grinned and held out his newspaper for inspection as if nothing had happened.

'Mabbott wanted to publish it as *The Moderate Intelligencer* after John Dillingham's paper of that name was suspended, but he couldn't get permission. So he's called it *The Moderate* instead . . . and personally, I prefer it.' He paused to push back the lock of hair that tended to stray perpetually across his brow and then said, 'I don't want it to sail under false colours, Bryony. I want it to make its own mark and become something more than any other paper has ever been. Is that presumptuous?'

She sat down, sorry that he hadn't kissed her properly but unable to resist his enthusiasm. 'No. It's splendid. But how will you achieve it?'

'By making *The Moderate* social as well as political. I've persuaded Mabbott to collate pamphlets and newsletters and reports from all around the country – partly so that people here in London will know what is happening elsewhere but also to create some kind of overall picture. And, in case that's not enough to make us different, William Walwyn has agreed to compose a series of articles designed to *explain* things.'

'What sort of things?' asked Bryony.

'Anything people may have had difficulty understanding,' he replied, seating himself beside her on the settle. 'The reasons for the first war, for example.'

'Goodness!' She smiled and tucked her hand in his. 'If Mr Walwyn can explain *those*, he must be a genius. Will you have space enough in your paper, do you think?'

Sam laughed. 'Since we're to publish six pages every Tuesday, it shouldn't be a problem. Well? What do you think of having a full-blown Leveller newspaper? It's my own concept, of course, and one I've been peddling in certain quarters for so long I'd given up hope of having it taken up. I must write to Abby. She'll be proud of me.'

'*I'm* proud of you too,' said Bryony. Then, pulling her hand free and sitting up very straight, 'Who's Abby?'

The dark eyes gleamed. 'Wouldn't you like to know?'

'Yes,' came the tight reply. 'And – and if you don't tell me this minute, you can go away and never come back!'

Sam shrugged. 'Suit yourself,' he said. And got up.

Bryony surged to her feet, almost oversetting a bowl of roses in her haste to grasp his arm. 'Wait! I didn't mean it. You know I didn't. I just thought . . .'

'Thought what? That I've other irons in the fire, so as to speak?'

She flushed. 'Y-yes. And have you?'

He let her wait for a moment and then said, flatly, 'No. Abby is my sister.'

Her eyes widened. 'But you haven't got a sister!'

'Yes I have. Two, as it happens.'

'Then why haven't you ever mentioned them? God knows you've talked enough about your horrible brother Jonas.'

Sam sighed, frowning a little. 'Talking about Jonas is easy. He's a sort of macabre joke. And my eldest sister, Ruth, is like enough to him to make any description of her superfluous. But Abby . . . Abby is different. And I suppose the truth is that I still miss her.'

Bryony sank slowly back on to the settle.

'Is she still at your home in Banbury?'

'No. She's married to a Royalist gentleman who lives near Newark.'

'Oh.' She thought for a moment. 'And you don't like him?'

'On the contrary. He's one of the best fellows I ever met and, judging from her letters, he's making her ecstatically happy. And that,' Sam finished pleasantly, 'is all I have to say on the subject. Unless you'd like me to add that you more than fulfil any need I have for feminine companionship and that I have never, in the last year or so, even glanced at another girl?'

'I'd like it very much,' agreed Bryony with a coquettish smile. '*Are* you adding it?'

'Not at the moment. But if you refrain from plaguing me, I might get round to it eventually.'

As often happened, she found herself torn between laughter and calling him something very rude. The result, on this occasion, was that she did both and then asked lightly, 'Where are you printing *The Moderate*?'

'Wapping.' He grinned and reached for his hat. 'You still haven't said whether or not you're pleased.'

'Oh *Sam*.' She rose again to face him, her expression suddenly very earnest. 'You *know* I'm pleased. How could I not be? Every other faction has its own newspaper, so why not us? Only . . . well . . .'

'Uncle Jack may not like it?'

Bryony stared at him while a tide of rare anger washed over her. Finally she said, 'If that's the only logic you consider me capable of, I think you'd better go.'

This time it was perfectly plain that she meant it and an odd gleam of satisfaction lit Sam's eyes. He said, 'And what should I think?'

'You know very well.' She drew a slightly ragged breath and spread her hands in a gesture at once impatient and appealing. 'I know you won't marry me yet or even s-say that you care – and I can understand why. But I *do* need to know that you're safe. I've been scared silly these last few weeks, not knowing where you were or being able to find anyone who'd seen you. And I – I *hate* it!'

Her voice ended on a distinct sob and there were tears on her lashes. Feeling rather lower than the rat she had just called him, Sam forced himself to say dispassionately, 'You hated it when the Colonel went off to marry the lovely Venetia, but you seem to have got over it fast enough.'

'Because I never loved him!' cried Bryony, stamping her foot. 'You know I didn't. You knew it before me. He – he seemed so glamorous and sophisticated and I'd never seen anyone else like him so I – I conceived a stupid fancy for him. But that's all it was. Just a silly infatuation. For I never really knew him – and still don't.'

Impassive black eyes met drenched brown ones.

'Go on,' said Sam.

She looked disconcerted. 'What?'

'Go on. You're implying that what you feel for me is different – but you haven't said *how*.'

'Haven't I?' She brushed the tears away, frowning as if confused. 'Well, then. It's different because it's more than just love. We're friends as well. And you're like the other half of me. Does that make sense?'

Seconds ticked by in silence before a slow smile curled Sam's mouth. Then, laying his hat carefully back on the table, he said simply, 'Oh yes. It's what I've felt myself ever since that night at Wapping.'

Bryony's heart gave a single, loud thud. 'T-truly?'

'Truly.' The smile altered and he shrugged a little. 'If I've made you miserable, I'm sorry. But, even though I'm neither

312

glamorous nor sophisticated, I had to be sure you weren't just exchanging one infatuation for another.'

She swallowed rather hard. 'And now you are?'

'I believe so. Though it has to be said that one way and another you're getting a rather poor bargain.'

'I don't agree.'

'No. I realise that. Now.'

'I'm glad to hear it.' A smile trembled into being. 'So why don't you kiss me?'

The dark brows rose. 'Because I was waiting to be asked,' said Mr Radford politely. And then swept her into an embrace that wasn't polite at all.

June wore by on leaden feet. Major-General Lambert bottled Sir Marmaduke Langdale up in Carlisle, the Prince of Wales sailed to Holland in readiness for an eventual landing in England and the Duke of Hamilton's recruiting problems were solved when the Scots Parliament handed power over to the Committee of Estates, on which his Grace ruled supreme. Meanwhile, the siege of Colchester moved into its third week and my lord Holland, having spectacularly failed to mount a relief force on horses smuggled out of London, began an ill-fated rising in the streets of Kingston on July 5th.

It lasted a mere forty-eight hours. Although the Earl's company included the Duke of Buckingham and John Dalbier – the experienced Dutch mercenary who had helped Cromwell take Basing House – it was no more than six hundred strong in all. Nor, as he found to his cost, was it easy to increase it. When he tried to take Reigate castle, the townsfolk declined to support him and, when he withdrew to Dorking, he learned that a division of the New Model was already in hot pursuit.

It overtook him at Ewell, drove his little force back into Kingston and eventually forced a full-scale confrontation on Surbiton Common – where, although his men fought well, the outcome was never in doubt. By the morning of July 8th, Lord Holland knew himself beaten. With the two hundred staunch fellows left to him, he made his way as far as St Neots where Dalbier was killed and he himself captured in a surprise attack during the early hours of the 10th. The Duke of Buckingham – cleverer or perhaps just more fortunate – slipped the net and escaped abroad.

To the Northern Royalists, counting on a necessary diversion while the Scots invaded and to those at Colchester, knowing they could not hold out indefinitely without relief, the failure of Lord Holland's enterprise was a bitter blow. And to Venetia Brandon, anxiously evaluating every scrap of news, it was somehow the catalyst she had been subconsciously waiting for. As soon as she heard the outcome of the skirmish at Surbiton, she sought out Jack and Annis and said, 'I hope you won't think me ungrateful – but I've decided that it's time I went home.'

Startled concern filled Annis's eyes and Jack said bluntly, 'I don't think that's a very good idea. With unrest and uprisings all around us, this is no time to be making a long journey. And if the Scots cross the border—'

'*If* they do,' cut in Venetia bitterly. 'Personally, I'm beginning to wonder if his Grace of Hamilton's army isn't merely a myth. But if it's not – and if it ever marches South – that's all the more reason why I should be at home with my own people instead of wasting my days here.'

'But Gabriel said—'

'Quite. And I've lingered here two full months since he said it. But our flax should be ready for pulling, this spring's wool ought by now to be nearly all woven, and, before we know where we are, the harvest will be upon us. And that being so, I imagine Gabriel would be relieved to know that I am taking care of matters in his absence.' She paused, smiling wryly. 'For what it's worth, I believe all that to be true. But the simple fact is that I intend to leave for Yorkshire tomorrow for no better reason than that I've already stayed away too long.'

'Your mind is obviously made up,' observed Jack. 'But how exactly do you propose to travel?'

Her brows arched. 'The same way we came. The coach is still here and we have Sym. But if it will set your mind at rest, I suppose I could also hire a couple of outriders.'

'If you expect to leave here, you most certainly *will* hire some outriders. The countryside's bristling with footpads, thieves and sundry groups of resurgents. And if something happened to you, I'd never forgive myself – let alone survive what Gabriel would do to me.'

Venetia gave a sudden, genuinely amused laugh.

'You know very well that Gabriel would say it was entirely my own fault – as, indeed, it would be. But nothing is going to happen to me. And, if it did, I am more than capable of taking care of myself. I've had years of practice. So there's no need to worry. None at all.'

Jack thought about it for a moment and then came to the reluctant conclusion that it was time to speak or forever hold his peace. He said, 'And what of Gabriel's half-brother? Have I no need to worry about him either?'

The laughter vanished from her eyes leaving them suddenly cool. 'Ah. I should have guessed. You're less anxious about me being robbed or otherwise molested *en route* than about what mischief I may get up to when I arrive.'

'Stop putting words in my mouth and answer the question.'

'What do you want me to say? That I don't know where Ellis is? I don't. That I've no intention of co-operating in any of his schemes? I haven't. That I'm not going to leap into bed with him? Guess. I wouldn't want to spoil your fun and it's none of your damned business anyway.'

'Perhaps not.' It was Annis who spoke. 'But Gabriel's well-being is. And I'd like you to understand that he's no more impervious to hurt than anyone else.'

'I *do* understand it.'

'Do you? Sir Robert complicated Gabriel's childhood by telling him both more and less than any thinking person would deem necessary; then, twenty years later – and without apparently stopping to wonder if it would be welcome, he made a Will which effectively re-arranged Gabriel's adult life. At best all this could be called inconsiderate; at worst, it's simply cruel. For Gabriel never wanted Brandon Lacey – or your lands either. And if you've never been sure of that in the past, it's time you started believing it now.'

It was probably the longest speech Venetia had ever heard Annis make and, when she stopped speaking, there was a long, almost airless silence. Finally, however, Venetia said slowly, 'You might equally, with perfect truth, have pointed out that he didn't want to marry me any more than I wanted to marry him. But, regrettable as that is, it at least has one saving grace.'

'Which is what?' asked Jack.

The violet eyes surveyed him with a complete absence of expression. 'Isn't it obvious? You can only be hurt by someone you care for. And Gabriel regards me with total indifference occasionally verging on irritation.'

Venetia left Shoreditch the following day with Phoebe, Sym, her maid and the two outriders engaged by Mr Morrell to protect them all on the arduous journey back to Yorkshire. She still did not quite understand the sense of unease that had taken possession of her or know why it suddenly seemed so important to get home again, only that both were unequivocably true.

It was not until they arrived in Oxford that she learned that the Duke of Hamilton's far-from-mythical army had crossed the border at last and was reputedly moving slowly but surely southwards.

The Rising Tide

August to December, 1648

Or love me less or love me more
    And play not with my liberty,
Either take all or all restore
    Bind me at least or set me free;
Let me some nobler torture find
    Than of a doubtful, wavering mind,
Take all my peace, but you betray
    Mine honour too this cruel way.

'Tis true that I have nursed before
    That of hope of which I now complain,
And having little, sought no more
    Fearing to meet with your disdain;
The sparks of favour you did give
    I gently blew to make them live;
And yet have gained by all this care
    No rest in hope, nor in despair.

Sidney Godolphin

One

By the time the Northern Army settled down at Barnard Castle in the latter part of July, Colonel Brandon and Major Maxwell agreed that they were heartily sick of hot-footing it around the remoter parts of the kingdom, through the rain and mud, and would be glad to see some real action. Certainly, unless one counted a few skirmishes with Sir Marmaduke Langdale's outposts, there had been precious little of it before the Scots crossed the border, or even, as things had turned out, since. It was just a constant game of retreat, wait and retreat again.

The problem, of course, was one of numbers. With detachments tied up in Northumberland and others besieging Pontefract (which the Royalists had seized sneakily, by sending in an advance-party disguised as peasants), Major-General Lambert was left with only four and a half thousand men to face the invasion. And the Duke of Hamilton, having entered England with an army of roughly ten thousand Scots, had since combined with Sir Marmaduke's three thousand English Cavaliers. Of course, numbers weren't everything – and every report Lambert received on the condition of the Royalist forces spoke of raw Scottish recruits, a lack of the most basic supplies and no artillery at all. On the other hand, when the odds were three to one in the enemy's favour, a little caution was undoubtedly necessary.

Although Gabriel understood this perfectly well, it didn't make the next two weeks any easier. After politely inviting Lambert to surrender and receiving an equally polite refusal, Hamilton had marched south on July 8th to join Langdale at Carlisle, while Lambert kept a watchful eye on them from Penrith. A week later, the Royalists advanced towards Penrith and Lambert withdrew to Appleby – where Colonel

Brandon spent his thirty-fifth birthday indulging in a little hand-to-hand combat when the Scots' advance guard made the mistake of overtaking them. Then, just as Gabriel was beginning to enjoy himself, Lambert ordered a further retreat on Barnard Castle.

There were two excellent reasons for this. The first was that Hamilton's line of march led Lambert to believe that he intended to cross into the West Riding of Yorkshire by way of Brough and the Stainmore Pass – a move which Lambert hoped to prevent by placing himself squarely in the way; the second was that Cromwell, having finally succeeded in taking Pembroke, had dispatched his own 10th Horse northwards to reinforce Lambert while he himself followed on more slowly with the infantry. And Barnard Castle was as good a place to rendezvous with the expected cavalry as it undoubtedly was to stop the Scots.

Gabriel knew this but had never been one for kicking his heels. Eden knew it, too, and cursed the inactivity which gave him more time than he wanted to dwell on his personal concerns. These, in fact, had been weighing upon him since just before they had left Windsor; and, though he had not uttered a word about them, he had been growing progressively moodier – with the result that, by the time Cromwell's cavalry eventually arrived on the 27th, Gabriel was tired enough of black looks and monosyllabic answers to say crisply, 'All right. What is it this time?'

'I beg your pardon?' The hazel gaze was warily cool.

'And so you should. I'll admit that my own *joie-de-vivre* is at a fairly low ebb, but watching you gnaw away at yourself with such dedication is enough to give anyone the marthambles. So I'll ask you again – and for the last time. What's the matter?'

Eden frowned, opened his mouth on a blighting denial and then appeared to change his mind. Shrugging as if the matter was of small importance but speaking in a voice which could have cut bread, he said, 'Felicity's marrying Ralph Cochrane at the beginning of September. And notwithstanding the fact that the entire family is to be gathered together for the event – including Kate and Felix all the way from Genoa – Felicity wants me to be there as well.'

320

Gabriel leaned back and contemplated his Major over folded arms. 'And what answer have you given her?'

'None.'

'Then don't you think you should?'

'Probably. But what can I say?'

'What do you *want* to say?'

'No! But I can't do it,' replied Eden bitterly. 'With Father dead, I ought to be there – not just for Felicity but for Mother. And Ralph is one of the best friends I ever had. I can't just refuse.'

'Then go.'

'I can't do that either – or, at least, I don't think I can. I'm not ready for a full-scale family reunion. Particularly not one that's bound to take place in a positive welter of euphoria.' He paused. 'I've been hoping I'd be safe in saying I'd be there if my duties permitted it. But now Pembroke's fallen and Cromwell's on his way, I could get caught out on that one.'

'Meaning that once Old Noll gets here, he'll want to bring the Scots to battle without delay and that, if we win at the first stroke, you could find yourself free as a bird before the end of August?' suggested Gabriel dryly.

'Quite. With Cromwell here, the odds will be greatly reduced; we are properly equipped for the task in hand – whereas Hamilton's men are having to pick up food and ammunition along the way because they haven't sufficient horses to pull their supply wagons; and our fellows are experienced campaigners – not green boys who've never handled a pike or a musket before. All in all, I think we'll trounce them. Don't you?'

'I think it very probable,' agreed Gabriel. 'I don't know very much about Hamilton but the popular view seems to be that he's willing rather than able – and monumentally unlucky. Also, Lambert suspects that he may be having certain difficulties with his second-in-command.'

'Callander?' said Eden. 'That wouldn't surprise me. They say he's not a great one for taking orders. Mind you, we might have a similar problem ourselves when Cromwell turns up. After all, Lambert is no tyro – and a local lad, to boot. He may not be especially eager to hand over the reins to Old Noll just like that.'

'Possibly not. But he'll do it. He's too professional to do otherwise.'

'Pity poor Hamilton, then.' Eden sought a means of keeping the conversation on an impersonal level and found it. 'How do you rate his chances of getting help?'

'From abroad? Not very high. Now Spain has made peace with the Dutch and is able to pursue its hostilities with France instead, Mazarin is unlikely to spare any French troops. And William of Orange appears determined to remain strictly neutral. So provided the Irish continue squabbling busily amongst themselves over religious matters and the terms of the Cessation, I'd say Hamilton is going to have to face us as he now stands.' Gabriel held the Major's gaze with a faintly satiric one of his own. 'However. None of this alters your fundamental problem, which is not whether you'll still be fighting the Scots on the day your sister is married but whether you're ever going to summon up enough nerve to face up to your past. And, on present showing, it's beginning to look as if you won't.'

A hint of colour stained the scarred face and Eden said furiously, 'I have faced up to it. What I *don't* want to do is bloody well *wallow* in it.'

'I wasn't aware that anyone was asking you to.'

'Felicity is, and Kate will too, given half a chance.'

'Then let them,' came the calm reply. 'Let them and be done with it. You've been ducking the issue for three years and that's more than enough. Moreover, if you don't deal with it now, you never will and it will rule your life. Is that what you want?'

'No.' Eden arose with sudden violence. 'And I don't want a barrage of well-meaning platitudes either.'

The dark brows rose and Gabriel's expression became one of acute irritation. He said, 'In that case I suggest you keep your bouts of self-pity well-hidden in future and refrain from wasting my time.'

'My pleasure!'

'Good. Then, since it's our night for sentry-duty, you may now do a round of the out-posts and check that no one is getting slack. That will be all, Major.'

The tone was one Gabriel very rarely used and it pulled

Eden up short. For a moment he hesitated and then, with a small, crooked smile, inclined his head and saluted.

'Colonel,' he said correctly. And strode from the room, closing the door behind him with a distinct snap.

Over the next few days, this conversation was never again referred to and, though their working relationship continued precisely as usual, a blanket of reserve – which neither tried to remove – settled over their friendship. Eden spoke of it to no one, for the simple reason that no one was close enough to him to ask. And when Wat Larkin tried probing the situation with Gabriel, he was promptly told to mind his own business for once.

As July drew to a close, Hamilton at last received his artillery, along with four thousand reinforcements and proceeded to take Appleby Castle. Then, at the beginning of August, they took to the road again, marching, as Lambert had expected they would, towards Brough and the Stainmore Pass. Scouts were sent out from Barnard Castle and all proper measures taken. Consequently, when misfortune struck, it was hard to say quite how it had come about.

The first Gabriel knew of it was when he was summoned to an urgent council of officers and, in a voice tight with temper, John Lambert said, 'The unthinkable has happened, gentlemen. We appear to have lost touch with the enemy.'

A distinct chill invaded the room and, for a time, no one spoke. It was the first rule of warfare. Always keep track of your enemy's movements.

Gabriel finally broke the silence.

'How?' he asked.

'I don't know yet – though you may rest assured that I shall be finding out,' replied the Major-General grimly. 'We know they reached Brough. But then they appear to have turned south towards Kirkby Stephen from where they could choose to go on into Lancashire, or cross the Pennines by way of Wensleydale or Skipton. And since we still can't risk bringing them to battle and are condemned to wholly preventative measures, we must now consider moving our own position; to which end I wish to withdraw to a point between Knaresborough and Leeds. From there we can keep an eye on Skipton, Wetherby and the main road south.' He rose and regarded them all stonily. 'We are going to Otley, gentlemen – and as soon as possible.'

It was a long march and the route took them within three miles of Brandon Lacey. Gabriel experienced a surprisingly strong desire to pay a flying visit to Sophia and seek out Dick Carter, but reason told him that this was no time to be asking for leave of absence, no matter how briefly; and, in any case, he wasn't in the habit of abandoning his men.

It wasn't until after they reached Otley that he realised there was another, perfectly simple solution and, when he did, he wasted no time in putting it into effect.

'Go to Brandon Lacey?' echoed Wat. 'Me? Why?'

'Because you've got the time and I haven't,' came the succinct reply. 'I want to know how everything's going – the weaving, the flax, the preparations for the harvest. Everything. And if Carter has any problems he feels I should know about, I want to hear what they are.'

'So I can go back again with your orders?'

A gleam of humour warmed the grey eyes. 'Probably.'

'I see.' Wat spat into the fire. 'There's nothing else you want me to do while I'm at it, is there? Take a message to Shoreditch – find the Scots for you – stick a broom up my arse and sweep the roads?'

'Not at the moment,' said Gabriel. 'But I'll give the matter some thought. Meanwhile, you needn't break your neck to get back here today. Tomorrow will do well enough.'

Mr Larkin snorted and stamped out. It was hard to tell whether or not he was laughing.

He returned late the following evening just as the Colonel concluded an exhausting day making sure the regiment was better housed and fed than it had been the day before.

'Well?' asked Gabriel, stripping off his wet cloak and crossing the room in search of the ale-jug.

'Is it?' grumbled Wat, throwing his equally sodden hat down beside the hearth. 'God rot the North! It never does anything but bloody rain!'

Gabriel shoved him unceremoniously into a seat by the fire and handed him a pot of ale.

'What did Carter have to say?'

324

Wat half-drained the tankard, belched and looked back sourly. 'Nothing. I didn't see him.'

There was a small pause. 'May I ask why not?'

'Because your lady-wife's back in residence – that's why not.'

An extremely strange sensation took place behind Gabriel's ribs. He said blankly, '*Venetia?*'

'She's the one you married, isn't she?'

'But what is she doing here in Yorkshire?'

'How should I know? She said the wool's ready for market, the flax is late and pretty well everything else looks like rotting on the stalk.' Wat fumbled in his pocket. 'But you needn't take my word for it. She sent you this letter.'

Gabriel accepted the sealed missive with a mixture of totally unexpected emotions which he was reluctant to name and most definitely did not want Wat to see. He said, lightly, 'Did she say if there was anything I could do?'

'Not unless you can stop it raining.'

'Ah. Then, in that case, I'll read it later.' He tossed the letter casually down on the table and brought the ale-jug back with him to the hearth. 'I suppose you've heard the latest news? Hamilton is at Kendal, where he's been reinforced by three thousand men from Ireland under Sir George Monro. Scarborough has declared for the King but Walmer Castle has surrendered; the Prince of Wales has sailed into the Downs and seized several merchant vessels for which he's demanding ransom from the City; and both Houses have agreed on holding fresh talks with his Majesty on the Isle of Wight – while the Army is occupied elsewhere. There is also a rumour that a petition has been presented to the Commons for the release of John Lilburne.'

'Fancy,' grunted Wat, not in the least deceived. 'And Lieutenant-General Cromwell?'

'Is apparently somewhere in the vicinity of Doncaster, waiting for artillery,' replied Gabriel with what he knew was just a shade too much vivacity. 'More ale?'

'No. Or not here, at all events.' Mr Larkin rose and picked up his gently steaming headgear. 'I reckon I'll go and find a good tavern. You'll be able to read your letter then, won't you?'

After he had gone, Gabriel communed silently with the ceiling for a few minutes. Then he did what he had been wanting to do since Wat had placed the thing in his hand. He rose and broke the seal on Venetia's letter.

It was impersonal and to the point – if, at times, slightly ironic. Once the weaving was completed, she had sent the cloth to be dyed by John Warner in Knaresborough and she was now planning to take it to York in the next week or so – Lambert and Hamilton permitting. The incessant rain looked like turning the corn harvest into a disaster – but she and Mr Carter still hoped to salvage the flax and intended to start pulling it as soon as God sent a dry day. For the rest, Phoebe was busy ridding Ford Edge of a clutch of leech-like relatives; and Sophy, suffering from a slight fever, was trailing even more shawls than usual.

'One thing more,' Venetia had concluded, sardonically, 'I did not come home for any nefarious reasons of my own. Neither did I come because of any quarrel with Jack or Annis or even Mistress Bryony – who, incidentally, is glowing like a dozen candles these days, for reasons which can only be guessed at. I came because I felt that, in times like these, my place is here amongst our own people. And if his Grace of Hamilton should arrive in search of assorted livestock, he will get the same reply I'd give to Lieutenant-General Cromwell.'

A faint smile curled Gabriel's mouth as he finished reading and then he walked slowly back to the hearth to stare into the fire. There was not a single word in the letter that might not be read by anyone; but he had expected that . . . which was why his peculiar reluctance to open it in front of Wat made so little sense. As for the wholly unexpected surge of pleasure he'd felt on learning that Venetia was both close at hand and had taken the trouble to write to him, that was downright bloody ridiculous. He was thirty-five years old, not twenty, and he couldn't remember a woman having such an effect on him in years. Or not, at least, with so little apparent cause.

Still, upon due reflection, it was undoubtedly true that something had changed during the course of that last night in Shoreditch. She had tended his wounds – with remarkable efficiency, too – and permitted him to sleep in her bed. To anyone else, those would be the significant factors . . . but Gabriel knew better. What counted – and what had made the difference, if difference there indeed was – was the fact that they had talked, honestly and with neither hostility nor flippancy, for the first time. And the result was that they had found themselves less seriously divided than they had previously thought.

He sat down and forced himself to grasp the nettle. Was it really possible, even now, for Venetia and himself to achieve a relationship consisting of more than strained tolerance? Because if it was, it raised an immediate and rather delicate question. He had deliberately refrained from consummating his marriage so that, if circumstances ever made it desirable, it could be nullified without undue difficulty. Until now, this had made perfect sense and been no particular hardship; and it would be stupid to change it without very careful consideration indeed. But if he wished to commit himself to Venetia, it was an omission which probably ought to be rectified as soon as possible.

Realising that he was going too far and too fast, Gabriel put an abrupt curb on his thoughts. All he could be sure of at this stage was that he was looking forward to his homecoming and that his next meeting with Venetia would be fraught with possibilities. He folded the letter and slipped it carefully into his pocket. Then he poured himself another pot of ale and forced himself to concentrate on Major Maxwell's meticulously tabulated duty-rosters.

Lieutenant-General Cromwell arrived two days later and Lambert's troops greeted their exhausted colleagues with a heartening cheer. What went on between the two commanders, however, went on strictly in private – and, if Lambert felt in any sense aggrieved, he was wise enough not to show it. At any rate, the next thing Gabriel and his fellow-officers knew was that it had been decided that they would all march westwards, across the Pennines, and attempt to intercept the Scots on their progress south.

It was the kind of gamble, observed Gabriel to Eden, that only Cromwell would have suggested. Their combined strength was now roughly nine thousand, compared to the estimated twenty thousand possessed by the Duke – and the sensible course would have been to send out scouting parties to track Hamilton whilst also covering the approaches to London. Eden agreed but with reservations. It wasn't enough, he said, just to contain the Scots; it was necessary to put an end to the present danger by defeating them. Gabriel contented himself with a thoughtful glance and said nothing more. Eden was still plainly one of the Lieutenant-General's more whole-hearted admirers. Gabriel knew how that felt. He'd been one himself until Basing House. But perhaps Eden – with other things on his mind that day – hadn't suffered the same disillusion.

With a rough march ahead of them, they left the artillery at Knaresborough Castle and set off across the moors for Skipton and the west. Rain had turned streams into raging torrents and roads into quagmires of mud but they reached Gisburn on the night of August 15th and, on the following day, held a Council of War at Hodder Bridge. According to their latest information, Hamilton had reached Preston and showed every sign of continuing south – but Monro's force was at some distance to the rear and Lieutenant-General Middleton was even now apparently taking the main cavalry across the River Ribble in the advance of the infantry. This scattering of the Royalist army was too advantageous to be ignored. But the most vital question of all was whether the New Model should stay on the south bank of the Ribble to prevent Hamilton advancing further into England – or whether it should follow the north bank in order to separate Hamilton more securely from Monro and cut the Scots off from their homeland.

It was another thorny choice and the stakes this time were enormous. If a battle was fought and won, the Scots were completely undone; if it were fought and lost, they were at liberty to continue their marauding march on London. Cromwell argued in favour of the north bank and eventually got his way. Gabriel kept his tongue between his teeth and confined himself to issuing the necessary orders.

After a chilly, uncomfortable night spent in the grounds of Stonyhurst Park, the Army arose on the morning of

Thursday August 17th to another grey and inevitably wet dawn. Tents were dismantled, pikes, muskets and swords resumed, and marching columns grumblingly re-formed. Then they embarked once more on the weary road to Preston . . . until, that was, their advance guard collided with Sir Marmaduke Langdale's van.

Langdale had formed his troops up across the New Model's line of march and was apparently prepared to contest its passage whilst awaiting reinforcements from the main army.

He'd positioned himself well, too, decided Gabriel, clinically, when he had the chance to observe the lie of the land. But that was only to be expected. Langdale was a professional; a raw-boned Yorkshireman who'd fought throughout the first war and become known as 'The Ghost' on account of his talent for appearing where least expected. And today he had demonstrated his quality by drawing up his three thousand or so men, only a small portion of whom were cavalry, amidst the hedged fields which surrounded the lane leading to Preston.

By the time Cromwell's dispositions were complete, with his own Horse and Colonel Harrison's commanding the approach to the lane and a line of Foot stretching out a thousand yards, the afternoon was well-advanced. Gabriel's regiment was on the right wing and had the task of protecting the infantry while it dislodged Langdale's men from their hedges.

This, as it turned out, was easier said than done. Impatient to enter the fray but with little to do as yet except command, Gabriel watched the best soldiers in the world hurling themselves again and again on the Royalist position only to be repeatedly repulsed by a hail of musket-fire and fierce hand-to-hand combat. No one, he thought grimly as the day wore on, could deny that the Cavaliers were acquitting themselves like heroes. And the unfortunate truth was that they needed to. For, with the exception of a few Scottish lancers – amongst whom, if the flag was to be believed, was his Grace of Hamilton in person – no reinforcements came up to aid Langdale in his unequal struggle and he was left to stand or fall as best he might.

He and his little army held their ground for four long hours before finally falling back upon the town. And that was when Gabriel said crisply to Eden, 'Bring up all our troops that haven't been engaged so far. I want to follow Cromwell down the lane.'

'So as not to miss the fun?' asked the Major.

'No. So as to try and make sure that if a surrender is offered, it's accepted,' came the austere reply.

They poured into the narrow streets of Preston in pursuit of Langdale's infantry, gradually turning the retreat into a rout. With few options left to them, the Royalist Foot surrendered virtually *en masse*; and Gabriel, insinuating his own men in amongst Thomas Harrison's, made sure that – unlike at Basing House – there was no question of surrenders not being accepted. Most of the Royalist Horse, meanwhile, slipped away to find Monro, leaving Sir Marmaduke and Hamilton to struggle across the swollen Ribble with a mere handful of their respective followers.

While Cromwell swept down on that part of the Scottish army which was still trying to cross the river, Gabriel gained Lambert's permission to undertake a mopping-up operation in Preston itself where a few intrepid Royalist officers were trying to round up sundry groups of panic-stricken troopers. And that was how, as dusk was just falling, he came face to face with his half-brother.

There was noise and confusion all around them but neither was aware of it and, for a moment, they eyed each other mutely. Ellis – soaked, dirty and dishevelled and mounted on a horse he'd just stolen from someone's stable; and Gabriel – equally wet and lightly mud-spattered but otherwise remarkably tidy. Then Ellis said venomously, 'Well, *brother*. It seems you're destined to be forever in my way.'

'So it appears,' agreed Gabriel. 'What are you going to do about it?'

'Not what I'd like, unfortunately.' Ellis had discarded his pistol after his ammunition ran out and, with Roundheads swarming throughout the town, wasn't prepared to waste time and court capture by drawing his sword. Characteristically, however, he could not resist saying, 'And what of you? What are *you* going to do? Shoot me in cold blood? No. I don't somehow think so. Arrest me and damn the consequences? Yes – perhaps. But it really wouldn't be very wise, you know.'

'You fascinate me,' said Gabriel – who, since there was little point in asking a man if he'd tried to kill you and expecting a truthful answer under the present circumstances, would have much preferred to avoid this encounter altogether. 'What consequences? In case you hadn't noticed it, this is war – and you and I are enemies.'

'So we are. But not, you'll agree, because of the war.' Ellis's teeth gleamed in a malicious smile. 'Just consider. If you make yourself personally responsible for my capture – what *are* you going to tell Venetia?'

'The truth.' Gabriel allowed his gaze to drift past Ellis to the fight taking place between some of his own fellows and half-a-dozen Cavaliers about twenty-five yards away at the end of the road. Then, looking coolly back at his half-brother, he said, 'Since you're heading North, I assume you're not intending to join in the general retreat?'

'In this weather? No. I don't think so. And I've already done as much for the Cause as I can today.'

'Ah well. I don't suppose they'll miss you,' came the derisive reply. 'However . . . Since I'm sure the answer would be disappointing, I won't ask where you *are* going. I'll simply point out that you'd better go now – before I'm left with no option but to stop you.'

Ellis's hand clenched hard on his reins.

'You think I want favours from you?' he spat.

'I'm not doing you any. I'm merely saying that I'd prefer to have as little to do with you as possible but that I'm not prepared to risk my reputation by letting you go under the eyes of my men – who, by the way, are getting rather close.' A chilly, impersonal smile touched Gabriel's mouth and then was gone. 'For future reference, on the other hand, you should know that my toleration won't last forever. And if we meet again, there's likely to be a reckoning.'

'Behold me – positively shaking with fear!'

'I'd rather not behold you at all.' The fight eddied back down the street again but Gabriel did not expect the retreat to last. 'Make up your mind. Are you going or not?'

'Yes.' Kicking his horse into motion, Ellis rode a little way past him and then paused again. 'But before I do, just answer me one question. If you don't sleep with your wife – who *do* you sleep with, Colonel? Whores – kitchen sluts – boys? Or are you just incapable?' And then, as Gabriel swung to face him, 'After all, a man who can resist such a tempting armful to the point of failing to consummate his marriage must have *some* reason for it. And Venetia's no coy little virgin waiting to be seduced . . . as I, of all people, should know.'

Something shifted in Gabriel's stomach and his hands clenched involuntarily. 'Get out of my sight!' he said.

'What's the matter? Surely the possibility must have occurred to you.' Ellis smiled tauntingly. 'We were betrothed for five years – and there was a war on. Did you really think we'd never done more than hold hands and exchange the odd, chaste kiss? Venetia's not the ice-maiden she appears, you know. But then – despite having been married to her for eight months – you've yet to—'

'If you talk much more,' said a light, deadly voice from out of the gloom beside them, 'the Colonel is likely to shoot you in the head or expire from pure boredom. I myself wouldn't blame him for either one.'

Ellis jerked his head round and swore. Gabriel turned slowly and found himself looking down into the barrel of a pistol. Its owner – a brown-haired man in shabby buff leather and a frayed blue sash – grinned faintly and said, 'I apologise both for my unintentional eavesdropping and my interruption. As for my unknown colleague's big mouth . . . I'd be more than delighted to give you time to shut it for him, except that I'm in something of a hurry to acquire your horse before your troopers arrive to prevent me.'

Beneath his mingled rage and disbelief, Gabriel was aware of distant amusement. He said, 'And you really imagine I'm going to give her to you?'

'Oh yes. I'm the one with the pistol, you see.'

'Why don't you just shoot him and have done with it?' demanded Ellis, furious at being deprived of the reaction he'd hoped for.

'And advertise my presence unnecessarily? Try not to be a

bigger fool than you can help,' returned the stranger. Then, 'Are you lost? If you're looking for what's left of our army—'

'To what end?' snapped Ellis bitterly. And, since there was plainly no further point in staying, set spurs to his horse and galloped off.

'He who fights and runs away . . .' murmured Gabriel, reaching stealthily for his own pistol while the Cavalier was apparently still watching Ellis's retreating back.

'Is probably wise but somehow not the sort you'd like your sister to marry. I really wouldn't do that if I were you.' Even in the gathering dusk, the expression in the light, clear gaze was unmistakable and Gabriel's hand stilled. 'Now. Your horse, if you please.'

Although he rather admired the stranger's nerve, Gabriel was not about to sacrifice his favourite mare. He said, 'It may have escaped your notice, but your fellows appear to be surrendering to mine. And, that being so, I'm afraid you'll just have to risk it and shoot me.'

'Ah.' A quick glance verified the truth of Gabriel's statement. 'Is that your last word?'

'Absolutely.'

'Pity,' came the half-regretful, half-cheerful reply. And then, with a tiny shrug as he turned to vanish into the murky alley he'd first sprung from, 'You win. The damned thing's not loaded anyway.'

With a thousand of their number dead and four thousand captured, the Scots used the hours of darkness to make a desperate march to Wigan and were three miles on their way before Cromwell found out they'd gone. Leaving the Lancashire levies to hold Preston and instructing their commander to put his prisoners to the sword at the first sign of Monro's troops, the Lieutenant-General set off in belated pursuit – and had the immediate satisfaction of finding Hamilton's entire stock of powder and bullets which someone, unbelievably, had failed to destroy.

Rain streamed down incessantly and the New Model was constantly harried by the Scottish cavalry – apparently eager to make up for its lack of activity the previous day and justify its presence on English soil. Responding with an ease born of

333

long practice, Gabriel formed and re-formed his men to meet each successive sally and told himself that he was enjoying himself. The truth, however, was that he wasn't – mainly because, thanks to Ellis, he had other things on his mind. And the only really bright spot in the whole day was discovering that, amongst a host of other captives, was Colonel Hurry – the man famous during the first war for changing sides more often than anybody else.

By the time they struggled through the mud to Wigan, the starving Scots had already been through it like a plague of locusts and moved on. The New Model – dirty, weary and wet – spent another miserable night in fields just south of the town; and Gabriel came to the conclusion that he should have taken his lying, malicious half-brother by the throat and shaken him until the truth emerged.

August 19th dawned and the chase continued to within three miles of Warrington before the Scots finally turned and gave battle – selling their lives dearly and standing their ground through several hours of tightly-knit charges and close combat until, with a further thousand killed and two thousand more taken, they disengaged and resumed their dispirited retreat. And by then, as Gabriel pointed out somewhat hazily to Eden, their own fellows were so tired they could have slept standing up.

Surrender finally came before nightfall that day at Warrington and both sides were unreservedly glad of it. Hamilton and Langdale slipped away south with a body of Horse; and four thousand more prisoners fell into the Lieutenant-General's already over-full hands. It was over.

'*Surely,*' wrote Cromwell that night to Speaker Lenthall, '*this is nothing but the hand of God; and wherever anything in this world exalts itself, God will put it down.*' And later, '*Take courage to do the work of the Lord in seeking the peace and welfare of this land . . . and they that are incapable and will not leave troubling the land may speedily be destroyed out of the land.*'

While Cromwell was writing his letter, Colonel Brandon sat beside a cosy fire for the first time in several days and forced himself to face the possibility that Ellis might – just might – have been speaking the truth. Given his and

334

Venetia's circumstances at the time, it was by no means impossible; and nor, if it *were* the truth, had he himself any right to feel betrayed by it – except, perhaps, in one particular. She ought to have told him.

Two

It seemed to Venetia that the only thing which had gone right in recent weeks was the sale of the cloth. She and Dick Carter had taken it to York and it had fetched a good price – for which she thanked God. But incessant rain threatened to ruin the corn and had so far prevented them from pulling more than half of the flax; every lane on the estate had become a sea of mud in which carts inevitably got stuck; and the local physician said that Mistress Sophia was suffering from Doctor Harvey's 'influenza'.

Sophy was certainly suffering. So too, in different ways, was Venetia. When not closeted with Mr Carter or out and about getting soaked, she spent her time helping to nurse the invalid and trying to stop the sickroom filling up with Sophy's motley collection of pets. Neither was easy and, as fatigue started to set in, she could feel her temper beginning to shorten. From time to time, she even contemplated asking Phoebe to come and help her but she never did. The harvest at Ford Edge would be no better than the one at Brandon Lacey.

The news from outside was fragmentary and mostly depressing. The Parliament continued to toy with the idea of opening fresh talks with the King – but announced that all who had aided the Prince of Wales in his piratical adventures in the Downs were to be regarded as traitors; those incarcerated in Colchester and Pontefract continued to hold out but small rebellions in Portsmouth and Oxford were soon suppressed; and while John Lilburne was finally freed from the Tower, his brother Henry declared for the King at Tynemouth – and died in a surprise assault the next day.

Then, within forty-eight hours of the event, news of

Preston put the final, catastrophic seal on all Venetia's hopes. She had not wanted a second war – but once it began, she had not been able to help praying that it might end with the King's restoration. But that chance now looked very slender indeed; and, as if that were not quite bad enough, she was also aware of an inexplicable and apparently involuntary concern for her husband's safety.

By the evening of August 20th, the only bright spot in Venetia's life was the fact that Sophy was gradually improving. Everything else, she decided gloomily, was about as dire as it could possibly be. Wearily clutching a candle, she went back to the little room where she kept her ledgers for another unrewarding tussle with the household accounts – and found Ellis sitting there.

The candlestick dropped from her fingers, splashing her with hot wax and plunging the room into darkness. For a moment there was total silence and then Ellis drawled, 'My apologies. I'd have warned you if I'd known how.'

Venetia re-inflated her lungs.

'Why didn't you just ride up to the front door?' she hissed. 'You might as well have done. This is insane!'

'Yes. Well, when you're as wet and hungry as I am and you haven't a groat to your name, you tend to look favourably on the odd risk,' he replied. 'I'm not complaining, of course, but do we *have* to talk in the dark?'

'Keep your voice down!' She knelt to try and locate the candle and found that her hands were shaking. 'There's tinder on the table beside you – if you can find it.'

Neither of them spoke again until there was light and then Venetia said abruptly, 'How did you get in here?'

'Through the side door. It wasn't too difficult. You don't seem to keep many servants these days.'

'Fortunately for you, we can't afford them.' She paused, absorbing the marks of exhaustion on his face and the small puddles forming around him on the floor. 'You were at Preston?'

He nodded. 'It's over. The army was in full retreat when I left it and in no state to fight again.'

Her brows narrowed. 'But Hamilton hadn't surrendered?'

'Not then, no. But I daresay he has by now.'

'Yes.' A new anger gripped her. 'If all his soldiers wander off when the mood takes them, I daresay he has.'

'Don't judge me!' he flashed back. 'It was a fiasco from the start – no artillery, no provisions, no horses to pull the baggage-wagons. Every time Hamilton made a half-sensible decision, the Earl of Callander talked him out of it; and because Monro wouldn't serve under Callander, three thousand men were left in the rear as reserves. On the morning of the battle, the infantry were still in Preston but the cavalry were nearly in Wigan. And the result was an absolute debacle – to which my continued presence wouldn't have made one whit of difference.'

The fact that this was probably true didn't somehow make it any better, but Venetia saw little point in saying so and instead coolly asked what he expected her to do for him.

'I should have thought that was obvious, sweetheart. To begin with – a change of clothes, some food and a place to sleep. Then, in due course, some money and a fresh horse.'

She stared at him irritably. 'You can't stay here! You must know that. Someone would be bound to find out.'

'Not necessarily. This is a big house and you've always been resourceful. I'm sure you'll work something out. And it will only be for a couple of days, after all.' Ellis smiled at her and reached for her hand. 'My dear, can't we discuss this after I'm out of these clothes and have some food inside me.'

'And how do you suggest we achieve that? I can't do anything about the food until the servants are all abed; and, though I presume some of your clothes are still in your old room, it will look very odd if I'm seen crossing the hall carrying an armful of them.' She paused, frowning a little. 'There's nothing else for it. You'll have to stay here for now. But if you want to take off your coat, I'll fetch a cloak to keep you warm while you wait.'

None of this was quite what Ellis had hoped for.

'Don't put yourself out, will you?' he muttered sulkily.

'No,' said Venetia. 'I won't. And let's get one thing straight. It's iniquitous of you to have put me in this position and, since the risks are mostly mine, you should be grateful I'm doing anything at all. Now. Sit down and be quiet until I get back.'

It was a further two hours before she decided it was safe to move him to a small, ill-furnished bedchamber in a little-used part of the house – and, by then, Ellis was becoming distinctly fractious. But once she had fetched him a dry suit of clothes and produced half a loaf, a steaming bowl of stew and a bottle of wine, he regained most of his customary insouciance and said, 'Well, well. Isn't this cosy? Quite like old times, in fact.'

'Not from where I'm standing,' came the acid reply. 'Quite apart from this being positively the worst place you could have come to – do you think I haven't enough to worry about already with Sophy ill in bed and—'

'Is she? How very convenient.'

'Your concern overwhelms me!' she snapped. 'But since you're here, you can tell me whether or not you hired a band of bravos to cut Gabriel's throat before he left London.'

There was a long, thoughtful silence and, in the shadows of the room, it was hard to read his expression. But finally, in a tone of pained affront, he drawled, 'Hired ruffians, my loved one? *I?* What a repulsive thought!'

'You're saying you didn't?'

'I don't think I need to. The mere suggestion is offensive.' He sat up so that more light fell on his face. 'But do tell me. Did someone damage the bastard's health?'

It did not occur to Venetia to wonder why he didn't ask if Gabriel's throat *had* been cut. She was too busy evaluating the look on his face. 'You could put it that way.'

'Really?' A malicious smile dawned. 'Well, you can't expect me to shed any tears over that.'

'I don't expect it.' She was deathly tired and her temples were beginning to pound. And since she was also beginning to experience a strong urge to box Ellis's ears, she said, tonelessly, 'I'm going to get some sleep and I suggest you do the same. But I'll be back before dawn to—'

'Back?' Ellis sprawled suggestively against the pillows and smiled at her. 'You mean you're not staying?'

'Hardly.' She crossed to remove the key from the door. 'What's more, just in case you get any urge to wander during the night, I'm going to lock you in. Goodnight. Sleep well.'

Venetia arose before it was light with a firm determination

to speed Ellis on his way – only to discover that he had no intention of budging. Still tired and taut with strain, she promptly lost her temper but was wise enough to do it quietly. Ellis merely demolished the bread and cheese she had brought and let her diatribe run its course. Then he informed her that he would go when he felt sufficiently rested, probably that night, but, in the meantime, he needed her to pay a call on Lawyer Crisp for him.

There was a long, blistering silence. Then, when she felt able to control her voice, Venetia said, 'Really? And how am I to do that without revealing that I've seen you?'

'It doesn't matter if you do reveal it.'

'*Not matter?* Of course it damned well matters!'

'Oh.' Ellis thought for a moment and then said nonchalantly, 'You're thinking old man Crisp may put two and two together and tell the bastard I was here? I doubt if he will. But if you're worried, you can simply say I've contacted you through a third party.'

Venetia gripped the frayed edges of her patience. 'And why didn't you send your third party direct to Mr Crisp?'

'Oh . . . any one of a dozen reasons,' he shrugged. 'I'm sure you'll think of something.'

'Not this time. I'm not having anything to do with it.'

Ellis lay back on the bed and folded his arms behind his head. 'I thought you wanted me to leave?'

'I do – and you will.'

'Not,' he replied suavely, 'until I've had word from Lawyer Crisp. And, before you tell me to go myself, allow me to point out that I can't. Half the country is looking out for fugitives from Preston and if I'm recognised in Knaresborough, it will create exactly the kind of furore you want to avoid.' He smiled with overt, deliberate charm. 'It's important, my heart. Otherwise I wouldn't ask.'

The thoughtless certainty of his attitude brought revelation bursting over Venetia like a blinding light. She said unevenly, 'Don't start showering me with endearments. If you cared about me at all, you wouldn't be here wreaking havoc with my life.'

The smile remained pinned to his mouth long after it had faded from his eyes. He said, 'You're overwrought.'

'No. I'm just giving you fair warning that, from this moment on, there is a limit to what I'll do for you.' She held his gaze and when he did not reply, said, 'I can't stay long. The house will be stirring. You'd better tell me what you want from Lawyer Crisp. Money?'

'Obviously.' Ellis sat up and swung his feet to the floor. 'But I also want to know if he's found me a tenant for Steeple Park yet.'

Her brows soared. 'You're leasing it?'

'What else can I do? I can't live there without bringing a sequestration order down on my head and, by the time the taxes are paid, there's not enough left over to make the place worth keeping. I'd prefer to sell it, of course, but with so much land on the market as a result of people trying to meet their composition fines, Crisp says it could take an age to attract a buyer and wouldn't fetch a high price. So my best option is to install a tenant and—'

'Wait a minute.' Venetia eyed him suspiciously. 'You've plainly already discussed this with Mr Crisp, which, considering you were all for staying out of his sight—'

'That was before the bastard and I had met.'

'Ah. Of course. Once Gabriel had seen you, there was no further point in being discreet. Yes. I should have realised that.' Sarcasm dripped from her voice like honey. 'And so that was when you sought out Lawyer Crisp?'

'More or less. I'm afraid I can't remember the exact date,' responded Ellis, devoutly hoping that Mr Crisp would not recall it either. Then, coaxingly, 'You're in a foul mood, sweetheart. Things aren't that bad, surely?'

'Work it out,' said Venetia, stalking to the door. 'Since I've to go into Knaresborough, your next meal may be somewhat delayed. But I'm sure you won't mind.' And she swept out, once more locking the door behind her.

The sudden discovery that, if she ever had loved Ellis, she certainly did not do so now, occupied Venetia's mind all the way into Knaresborough and half the way home again. And, in between, Isaiah Crisp listened to her carefully-phrased request with only partially-veiled cynicism before telling her that she might inform Sir Ellis that a potential occupant for Steeple Park was in view – if not, due to the size of the rent involved, securely hooked. Venetia promised to explain the situation to Sir Ellis's *friend* and, maintaining her most limpid expression, complimented the little lawyer on finding a possible tenant so quickly. Mr Crisp replied that he had certainly done his best but that he did not consider seven months particularly rapid.

By the time she had ridden back to Brandon Lacey, Venetia found that her mind was very clear indeed on certain points. Ellis was not, and never had been, the least bit reliable. She had always known that. But, until today, she had never allowed herself to recognise that there was nothing in the world as important to him as he was to himself; that he was arrogant, selfish, mischievous and patently untruthful. It was not a pleasant discovery and, for a moment or two, it made her feel slightly sick. She had known him since childhood without ever really knowing him at all. Worse still, she had spent five years or more telling herself that she loved him and wanted to be his wife, only to find that, had she been given her wish, it would have been the most catastrophic mistake of her life.

Well, she was free of all that now. Free not just of the love she'd believed in and clung to so stubbornly, but also of the hairshirt of self-imposed loyalty she'd been wearing since the day Sir Robert's Will had been read. She no longer owed Ellis anything and felt a huge burden was suddenly gone from her shoulders. She was free.

But for what? That was the question. To make a life with Gabriel? He was her husband, after all, and it had been plain for some time that he had his good points. Rather a lot of them, as it happened. She felt the beginnings of a smile disturb her mouth and instantly quelled it. This would never do! She was not so feeble-minded that she had to instantly replace one man with another . . . and sufficient unto the day was the evil thereof. The only thing she was willing to admit to herself was that, for several months now, her feelings towards Gabriel had not been what they once were; that the thunderous '*Never!*' had somehow become a small, whispering '*Perhaps*'.

Having changed out of her muddied riding-dress and decided that it would do Ellis no harm to wait a little longer,

Venetia went upstairs to see Sophia. She found her sitting up in bed with the inevitable cat in her lap and Trixie curled up at her feet. She also found her claiming to feel perfectly well again and wanting to get up, which, as far as Venetia was concerned, was something best prevented and caused her to spend the next half hour persuading Sophy that it would be silly to take any unnecessary risks. Then she went slowly back to her own room, told her maid she had a headache and asked for some food to be brought up to her on a tray.

By the time she considered it safe to look in on Ellis, the afternoon was well-advanced and she had decided precisely how best to be rid of him without further delay. She therefore slipped along the passages which led to the east wing and entered his room to find him pacing back and forth like a caged lion.

'Where the devil have you been?' he demanded. 'My God – you could have been to Leeds and back by now!'

Venetia placed the plate of food on the table and said coolly, 'I have other demands on my time.'

'So you keep telling me.' The brown gaze was distinctly irritable. 'Did you see him?'

'Lawyer Crisp? Yes.'

'And?'

'And I'll tell you about it later,' she replied calmly. 'Tonight – when you're on the point of leaving here.'

For a moment, Ellis was completely taken aback. Then he said angrily, 'Don't play games with me, Venetia.'

'I'm not. I'm just stating a fact. *You* want to know what Mr Crisp said and *I* want you out of the house. But if I tell you now, you could be here for days yet and I can't risk that.' She paused and awarded him a small, sardonic smile. 'I'll get you a warm cloak, food, money and a horse and I'll be back shortly after midnight to escort you from the premises and satisfy your curiosity. Agreed?'

Scowling, Ellis recognised that he didn't appear to have much choice. This was the side of Venetia he'd always liked least; this ruthless implacability which nothing dented. No woman, in his opinion, had any right to be so bloody unyielding. He thanked God that the war had come in time to stop him marrying her and said, huffily, 'You're not the girl I used to know. I just don't understand what has got into you these days.'

'No,' she agreed. 'Of course you don't. And wouldn't even if I tried to explain it.'

As she had done the night before, she waited until the servants were safely in bed before she began her preparations. She bundled up the clothes Ellis had arrived in, collected a thick cloak from the closet in his old bedchamber and made up a generous parcel of food – all of which she stowed neatly in the saddlebags she'd left hidden in the hall chest. Then she went out through the darkness to the stables and deftly saddled up a sturdy roan whilst trying to work out how best to explain its loss.

When everything was finally ready, she went to fetch Ellis and was relieved to find him fully dressed. Without giving him time to open his mouth and carefully shading the candle with her hand, she led him down through the silent house to the little side door – and from there to the shadows beneath the gate-house where she'd left the roan.

Ellis heaved himself into the saddle, saying sulkily, 'Now. Tell me what old man Crisp said.'

Venetia smiled faintly and did so. 'I imagine you'll get your tenant, but not for quite such a fat rent as you seem to have had in mind,' she finished dryly. 'At any rate, I wish you luck.'

He looked down at her face, shimmering like a pearl in the moonlight. 'Is that all?'

'Yes. What else is there?' She hesitated briefly and then said, 'Goodbye, Ellis. Our paths lie in different directions from here on. I think you know that.'

His brows rose and he smiled with all his old, malicious charm. 'You're going to settle for the bastard?'

'If I am, it's no one's affair but my own. And I think it's time you stopped calling him that.'

Ellis laughed. 'You've changed your tune, haven't you? But perhaps, having made your bed, you're preparing to lie on it. So I wish you joy of him, my dear. Not, it has to be said, that I think you'll get much.' And, kicking his horse into motion, he rode away into the night.

It wasn't until Venetia turned back into the courtyard that

she realised that Sophia, with an ancient fur-trimmed mantle over her night-rail, was standing there watching. Her heart gave an abrupt lurch and she said breathlessly, 'Sophy – what on earth are you doing? You'll catch your death!'

'Trixie needed to be let out,' came the characteristic reply. And then, 'Don't tell me who that was or what you were doing. I'd rather not know.'

'And I'd rather not tell you.' Venetia walked slowly up to the older woman. 'But there are certain things I must explain. First, that I neither asked nor wanted him to come; second, that I've done nothing I need be ashamed of; and third, that it will not happen again.'

Sophia gazed at her myopically for what seemed like an eternity. But finally she smiled and said, 'You're free of him, aren't you? I'm glad. And now I'd be grateful if you'd find Trixie and bring her inside. She's breeding again, you know.'

Venetia collapsed into bed, slept like a log and arose much later than was usual. And that was how it came about that she and Sophia were just finishing breakfast when Gabriel walked in.

Caught in the act of swallowing a morsel of bread, Venetia promptly choked. Sophia merely froze, one hand poised above the ham and her mouth slightly ajar. Gabriel looked quizzically from one to the other of them and then strolled around the table to pat his wife helpfully on the back. 'What's the matter? Did someone tell you I was dead?'

Cheeks flushed and eyes watering, Venetia managed to stop coughing but still dared not trust her voice. Sophia blinked, made a vague sort of half-gesture and said earnestly, 'Dead? Oh no, dear. If we'd thought *that*, I'm sure we wouldn't be sitting here as though nothing had happened.'

'Why not?' He stripped off his gloves, tossed them on to the dresser and took a seat at the board. 'One has to eat, after all.' And, with a deceptively casual glance at Venetia, 'Was my arrival really such a shock – or just inopportunely timed?'

'B-both.' Taking refuge in her kerchief on the pretext of mopping her eyes and still reeling from her hairsbreadth escape, Venetia struggled to pull herself together. 'We assumed you were still somewhere south of Preston.'

'I was. But once the Scots disintegrated into full flight after Warrington—' He stopped and, without appearing to do so, read her expression. 'You haven't heard about that?'

She shook her head. 'Tell us.'

'There's not a lot to say. They made a second stand at a place called Winwick, but they were badly equipped from the outset and no longer in any condition to fight. So they retreated to Warrington where, rumour has it, the Earl of Callander insisted that their only option was surrender.' Gabriel paused again and then added dryly, 'The truth is that, by then, it probably was. But from what I've heard, the blame for that rests securely on Callander himself.'

'Yes. It certainly looks that way,' agreed Venetia.

The grey eyes trapped hers. 'Why do you say that?'

Her stomach lurched and she cursed her own stupidity. Then, in the nick of time, Sophia said vaguely, 'You know what it's like. People love to gossip.'

'And say what, precisely?'

Sophia's gaze became curiously unfocused and, seeing it, Venetia said lightly, 'All the usual things – along with the suggestion that Callander undermined Hamilton's decisions. Isn't that what you meant?'

'Yes. That's precisely what I meant.'

'So it's true then?'

'Very probably.' Apparently satisfied, Gabriel reached for some bread and a slice of ham and, folding one around the other, said bluntly, 'This can't be easy for you. I know you didn't want this war . . . but you wouldn't be human if you hadn't hoped it might end differently.'

Venetia shrugged and kept her relief well-hidden.

'I won't pretend I didn't. But perhaps it's better this way. Aside from Colchester, all the risings in the south have come to nothing, so Hamilton would have found little enough support waiting for him if he *had* managed to get that far. And the entire country would have been turned upside down for the same result that we have now.'

He nodded and then, as Sophia rose from her stool, said, 'Don't go. I've brought you a present.'

She smiled. 'Have you, dear? How nice.'

'Isn't it, though?' He pulled a rather battered leather flask from his pocket and offered it to her, grinning. 'I understand you've been ill. So since I was passing quite close by the Tewit Well at Haregate-head, I thought—'

'Oh, *did* you indeed?' Mingled indignation and laughter combined to produce a surge of rare animation. 'And have you tasted it yourself at all?'

'Well, no. To be frank with you, the smell was enough.'

'Exactly!' Sophia sailed to the door, her scarves flying like pennants. 'And anyone who uncorks it in my presence had better be prepared for the consequences.'

Gabriel continued laughing for several moments after she had gone. Then the realisation slowly dawned on him that he was alone with his wife, without any idea of what to say. He had felt awkward when he'd walked in – but the comic nature of his reception had temporarily banished it. And now he was more aware than ever of the sheer impossibility of saying, 'Ellis tells me you slept with him. Is it true?'

Equally ill-at-ease, Venetia said, 'We've strayed from the point somewhat, haven't we? You were about to explain how you come to be here and not chasing the Scots.'

'I asked for three days' leave of absence and was granted it.' Gabriel crossed to the dresser and poured a cup of morning-ale from the jug. 'My regiment is still moving south with Lambert, trying to round up Hamilton and Langdale and I've to be back at my post the day after tomorrow.'

She digested this; and then said, staring at him, 'You mean you've ridden here overnight?'

'More or less.' He turned and, grinning faintly, gestured to the disreputable state of his uniform. 'It shows, doesn't it?'

'Very slightly,' agreed Venetia. And suffered her second shock of the morning from the realisation that, until this moment, she had noticed nothing except that his hair was slightly longer than she remembered it and his eyes were shadowed with fatigue. In short, the tawny, Parliamentarian sash she'd hated so much had for the first time made no impression whatsoever. She drew a small, unsteady breath and then said quickly, 'You'll want to rest, then.'

'Presently, perhaps.' Gabriel moved back to the table and sat down again. 'First I'd like to hear how things have been with you here.'

'Much the same as they were when I wrote to you,' she shrugged. And briskly recited the litany of her daily concerns. Then, 'It's going to be another bad year and there's very little we can do about it. The wool fetched a good price, it's true; but, as you said yourself, we need the flax as well if the operation is to succeed – and Carter is beginning to have severe doubts on that score. But he'll tell you that himself later, I daresay.'

'Quite.' Gabriel frowned into his ale and then looked up at her. 'So. No other problems I should know about?'

A tiny tremor made its way down Venetia's back.

'I'd have thought those I've mentioned would be enough.'

'They are. More than enough.' He paused. 'Are you afraid we won't be able to meet the taxes?'

'Yes. And when you've seen the ledgers, so will you be.'

'If you want the truth, I'm afraid of it already and praying that something will turn up.' He rose again and paced restlessly away from her. Then, without turning, he said abruptly, 'I was glad of your letter. I'd have sent Wat with a reply if there had been time . . . or no. That's not strictly true.' He swivelled smartly to face her. 'I didn't know what I wanted to say to you. And still don't.'

The air shifted about Venetia and she suddenly felt very odd. She said, 'What do you mean?'

'I mean that I sense we're no longer enemies, but I don't know how far we've progressed towards becoming friends,' replied Gabriel carefully. 'Perhaps you don't know that either. Or there again, perhaps you'd say that the idea there's been any change, however small, is all in my mind.'

Silence stretched out to the edges of the room while Venetia tried to unscramble her wits and frame some sensibly noncommittal reply. Then, giving way for once to sheer impulse and aware neither of her smile nor the effect it was having on Gabriel, she heard herself say, 'It's not in your mind. And I would like to think that friendship is not beyond us – though it may take more than a day.'

Over the odd disturbance in his chest, Gabriel made one more bid to lure her to confide in him. 'And trust?'

She nodded. 'That, too.'

He found himself facing a brick wall. He could no more

ask if she had anything she'd like to tell him than he could come straight out and ask if she had lain with Ellis. And suddenly he realised that it really didn't matter. Just as he was no idealistic boy of twenty, she was no sheltered seventeen-year-old, and her past life belonged to no one but herself. Consequently, the only thing to regret was that – out of all the men in the world – she'd been betrothed to the one whom he personally held in total contempt and whom he once more suspected of telling him a pack of lies.

Venetia watched him, waiting for him to speak and unable to interpret his expression. Then the harsh lines of his face dissolved into an unexpectedly charming smile and he said, 'I'm glad – and I'll look forward to furthering our acquaintance. Beginning, perhaps, over supper?'

Gabriel spent what remained of the morning with Dick Carter and most of the afternoon taking a lightning tour of the estate, which gave Venetia plenty of time in which to thank Sophia for her discretion and also to confront the head groom over the subject of the missing roan. Then, when both matters were satisfactorily dealt with, she consulted with Cook, summoned her maid and devoted two relaxing and extremely enjoyable hours to her appearance.

Downstairs again and still with time on her hands, she made sure a fire had been lit in the parlour and checked that there was wine ready and waiting. She was not sure why she was going to so much trouble or even what she hoped would come of it; she only knew that this was the first time she and Gabriel would sit down to a meal without hostility joining them at the board. And that there was a small but distinct flutter of excitement somewhere behind her bodice.

When the parlour door finally opened, she turned with a half-smile, expecting to see Sophia and then froze.

It wasn't Sophia. It was Gabriel, in his shirt-sleeves, with one hand resting on the door-latch and the other clenched on something at his side. Suddenly acutely self-conscious, Venetia rose in a rustle of dark green taffeta and embarked on some flippant remark about her unaccustomed finery, only to have the words wither on her lips before the blazing anger in his face.

The grey eyes swept over her intricately-arranged curls and flowing, décolleté gown. Then, his voice ragged with temper, he said, 'Well, well. I suppose I should be flattered. But though it's ungrateful of me to find fault, I can't help thinking red would have been more apt.'

One hand closed hard over the other. 'What's wrong?'

'Wrong? Now what could possibly be wrong?' Gabriel released the door, slammed it shut with his foot and crossed the room towards her. 'Think carefully. You never know – you may even come up with the answer.'

With her conscience far from clear, Venetia hovered between blurting out the truth while she still had the chance – and hoping that the cause of Gabriel's wrath was something quite different. Then, just as she opened her mouth to speak, he said, 'No? Then perhaps this will jog your memory.' And he hurled a lavishly embroidered glove down on the floor at her feet.

It was very much the worse for wear but she recognised it immediately. Indeed, it was difficult not to – for, with his usual extravagance, Ellis had caused his monogram to be picked out in silver thread amidst a profusion of leaves and flowers. Venetia stared down at it thinking stupidly, But I was so *careful*! And discovered that she felt sick.

The silence stretched on and on; and finally – steeling herself to meet the glittering grey gaze – she said tonelessly, 'Where did you find it?'

'You mean you don't know? My God – how many options are there? This room? The gallery? My bedchamber? Yours?'

'Of course not!' she began. And then, the answer suddenly presenting itself, 'Oh. The bookroom.'

'Hallelujah!' said Gabriel grimly. 'The bookroom. What was he doing? Going through the accounts? No doubt he found them stimulating reading. Not that it matters. The point at issue is what he was doing in this house at all. And don't try convincing me that glove got here except on my half-brother's hand – and recently, too – because I won't believe it. The damned thing's still damp!'

Venetia tried to stop telling herself that she ought to have checked the bookroom after she'd taken Ellis upstairs. It was pointless; and what mattered now was to try and convince Gabriel of the truth. She said flatly, 'He came here the night before last. I went into the bookroom and found him. He was tired and wet and hungry—'

'Spare me the pathos and stick to the facts.'

'Very well. I – I hid him in the east wing while I got him some food and dry clothes.' She swallowed hard. 'I didn't want him here. I—'

'No, no. Of course you didn't.' His temper simmering gently, Gabriel regarded her over folded arms. 'Let's get to the interesting bit. When did he leave?'

Her heart sank. It was going badly and she didn't know how to mend it. 'In the early hours of this morning.'

His eyes bored into her like flints and an unpleasant smile curled his mouth. 'So,' he said, at length. 'Ellis spent the night here. That must have been cosy for you.'

She was about to hotly deny it, but then something in the tenor of his voice stopped her and, drawing a short, painful breath, she said, 'What exactly are you suggesting? That I . . . that I *lay* with him?'

'Didn't you?' Gabriel paused with icy deliberation. 'After all, it wouldn't be the first time, would it?'

The parlour floor rocked beneath Venetia's feet and ice invaded every vein. No wonder it was going badly. It was worse . . . so very much worse than she had thought. In a thread-like voice, she said, 'Who told you?'

'Not, obviously, the one person who should have done. Do you deny it?'

Venetia sank slowly back into her chair.

'No.' She frowned down at her hands. They were bloodless and shaking. 'How long have you known?'

'Long enough. But I only started *believing* it when I found *that*.' The raw, eviscerating anger which Gabriel thought he'd suppressed erupted again and he kicked the glove savagely into the heart of the fire. 'I could have accepted the fact that you'd slept with him during your betrothal. I could even excuse you for not telling me that you had. But what I *can't* forgive is that you could talk so glibly to me this morning about trust – when the bed you and he had shared was barely cold!'

'But it wasn't! I mean – we *didn't*!'

'And I'm supposed to believe that, am I? Christ! You must think I came down with the last shower – behaving like a perfect bloody gentleman when all the time—' He stopped abruptly, breathing rather hard. 'It's a good joke, isn't it? Did you enjoy sharing it with Ellis?'

Formless suspicion sent the tremors that had been afflicting Venetia's hands into every nerve and sinew. Speech was beyond her but she managed a small gesture of denial and instantly regretted it as Gabriel closed the space between them. He leaned over her, his hands resting on the carved arms of her chair. He was so close that she could see the pulse hammering in his throat. Then he said, 'Don't lie. There's been enough of that already. And don't give me any excuses. Just tell me one thing. Do you love him?'

She shook her head. 'No.'

'No? You're sure?'

Her mouth was bone dry. 'Perfectly sure.'

'I see.' He released her chair and straightened his back. 'Well, that simplifies matters no end. For if you can lie with Ellis without loving him, you can't have any objection to lying with me – now can you?'

For a moment, Venetia couldn't believe she'd heard him correctly. She said hesitantly, 'You – you don't mean it.'

'I do.' Gabriel smiled again, that chilly purposeful smile. 'After all, why should Ellis have all the fun? And at least he won't be able to call me a eunuch when next we meet. So get up, my sweet, and let's go to bed.'

With only one thought pounding in her brain, Venetia could not have moved if her life had depended on it.

'Ellis,' she whispered. '*Ellis* told you?'

'Who else? But we've talked enough. Get up!'

She shook her head again, trying to clear it.

Gabriel's hand immediately closed about her wrist, pulling her out of the chair and propelling her with him across the room. Jerked into sudden awareness, Venetia tore at his grip and shouted at him to wait; but he merely continued hauling her with him and did not speak until he threw open the door and almost collided with Sophia.

'Our apologies,' he said, barely breaking stride and

353

heading for the stairs. 'You'll have to sup alone tonight. My wife and I have unfinished business to attend to.'

Venetia opened her mouth to ask Sophy to help, recognised the futility of it and stumbled blindly on in the Colonel's wake, clutching a handful of green taffeta. Then, when he catapulted her into his room and turned to slam the bolt home, she said breathlessly, 'There's no need for this! I haven't slept with Ellis in four years.'

'Why should I believe that?' Gabriel pulled his shirt off over his head and advanced on her. 'You're wasting time. Are you going to remove that gown or shall I?'

She backed away from him, still convinced she could make him listen. 'It was in June of '44 in Oxford. I—'

'Suit yourself.' He grasped her elbow and spun her round. Then, when she tried to get away from him, he hooked his fingers into her neckline and, picking up a pen-knife from the table at his side, sliced through her laces. Venetia gasped and made a quick grab for the gown as it slid from her shoulders – but Gabriel was even quicker. One sharp tug sent it slithering to her feet while he dealt equally ruthlessly with stay-laces and petticoat ties. He threw the knife back on the table and released her.

The whole business had taken only seconds. Reduced to her shift, Venetia turned slowly amidst a heap of taffeta and cambric to meet his eyes . . . and finally accepted the reality of the situation. Something, her own guilt perhaps, robbed her of the right to fight back and she said haltingly, 'You've every right to – to be angry. But—'

'That's generous of you.' He was already sitting down to pull off his boots. 'Get into bed.'

'But are you sure that this is going to help?'

'You mean – won't I hate myself in the morning? Possibly. But, to be frank, I don't much care. *Get into bed.*'

It was the tone five hundred troopers obeyed without question and, shaking from head to foot, Venetia shot between the sheets. Oddly enough, she was not frightened that he would hurt her; the thought had still not occurred to her. Nor did she blame him for taking what he could have taken long ago. But she was suddenly and inexplicably afraid that, in deliberately stripping the occasion of every grace, he would also destroy any chance of kindness between them in the future. Argument or resistance would only make things worse but she could not help saying, 'You once told me that you d-didn't approve of rape.'

'No more I do.' His breeches followed his boots and, for a moment, he stood looking at her, breathing rather fast. 'But this isn't rape. It's the long-delayed consummation of our marriage and it needn't be unnecessarily unpleasant unless you make it so.' He paused and then, when she simply went on staring at him as if mesmerised, said abrasively, 'Well? How *do* I compare with Ellis?'

Venetia started, averted her eyes and turned scarlet with humiliation. She wasn't sure what had come over her. True, he had a magnificent physique but that was no reason to gawk like a moonstruck adolescent. She bent her head, hugging the bedcovers to her chest . . . and felt her breath leak away as the mattress dipped beneath his weight.

For a few seconds there was silence and stillness before his arm reached out to sweep her down beside him. He loosened the string of her chemise and drew it briskly from her shoulders. Then he paused, looking at her. Venetia shut her eyes, clamped her teeth together and waited for the inevitable assault. It did not come. Instead, after what felt like an age, his hand traced the contour of her hip and moved unhurriedly up towards her breast. Her eyes flew wide and she found herself impaled on an impenetrable grey gaze. She said, jerkily, 'Since it's too late to woo me – why don't you get on with it? Unless you've changed your mind.'

'Dear me,' responded Gabriel aridly. 'Did you expect a three-minute wonder? If so, you're about to be disappointed. There's been nothing so far to make me that eager.' And, pulling her smoothly against his body, he brought his mouth down hard on hers.

Flesh met flesh and Venetia gasped, her hands pressed flat against the warmth of his chest. Without warning, an unexpected and wholly unfamiliar sensation budded and blossomed inside her and half-alarmed, half-seduced, she did not know whether to struggle or melt. His kiss – a little rough and undeniably demanding but somehow wickedly enticing – seemed to go on forever and elicited a response that startled her. For perhaps a minute, she tensed against him, trying to stamp out the sparks of excitement that were beginning to rush through her veins; then his hands resumed their insistent and no longer leisurely exploration – and the sparks erupted into a blaze.

All her proud notions of remaining dutifully passive promptly perished. Her bones dissolved, her arms closed about him and her fingers slid over the muscles of his shoulders and back before entangling themselves in the long, crisp hair. She thought hazily, *This is all wrong. I shouldn't feel like this. Not yet.* But she said nothing; and could not anyway, for her breathing was completely disrupted.

She heard Gabriel murmur sardonically, 'Not that it makes the slightest difference . . . but I take it you're not saying no?' And then, blotting out her answer with his mouth, brought all discussion to a summary end.

Venetia awoke early in the morning to a curious sense of well-being which intensified as memory came flooding back. She stirred lazily, smiling to herself; and then she opened her eyes to find Gabriel standing over her – fully-dressed and with an expression bleak enough to make hell freeze.

Most of her own pleasant anticipation drained away and she sat up quickly, clutching the sheet to her chest. She had been foolish to think last night might have changed the way he felt. Why should it? In fact, all things considered, he probably thought she was little better than a whore.

As usual, what Gabriel thought was not immediately apparent and he seemed in no hurry to speak. But finally he said curtly, 'As you know, I have to go back to the Army. With the harvest due – and a bad one at that – I'd naturally prefer to leave you here to look after things. But since I've a particular aversion to having Ellis keep my bed warm for me, I can't do it. No.' This as Venetia would have spoken. 'Don't interrupt. I intend, as before, to take you with me. But this time there will be no carriage, no maid and no Phoebe. We are going to ride fast, just you and I. And you may take only what can be carried on a pack-horse. I trust I make myself clear?'

She swallowed and kept her head very high. 'Perfectly.'

356

'Good. Then I suggest you get up and make ready while I speak to Sophy. I want to leave within the hour.'

Three

It was an arduous, unpleasant ride and it ended up taking longer than Gabriel had expected – partly because, with Lambert in hot pursuit of Hamilton, it was necessary to follow the trail of messages which Wat had left at every halt – and partly because Venetia was with him.

Not that she ever complained. In fact, Gabriel got the distinct impression that she'd have bled to death sooner than do so. But when he could see her growing gradually white with fatigue, he told himself that it was only sensible to pause for refreshment or stop for the night rather earlier than he'd planned. After all, it would cost an even bigger delay if she collapsed in the saddle.

They crossed the Pennines by way of Leeds, Huddersfield and Oldham to Manchester – where they shared a mediocre and largely silent meal at a noisy and not especially comfortable tavern. Gabriel retreated behind a mask of granite-like courtesy and said nothing of the fact that he'd hoped to be in Warrington by now. Venetia pushed her food around her plate, tried not to show that her back was aching and wondered why all her usual confidence had deserted her. Then they bade each other a formal goodnight and retired, in equal confusion, to their separate chambers.

Since communication between them had been reduced once more to its most basic level, Gabriel did not know that Venetia was far from averse to making this journey with him. He only knew that, in dragging her off to his bed, he had somehow made matters worse rather than better. As yet, he was too wrapped up in his own feelings to even begin wondering what hers might be.

The moment in which he had found and recognised Ellis's

359

glove was trapped in his mind like a fly in amber. Savage disillusion and a sense of betrayal had sliced through him, bringing something akin to physical pain and then sheer, blinding rage. And rage, of course, had been responsible for everything which had followed.

In all his life, Gabriel could not remember ever totally losing his temper. But when he had walked into the parlour and heard Venetia admit that Ellis had been her lover he had lost it with a vengeance. Caution, common-sense and even the most rudimentary self-control had flown, leaving only a white-hot need to cure a few of his ills by teaching his exquisite, lying wife a sharp lesson.

Well, he'd done that all right. He'd let his tongue run riot and forced her into bed. Thus far, it had been ugly, shameful and potentially dangerous; all the things he'd thought he wanted. Only then she'd melted into his arms as if being there obliterated everything else and her mouth had breathed wild hunger into his; and, even when he'd taken her with rather less consideration than he would have shown a whore, she had still responded to him as though . . .

He reached abruptly for the bottle and poured himself another drink. It did no good to remember how she'd reacted in his arms. She had proved that she wasn't to be trusted – and was probably as accomplished an actress as she was a liar. Either that or she didn't much care *which* man was in her bed. But no. He frowned down into the amber liquid. He could not believe – could not bear to believe – it was that. And if she'd been acting, it had been a truly remarkable performance – that, or he was more gullible than he'd thought.

All this, however, was almost beside the point. The trick now was to put it to the back of his mind and recover his self-possession. But that was easier said than done when the scent of her hair lingered in every breath he took . . . and the softness of her skin and every slender curve of her body were indelibly imprinted on his fingers.

He fell asleep wondering why nothing seemed to go quite right; why, instead of exorcising his growing attraction to Venetia, he had managed instead to weave a web for himself. And by the time they halted the following night, after

360

another crippling day's ride and still seemingly some distance behind Lambert, he was acutely aware of two damnably incompatible facts. The first was how badly he wanted her – and the second was that it would be a cold day in hell before he laid a hand on her again; because whichever way one looked at it, only a complete idiot would risk becoming emotionally involved with a woman he couldn't trust.

The end of the third day brought them wearily to Uttoxeter and journey's end. By the time she had ridden through the scattered, grinning ranks of the Colonel's regiment and been deposited like superfluous baggage at a small inn bustling with officers, Venetia cared for nothing except her chances of persuading someone to bring up sufficient hot water for a bath. Gabriel, meanwhile, went immediately in search of the Major-General to report his return and apologise for having arrived twenty-four hours late – only to find, as Eden Maxwell later put it, that he'd missed all the fun. The Duke of Hamilton had surrendered to them earlier that day and was even now in dignified custody.

Gabriel nodded. 'So I've been told – along with the fact that Callander continues to elude you.'

'And Langdale,' said Eden.

'Quite. But Sir Marmaduke has my very good wishes for a fair wind to France. Callander doesn't. In short, since he's largely responsible for Hamilton's current predicament – he ought to have the decency to be here sharing it with him. But life, as they say, is rarely fair.'

The crisp voice held a note of unusual bitterness and Eden took a long, thoughtful look at his Colonel. He said, 'If you don't mind me saying so, you look bloody awful. Have you managed to find yourself some quarters?'

The lean mouth curled slightly.

'After a fashion. I've thrown out Ned Moulton and Lieutenant Billings. It's one of the privileges of rank.'

Eden grinned. 'Obviously. But when did you grow too grand to fit into one room?'

'When I decided to bring my wife with me,' came the cool reply. And then, before the Major had recovered his breath, 'You won't know it yet, but Lambert is taking the bulk of the

Army to join up with Cromwell for a march into Scotland. I, on the other hand, have been ordered to take two troops and escort Hamilton and a handful of others to London. If you want to attend your sister's wedding, you can come with me; if not, I'll take Captain Massey. It's entirely up to you. And now I'd like to get some idea of the number of prisoners who are being assigned to my chaperonage.'

Not unnaturally, Eden was unsure how best to answer this and therefore confined himself to guiding Colonel Brandon to the house where, with the exception of his Grace of Hamilton, the London-bound captives were lodged. There were four of them. Three were minor Scottish nobility; the other was the fellow who Gabriel had last seen disappearing into the dusk of Preston with an empty pistol.

Across the heads of the gloomy, disdainful Scots, two pairs of grey eyes – one as light and clear as spring water and the other dark as threatening storm-clouds – met and locked. Then, without a hint of recognition, the Cavalier said, 'If you're staying, I hope you've brought some dice.'

'Unfortunately, not,' replied Gabriel evenly. 'But I daresay Major Maxwell can oblige you.'

While Eden was good-humouredly searching his pockets under the Royalist's suddenly acute stare, Colonel Brandon faced the officer outside the door and said briskly, 'Who's the Englishman?'

'We're not sure, sir. He *says* his name's Ambrose and that he's just a common soldier, serving as a Colonel under Sir Marmaduke Langdale. But there's some as think he's a rich, Midland lord who's broken his parole.'

'Is that why he's being sent to London?'

'Not altogether, sir. There's also a rumour that he's the one as planned the scurvy trick what took Pontefract.'

'I see,' said Gabriel. And thought irritably, *Christ! Out of the whole damned Royalist army, why did it have to be him?* Then, as Eden materialised at his elbow, he said, 'Let's go. I've seen all I need to. And now I suppose it behoves me to find Wat and send him to guard Venetia's door from the nasty, drunken soldiers. Do you know where he is?'

'Hardly,' shrugged the Major, following him out into the

street. 'You know Wat – the unofficial commissariat, always busy turning the odd coin on illicit supplies.' He cast a slanting glance at Gabriel's profile and said lightly, 'Dare I ask why you don't go and guard Venetia's door yourself?'

The dark brows soared. 'Because – after the hellish journey I've just had – I intend to become nasty and drunken myself as fast as possible. Why do you think?'

'Oh.' Eden walked along in silence for a moment, wondering how best to find out if the last few days had mended the rift between them. 'Then perhaps you'd care to share some ale with me while I send someone to look for Wat?'

'That,' responded the Colonel, 'is the best offer I've had all day.'

Throughout several flagons of beer, Gabriel kept to strictly neutral topics such as the state of the roads and the Parliament's recent repeal of the Vote of No Addresses – with the result that Wat arrived to find him in the early stages of inebriacy and, fixing a deeply disapproving gaze on him, said dourly, 'Having a liquid supper, are you?'

'You sound like somebody's mother.' Gabriel tossed some coins down on the table, waved a vague farewell to Eden and bore his henchman back out into the night. 'Or so I imagine. I can't speak from experience, of course.'

Mr Larkin's habitual scowl turned imperceptibly into real anxiety. 'What's happened?'

'Happened? Why, nothing very much. I just rode to Brandon Lacey and came back again, that's all.' Gabriel continued his slightly weaving progress up the street. 'Ah yes. I almost forgot. I brought my lovely wife – my faithful helpmeet, my pearl beyond price – back with me.'

'You did *what*?'

'You heard. She's snug as a bug in her virtuous bed at the Rose and Crown. Or at least I hope she is. It's never wise to take these things for granted, is it?'

Wat caught hold of his arm and pulled him to a standstill against a water-butt. Staring grimly into the shuttered face, he said, '*What's she done?*'

There was a small pause and finally Gabriel said remotely, 'I'm not sure it's what *she's* done that matters.'

363

'God's teeth!' muttered Wat. 'All right. Have it your own way. What have *you* done?'

Another silence. Then, his nonchalant facade suddenly shattering, Gabriel said, 'I'm not sure. I wish I was. But on balance, I'd say I've made one catastrophic mistake on top of another. And I don't know what I can do about it.'

After an extremely restless night, Venetia spent the bulk of the following day staring out of her window and wondering whether Gabriel was avoiding her on purpose or had simply forgotten she was there. In the end, she jettisoned her pride, summoned Mr Larkin and asked if the Colonel was likely to join her for dinner. Wat curbed an impulse to spit and told her – with perfect truth – that he hadn't the least idea. Then he stumped back out to the pile of wood-shavings he'd been methodically creating in the taproom.

Gabriel stayed away from Venetia all of that day and most of the next – by which time her deep depression was becoming tinged with natural indignation. Then, just as she was rehearsing some of the things she'd like to say to her damnably difficult husband, Wat stuck his head round the door and announced that the Colonel would be grateful for five minutes of her time downstairs in the parlour.

Venetia considered informing Mr Larkin that if the Colonel wanted to see her, he knew where she was and then, deciding against it, sailed down to the parlour with a fast-beating heart and a degree of well-simulated confidence.

Gabriel was sitting on the edge of the table, frowning down at his hat and idly swinging one booted foot. Venetia said abruptly, 'Don't tell me. You're not staying.'

He rose and faced her unsmilingly. 'I'm busy.'

'So I've gathered. But you must eat some time?'

'I do. Do you want a list of what and when?'

A chill invaded her bones. 'No. I just want to talk.'

'Do we have anything to say to each other?'

'Yes. Unless you're suggesting we – we forget everything that's happened?'

'I will if you will,' shrugged Gabriel. 'But I haven't time for this now. I merely came to say that we're leaving here tomorrow morning with a hundred of my men and five prisoners of war. So it would be helpful if—' He stopped in response to a knock at the door and bade whoever it was to come in. Then, looking with faint annoyance at Eden Maxwell, he said curtly, 'I hope this is important.'

'It is.' Eden accorded Venetia a swift bow and an apologetic smile before turning back to the Colonel. 'I hear you're leaving for London tomorrow.'

'Well? What about it?'

'I want to come with you,' came the tense reply. 'In short, I'll go to Thorne Ash and attend this damned wedding – if you'll come as well to dilute the inevitable sentimentality of it all. With Mistress Venetia, naturally.'

'Naturally,' agreed Gabriel dryly. And with a brief, hard laugh, 'Well, why not? If you don't mind turning up with a hundred motley ruffians at your back – who am I to quibble? And if there's one thing my lady-wife and I are good at, it's stifling the merest hint of sentiment.' The dark eyes swept over Venetia and then returned to the Major. 'Very well. We'll come. And now, if you don't mind . . . ?'

'Consider me gone,' said Eden briskly. And went.

Scarcely waiting for the door to close behind him, Venetia said flatly, 'I'm not sure what all that was about – but I do know one thing. Wild horses won't take me to any wedding at Thorne Ash.'

He regarded her impassively. 'You haven't a thing to wear? Don't worry. I'm sure the mere fact of your presence will outweigh any sartorial considerations. Now. I was about to say that you should be ready to leave by ten o'clock – and that I've arranged for the wife of one of my sergeants to ride with you in order to preserve you from impertinence. Not,' he finished simply, picking up his hat, 'that I think you'll be subjected to any.' And with a small, perfunctory bow, he walked calmly out of the parlour – leaving Venetia staring speechlessly after him.

With abundant time in which to get to Banbury, Gabriel ordered a leisurely march as far as Warwick and spent most of it riding beside the Duke of Hamilton – that unfailingly polite gentleman who had been an unqualified disaster both as a soldier and as a diplomat and who, according to the satirists, had such an ingeniously subtle brain that he couldn't follow its workings himself. Gabriel found him pleasant but ponderous company and was glad when Warwick came into view. Then, as soon as his prisoners and his wife were suitably bestowed, he decided to exchange a few private words with the gentleman calling himself Colonel Ambrose.

Making sure that both Wat and Eden were occupied elsewhere, he had the Cavalier brought to his quarters and, as soon as they were alone, said bluntly, 'I suppose I should thank you for your discretion.'

Colonel Ambrose lifted one cool brow. 'Unnecessary. Your personal life is no one's affair but your own.'

Gabriel surveyed his guest thoughtfully. The austere, severely-sculpted face gave nothing away but the buff coat had plainly seen a lot of wear and the tattered blue sash was flamboyantly-tied. He said, 'Who are you?'

'Ah.' A sudden, gleaming grin appeared. 'Everybody's favourite question.' And then, sweeping the floor with the bedraggled plume of his black felt hat, 'Justin Ambrose. A humble soldier-of-fortune.'

Experiencing again that odd tug of liking, Gabriel waved him into a chair and poured two cups of wine. 'Humble? I wouldn't say that. They tell me you are a Colonel.'

'Oh – that.' Justin accepted the wine with a tiny nod of thanks. 'I wouldn't set too much store by that, if I were you. I fought all through the first war with one eye on promotion and ended it a mere Captain. I present myself for service at the beginning of the second and suddenly I'm a Colonel. It's called desperation.'

Gabriel didn't think so. If what they said about Pontefract was true, the fellow was good. He said, 'If you fought under Langdale, why didn't you leave with him?'

'Because, having respect for Hamilton's personal courage, I had some idea of trying to mend his luck. My mistake, obviously.' The tone was suddenly bitter and acutely restless. 'Why did you send for me? You didn't need to.'

'Unfortunately, I did,' replied Gabriel. 'There are at least three people in this convoy who would like to know precisely what my half-brother said that night in Preston.'

'Your half-brother?' The light grey gaze sharpened. Then, with a small, mirthless laugh, 'Well, well. In that case, you may be absolutely assured of my silence.' Justin drained his cup and stood up. 'Do you mind if I ask why we're travelling so slowly.'

'Family matters. Major Maxwell has a wedding to attend near Banbury. And it's my self-imposed duty to see he gets there.'

An extremely peculiar expression crossed Justin Ambrose's face and then he dissolved into sardonic laughter.

'Oh God,' he said breathlessly, at length. 'Banbury. That's all I need. Get careless with me there, Colonel, and the Parliament could be saved the expense of putting me on trial. But it's an ill-wind, as they say. At least there'll be plenty of people desperate to tell you who I am – not excluding the Major's strong-minded sister.'

Gabriel's brows rose. 'You know Kate?'

'In a manner of speaking. I inherited the task of collecting Thorne Ash's rents during the latter part of the war. Some of them, anyway. Mistress Kate cheated, you see – and prevented me from curtailing her little game by informing me that my predecessor had run off with her elder brother's wife.' He paused, meeting the suddenly frowning gaze. 'The plot thickens, doesn't it? But don't worry. The Major's secrets are as safe with me as yours are – and there's no reason why he should even guess that I know.'

On the following afternoon, Gabriel stopped his cavalcade just short of Banbury and rode into the town to consult with the County Committee about suitable quartering for his men. Then he returned with what he personally considered an admirable solution, expounded it to Major Maxwell – and found he had conjured up a storm.

'Far Flamstead?' echoed Eden wildly. 'You want to billet us all at *Far Flamstead*?'

'Why not? It's under sequestration and close to—'

'Do you know who it belongs to?'

'The Earl of Wroxton – currently in exile,' sighed Gabriel patiently. 'Is he a friend of yours?'

'He's Celia's father!' Eden struggled to control his

breathing. 'And Far Flamstead was where she slept with Hugo Verney. So if you think I'm setting foot in the place, you can think again! It's worse than going to Thorne Ash.'

Gabriel could well understand this. But because it did no good to sympathise he said quietly, 'Then, if you can face that – you can face anything. And, having come this far, it would be a pity to let the ghosts win now.'

After six years of neglect and the visits of more than one looting party, Far Flamstead was no longer the elegant house it had once been. Eden entered it white-faced and silent . . . and started issuing orders in a tone which soon had a hundred men scurrying about like mice. Gabriel left him to get on with it and reluctantly turned his own attention to finding a suitably habitable room for his wife. He did not know that she, too, felt less than comfortable about invading Far Flamstead – and Venetia saw no point in telling him. She merely went where she was told and set about trying to get the creases out of her only silk gown in readiness for making an appearance at Thorne Ash.

With the prisoners secure in the charge of Lieutenant Billings and no further excuses remaining to him, Eden Maxwell left Far Flamstead on the following morning accompanied by Colonel and Mistress Brandon, and reluctantly rode home for the first time in two years. Gabriel punctuated the journey with light talk and Venetia was strangely silent but Eden, less sure than ever why he had decided to come home, noticed neither. He only knew that, more than anything else, he was dreading the moment when he would have to greet four-year-old Viola Mary . . . who was more likely Hugo Verney's daughter than his own.

Thorne Ash slid into view at the end of the lane, tranquil and unpretentious as ever – and he felt a sharp tug of nostalgia. Then they were riding into the courtyard and his mother, closely followed by Felicity and Kate, erupted from the house to congeal in a small huddle in front of it. Disconnected and paralysed, Eden remained ramrod-stiff in the saddle. It had been too long. He didn't know what to say – and he was afraid that the first unwary word might shatter him like glass. So he sat like a stone until Kate drew their mother gently forward saying aridly, 'It's not enough just to show that you're still alive, Eden. You have to *speak* as well.'

The spell dissolved and he dismounted slowly, his eyes fixed on Dorothy. The lovely dark red hair was lightly touched with silver and the tawny-green eyes were dilated with shock, but otherwise she looked exactly the same. Then a swift, heart-stopping smile lit her face and she held out her hands, drawing him into a warm, scented embrace.

'My dear, my dear,' she finally said unsteadily, 'I'm so glad you decided to come. Thank you.' And released him, with reluctance, to Felicity's bubbling exuberance and Kate's merciful astringence.

Eden wasn't sure what either he or they said. He was just glad that he had a distraction to hand. As soon as he was free to do so, he turned with a small gesture which encompassed both Gabriel and Venetia and said baldly, 'As you can see, I've brought some friends. Mistress Venetia needs no introduction to any of you, of course. But I believe that her husband – Colonel Brandon – is known only to Kate. And since it's he who is largely responsible for . . . for my presence here today, I thought you might like the opportunity of congratulating him.'

It worked, of course. He had known it would. And despite both the air of barely-concealed tension between Kate and Venetia and the fact that he himself was bracing himself for what presumably lay ahead in the parlour, they were all swept inside on a tide of pleasure and excitement.

The hall and the parlour were just as he remembered them – and mercifully empty. Eden looked around him and said with careful lightness, 'Where is everyone?'

'Making themselves scarce,' grinned Felicity. 'I saw you coming and Kate thought you might find it easier to deal with us in instalments. So Ralph's taken Geoffrey and Luciano out riding, Felix got the job of coaxing the children back to the nursery – and Amy is changing her gown.'

Eden smiled faintly and looked at Kate. 'I thought Luciano was prohibited from leaving Genoa by his uncle's ill-health?'

'And so he was.' Exquisitely clad in costly bronze silk, Kate finished pouring wine and moved amongst them handing out glasses. 'Sadly, however, Vittorio died two months ago . . . and that rather changed things.'

'Oh. I see.' He paused and then, less tactfully than he meant, added, 'So Luciano is now his own master.'

'Luciano has always been his own master,' came the characteristic reply. 'I thought you knew that.'

No longer able to read her son accurately, Dorothy said quickly, 'Venetia, my dear, I don't know where you've all sprung from but I sincerely hope that, having brought Eden to us, you and the Colonel are going to accept our hospitality until after the wedding.'

Venetia smiled. 'That's kind of you, but I'm afraid it will depend on whether Gabriel can leave his prisoners.'

'Prisoners?' Felicity turned an awed grey gaze on the Colonel. 'Are they Scots from the battle at Preston?'

'Four are,' responded Gabriel. 'The fifth is a Cavalier Colonel who was once attached to the Banbury garrison. He says his name is Ambrose.'

'*Justin* Ambrose?' asked Kate sharply. And, when Gabriel nodded, said, 'Goodness! He used to collect our taxes.'

'He's also,' grinned Felicity, 'the gentleman who seduced Abigail Radford. Or so they say.'

Venetia's eyes widened but she said nothing. Gabriel looked at Eden and said, 'Radford as in *Sam* Radford?'

'His sister.' Eden gave a short laugh. 'My God! Are you going to ask Ambrose if it's true?'

'Why should I? It's no affair of mine.'

'Quite,' said Felicity. 'But where is he now?'

There was a small, awkward pause and then, in as few words as possible, Gabriel told her. Dorothy stared speechlessly at her son, plainly horrified, and Felicity narrowly avoided choking on her wine. Kate, on the other hand, fixed Gabriel with a jewel-bright stare and steered the conversation clear of catastrophe. 'I assume you're taking Colonel Ambrose to London. Have you a good reason for it?'

Gabriel shrugged. 'It's not my decision. But my superiors apparently think they have sufficient cause. Why?'

'Because, despite his mission here, I didn't dislike him,' came the direct response. 'And, after what happened at Colchester, one can't help but feel a certain concern.'

370

Gabriel and Eden exchanged quick glances and Venetia said sharply, 'Why? What *did* happen at Colchester?'

'Haven't you heard? It surrendered four days ago – having eaten all the horses and most of the dogs and cats,' replied Kate. 'And twenty-four hours later, Sir Charles Lucas and Sir George Lisle were put against a wall and shot.'

Some of the colour drained from Venetia's skin but she kept her face carefully blank, not realising that the two people who knew her best were watching her hands.

Kate looked from the tightly-latticed fingers to the cold cynicism in Colonel Brandon's eyes and recognised that, in sidestepping one quagmire, she appeared to have uncovered another. Fortunately, however, Eden said quickly, '*Shot?* Are you sure? That doesn't sound like Fairfax.'

'Ask Geoffrey,' shrugged Kate. 'He brought three accounts of it, in various newspapers, from London yesterday.'

'Which you may read at your leisure,' interposed Dorothy smoothly. 'Right now, however, I'd like to repeat my invitation to Colonel Brandon, and hear his answer.' She smiled at Gabriel. 'Well, sir? Will you stay with us?'

He hesitated and then said, 'We'd be honoured, madam, though I can't leave my lieutenant completely to his own devices. And no.' This as Eden would have spoken. 'I shan't need you and hereby give you two days' leave.'

'For which *I* thank you – if Eden does not.' Dorothy arose, feeling that she had now been as patient as courtesy demanded. 'Come and go as you please, Colonel – but do try to join us for supper. Meanwhile, Kate will take Venetia upstairs . . . to the yellow room I think, Kate. And Fel—'

'Felicity will go and see if Felix needs rescuing,' said that young lady, moving good-humouredly to the door. 'Never let it be said that I don't know when I'm not wanted!'

Eden sat very still and watched them all leave the room. Then he looked at Dorothy and said bluntly, 'I'm here because Gabriel made me see that I would never mend anything by staying away. But, as yet, nothing is fundamentally changed. And I still can't talk about it.'

'Do you think we haven't learned that?' She sat beside

371

him, resisting the impulse to take his hand. 'No one will mention the past to you or push you against your inclinations. We made that mistake before, if you recall. And, for now, it's enough that you're here.'

Bleak hazel eyes searched her face and appeared to relax slightly. 'Then what *do* you want to talk about?'

'Everything. Good heavens – we've two years to catch up on. I want to know where you've been and doing what with whom . . . and how come Venetia Clifford is married to your commanding officer,' replied Dorothy, for all the world as if there were not a hundred questions she would much rather ask. 'Go on. I'm listening.'

Upstairs, Venetia followed Kate into the yellow bedchamber and wondered whether Gabriel intended to preserve appearances by sharing it with her or whether he expected her to put herself in the embarrassing position of asking for a second room. Before she could decide which it was to be, however, Kate turned to her and said unexpectedly, 'I didn't care to mention it in front of the Colonel . . . but I had the feeling that you know somebody who was in Colchester.'

'I do.' Venetia turned away to lay her cloak on the bed. 'And so do you. Francis Langley. I saw him in London in May and he was off to join Lord Norwich. But, as you so rightly assumed, Gabriel knows nothing about it.'

With so much still unsaid between them, Kate refrained from remarking that – judging by the look in his eye – Gabriel knew more than Venetia supposed. Instead, she said cautiously, 'Francis will be all right. He was born lucky. But I'm sorry I threw the news at you that way. I just assumed you knew. And, of course, I was trying to keep the conversation away from unsuitable topics for Eden's sake.'

'I know.' Venetia decided that it was time to grasp the nettle. 'And is that what you and I are doing?'

Kate smiled wryly. 'It looks like it, doesn't it? I'm all too aware that this can't be easy for you.'

'It isn't easy for either of us.' Venetia paused and drew a steadying breath. 'I read the letters you wrote to me after Kit died but there seemed no point in replying simply to say I couldn't forgive you. Now, however, I rather wish I had. I might have realised sooner that suitability isn't everything . . . and that we all make mistakes. Nor are our emotions fixed in lead. And that being so, I'd like to salvage what remains of our friendship. If that's possible?'

Kate sank down on the windowseat, grinned and decided that a more mundane tone was needed before they ended up falling on each other's necks. 'I don't foresee any problems. Particularly if you'll sit down and tell me how you came to exchange one Brandon for another!'

Venetia laughed and immediately felt better for it.

'It's a long story – but I suppose you think I've got the better bargain.'

'Actually, yes. I never really took to Ellis . . . whereas, despite the unfortunate circumstances of our first meeting, I found your Colonel quite—' Kate stopped as Venetia suddenly sat down beside her. 'What have I said?'

'Nothing – yet.' Venetia frowned down at her hands, caution warring with a desire to talk. 'Kate . . . tell me about Basing House.'

A familiar chill slid down Kate's back but she said, 'If you're asking me about the atrocities which took place during the surrender, I didn't see very much of them.'

'You must have! You were *there*.'

'Yes. I was.' She hesitated briefly. 'If you really want to know, I was shut in the Marquis of Winchester's library, watching Luciano blow Cyrus Winter's head off.'

Venetia stared at her. 'Literally?'

'Literally. But since that, too, is a long story, I think we should deal with one thing at a time. Such as the fact that, so far as I'm aware, Colonel Brandon's men were not amongst those permitted to run amok that day. I take it that *is* what you wanted to know?' Kate waited; and then, when Venetia merely nodded mutely, said, 'You know, I can't help feeling there must be something very wrong if you needed to ask me that question.'

'I don't think I really *did* need to ask it. But you're right, of course. Things are far from perfect between us.'

'And you're miserable,' said Kate flatly. 'I sensed it as soon as I saw you. So why did you marry him?'

'Because I had no choice,' replied Venetia, and embarked

on a swift, colourless account of the circumstances surrounding her marriage. 'So you see,' she said, her voice becoming a trifle uneven, 'we began badly. But it might still have been all right if only I hadn't been so stupid.'

'And were you?'

'Oh yes.' She gave a small, brittle laugh. 'Yes. In the beginning, I sneered at his birth, his integrity and his profession. And then, just when I'd begun to realise my mistake and there was actually some hope of starting again, I—' She stopped, staring despairingly into the attentive green eyes. 'Oh God! I've made such a mess of it, Kate – and I'd give anything to put it right. But I'm very much afraid that, this time, he's not going to let me.'

When Kate finally left Venetia's room some time later, she met her eldest brother crossing the gallery and immediately said, 'Eden – how well do you know the Colonel?'

His brows rose. 'As well as he allows – but not well enough to stick my nose into his personal affairs. Why?'

She shrugged. 'I just thought he might like to know that his wife's in love with him, that's all.'

Eden eyed her sceptically. 'Has she said as much?'

'Not in so many words, no. But—'

'I thought not. You can take it from me that, whatever their relationship is, love has very little to do with it. So the best thing you can do is to follow my example and leave well alone.' He smiled suddenly. 'Unfortunate as it may seem, not everyone's marriage is as blissful as yours. Or am I making an assumption?'

'You know you're not.' She laughed and, linking her arm with his, said simply, 'Luciano is . . . everything I want. And I hope you're going to be polite to him for once.'

'And spoil his fun? Not I!'

'My husband,' announced Kate severely, 'does not enjoy being rude to people.'

'Yes he does. If he didn't, he wouldn't be so bloody good at it,' retorted Eden. And then, his expression altering subtly as they approached the nursery door, 'I understand the house is brimming with little Maxwells – not excluding your own. What's he called, by the way?'

374

'Alexander Richard or Alessandro Ricardo – depending on the obvious. Fortunately, at only eighteen months, he's too young to be confused by it.' She paused and added helpfully, 'You'll find Bess there too – Amy's little girl.'

'Yes. Mother told me.'

Kate knew what was wrong but did not know how best to help him. 'Do you want me to come with you or go away?'

'I don't know. Go away, I think.' And then, for the simple reason that she had not asked, he said abruptly, 'I don't know how I'm going to handle this, Kate, or even if I can. Does she still look like Celia?'

'Yes. But her disposition is quite different. She's gentle and shy, and, I suspect, intelligent.' Kate hesitated again. 'As for Jude, he remembers you and thinks you are a great hero – but it's his Uncle Ralph who takes him fishing and riding and lets him dismantle his pistol.'

'So I shouldn't expect too much. Quite.' Eden squared his shoulders and drew a long, bracing breath. 'Oh well. It's no good putting it off any longer. Boot and saddle.' And he set his hand to the latch and went in.

The babble of voices dwindled into silence while four pairs of wide young eyes glued themselves to his person and Felix, Felicity and Meg Bennet, the nursery-maid, got hurriedly to their feet. The only one who took no notice of him at all was Alessandro Ricardo Falcieri del Santi – single-mindedly banging a wooden spoon on the floor.

Felix surged across the room, grinning from ear to ear. Like Felicity, he had grown to adulthood in the last two years and, at eighteen, was nearer his late father's height than his brother's. Now he grasped Eden's hand and said, 'My God – you took your time, didn't you? I've been having nightmares about having to fill your shoes tomorrow!'

'They'd never fit you,' retorted Eden. 'But I apologise for cutting it so fine. My only excuse is that I was busy.'

'Saving the nation,' nodded Felix. 'We know.'

Eden's eyes strayed involuntarily to the red-headed seven-year-old staring at him from the hearth and the small girl peeping past his shoulder. Felicity said quickly, 'Come on, Felix – and you, Meg. Let's take Bess and Eve and Alex into the garden for an airing before it rains again.'

Meg scooped up little Alessandro and took her own child by the hand. Felix opened his mouth to demur but found young Bess being smartly deposited in his arms. Then Felicity opened the door and ushered them all briskly through it, leaving Eden alone with his children.

He felt his throat close and realised he couldn't think of anything to say but finally he managed a tight smile and said, 'Well . . . what's this? Never say you've forgotten me?'

Jude shook his head and came a few steps closer, Viola Mary clinging limpet-like to his sleeve. He said, 'Father?' And then, a huge smile creasing his face, 'You came! I knew you would – I knew it!' And flew across the floor, dragging his sister with him.

Eden dropped on one knee and met the onslaught as best he might. He said unsteadily, 'You've grown.'

'Yes. Uncle Ralph says I'm big enough for my own pony now,' came the proud reply. And, hauling his sister forward to receive her share of notice, 'Mary's grown too. But she can't have a pony yet because she's only four.'

Trapped by a huge pair of pansy-blue eyes, Eden felt as though he might suffocate and had to force himself to remain still. It was not her fault that she wasn't his – any more than she could help resembling Celia; but the plain truth was that he couldn't look at her without re-living the day on which his life had been irrevocably shattered. And, with the best will in the world, he didn't know how to hide it.

As though sensing something amiss, Jude said excusingly, 'She's shy.' And, nudging Viola Mary with his arm, 'This is our father. I told you he'd come when he'd finished fighting with the Scots. Say hello and don't be a baby.'

She whispered something indistinguishable and hung back, nibbling one finger. Seizing his opportunity, Eden got up and tried to pull himself together. Ruffling his son's hair, he said lightly, 'So you can ride, can you?'

'*And* jump,' replied Jude. 'I'll show you, if you like.'

'I'd like that very much.'

'Come on, then.' The boy grabbed his hand and made a dive for the door. 'We can take Mary to Grandmother. Then we won't have to hurry up because of her being cold.'

Eden knew it was the coward's way out but he couldn't

resist it. He kept his mouth shut and let himself be towed away downstairs.

After that, meeting Ralph and his brothers-in-law was mere child's play. Blond and massive as ever, Mr Cochrane slapped him painfully on the back and asked him how it felt to be one of Old Noll's up-and-coming young heroes; Geoffrey Cox shook his hand and murmured something banal; and Luciano Falcieri del Santi gave him a lurking smile and made the kind of typically cryptic remark to which, as usual, there was no answer whatsoever.

By the time the Colonel returned from Far Flamstead, Ralph's mother and elder brother had joined the party and everyone was gathered in the parlour, enjoying a glass of wine. Venetia looked up as Gabriel came in and felt her nerves tighten; then she forced herself to continue attending to Amy Cox's pretentious prattle. After all, he had been sedulously avoiding her ever since they had arrived in Uttoxeter and was therefore unlikely to seek her out now.

She was wrong. As soon as Amy drifted away and the company began to assemble for supper, Gabriel materialised unsmilingly at her side to ask why in Hades she hadn't had the sense to have them placed in separate rooms.

Quite without warning, Venetia experienced a sudden gust of temper. 'Because, thanks to recent events, I couldn't be sure that was what you'd want. And if I'd taken it upon myself to have you lodged elsewhere, you'd probably be accusing me of having improper designs on Eden or Felix – or the damned steward.'

'Oh no,' murmured Gabriel, lethally. 'I might have my doubts about your friend from Colchester if he were here. But only after I'd found his boots under my bed.'

Her breath caught. '*What* friend?'

'You tell me. Of course, it's probably all perfectly innocent. But then you said that about Ellis, didn't you?'

'And it was true!'

'Was it?' The grey eyes were utterly impervious. 'Then why did you do your damnedest to keep his visit secret?'

'Not for the reasons *you* have in mind,' snapped Venetia edgily. 'But if it will stop you dragging me off to bed and ravishing me, you can be sure I'll tell you next time.'

His smile was deliberately insulting. 'There had better not *be* a next time. And your memory is at fault. I didn't ravish you. You damned well enjoyed it.'

Hot colour washed over her and, without stopping to think, she said shakily, 'You *bastard*!'

For one tiny, frozen moment, she thought he was going to hit her. Then he said, gratingly, 'Well, of course. But you've known that all along, haven't you?'

While the evening generally passed on wings of laughter and music, Venetia existed in a black void of mingled anger, humiliation and regret. She kept away from Kate so she wouldn't be tempted to blurt out the whole, sorry story. And she made sure she never met Gabriel's eyes – nor went within two yards of him unless someone else was at her side.

She never knew where he slept that night. She only knew it was not with her . . . and, for the first time in a week, she was grateful.

The wedding went well. Attended by her sisters and wearing a gown of sprigged primrose silk, Felicity Maxwell walked down the aisle of Thorne Ash's chapel and was duly joined in wedlock with Ralph Cochrane. Then everyone went merrily back to the hall for the wedding-breakfast and the dancing. Venetia pinned a smile to her face and tried, somewhat unsuccessfully, not to let her eyes follow Gabriel. Then, just when she was least expecting it, Kate emerged at her side and said baldly, 'What's wrong? Another quarrel?'

'No. Just a continuation of the same one.'

'And which you're still determined not to talk about.'

'Quite.' Venetia smiled wryly. 'I'm sorry, Kate. But it's not something I can discuss with anyone. Even you.'

'Then I won't ask. I'll simply observe that, if you want to mend matters, you're going to have to talk to him.'

'I know. I keep hoping against hope that his temper will cool and he'll go back to being reasonable. But if I wait till we reach London, we'll never have a moment alone. Gabriel will stay with his men and I'll doubtless be thrown back on his foster-family in Shoreditch.'

The green eyes considered her thoughtfully.

'That doesn't sound very satisfactory.'

'It isn't. But what can I do?'

'Leave it to me,' said Kate unexpectedly. 'I can't promise anything. But I think I just may have a solution.'

Hauled without explanation into the privacy of the bookroom, Signor Falcieri del Santi naturally made the most of his opportunities, which made it rather difficult for his wife to tell him what she wanted. And when, between laughter and languor, she finally managed to do so, he went on to raise some half-dozen objections purely for the pleasure of prolonging the moment. Then he grinned, told her to leave the matter with him, and permitted her to tidy her hair.

Luciano waited until the bridal pair were being noisily escorted to bed and then, taking a bottle and two glasses, went in search of Eden. He found him standing at the window of the winter parlour, staring out into the darkness.

Turning slightly and looking as though he'd have preferred to be left alone, Eden said, 'Why aren't you upstairs making bawdy jests with the rest of them?'

'For the same reason you're not, I imagine.' Luciano filled the glasses and handed one to his brother-in-law. 'Or do you still believe we have nothing in common?'

'Odd as it may seem, I don't give it much thought. But I suppose, if I were honest, I'd have to admit to possibly having misjudged you in the past.'

A gleam of humour appeared in the night-dark eyes.

'And I'll admit that you may have had cause.'

Eden smiled faintly. 'My God. *Aren't* we being civilised? It's a pity Kate's not here.'

'You can rely on me to tell her.' Luciano paused briefly and then decided to come to the point. 'In the meantime, however, she – and I – need your help. For reasons which I haven't quite fathomed, Kate is convinced that the state of unholy discord which plainly exists between your Colonel and his lady can be transformed into heavenly harmony by simply trapping them under the same roof.'

'I doubt it,' said Eden caustically.

'So do I. But Kate has asked me to put the Cheapside premises at their disposal for as long as they are in London – and, since it will be some time before Felix is ready to set up his sign there, I've agreed to do so. My difficulty, however, lies in offering rent-free lodgings to a man I barely know. And that's where you come in.'

For a long time, Eden regarded him without speaking. Then he said resignedly, 'Is *nothing* you do ever simple?'

'Apparently not,' shrugged Luciano. And, with a sudden, genuinely amused laugh, 'But look on the bright side. At least no one's in any physical danger this time.'

Four

Though less than ecstatic about continuing to reside with his wife, Gabriel considered it preferable to having his domestic problems picked over in Shoreditch. So when, after leaving Thorne Ash to resume their journey, Eden dangled the keys of the Cheapside premises before him, he merely said that, since they were likely to find themselves guarding either the Tower or Whitehall until the rest of the regiment returned from the North, Eden should live there, too. Then he sent Wat down the column to inform Venetia of the arrangement and went back to exchanging meaningless courtesies with the Duke of Hamilton.

Having been forewarned by Kate, Venetia accepted the news without comment and with a well-concealed quiver of apprehension. She suddenly realised that it was one thing to stop Gabriel avoiding her but quite another to predict what would happen when he did. Also, if she handled her next opportunity as badly as she had the last one, the results were likely to be catastrophic.

They arrived in London two days later; and while Gabriel completed the mission which, since he'd heard about Lucas and Lisle, had become more than ever distasteful to him, Eden and Wat escorted Venetia to the house in Cheapside.

It was larger than she had expected . . . and she was glad that someone had thrown sheets over most of the furniture. But, after nearly three years of disuse, there were cobwebs in every corner and a faint but all-pervading smell of damp. Venetia followed Eden from room to room while he unbolted shutters to let the light come flooding in. Then, when she had taken in the full scale of the problem, she cast aside her cloak and started giving Wat a list of her requirements.

By the time the Colonel returned at a little after ten that evening, they had wrought a semi-transformation. Fires were burning in all the bedchambers, with mattresses and linen airing in front of them; the parlour had been denuded of cobwebs and dust-covers; and a substantial meal from the nearest cook-shop stood ready and waiting on well-scoured platters. Gabriel, however, merely helped himself to a piece of pie and remarked dryly that he was glad the three of them had managed to make themselves so comfortable.

Venetia could have hit him. And because she immediately stalked grimly from the room to go and start making up beds, she did not know that, for once, she wasn't the only one. As soon as she had gone however, Wat said dourly, 'Comfortable we may be – but we've had to bloody work at it. And an extra pair of hands wouldn't have gone amiss.'

'You're wondering what kept me?' Gabriel subsided into the large, carved chair vacated by Venetia. 'I've been delivering his Grace of Hamilton to Windsor. His less-exalted fellows, of course, are snug in the Tower – along with a handful of similarly unfortunate gentlemen from Colchester and elsewhere. And we are to have the privilege of helping to make sure they all stay there.'

The cutting edge was more evident than Eden had ever seen it. Exchanging a brief, expressionless glance with Wat, he said lightly, 'Well at least we'll find this place a reasonably convenient billet. Only I think perhaps we ought to engage a couple of servants, don't you? After all, it's hardly fair to expect Venetia to do everything herself.'

The grey eyes examined him with cynical interest.

'Her idea or yours?'

'Mine.'

'Good. Then you won't mind seeing to it, will you?'

'*I'll* see to it,' growled Wat. 'I've not had much time for your lady in the past – and I still think it's a pity you married her. But she's ridden all the way here without complaining, and today's proved that she's not afraid to dirty her hands neither. So I reckon she's maybe earned a touch more consideration – and a few less megrims.'

'I see.' Gabriel cast the remains of his pie into the fire and came abruptly to his feet. 'Then allow me to inform you that

– inconsiderate as I am – I sent a couple of fellows back to Brandon Lacey before we left Banbury to fetch both Venetia's maid and a goodly portion of her wardrobe. And now I'm going to take my megrims off to the less censorious atmosphere of the nearest tavern. Goodnight.'

For a long time after the door had slammed shut behind him, Eden and Wat contemplated each other in silence. Then Eden said simply, 'Something nasty happened at Brandon Lacey. Do *you* know what it was?'

'No.' Mr Larkin's seamed, brown face settled into lines of pure anxiety. 'He won't talk to me. And it's the first time in sixteen years that's happened.'

While Venetia attended to purely domestic matters and discovered, with some relief, that she was definitely not pregnant, Sir Marmaduke Langdale was captured near Nottingham and the Prince of Wales sailed dispiritedly back to Holland. And while the Parliament, once more under the sway of Denzil Holles and the Presbyterians, prepared for its forthcoming talks with the King, John Lilburne and his associates presented it with a petition calling for constitutional reform and religious toleration along with the abolition both of his Majesty's veto and that of the Lords.

Not surprisingly – and despite its forty thousand signatures – the *Humble Petition* met with the usual fog of indifference. And when Bryony Morrell was told of its failure on a visit, with Sam, to the Lilburnes' new lodgings in Brewer's Yard, she immediately said worriedly, 'They won't put you in prison again, will they?'

Free-born John's face – still alarmingly thin in spite of nearly six weeks of Elizabeth's cosseting – creased into its usual attractive smile. 'No. At the moment, the Commons is still busy trying to buy my goodwill with the lands of so-called Delinquents who never did me any harm. And, of course, there's still hope in certain quarters that I'll second this charge of opportunism and over-ambition that's been laid against Cromwell.' He shrugged slightly. 'All I can say is that those who think so don't know me very well.'

'You don't think it's true?' asked Sam dryly.

'On the contrary. During the course of my recent visit to

County Durham, I took the opportunity to observe Oliver's northern progress – and everything pointed to a man dedicated more to self-aggrandisement than the welfare of his nation. But if and when I *do* choose to strike at him, you may be sure it won't be behind his back.'

Sam grinned. 'Can I quote that in *The Moderate?*'

'If you like. I've already written as much to Oliver himself – so it's no secret,' replied John. 'How is the newspaper doing, by the way?'

'Very well. We're selling every copy we print and making a reasonable profit into the bargain. So much so, in fact, that I now earn enough to afford a decent lodging.'

'He's moved to rooms on Tower Street,' said Bryony proudly. And then, sighing, 'The only trouble is that he works so hard I scarcely ever see him.'

Free-born John looked from one to the other of them with an air of mild discovery. Then he said, 'Well, there's a very simple solution to that, isn't there? Perhaps it's time you considered getting married.'

A little later, Sam and Bryony walked down to Westminster Stairs in thoughtful silence – until, unable to keep the words back any longer, Bryony said, 'He's right, you know. We've known each other over a year and been in love for months – so why *shouldn't* we be married?'

'Uncle Jack,' replied Sam succinctly. 'You know he won't hear of it. And who's to blame him? I've only been in prison once but there's no guarantee I won't end up there again one day. And though it's true we could probably manage on what I earn, it would be pretty hand-to-mouth.'

'I know. But it would get better in time and at least we'd be together,' she argued. 'Then again, we're never going to talk Uncle Jack round unless we start trying. And though he'll say no to begin with, he can't go on saying it forever, can he?'

'Don't count on it,' advised Sam. 'And what if he orders me never to darken his door again?'

'He won't.'

'Considering that he warned us both to avoid this particular complication, I don't see how you can be so sure of that. But what I'm really asking is whether or not you're willing to take the risk?'

Bryony's breath leaked away and she came to an abrupt halt, staring at him out of suddenly luminous eyes. 'Yes. Are you . . . do you mean you'll do it?'

He smiled back crookedly. 'I suppose I'll have to, won't I? But don't be surprised if he kicks me out. Looking at it from his point of view, he'd be mad if he didn't.'

Having decided that it would be foolish to form any sort of friendship with a man awaiting trial for open rebellion against Parliament, Colonel Brandon had carefully avoided Justin Ambrose ever since Warwick – only to break his resolution within a week of assuming his duties at the Tower. There were two reasons for this. The first was that the summary executions of Lucas and Lisle continued to worry him because they spoke of vengeance rather than either necessity or normal military practice; and the second was that, with little enough to occupy his mind these days, anything was better than facing up to the real reason why he was finding Venetia's betrayal so hard to accept.

So he sought out Colonel Ambrose and spent an hour discussing the Preston campaign and the Parliament's chances of reaching agreement with the King, whilst trying to establish why the fate of this one man should concern him. Then he rode thoughtfully off to Shoreditch to announce his return to Jack – and make a few tactful inquiries of Bryony.

She was prowling moodily up and down the hall when he arrived and lost no time in dragging him into the seldom-used back parlour, saying baldly, 'You can't go in yet! Sam's asking Uncle Jack if he can marry me – and I don't want them interrupted. It could be *critical*.'

Gabriel had not felt like laughing in two weeks or more and now, unfortunately, was not the time. He therefore said gravely, 'Dear me. This is rather sudden, isn't it?'

'Not to Sam and me.'

'I see. And have you thought about it properly?'

'Yes.' Bryony hovered on the threshold, her eyes glued anxiously to the door on the other side of the hall.

Gabriel surveyed her over folded arms.

'How much do you know about him?'

'As much as I need to. I love him!'

'Yes. I've rather gathered that. But what do you know about his background . . . his family?'

She shrugged impatiently. 'It's in the cloth trade and as respectable as ours. His father died years ago but his mother is still alive and he has a brother and two sisters.'

The grey eyes sharpened. 'Go on.'

'What more is there? And why should you care?'

'Humour me. Are his sisters married?'

'Yes. Ruth to a tradesman just outside Banbury, and Abby to a Cavalier with an estate near Newark,' she replied edgily. 'And now will you please stop distracting me with silly questions? I've got more important things on my mind.'

Gabriel frowned down at his hands. It was beginning to look as if Justin Ambrose was by no means the unprincipled libertine everyone seemed to think – and that raised a number of delicate questions. He opened his mouth to ask how Sam felt about his Royalist brother-in-law, but was forestalled as Jack threw open the parlour door, saying testily, 'You can come in now, Bryony. I haven't killed him.'

Bryony picked up her skirts and ran straight to the shelter of Sam's arms, leaving Gabriel to stroll unhurriedly after her and lean against the door-jamb. From inside the room, Jack and Annis stared at him blankly and even Sam, pre-occupied as he was, looked faintly startled.

'Don't mind me,' said Gabriel laconically. 'This is one day when I'm in no particular hurry. And if Bryony has to wait much longer for your verdict, she may well burst.'

Jack grinned, crossed to shake his hand and said, 'I can't think why. However. Let's get the recriminations over with as quickly as possible.' He turned back to his niece. 'The answer, quite simply, is no – and you know why. I explained it all back in January, on the day you both assured me that there was no question of this ever happening.'

'But everything's changed since then!'

'So I've been told. But Sam's beliefs mean that though he's respectable today, he may be less so tomorrow. And you'll probably be passionately in love with someone else six months from now.'

'I won't!' cried Bryony angrily. 'I love Sam. I do!'

386

'It's no use telling him,' remarked Mr Radford bitterly. 'He's not taking us seriously.'

'Be grateful,' advised Jack. 'If I was, I'd be forbidding the two of you ever to see each other again – instead of merely saying that you may only meet here in this house.'

Relief weakened Bryony's knees. 'Oh! Do you mean it?'

'Of course he does,' said Sam ironically. 'He and your aunt have decided that your infatuation will wear out more quickly if you don't start seeing yourself as a sort of modern-day Juliet. Clever, don't you think?'

Bryony looked at Annis. 'Is that true?'

'Well, yes. I'm afraid it is,' replied Annis ruefully. 'You've always hankered after what you couldn't have – but it doesn't last. And that's the point we're making.'

'I see.' Bryony faced her uncle squarely. 'And what happens when you find out that what Sam and I feel for each other is different – that it *will* last?'

'We'll cross that bridge when we come to it,' he replied calmly. 'But somehow, I don't think we will. And that is all I have to say on the subject. You may discuss this at length with Samuel in the other room, if you wish, but you may not, in future, leave the house with him or meet him elsewhere unless you want me to impose even more restrictions. Do I make myself clear?'

'Perfectly,' she sniffed. And then, pulling Sam towards the door, 'Come on. Since we're to be treated as children, we may as well go and play.'

'One moment.' Arriving, almost without realising it, at a decision, Gabriel detached himself from the door-frame and fixed Mr Radford with an impassive grey gaze. 'I spent part of this morning with a gentleman I think you may possibly know. His name is Justin Ambrose.'

Sam was suddenly very still. He said, 'Where?'

'I regret to say in the Tower. He's to be tried for his part in the recent war.' Gabriel paused and then, when the younger man merely stood ramrod straight, his face pale and set, said, 'Do you want to discuss this in private?'

'No,' said Sam baldly. 'I want to see him. Can I?'

'Of course. If you present yourself tomorrow, I'll—'

'Not tomorrow. Now.' Sam drew a long breath and met

Bryony's bewildered eyes. 'I'm sorry. But it's for Abby, you see. Justin is her husband and—'

'And you like him,' she nodded. 'Yes. I know.'

'Like him? Just at this moment I could *murder* him!' Sam turned back to Gabriel. 'I'm sorry to be importunate—'

'But you regard this as an emergency. Quite.' Sighing, the Colonel replaced his hat and directed a mocking smile at his foster-brother. 'Sorry, Jack. Aside from telling you that I'm living on the corner of Friday Street and Cheapside, everything else will have to wait till another day. And meanwhile I'm sure you won't mind lending Mr Radford a horse. I draw the line at having him ride pillion on mine.'

By the time they arrived within the cold, stone precincts of the Tower, Gabriel had told Samuel more or less the whole story and discovered that an unlikely but very real bond appeared to exist between the Cavalier and the Leveller. Once inside, however, he simply led Mr Radford past the guards and along a short, vaulted passage to the cell occupied by Colonel Ambrose and unlocked the door.

Justin was lying full-length on his pallet with his arms folded across his face and, when the door opened, he did not immediately move. Then Sam said, 'I thought *I* was the one who was supposed to end up here.' And the hidden face was suddenly uncovered to reveal an expression of torment, slowly shifting into shock.

'*Sam?*' Justin catapulted to his feet. 'My God. How—?'

'Blame it on the Colonel,' said Samuel, jerking his head in Gabriel's direction. And then, coming to the point with a vengeance, 'Does Abby know where you are?'

'No.' The tone was flat and cold but the light grey eyes were haunted. 'She must be frantic by now.'

'It's nice of you to realise it. Of course it would have been even nicer if you'd stayed at home where you belong and left the King to sink or swim on his own . . . but I suppose you couldn't resist making the grand gesture.'

'Stop it, Sam.'

'Why should I? I trusted you to look after her, damn it, not go running back to the wars as if—'

'*For Christ's sake!*' The sculpted face was perfectly white.

'All right. I made a mistake and let myself get caught – and you can't possibly say anything I haven't said to myself a hundred times over. But blaming me won't help Abby.' He drew an unsteady breath. 'It's worse than you realise. She's almost six months pregnant.'

For a moment Sam stared at him as though he couldn't trust his voice. Then he said wildly, 'And you *left* her?'

'Obviously. But I didn't bargain for being shut up in this place – or for what's likely to happen next.'

'And what *is* likely to happen next?'

'How the bloody hell should I know?'

Gabriel stepped through the door and closed it behind him. He said, 'It depends what they can charge you with.'

Colonel Ambrose gave a short, sardonic laugh.

'I'm dead, then.'

There was an airless silence. Then Sam said, 'If that's your idea of a joke, it's not funny.'

'No. It isn't, is it? And neither is this. I want you to go to Trent with a letter for Abby.'

'You think I needed to be asked?' Sam turned an opaque black gaze on Gabriel. 'Can't *you* do something?'

'Unfair, Sam,' said Justin sharply. 'He's already helped by bringing you here. You can't ask him to save my neck as well.' And, to Gabriel, 'I owe you the truth – and somehow I don't think you'll misuse it. They'll charge me, quite legitimately, with devising the ruse which took Pontefract. And if they find out who I am, they'll also accuse me of breaking my parole not to fight again.' He shrugged slightly. 'It's a technicality . . . but Justin Ambrose never took the oath. The man who did was the eighth baron Templeton of Trent. And that, I'm afraid, is who I now am.'

While Colonel Ambrose was writing to his wife and Colonel Brandon was trying to decide how much further he was prepared to involve himself in the affairs of a man who had crossed his path purely by chance, Venetia was staring moodily out of the parlour window on to Cheapside wondering how to pass the rest of the day.

Her maid had arrived, along with her clothes, for which she was extremely thankful; she had a cook and a sturdy girl

389

to help with the cleaning; and, with the exception of the downstairs room which had plainly once been Luciano del Santi's workshop, the rest of the house was now in pristine order. She had even replied to Sophia's letter about the depressing quality of the harvest. In short, everything was going beautifully – except for her relationship with Gabriel and the desert it seemed to be creating in her soul.

She heaved a morose sigh and wondered, for perhaps the hundredth time, why she didn't seem able to pull herself together. Then her eye alighted on a familiar, flamboyantly-cloaked figure and, without any warning at all, she discovered that one's blood really could run cold. For a mere fraction of a second, she froze. Then she flew out of the room and down the stairs into the street.

Catching up with her quarry from behind, she hauled viciously on his cloak, half-strangling him in the process, and said furiously, 'You malicious bastard – how *dare* you tell Gabriel that you were my lover?'

Ellis continued coughing for rather longer than was necessary while he assembled the fragments of his customary *sangfroid*. This, of course, was a mistake – for it enabled Venetia to launch a breathless and vitriolic assault on his manners, his morals and his intelligence. Then, still without allowing him to speak, she demanded to know whether wrecking her life was his sole, self-imposed mission.

Seeing no point in wasting his charm, Ellis said sulkily, 'I don't know why you should think I'm here on your account. As far as I knew, you were still in Yorkshire.'

'And but for you, I would be!' she snapped. 'Well? What *are* you doing here? Rescuing the Royalists in the Tower? Arranging to blow up Parliament? Planning to assassinate Cromwell? I'm sure it's bound to be something spectacular.'

He shrugged. 'Not this time. I'm merely attending to a small business venture of my own. I've spent months setting it up – in between doing my best for the Cause – and I'm damned if I'm going to kiss it goodbye just to suit you.'

'I see.' The violet eyes regarded him witheringly. 'Tell me something. Did you return to England to fight for the King or to make money?'

'Both – and why not? The revenue from Steeple Park

barely keeps me in boot-polish and I can't go back to Paris unless I can pay off some of my debts.'

'Ah! At last I'm beginning to understand.'

'No you're not. You don't know what it's like. I can put up with exile but not with penury as well. And why the hell should I? Brandon Lacey is mine by right; and if the King regains his throne, I'll have it back.'

'Yes. I can just imagine what you'll do with it, too,' said Venetia bitterly. Then, 'There's no point in continuing this conversation, except in one particular. Gabriel and I are living just across the street and if you interfere any more – or even come near us – I won't be responsible for my actions. Do you understand me?'

He laughed. 'Oh yes, sweetheart. I understand. You've fallen in love with the bastard. I'm disappointed in you – really I am. I thought you had more discrimination.'

For a moment, she stared at him so oddly that he thought she was about to faint. Then, with a complete disregard for the passers-by, she struck him hard and accurately across the face and walked away, leaving him to become the butt of a good deal of coarse humour as the imprint of her hand flamed on his skin.

Back in Luciano del Santi's parlour and shaking in every limb, Venetia finally acknowledged the fact that – for once in his life – Ellis had spoken no more than the truth. She loved Gabriel; and, in some small, locked chamber of her mind, she had known it for some time but been afraid to face it.

Well, it was out now – and part of her was glad. At least it went some way to explaining her damnable stupidity at Thorne Ash and her uncharacteristic cowardice since. She loved him and wanted him and was frightened as much by the sheer intensity of it as by the knowledge that, short of a miracle, she couldn't tell him. For though Gabriel's whole life was a testament to fair play, he wasn't the man to let himself be made a fool of twice; and a declaration of love at this stage was likely to produce exactly the kind of reaction she most dreaded.

Eden appeared in time for supper but Gabriel didn't. Venetia was not surprised. She had become used both to his frequent absences and the fact that he made sure they were never alone together. So she sat down with Eden, picked listlessly at her food and, gradually becoming aware that the Major was doing exactly the same, eventually summoned enough interest to ask what was wrong.

'What?' The hazel gaze focused slowly on her face. 'I'm sorry. I was just thinking about a mutual friend whom I discovered this morning amongst our captives, but almost failed to recognise because he looks so ill.'

Venetia laid down her knife. 'Francis?'

'You *knew*?'

'I . . . wondered. Was he at Colchester?'

'Yes.' Eden pushed back his chair and stood up. 'He says it was a sort of hell and I can well believe it. But I don't know what I can do about his present predicament.'

'I suppose that depends on how many risks you're prepared to take,' remarked Venetia. 'As I recall it, he was once your best friend.'

'I'm more than aware of it. But that was six years ago and the war has created a huge chasm between us.' He saw no reason to add that Francis's attempts to talk of Celia had done nothing to bridge the gap. 'And though I'd like to help him – for old times' sake – I can't just free him. It would finish my career.'

'Only if you allow yourself to be implicated. But it's entirely up to you, of course. I'm just glad Francis never promised not to fight again, otherwise he might have gone the way of Lucas and Lisle instead of merely spending the next few years in prison.' She raised one cool brow. 'I suppose you realise that Sir Lewis Dyve is still in the Tower for his part in the *first* war?'

'Yes, damn it! But arranging an escape isn't as easy as you seem to think,' began Eden. And then stopped abruptly as the door opened and Gabriel came in.

'Dear me,' he said gently. 'I do hope you haven't been waiting for me?'

Venetia felt her insides turn into something closely resembling a butter-churn and stayed sensibly silent.

'No.' Eden dropped neatly back into his chair and poured himself another glass of wine. 'If we did that, we'd starve. However. May we ask where you've been?'

'By all means.' Gabriel discarded his hat and gloves and took his place at the board. 'I've been talking to Henry Ireton – or, to be more accurate, *he* has been talking to *me*. He's not happy about Denzil Holles's renewed presence in the Commons or the forthcoming talks with the King – or Fairfax's refusal to do anything about either. In short, he's seriously concerned about a myriad of things and that makes it very difficult to get a word in edgeways.'

'And what word,' asked Eden, 'were you striving for?'

'Ransom,' came the succinct reply. And then, in response to his Major's uncomprehending stare, 'After Colchester, Fairfax allowed every regiment its share of prisoners to be held for ransom or to be sold to the galleys. And since what's good for one ought to be good for all, I asked to be allocated two gentlemen on a similar basis.'

Eden choked on his wine. 'You're joking!'

'What makes you think that? It's a simple scheme which benefits everyone.'

'Then I hope your chosen prisoners agree with you.'

'I daresay they will,' came the negligent reply. 'But it might be more useful if you hoped they were rich.'

There was a small silence during which Venetia cautiously unlocked her tongue.

'I can't believe you're only doing this for the money.'

Gabriel surveyed her expressionlessly. 'Why not?'

'Because it's not the way you do things.'

A glimmer of surprise touched his eyes and then was gone. He said abrasively, 'It is now. With my pay substantially in arrears and Brandon Lacey hanging around my neck like the proverbial millstone, I'm lining my pockets as best I may.' A deliberately mocking smile bracketed his mouth. 'I'm sorry to disappoint you – but blood will tell, as they say. And I thought I'd already given you ample demonstration of the fact that I'm no gentleman?'

A tide of colour stained Venetia's skin and, for a moment, she simply stared at him. Then, because Eden's presence prevented her answering as she would have liked, she rose abruptly from the table and stalked from the room.

The door slammed shut but Gabriel remained oddly still, frowning into space. Eden tolerated the ensuing silence as long as he could and then said impatiently, 'All right. I give up. None of this is what it seems. So are you going to tell me what the hell you're up to or aren't you?'

'Since you ask so nicely – why not?' Gabriel pulled a document from his pocket and laid it before the Major. 'For reasons too complex to explain, I'm trying to ensure that there's no question of Justin Ambrose going to the gallows. But so my request didn't look too personal – and because one might as well be hung for a sheep as a lamb – I asked Henry for permission to select a second prize.' He paused. 'You'll notice that the other name has been left blank.'

Eden was suddenly very still. 'Why?'

Gabriel sighed. 'So that you may tell me what to write.'

There was a short, airless pause while Major Maxwell came to terms with his Colonel's unexpected knowledge. Then, shortly, 'It's Francis Langley – Celia's brother. And I doubt he's got sixpence to scratch with, let alone the means of ransoming himself.'

The grey eyes sharpened. 'Does Venetia know him?'

'Yes.' Eden debated outlining his conversation with Venetia – and tactfully decided against it.

'Good.' A strange, sardonic smile dawned. 'Then once we have Messrs Langley and Ambrose locked up downstairs, the question of money may possibly become academic.'

This time the silence reached epic proportions.

'Are you saying what I think you're saying?' asked Eden weakly.

'I'm not saying anything at all. I'm merely keeping my options open.' Gabriel reached for the wine-jug and placed it at the Major's elbow. 'Have another drink,' he invited. 'You look as though you need it.'

On September 18th, a group of Parliamentary commissioners which included Denzil Holles, Harry Vane and Lord Saye and Sele opened forty days of controversial negotiation with his Majesty at Newport on the Isle of Wight. And, in Cheapside, Colonel Brandon coolly informed his wife that he was installing two Royalist gentlemen in the empty workroom and a round-the-clock guard in the passage outside it.

'For how long?' she asked.

'As long as it takes our guests to purchase their freedom. But don't worry. Wat will see that the place is made habitable for them and the guards will serve their meals – so there will be no need for you to see them. At all.' He paused, eyeing her blandly. 'You're remarkably incurious. Don't you want to know who I've decided to milk?'

Venetia shrugged. 'Of course. But I'd rather got the impression that I wasn't supposed to ask.'

'Now, why should you think that?'

'My fevered imagination, obviously. So who are they?'

'One is the Cavalier inaccurately credited with the seduction of Samuel Radford's sister. And the other, I suspect, is your mysterious friend from Colchester.'

Venetia's breath caught. Then all the tumblers clicked into place and the door to understanding swung partially open. Her instinct had been right. He wasn't doing this for money. He was doing it to save two men from Parliamentary justice but, for some reason she couldn't quite fathom, he was intent on making her think otherwise.

Allowing just the right degree of sarcasm to enter her gaze and with the first flicker of inspiration she'd felt in a month, she said, 'I see. Then that will give you ample opportunity in which to establish whether or not you've any reason to be jealous of him, won't it?'

'*Jealous?*' echoed Gabriel. 'It's a joke!'

'Is it? Since there's not a shred of truth in your suspicions – I can't imagine what else could cause them.' She smiled kindly. 'But of course I don't expect you to admit it. And now I wish to change my dress and go out – unless I'm supposed to apply for leave of absence?' And she drifted away, leaving him staring at her retreating back.

In truth, she had not previously had any intention of going out – but a natural reluctance to let Gabriel know it, coupled with a small but undeniably exhilarating sense of triumph changed her mind. And two hours later she was inside one of the elegant houses in Inigo Jones' Covent Garden *piazza*, asking if Lady Gillingham was at home.

The room into which she was shown was light, well-proportioned and exquisitely-furnished. A king's ransom in books lined one wall and a glowing French tapestry adorned another; a portrait of the late Earl by Van Dyck hung over the fireplace and an impressive array of English silver and Japanese porcelain graced the carved, oak court-cupboard. Venetia found herself wondering why Isabel continually pleaded poverty when – no matter how high the composition fine on the Gillingham lands had been set – the books alone would probably pay it twice over. Then the door opened and her ladyship shot in looking oddly harassed.

'This *is* a surprise,' she said, her voice both breathless and faintly brittle. 'I didn't know you were back in London. If you'd sent me word, I'd have called on you.'

Venetia's brows rose almost imperceptibly.

'I'm sorry. Have I come at a bad time?'

'No, no. I'm delighted to see you – truly. Only you know the problems I have.' Isabel arrived at Venetia's side and lowered her voice confidentially. 'My mother-in-law's here – and I know just how it will be if she meets you. She'll say the most terrible things and you'll believe her. Everyone does. She – she *bewitches* people.'

'Then perhaps I should go,' offered Venetia.

'No! No – not just yet. Not before you've told me some of your news.' Catching Venetia's hand in a feverish grip, Isabel drew her to a chair and sat down beside her. 'How do you come to be here again so soon? I thought you were to stay at Brandon Lacey for the harvest.'

'I was. But Gabriel's duty brought him south and so—'

'He's with you?' The words cracked like a pistol shot.

Venetia blinked. 'Why yes. He brought the Duke of Hamilton and some other prisoners to London. And since the bulk of his regiment is still in the North, he's been temporarily assigned to guard-duty at the Tower.'

'Dear me,' murmured Isabel reflectively. 'Dear me. And doubtless you are once more living with the Morrells?'

'Not this time.' Venetia gave the ghost of a smile and explained about Luciano del Santi's offer.

For once, Isabel listened without interrupting. Then she drawled, 'Well, I suppose Cheapside is *some* improvement on Shoreditch. But surely you didn't walk here unattended?'

'Why not? It's hardly the other side of the earth, after all. And being country-bred, my maid is—'

'You mean you haven't even a groom? Good God! Then who carries your messages?'

'I haven't had occasion to send any. But I suppose I could ask Wat Larkin. He's been remarkably helpful of late.'

'I daresay. But do you *trust* him?'

'In a way,' began Venetia. And then, suddenly thinking of Ellis and the fact that if he materialised again she might be glad of a go-between. 'Or no. Perhaps not.'

'There you are, then. You need someone you can rely on. And I,' announced Isabel earnestly, 'know just the man. He's always been loyal to me, so much so that the Dowager is set on dismissing him. And she'll do it, too. She always gets what she wants. So if you can find a use for him, you'd be doing me a favour.'

Venetia shook her head. 'I only need someone while I'm here in London. After that—'

'After that, if you can't keep him on, I'll find him another position. So what do you say?'

Feeling rather like a piece of rolled-out pastry, Venetia hesitated briefly and then gave in. 'Thank you.'

'Good. I'll see that he's ready to leave with you.' Her ladyship rose, shook the creases from her cornflower taffeta and, with no warning whatsoever, said, 'You're dreadfully pale, my dear. You're not pregnant, are you?'

Caught unawares, Venetia replied unevenly, 'No! No – of course not. I – I'm just a bit tired.'

For a moment, the too-vivid gaze gave the uncomfortable impression of seeing right through her. Then Isabel said, 'You should take better care of yourself. I'll tell Harris of our arrangement and give him some of my special cordial for you. I'm sure you'll find it most beneficial.'

The door clicked shut behind her and Venetia gave a sigh of relief. She could tell no one what had happened between herself and Gabriel – not even Isabel; but she had just come perilously close to giving herself away through sheer clumsiness. And that, when she had always prided herself on having a cool head, was downright frightening.

Unable to sit still, she crossed the room to examine the books. And then the door opened again and a woman came in.

Though of moderate height and slender build, she was by no means young – for the black hair was stranded with silver and there were lines and shadows about the liquid dark eyes. But it was obvious that she had once been a great beauty; and she still had the kind of elegant simplicity that most women envied but few could achieve. Venetia closed the book she was holding and expelled her breath. This, presumably, was Susannah, Dowager Countess of Gillingham. And she wasn't at all what one might have expected from Isabel's tales.

Unsmilingly but in a rich, warm contralto, the Dowager said, 'You must be a friend of my daughter-in-law.'

Venetia replaced the book and curtsied.

'Yes, Madam. My name is Venetia Brandon and I—'

'Brandon?' The echo was quick and soft. Then, with a slight shrug, 'Ah – the Suffolk branch, no doubt?'

'No.' Unwilling to enter the realms of genealogy, Venetia said, 'My late father-in-law was a Yorkshireman.'

'I – see.' The Dowager paused, eyeing her with a strange sort of remoteness, 'So you are married. To whom?'

'A Colonel in the New Model Army,' said Venetia, tiring of the interrogation and determined to put an end to it. 'You must be wondering where Isabel is. But I'm taking on one of her servants, you see and she's just—'

'Which one?' The musical voice sharpened suddenly.

'I believe his name is Harris.'

'Ah.' A frown appeared but, as ever, she seemed in no hurry to speak. Then, 'Tell me . . . do you know Isabel well?'

'Well enough. We served the Queen together.'

'At Whitehall and in France and Oxford,' added Isabel gratingly from the door. Her knuckles glowed white on the latch and the blue eyes were no longer empty. 'So all your lies will be wasted – for Venetia will not believe them.'

'Lies?' The Dowager turned with sudden, bitter weariness. 'What lies could surpass the truth?'

Impaled by the china-blue gaze and feeling intensely uncomfortable, Venetia said hastily, 'I'm sorry – but I really must leave, Isabel.'

'Of course you must. It's no good staying, after all. *She'll* spoil everything. And Harris is waiting in the hall to escort you. You'll like him. I know you will. And when he returns for his belongings, he can tell me where to find you so I can call. You will let me call, won't you?'

'Of course I will.' Venetia curtsied briskly to the Dowager. 'I am pleased to have met you, madam.'

'Polite – but untrue, I fear,' came the oblique reply. 'And I think that, just this once, I am sorry for it.'

Out in the hall Isabel disintegrated into another impassioned torrent and it was therefore several minutes more before Venetia reached the safety of the street with Harris following a correct two paces behind her. From the little she had seen, he was a large, softly-spoken young man with dun-coloured hair and a very helpful demeanour. Venetia wondered what the Dowager had against him; and then, recalling Isabel's past history, decided that it was probably better not to know.

With two Royalist gentlemen confined below stairs and a host of other problems, Gabriel accepted the addition of Tom Harris to the household with no more than a lifted eyebrow and a pithy remark. Wat, on the other hand, conceived an instant and apparently unreasoning dislike of the newcomer and, when not occupied elsewhere, took to keeping him under subtle surveillance – until, that was, a severe attack of colic unexpectedly confined him to bed.

On the day Mr Larkin fell sick, Venetia received an airy, apologetic visit from Isabel and a letter from Phoebe, gleefully announcing the departure of their aunt and cousins from Ford Edge. On the following morning, however, learning that the invalid was no better, she climbed the stairs to see for herself. Wat, consumed with stomach pains and feeling as sick as a dog, greeted her with apparent loathing. Venetia told him to hold his tongue or she'd leave him to suffer. Then she assessed his condition, brewed a concoction of mint and balm and stood over him until he drank it.

By the time she reappeared with a second cupful, Wat was feeling sufficiently improved to swallow the mixture without argument. Then he said bluntly, 'I reckon it's time you and me had a bit of a talk.'

'About what?'

'About what's going on in Gabriel's head.'

Venetia kept her gaze carefully blank. 'I'd have thought you would know more of that than I.'

'Yes – and time was when I *would* have. But whatever's gnawing at his vitals now, it's something he can't bring himself to tell me. So I thought maybe you might.'

'And why would I want to do that?'

'Because it's gnawing at you as well, lass, and has been ever since Uttoxeter.'

Understanding from Mr Larkin was the very last thing Venetia had expected and, to her horror, she felt tears pricking at her eyes. Blinking them away, she said uncertainly, 'Haven't you guessed? He thinks I've . . . done something terrible.'

'Ah.' Wat fixed her with a shrewd stare. 'And have you?'

'No! I've been stupid and blind and unfair – I admit that. But I've done nothing else I need be ashamed of.'

'And have you told *him* that?'

'I've tried. At first he wasn't in the mood to listen; and lately he hasn't stood still long enough.' She paused and then, looking at him, drew a slightly uneven breath. 'You know, don't you? You know what he thinks I've done.'

'I could take a fair guess,' agreed Wat, neutrally. 'But what I haven't worked out is what he *did* about it.'

Venetia coloured. 'He – he lost his temper. But I don't blame him for that.'

'No. But he might blame himself.' Wat winced as a fresh spasm of cramp attacked his stomach. 'Was he violent?'

'No.' She turned restlessly away towards the window. 'I can't discuss this, Mr Larkin. It wouldn't be right. All I can tell you is that Gabriel has nothing to reproach himself with – or to apologise for.'

Having by now acquired a surprisingly accurate picture, Wat fired his final salvo. 'Do you love him?'

Shock caught her by the throat. 'Yes.'

There was a long, thoughtful silence. 'Then you'd better get used to calling me Wat, hadn't you?' he said.

Venetia turned slowly and met a deceptively irritable scowl. 'And you,' she remarked, 'had better start eating at home, where we know one mushroom from another.'

The scowl turned into a look she couldn't identify.

'Are you saying,' asked Wat, 'that I've been poisoned?'

Since she had been saying nothing of the sort, Venetia's first impulse was to observe that if he had been, someone had made a shocking poor job of it. Then, upon due reflection, she said, 'Given your symptoms, I suppose it's not impossible. But it's hardly likely, is it? Unless, of course, you've upset someone by winning at dice a bit too often – or got your lady-friends mixed up?'

Mr Larkin eyed her with a sort of disgusted approval.

'I said you could call me Wat,' he remarked. 'I didn't give you leave to be cheeky.'

Five

Having served together under Prince Rupert in the early part of the first war, Francis and Justin had less difficulty settling amicably into Luciano del Santi's workroom than they had in agreeing why Colonel Brandon seemed in no hurry to discuss money. Francis maintained that it was because Eden knew perfectly well that he himself didn't have any. Justin, less sanguine and worried about his wife, pointed out that it didn't make any difference. The Colonel was supposed to be ransoming them on behalf of his regiment; and, unless he wanted to face a charge of corruption, he was going to have to do it.

By the time ten days had passed, Gabriel was beginning to think so too. He had chosen guards who were not exactly over-burdened with intelligence, ordered Venetia to stay away from the prisoners and done his damnedest to make her believe that he'd sell them to the galleys if the price was right – but all to no avail. She merely behaved as if the Cavaliers downstairs didn't exist and continued looking at him in a way that was beginning to haunt his sleep.

He knew, of course, that sooner or later they were going to have to talk about what had happened at Brandon Lacey. The trouble was that now his anger had gone he had fallen victim to an emotion that was infinitely more dangerous – and which he did not know how to fight. So he went on avoiding her . . . and would probably have continued doing so had not Wat taken a hand in the matter by helping Venetia to trap him in the parlour one evening when Eden was out.

She shut the door and then leaned against it, her hand still resting on the latch. Then she said simply, 'I can't go on like this. Either talk to me – or send me home.'

Gabriel stood very still and controlled an impulse to push past her and walk out. Then he said, 'Why should I?'

'Because I don't deserve this. I've made a good many mistakes during the course of our marriage but adultery isn't one of them. I slept with Ellis just before I left Oxford in 1644 – but never since then. As for his visit after Preston, I neither wanted nor invited it and I sent him packing as soon as I could. And I will swear to that on anything, or before anyone, you care to name.'

The violet eyes met Gabriel's with every appearance of candour and the temptation to believe her was almost irresistible. Forcing himself to concentrate on saying nothing he might regret, he said coolly, 'Isn't it a little late to be telling me all this? If you had revealed your liaison when we were first married, I would have had fewer misconceptions and Ellis, less scope for his malicious remarks. And if his stay at Brandon Lacey was as innocent as you say – why didn't you apprise me of it as soon as I arrived?'

'Because I knew how it would look to you,' she replied. 'And because I – I was afraid it would destroy the foundations which you and I had only just begun to build and which mattered a great deal to me. As they still do.'

'Do they?' An ironic, faintly incredulous smile curled his mouth. 'Then it's a pity we built them on sand.'

'We didn't! We just . . . haven't trusted each other as much as we perhaps should have done.'

'My God!' Gabriel gave a short, harsh laugh. 'That's the most thundering euphemism I've ever heard. You've never trusted me *at all*. I'm just the Roundhead bastard you were forced to demean yourself by marrying.'

Venetia flinched. 'That's not true any more. But after what I said at Thorne Ash, I can't blame you for thinking it. All I can say is that I didn't mean it the way it must have sounded – and that I deeply regret it. My only excuse is that my nerves were raw.'

'So, as it happens, were mine.'

'I know. I'm sorry.'

He stared at her across the width of the room, wishing his sense of proportion had stayed buried. Then he said abruptly, 'Why? I provoked you and we both know it. Also,

404

if apologies are the order of the day, I most certainly owe you one for my lack of self-control at Brandon Lacey. It was, of course, entirely inexcusable.'

'But not unreasonable.' Venetia coloured faintly. 'Also – as you yourself pointed out – it was not rape.'

'No. But it might have been.' Turning away slightly, he leaned his elbow on the mantelpiece and frowned down into the fire while he grappled with the most difficult question of all. 'You didn't fight me. Was that because you were afraid of what might happen if you did?'

'No.' Her voice was low and strained. 'It was because I didn't want to. And I think you know it perfectly well.'

He looked at her then, the frown still lingering in his eyes. 'If there is logic in that, I can't see it.'

'Then perhaps,' suggested Venetia, with a crooked smile, 'you're just not looking in the right place.'

Gabriel's breath caught and he made a small, involuntary movement. Then, placing every nerve and muscle under rigid control, he said, 'I think this has gone far enough.'

'I don't. I was rather hoping, you see, that we . . . that we could go back to being civil to one another.'

'You mean you'd like *me* to be civil.' He eyed her sardonically for a moment and then shrugged. 'Very well. If you'll move away from the door, I promise I'll do my best.'

Very slowly, Venetia did as he asked. She said remotely, 'You're going out?'

'No. I'm going to introduce you to our guests. It's about time, after all. And though *you* may be ready for a cosy evening à deux, I'm afraid I'm not.'

Since it was necessary to preserve appearances, this was the first time Gabriel had removed both his prisoners from their makeshift dungeon simultaneously – and he knew that it wasn't an especially good idea. Nor was he really sure why he had decided to do it. He merely watched the cautious greeting which Venetia exchanged with Captain Langley, presented her to the man he was continuing to call Colonel Ambrose – and turned away to pour wine for them all.

Justin bowed over Venetia's hand and concealed his

inevitable reflections as well as she was concealing hers. Francis, still rather gaunt but otherwise largely restored, said lightly, 'Venetia, my loved one . . . after so long, there are doubtless a thousand questions to be asked. But just at this moment, I can only think of one. Is there the remotest chance that you can find me some poetry to read?'

Venetia recognised that, in his own inimitable manner, he was telling her that he had said nothing to Gabriel of their more recent meetings. Smiling to show that she had understood, she said, 'There are some books upstairs belonging to Luciano del Santi – though I imagine there's nothing amongst them that you haven't already read.'

'He won't mind,' grinned Justin Ambrose. 'He'll just be grateful for any alternative to my conversation.'

'True,' nodded Francis. 'Very true. I'm tired of re-fighting Preston and Colchester. It is not my idea of fun.'

'Then I'd better see if I can find you a new source of entertainment, hadn't I?' said Venetia, moving to the door. 'God forbid that you should find our hospitality lacking.'

'And God forbid that we should find any cause for complaint,' remarked Justin dryly as she left the room. And, to Gabriel, 'It's probably a silly question . . . but are you ready to name your price yet?'

'I'm sure we'll all have a much more pleasant evening if I don't.' Gabriel handed both men a glass and then leaned negligently against the fireplace, smiling faintly. 'And you never know. These talks at Newport may finally result in the kind of agreement which will radically alter your position – though I have to say I wouldn't like to rely on it.'

'Neither would I,' said Francis, abandoning his languid tone. 'Have they made any progress worth mentioning?'

'Not yet. The Parliament is once more offering the so-called Hampton Court Propositions – which, as we all know, are merely the old Newcastle Propositions, thinly disguised. The King naturally began by objecting to the preamble's assertion that both Houses were "*necessitated to undertake a war in their just and lawful defence*" – but has since withdrawn his opposition on condition that his acceptance of that or any other point shall be considered invalid if an over-all agreement is not reached.'

Colonel Ambrose lifted one openly sardonic brow.

'Which is basically as good as admitting that he has no intention of putting his name to anything.'

'That is certainly the general feeling in the Army,' agreed Gabriel. 'For the rest, Holles appears to have begged on bended knee for his Majesty to conclude a treaty before Ireton gets the Army to purge Parliament of the Presbyterians; and Harry Vane has been doing his best to promote the *Heads of the Proposals*. Neither, so far as I am aware, have had much success.'

'And they won't,' said Francis. 'The King won't compromise on religion. He'll go on refusing to turn England Presbyterian even if it costs him his crown.'

'It could cost him more than that,' murmured Justin Ambrose flatly. And then stopped as the door opened and Venetia returned with an armful of books.

A little later, when Francis and Venetia were apparently debating the rival merits of Marlowe and Spenser, Gabriel drew Colonel Ambrose to one side and said quietly, 'What, precisely, were you suggesting just now?'

'Isn't it obvious?' The light grey eyes were bleak. 'If the King goes on pitting the factions against each other and refusing to stick to his word . . . I think they'll kill him.'

There was a long, eviscerating silence.

'They can't,' said Gabriel.

'They'll have to. What choice have they got? He won't give up, he's a focus for rebellion – and he's brought about a second war. They won't forgive him for that. So his only security lies in making terms – and fast.'

'Security from what? Assassination?'

'Only if all else fails,' replied Justin cynically. 'Or perhaps I'm mistaken in thinking that Ireton isn't the only one who wants the King put on trial?'

'No,' said Gabriel slowly. 'You're not mistaken. But there is no provision within the law for such a trial – and even John Lilburne has set his face against it. Also, I hope and believe that there are still enough moderate men in the Army to prevent it happening at all – let alone imposing a death sentence.'

'And what if there aren't?'

'If there aren't, I, for one, am going to have to seriously consider my position. I want no part in regicide. And though I hold no brief for Charles Stuart, the possible alternatives horrify me.'

'My thoughts exactly,' agreed Justin. Raised voices outside the room assailed his ear and he grinned faintly. 'It sounds as though your guards have fallen out over the dice-box again. Are they really the best you could find?'

He did not receive an answer. The door opened and Gabriel swore furiously under his breath. It was Eden Maxwell, closely followed by Samuel Radford.

Silence filled the room. Then Justin came abruptly to his feet and said, 'At bloody last! What took you so long?'

'What do you think?' retorted Sam. And stepped aside to reveal a dainty, dark-haired girl in a shabby blue cloak.

Shock drove the blood from Justin's skin and he seemed to stop breathing. Then, in a voice which cracked, he said, '*Abby?*' And moved uncertainly towards her.

Sam's sister did not wait. Half-laughing, half-crying, she met him half-way and when his arms closed around her, she reached up to touch his face as if convincing herself of his reality. For a long, timeless moment, they remained absolutely motionless, drowning in each other's eyes. Then, very very slowly, Justin gathered her still closer, his hand sliding up into the curling, night-dark hair to cradle her skull and with a hunger tempered by exquisite tenderness, his mouth found hers.

For the others in the room, the spell which had bound them gradually dissolved. Francis turned away to the fire, Sam pushed the door to in the face of the grinning troopers and Venetia, her throat full of ridiculous tears, looked across at her husband. His eyes were locked with those of Eden Maxwell and he looked positively thunderous.

Justin and Abigail remained frozen in the centre of the floor. Ignoring them and turning his attention to Mr Radford, Gabriel said softly, 'This isn't clever, Sam.'

'I know that, damn it! But—'

'You know nothing!' Realising that Eden had finally noticed that the door was still partly ajar, Gabriel gave a curt shake of his head to prevent him from closing it. Then with crisp, deliberate clarity, he said, 'I sincerely trust that this unlooked-for arrival means we may soon expect Colonel Ambrose's ransom payment?'

Reluctantly and without releasing his wife, Justin raised his head; but before he could speak, Samuel said, 'Ransom? Major Maxwell said something of that – but I didn't believe him.'

'Then you should have done,' responded Gabriel crisply. 'After all, you can't surely have imagined that I've put myself to the trouble of bringing Colonel Ambrose here purely for the good of his health?'

Venetia's eyes narrowed thoughtfully, Francis looked somewhat startled and a small snigger, swiftly checked, made its way around the door. Staring fixedly at Gabriel, Samuel said, 'I did think that, yes. I had the idea, you see, that you weren't the sort to prey on the misfortunes of others. My mistake, obviously.'

Abigail looked up at her husband. 'What's happening?'

His arm tightened about her and he gave her a clear, untroubled smile. 'Don't ask me, sweetheart. Colonel Brandon is the man with all the answers.'

She turned, half-shyly, to Gabriel.

'Are you really holding Justin for ransom?'

'I am indeed. What else would I want with him? Neither I nor my regiment has been paid for some considerable time – and we all have to live. Also, I should have thought that sparing Colonel Ambrose the inconvenience of a trial would be worth some small remuneration.'

'*How* small?' muttered Samuel bitterly. 'He sold half of his lands to meet his composition fines after the first war – he's barely got two sovereigns to rub together.'

'Not according to my information,' shrugged Gabriel. Then, clinically appraising Abby's waistline, 'And since he appears to need his freedom fairly urgently, I'm sure he'll contrive something.'

Sam swore, Eden frowned uncomfortably at his feet and Francis said, frigidly, 'In my opinion, that remark was neither courteous nor necessary.'

'Your views are a matter of the supremest indifference to

me,' returned Gabriel blightingly. 'In fact, I think we can dispense with your presence altogether. Major Maxwell?'

Aware that Venetia had silenced Francis with a jab of her elbow, Eden came smartly to attention. 'Sir?'

'Take the prisoners back where they belong. And if Troopers Baxter or Willis are anything less than sober, put their heads under the pump.'

There were more sounds from without and Eden grinned. 'My pleasure, Colonel.'

Still clinging to her husband, Abigail turned a disbelieving gaze on Gabriel. 'You can't send him away yet!'

'Watch me,' came the laconic reply.

'Then lock me up with him,' she begged.

'Out of the question.' Gabriel strolled across the floor towards them. 'You and I, Mistress, are going to have a little chat about the Colonel's future – or lack of it.'

Abigail stared despairingly up at Justin. He still looked relatively unconcerned and was even smiling a little. She said, 'How can you be so—'

He stopped the words with a tantalisingly unhurried kiss. 'Do you know how much – how very much – I love you?' he murmured. And then, in his usual distinct tone, 'We have to do as Colonel Brandon says, my heart . . . or the consequences could be very unfortunate. For all of us.'

No more than two paces away, Gabriel met the light, gleaming gaze with one of almost imperceptible amusement. 'Thank God someone is following the plot!' he breathed. And, aloud, 'Major Maxwell – do I have to wait all night?'

It was some moments before the door clicked shut behind Eden, Francis and Justin . . . and even then Gabriel held up a warning hand to prevent anyone speaking until he was sure they could not be overheard. Then he said briskly, 'You'd better sit down, Lady Templeton. You look worn to the bone.'

Abigail sank gratefully into the nearest chair.

'I'm also more than a bit confused,' she said.

'So am I,' murmured Venetia. 'Did you say *Templeton?*'

'I did. Justin is Lord Templeton of Trent,' replied Gabriel. 'But since it will do him no good at all to have anyone outside this room discover it, we had better all go on calling him Colonel Ambrose.' His gaze returned to Abigail. 'I'm sorry I had to part you from him so abruptly – but it was the only way to get rid of Willis and Baxter. They may have less than half a brain between them but they are still capable of repeating what they hear.'

There was a short, airless silence. Then, 'Are you saying,' asked Sam blankly, 'that all this has been part of some sort of *act?*'

'Yes. And a fairly convincing one, I hope.' Gabriel moved to pour wine for them all. 'Neither Eden nor I are particularly anxious to ruin our careers over this business – and I'd have preferred to conclude it without anyone else being any the wiser. But your sister's arrival has made that rather difficult – mainly because it's not going to be easy maintaining Justin's incognito if it becomes clear that his wife and brother-in-law are known to me.'

Absently accepting the wine he offered her, Abigail said remorsefully, 'I shouldn't have come. I'm sorry.'

'Why?' asked Sam. 'You didn't know about this ransom scheme – any more than I did. And we still don't know how it was supposed to work.'

Feeling as though the last piece of the puzzle had finally dropped into place, Venetia met Gabriel's eyes and smiled faintly. 'You're going to have to explain it to them.'

'But not to you, I gather?'

'No.' She drew a long, bracing breath. 'I've always known you didn't want the money – and of course you can't just let Francis and Justin go. So the only possible solution is for . . . someone . . . to help them escape. And that's what you hoped would happen.'

'Is that true?' asked Samuel sharply.

'Perfectly.' Gabriel continued to look at Venetia. 'It seems, however, that I miscalculated.'

She nodded gravely. 'Yes – and I hope you know why.'

Samuel drew an irritable breath. He said, 'I can't pretend to understand what's going on here. But if Justin's supposed to escape, it seems to me that we need a plan.'

'I already have a plan,' sighed the Colonel. 'I was just hoping I could avoid using it.' Then, as the door opened and Major Maxwell came in, 'But since time – as well as

411

discretion – is now of the essence, I suppose I'd better take you all into my confidence.'

'That,' remarked Eden, helping himself to wine, 'would be a relief. After tonight's debacle, I for one am sick of playing blindfold.'

'Then you'd better sit down and listen.' Gabriel perched himself on the edge of the table and surveyed his troops. 'We're going to do this as simply as possible – hopefully the night after tomorrow. Wat will have horses ready for our friends at the Blue Boar in Holborn – and Sam will wait with Mistress Abigail at some convenient inn roughly five miles north of London. Venetia will help me to drug Willis and Baxter . . . and in due course I shall unlock the door and allow myself to be overpowered.'

'And what,' asked Eden, 'will I be doing?'

'Since there's no point in us both putting our necks in the noose, you will be conspicuously on duty at the Tower.'

'While you're inviting Colonel Ambrose to hit you?'

'Exactly. You've some objection?'

'Only a dozen or so.' Eden grimaced wryly. 'But at least he'll probably make a better job of it than Francis.'

'Justin,' offered Abigail, on an unexpected quiver of laughter, 'is nothing if not thorough.'

'God, yes.' Samuel grinned. 'He laid our brother Jonas out cold in the middle of the parlour with a single blow. It was one of the most enjoyable moments of my life.'

'I wonder,' remarked Gabriel gently, 'why I don't find that information particularly comforting?'

'You're worried you'll lose some teeth,' replied Eden. 'I, on the other hand, am more concerned about how you're going to come out of all this looking innocent.'

'Since you and Wat won't be here to render your assistance at the crucial time, that shouldn't be a problem.'

'And I can make sure that the guards are well-fuddled with drink before I take them the jug containing the opiate,' volunteered Venetia.

'Yes. That would help,' agreed Gabriel. 'Also, Justin and Francis can leave me locked in the workroom – from which I shall presently raise the alarm and be released by the servants. Then I take Baxter and Willis limb from limb for

412

being drunk on duty and visit Commissary-General Ireton to show him my cuts and bruises. Simple.'

'Is it?' asked Eden, dubiously.

'Oh yes. Henry has weightier matters on his mind than the loss of a couple of prisoners.' Gabriel came to his feet and raised an inquiring brow at Samuel. 'Have you somewhere for your sister to sleep tonight?'

'Yes. There's room in my lodging in Tower Street.'

'Then I suggest you take her there. Do not, under any circumstances, come back here. Just find the inn I spoke of earlier – and meet me in Shoreditch the day after tomorrow to let me have the necessary details. Also, if you're going to introduce Mistress Abigail to Bryony be careful what you say. Clear?'

'Clear,' agreed Samuel cheerfully.

Abigail rose and awarded Gabriel her spectacularly sweet smile. 'I don't know why you should go to so much trouble for us . . . but I'm more grateful than I can say.'

'Then let's leave it at that, shall we?' he replied pleasantly. 'I'm about to have Major Maxwell show you out – so an appearance of being overcome with emotion as you leave would probably be no bad thing. Sam . . . you can mutter about the extortionate nature of my demands.'

Mr Radford eyed him speculatively. 'I don't suppose you'd care to turn your ingenuity towards persuading Mr Morrell into admitting me to the family?'

'No,' agreed the Colonel. 'I wouldn't. Some things, as they say, are easier than others. And now – goodnight.'

When at last Venetia was left alone with her husband, she said lightly, 'Sam wants to marry Bryony?'

'And *vice versa*. Jack, however, is not enthusiastic.'

'No. I suppose he wouldn't be.' She hesitated, feeling her way. 'This has been quite a night, hasn't it?'

'It's been bloody long, if that's what you mean.' Gabriel laid his fingers on the rim of the table and stared meditatively down on them. 'I must be losing my touch. You never believed the ransom story at all?'

'Not a word. It may have taken some time, but I think I know you better than that.'

'Better, perhaps, than I know you?' His eyes rose

enigmatically to meet hers. 'What's the matter? Don't you want to berate me for misjudging you?'

'Not particularly. You thought you had cause.' She smiled crookedly. 'And truth to tell, six months ago I believed you every species of villain – and would have had Francis out of your evil clutches like a shot.'

'So what's changed?'

'Don't you know?' Venetia moved gracefully towards the door. 'I have.' Then she was gone.

Escorted by Ben Harris, Venetia spent most of the following morning trailing from apothecary to apothecary, discreetly harvesting the ingredients she needed to make a reliable, fast-acting sleeping potion. Then, remembering that Isabel had promised to call that afternoon, she sent Harris off to Covent Garden with a message designed to put her ladyship off for a few days. And all the time, she was aware of feeling foolishly optimistic . . . as if a great weight had been lifted from her shoulders.

Half an hour later – and from a source that she had all but forgotten – it was back with a vengeance. Venetia stared at the note with a sensation of sick rage, before crumpling it savagely in her hand. Then she went in search of Mr Larkin and, when she found him, said baldly, 'Read that – and tell me what you think.'

Wat subjected her to a long, inscrutable stare, smoothed out the paper and squinted at it from arm's length.

'I think,' he grunted eventually, 'that Sir Ellis needs a kick up the arse. What does he want to meet you for?'

'How should I know? And what difference does it make? I *can't* meet him. But neither can I just ignore him and hope he'll go away – because he won't. He never does, damn it.' Venetia drew an unsteady breath. 'Shall I tell Gabriel?'

The seamed brown face creased thoughtfully.

'I reckon that depends on what happened last night.'

'He hasn't told you?'

'I haven't seen him,' shrugged Wat. 'Well?'

'It's a long story,' she replied. And gave him the gist of the previous evening's events – none of which Wat appeared to find particularly surprising. Then she said, 'I'm not sure I really want to muddy the waters by dredging up Ellis again right now. And Gabriel could certainly do without it. He's got more important things to think of.'

'So where does that leave you then?'

For the first time since she had entered the room, a faint, wry smile touched her face. 'With only one alternative. I write a reply to Ellis and you deliver it – along with a kick up any part of his anatomy that pleases you.'

Wat regarded her with a sort of caustic indulgence.

'Now why didn't you say that in the first place?' he asked.

Venetia wrote a brief, pithy reply to her former betrothed and made Mr Larkin read it before he set off for his rendezvous amongst the bookstalls in St Paul's churchyard. Then she prowled restlessly about the parlour until Gabriel walked in and unwittingly frightened her silly.

He said, crisply, 'I can't stay. I've been summoned to a meeting at Army headquarters in St Albans and probably won't be back until late tonight. I was hoping to catch Wat. Since, however, he appears to be out at the moment, I'd be grateful if you could brief him for me.'

Venetia's nerves were vibrating like lute strings but she kept her voice perfectly even. 'Of course.'

'Thank you. And one more thing. Our friends downstairs need to be informed of what we intend, but I don't want any of us to be seen communicating with them. So I'd like you to write down the basic outline and put it inside a book for Francis: preferably, the kind he'd never normally open. Eden will then make sure it's passed over intact after the day guards come on duty tomorrow. Can you do that?'

She nodded, suddenly acutely conscious of the well-defined planes of his face and the rich timbre of his voice; of the way his hair curled against his collar. Then, striving to concentrate on the matter in hand, she said, 'In French, if you like. I know Francis speaks it.'

'Better still,' said Gabriel. And, entirely without warning, he smiled – that rare, singularly attractive smile which Venetia had not seen in more than a month and which had the immediate effect of turning her bones to water. 'Tell me. Are you enjoying all this?'

'Of course,' she replied simply. And thought *How could I*

not be? It's made you talk to me. But had the sense, still, not to say it.

Wat returned half an hour later with a distinctly irritable glint in his eye.

'Well – I've seen him,' he said sourly. 'All prinked out like a candied tart, with nice shiny buttons and a jewel in his ear. I gave him your letter and watched him read it, and he wasn't best pleased. Then I told him what the upshot'll be if he comes sniffing round here again and he didn't like that neither.'

'No. He wouldn't. But will he take notice of it?'

'I wouldn't put money on it. He's so full of himself he thinks a bit of charm can fix anything.'

'The unfortunate truth being that, in Ellis's case, it usually does,' sighed Venetia. 'Did he say what he wanted?'

'In a manner of speaking. He sent you this.' Wat pulled a purse from his pocket and tipped a stream of shiny sovereigns into her lap. 'Said he owed it to you.'

Venetia stared blankly at the money for a moment and then said flatly, 'Now I *am* worried. In all his life, Ellis has never paid a debt unless he was forced to. So why is he doing this? There has to be a reason.'

'Devilment, I reckon.' Wat stirred through the heap of coins, selected two of them and placed one in each of her hands. 'What do you make of those?'

'Is this a game?' she began. And then, automatically weighing one against the other, 'This one feels heavier.'

'That one *is* heavier,' came the grim reply. 'Not much – but enough to give the game away.'

The amethyst eyes widened slowly.

'It's *counterfeit?*' said Venetia, disbelievingly. And when he nodded, 'But . . . but where did Ellis get it?'

'Where do you think?' demanded Wat irritably. 'He must be in it up to his bloody ear-ring with the clever fellow who's doing the coining. And if he don't watch his step, they'll be stretching his neck at Tyburn one of these days!'

While Venetia bestowed twenty-five lawful sovereigns on Wat for the purpose of acquiring two horses and hid the same

416

number of illegal ones at the back of a drawer, Gabriel was sitting in St Albans listening to the boiling discontent of his colleagues. Then, deciding against a late ride home, he spent the night with the Army and departed on the following morning for Shoreditch and his appointment with Sam Radford.

It went off reasonably well. Abigail Ambrose sat quietly in a corner with Bryony and behaved as if she had never laid eyes on him before; Jack made a number of provocative remarks about his protracted absence; and Sam discreetly passed him a small slip of paper containing the name of an inn at Barnet. Gabriel drank a glass of wine, thanked God that neither Samuel nor his sister had revealed the fact that Justin Ambrose was currently residing in Cheapside and then left to return to his duties at the Tower.

He stayed there, as arranged, until Major Maxwell arrived at about nine in the evening. Then, with little more than a faint smile and a nod, he walked out into the night air and strolled unhurriedly back to Cheapside.

Venetia was in the parlour, brooding over the remains of supper. Absorbing the tension in her face, Gabriel said deliberately, 'I wish, just once, I could come in to a meal that Eden hasn't already picked over.'

'You ought to try being more punctual, then,' she retorted edgily. 'Where the devil have you been all day?'

'Staying out of the way. Why? Did you need me?'

'It would have been all the same if I had, wouldn't it? But no. As it happens, I didn't.'

'That's what I thought.'

Venetia drew a fulminating breath and then encountered the gleam in his eye. The strain of the past hour slid miraculously away and she gave a tiny choke of laughter.

'That's better,' approved Gabriel, unwinding his sash and preparing to unfasten his coat. 'Now. Why don't you pour us both some wine and give me a progress report?'

'I thought you'd never ask.' She crossed to the dresser in search of a clean glass. 'Wat arranged the horses this afternoon and set off back to Holborn shortly before you came in – having spent the last hour drinking with Willis and Baxter. I then made sure that two jugs of wine were sent down with their supper and am fairly confident that Nan will presently refill them – in order to continue making eyes at Trooper Willis.' She paused, handing him the glass and trying not to notice how well the loose-fitting white cambric shirt suited him. 'The only thing I can't be sure of is whether or not Francis has read my note. Eden passed it over inside a copy of Machiavelli's *Prince*.'

Gabriel dropped carelessly into a large, carved chair near the hearth. 'Do you think that was a big enough clue?'

'I hope so.' A sudden, vivid smile transformed her face. 'It was in Italian.'

He looked at her. The silver-gilt hair gleamed in the candlelight, her skin was creamy-pale against the dark blue of her gown and the pansy-coloured eyes were bright with laughter. She was, without doubt, the most beautiful woman he had ever seen; and the fact that he also knew her to be capable, intelligent and, above all, damnably responsive, made it very hard indeed to continue being cautious.

'Ah. Then that should do it.' He hesitated, seeking some means of keeping the conversation neutral. 'You've heard, I suppose, that the Commons has acceded to his Majesty's request that no single concession at Newport be considered binding unless total agreement is reached?'

Venetia nodded and seated herself facing him. 'As I understand it, they fixed the debate for a day when there was a call of the House – knowing that all the normally absent Presbyterian members would turn out in force to avoid being fined for non-attendance.' She paused, thoughtfully sipping her wine, and then said, 'I don't imagine that the Army is especially happy about it.'

'It's not. The general feeling is that there's no point in bending over backwards to make terms with a king who appears to have no regard for peace and whose word cannot be relied upon.' He met her gaze wryly. 'The result is a widespread demand for the Army to purge Parliament of the Presbyterians so that the Newport talks can be brought to a summary end. Fortunately, however, it's a demand which the Lord General has so far managed to resist – much to the disgust of Henry Ireton who, having had his resignation refused, has taken himself off to Windsor in a huff.'

'Good,' said Venetia tersely.

The dark brows rose. 'Not from my point of view it isn't. You may have forgotten – but I have to present myself before him tomorrow; and I'd as soon not have to ride ten miles in order to do it.' He paused, watching her recollect what lay ahead of them. Then, without giving her time to speak, he turned the talk first to Bryony's unquenched desire to marry Samuel Radford and from there to mundane matters concerning the management of Brandon Lacey.

An hour passed almost without her noticing it. But finally Gabriel said calmly, 'I think it's time you took Willis and Baxter their brew.'

Venetia's eyes seemed to refocus. Wordlessly, she crossed to the dresser, withdrew a small pot of brownish powder from the drawer and poured it into the earthenware jug of wine which stood ready and waiting. Then, stirring it, she said, 'It should take effect within the hour.'

'Good.' He rose, smiling faintly. 'You realise that I'll never again accept wine from your hands without a certain amount of trepidation?'

'Yes. But I wouldn't let it worry you.' She walked, jug in hand, to the door and turned to fix him with a wicked amethyst gaze. 'If I ever drop a little something into your malmsey, you may be sure it won't be a sleeping-potion.' And she was gone, shutting the door with a gentle click.

When she re-appeared five minutes later, all traces of flirtation had vanished beneath layers of bountiful satisfaction. 'They're already so fuddled that they're unlikely to remember I was ever there,' she announced cheerfully. 'And they started drinking before I turned my back.'

'Good.' Gabriel surveyed her lazily from the hearth. 'Then you may now go to bed and attempt to get some sleep.'

'*Sleep?*' echoed Venetia. 'Don't be silly! How can I? And don't, please, give me the obvious, flippant answer.'

'I wasn't about to. The truth, if you want it, is that you can do nothing about what happens next. And if anything goes wrong, I'd prefer you to be able to emerge – suitably startled and in your night-rail – from your room.'

'But—'

'No.' His tone was pleasant still but utterly final. 'I thank you for your help, but your part is done and now I'd like you to leave me to do mine. Goodnight.'

She hesitated, knowing that he was right but reluctant to leave him. Then, realising that it would be stupid to spoil the companiable intimacy of the last hour by arguing, she shrugged slightly and said, 'As you wish. But you . . . you will take care, won't you?'

The note of anxiety surprised him but he refused to let it deflect him. 'I always do,' he said. And waited, with courteous patience, until she finally left the room.

Once alone, the time seemed to pass very slowly and Gabriel found he was thinking more about his wife than the task ahead. But eventually midnight arrived and, glad of the prospect of some action, he trod silently down the stairs and into the corridor leading to the rear of the house.

Trooper Willis was slumped, snoring, across the table and Baxter had slipped into an inert heap on the floor. Gabriel smiled dryly to himself and unhooked the keys from the wall. Then he unlocked the workroom door and went in.

In the shadowy light of a single oil lamp, two pairs of eyes encompassed him wordlessly. Colonel Ambrose was lying upon his pallet with his arms behind his head and his ankles crossed and Captain Langley leaned negligently against the wall. Then Justin came smoothly to his feet and Francis murmured, 'So it's true, then. May I ask why?'

'Because I don't believe a soldier should face trial for merely doing his duty,' responded Gabriel briskly. 'Are you ready to go?'

'As soon as you like,' said Justin. 'I presume you want this to look like an escape?'

'Since I'd as soon not be court-martialled – yes,' agreed Gabriel with a glint of acidic humour. 'The guards are out cold and will stay that way for some hours. When you leave here, take their pistols, lock me in and drop the keys in the passage outside. As you're aware, Wat has horses ready for you in Holborn – and I suggest you make good use of them.'

'You can rely on it,' said Francis. 'Speaking for myself, I intend to board the first boat sailing out of Harwich for either France or the Netherlands.'

'Then you'll need this.' Gabriel tossed each of them a small purse. 'It's not much but I hope it will help.' And to Justin, 'You'll find your wife at The Partridge in Barnet with her brother. She's expecting you.'

A hint of colour touched the austere face.

'I'm grateful. I just hope you don't suffer by this.'

'So do I – but I suspect I will,' came the mordant reply. And, with a sigh, 'You're going to have to hit me.'

Silence. Then, 'Rather you than me,' murmured Francis.

'Now?' asked Justin, calmly.

'Now. And make it good.'

'I will.' Smiling remotely, Justin held out his hand. 'But since we're unlikely to meet again – at least allow me to thank you for all you've done. I shan't forget it.'

Gabriel smiled back and accepted the outstretched hand. For a moment, their fingers gripped and a look of perfect comprehension passed between them. Then Gabriel was sent staggering backwards by a crashing blow to his jaw.

'Christ!' he breathed. 'You might have warned me.'

A fist like a sledgehammer took him in the stomach, depriving him of breath. He heard a voice say coolly, 'Better not. It would have hurt more.' And then a second, perfectly controlled punch connected with the side of his face, sending him ricocheting painfully against the wall and causing him to skin his knuckles. Half-dazed and gasping, he dropped to one knee, feeling his throbbing jaw. Amazingly enough it did not appear to be dislocated and, as far as he could tell, he still had all his teeth. Keeping his head bent and summoning his resources, he said thickly, 'I think that will do. Now knock me out.'

There was a second or two of silent hesitation before he heard Justin murmur, 'I can't see the need but I won't argue. My apologies – and my thanks.' And then something came down on the base of his skull and he knew nothing more.

It was the coughing that brought him round. A searing, relentless cough that he eventually realised was emanating from himself . . . and which tore at his lungs and made his ribs ache. For a moment or two he merely lay where he was with his eyes closed, fighting unsuccessfully against it. Then, as his brain slowly resumed its function, he became aware that something was very wrong; and forcing himself into reluctant activity, he opened his eyes.

One side of the room was ablaze and the air was full of smoke. Flames had all but consumed one of the straw mattresses and were fastening greedily on to the other; Luciano del Santi's workbench was already smouldering and sparks were beginning to ignite the wooden shelving above it. As far as Gabriel could see, the only thing that wasn't going to catch fire in the next few minutes was the door. And by the time it did, he'd be unconscious again.

The door. The most sensible thing to do, he decided, was to check the door. He heaved himself first to his knees and then to his feet, hoping against frail hope that Justin and Francis had forgotten to lock it. They hadn't . . . but desperation made him waste a good deal of effort tugging fruitlessly at the latch until a violent fit of coughing overtook him. He dropped to his knees again, crippled by the raw agony in his chest. His eyes smarted painfully and he tried wiping them on his sleeve. And that was when he noticed the ewer.

Miraculously, it was half full of water. Not knowing whether, in the end, it would help very much, Gabriel set about using it to soak his hair and shirt. Then, sensibly deciding that there was little he could do about the fire and holding a fold of his shirt over his mouth, he picked up the empty pewter jug and started banging it against the heavy, oak door in the hope of summoning help.

He didn't know how long he continued doing it. He was only aware of the encroaching heat from the flames, the occasional spark touching his face or hands, the dense, suffocating smoke . . . and, more than all of this, the dizziness and pain that finally made him stop. Vaguely and with something akin to surprise, he thought, *So this is it, then*. And drifted, uncaringly, into oblivion.

There were knives grinding inside his head and a blistering inferno in his lungs. The cough was tearing at him again and he wanted to be sick. Then he was sick – and that hurt more than all the rest put together. He swore to himself and relapsed once more into blessed darkness.

The next time he awoke, it was to the awareness of cool, steady hands and a voice calling him.

'Gabriel? Wake up now. You can hear me, can't you? Open your eyes and let me give you something to drink.'

He didn't want to open his eyes or to move or to do anything at all, but the voice was insistent. Slowly, and with overwhelming irritation, he did as it asked and opened his eyes. The first thing he saw was a blurred curtain of silver-gilt and then, as his sight cleared, a frowning violet gaze set in a face streaked with dirt. And then it struck him that he wasn't dead after all.

A cup touched his lips and warm honey slid like silk over the burning torture in his throat. Gradually, the fog inside his head started to clear. He wondered why he appeared to be lying on the floor of the parlour . . . and then remembered. With careful economy, he croaked, 'The fire?'

'It's out. Don't worry. How do you feel?'

'Bloody awful.' He dissolved into a fresh paroxysm of coughing. 'What happened?'

'Can't it wait?' asked Venetia.

'No.'

Sighing, she pushed back the tangled fall of her hair and offered him the cup again. 'I smelled the smoke. So, fortunately, did Harris – as we went downstairs, we heard you banging on the door. Then Wat came in. He and Harris pulled you out while I roused the servants. We managed to douse it between us, but we were only just in time. A few minutes more and the whole house would have gone up.'

Gabriel's brows were furrowed with concentration. He said, 'What about Baxter and Willis?'

'They came round eventually. You don't need to see them. Wat's already played merry hell with them for being drunk.'

'Has he kept them here?'

'Yes.' Venetia sank back on her heels and gave up trying to sound calm. Finding him unconscious inside that blazing, smoke-filled room had been the single most terrifying moment of her life. 'Will you stop worrying about the thrice-blasted escape? Considering that Justin Ambrose was so damned thorough he left you to be roasted alive—'

'He didn't.' Very cautiously, Gabriel sat up. 'He wouldn't

have been that careless. Nor, I think, would Francis Langley.'

'Then how do you account for it?'

'I can't.' He pressed the heels of his hands over his smarting, bloodshot eyes. 'I asked Justin to knock me out and he did. When I came round, the place was on fire. I can only suppose that the lamp was somehow overset.'

'But the door was locked,' said Venetia slowly. 'If neither Francis nor Justin knocked the lamp over and you were unconscious . . . that only leaves two possible explanations. Either it fell over by itself – or someone else came in and deliberately upset it.'

This was something that Gabriel had already worked out for himself but did not want to discuss. He said, 'Each being equally unlikely. Do you think you could help me up? This floor's damned hard; and I have bruises in places I can't mention.'

Venetia's insides were knotted with cramp pains but she forced herself to do as he asked. The effort of moving made him cough again; but when he was safely ensconced in a chair, she said unevenly, 'Do you think that someone – that someone may be trying to kill you?'

'I sincerely hope not.' He contemplated the profusion of grazes and small burns on his hands. 'Why should they? Accidents do happen, you know.'

'I know. But this one nearly cost you your life.'

Gabriel looked up. Beneath the dirt, her face was green with fright. He felt unequal to coping with whatever that implied. 'You're making too much of it. No real harm was done. I'm just desperately tired, that's all. And since I've to be fit enough to travel to Windsor tomorrow, I'd like to get some sleep.'

Venetia stared at him explosively. 'You're in no state to go anywhere. Have you any idea how *ill* you look?'

'I could hazard a guess.' He achieved a hint of his usual sardonic smile and then turned as the door opened and Mr Larkin came in, soaked to the skin and indescribably filthy. 'My God! You've obviously been having fun.'

'Not as much as you, I reckon,' grunted Wat, his eyes at distinct variance with his tone. 'How did it start?'

'He doesn't know,' said Venetia. 'And the important thing now is that he says he's going to Windsor tomorrow.'

'Correction.' Gabriel hauled himself to his feet, grimacing slightly. 'I *am* going to Windsor tomorrow.'

Wat folded his arms. 'Don't be so bloody silly. You can barely stand. Send Major Maxwell.'

'No. Ireton will want a first-hand account. And seeing me in this condition ought to answer all his questions.'

'Then let him come here.'

Gabriel drew an impatient breath and immediately regretted it. Over the hiatus in his chest, he gasped, 'Now who's being bloody silly? We don't want the Commissary-General here, questioning everybody in sight; and I . . . I'll get a much more sympathetic hearing if I arrive in Windsor looking like a death's head. And now,' he finished, leaning heavily on the back of the chair and looking at Wat, 'will you please get me to bed – before I disgrace myself by passing out again?'

Six

In the end, Wat rode to Windsor, too – for which Gabriel was quietly grateful. Thanks to Justin Ambrose, he had a jaw as stiff as last week's bread and a quantity of miscellaneous bruises; thanks to other sources entirely, his throat felt as though someone had taken a razor to it and every breath excoriated his lungs. The result was that he felt a good deal more fragile than he cared to admit – and found it comforting to know that if he passed out in the saddle there would be someone to pick him up again.

Of course, it was too much to expect Mr Larkin to ride ten miles or so without taking the opportunity to thoroughly investigate the previous night's fire. And when all his questions had been answered, he said broodingly, 'You're right about the lamp. We found it amongst the remains of one of the pallets. But a thing that heavy don't tip up of its own accord. And that only leaves one explanation.'

'That someone gave it a helping hand,' agreed Gabriel. 'My difficulty, however, is that without any obvious motive or culprit, I can't quite believe it.'

'Why not? In case you've forgotten, you've already been set upon by three fellows you didn't think were footpads.'

'Ah.' A wry frown gathered behind the grey eyes. 'Yes. And that is the only thing suggesting that this isn't quite as far-fetched as it otherwise seems.'

Wat thought about it. 'Who gains by your death? Ellis?'

'Not directly. He can only inherit Brandon Lacey through his children and, as far as I'm aware, he has none.'

'Would he kill you just for spite?'

'It's a possibility.' Gabriel's mouth closed over the words like a steel trap and it was some time before he spoke again. Then, he said curtly, 'You're missing the point, you know. If

427

someone tried to fry me last night, they did so knowing that I'd be out cold on the workroom floor – which means that one of our fellow-conspirators is either a would-be assassin or possessed of a very loose tongue. And, speaking for myself, I can't think of any likely candidates.'

Neither, unfortunately, could Wat. He said, 'So where does that leave us?'

'Back where we started,' replied Gabriel. And relapsed into silence.

By the time they reached Windsor, he was exhausted – and it showed. Commissary-General Ireton took one look at the ghastly pallor lying beneath the marks of violence and was shocked enough to send for wine before listening to Gabriel's report. Then he said austerely, 'These are plainly very dangerous fellows. Do you need help in recovering them?'

'My Major already has the matter well in hand,' replied Gabriel mendaciously – the truth being that Eden was still wondering how to explain the destruction downstairs to Luciano del Santi. 'I came only to inform you of the incident – and to say that I accept full responsibility for it.'

Ireton pulled a quill thoughtfully through his fingers, inwardly acknowledging the difficulty of disciplining the Colonel after his assistance in the matter of the King's letter. Finally, he said slowly, 'You obviously did all you could to prevent your prisoners escaping – at some cost, it seems, to your health. And since you are clearly unfit for duty, I suggest that you consider yourself officially relieved . . . and take a few weeks' leave to recuperate.'

Informed, on the way back to Cheapside, of the Commissary-General's generosity, Mr Larkin subjected Gabriel to an astute, black stare and said, 'Well, I'm glad you got what you wanted. It'd have been a pity if you'd half-killed yourself for nothing, wouldn't it?' Then, when no reply was forthcoming, 'Going to Brandon Lacey, are you?'

'Where else?' Gabriel was beginning to have severe difficulty remaining upright in the saddle but he still managed to smile faintly. 'Do you want to come?'

Wat considered it for a moment. Then, deciding that there

were a few things in London which would bear looking into, said sourly, 'Not especially. If you want the truth, Yorkshire gives me the bloody marthambles.'

'*Everything* gives you the marthambles,' murmured Gabriel. 'It's what keeps you going.'

Informed that they were leaving for Brandon Lacey in two days' time, Venetia's immediate response was to point out that – on present evidence – Gabriel had about as much chance of riding two hundred miles as flying to the moon.

'But I don't intend to ride,' he replied with acidic kindness. 'I intend to hire a coach. And that, hopefully, should satisfy you, Wat, and every other busybody.'

Effectively silenced but by no means downcast, Venetia set about preparing to depart. She told Tom Harris that she no longer needed his services, wrote a letter of recommendation for him and sent him back – surprisingly long-faced – to Isabel. She helped Jane with the packing, supervised a clearing-up operation in the workroom and found time for a private chat with Mr Larkin. Then, on the morning appointed, she left Cheapside without a backward glance.

It was long, tedious journey – and Jane's presence in the carriage had a distinctly limiting effect on the conversation. Or so Venetia thought. Gabriel, on the other hand, seemed perfectly happy confining himself to discussing the news they picked up at each halt – so it was perhaps fortunate that the Newport negotiations provided him with plenty of scope.

Having been asked, yet again, to consent to the abolition of both Prayer Book and Episcopacy and also to allow a Presbyterian system which required everyone in the realm to take the Covenant, his Majesty had replied (yet again) with his own set of counter-proposals. He was willing, he said, to agree to three years of Presbyterianism – provided that toleration was granted not only to himself but also to '*any others who could not in conscience submit themselves thereto.*' He was not, however, willing either to take the Covenant himself or have it forced on others.

Venetia thought this attitude a good deal more reasonable than the Parliament's outright rejection of it. Gabriel agreed with her, but somewhat wryly pointed out that the question in most people's minds was whether his Majesty intended to use the three years to achieve a sensible compromise or whether he would merely assemble enough power to enable him to go his own way in the fourth.

The road fell slowly and uneventfully away behind them, along with the first week of October. Then, on a bright, chilly day when they were no more than twenty miles from home, a couple of shots tore the air, the coach lost speed and Gabriel snatched the pistol from the holster beside him.

'*Highwaymen?*' breathed Venetia, disbelievingly.

'What do you think?' came the sparse reply. And then, as Jane cowered back in her seat rapidly reciting the Lord's Prayer, 'Tell her to try "When the King Enjoys his Own Again". It's likely to have more effect.'

Venetia opened her mouth on a suitably pithy retort, then closed it again as the coach drew to a halt and a fellow swathed in a cloak, with his hat jammed low on his head and a black kerchief hiding the lower part of his face, dropped neatly from a powerful chestnut to throw open the door. Pointing a pistol at them, he said cheerfully, 'Well, now . . . what have we here?'

Venetia's lungs malfunctioned. This, she decided on a faint bubble of hysteria, was really all she needed – but with a second pistol in Gabriel's hand, now was no time to think of it. She leaned forward so that she could be seen and, with neither subtlety nor grace, said swiftly, 'See for yourself. *I'd* call it a monumental mistake.'

'Hell's teeth!' Over the mask, a pair of silver-green eyes widened a little and then filled with laughter.

'Quite,' she replied tartly. 'And you can stop waving that gun in my face. It's frightening my maid and annoying my husband – who, by the way, is quite likely to shoot you if you go on with this silly charade!'

For a moment, Ashley Peverell looked completely nonplussed and Venetia held her breath. Then, on a note of gentle inquiry, Gabriel said, 'Friend of yours, Venetia?'

'In a manner of speaking.'

'But not – given his present occupation – one you're particularly eager to introduce?'

She surveyed him witheringly and declined to reply.

Sighing, Captain Peverell lowered his pistol.

'All right,' he said. 'Have it your own way. I know you and you know me – and we both know I'm not about to rob you. But you might have upheld the pretence.'

'You heard her,' said Gabriel pleasantly. 'She didn't want me to shoot you. Whether that's a tribute to my reflexes and marksmanship or something less flattering, I haven't yet worked out.'

'Oh – she knew I wouldn't shoot you.' Ashley turned casually to his accomplice who was still covering the coachman. 'You can stand down, Jem. We can't steal from one of the Queen's ladies.'

Jem was heard to observe that the Captain was a damned sight too choosy – and that if it was to carry on, they might as well stay at home with their knitting. The Captain grinned and ruefully informed Gabriel and Venetia that he was having trouble getting Jem to adopt the right attitude.

'*I'm* trying to rob the Roundheads in order to give to the Cavaliers – and *he* just wants to rob everybody.'

'We've gathered that,' said Venetia. And, on a faintly irritable sigh, 'You're playing with fire, you know.'

'No more than usual. And what else is there to do?' Bitterness shadowed his eyes and then was gone. 'Pleasant as this is, I'd best be on my way. My apologies for not unmasking, Colonel – but I'm sure you see my difficulty.'

'Vividly,' agreed Gabriel gently. 'As you, I hope, will appreciate mine – if I happen to hear of any hapless travellers being held up within five miles of Brandon Lacey.'

'Is that a warning?'

'Yes. Heed it . . . and today never happened.'

'I see. Well, you can't say fairer than that, can you?' Ashley set his foot in the stirrup and rose effortlessly back into the saddle. Then, holding Venetia's gaze with his own, 'You may wish to know that our mutual friend was in the vicinity fairly recently – though I think he's gone now.'

Venetia coloured slightly. 'If you mean Ellis – I don't care *where* he is so long as he stays away from me.'

'Ah. Like that, is it?'

'Yes. And if you say "I told you so" – I'll hit you.'

'I wouldn't dream of it.' The green eyes looked reflectively at the Colonel. 'It may be unnecessary advice . . . but it would probably pay you to keep an eye on Ellis.'

Gabriel's expression remained completely unchanged. 'He's a bad man?' he suggested lightly.

'Not exactly. He's just got an unerring instinct for mischief and a tendency to think with his stomach.' Captain Peverell gathered his reins and wheeled his horse in readiness to depart. Then, with a wry laugh, 'Actually – if you want my opinion, the man's a walking bloody disaster.' And he cantered away calling for Jem to follow.

Gabriel watched him go and then fixed Venetia with a bland stare. 'You haven't any other similarly picturesque acquaintances you'd like to warn me about, have you?'

'Not that I know of,' she replied warily. And, as the coach lurched into motion again, 'You – you're taking this very well. Don't you want to ask me about him?'

'Not particularly.' Gabriel wedged himself comfortably into the corner and folded his arms. 'Unless, of course, your association with the gentleman is likely to continue?'

'It isn't.' Venetia met his gaze squarely and took a deep breath. 'He used to be a Royalist agent – as, in a very minor way, was I. But that's all over now.'

'Good.' He closed his eyes and let his chin sink on to his chest. 'Then there's no more to be said, is there?'

'You – you *believe* me?' she asked uncertainly.

'Why not?' The merest ghost of a smile touched Gabriel's mouth and he added urbanely, 'For the moment, anyway.'

Sophia was unreservedly glad to see them. She was also, Venetia thought, rather less ephemeral than usual, and, as soon as the two of them were alone, she said simply, 'I take it Gabriel found out that Ellis came here after Preston?'

Venetia nodded. 'He didn't tell you before we left?'

'Not a word. He merely said you were travelling south with him. And he was in such a black mood, I didn't dare inquire further.' Sophia paused and then, with slight awkwardness, said, 'Did what I saw the night before you left mean what I thought it meant?'

'Yes.' Venetia would have preferred to leave it at that but

432

the look in Sophy's eyes made her add baldly, 'It's all right. He didn't force me and he hasn't laid a hand on me since. But the mood you saw has only just lifted.' She paused. 'It – it was like living with a stranger.'

'And that mattered to you?'

'Yes. Very much, as it happens.'

'I see.' The short-sighted gaze grew oddly speculative. 'Then perhaps Ellis wasn't such an ill-wind after all.'

'How do you work that out?'

'Because, in addition to teaching you that Gabriel is everything he is not – he's also given you the chance to learn something rather interesting about Gabriel himself.'

Venetia stared at her blankly. 'Has he?'

'Well, of course,' came the patient reply. 'After all – for a reasonable, well-balanced man – Gabriel's reaction to Ellis's presence here was somewhat extreme. And that being so, there has to be a reason for it.'

'There was. He felt he'd been made a fool of.'

'Yes, dear. I'm sure he did. But I doubt very much if that was all.' Sophia drifted towards the door and then turned with a vague smile. 'Think about it. And, in the meantime, I suppose I ought to mention that your Uncle James will very likely be here for the noonday meal tomorrow.'

Venetia blinked. 'He will? Why?'

'No particular reason,' replied Sophia. And was gone before Venetia could decide whether or not she was blushing.

Although the corn harvest had been a near-disaster, Gabriel discovered that Dick Carter had not only managed to save most of the flax but also turned the wet weather to good account by having the pulled crop laid out in the fields to ret naturally in the rain. Then, after it had been brought inside to dry, he'd sent it down to Scar Croft to be dressed – with the result that, by the time Gabriel arrived, the process was already well-advanced. The stalks had been crushed to separate the fibres from the outer bark and the scutching – beating the flax against a board to remove any broken straw – was almost complete. All that was left, therefore, was the heckling . . . and Gabriel was glad he wasn't going to miss that as well.

In between making a comprehensive tour of the estate, he spent hours watching the men patiently passing the long greyish fibres through a series of combs, while the women gathered up the tow – shorter strands which were no use for weaving linen but could be made into a coarser fabric known as harden. Then, while the yarn was being bleached in a potash solution, he shut himself in the bookroom with his ledgers and tried to work out some means of paying the next quarter's taxes. Gabriel rarely saw his wife before suppertime and was rarely alone with her, but he was nevertheless acutely conscious of two things. The first was how much he enjoyed telling her about his day and hearing about hers; and the second was that, despite all his attempts to subdue it, the intensity of his physical desire for her was becoming increasingly difficult to resist. It was a potentially explosive combination . . . and he was no longer sure where he wanted it to end.

Unaware of her husband's dilemma, Venetia worked out and then set aside Sophy's theory concerning him. After all, there was no point in letting her hopes build up only to have them shattered . . . and if Gabriel *did* care for her, he certainly didn't show it. So she filled her days with mundane activity and lived for those precious hours after supper when they discussed everything from the progress down at Scar Croft to the contents of the latest news-sheets; and she concentrated on hiding the fact that the enemy soldier she had not wanted to marry was now the core of her being.

She visited Ford Edge, was given her mother's cheek to kiss and then subjected to a lengthy catalogue of my lady's complaints. Phoebe, on the other hand, was plainly delighted to see her and bubbled over with questions about Gabriel and London and Bryony Morrell. Venetia answered these as best she could until Lady Clifford unwittingly helped her out by saying, peevishly, '*Must* we talk of these vulgar people?'

Phoebe sighed. 'The Morrells aren't vulgar, Mother.'

'Of course they are! They're in trade,' responded her ladyship as if that settled the matter. Then, to Venetia, 'And never – *never* did I think any daughter of mine would so much as set foot in a usurer's establishment!'

'Dreadful, isn't it?' sympathised Venetia. 'But look on the bright side. If we ever need a loan, we'll know who to approach. And Ruth Knightley needn't know how seriously I've demeaned myself unless you tell her.'

There was a tiny, frozen silence before, in a timely attempt to divert her mother's attention, Phoebe said swiftly, 'Good heavens! We haven't told you about Elizabeth yet, have we? Tom rode over yesterday with the news.'

'Ah yes.' Her ladyship's annoyance disappeared beneath a complacent smile. 'My sweetest Bess is expecting a happy event in the spring. Of course, I always assumed *you* would provide me with my first grandchild. But that was when you were betrothed to dear Ellis. Everything is changed now.'

The violet eyes narrowed dangerously. 'In what way?'

'Isn't it obvious?'

'Yes. But I'd like to hear you say it.'

'Well, I wouldn't!' Rising from her seat, Phoebe looked from one to the other of them. 'There's no point to this – and, if you *must* argue, I can think of better topics.'

'Such as what?' asked Venetia.

'Such as the fact that I'll be eighteen next week and Lawyer Crisp will be bringing me the deeds to Ford Edge.' She paused and took a deep breath. 'What I want to know is whether or not you still want him to do so, because there's no need for it and never was.'

Venetia smiled faintly. 'I know.'

Phoebe sat down again with a bump. 'You do?'

'Yes. In contrast to "dear Ellis", Gabriel wouldn't touch Ford Edge if he was down to his last groat.'

Lady Clifford stiffened. 'You can't possibly know that. And I don't know what you're implying about Ellis but—'

'I'm not implying anything. I'm stating a fact,' sighed Venetia. 'Ellis would sell the roof over your head without a second thought – and if he owned Brandon Lacey, he'd probably sell that, too. But we're straying from the point. Since Ford Edge needs no protection from Gabriel, there's no reason why I shouldn't retain ownership myself. But—'

'You can't!' Lady Clifford's voice lost much of its customary languor. 'It wouldn't do at all. And besides, you promised Phoebe. You know you did.'

'Yes. But if *I* don't mind – I don't see why *you* should,' argued Phoebe reasonably. 'You never wanted me to have Ford Edge anyway. You were happy enough for Venetia to own it before – so why not now?'

'Because of Gabriel, of course.' Venetia's smile was grimly sardonic. 'Until I suggested making Ford Edge over to you, Mother hadn't given a thought to the fact that – as my husband – he could still lay claim to it. But now she has and naturally she'd rather it belonged to you than to me. Isn't that so, Mother?'

'Yes,' came the pettish reply. 'It is. And it's not so long since you thought the same thing yourself.'

'Quite. But I've already admitted that I was wrong. Gabriel is as honourable as any man I ever met – and more so than most of them. He doesn't want Ford Edge. He never did. That's why he married me.'

'So you say. I, on the other hand, find it difficult to place my trust in a – a baseborn rebel.'

This time the silence reached epic proportions and Phoebe held her breath. Then, in a voice like splintering glass, Venetia said, 'And one, moreover, whom you consider totally unfit to father your grandchildren.'

Her ladyship flushed. 'I didn't say that.'

'No, but you might as well have done.' Venetia rose and shook out her skirts. 'However. You will be happy to know that there is no question of me keeping Ford Edge. Since Phoebe is the one left to care for it, Phoebe is the one it should belong to. And my place is at Brandon Lacey. But there is one thing you should recognise. Gabriel is my husband and I respect him. Consequently, from now on I shan't visit you until you are prepared to accord him the courtesy he deserves.' She held her mother's gaze for a moment. Then, when no reply was forthcoming, she made a small, formal curtsy and walked calmly from the room.

Phoebe caught up with her in the hall. She said uncertainly, 'You – you didn't mean that, did you?'

'Every word – and not before time. But don't worry. You know you'll always be welcome at Brandon Lacey. In fact I'm surprised you haven't ridden over with Uncle James. He all but lives with us these days.'

'I know,' nodded Phoebe. 'At first he only did it to escape from Aunt Margaret but then he carried on going after she left. Do you think he's courting Sophy?'

'It's hard to tell.' Venetia grinned suddenly. 'Sophy sits there picking fleas off whichever animal comes to hand and Uncle James reads *The Canterbury Tales* with all the voices.' Venetia grinned suddenly. 'And if you don't believe me, you can ask Gabriel. He walked in on them the other day and came out laughing himself silly.'

Phoebe thought for a moment and then cast caution to the winds. 'You seem to like Gabriel a lot more than you ever thought you would.'

The grin turned into a faintly wry smile. 'I do. The only trouble is that I'm not sure it's mutual.'

While, in Europe, the Thirty Years War finally ended in the Treaty of Westphalia, England seemed to lie under a strange pall of domestic expectancy. And at Brandon Lacey the days of October drifted by in a barely-ruffled rhythm – punctuated by news from only two sources.

In Scotland, the Covenanting Duke of Argyll (who had disliked both the Engagement and the recent war only marginally less than he disliked the Duke of Hamilton) had spent September struggling to regain his lost power; and when a multitude of Presbyterian peasants rejoicing under the name of Whiggamores seized Edinburgh and threw out the Committee of Estates at pitchfork-point, he finally achieved it. The result was that Lieutenant-General Cromwell – having crossed the Tweed on the 21st – asked for and was given peaceful repossession of Berwick and Carlisle before the end of the month; and by October 5th, he was conferring amicably with Argyll in Edinburgh about the desirability of all Engagers being removed from public office. Then, leaving Major-General Lambert behind to prop up Argyll's regime, he turned south again towards Yorkshire and the only two remaining Royalist strongholds of Scarborough and Pontefract.

On the Isle of Wight, meanwhile, the forty days of negotiation trickled slowly away like sand in a glass. The Parliament proposed that thirty-seven leading Royalists and all Catholics who had taken up arms for the King be exempted from pardon. His Majesty flatly refused to consider it. The King made renewed proposals concerning Church government and the episcopacy. Parliament rejected them out of hand. And so it went on. Proposal and counter-proposal, rebuttal and refusal. Parliament was working against the clock to effect a settlement before Ireton, still lurking in apparent semi-retirement at Windsor, managed to put a spoke in its wheel; and the King continued playing for time – in the hope that the Earl of Ormonde would succeed in uniting the Irish in his favour – totally unaware that a growing tide of suspicion and ill-feeling was rising against him.

This manifested itself not only in the number of petitions being delivered to Westminster but in the various pamphlets and news-sheets being delivered to Brandon Lacey. Then, on the last day of the month, Gabriel came home with news that the Royalists holding Pontefract had attempted to kidnap Thomas Rainsborough from his quarters in Doncaster and, when he refused to go with them, they'd shot him dead.

Sophia tutted disapprovingly and continued stroking the cat. Venetia absorbed the grimness in her husband's face and said slowly, 'Why do I get the feeling that that's more significant than it appears?'

'Because it is.' Tossing his hat and gloves down on the sideboard, Gabriel poured himself a glass of wine and turned back to face her. 'Rainsborough may have been a disaster as Vice-Admiral and a thorn in the side of the Army Council; he may even have been partly responsible for the executions of Lucas and Lisle at Colchester – and thus made himself a target for retribution. But none of that will matter now. The Independents will see his murder as one Royalist atrocity too many. And they'll unite behind Ireton in his desire for what he calls "justice without respect of persons".'

Venetia swallowed. 'Meaning the King?'

'Who else?' He paused to half-drain his glass. 'The way I see it, his Majesty needs to make terms fast and stick by them. But since he appears to be hoping that next spring will bring the Irish down on us just as last spring brought the Scots, it doesn't look as if he will.'

'No.' She thought for a moment and then said gravely, 'You once told me that you'd little personal respect for the King. So why does the thought of his trial worry you?'

'Because it can only be done by first getting rid of all those members of Parliament who might stand against it. And, at the very least, it will result in his Majesty being deposed. And that,' finished Gabriel grimly, 'leaves nothing in the balance to check the power of the Army.'

'I see.' Violet eyes remained locked with grey. 'What do you think Cromwell will do?'

'Aside from trying to reduce Pontefract Castle? God knows. I *hope* he'll use his influence to restrain Ireton. But if he doesn't – and the Army starts baying for Charles Stuart's blood – I may be left with no alternative but to resign my commission.'

On November 3rd, Phoebe celebrated her eighteenth birthday and became mistress of Ford Edge. On the 4th, she rode over to Brandon Lacey to see Uncle James entertaining Sophy and her menagerie with *The Wife of Bath's Tale*. She was not disappointed. Better still, as she was on the point of leaving, she met Gabriel in the stables.

He responded to her rapturous hug and grinned at her.

'Well, well. It's nice of you to remember us.'

'Isn't it, though?' retorted Phoebe. 'I wanted to come before. But there never seems to be any *time*.'

'I know the feeling. And are you enjoying yourself?'

'Yes. I didn't expect to – but I am. Odd, isn't it?'

'Not particularly. You began by worrying about your inexperience, only to discover that learning was half the fun. And now day-to-day involvement and the stimulation of meeting the challenge has taken over. Simple.'

She eyed him wonderingly and then laughed. 'You too?'

'Me too,' agreed Gabriel wryly. He waved the stable-lad away and deftly finished saddling Phoebe's horse. 'How's your mother responding to the situation?'

'A lot better since her quarrel with Venetia.'

His hands stilled and he looked up at her. 'Quarrel?'

Phoebe nodded. 'Didn't Venetia mention it? Mother said some rather unflattering things about you, so Venetia pointed out that you were more honourable than most men she knew and that she wouldn't set foot in Ford Edge again until Mother was prepared to welcome you as well.'

'I see.' Gabriel returned thoughtfully to his task.

'Is that all you've got to say?'

'What else would you *like* me to say?'

'Quite a lot of things,' came the candid reply. 'But I suspect you're not open to questioning.'

'I'm afraid not.' He offered his hands and lifted her into the saddle. 'But don't lose heart. Your interest is appreciated. And if I ever want to send Venetia a message, I'll certainly bear you in mind.'

Over the next couple of days, Gabriel found his thoughts turning again and again to Phoebe's disclosures. That Venetia had chosen to champion him was both surprising and more than he deserved. The last weeks had made it increasingly plain that the conclusions he'd jumped to on the night he'd found Ellis's glove in the bookroom were completely wrong. And, that being so, he owed Venetia a much larger apology than the rather limited one he'd offered back in Cheapside. The only difficulty was in knowing how best to do it.

With the flax once more hung up to dry after its bleaching, he returned from Scar Croft early one evening to find Venetia poring over the household accounts.

'Don't tell me,' he said resignedly. 'We can't afford wine and must start contenting ourselves with ale.'

'Something like that,' she sighed. 'I can't believe we spend this much on candles. And just look at the figure for coal! It's almost as high as during the war.'

Gabriel looked down on the ledger over her shoulder.

'Quite. Unfortunately, however, heat and light are two things we can't well do without.'

'I know – and we already burn as much wood as we can get. So the only other thing is to use more oil lamps.'

'By all means,' he said calmly. 'But not in this room, nor your bedchamber, or Sophy's.'

Venetia turned to look up at him and wished he wouldn't stand quite so close. It was playing havoc with her nervous

440

system. 'And what about yours? Or are you the only one permitted to suffer in the economic cause?'

'No. I'm just the only one who won't notice either the dingy light or the smell. And it seems to me that you're already making a few sacrifices yourself. When, for example, was the last time you had a new gown?'

'I can't remember – and it's really not important. Or not compared with meeting next month's taxes.'

Gabriel stared down into her face and felt the now familiar tightening of his throat. He said absently, 'Don't worry about that. We've got the wool money and the rents. And then there's my arrears of pay – if I ever get them.'

Something in his expression confused her but she found herself unable to look away. The air shifted about her and she said unevenly, 'Do you think it likely that you will?'

'No.' His eyes investigated the contours of her mouth. 'No. But one lives in hope.'

Venetia found it suddenly difficult to breathe and was dimly aware that, if she didn't do something sensible very quickly, she would probably do something extremely stupid. She came abruptly to her feet – and found herself no more than four inches from his chest. And it was that, had she but known it, that made the difference between Gabriel continuing to do what he had been doing for the last two months and doing, instead, what he *wanted* to do.

Slowly, almost tentatively, his right hand rose to stroke her cheek with the back of lightly-curled fingers which then spread to the curve of her neck, leaving the thumb poised beneath her chin. Venetia remained mouse-still but he saw her response in the widening of her eyes and the faint quiver that afflicted her breathing. Slightly pale, his hands no longer entirely steady, Gabriel slid his left arm about her waist and tilted her face. Then, still with a tantalising lack of haste, he bent his head and brushed her lips with his. She gasped and swayed against him, her hands reaching for his shoulders. For a moment longer, he looked down into the dilated violet eyes before drawing her close against his body and at long last allowing himself to possess her mouth.

The door opened and Sophia walked in.

To do her justice, she stopped dead as soon as she saw what

she was interrupting and would have left – except that it was already too late.

Being careful not to hurry, Gabriel released Venetia and strolled with studied nonchalance towards the hearth. A hint of colour stained his skin, betraying unaccustomed and faintly ridiculous embarrassment. Then, purely to break the silence, he said sardonically, 'It's all right, Sophy – you're quite welcome to come in and join us. In fact, I wish you would. The fire's starting to smoke.'

Supper was an uneasy meal. Gabriel maintained a flow of impervious banalities and avoided looking at his wife; Venetia – elated, regretful and, above all, confused – pushed her food around her plate and said virtually nothing; and Sophia decided to make a strategic withdrawal at the first opportunity.

She wasn't the only one. As soon as they rose from the table, Gabriel calmly announced that he was going out – and bidding both ladies a courteous goodnight, he went.

'Oh dear,' sighed Sophy. 'He's on the hoof again – and I'm very much afraid that it's my fault.'

Disappointed but not downcast, Venetia smiled at her. 'It doesn't matter,' she said simply. 'It was a beginning. And, if it meant anything at all, it will happen again.'

On the following morning, learning from one of the maids that the Colonel's bed had not been slept in, Venetia's optimism suffered a slight jolt. And by evening – with a letter addressed in Eden Maxwell's hand still lying unclaimed on the hall chest and bearing silent witness to Gabriel's continued absence – she was beginning to feel distinctly edgy. Then, just as she and Sophy were about to sit down to supper, Rob Skilbeck arrived to tell them that Colonel Brandon had been delayed in Knaresborough but would probably be home before the night was out.

Venetia fixed Master Skilbeck with a jewel-bright gaze.

'*Where* in Knaresborough?'

Rob shuffled his feet and crumpled the brim of his hat between his hands. 'At – at the Red Bear, Mistress. But he weren't drinking, thou knows. Not much, anyhow. I reckon he finished wi' that last night.'

Keeping her expression under rigid control, Venetia gave

him sixpence and let him go. Then she looked at Sophia and said, 'Don't! Just don't say a word. Any discussion and I'm likely to either have hysterics or throw a fit.'

Later, after Jane had prepared her for bed, she sat on the rug in front of her fire trying to fathom the workings of Gabriel's mind. In those few, fleeting moments the previous night, he had appeared to want her as much as she wanted him; and though she knew it had probably been no more than simple desire, still she had been glad of it. Only then Sophy had come in and the spell had been shattered . . . and, for reasons beyond Venetia's comprehension, Gabriel had apparently fled to the tavern and stayed there.

Both the fire and the solitary candle started to burn low but sleep was still a long way off. She debated going back downstairs and then decided against it. Waiting up wouldn't make Gabriel come home any quicker – and she would look a fool if he returned to find her lurking in the hall like the proverbial scold. No. The sensible thing was to put out the candle and go to bed.

A light rap on the door sent all her muscles into spasm. Then, before she could answer, the latch lifted and the door opened to reveal Gabriel, fully-dressed and holding Eden's letter in his hand. Without crossing the threshold, he said remotely, 'I'm sorry to trouble you so late, but I've something to tell you that won't wait.'

'Then you – you'd better come in.'

Having spent the previous night drinking rather more than he'd intended and half of today suffering for it, Gabriel closed the door behind him and remained just inside it, clinging both to the shadows and the shreds of his self-control. He had expected her to be undressed; what he had *not* expected was for her to be sitting in a pool of firelight, clad only in a flimsy night-rail and with her hair falling over one shoulder, loosely confined in a ribbon. And he wasn't sure he was up to dealing with it.

Gesturing to the letter, he said, 'I've got to go back to London. Eden says that Fairfax summoned a Council of Officers for the 7th to discuss a new document that Ireton has written – and which I suspect will contain his arguments in favour of bringing the King to trial.'

'Oh,' said Venetia hollowly. Then, striving to think of more than her own disappointment, 'But today is the 9th.'

'And the journey will take three days. Quite. But, knowing the Army's fondness for hearing half-a-dozen sermons before getting down to business, I may be in time to catch at least some of the debate. At any rate, it's worth a try.'

'So you're leaving in the morning?'

'At dawn,' he nodded.

'I see.' Venetia came slowly to her feet, aware of what she wished to do but afraid it might not work quite as she hoped. 'Was that all you wanted to say?'

Gabriel forced his eyes away from the nimbus of gold silhouetting her body and focused them on her face. 'What else is there?'

'I'm not sure.' She swallowed hard and summoned all the courage she possessed. 'But if . . . if you were to stay . . . we could explore the possibilities.'

His breath left him and for a time he neither moved nor spoke. Then he said, 'Is that an invitation?'

'Yes.'

There was another long pause before he finally moved towards her, into the light of the hearth. 'Even knowing that – if I accept – it won't be to talk?'

'Yes.' With hands that were by no means steady, she freed her hair from the ribbon and shook it loose. 'Especially knowing that.'

Something flared in the intense dark gaze and he managed a faintly crooked smile. 'Then I'll have to try not to disappoint you, won't I?' he murmured. And drew her, with dreamlike slowness, into his arms.

Venetia melted against the hard length of his body and the ribbon floated unheeded to the floor. Her mouth opened like a flower beneath his and her fingers slid up around his neck to bury themselves in the thick, dark hair. The moment stretched out into infinity and yet ended too soon. Gabriel was in no hurry. His hands drifted lightly over the curves of spine and hip while he feathered tiny kisses along her jaw and down the rounded column of her throat; and when his lips returned to hers, it was to brush them with the same wickedly erotic lightness he had demonstrated last night in the

444

parlour. Then, slowly and seductively, he kissed her again; and released a storm of mutual wanting that almost destroyed his resolve.

Made clumsy by impatience, Venetia's fingers struggled with the unfamiliar fastenings of his coat until, twining one hand in the gleaming mane of her hair, Gabriel raised his head to look at her. He said, 'Gently, my dear. We have all night. Let's use it well.' Then, briefly releasing her in order to untie his sash and shed his coat, he dropped them both on the rug and smiled at her.

Venetia's breath leaked away and her bones turned to water. Reaching out, she unlaced his shirt and then closed the small, unbearable space between them to lay her mouth against the warm skin of his chest. His hands gripped her waist and for one tiny, frozen second he remained utterly still. Then, sweeping her up into his arms, he carried her to the bed.

Lying entangled with her in the downy softness, he continued soliciting her senses until he could not tell her heartbeat from his own. He let her hands wander where they would, but fed her desire and controlled his own by preventing her from undressing him further. And by the time he finally disposed of the impediment of her night-rail, her body was shaking. With infinite care, Gabriel let one palm glide slowly downwards until it cupped her breast and then, after making her wait for a moment, followed its passage with his mouth.

Flames licked along Venetia's veins and she gave a small, sobbing gasp. His tongue pursued its enticing course while one hand investigated the smooth skin of her thigh, and she arched herself against him, incoherent words tumbling from her lips. His own hunger decently cloaked but equalling hers, Gabriel paused for a moment to read her face. And then, apparently satisfied, he withdrew himself gently from her hold and stood up.

Outlined by the dying glow of the fire, Gabriel swiftly discarded the rest of his clothes while Venetia watched out of wide, dark eyes until he returned to her and flesh met flesh in a tingling explosion of breath. Slowly but with increasing urgency, he resumed his exploration . . . seducing her with every art at his command, filling her with wild hunger and being consumed by it himself. Then, with the time for restraint long past, he entered the silken fire she offered him and brought the song of their loving to its passionate crescendo.

They slept, closely entwined amidst the flagrant disorder of the bed. And when Venetia awoke again in the ghostly pre-dawn light, it was to the enticing drift of his hands and his voice murmuring, '"*Rise up, my love, my fair one and come away. For lo, the winter is past, the rain is over and gone . . . and the voice of the turtle is heard in our land*".' Then, when she opened her eyes, he grinned and said, 'I don't know any Chaucer so I'm managing as best I can. Does it work?'

Venetia smiled back at him, flushing slightly as recollection returned and his touch became more intimate.

'If you need to ask,' she replied absently, 'perhaps you should persevere?'

'You think I don't know any more?' Laughter gathered invitingly behind the grey eyes. '"*Who is she that looketh forth, terrible as an army with banners?*"'

With mock-indignation, she pulled herself from his hold and sat up. 'That's cheating. You missed out "*fair as the moon and—*"'

'I know.' Gabriel's arm swept her down beside him again and kept her there while, propping himself on one elbow, his fingers resumed their exquisite assault. 'I know. I thought that went without saying.'

Venetia looked up at him and felt something melt afresh inside her. This teasing, wholly-relaxed man was a Gabriel she had never seen and one whom she did not now think she could live without. Love rushed through her like a torrent . . . but, because she was still not sure what his reaction would be if she told him, she lowered her eyes to his chest and concentrated on tracing the thin, white line of an old scar.

'Nordlingen – Wurttemberg, 1634,' said Gabriel helpfully. 'And here we have Roundway Down, Cheriton and Naseby. Less a torso, you might say, than a map. Interesting, isn't it?' He slid down beside her, his mouth seeking the hollow beneath her ear. 'Of course, the most interesting one of all is Breda . . . but you'll have to look elsewhere for that.'

The lean hardness of his body against hers and the delicious journeyings of his hands made levity almost – but not quite – unattainable. Presently, and with difficulty, she said, 'If this is it, you've got some explaining to do.'

'Very likely,' agreed Gabriel, his voice as uneven as her own. 'But not just now.'

When Venetia awoke again it was full light and the bed beside her was empty save for a couple of long, ebony hairs on the pillow and a small scrap of paper.

'"*I have gathered my myrrh with my spice and eaten my honeycomb with my honey. Behold, thou are fair . . . also our bed is green*".' And then, simply, 'Be patient, if you can. When next we meet, I hope to find words of my own.'

Seven

Gabriel arrived in London on the evening of Sunday November 12th and went straight to Cheapside.

'Congratulations,' said Major Maxwell. 'Wat didn't think you'd be here before morning and now owes me five pounds.'

'Which naturally accounts for your pleasure at seeing me,' grinned Gabriel, stripping off his gloves and tossing his hat to one side. Then, 'Where *is* Wat?'

'God knows!' Eden crossed to the dresser and returned carrying a bottle of claret and two glasses. 'I've scarcely laid eyes on him this last month and can only assume he's up to some nefarious business of his own which I'd be happier not knowing about.' He paused to pour the wine and then said, 'I did as you asked, by the way, and went to inform your foster-brother of your departure – but I'm not sure I made much impression. He and Sam Radford were going at it hammer-and-tongs when I walked in and Mistress Bryony was working up to a fit of hysterics.'

'So you left. Very wise.' Gabriel's coat followed his hat and gloves and, accepting the glass Eden offered, he dropped into a chair by the fire. 'Fascinating as all this is, it's not what I've ridden two hundred miles for. So tell me about Henry's latest masterpiece.'

'He's calling it the *Remonstrance of the Army*.'

The grey eyes gleamed. 'How original!'

'Isn't it?' Noticing that the Colonel was looking a good deal fresher and more relaxed than he had in several months but knowing better than to remark on it, Eden said, 'Ireton asked the Lord General to call the Army Council to discuss it – but Fairfax obviously decided it might be safer to omit the agitators and summoned only the Council of Officers. We sat through prayers and sermons on the 7th, spent the 8th and

449

9th talking about arrears of pay and Parliament's failure to make any provision for war-widows and orphans – and finally got to see the Remonstrance the day before yesterday.'

Gabriel leaned back in his chair and contemplated the ruby brightness in his glass. 'And?'

'And it largely revolves around two points,' responded Eden, sitting down on the other side of the hearth. 'The perils of continuing to negotiate with the King and the justice and importance of bringing him to trial. With regard to the first, Ireton says that the King has shown that he'll never leave the country in peace till he's restored to the throne; that to treat with him now is as good as saying that his position is independent of the nation; and that he's proved over and over again that he'll never be bound by any agreement he makes. As to the question of a trial, Ireton says his Majesty will be satisfied with nothing less than absolute power – and suggests that the only way to be free of such tyranny is to demonstrate that *no* king is beyond the reach of the law.'

'I see.' Gabriel frowned slightly. 'And what conclusion does Henry draw from all this?'

'That the Prince of Wales and Duke of York should be declared unfit to govern and sentenced to death if ever found in England; that certain leading Royalists from both wars be executed and others moderately fined; and that you and I should be honoured with our back-pay.'

Eden paused and, looking him in the eye, Gabriel said gently, 'Go on.'

Knowing how his next words were likely to be received, Eden grimaced ruefully.

'The Remonstrance concludes that "the person of the King – by whose commissions, commands or procurement and on whose behalf all our wars and troubles have been – may be speedily brought to justice for the treason, blood and mischief he is therein guilty of".'

There was a long, thoughtful silence. Then Gabriel said aridly, 'In short, Henry wants to clear the path for some settlement – as yet undisclosed – by means of charging the King with making war on the nation.'

'More or less. Do you consider that unreasonable?'

'Since the Parliament bears an equal responsibility for the

first war – yes. But, more importantly, I consider it dangerous. Don't you?'

'It's certainly a mammoth step,' agreed Eden cautiously, 'and it's already arousing opposition. Fairfax is against it, of course. Also a number of Colonels are worried about the Army being seen as a trouble-maker and would prefer that King and Kingdom be "knit together in a threefold cord of love". But the things Ireton says of the King are true. His word *can't* be trusted – and he'll carry on playing Westminster off against the Army till Doomsday. So how else can we make a lasting peace except by removing him?'

'We could stop making it possible for his Majesty to drive a wedge between ourselves and Parliament by thrashing out some mutually acceptable compromise. Then, if the King fails to accept it, Parliament could simply pass the necessary bills without further ado.' Gabriel's mouth curled in a sardonic smile. 'After all, compared with putting his Majesty on trial, forcibly removing his veto ought to be relatively easy. And it would at least have the merit of preserving something of the old order – instead of destroying it completely in favour of some mythical Utopia. Unfortunately, however, Henry Ireton is about as likely to reach agreement with the likes of Denzil Holles as he is to cast himself into the arms of John Lilburne.'

'Much *less* likely, actually,' murmured Eden. And then, meeting Gabriel's eyes, 'The Levellers won't support any move to either purge or dissolve Parliament until a suitable settlement has been drawn up. There was some mention of talks being held between them and the Officers' Council, in order to try and come to an understanding.'

The dark brows rose. 'Henry's wooing Free-born John? My God! I'd give a lot to see that.'

'Once Ireton knows you're back, you probably *will* see it. But the present situation is that, though the Council has agreed to abide by any treaty struck in Newport, it plans to send some proposals of its own directly to the King. If his Majesty accepts them, they'll be laid before the House; if not . . . well, I imagine we'll be back to looking at the *Remonstrance* again. And, in the meantime, the Council has adjourned itself until Thursday.'

'You're telling me that nothing more will happen for three whole days?' Sighing, Gabriel reached for the bottle and refilled both their glasses. 'What a shame. If I'd known that, I needn't have rushed.'

As it turned out, things continued happening in rapid succession. On the following day, while the House of Lords was agreeing to liberate the Duke of Hamilton in return for a paltry hundred thousand pounds, the Derby House Committee was learning of his Majesty's latest plans to leave the Isle of Wight and also discussing the worrying likelihood of the Royalist fleet, which was now under the command of Prince Rupert, joining forces with my lord Ormonde in Ireland. When Colonel Brandon dutifully presented himself at Headquarters, he was immediately invited to a meeting of officers and Levellers at the Nag's Head tavern in two days' time.

He finally saw Mr Larkin that evening and was accorded a shrewd black stare and the usual taciturn greeting. Undeceived by this, Gabriel said, 'Eden tells me you've been busy. Anything I should know about?'

'No.' Wat had no intention of admitting that, having wasted the last month dogging Ellis Brandon's every step, he'd signally failed to find anything that might link that gentleman to the mysterious fire in the workroom. 'I've just been minding my own business, same as always. And it'd be no bad thing if everybody else did likewise.'

'Meaning me, I suppose?'

'If the cap fits,' shrugged Wat. And then, casually, 'How's the missus?'

'Busy, I expect,' came the deliberately unhelpful reply. 'And that reminds me. Jane Skilbeck was asking after you.'

The seamed face expressed total disinterest. 'Was she?'

'Yes. But don't worry,' said Gabriel blandly. 'I told her you were still just as cantankerous as ever.'

His duties at the Tower not being particularly arduous, Gabriel decided to use the day before the meeting at the Nag's Head to pay a visit to Shoreditch and the Morrells. He arrived to find Annis and Bryony out on a shopping expedition and Jack busy in the workshop, putting the finishing touches to a particularly fine basket-hilt. For a moment or two, Gabriel looked on unobserved before strolling forward, saying, 'I'm glad to see business continues to thrive. Is that pretty toy destined for anyone I know?'

'Colonel Desborough,' replied Jack tersely. And then, laying down his work and turning a cool gaze on his visitor, 'I suppose you've come back because of this so-called *Remonstrance* we're all hearing so much about?'

'You suppose right. There's no need, of course, for me to ask your views on the subject.'

'None. As far as I'm concerned, the King should have been brought to London months ago to talk directly with Parliament, and the Army ought to keep its nose out of what doesn't concern it. As for this insane notion of bringing his Majesty to trial – words fail me. But I'll tell you one thing. Neither I – nor anyone I know – want our lives ordered by the likes of Henry bloody Ireton.'

'I entirely agree with you,' said Gabriel mildly.

Jack stared at him. 'What?'

'I said I agree. Unlike Ireton and a good many of his cohorts, I'm just a common mercenary. I didn't choose to fight for the Parliament out of any massive conviction, but because William Waller persuaded me that its cause was just. All I ever asked was that both I and my men should be paid and I still want that. But if the cost of it is going to be the King's head and a Parliament under military control, then the price is too high for me.'

'I – I see,' said Jack, faintly taken aback. 'So what are you going to do to stop it?'

'Use my vote on the Officers' Council and join forces with any others who feel as I do. It's not much, I grant you. But it's all that's open to me.' Gabriel continued to hold his foster-brother's eyes for a moment and then grinned. 'And now – if I've satisfied you on that point – perhaps we can discuss the things that are *really* bothering you. Such as the continuing saga of Bryony and Samuel, for example.'

Jack's response was a brief, irritable expletive.

'Ah! As bad as that, is it?'

'Worse. The house has become a battleground and they're driving Annis and me mad.'

'Well, of course,' sighed Gabriel. 'So why not put a stop to it by wishing them joy of one another.'

Jack's brows soared. 'There are times when I find your sense of humour misplaced.'

'I daresay. But, odd as it may seem, I'm not joking. No, just listen for a moment. Bryony and Sam have been consorting with each other for some sixteen months now and have considered themselves in love for the last six. Does that sound like an adolescent infatuation to you?'

'Bryony's too young to know her own mind.'

'She's eighteen, Jack. And as for Sam . . . your objections to his politics ought to be less than they were. The Levellers are almost respectable these days, you know – and right now they're using their influence to prevent the Army interfering with Parliament. You ought to be glad of that. You ought also to be glad that Sam's safely employed by Gilbert Mabbott and that – since the *Moderate*'s circulation reputedly rivals that of the *Diurnall* – our young friend can probably afford to support a wife.'

Mr Morrell looked back at him over folded arms.

'You're very eloquent today. Come to think of it – you're looking remarkably pleased with yourself as well. Things going well at Brandon Lacey, are they?'

A hint of rare colour touched Gabriel's cheekbones.

'In a manner of speaking.'

There was a small silence, broken only by the roaring of the furnace. Then, with a slow, knowing smile, Jack said, 'I see. And presumably Venetia feels the same?'

Gabriel thought of and discarded a number of smart answers. 'I . . . believe so. We haven't discussed it.'

'Why not, for God's sake?'

'Because I've only recently admitted to myself that I want to know,' came the wryly truthful reply. 'And because after eleven stormy months of marriage, it's really quite difficult to start telling your wife that you love her.'

Afterwards, it seemed that having admitted the basic truth to Jack made it easier for Gabriel to admit a host of other things to himself – such as the fact that he missed Venetia at every turn. By day, he missed her voice, her perfume – even the turn of her head; by night, he missed the warmth of her body and the exquisite, terrifying explosions of passion which neither of them seemed able to withstand. It was an unfamiliar sensation, and his only refuge lay in work.

By the time he walked into the oak-beamed room above the Nag's Head tavern, Gabriel was already aware that those officers who thought as he did were at that very moment holding a meeting of their own at the Bull's Head Inn. In certain respects, he regretted not being with them. On the other hand, the art of a successful campaign lay in good intelligence ... and where better to get it than here?

One look around was enough to tell him that he was without visible means of support amongst the officers – for Ireton was backed by Harrison and Desborough and a clutch of others who wholeheartedly supported the *Remonstrance*. But amongst those standing around Lilburne were John Wildman and William Walwyn; and, less well-known but equally conspicuous, Samuel Radford. Gabriel met a satirical dark gaze and gave an almost imperceptible nod of acknowledgement. Sam responded with a faint twitch of his brows and restored his attention to Free-born John.

Commissary-General Ireton opened the proceedings by expressing the hope that their deliberations might be attended by harmony and good-sense – and then went on to deliver a beautifully reasoned argument in favour of dissolving a Parliament that showed every sign of sitting forever. John Wildman then replied on behalf of the Levellers and calmly informed those present that the only object he and his friends had in supporting the war was in securing a just and stable government.

'Then we must first cut off the King's head,' called a soldier from the back. 'Cut off the King's head – and thoroughly purge, if not dissolve the Parliament.'

There was a rumble of assorted reaction into which John Lilburne rose and said bluntly, 'It is true that the King is an evil man in his actions, and others of his party as bad. But it is equally true that the Army has cozened us this last year and fallen from all its promises and declarations until it cannot rationally be trusted any more by us without good cautions and security.'

Gabriel sat perfectly still while the officers around him roared their disapproval. Sam Radford leaned back on his bench, folded his arms and grinned.

'That is not so!' said Ireton sharply.

'By your leave,' responded Free-born John dryly, 'it *is* so. Thus far the Army has done nothing for the liberty of the people or the settlement of the nation; it has merely extended its own power and influence. And, when there are two tyrants in the country, it is in the interest of the people to keep one to balance the other – until such time as we know for certain that the tyrant who pretends fairest will actually give us our freedom.'

There was another upsurge of disagreement which Ireton allowed to run its course before he spoke. 'Then how,' he asked coldly, 'would you suggest we proceed?'

'By drawing up the settlement we wish to achieve,' said Free-born John simply. 'If the King is beheaded and Parliament purged, the whole of government will devolve upon the will and swords of the Army. And therein lies no security that I can see. Indeed, our slavery in the future might be greater than ever it was in the King's time – and so our last error would be greater than our first. Consequently, I propose that we join together in drafting a second *Agreement of the People* – for, once that is done, we will be protected from tyranny by King, Army or Parliament.'

For a little while longer, Ireton and Harrison continued to argue in favour of bringing the King to justice first and settling the other affairs of the nation afterwards but Lilburne stood his ground – with the result that a committee of four-a-side was chosen to write the new *Agreement*. This came to grief almost immediately when fiercely Independent John Price refused to sit down with William Walwyn, causing Free-born John to declare that if there were no Walwyn, there should be no Lilburne either. But matters were smoothed over when both Price and Walwyn voluntarily agreed to withdraw and the remaining six sat down to begin their work over a jug or two of wine.

Strolling out into the street with Samuel Radford, Gabriel said quietly, 'I never thought to applaud Lilburne's good sense, but I do so now. He would be wise, however, not to place too much faith in any promises Ireton may make at this stage. Just to be on the safe side, you know.'

Sam shot him an acute glance. 'I'll tell him.'

'Do.' Gabriel paused briefly. 'You might also consider abating your assault on Jack. I suspect it's currently doing more harm than good. And, for what it's worth, I put in a word on your behalf myself yesterday.'

Sam stared at him. 'That was uncommonly good of you.'

'It was, wasn't it?' Gabriel smiled suddenly. 'But don't expect me to make a habit of it. What you do from here on is entirely up to you.'

'Then I'll take your advice and see what happens during the next month. After which – if Mr Morrell is still saying no – I'll do my damnedest to marry Bryony out of hand.'

'I didn't hear that. Neither do I wish to.'

'Point taken,' grinned Sam. And then, pausing briefly before following his colleagues, 'You might, however, wish to hear that my sister and her husband are safe and sound in their own home, blessing you thrice-daily.'

'Good,' said Gabriel, ambiguously. 'It's comforting to know that somebody is.'

While the Moderate officers at the Bull's Head were declaring their 'unanimous resolutions for peace', the committee of Independents and Levellers came to the reluctant conclusion that, since there was insufficient time for a new *Agreement of the People* to be drawn up before the King received and replied to the proposals being sent up to him by the Council of Officers, a suitable interim measure was needed. They consequently adjourned to St Albans where the Levellers set about adding a few vital paragraphs to the Remonstrance – on the strict understanding that no attempt should be made to dissolve Parliament until both sections of the committee were in total accord. Gabriel smiled wryly to himself and hoped that Sam had passed his message on to Free-born John.

The Council of Officers, meanwhile, sent the King the conditions on which he might be restored to a condition of 'safety, honour and freedom in this nation'. These wisely omitted all mention of religion and concentrated on asking for a permanent settlement, rather than the usual three years of this and ten of that. Parliaments were to be held biennially, the Militia placed under control of a Council of State and only five English Royalists were to be denied pardon. Gabriel thought the proposals eminently reasonable. Both Houses of Commons sniffed and declared that the King could only be restored if he accepted, unconditionally, the terms he'd been busily amending at Newport.

On November 17th, while his Majesty was being presented with the officers' proposals and preparing to celebrate his forty-eighth birthday, Commissary-General Ireton responded to the current clutch of escape rumours by writing to Colonel Hammond on the Isle of Wight and urging him to tighten security. On the 18th, the Council of Officers met to learn that the said proposals had met with the usual gently evasive rejection and immediately voted to adopt the *Remonstrance*. Only three voices were raised against it . . . and one of them was that of Colonel Brandon.

Gabriel's defection naturally won him an interview with the Commissary-General, during the course of which he confined himself to saying that, although the *Remonstrance* doubtless contained many worthy things, he could not reconcile his conscience to the paragraph concerning the King's trial. This, of course, was the right tack to take and also had the merit of being true. But Gabriel, who would have much preferred to make a more positive stand, found it left an unpleasant taste in his mouth.

Receiving the *Remonstrance* with a noticeable lack of enthusiasm, the Commons postponed consideration of it for a week and busied themselves instead with choosing seven Delinquents to banish and seven others to exempt from pardon. The first list contained the names of my lords Norwich, Holland, Capel and Loughborough, and the second those of Newcastle, Digby, Byron and Langdale. No one saw fit to dwell on the fact that Newcastle, Digby and Byron were already safely overseas – or that, living up to his sobriquet of The Ghost, Sir Marmaduke Langdale had recently escaped from Nottingham to join them.

While the Army transferred its Headquarters from St

Albans to Windsor and Colonel Hammond was recalled for refusing to increase the King's guards without orders from Parliament, his Majesty refused to make any further concessions in the matter of church government. And, on the 27th – a full month after the date originally set – Denzil Holles and his fellow commissioners brought their negotiations to an end and headed gloomily back to London.

Having spent the last week skirmishing with Hugh Peter and trying to drum up some resistance to the *Remonstrance* without bringing himself into open conflict with Ireton, Gabriel went back to Cheapside on that Monday evening wanting nothing more than a brief respite from the fray. He did not get it. Major Maxwell returned from Windsor with the news that, from far-away Pontefract, Cromwell had signified his agreement with Ireton's demand for justice without respect of persons; and this – since Eden agreed with it too – naturally provoked an argument. Then, almost before the dust had settled, Samuel Radford appeared with his hair all on end and Bryony clinging tearfully to his arm.

'Oh my God,' groaned Gabriel irritably. 'What now?'

'She won't go home,' said Sam. 'Mr Morrell found out that we've been meeting at the Lilburne's house in Brewer's Yard and there was one hell of a row which ended up with Bryony running to my lodgings. Only it wouldn't be proper for her to stay the night there, so I thought—'

'You thought you'd bring her here to me,' finished Gabriel blightingly. 'Quite. But if either of you imagines I'm going to tuck her up in bed while Jack goes frantic with worry, you've missed your mark. I won't.'

'But you must!' Bryony released Sam in order to cast herself on Gabriel's chest. 'Uncle Jack says I can't see Sam ever again – so I won't go back! I *won't*! And if you make me, I'll run away again and sl-sleep with Sam and then we'll *have* to be married!'

Gabriel gazed up at the ceiling and swore quietly. Smothering a grin, Major Maxwell rose from his chair and murmured, 'I think I'd better leave you to it.' And went.

Gabriel detached Bryony's hands from his coat and looked her in the eye. Then he said flatly, 'I'm taking you back to Shoreditch. And that is final.'

Bryony shouted that she'd sooner die and burst into tears. Gabriel retained his grip on her wrists and shook her. 'Stop it or I'll slap you!' he said. And, to Mr Radford, 'Go home, Sam. And thank you.'

Samuel hesitated, wanting to comfort Bryony but realising that staying would only make matters worse. Nodding at Gabriel, he said wearily, 'Try to understand, Bryony. It's not that I don't love you – and if all else fails, I'll willingly marry you without your uncle's permission. But I won't force his hand by compromising you. Not today, not ever. It's a matter of respect. And that's why I'm going to let the Colonel take you home. Goodnight, my dear.'

Bryony howled as the door closed behind him. She shrieked as Gabriel took her downstairs and threw her up before him on his horse . . . and she wailed all the way to Shoreditch. Consequently, by the time they walked in on Jack and Annis, Gabriel's temper was on a decidedly short rein and he was past the stage of being tactful.

Ignoring Annis's white face and Jack's muffled exclamation of relief, he hauled Bryony into the parlour and said crisply, 'Before you both overwhelm me with your gratitude, allow me to point out that the credit for her safe and unsullied return belongs, not to me, but to Sam Radford – who has more sense than the rest of you put together.'

Jack stiffened. 'I *beg* your pardon?'

'You heard – and I'm not staying to argue. Quite frankly, I could have done without riding here at this time of night altogether. But since I've been forced to do so, I may as well say this. What happened tonight will happen again – and though you can trust Samuel not to dishonour Bryony, there'll come a point when he'll agree to an elopement. And I, for one, won't blame him.'

Bryony crumpled abruptly on to a settle.

'Are you out of your mind?' snapped Jack. 'It's thanks to him that she's thick as thieves with Free-born John!'

'So? I can think of worse people for her to associate with,' came the cool reply. Then, to Annis, 'Do you *want* to end up locking Bryony in the attic?'

Her brows contracted. 'No. Of course I don't.'

'Then talk some sense into Jack. I've already told him why

it's not such an unsuitable match. Sam's got character and he knows how to handle her – which is more, just at the moment, than either of you do.'

'I don't think,' observed Jack, coldly, 'that I like your tone. And what makes you such an expert?'

'Common-sense,' returned Gabriel irascibly. 'You should try it some time.' And, turning on his heel, he walked out of the house, slamming the door behind him.

In the week that followed, the Lord General allowed himself to be persuaded that it might be as well to secure the King's person before Parliament could do so, with the result that Lieutenant-Colonel Cobbet and Captain Merryman were dispatched to the Isle of Wight. Meanwhile, Lilburne and Ireton continued to argue the case of liberty of conscience versus the repression of radical opinions and were only prevented from going their separate ways when Colonel Harrison told Lilburne that Ireton had agreed to his suggestion for a new committee of Levellers, Army officers, civilian Independents and MPs to draft the *Agreement*.

With this division temporarily healed and the Commons still postponing consideration of the *Remonstrance*, there was a sudden upsurge of activity. On November 30th, the Council of Officers issued a Declaration demanding the immediate dissolution of Parliament and announcing its intention to march on London; Fairfax asked the Lord Mayor for forty thousand pounds towards arrears of Army pay; and Officers Cobbet and Merryman were instructed to remove the King from Carisbrooke. On December 1st, the Commons listened to Denzil Holles's account of the final answers given by the King at Newport, ignored William Prynne's desire to declare the Army a collection of rebels, and authorised payment of the money Fairfax had asked for. On the 2nd, the Commons quaked as the Army entered London and established its headquarters at Whitehall. And on Monday 4th, it learned that the Army had once again seized the King, this time transferring him to bleak, inaccessible Hurst Castle on the Solent.

For a few hours on Tuesday 5th, Gabriel began to hope that, having the King securely in their hands, his more moderate colleagues would be tempted into a change of heart on the matter of the trial. Then, while the Officers' Council was busily amending Lilburne's *Agreement* (and being told that Free-born John would as soon write propaganda for the Turk as for the Army), the Commons voted that the King's answers at Newport be considered grounds 'to proceed upon for the settlement and peace of the kingdom'. Suddenly, everything was back in the melting-pot again.

Immediately summoned to a meeting of officers and MPs at Whitehall, Gabriel took a boat to Westminster Stairs and then strode up King Street in a mood of black preoccupation. He did not notice the initially startled and then frankly venomous gaze that followed him from across the street. There was, of course, no reason why he should.

The meeting was neither better nor worse than he expected. Ireton and Harrison urged the dissolution of Parliament in accordance with the recent Declaration of the Army, on the grounds that purging would merely create a 'mock power'. The Members replied by somewhat dryly pointing out that, since the bulk of the people still wanted the King restored, a general election at this stage was unlikely to produce the kind of result the Army wanted. And after hours of circuitous argument, it was finally agreed that – Parliament having forfeited its trust – it was the duty of the Army 'to endeavour to put a stop to such proceedings' by means of an immediate purge, closely followed by total dissolution. Another joint committee was appointed to establish the criteria on which members were to be excluded.

Leaving the rest to their deliberations, Gabriel slipped away unnoticed into the chilly night air and set off moodily back towards the river. A shadowy figure erupted from the Axe Yard and another detached itself from a doorway just in front of him. Steel gleamed dully in the fitful light. Gabriel stopped abruptly and drew his sword. Then the assailants closed in on him.

He dispatched the first easily enough with a swift, vicious thrust to the throat but the other was more tenacious. Also, Gabriel was grimly aware that it would be silly to kill the only man who could answer several burning questions. So he opened a fast but careful attack that pushed his opponent

462

gradually backwards whilst demanding curtly, 'Who sent you?'

The fellow reserved all his energies for the fight and declined to answer. Gabriel encouraged him by slitting his left sleeve from elbow to shoulder. 'Who sent you?'

'Wouldn't you like to know?' came the breathless reply.

Gabriel disarmed with him with a savage twist of his wrist and heard the sword clatter to the cobbles several feet away. Then, just as he was about to pin its owner to the wall, a group of noisy youths flooded inebriately into the street nearby from The Leg tavern and, in the split second that Gabriel's attention was diverted, his attacker wriggled from his grasp and bolted.

Gabriel swore and gave chase, running back past Whitehall and the Tiltyard towards Charing Cross. And there, inexplicably, his quarry vanished. Gabriel spent ten fruitless minutes searching alleys and doorways and then gave up. Ramming his sword home, he strode furiously to the river and hailed a boat. He'd had his chance and made a mess of it; and the most annoying thing was that it was no one's fault but his own.

He arrived back in Cheapside to find Wat sitting by the fire with a beef patty in one hand and a mug of ale in the other. For a moment, Gabriel debated keeping the evening's events to himself and then, deciding against it, pulled off his sword and laid it across a stool.

'Clean that, will you?' he asked negligently.

Mr Larkin froze, patty in mouth. Then, slowly removing it, 'What happened?'

'I was attacked by hired bravos. Again. So it looks as if you were right all along. Someone is trying to kill me.'

'Christ!' muttered Wat. He stared down at the remains of his supper and then threw it into the fire, wondering if he'd allowed Ellis to lull him into a false sense of security. He said, abruptly, 'Your half-brother was hereabouts the night you nearly fried – and for a few weeks after. But I don't know where he is now because I stopped watching him once you'd been back a week or so and he was still seemingly minding his own business.'

Gabriel sat down, a faintly arrested gleam in his eyes.

'And what,' he asked gently, '*is* his business?'

'Coining,' came the bald reply. 'There's four of 'em in it. The work's done near the Lion in Blackfriars.'

There was a long, reflective silence.

'You appear to know an awful lot about it. But what interests me is how come you were able to recognise dear Ellis – since I didn't think you'd ever seen him.'

'Ah.' Wat half-drained his tankard and then, since there wasn't much alternative, said grudgingly, 'He wrote to the missus the day before the fire, asking to see her – and she asked me to go instead and get rid of him. So I did.'

'That was nice of you.' Gabriel leaned back and folded his arms. 'And neither of you thought to mention it to me?'

'No. But if you'll cast your mind back, you'll know why.'

A faint smile touched the hard mouth. 'Perhaps.'

'There's no perhaps about it,' retorted Mr Larkin. Then, sourly, 'I'd better find Sir Ellis again – though how I'm to do that *and* guard your back, I don't know.'

'Then you'd better leave me to guard my own back, hadn't you?' Gabriel stretched out his feet to the fire. 'After all, the tools Ellis is using – if, of course it *is* Ellis – haven't been very efficient so far, have they? And though I'd as soon not go on repelling random attacks on my life, I'm not trembling with fear just yet.'

'Maybe not,' said Wat grimly. 'But from now on after dark, where you go, *I* go. And then we'll see, won't we, if we can't catch the murdering bugger red-handed?'

Eight

The following morning found Wat hammering on Gabriel's bedchamber door before it was fully light and then sticking his head round it to say tersely, 'I thought you'd want to know. Major Maxwell's just sent word that our boys have been ordered down to Westminster.'

Colonel Brandon was suddenly wide awake and out of bed, reaching for his clothes. 'Get my horse saddled – fast.'

Wat stared at him. 'You're going down there?'

'What does it look like?'

'Why?'

'To ram Eden's teeth down his throat,' came the not entirely flippant reply. And then, 'Are you going to stand there all bloody day?'

By the time Gabriel arrived at Westminster, two regiments were deployed in the surrounding area and the Trained Bands who normally guarded Parliament were being jocularly told to go home and see to their wives. Ignoring this, and narrowing his eyes against the driving sleet, Gabriel rode on until he found his own fellows outside the entrance to the Commons. Then, fixing Major Maxwell with a blistering gaze, he said, 'Do you *know* what's going on here today?'

Eden nodded warily. 'A purge of the House.'

'Quite. So – knowing my views as well as you do – why the devil did you bring my troops to assist in it?'

'What choice did I have? *You* may feel up to countermanding an order from the Commissary-General but I don't.'

Hard grey eyes locked with cool hazel ones. 'You mean,' said Gabriel silkily, 'that you didn't want to. Which means you have a problem, Major, because *I'm* ordering you to take our men back to the Tower. Now.'

The scarred face tightened fractionally and, for a moment, Eden looked as though he wanted to argue. Then, shrugging slightly, he said, 'On your head be it.'

'Certainly.' Gabriel glanced around him. 'Who's in charge of this foolishness?'

'Colonel Pride.' Eden jerked his head towards the steps of the House. 'He's up there with Lord Grey of Groby.'

Gabriel's brows rose slightly but he forbore to remark that the former drayman and the grinning dwarf made an odd combination and, instead, said smoothly, 'Then I'll inform the Colonel of my change in your orders. Meanwhile, Major, you may take the men back where they came from.'

The bells of St Margaret's were striking eight as he ran lightly up the steps and members of the House were already starting to arrive. They looked nervous, Gabriel thought, and he didn't blame them. The heavy military presence must have already told them what was afoot.

Outside the door to the lobby, with his hat in one hand, his list in the other and Lord Grey to identify those members he was not himself familiar with, Colonel Pride was politely arresting those who had either supported the previous day's motion that settlement could still be reached with the King or voted against declaring all who'd assisted in the Scots' invasion traitors.

Gabriel waited while William Prynne was hauled off, loudly protesting that he was but a member of the House doing his duty, and that this was 'a high breach of privilege of Parliament and an affront to the House.' Then, stalking up to Colonel Pride, he said curtly, 'I can't stop what you're doing, but I won't have my men used in it and have therefore had them removed. I shall also – in case you're wondering – be informing Henry of it.'

'I see.' Thomas Pride eyed him with acute disfavour. 'Then there's nothing more to be said, is there?'

'Only one thing. Does Fairfax know about this?'

'He will,' came the flat reply. 'When it's finished.'

A total of forty-one members spent the morning under guard in the Queen's Court while their colleagues in the House sent out demands for their release which eventually procured the liberty of Nathaniel Fiennes and Sir Benjamin Rudyard. The remaining thirty-nine (Sir William Waller and Sir Samuel Luke amongst them – but not, oddly enough, Denzil Holles) were told they were detained 'by the power of the sword' and, under the supervision of Hugh Peter, condemned to an uncomfortable night in an icy room below the Exchequer, satirically known as 'Hell'. By then, Henry Ireton's hand had been strengthened by more than a mere thirty-five inches of steel for, having left Major-General Lambert to prosecute the siege of Pontefract – some twelve hours after Colonel Pride had purged Parliament – Oliver Cromwell rode back into Westminster.

The following day, while the newly-culled Commons was formally congratulating the Lieutenant-General on his victories and also learning that it must answer the Army's demands before its restrained members could be freed, Colonel Brandon told the Lieutenant-General's son-in-law precisely what he thought of the purge.

'I don't accept that it is the Army's place to turn Parliament into a public joke by forcibly removing the duly elected representatives of the nation,' he said bluntly. 'And I don't see the difference between what was done yesterday and what the King did back in January '42 when he tried to arrest Holles and the others.'

'Your views on the subject have been well-noted,' responded Ireton pointedly. 'They are, however, insufficient grounds on which to supersede my orders with your own. And it is that which we are at present discussing.'

'I'm aware of it and have already expressed my regrets that it should have become necessary. But I don't care to be associated with unlawful interference in matters which lie outside my province as a soldier. Particularly when it has the ultimate aim of taking off the King's head.'

There was a frigid silence during which, beneath the ice-cold facade, Ireton's temper began to stir.

'The King,' he remarked, 'is the author of every trouble which has beset this nation for the last six years.'

'Is he? Did the King make war on Parliament – or was it the other way about? At best it's a moot point and I doubt you'll find one in twenty people across the country who are as convinced of his guilt as you are. Or perhaps the will of the nation isn't important?'

'Of course it's important! But the people's main desire is for a secure and stable government, without which they and their posterity have nothing.'

'Quite. But as far as the common man is concerned, stability is not to be found in a puppet King and Parliament whose strings are being pulled by the Army,' said Gabriel flatly. Then, 'Do you *know* how resentful and confused people are these days? *"There is no such thing as a Bishop or King – nor Peer but in name or show."* That's what they're singing, and it frightens them.'

'Do you think I don't realise that – or that I wanted the situation to deteriorate this far?' snapped Ireton. 'But the King has given us no choice. And *you* are in danger of sticking your neck out beyond what will be forgiven.'

Grey eyes met black.

'Are you relieving me of duty?' asked Gabriel evenly.

'Not yet,' came the clipped reply. 'But I suggest you put a curb on your tongue while you consider your position. And that, Colonel, is a warning you would do well to heed.'

Outside in the street Gabriel watched a gaggle of children skipping round in a circle, chanting.

> *Then let's have King Charles, says George,*
> *Nay we'll have his son, says Hugh,*
> *Nay, then let's have none, says jabbering Joan,*
> *Nay – we'll all be kings, says Prue.*

Smiling wryly, Gabriel wondered if Henry could hear them. Then he turned his face towards the river and went home.

During the course of the next week, Gabriel made an uneasy peace with Eden. Then, on the orders of the Lord General and with fifty men at his back, he coolly invaded the Weavers Hall and carried off twenty-eight of the forty thousand pounds that had been asked for to meet the Army's arrears of pay. It wasn't the kind of mission he would normally have enjoyed – but it made a change from the daily tedium of the Tower and the rounds of endless meetings; and then again, his share might just enable him to pay Brandon Lacey's taxes in full.

On December 10th, John Lilburne and his committee completed their work on the *Agreement of the People* and on the 11th they laid it proudly before the Officers' Council in the expectation of seeing it immediately sent out for signature – first within the Army and then to the country as a whole. Ireton, however, had other ideas and, backed by Cromwell, insisted on picking the document apart, clause by clause, in further debate.

Though plainly furious at what he saw as Ireton's trickery and procrastination, Lilburne began by keeping a tight rein on his temper. Wildman and Walwyn followed his lead and Sam Radford kept his head down, apparently taking copious notes of the proceedings. Gabriel, sitting at the back amongst his fellow officers, folded his arms and waited, with interest, for the inevitable explosion.

By noon, when they were still debating which matters should be placed outside Parliamentary control, he had come to the conclusion that, if it hadn't been so time-consumingly tedious, it would have been funny. Ireton, though he frequently prefaced his speeches with 'I desire only one word', was rarely on his feet for less than half an hour; Colonel Harrison halted progress for some time by querying the precise wording of the clause in question; and John Goodwin persisted in dragging the debate into the misty realms of deep theology while some of the younger, less patient men present called every now and then for a vote.

They never took one. During the course of the afternoon, tempers started to fray and harsh words passed between the Levellers and the officers over whether, having found favour with all sections of the committee which had drafted it, the *Agreement* should or should not now be accepted without further delay. And when someone flung one insult too many at Lilburne's head, he responded by challenging the speaker to a duel.

Men from both sides surged to their feet, all shouting at

once and, for a moment, it seemed that a fight was about to develop. Sam Radford laid down his quill, looking optimistic, and Sir Hardress Waller bellowed for order. Then, as soon as the din abated somewhat, Free-born John said cuttingly, 'You are a pack of dissembling, juggling knaves – with neither faith, truth nor common honesty amongst you!'

The uproar broke out afresh but Lilburne stood his ground, his expression utterly contemptuous. 'You have cozened and deceived us with your promises and you have turned the Parliament into a mock-power who will fly to your swords for protection and bid us shake our ears for our *Agreement*. But no more, gentlemen! No more, I say. From now on, I discharge myself from meddling with so perfidious a generation of men . . . especially the cunningest of all Machiavellians, Commissary Henry Ireton!' And, ignoring the tumult around him, he strode to the door and walked out.

Messrs Wildman and Walwyn followed hard on his heels, leaving Mr Radford hurriedly scooping up his writing materials and notes. Gabriel rose from his bench and stretched his cramped muscles; then, when the younger man drew level with him, he walked out of the room beside him saying softly, 'Why do I suspect there's more to Lilburne's withdrawal just now than meets the eye?'

'Because there is,' Sam grinned cheerfully. And, when he was sure of not being overheard, 'What happened today wasn't exactly unexpected. Consequently, he's already begun arrangements to have the *Agreement* published.'

'In an attempt to expedite matters – or so that the public will know what he was trying to do for them?'

'Both.' Sam paused, eyeing him obliquely. 'You have objections – to the articles themselves, I mean?'

'No. In many respects, they seem a rather neat composite between the original *Agreement* of a year ago and Ireton's own *Heads of the Proposals*. I do, however, suspect that a document which requires the signature of every man with the vote is not especially practical. And I can't help but wonder if Mr Lilburne isn't being a little naïve in placing so much faith in the goodness of individual consciences.'

'Perhaps so. But to do anything else would be to leave the way open to restriction and repression,' returned Sam. Then,

'I haven't had the opportunity to thank you for what you said to Mr Morrell the other night.'

Gabriel gave a brief, sardonic laugh.

'I'm not sure thanks are in order. Did it work?'

'Better than anything else has so far. He's continued letting me visit Bryony and stopped ranting about my having introduced her to Free-born John. And, yesterday, he interrogated me about the state of my finances.'

The dark brows rose over eyes full of lazy amusement.

'What you're really saying is that you're cautiously optimistic.'

'That,' agreed Sam, with a sudden, wide smile, 'is exactly what I'm saying. Bryony, of course, is already planning her wedding gown.'

'Then let us hope that she's not going to be disappointed,' said Gabriel. 'But if she is, don't bring her to me. At the end of a day such as today, I don't respond especially well to youthful histrionics. And I really do have other, more important things on my mind.'

'So I've heard. They say, for example, that you fell foul of the Commissary-General over the purge. Is it true?'

'Perfectly.'

'Then you'd better watch your step, hadn't you?' Sam surveyed him with a gleam of characteristic humour. 'After all, it's going to be rather embarrassing if you end up in the Tower. Who is going to get *you* out?'

As it happened, Sam's optimism was better-founded than he knew, for Jack was actually much closer to giving in to Bryony's wishes than he was as yet prepared to reveal. Most of the reasons for this were things he preferred not to contemplate; but Bryony's unsuccessful attempt to fly the coop undoubtedly had a lot to do with it. And then, of course, there were the gentle persuasions of Annis.

'This can't go on, you know,' she had said reasonably, as soon as Jack's temper had cooled after the Colonel's last visit. 'Whether you like to admit it or not, Gabriel is right. We can't keep Bryony under lock and key – nor do we wish to try. So if we don't want her to run off again, there's really only one solution. And it's not as though you dislike Sam, is it?'

471

'No. That's just the trouble,' said Jack ruefully. And then, 'Are you convinced he loves her?'

'Of course. Aren't you?'

'Yes. If I'm to be honest, I was sure of *his* feelings long before I became sure of Bryony's. But his politics still bother me. The Levellers may be respectable today but I doubt it will last, not now the Army has got Parliament under its thumb. And if Lilburne continues standing in Ireton's way, Sam may find himself in even bigger trouble than he was before.'

'It's a possibility,' agreed Annis mildly. 'And one that Bryony is fully aware of.'

He met her gaze in silence for a moment and then grinned. 'You're saying I should set my reservations to one side for a time and try talking to her.'

Smiling back at him, Annis rose from her seat and crossed the hearth to sit on his knee. 'I wasn't saying anything of the sort . . . but it's an excellent idea. And just think how much we'll enjoy the peace and quiet.'

Battening down his own anxieties, Jack encouraged Bryony to talk about her hopes and the feelings she cherished towards Sam, and also set about discovering whether Mr Radford had both the means to support a wife and suitable lodgings in which to install her. Then, having discussed his findings thoroughly with Annis, he took himself off to Cheapside to confront his foster-brother.

He found Gabriel buckling on his sword whilst indulging in a typically terse argument with Wat Larkin.

'Haven't you been listening?' snapped Wat.

'Yes. You say you can't find him, which probably means he isn't here,' returned Gabriel irritably. 'Personally, I don't give a tinker's curse either way. I can look after myself. And what I *don't* need is a bloody nursemaid!'

'Who thinks that you do?' Jack strolled over the threshold, smiling faintly. 'Not Wat, surely?'

Two pairs of eyes encompassed him briefly and then locked with each other.

'I'm afraid so,' said Gabriel blandly. 'Old age is bringing out the mother in him.'

Wat spat hard into the fire. 'Nice try,' he grunted. 'But

you'll have to do better than that if you want to get rid of me.'
And he stamped across the room and went out.

The door slammed and, for a moment, there was silence.
Then Jack said cautiously, 'What was all that about?'

'Nothing in particular. Just daily life in the bear-pit.'
Waving him towards a chair, Gabriel turned away to pour
wine. 'Aside from apologising for my recent ill-humour –
what can I do for you?'

'You can come to supper next Thursday.'

Gabriel's brows rose slightly. 'Any special reason?'

'Yes. I'm going to give Bryony and Samuel my blessing,'
replied Jack, accepting the glass. 'And don't flatter yourself
that it's all your doing. It's not.'

'No.' Gabriel grinned suddenly. 'The credit doubtless
belongs to Annis.'

Jack laughed. 'Quite. So you'll come, then?'

'If I can.' The grin faded. 'Events are on the march again,
with the result that I don't know what I'll be doing
tomorrow, let alone next week. But I'll try.' He paused.
'You'll have heard that the Commons has re-instated the
Vote of No Addresses, annulled the Newport talks and
changed its mind about merely fining or banishing the
Royalists?'

'Yes. Though with a hundred or so members turned out by
the purge and quantities of others refusing to sit in protest
because of it, I'm surprised there are enough of them left to
form a quorum.'

'Some days there aren't,' said Gabriel dryly. 'But the
strength of the Army more than makes up for it. Three
days ago, Denzil Holles was expelled yet again and William
Waller was placed under arrest. And this afternoon the
Council of Officers voted to bring the King from Hurst to
Windsor.'

'To what end?' Jack frowned. 'The Vote of No Addresses
means that further negotiation is out of the question.'

'Yes. But only, you will realise, between his Majesty and
Parliament.' The grey gaze grew openly derisive. 'And that's
not all. In what I can only assume to be an attempt to shake
the King's nerve, they've given the duty of transferring him
from Hurst Castle to Thomas Harrison – whose well-known

473

desire for the King's death was what caused his Majesty to escape from Windsor in the first place.'

Mr Morrell stared broodingly into his wine. Then, meeting the Colonel's eyes, he said, 'No court in this land has the power to try a king. Have they thought of that?'

'Constantly.'

'But they're still set on it.'

'Some are – some aren't,' replied Gabriel. 'At this stage, I wouldn't like to predict what will happen – and am still hoping for the best. But the King is his own worst enemy. In the last three years he's been offered terms from both the Army and Parliament . . . and it would have saved a lot of trouble if he'd stopped playing games and simply said yes to one or the other of us.'

While Colonel Harrison was at Hurst Castle arranging the King's journey to Windsor, Lieutenant-General Cromwell conferred quietly with Bulstrode Whitelocke and veered gently away from the notion of regicide. And, by the time Harrison and his royal charge reached Winchester, the Earl of Denbigh had received Fairfax's permission for a final, informal attempt to make his Majesty see reason.

On Thursday December 21st, Gabriel sat through a prolonged meeting of the Officers' Council – for once without noticing that darkness was falling or even becoming unduly concerned by the knowledge that he was supposed to be supping in Shoreditch. For the question being debated was that of the fate of the King and the last few days had seemingly brought about a significant shift of opinion.

Ireton, though he continued to demand the King's immediate trial, was no longer asking for blood. He would be content, he declared, for his Majesty to be imprisoned until such time as he consented to abjure both his veto and the Scots. Cromwell went even further. He suggested that the King's trial be postponed until after those of Hamilton, Norwich and Holland. And, when a vote was finally taken, the Council rejected the notion of executing the King by a slender majority of five.

Gabriel ran lightly down the steps and out into freezing night air, feeling more optimistic than he had in a month.

'You took your time, didn't you?' grunted Mr Larkin.

'Oh hell!' He stopped abruptly, staring at his henchman with mingled amusement and annoyance. 'Can't you take a hint? Or is it just that you haven't anything better to do?'

'Some people are never grateful,' observed Wat, setting off in the direction of the river.

'And some others are just naturally bloody-minded,' retorted Gabriel, falling into step with him. Then, 'I'm going to Shoreditch, you know, and I'm late. Fortunately, I took the precaution of leaving my horse at the Tower.'

'So did I,' said Wat. And, with a sour grin, 'Old I may be; senile I'm not. So let's go – while the tide's with us.'

Since only young men with more bravado than sense took a boat through the lethal currents of London Bridge, Gabriel instructed the waterman to take them to the Old Swan stairs and then settled back to tell Wat about the Council's latest vote while the Savoy Palace, Essex House and Puddle Wharf drifted away behind them. Then, as they approached the Three Cranes and the boatman began drawing his craft towards the bank, Gabriel asked Wat, with levity, if he'd had time to read the newly-published *Agreement of the People*.

He never got an answer. Something cold and deadly whistled through the air from the shadows of Dowgate and impaled the waterman through the chest. He slumped with an odd, gurgling sound and the oars disappeared overboard.

Wat was startled into a single, monosyllabic expletive before Gabriel sent him sprawling into the well of the boat and dropped down beside him, saying succinctly, 'Crossbow.'

'So I notice.' Mr Larkin peered awkwardly across at the waterman. 'He's dead, I reckon. What did they want to go and shoot him for, poor bugger?'

'To be on the safe side. We're caught in the current and being sucked down to the Bridge. If they don't shoot us, we drown – or get battered against the stanchions.'

Wat lifted a cautious head to verify this statement. Already gathering speed, the boat was being towed back into midstream and down towards the twenty narrow arches of London Bridge – while moonlight glancing off metal revealed that the marksman was keeping pace with them from the Steelyard. Ducking back as a second bolt bit into the side of the boat, Wat said, 'Sod it!' And reached for his pistol.

'Quite. What are you doing?'

'What does it look like? I'm going to take a shot at that bastard on the bank while I've got the chance.'

'You won't do it. We're moving too fast.'

'So? It'll at least give him something to think about, won't it? And meantime, *you* can get your boots off.'

It was sound advice – if a trifle difficult to follow from a semi-prone position – and by the time Gabriel achieved it, Wat had taken his first shot, missed and was busy reloading. 'God damn it!' he muttered. 'Can't somebody come up with a pistol that fires more than one bullet? Better get rid of your sword and coat as well.'

'Stop worrying about me and keep your head down!' snapped Gabriel, his fingers already struggling with the laces of his buff leather. The Bridge, so far as he could see, was roughly forty yards away and closing fast. Casting off his coat, he began trying both to calculate the odds and work out some means of improving them.

Wat, meanwhile, had finished reloading and was taking careful aim at the shadowy figure in the Steelyard – now once more rewinding his bow. In the poor light and with the distance steadily increasing, Wat was aware that his best chance would occur as the fellow stood upright again. Heaving himself on to his knees, he levelled his pistol and waited for the right moment. It was just plain bad luck that, when it came, the boat was seized by the current.

The little craft dipped, shuddered and tilted sideways, throwing Wat against the gunnel and causing him to hold his fire. Then, in the brief second that the boat steadied again and he tried to regain his aim before they were sucked into the torrent raging about the Bridge, the marksman on the bank shot his final bolt.

Seeing it coming, Gabriel shouted – but too late. With wicked, glittering grace, it tore through the night to embed itself in the flesh and sinew and bone of Wat's shoulder. He screamed and crumpled against the gunnel at the precise moment that the boat hit the fast-surging foam. Gabriel hurled himself forward and reached out to grab his friend but was knocked off-balance as the water hurled them against the stanchion to their right. For an instant, London Bridge loomed high and sheer above them. Then, with a sickening downwards lurch, the boat ricocheted back into the tide – and Wat was tipped out into the river.

Deafened by the roar of the water and blinded by the rank-smelling darkness under the Bridge, Gabriel had to use every ounce of control he possessed not to immediately dive in after him. The boat scraped against stone, slowed, half-turned and picked up speed again. Then the Bridge was behind him and there was light. Frantically, Gabriel's eyes scoured the surface of the water and were rewarded with a glimmer of something that surfaced, vanished and then surfaced again a few yards to his left. He wasn't sure it was Wat – he couldn't be; but it was his best hope. Rising to his feet, he cast himself into the icy blackness of the river and struck out towards it.

Swimming across the current was slow, gruelling work and the cold sapped his energy quicker than he had expected. But it *was* Wat. He was sure – almost sure – of that now; and in another dozen or so strokes, he would reach him. He *must*.

The tide bore him on past Botolph's Wharf. Waves slapped him in the face, blurring his vision and, when his sight cleared again, there was nothing ahead of him but dark, empty water. Harnessing what remained of his strength, he took an immense gulp of air and dived down into a blackness so dense that he could not even see his own hand. He swam blind until his lungs were bursting, hoping against hope that he could find what he sought by touch; by the time he surfaced again, he found himself unable even to shout.

Common-sense receded in the face of desperation and he continued to swim about long after it was safe to do so. Lethargy invaded his limbs and numbed his senses. He saw nothing, heard nothing and knew only that the effort of simply keeping himself afloat was becoming intolerable. He slipped beneath the surface and arose choking. And then, just as he was about to give in, a boat-hook clawed painfully at his shoulder and dragged him back to consciousness.

The lightermen – who had been bellowing at him for some minutes as they rowed swiftly towards him from the Custom

House – hauled him roughly aboard and threw him face-down in the bottom of their craft. Gabriel tried to speak – tried to tell them they must look for Wat – and collapsed, retching. One of the men said something to him but he did not hear what it was . . . or, in fact, anything at all until he had been lifted from the boat and dumped ashore. Then, propping himself up on one elbow, he managed to say feebly, 'My friend. I was looking for my friend.'

The lightermen exchanged glances and the one who had spoken before said uncomfortably, 'You won't find him now, Captain. If there'd been something out there to see, we'd have seen it – like we saw you. Sorry.'

Although it was no more than he already knew, the sense of it seemed to take a long time to reach him. When it did, pain ripped through him like a knife. Incapable of withstanding it, Gabriel drew his knees up hard against his chest and dissolved into violent, uncontrollable shuddering.

Nine

Wat's body was washed up at Wapping on Christmas Eve and buried at St Mary-le-Bow two days later. Gabriel made the necessary arrangements, attended the funeral and remained locked in some solitary, frozen wasteland. Jack brought a new sword to replace the lost one but learned nothing of what had happened on the river; Annis came with pies and potions which went untasted; and Bryony and Samuel arrived handfast and glowing, only to be summarily shown the door. Then on the 27th, Major Maxwell decided to take a hand.

He found Gabriel in the parlour, staring unseeingly into the fire. He wasn't drinking – but that was no surprise. As far as Eden was aware, he hadn't touched a drop since the night he'd come home soaked to the skin, half-dressed and with a look in his eyes nobody recognised.

Frowning a little, Eden poured two glasses of brandy and set one down at Gabriel's elbow. Then he said crisply, 'The King has refused to receive Denbigh.'

Gabriel did not reply.

'Did you hear what I said? Denbigh's mission was the final attempt to present terms. Cromwell spent Christmas Day persuading all but six officers to stop howling for a trial and the King has promptly slammed the door in our faces.' Eden paused and then, when Gabriel still said nothing, added trenchantly, 'I hope his Majesty's satisfied. He's wiped out every vestige of goodwill in both Council and Commons and will wake up to find that his household has been reduced and that he's no longer being served on bended knee.'

Stirring slightly, Gabriel said indifferently, 'That will teach him, won't it?'

'Don't you care?'

'Not particularly.'

Eden sighed and gave up. He said, 'It's been six days, Gabriel . . . and you haven't said a word to any of us about how it happened. You can't go on like this.'

The bleak grey eyes turned slowly to encompass him.

'No. I'm leaving for Brandon Lacey in the morning.'

Eden stared at him. 'Just like that? Without formally applying for leave of absence? You can't!'

'Why not?' Gabriel rose from his seat and walked to the door. Then, turning, he said distantly, 'As far as I'm concerned, this Army is no place for soldiers any more, so you can tell Ireton what the hell you like. I really don't mind. And you won't find him sorry to lose me. Indeed, if you're lucky, he'll promote you into my place. Goodnight.'

On the following morning, he left Cheapside early and made his way to a narrow house near the sign of Lion in Blackfriars. The fellow who peered at him through a crack in the door seemed disinclined to let him in so Gabriel rammed his shoulder against it, slammed it behind him and pinned its guardian with a bruising grip to the throat. Then, establishing that there was no one else there, he dragged his captive from room to room until he found what he was looking for.

Dies, presses, vats and a small furnace; all the equipment necessary to make counterfeit coin. Gabriel took a good look at it, a slow unpleasant smile bracketing his mouth. And finally he said coldly, 'Where is Ellis Brandon?'

Ashen with fear and convinced he had fallen into the hands of the authorities, the man simply stared at him, gibbering. Gabriel shook him like a rabbit and repeated the question. *Where is Ellis Brandon?*

'I – I d-don't know. He t-travels about.'

'Spreading your work around the country so it will attract less attention, presumably. And he's travelling now? Outside London? You're sure about that?' The questions gathered speed, leaving the coiner time only to nod. Then, 'Where was he a week ago?'

'A week ago? I d-don't know. I can't remember.'

Merciless fingers twisted his collar, half-strangling him. 'Try,' advised Gabriel.

'Here,' came the gasping reply. 'He was here!'

Something infinitely dangerous flared in the cold grey eyes before Gabriel finally relaxed his grip and let the fellow collapse into a choking heap. Then, once more looking around the workshop, he said, 'And doubtless he'll be back. In which case, given the right incentive, you and he can save me a great deal of trouble.' And, picking up a small hammer from the workbench, he brought it crashing down on the exquisitely-made currency dies.

He destroyed the presses next and then the neat array of small tools. There was temporary satisfaction in the exercise but no real relief. And, when it was done, he said flatly, 'My name is Gabriel. If Ellis wants to thank me for saving him from the gallows, he can find me in Yorkshire. I'll be waiting.'

The journey was appalling. Not knowing whether he was running away from something or towards it, Gabriel rode on long after it was dark each day and set out again before it grew light; he forced himself to eat but never managed more than an hour's sleep without waking drenched in icy sweat. And when, late in the evening of the 30th, he finally walked through the front door of Brandon Lacey, it was to the paralysing realisation that he shouldn't have come.

Venetia stared down from the turn of the stair while surprise melted into a maelstrom of delight. Then, afraid to take anything for granted, she continued her descent saying somewhat breathlessly, 'If you wanted the fatted calf, you should have got here by Yule.'

He remained quite still, just inside the door.

'It wasn't possible.'

Neither his words nor the flat tone in which they were uttered were what she had expected but worse was to come. As she approached him and he removed his hat, she saw what the shadows had previously concealed; a face white and drawn with fatigue and eyes bleak enough to make hell freeze. Stopping as if she had walked into a wall, Venetia said, 'You look exhausted. What have you been doing?'

'Oh – this and that, you know.' He concentrated on removing his gloves and pulling off his sword. 'Going to council meetings; arguing with Henry Ireton; stopping Bryony throwing her cap over the windmill; burying Wat.'

For a moment, Venetia couldn't believe she'd heard aright but then the look on his face and the desperate unsteadiness of his hands convinced her that she had.

'Wat's *dead*?'

'Yes.' Knowing that if he did not tell her now, straight out, he wouldn't be able to tell her at all, Gabriel said tonelessly, 'Someone who wants to kill me, killed him instead. He drowned a week last Thursday.'

Venetia's stomach heaved and she felt suddenly very sick. Clasping her hands over her mouth, she mumbled, 'I'm sorry – I'm sorry.' And fled to the privacy of the close-stool.

Under the circumstances, the nausea wasn't especially surprising, but by the time she'd got rid of her supper, Venetia knew that this wasn't the moment to tell Gabriel why. The only thing that mattered now was to help him cope – and judging by what she had seen so far, it wasn't going to be easy; so she conquered her weakness, pulled herself together and walked slowly back to the parlour.

He was sitting by the fire with his eyes closed. She knew he wasn't sleeping; what she *didn't* know was how best to begin. And, as if aware of it, Gabriel filled the silence for her by saying, 'Forgive me. Subtlety is beyond me just at present. Are you all right?'

'More so than you think.'

He neither replied nor opened his eyes. Venetia said uncertainly, 'There is food, if you want it. Shall I—?'

'No. I've already eaten.' Easy to say – and true, if one counted the bread and cheese he had forced down at Leeds.

'Oh. Wine, then?'

'Better not.' His lids lifted slowly, as if in response to some massive effort. 'If I start drinking, I may not stop. The same is true of talking. And that's why I can't tell you about it. Not yet. I'm sorry.'

Her throat ached. 'How can I help?'

'By sparing me the task of explaining to Sophy.'

'Of course.' Venetia paused. Then, 'You look as though you haven't slept since – since it happened. If I brought you something that might help, would you take it?'

Recognising her concern but unable, as yet, to respond to it, Gabriel shrugged slightly. 'Why not? If you can drug me as efficiently as you drugged Baxter and Willis, I'll be forever in your debt.'

'I'll do my best.' Like him, Venetia found even the mildest attempt at humour impossible. 'I'll go and get it, then. But you should go to bed.'

'Presently.' The strain of choosing his words was beginning to show. 'Perhaps you could leave it in my room?'

He was telling her that he wished to be left alone – and it hurt. But she said merely, 'As you wish.' And left the room without a backward glance.

She lay awake, grieving silently for the odd little man whose friendship she had earned too late and grappling with the terrifying knowledge that someone wanted Gabriel dead. Tonight – for the first time since she had become sure – there were no thoughts of the unborn child and no rehearsals of how she was going to tell Gabriel. All that must wait. There were other tasks to perform.

She arose early and discovered that Gabriel had already gone down to Scar Croft to see Dick Carter. Faintly disappointed but not surprised, she picked listlessly at her breakfast and waited for Sophia to appear. Then, without wasting words, she told her everything she knew.

Sophy's short-sighted eyes filled with tears and she pushed her plate away. 'Poor man,' she said. 'We'll miss him. And Gabriel . . . Gabriel must be distraught.'

'Yes. He is. But he's not ready to talk yet. Truth to tell, I don't think he can bear it. So you mustn't ask, Sophy. Even though . . . even though—' Venetia stopped, closing one hand hard over the other.

'Even though the matter isn't ended,' supplied Sophia, wisely avoiding the words that had stuck in Venetia's throat. 'Yes. But he should be safe enough here with us.'

'I don't see how you can be sure of that.'

'I'm not. But since all the other incidents you mention took place in London, it seems a reasonable supposition.'

Not for the first time, Venetia found herself taken aback by one of Sophia's lightning bursts of logic. She said abruptly, 'Why do you pretend to appear so vague?'

'Habit. I started doing it when Robert's wife was trying to marry me off and it sort of stuck. Also, when one is no longer young and has never been pretty, eccentricity is all that's left.' She stood up, grabbing automatically at her shawl and, without altering her tone, said, 'You love him very much, don't you?'

'Yes. Yes, I do. Very much.'

'Have you told him?'

'No. I – I haven't known how . . . or whether he'd welcome it,' responded Venetia truthfully. 'And now isn't the time.'

'No?' Sophia meandered to the door. 'I'd have thought now was *just* the time. And the results may surprise you.'

Gabriel re-appeared just in time for supper, wearing an expression of rigid control and apparently intent on talking of everything except Wat. He described the proceedings in the Officers' Council and the Army's dealings with the Levellers, Pride's Purge and Cromwell's recent efforts to moderate the extremists; and finally, he spoke of the King's refusal to receive Lord Denbigh – and the resultant hardening of attitudes in both Council and Commons. Then, meeting his wife's troubled eyes, he said bluntly, 'Everything that can be done *has* been done, but his Majesty seems hell-bent on digging his own pit. And I doubt that anyone can save him from standing trial now; not even Cromwell.'

'But no court can try him! It isn't *legal*.'

'My objections precisely. Amongst other things, Parliament fought the King because he was bending the law to his will. Then, when the war was over, it instantly did precisely the same itself. And now the Army is throwing law out of the window to rule by the sword. Personally, I suspect that Lilburne has it right. We've exchanged one tyrant for another. And, if that's so, I consider myself well out of it.'

Venetia's breath caught and, seeing it, Sophia asked the obvious question for her. 'You're not going back?'

'To the Army? Not unless circumstances change.' Gabriel paused and continued pushing food aimlessly around his plate. Then he said, 'But I may well have to return to London. It all depends on Ellis.'

'Ellis?' echoed Venetia, sharply.

The heavy grey gaze rose to meet hers.

'Yes. Since I can't think of anyone else who might want to kill me, I've done my best to make him follow me here. If he does, we may get some answers.'

'And if not, you'll go looking for him?'

'Naturally.' He pushed back his chair and stood up, his face like granite. 'It would be stupid to leave it alone, after all. And I don't want to. Not now.'

As soon as the meal was over, Sophia drifted tactfully away, leaving them alone. Venetia lingered for another hour or so – hoping to find some small fissure in the wall of ice Gabriel had built round himself but discovering only that he had divided his day between watching the linen growing on the looms and riding into Knaresborough to pay the quarter's taxes. And finally, when it was plain that he still didn't want to talk, she bade him goodnight and went to her room.

She fell into a restless doze only to wake again shortly after midnight. For a time, she lay wondering what had roused her. Then, without quite knowing why, she got up, pulled on her robe and walked out into the silent corridor.

It was dark as pitch but Venetia did not find that a handicap. She paused briefly at the head of the stairs and then moved on until she arrived at Gabriel's door. It was shut and no light showed beneath it. Still following her instincts, she set her hand to the latch and went in.

Illuminated only by the dying glow of the fire and still clad in his shirt and breeches, Gabriel sat on the side of the bed, staring down at his tightly-latticed hands . . . and although he must have known she was there, he gave no sign of it. For a second or two more, Venetia continued to hesitate. Then she closed the door gently behind her and walked over to stand beside him, saying softly, 'Gabriel . . . you can't handle this alone.'

A violent shudder passed over him.

'Why not? It's my fault, after all.'

The words were barely audible. Dropping to her knees, Venetia laid her hands around his and looked up into the haggard face. 'No. That's not so.'

'It *is* so. He was only there because of me – and I let him die.' A pulse hammered in his throat and he was breathing as if it hurt. Then, without warning, the dam burst and the words came tumbling over each other. He told her everything in the exact, devastating detail that he remembered it. And, at the end, he said unevenly, 'Sixteen years. He'd been with me for sixteen years, since I was an ignorant boy on my first campaign. He patched me up when I was wounded, bolstered me in defeat and told me what he thought of every move I made whether I liked it or not. He couldn't have done more if I'd been his own son – and I let him down.'

'You didn't.' Venetia's face was wet. 'Name one thing you could have done and didn't?'

'Stopped him taking pot-shots at the archer; grabbed him before he went overboard; dived straight in after him instead of waiting to get clear of the Bridge.' Gabriel rapidly recited his ten-day-old litany. 'Better still, I could have made bloody sure he stayed at home.'

'Could you? Do you think he'd have listened?' She shook him slightly. 'Look at me. Can you honestly say that Wat ever took an order that didn't suit him?'

He drew a long, ragged breath and focused his eyes on her face. 'No. Perhaps not. I don't know.' And then, dropping his brow against his hands and hers, 'Oh God! I'm sorry. I shouldn't be inflicting all this on you. I never meant to. You'd better go. My self-control doesn't seem to be functioning very well tonight.'

'Then let it go completely,' said Venetia. 'You may as well – because I'm not leaving till you're asleep.'

'You'll be here all night, then – because I'm damned if I'm going to start relying on opiates.'

'No. But there are other things we might try.' Smiling a little, she stood up and drew him to his feet. Then, throwing back the coverlet, she said, 'Nightmares are worse when you're alone. So let's see what company will do.'

Not convinced that this was what he wanted, but too weary to argue, Gabriel let her have her way. And, when he was lying with her arms about him and his head on her shoulder, he said hazily, 'This wasn't in the contract.'

'Then we'll add a clause to cover it,' she responded. And said nothing more.

He fell asleep almost immediately; and when, after an hour or so, he started growing restless, she murmured soothingly to him till he was quiet again. Then, because the sound of her voice seemed to help and because she knew he could not hear her, she told him some of the things she had never previously dared say. And, so doing, slid imperceptibly into sleep.

When she awoke, it was full morning and Gabriel was propped up on one elbow, looking at her. Though not banished completely, the shadows in his eyes had lessened and the merest ghost of a smile touched his mouth as he said, 'Don't worry. I haven't been watching long and I slept remarkably well. But you already know that, don't you?'

Finding this difficult to answer, Venetia confined herself to saying cautiously, 'You look a little better.'

'I feel it.'

'I'm glad.' Muted sounds of activity told her that the house was going about its daily concerns. 'Is it very late?'

'Very,' agreed Gabriel, without moving an inch. 'The church clock struck noon just before you woke.'

Her eyes widened and she sat up. 'My God! Phoebe and Uncle James will be here. And—'

'Uncle James? He's still coming, then?'

'Yes. He's given up *The Canterbury Tales* in favour of *Troilus and Criseyde*. But—'

'Is that significant?'

'It's pure passion,' said Venetia with a fleeting grin. Then, before he could interrupt again, 'I'll have to get up. Everyone will be wondering where on earth I am.'

'I imagine that everyone has worked out *precisely* where you are. But no one will come to look.' Behind the wry indifference, his expression was curiously intent. 'Another hour or so at this stage won't make any difference whatsoever. And I'm happy where I am. Aren't you?'

'Y-yes.' Happy, she thought, but confused. And far more aware of the closeness of his body than was seemly.

'Good.' The grey gaze continued to hold hers in silence for a moment. Then, as if it made perfect sense, he said, 'Why don't you tell me now?'

Her lungs malfunctioned. 'Tell you what?'

'You don't know?' His fingers toyed idly with a strand of silver-gilt hair. 'I can't believe that. You've shown it in every conceivable way – both in bed and out; and last night, unless I was dreaming, you finally put it into words. So why not say it now, while my eyes are open?'

A tide of colour stained Venetia's skin. She said feebly, 'You – you were listening?'

'Let's say that I heard – or thought I did. I'm still waiting to have it confirmed.'

Somewhere deep inside her was relief that at least she'd said nothing about the baby. Everything else was lost in a wave of crippling shyness . . . and the only words that came to mind were, 'I can't!' Then, as she struggled to say them, something changed. Perhaps it was due to Gabriel's utter stillness, or the distant echo of Sophy's words on the previous day. Venetia didn't know. She was merely aware of a sudden feeling of calm; and, reaching out to touch his cheek, she said simply, 'I love you.'

For several seconds he did not even seem to breathe, then his hand captured hers. 'You're sure?'

'You know I am.'

'Perhaps. But it's not the same as hearing you say it.' He looked at her, his eyes dark and strangely compelling. Then, just as he opened his mouth to speak, the spell was shattered by running feet outside in the corridor and a fist hammering hard upon the door. Gabriel expelled a breath of furious irritation.

'Hell's teeth! Is there no damned peace in this house?'

'Gabriel? *Gabriel!*' It was Phoebe's voice and presumably Phoebe's fist which beat again on the panels. 'Wake up, for God's sake! Ellis is on his way to the door.'

Suddenly-alert grey eyes locked with stunned amethyst ones. Then, 'Hallelujah' murmured Gabriel. And, dropping a brief, hard kiss on Venetia's lips, 'Sorry, sweetheart.'

He left the bed in one lithe bound and began pulling on his boots, shouting, 'All right, Phoebe. I'm on my way.'

'And about time, too,' she retorted. 'Sophy doesn't know whether to load a gun or send for the cherry cordial.'

'Neither. I want her out of the way. See to it.'

Phoebe's footsteps receded and Venetia sat up, pushing

back her hair. Then, striving to conceal her anxiety, she said severely, 'You can't meet Ellis in a shirt you've slept in. Have you *no* sense of occasion?'

'None, I'm afraid.' He gave her a swift, heartening smile. 'Don't worry. If anyone dies today, it won't be me.' And snatching up his sword from the corner, he was gone.

Venetia waited for one wholly unpleasant minute before running back to her own room so that she could be sick. Then, without bothering to call for her maid, she started throwing on her clothes and dragging a comb through her hair. If Gabriel thought she was going to stay discreetly out of the way, he was mistaken.

Downstairs in the parlour Phoebe was saying much the same thing. 'I've got rid of Sophy and Uncle James for you,' she announced, 'but I'm staying.'

'You're not.' Gabriel turned away from the window.

'I am, you know. Wild horses couldn't drag me away.'

With Ellis already riding into the courtyard, Gabriel didn't have time to argue. 'Maybe not,' he said, 'but I can!' And, throwing her unceremoniously over his shoulder, he carried her to the bookroom.

Phoebe squawked and beat a tattoo on his back. Gabriel ignored her and locked her in. Then he strode back across the hall just as the door opened and Ellis walked in.

For a moment they faced each other silently, as they had done in Preston; Ellis, elegant in scarlet under a fur-trimmed cloak – and Gabriel, coatless and faintly dishevelled in a creased, half-fastened shirt. Then Ellis drawled, 'Dear me. I thought you were expecting me.'

'Dear me,' countered Gabriel, smoothly. 'What a pity no one ever taught you to knock.'

'On my own door? Hardly.' Ellis strolled forward, removing his extravagantly-plumed hat. 'You don't belong here, you know. And your stay will be a short one.'

'Is that a threat?'

'A prophecy.'

'Then I suggest you don't hold your breath.' Gabriel gestured towards the parlour. 'Shall we continue this in private? After all, I'm sure you don't want too many people knowing what brought you here.'

Ellis cast him a malevolent glance and followed his suggestion. Then, tossing his hat on the table and leaving Gabriel to shut the door, he said pointedly, 'I didn't come to talk. But, before we settle our differences, I'd like to know why the hell you decided to ruin my business.'

'Two reasons. Firstly, it was the surest way of getting you here; and secondly, coining is a capital offence.'

'Only if one gets caught.'

'Which you would have done. And I couldn't risk that happening before we'd had a little talk.'

The brown eyes narrowed. 'Why not?'

Gabriel stared intently back at him, his face slightly pale but perfectly controlled. 'You don't know?'

'Supposing you tell me.'

'Very well. Someone has made four attempts to kill me – with a resounding lack of success that naturally led me to suppose it might be you.'

Ellis's brows soared and he gave way to contemptuous laughter. 'My God! You're scared, aren't you?'

'No,' came the chilly response. 'I'm looking for blood. Because, instead of facing me man-to-man, some feeble-minded coward has been attacking me by proxy in the dark. And he has murdered my friend.'

'Then he can't be totally inept, can he?' came the indifferent reply.

Gabriel's hands clenched at his sides and he experienced a wild urge to smash one of them into his half-brother's smugly amused face. Then, while he was still trying to subdue it, the door opened and Venetia walked in.

'Christ!' breathed Gabriel, savagely. 'Go away. Now!'

She planted herself stubbornly beside him. 'No.'

Ellis examined her from head to foot – absorbing the simple, hastily-donned gown and the loose, gleaming mantle of her hair – and drew the obvious conclusion. This time his laughter was faintly brittle but he still managed to say insultingly, 'Well, well . . . it seems I timed my arrival better than I thought. Was the bastard trying to bed you, my loved one? I didn't think he had it in him.'

'That's it!' Gabriel shook Venetia from his arm and crossed the room in three swift strides to pick Ellis up by his collar.

490

'Confine yourself to the matter in hand! My wife and my bed
are no concern of yours, nor will they ever be. I want one
thing from you and one only; and if you're wise, you'll tell me
now before I start breaking your bones. *Have you been trying
to kill me?*'

Ellis clawed uselessly at the iron grip.

'Fight me and find out,' he invited.

'Don't!' said Venetia urgently.

Gabriel's gaze, harsh and purposeful, remained locked
with that of his half-brother. 'Fight you? Why should I?
You'll tell me what I want to know without that.'

'Damned if I will!'

The fingers shifted slightly and increased their pressure.
Turning gradually red and choking a little, Ellis managed a
derisory grimace and kept his mouth firmly shut. Gabriel
held him for a moment longer and then, with an exclamation
of mingled irritation and disgust, dropped him neatly into
the nearest chair.

'All right,' he said crisply. 'You want to fight me? You
shall. What did you have in mind?'

Having succeeded in loosening his collar, Ellis stared
back, breathing rather hard. 'Swords. It's a gentleman's
weapon, of course, but you must have picked up some
knowledge in King Noll's Army of bakers and brewers.'

Venetia grasped Gabriel's arm. 'Don't do it!' she begged
again. 'He won't fight fair. He never does. And he's trained
with every fencing-master in Europe.'

'And I on most of its battlefields,' returned Gabriel, still
watching the other man. 'Very well. Nasty and common as I
am, I'd much prefer to ram your teeth down your throat. But
I suppose one can't have everything – so swords it is. In the
courtyard, as soon as you like.'

'Now, then.' Ellis stood up, throwing off his cloak with an
exaggerated gesture and unbuckling his baldrick.

With no preparations to make, Gabriel turned to Venetia.
'Phoebe's locked in the bookroom. Leave her there. And stay
inside yourself. You hear me? I don't want you to watch.'

Ellis laughed. 'What's the matter, *brother*? Afraid to let her
see you humiliated? For you will be, you know. I'm looking
forward to it.'

'I daresay. But, as I believe I told you once before, these things rarely live up to one's expectations,' replied Gabriel prosaically. 'Shall we go?'

He lifted Venetia's hand as he passed her and dropped a swift kiss in her palm. Then, closing her fingers tightly over it, he smiled briefly and walked out into the hall to pick up his sword. Following closely behind him, Ellis swept his one-time betrothed an extravagantly mocking bow and murmured, 'I'm disappointed in you, my dear. You used to be so fastidious.'

'I still am,' she replied witheringly. 'And have learned to distinguish gold from glitter.'

Lost for an answer, Ellis stalked on. Venetia remained where she was for a moment and then followed as far as the door. She knew it wasn't what Gabriel wanted, but she couldn't help that. She had to see for herself.

Outside in the courtyard, the breath of both men smoked on the frosty air as Ellis opened with a quick, sweeping pass that Gabriel avoided by simply stepping back. Then Gabriel replied with an equally swift lunge which Ellis was forced to parry – and the blades exploded together in earnest. Steel rang on steel, slithered to a disengage and began again. Venetia shivered.

Gabriel had a soldier's training and sixteen years in the field. Ellis had acquired tricks from every part of the Continent to perfect a unique blend of styles of which he was justly proud. He also had the advantage of knowing that Gabriel would not kill him before he talked.

Ellis produced a cunning flanconade and Gabriel received a savage gash to the forearm before he managed to parry it. Gabriel responded, quicker than expected, with a superb counter-riposte which forced Ellis to retreat a little and there was a violent scraping of blades before both of them withdrew to start afresh. Blood began to drip down Gabriel's left hand and Ellis circled slowly, keeping him at a distance with a series of vicious little jabs.

Her eyes never leaving them, Venetia suddenly became aware that Phoebe had materialised at her elbow – thanks, no doubt, to Sophia and Uncle James who were standing a pace or two behind.

'Don't make a sound,' Venetia hissed. 'Don't even *breathe*.'

Gabriel had his back to them. Ellis hadn't and he said jeeringly, 'You poor bastard! Is this the best you can do?'

Entirely without warning, Gabriel engaged the playful blade in a precise, fast-moving attack that drove Ellis back across the cobbles while he strove to counter it. Gabriel completed the sequence with a time-thrust that pierced his half-brother's upper arm – and Ellis went sprawling as he collided with the ancient stone dovecot. One of the crumbling, lichen-encrusted supports gave way and disintegrated into a shower of masonry.

Gabriel stepped back, a chilly smile bracketing his mouth. 'Better?' he asked.

Ellis scrambled to his feet. Maintaining his guard and biding his time, he said, 'Brutish and unimaginative. But it impressed your audience.'

Refusing the bait, Gabriel refrained from turning his head to look. Instead, he tempted Ellis with a feint against his left hand and the game erupted into a rapid succession of clamouring chimes. Then, at the next brief respite and with the crowded doorway in full view, Gabriel said bitingly, 'Why don't you just invite the whole bloody village? You could sell tickets.'

Phoebe managed a tense grin; Venetia merely leaned against the architrave, white as a sheet and with her arms folded hard across her body. But James Bancroft said sternly, 'This does neither of you any credit. Remember you are brothers and desist now, before it is too late.'

'It's already too late,' remarked Ellis breathlessly. 'My father made sure of that when he gave my birthright to his gutter-bred by-blow!' And he made a vicious pass which nearly cost Gabriel the use of his right hand.

Countering deftly, but not fast enough to stop his knuckles being scraped bare, Gabriel said gratingly, 'If you want to talk, tell me about the marksman by the river.'

'Make me!' snapped Ellis, deflecting a low thrust.

Forte locked with forte, over which grey eyes met brown. 'If you insist,' said Gabriel. And, stepping back, launched the most relentless, complex attack of his career.

Startled by the ferocity of it, Ellis summoned the full extent of his skill but found that it was somehow never quite enough to break through Gabriel's guard. Then, just as his sword-arm was beginning to feel like a lead weight, he saw the opening he had been searching for. His point darted unerringly towards Gabriel's heart while his own thudded against his ribs; and, in the same vital instant, a savage and wholly unexpected twist jarred every bone in his wrist and his sword went spinning from his hand.

Even before it had clattered to the cobbles Gabriel's blade was at his throat and his voice was saying unevenly, 'All right. The fun's over. Tell me what I want to know.'

'Or what?' asked Ellis, his chest heaving.

'Or I'll start taking you apart, piece by piece.' The sword-point moved from throat to sternum with just enough pressure to pierce the scarlet satin. 'Talk. Now.'

Since there appeared to be no alternative, Ellis shrugged slightly and then froze as steel bit his skin. 'All right – but if all you want is a confession, you'll be disappointed. I know nothing about any attempts on your life – though I'd shed no tears if one were to succeed. And I've better uses for my money than paying others to do what I'd rather do myself. Does that answer you?'

A pair of granite-like eyes scoured his face in chilling silence. Then, against all expectation, the sword was withdrawn from his chest and Gabriel said, 'Yes.'

Ellis's jaw dropped. ' 'Wh-what?'

'You heard me.' Gabriel stepped back, wiping the sweat from his eyes in order to take a cursory look at his blood-soaked forearm. 'I suspected it wasn't you from the moment you were ready to let me throttle you rather than answer.'

'You *knew*? Then why—'

'Why go through all this? Because something of the sort had to happen eventually and today was as good a time as any.' Gabriel surveyed him with annihilating indifference. 'You wanted to see my blood and now you have. Collect your things and leave. Personally, I hope I never see you again.' And he turned on his heel and walked away.

It was all Venetia had been waiting for. With a tiny, half-strangled sound, she snatched up her skirts and ran to him.

He caught her in his sound arm and held her in a hard, wordless embrace while Phoebe trudged across the yard to deposit Ellis's cloak and hat in his arms.

'Don't be too upset,' she said indulgently. 'No one can win all the time, you know.' And she, too, walked away.

Gabriel let Venetia draw him into the house and then stopped dead in the doorway of the parlour. The table was laden with food and the air was filled with the scent of it.

'I thought,' volunteered Sophia from behind him, 'that we might all be glad of some sustenance. And preparing it kept the servants from peering out of the windows.'

'It looks like a damned funeral feast,' remarked Gabriel aridly. 'And, for all you knew, it might have been.'

'Sit down and let me see to your arm,' said Venetia abruptly. 'You're bleeding all over the floor.'

He shot her an acute glance, then did as she asked. And, as soon as she knelt beside him, he tilted up her chin and said softly, 'It's all right. Stop worrying.'

'How can I? It's *not* all right, is it? You're safe now – but for how long? For if it isn't Ellis – who is it?'

'I don't know. But I promise you I'll find out.'

'If it's the last thing you do?' she said on something suspiciously like a sob. And, when he did not answer, 'I'm sorry, I'm sorry. You've been through enough today without me having hysterics all over you as well.'

He smiled a little. 'I'd certainly rather you didn't. But, at need, I daresay I can cope with it.'

She shook her head and set about dressing his arm. Phoebe came up with a glass of wine and the news that Ellis had gone, then stayed to talk excitedly about the fight; Sophy brought him a plate of food and murmured distressfully about the damage to the dovecot. Venetia finished bandaging his arm and watched him trying to eat and drink one-handed, whilst simultaneously responding to two different conversations. Amusement crept in and her nerves started to settle.

Gabriel tolerated it as long as he could – and then his patience snapped. Coming abruptly to his feet, he said, 'Phoebe – take your uncle and go home. It will be dark before you get there as it is. Sophy – do what you like about the blasted dovecot. For myself, I don't care if the ugly thing crumbles into dust. In fact, all *I* want right now is some bloody privacy.' And, grasping Venetia's hand, he strode off in the direction of the stairs, taking her with him.

He paused at the top and met the laughter in her eyes.

'It's not funny. Neither is this constant shuttling between your room and mine. But since yours is equipped with both lock and bolt, we'd better go there. Get rid of your maid and I'll join you in just a minute.'

A fire was burning in the hearth but no candles had been lit as yet and Jane was not in evidence. Venetia peered at herself in the mirror and attempted to tidy her hair. Then Gabriel came in, having replaced his bloodstained shirt with a clean one. Wordlessly, he barred the door and turned the key in the lock; and then, smiling, drew Venetia into his arms.

By the time his mouth finally left hers the alarms of the day had receded and she had only one thought in mind. But Gabriel appeared to have other ideas for, instead of continuing what he had begun, he sat on the edge of the bed and pulled her down beside him, saying, 'Before Ellis interrupted us, you were telling me that you loved me. You may recall, however, that I did not return the compliment.'

His eyes contained an expression she did not recognise and a tiny tremor made its way down her back. As lightly as she was able, she said, 'No. But it isn't obligatory.'

'I'm glad you realise that.' He paused, still holding her gaze. 'You think I'm here with you now because I want your body – and you're right. I do. In truth, I've never wanted any woman a tithe as much as I do you, or found a fraction of the joy we bring to each other. But, important as that is, it's by no means all. For I honour your courage, your beauty and your mind; and everything you feel for me, I also feel for you.'

Half-believing him but suddenly afraid, Venetia said raggedly, 'You can't. How can you? Do you think I've forgotten the things I said to you or the way I behaved?'

'None of that matters.' Gabriel gathered her back into his arms. 'If it did, how could you want me near you after I accused you of adultery and all but raped you?'

'That was different. You had more reason.'

'No. I was jealous and angry and hurt – and too stubborn to

admit it. But not any more.' His fingers twined themselves in her hair. 'I love you. Do you believe me – or must we spend the rest of the night arguing about it?'

Inexplicably, the warmth of certainty flooded through her veins and she slid her arms about his neck. 'I believe you. But I wouldn't mind a little extra convincing.'

'I know that,' grinned Gabriel. 'If it was left to you, we'd never do any talking at all.'

It was several minutes before Venetia found the breath to reply and by then she was lying half-naked against his chest. 'I don't notice you objecting,' she said.

Silence. Then, 'No,' agreed Gabriel. 'And you won't.'

Later, languorously entwined in the firelight, they exchanged murmured endearments and small, foolish jokes. And, later still, Gabriel forced himself to say gently, 'You know I'll have to leave you for a time, don't you?'

A chill struck Venetia's skin and she shivered.

'I know you believe you must and I understand why. But surely there's no point? Ellis was your only suspect. So how can you possibly know where to look?'

'I can't. But sooner or later, whoever it is will try again. And next time I'll be ready for them.'

She pulled herself up on one elbow to look at him.

'You mean you're prepared to use your life as bait?'

'I don't have a choice.'

'You do!' Her eyes were stark with fright. 'You can stay here. As Sophy says, these attacks only happen in London. If you stay at home, you'll be safe.'

Gabriel reached up to touch her cheek. 'Sweetheart, no. If I stay here and do nothing, we'll spend the rest of our lives worrying about what's around the next corner. And, just because nothing has happened here yet, doesn't necessarily mean that it won't.'

Despite the flawless logic of it, Venetia sought for ways to stop him going. Consequently, although she had meant to wait for a few more days before telling him about the baby, she said tensely, 'There's something you should know before you decide.'

His hand stilled against the curve of her hip. 'Oh?'

'Yes.' Drawing a deep breath, she opened her mouth to tell

him only to be distracted by the clatter of hooves in the courtyard, immediately followed by a distant, thunderous hammering.

'Bloody hell!' breathed Gabriel. 'What now?'

The hammering persisted and then was abruptly replaced by a staccato voice and the tramp of feet. Gabriel frowned and swung himself out of bed, reaching for the tinder and swiftly lighting a candle. 'It sounds like half a troop of Horse. And Sophy's let them in.'

'But it's the middle of the night!'

'No. It's probably no more than eight or nine of the clock,' he replied, crossing the room in search of his clothes. And then, in response to the sound of booted feet running smartly up the stairs, '*Christ.* What in Hades do they think they're doing?'

There were voices outside and someone rapped on the door with a pistol-butt. 'Colonel Brandon? Open up!'

Colonel Brandon pulled on his breeches and unlocked the door in a manner which boded ill for whoever was on the other side of it – and was immediately pushed back into the room, an officer and three helmeted troopers crowding after him. Venetia sat up, clutching the sheet to her chin.

'Colonel Brandon?' said the officer.

'Yes,' snapped Gabriel. 'And who the devil are you?'

'Major Nathaniel Barton of the Commissary-General's regiment. And it is my duty to inform you—'

'It's your duty to salute a superior officer! Unless Henry doesn't insist on such formalities?'

A hint of dull colour invading his face, the Major clicked his heels and stood ramrod straight. 'Sir!'

'That's better. And now you can take yourself and your men out of my wife's room. I'll receive both your apologies and your explanations downstairs presently.'

His colour deepening and carefully avoiding the collective gaze of his troopers, Major Barton said uncomfortably, 'I'm sorry, Colonel. I can't do that. My orders were to – to secure your person.'

Venetia's stomach plummeted and there was a sudden, airless silence. Then, his tone crisp as ever but carefully expressionless, Gabriel said, 'You're arresting me?'

'Yes, sir.'

'On what charge?'

The Major pulled a document from his pocket.

'Being absent without leave; countermanding orders; taking advantage of your position to liberate justly imprisoned Delinquents; conspiracy to defraud; collusion with Royalist agents,' he muttered rapidly. 'It's all here, Colonel. See for yourself.'

Gabriel took the warrant and scanned it. Then, impaling Nathaniel Barton on a razor-sharp stare, 'It says "as a result of information received". From whom?'

'I don't know, sir. It wasn't necessary that I should.'

'No.' Gabriel drew a long, thoughtful breath. 'No. I suppose not.' He directed a brief glance at Venetia, sitting white-faced and frozen amidst the flagrant disorder of the bed, and then turned back to the Major. 'Very well. I won't offer any resistance. So you may now wait outside the door while I have five minutes alone with my wife.'

Major Barton hesitated and then came to the conclusion that there was probably no harm in it. 'Five minutes, then,' he said. And shepherded his men out.

Gabriel waited till the door was shut before returning to the bed. Venetia clung to him, willing herself not to cry and said, 'It's starting again, isn't it?'

'I'm afraid so.'

'Where will they take you?'

'I don't know. Hopefully, to the Tower.' She stared at him and he smiled crookedly. 'Eden is there. Or was. And he'll be able to make some inquiries for me. He'll also tell Jack what's happened, and Jack will tell Sam Radford. Before you know it, Free-born John will be getting up petitions on my behalf.'

Venetia wasn't comforted, 'God help us, then.'

'Don't.' Gabriel hugged her close. 'It's not as bad as it seems, you know. The charges sound impressive but, given my previously unblemished record, they're unlikely to result in anything more than a court-martial. So stop upsetting yourself and tell me whatever it was you were going to say before our friends arrived.'

She pressed her face against the warm skin of his shoulder

and, because he already had enough to worry about, lied. 'It was nothing. I was just grasping at any straw that might keep you here. It hardly matters now.'

'You're sure?' There was another knock at the door and his muscles tensed. 'We haven't much time.'

'I'm sure.' Venetia lifted her head to look up at him. 'I love you so much. And I'm scared silly.'

'I know.' His kiss was lingering and edged with desperation. Then he tore himself from her and stood up. 'I'll have to go and dress. Will you – will you come downstairs?'

She tried to smile. 'Need you ask?'

By the time Gabriel descended the stairs, correctly attired in full uniform and escorted by Major Barton, Venetia had thrown on her night-rail and chamber-robe and was standing beside Sophia under the appreciative eyes of twenty or so troopers. Gabriel smiled at her and murmured, 'You're doing wonders for my reputation. But do you think Henry has sent enough men to hold me?'

'It's marginal,' she replied. 'My only regret is that he didn't come himself.'

'I daresay. But it's probably just as well. Under present circumstances, bobbing the Commissary-General on the noll wouldn't necessarily be a help.'

Major Barton gave an apologetic cough and Sophia told him to be patient or she'd box his ears. Gabriel turned to her, laughing, and let her hug him. Then, kissing her cheek, he said, 'You're a wonderful woman, Sophy. Look after Venetia for me, won't you?'

'You know I will. You just take care of yourself.'

'I always do.' The grey eyes returned to Venetia and his arms closed hard about her. Against her mouth, he breathed, 'I love you – and I'll be back. Don't worry.'

Her throat ached with unshed tears but she forced herself to neither weep nor cling and, when he stepped back from her, even managed a smile. Gabriel held her eyes for a moment more. Then he turned and strode away to the door, leaving his captors to follow as best they could.

The door slammed shut behind them and Venetia collapsed abruptly on the foot of the stairs, her hands pressed over her mouth. Knowing better than to offer fatuous words of comfort, Sophia sat down beside her and said, 'Cry, my dear. And then, later, we can think what's best to be done.'

Painful, wracking sobs tore Venetia's body and she gasped, 'I'm going to London. I *must*.'

'Of course,' agreed Sophia calmly. 'When do we leave?'

Drenched violet eyes rose to her face. '*We*?'

'Well, of course. I love him too, you know.'

Venetia's mouth quivered and she hurled herself against Sophia's shoulder. She said, chokingly, 'I'm pregnant, Sophy! I'm pregnant – and he doesn't know. Who can hate him this much. *Who*?'

Said Algernon Sidney, '*The King can be tried by no Court;
and no man can be tried by this Court.*'

'*I tell you,*' replied Cromwell, '*we will cut off his head
with the Crown upon it.*'

The
Incorruptible
Crown

January to March, 1649

*I'll Crown thee with a Garland of Straw then
   and I'll Marry thee with a Rush ring;
My frozen hopes shall thaw then
   and merrily we will Sing:
O turn to me my dear Love
   and prithee love turn to me,
For thou art the Man that alone canst
   procure my Liberty.*

Sir William Davenant

One

Setting off thirty-six hours after Gabriel and travelling in the ancient family coach over roads made mercifully hard by a succession of frosts, Venetia and Sophy arrived in Cheapside on Monday January 8th. The first Eden Maxwell knew of their coming was when he walked in at suppertime to find them wearily ensconced in the parlour; and, not having previously supposed that Gabriel's wife cared enough to travel even two miles for his sake let alone two hundred, he said blankly, 'My God! Where did you spring from?'

'Yorkshire,' replied Venetia tersely. 'Where's Gabriel?'

'In the Beauchamp Tower.'

'You've seen him?'

'Every day since he came,' said Eden, slowly absorbing the shadows under her eyes and the way her hands wouldn't stay still. 'He's well enough – and as comfortably-housed as one can be in there.'

A tiny, shivering breath ran through Venetia's frame and Sophia reached out to grasp her fingers, saying calmly, 'There – you see? He's not chained to a damp wall or being starved to death. Major Maxwell wouldn't permit it.'

'Hardly!' Eden turned away to pour wine. 'But though I'm aware of its advantages, I can't say that I find acting as my best friend's gaoler particularly enjoyable.'

Venetia accepted the glass he offered her and, meeting his eyes, said, 'What do you know about this business?'

'Not as much as I'd like. Someone laid information – presumably about Francis and Colonel Ambrose; but, for obvious reasons, Ireton isn't about to give *me* any details. And though he hasn't attempted to remove me from the Tower, I suspect he's keeping a very close eye on me.' He shrugged wryly and sat down. 'I'd willingly admit my share of the guilt if it would help, but Gabriel says I'm more use to him as things are. In which he probably has a point. Certainly, I can do very little about the other charges – except to explain precisely *why* he went off as he did. And naturally, I've already done that.'

Venetia nodded slowly and Sophia said, 'Gabriel was of the opinion that the whole indictment would amount to nothing worse than a court-martial. Do *you* think that?'

The scarred face tightened fractionally and Eden took his time about answering. 'I don't know. They searched the house, you see.'

Venetia's brows contracted. 'So?'

'So they found twenty-five counterfeit sovereigns at the back of a drawer in your bedchamber.'

She lost what little colour she had and stared back at him so oddly that he thought she was going to faint. Then she said stonily, 'Does Gabriel know?'

'Yes.'

'Then he'll have guessed where they came from.'

'And where *did* they come from?' asked Sophia.

'Ellis.' Venetia took a gulp of wine. 'They came from Ellis. Wat told me they were false and I just – I just pushed them out of sight. I'd forgotten they were there. But Ireton can't accuse Gabriel of coining, he *can't*!'

'He's not accusing him of it – or not yet, anyway. He's merely said that the matter requires proper investigation,' remarked Eden. 'For what it's worth, I think he knows how ludicrous such a charge must be in Gabriel's case. But, just at the moment, it doesn't suit him to admit it.'

'Why not?' asked Sophia.

'Because Gabriel has made his feelings about the King's trial abundantly plain – and any reduction in the opposition is better than none,' came the arid reply. Then, meeting Venetia's shocked gaze, 'You didn't know that arrangements for the trial are already under way?'

She shook her head. 'Since when?'

'Two days ago. After six years of enacting its legislation through Ordinances, the Commons has passed its first Act of Parliament since the start of the first war – and without the agreement of the Lords, moreover.'

Venetia did not need to be told that the purged House of Commons was demonstrating both its willingness and its ability to act without reference to either King or peers. She said, 'And what does this Act say?'

'That for the prevention of new "commotions, rebellions and invasions" and so that no one in authority may hereafter "contrive the enslaving or destroying of the English nation and expect impunity for so doing", one hundred and thirty-five commissioners are to form a special High Court of Justice to try "Charles Stuart, the now King of England".'

'Commissioners?' echoed Venetia sharply. 'No Chief Justices or senior judges?'

'No.' Eden paused, reluctant to admit that the three Justices chosen, one of them being Cromwell's own kinsman, Oliver St John, had refused to serve. 'Those named held their first meeting today in the Painted Chamber at Westminster, but rumour has it that only fifty-three of them turned up.'

'Are you surprised?' asked Venetia. And then, contemptuously, 'Doubtless Ireton was there?'

He nodded. 'And Cromwell – and Fairfax, surprisingly enough. Also Colonels Pride, Harrison and Whalley – Lord Grey of Groby, Harry Marten and John Lilburne's brother, Robert. Free-born John himself has apparently refused point-blank to have anything to do with it.'

'Good. And where do *you* stand?'

Eden met her eyes and grimaced wryly. 'I regard it as an extremely regrettable necessity which the King has brought upon himself. And though I'd sooner see him deposed than executed, I won't oppose the court's decision.'

There was a long silence into which Sophia finally said, 'Then – since the two of you are unlikely to agree – there's no point in discussing it further, is there?'

'None,' agreed Venetia, still looking at Eden. 'How soon can I see Gabriel?'

'I don't know. I'll do my best, of course – but so far he's been refused visitors. I wasn't even able to admit Mr Morrell. And Sam Radford didn't get past the main gate.'

A hint of colour seeped back into her skin and she rose abruptly from her seat. 'Are you telling me that Henry Ireton can stop me seeing my husband?'

'He can but that's not to say he *will*. I'll ask him.'

'Do that,' said Venetia. 'And while you're about it, tell him that I want to see him. Soon.'

With nothing to do except kick her heels while Eden spoke with the Commissary-General, Venetia decided to spend the next day taking Sophia to meet the Morrells. They were just stepping into the carriage when the Sergeant-at-Arms, together with six trumpeters and two full troops of Horse, appeared in Cheapside to proclaim that Charles Stuart – having tried 'to introduce an arbitrary and tyrannical government' and 'levied and maintained a cruel war' – was to be tried by a High Court of Justice appointed for the purpose. Like the rest of the assembled crowd, Venetia and Sophia listened in appalled silence. Then, with an absence of remark that was its own comment, they instructed the coachman to set off for Shoreditch.

Annis received them with surprised pleasure – and Jack, recalling the white mouse once bestowed on Gabriel, asked Sophia if she had any idea how jealous he himself had been at the time. Bryony, however, merely sat down beside Venetia and held her hand rather hard, saying simply, 'If you didn't love him, you wouldn't be here. And that being so, I know exactly how you must feel.'

Jack sighed. 'Well done, Bryony. So much both for the courtesies and my own feeble attempts to lighten the gloom.' Then, bluntly, to Venetia, 'Does anything about this situation make sense to you?'

'In a way,' she replied tonelessly. 'It seems that Gabriel has an anonymous enemy; one who wishes to kill him – and *did* kill Wat Larkin – and who has now laid information regarding the escape of Francis Langley and Mr Radford's brother-in-law.'

Silence lapped the edges of the room and three pairs of horrified, incredulous eyes glued themselves to her face. Finally, stalking away to the window, Jack said, 'And why the hell didn't Major Maxwell tell us any of this?'

'I suspect – because he doesn't know it – though I won't be sure until I'm able to speak with Gabriel. And that, of course, may not be as soon as I'd like.'

Annis said, 'They can't stop you seeing him, surely? Jack was refused on the excuse of not being blood-kin. But you're his *wife*, for heaven's sake!'

'Quite. And if Eden can't get the permission I need, I'll be pointing that out to Henry Ireton personally.'

'Tell him that keeping husband and wife asunder is contrary to God's law,' advised Bryony abruptly. 'If it worked for Elizabeth Lilburne, it ought to work for you.'

Venetia smiled grimly. 'Thank you. I will.'

Jack swung back to face her. 'Speaking for myself, I can only think of one man likely to wish Gabriel harm.'

She held his gaze. 'It isn't Ellis. Gabriel is quite sure of that.'

'Oh.' A pause. 'Are you sure he's not mistaken?'

'Yes. Ellis isn't clever enough to fool Gabriel and particularly not after Wat's death. Also, paid assassins aren't his style. He likes an audience.'

'But if it isn't him,' objected Bryony, 'who *is* it?'

'Someone who knew that Francis Langley and Justin Ambrose didn't escape without help,' replied Venetia. 'To whit; Eden Maxwell, Sam Radford and his sister – and myself. Except, of course, that it isn't any of us.'

Bryony stared at her uncertainly. 'You're saying Gabriel let Sam's brother-in-law go and that Sam *knew*?'

'Just that.'

'But he never breathed a word to me!'

Annis looked at her husband. 'Did *you* know?'

'No.' Jack frowned thoughtfully. 'Gabriel played his cards close to his chest but not, it seems, closely enough. Because since we can acquit those who were actually in on the plot, someone else must have found out.'

'It's hard to see how,' remarked Venetia. 'We were so careful – and I drugged the guards myself.'

'They might have worked it out afterwards.'

'I doubt it. But even if they did – what then? Who did they tell? For if the attack in Moorfields was part of the pattern, Gabriel's enemy has been busy since last May. And the fire in the workshop happened on the same night as the escape – which means it had already been planned.' Venetia drew a long, bracing breath. 'But you're right, of course. We have to

509

start somewhere. So I'll ask Eden to interrogate the guards – and I'll see Henry Ireton in the hope that he'll tell me the name of his informant. It's not much but it's all we've got. And, surely to God, whoever it is can't be so clever that they haven't left a clue somewhere?'

Eden returned to Cheapside that evening with the information that the House of Commons had commissioned a new Great Seal and the Lords had resumed their feeble opposition to the trial. He also told Venetia that Henry Ireton had refused her request to visit her husband, but was willing to spare her a few minutes of his time on the following afternoon at Whitehall. To his surprise, she accepted this with perfect calm and the merest hint of a smile. He was relieved. Sophia, on the other hand, said baldly, 'Venetia – I know how you feel and I sympathise. But it won't do any good to lose your temper with the Commissary-General.'

'I'm not planning to lose my temper,' came the remote reply. 'Then again, I can't promise I won't.'

Having steadfastly refused to let Sophia accompany her, Venetia duly presented herself outside the room Ireton had appropriated as an office and was kept waiting for almost half an hour. She had, of course, expected this; what she *hadn't* expected was the sudden rush of emotion produced by Whitehall itself. The ghostly echoes of music, the rustle of silks and the murmur of long-gone voices all drowned out by booted feet ringing on the stone; the shades of a small, dignified King and his vivacious, sharp-eyed Queen, banished by uniformed soldiers and black-clad lawyers. The past; gone forever.

Commissary-General Ireton received her with chilly courtesy and a repetition of his earlier refusal. Venetia smiled sweetly, accepted a chair he hadn't offered and suggested that perhaps he had not considered the matter sufficiently. Then she used the argument proffered by Bryony and watched him recognise it.

'Like the devil, Mr Lilburne has a quantity of good tunes,' he remarked sardonically. And then, 'Very well, Mistress Brandon. You may have an hour with your husband tomorrow – and I will send the necessary instructions to the Tower. I trust that satisfies you?'

'It's a start,' agreed Venetia. 'Thank you.'

'Not at all. And now, if you will excuse me, I have a meeting of the Officers' Council to attend.'

Her mouth curled derisively but she repressed the urge to remark that since it now formed the effective government of the kingdom, the Council was doubtless kept suitably busy, and said instead, 'There's something else.'

The dark eyes surveyed her impatiently. 'Indeed?'

'Yes. To begin with there's the matter of the twenty-five counterfeit sovereigns. They were sent to me in payment of a debt; and I, doubting their origins, put them away where they could do no harm. Gabriel knew nothing about them.'

'I see.' Ireton pulled a quill thoughtfully between his fingers. 'And you can substantiate this?'

'No. The only other person who knew of it was Walter Larkin. And, as I believe Major Maxwell has already informed you, he is now dead. Murdered, in fact.'

'By whom?'

'Presumably by the same person who caused Gabriel's arrest by approaching you with wild, unfounded accusations about his supposed complicity in Royalist plots.'

'Are they so wild?' A faint, icy smile dawned. 'Your own allegiances are well-known, Madam – and Colonel Brandon would not be the first man to be swayed by a pretty wife.'

Venetia raised scornful brows. 'If you think that, you can't know him very well.'

'Perhaps not. But then, I am basing my inquiries less on my knowledge of the Colonel's character than on various facts. Such as his flouting of my orders during the recent purging of Parliament, followed by his subsequent desertion of his post.' He tossed the quill down on the table and stood up. 'As for the implication that he may have contrived the release of two Royalist officers – that is something which I cannot discuss until the necessary inquiries have been completed.'

'I wasn't asking you to discuss it,' said Venetia tartly. 'I was asking where the said implication came from.'

Henry Ireton expelled a breath of pure irritation. He had spent the bulk of the day in the Painted Chamber with eight fewer commissioners than had turned up before and no sign,

511

this time, of the Lord General. He had now to continue patiently discussing the thrice-blasted *Agreement* with the Council of Officers. And, if that wasn't enough, he also had Gabriel Brandon's tiresome wife sitting in front of him with every appearance of growing long roots.

Fortunately, there was a way to be rid of her. Crossing to the door, he said, 'You are wasting your time. Contrary to your assumption, the information to which you refer came, not to me, but to Lieutenant-General Cromwell. And since I had no reason to query its source, I am very much afraid that I can't help you.' He lifted the latch and let the door swing wide. 'I have the honour to bid you good-day, Madam. Unless you'd like me to call an escort for you?'

He was threatening to have her thrown out; and because Venetia did not doubt that he would do it, she bowed to the inevitable and rose, shaking out her skirts. Then, pausing to look directly into the cold, clever eyes, she said, 'The corridors of Whitehall are no mystery to me, sir. But I thank you both for your offer and your advice – and will take my enquiries to the Lieutenant-General as soon as maybe.'

Major Maxwell listened to Venetia's account of her conversation with Ireton and then told her bluntly that Cromwell was unlikely to reveal anything to her which he'd apparently withheld from his son-in-law. Venetia agreed that this was probably true but maintained that it was still worth a try. Then she asked how soon she could see Gabriel.

Unlike Whitehall, the Tower of London had hitherto lain outside Venetia's experience and she would have been happy for it to have remained so. She did not know which chilled her most – its cold, vaulted passages or its grim reputation – and the thought of Gabriel being locked away in such a place was horrible to her. She shivered and, seeing it, Eden drew her hand through his arm and said, 'He isn't expecting you. Since he clearly assumed you'd stay in Yorkshire and await developments, I thought it might be best if you did your own explaining.' Then, with a grin, 'In short, I'm keeping well clear of the potential explosion!'

There was no explosion. Gabriel rose from his pallet as the door opened and froze, drowning in Venetia's eyes. Then she was in his arms and, smiling a little, Eden closed the door and left them alone.

After a time, Gabriel said, unevenly, 'You shouldn't be here! Why did you come? It's madness to make such a journey at this time of year when there's nothing to be gained from it. I thought you were safe at home. You *should* be safe at home. And I should be flayed for being glad you're not.'

She shook her head. 'Did you think I'd sit meekly by the hearth? You should have known better. And there *is* something to be gained – or, at least, I hope there is. I've already spoken to Ireton; and tomorrow I'll set about trying to get an audience with Cromwell.'

A faint frown gathered behind his eyes and he drew her down to sit beside him. 'I think you'd better start at the beginning. What exactly have you said to Henry?'

Concentrating on his face and trying, as yet, not to see the sombre, ill-lit room around her, Venetia told him. Then, at the end, she said, 'I'm not convinced that Ireton doesn't know but I couldn't very well call him a liar.'

'You're too modest,' grinned Gabriel. 'Given the right incentive, I'm sure you're more than capable of calling him all manner of things. But I applaud your restraint and suggest you also employ it with Cromwell. If, that is, he agrees to see you – which is by no means certain.'

'He'll see me,' stated Venetia flatly. 'If necessary, I'll sit on his doorstep till he does. And since he can hardly pretend that *he* knows nothing either, there is just a chance that he'll tell me the truth.'

'Don't count on it.'

'I have to.' The amethyst eyes met his, stark with distress. 'Don't you see? It's all I have. I can't bear the thought of leaving you in this place. And if I don't do something, I shall go mad!'

Gabriel's arm tightened about her and he said, 'It's not as bad as all that, you know. And the company is excellent. Where else could I take the air with the brother of an earl?' He paused and, in response to her inquiring look, added, 'Sir William Compton – who, incidentally, served in Banbury with Justin Ambrose and in Colchester with Captain Langley. Small world, isn't it?'

'It is, in here,' she sighed. And then, finally taking in the meagre furnishings of the room, 'Eden said you were comfortably housed. It doesn't look so to me.'

'Probably not. But then *you* haven't spent most of your adult life in army quarters. And everything's relative.'

'In other words, you've nothing to complain about?'

'I wouldn't say that exactly.' Laughter stirred in his eyes and his mouth curled in a rare, singularly attractive smile. 'But the comforts I'm lacking are the sort which, under present circumstances, it's better not to dwell on.'

Responding involuntarily to his smile, she murmured, 'Self-restraint is a wonderful thing.'

'Freedom would be better,' he murmured, kissing her. 'Unfortunately, it would be foolish to expect that to come soon. The powers-that-be are much too busy with the King's trial to bother about mine. And, that being so, you may wish to consider going home.'

'Not until you can come too,' said Venetia flatly. 'Dick Carter can manage the estate perfectly well on his own for a time . . . ah. Did I mention that Sophy is here too?'

'No. You didn't.' His brows rose in faint surprise. 'I always thought it would take an act of God to move Sophy so far from Brandon Lacey. Does she think I'm going to die?'

'Of course not!' She kept her eyes guilelessly wide. 'She's just as eager to see you home again as I am. And, if I'd stayed in Cheapside with just Eden for company, Jack might have got the wrong idea.'

'Very likely,' agreed Gabriel. And then, 'How is he viewing the arrangements for the King's trial?'

'We didn't really discuss it. But, in common with a lot of other people, he seems to be clinging to the hope that it's all a huge charade, aimed at frightening his Majesty into making all the concessions he's hitherto refused.'

The dark grey gaze rested on her thoughtfully.

'And what do *you* think?'

'That it may well be so but that it won't work. His Majesty will never abandon what he sees as his God-given right to govern; and the trial will go ahead because the Army has passed the point of no return.' She paused and met his gaze with a hint of wry apology. 'I should also say that, if I'm still

514

here when it happens, I shall attend. The King may not always have been wise but he doesn't deserve this. And though I can't help him, I can at least be a friendly face in the crowd.'

'It won't be a pleasant experience,' warned Gabriel grimly. 'But since I can understand your motives, I won't try to dissuade you so long as you promise to be careful.'

'I promise. Of course I do.' She smiled at him. 'On the other hand, if I make a complete and utter nuisance of myself, they may let us share the same cell.'

Getting to see Oliver Cromwell, remarked Venetia irritably to Sophia two days later, was about as easy as catching a flea. Every time you thought you had him he shot off in a direction you hadn't anticipated, dividing his time between the High Court of Justice, the House of Commons and the Council of Officers with barely a pause in between. And Betty Cromwell could rival St Peter in the art of door-keeping any day of the week, but most especially when the visitor was someone who'd previously been silly enough to offend her. 'In short,' finished Venetia crossly, 'I'm running about like a lunatic and achieving nothing!'

It was this – coupled with Eden's pronouncement that Troopers Baxter and Willis had no more idea what was going on than a pair of sheep – that finally made her decide that desperate situations required desperate remedies. And, on the morning of the 15th, she donned her best cornflower silk and set off for Covent Garden. Inigo Jones's splendid *piazza* was looking a good deal less elegant than when she had seen it last – having been turned into a sort of makeshift stable where common soldiers tethered their horses to gentlemen's door-knockers. Ignoring the appreciative whistles and good-humoured ribaldry around her, Venetia trod purposefully up to Gillingham House and demanded to see the Countess.

Plumper than ever and extravagantly gowned, Isabel received her with rather less surprise than might have been expected; and when Venetia remarked upon it, she drawled, 'Well, of course, my dear. It's the trial, isn't it? All the world and his wife will want to be there.'

'I daresay,' replied Venetia tersely. Then, coming directly

to the point, 'I'm in trouble, Isabel. Gabriel is in the Tower and I need to speak with Cromwell. But—'

'In the *Tower*?' echoed her ladyship. 'Good heavens! How has that come about?'

'Mostly through Gabriel's opposition to Ireton during the course of the Whitehall debates and over the Purge. But there are other charges as well – and it's vital that I talk to Cromwell before things get any worse. The only problem is finding the opportunity. This isn't the kind of thing that can be discussed on the steps outside the Commons or scuttling between the Painted Chamber and Whitehall – and his wife doesn't like me. So I was hoping *you* could persuade her to name a time when I might call on King Street.'

'I – see.' The vivid blue gaze rested on her in silence for a moment. Then Isabel said regretfully, 'I'd like to oblige you, dearest. I really would. But, to be absolutely frank, I let my friendship with Betty dwindle a little as soon as the Lieutenant-General had looked into the matter of our composition fines and it would be a trifle difficult to revive it now purely in order to ask another favour. I'm truly sorry. But if there's anything else I can do, anything at all, I'd be more than happy.'

A lead weight settled in Venetia's chest. She said tonelessly, 'Thank you, but there's nothing. The only person who can help is Cromwell himself – if he chooses to.'

'Well, I'm sure that if you get to see him he'll do his best. But the Colonel can't be in any danger, surely? A senior officer who's served throughout both wars, doubtless with some distinction? It would take more than a little brush with Henry Ireton to cancel *that* out.'

'They've *got* more. And there are other, even greater dangers that I'm not at liberty to discuss.'

'It's really as bad as that?' asked Isabel, shocked.

'It's damnable,' responded Venetia. And then, with rare candour, 'You see – despite all my brave words to the contrary, I love him. And he loves me. And if anything happens to him, I don't know how I shall bear it.'

While Venetia was in Covent Garden, the High Court of Justice finished drafting the King's indictment and the

Council of Officers (no longer working in consultation with the Levellers) put the final touches to the *Agreement of the People*. The combined result, according to Major Maxwell, was that Venetia ought to find it easier to catch up with the Lieutenant-General . . . and, after three seemingly endless days, he was finally proved right.

Venetia achieved her goal by the simple but risky expedient of waylaying Cromwell outside his own front door and, without giving him time to open his mouth, saying rapidly, 'Sir – I know how busy you are and I apologise for my intrusion. But I beg you to give me just five minutes of your time on a matter of the utmost urgency. Please?'

For a moment he simply surveyed her out of slightly narrowed eyes and without a trace of the geniality she had seen last time they met. Then he said brusquely, 'Very well, Mistress Brandon. Five minutes, but only on the understanding that you henceforth stop dogging my every step. I trust I make myself clear?'

'Very clear,' agreed Venetia readily, following him first into the house and then to a small room, overflowing with documents and correspondence. 'If you have spoken to Commissary-General Ireton, you will know what I want.'

'I know precisely what you want. But first I'd like to hear you explain why you want it.'

She gripped her hands together, suddenly aware how cold she was and praying her teeth wouldn't start to chatter.

'Someone is trying to harm my husband and I don't know who it is. So far this person has attacked him twice in the street and once on the river; they have killed his oldest friend, plunging him into grief and causing him to temporarily absent himself from duty; and they have laid wicked accusations which have resulted in his imprisonment.' She paused briefly, trying to gauge his expression; and, failing, continued simply, 'I haven't come to plead his innocence or assure you of his loyalty – or even to beg you to investigate his case personally. I am here purely to ask you to help me save his life by furnishing me with the name of his accuser.'

There was a long silence when she had finished speaking and the echo of her words seemed to hang upon the air. Finally Cromwell said, 'The Lord has given Colonel Brandon

517

a great gift and your sentiments do you credit. But I'm afraid I can't tell you what you want to know – nor would it help you if I did. For the person who informed me that your husband went out of his way to free the Royalist officer responsible for the loss of Pontefract is most certainly *not* in any way connected with these attempts on his life.'

Venetia's nails dug into her palms. Swallowing hard, she said, 'Excuse me for asking – but how can you be so sure?'

'It is simply not possible. But you'll just have to take my word for that.' His tone was utterly final and his expression forbade further questions. Then, entirely without warning, he said, 'Tell me . . . what are your feelings on the projected trial of the King?'

Just now, it was the very last thing she wished to discuss but she said coolly, 'I am opposed to it, sir.'

'On what grounds?'

'On the grounds that, according to law, the King can be tried by no court at all, let alone one virtually bereft of the judiciary. And because, irrespective of his faults, I was reared to respect the Lord's Anointed.'

He nodded slowly. 'But this King's faults have been many and the Lord has witnessed against him . . . that much is clear. God revealed his judgement on Charles Stuart when He allowed his armies to be defeated in the field.'

'Perhaps so,' agreed Venetia. 'But at what stage did He appoint the Army to be his executioner?'

A burning gleam entered the Lieutenant-General's eyes and he said, 'If any man whatsoever had carried on the design of deposing the King and disinheriting his posterity, he would be the greatest traitor and rebel in the world! But since the Providence of God has cast this upon us, I cannot but submit to it. In short, Madam, I and my colleagues are doing the Lord's work'

She tried to curb her tongue but the temptation was too great. 'Certainly you are serving the Lord's *purpose*. But since God knows how to use His enemies as well as His friends, the same could equally be said of Nebuchadnezzar.'

Cromwell's nose glowed and there was a brief, chilly silence. Then he said, 'You are a brave woman but not very wise. Or have you forgotten you're seeking a favour?'

'Not at all. But if you didn't want my opinions, you shouldn't have asked for them,' replied Venetia. 'Also – though I may loathe what you're doing – I believe you to be possessed of strong, personal integrity. And I don't think you would stoop to punish Gabriel for my faults.'

This time the pause was longer and, at the end of it, the Lieutenant-General said dryly, 'My mistake, Madam. You're cleverer than I thought.' Crossing to his writing-table, he pulled a piece of paper before him, scrawled a few lines and sealed it. Then, offering it to Venetia, he said, 'Give that to Major Maxwell. It's not what you came for – but it's the best you'll get. And now go home. The weather's too raw for the kind of antics you've been up to – and I want my supper.'

Arriving back in Cheapside to discover that Eden had sent word saying he'd be late, Venetia ground her teeth and placed the Lieutenant-General's missive, unopened, on the dresser. Then Sophia appeared to ask about her day and, with startling brevity, Venetia told her. At the end she said, 'I've no idea what he wrote but I doubt it will be much use. As far as I can see, Oliver Cromwell is the sort who only functions in response to divine inspiration, with the result that he doesn't know what he'll do from one minute to the next. And bad as that is for Gabriel, it's worse still for the nation as a whole.'

Sophia stared dreamily into the heart of the fire.

'Then perhaps it's time to approach someone with greater authority and a more sympathetic attitude,' she remarked gently. 'The Lord General, for example.'

'Fairfax?' Venetia wrinkled her brow. 'That's not such a bad idea, I suppose. He certainly ought to be able to do something if he chose . . . and though I've never met him, he *is* a Yorkshireman. Then again, getting to see him will probably be as difficult as getting to see Cromwell.'

'Not quite,' said Sophia. 'You see, I knew his wife when she was a girl. She's much younger than I am, of course, but her father and mine were very friendly at one time.'

'And she'd remember you?' asked Venetia hopefully.

'She *does* remember me. I called on her this afternoon and

we spent quite a pleasant hour together.' Turning slightly, she smiled apologetically at Venetia. 'You're wondering why I didn't mention it before; the answer is that I didn't want to raise your hopes before I was sure she'd agree to receive you.'

'And *has* she agreed?'

'Yes. Not tomorrow, unfortunately, but on Saturday. She's become a woman of character and is quite as opposed to the trial as you are. I think you'll like her.'

'If she persuades the Lord General to help Gabriel, I'll *love* her,' vowed Venetia. 'But can she? Black Tom hasn't exactly been conspicuous of late, has he? And if his views coincide with those of his wife, he ought to be standing his ground, not retiring into semi-obscurity and leaving all the running to Cromwell.'

'Doubtless he has his reasons,' said Sophia cautiously. Then, as the door opened and Eden came in. 'Ah. At last.'

He grinned at her. 'You look remarkably pleased to see me. I wonder why I'm not flattered?'

'Guess,' said Venetia, fetching the note and handing it to him. 'It's from Cromwell.'

Eden shot her an acute glance, then swiftly broke the seal. He frowned over the Lieutenant-General's scribble and, when he'd mastered its contents, read it again to make sure. Then, looking up with an expression of faint bemusement, he said, 'He's ordering an immediate investigation into the charges against Gabriel and wants to see all the relevant information personally. He's also given you permission to visit the Tower for one hour each day.'

It was more than Venetia had expected and she sat down rather abruptly. Sophia continued gazing myopically at Eden and said, 'And who is to handle the investigation?'

The hazel eyes gleamed. 'Me.'

Venetia and Sophia stared at one another, first with dawning hope and then sharing another, quite separate thought. Venetia said slowly, 'You'd better sit down, Eden. There's something Gabriel hasn't told you.'

He remained where he was. 'And what is that?'

'The fact that, for over a year now, someone has been trying to kill him.'

Two

By Saturday January 20th – the morning of Venetia's appointment with Lady Fairfax – all London knew that the trial of the King was to begin later that day in Westminster Hall and Venetia had every intention of being there. She therefore presented herself at the Lord General's residence at a little after eleven . . . and immediately discovered that, having precisely the same resolve as herself, my lady had arranged matters accordingly.

As Sophia had said, Anne Fairfax was a woman of character. She also worked with amazing speed; and, having explained that she had reserved seats for herself and certain friends in one of the public galleries at the south end of Westminster Hall, she briskly issued an invitation for Mistress Brandon to join her.

'Thank you,' said Venetia, gratefully. 'I had half-resigned myself to the thought of the public benches.'

'Most unsuitable – and I doubt you'd have got in anyway. Half of London will be queuing already,' came the reply. 'So you are married to Sophy's illegitimate nephew. I never knew Robert Brandon very well, of course, but I confess I find his lapse surprising. Not that *that* matters in the least. What concerns us now is how best to help your husband. And, though I'm not sure what Sophy expects of me, I did promise her that I would try. I was very fond of her when I was a girl, you know.'

'No.' Venetia's brows rose. 'I didn't know. She wasn't even convinced you would remember her.'

'Then she should have been.' A sudden smile dawned. 'I suspect that few people ever forget Sophy. She has a sort of magic that is entirely her own. However, let us address the matter in hand. I understand that Colonel Brandon is a soldier of exemplary record, that he has incurred the enmity of some person or persons unknown and that he has fallen foul of Henry Ireton over the purging of Parliament and the King's trial. Is that an accurate picture?'

'Yes. The Lieutenant-General has recently ordered an investigation of the charges, but—'

'But you are wondering how prompt he will be, under the present circumstances, to recognise your husband's innocence and release him. Quite. But there is also, I believe, the matter of some counterfeit coin?'

Venetia nodded and explained. Then she said, 'Major Maxwell is fully aware of all this and I've signed the necessary declaration. As for Gabriel's alleged release of the two Royalist officers, the troopers on guard-duty that night have sworn that the prisoners escaped by their own endeavours, leaving my husband to be burned alive.'

'I see. So what you are saying, I take it, is that it only remains for someone to drop the appropriate word in the Lieutenant-General's ear – and you are hoping I may persuade Tom to do it,' remarked Lady Fairfax crisply. Then, without waiting for a reply, 'And so I may. But I make no promises. Tom has a lot on his mind these days – such as deciding how far Cromwell means to go in this business of the King and working out how much damage will be done by openly opposing him in it. Then again, there is the Officers' *Agreement*, which is being presented to the Commons even as we speak. But if he can help your husband, I'm sure he will. And now we must go. My friend, Mrs Nelson, will be waiting and someone is likely to occupy our places if we don't arrive early enough to prevent them.'

The precincts of Westminster were swarming with people hoping to get into the great Hall and, by the time Lady Fairfax had shepherded her guests to their seats, the public benches were already crowded with spectators, stairways were jammed and a few intrepid persons were even perched crow-like on the window-ledges. Amidst the well-dressed throng in the opposite gallery, Venetia recognised Lady Gillingham . . . and then, with surprise, her old friend Kate D'Aubigny. So far, neither appeared to have seen her; and, leaning both elbows on the parapet, she forgot all about them as she stared down on the scene directly below her.

It was empty as yet – like a stage-set waiting for the play to begin. Tiered benches covered in red baize had been erected beneath the huge south window and, in the front row, a large raised chair with a writing-desk set before it waited for the Lord President of the Court. A little way in front of that was another table covered with a rich Turkey carpet; and a few feet away, draped in red velvet and standing with its back to the body of the Hall, was the chair which had been placed for the King. A double barrier lined with pikemen divided the Court from the public benches – where more troopers lined the walls and guarded the doors. The Army, it seemed, was taking no chances.

The wait was a long one but eventually, at a little after two o'clock, in the wake of twenty halberdiers and officers carrying the sword and mace, the Commissioners filed into their places. The articles of state were laid on the carpeted table, two Clerks of the Court took their places behind it and a man in a black, steeple-crowned hat ascended to the raised chair.

Venetia turned to Lady Fairfax. 'Who is presiding?'

'One John Bradshaw, the Chief Justice of Chester. Rumour has it that his hat is lined with steel for fear of assassination.' Anne kept her voice low but disdained to whisper. 'The Clerks are John Phelps and Andrew Broughton. And the fellow over there in the fur-trimmed robe is John Cook – a barrister of Gray's Inn and a convinced republican. Scarcely an illustrious collection.' Her gaze moved to the assembled rows of Commissioners – amongst whom sat Cromwell, Ireton, Lord Grey and a miscellaneous clutch of Colonels. 'But as you can see, the power is all behind them.'

Gradually, the Court fell more or less silent and, on a signal from Lord President Bradshaw, John Phelps arose to read the Act of Parliament empowering the Court. Being already aware of its contents, Venetia chose to count the Commissioners. There were sixty-eight of them; not, she decided, a particularly brilliant showing when everyone knew that a hundred and thirty-five had been chosen.

After the Act had been read, Bradshaw commanded that the prisoner be summoned to the bar and ordered the names of the Commissioners to be called. Lesser Court officials fussed nervously with the exact positioning of the King's chair and Venetia's mouth curled derisively. Then she nearly jumped out of her skin as Mr Phelps reached the name of the Lord General and Anne Fairfax shouted, 'He has more wit than to be here – and you do wrong to name him!'

Startled faces looked up from below and the soldiers' hands clenched on their muskets. Then the King appeared, under heavy guard . . . and all else was forgotten.

Dressed wholly in black and wearing the jewelled order of the Garter on his cloak, he walked briskly to a velvet-covered chair and sat down without troubling to remove his hat. Venetia's breath caught in her throat. She had not seen him in four years – but he had aged ten. Only his expression was familiar; rigid, impassive and entirely without curiosity.

Regarding the King with a steely eye, Bradshaw said portentously, 'Charles Stuart, King of England; the Commons of England assembled in Parliament, being sensible of the great calamities that have been brought upon this nation which are fixed upon you as the author of them, have resolved to make inquisition for blood and have constituted this High Court of Justice before which you are now brought.'

John Cook arose, holding the indictment. 'My Lord, on behalf of the Commons of England and all the people thereof, I do accuse Charles Stuart here present of high treason and high misdemeanours; and I do desire the charge may be read to him.'

The King stirred in his chair. 'Hold a little.'

Cook ignored him and continued unrolling the indictment. Reaching out, Charles tapped him lightly upon the arm with his silver-headed cane and there was a sudden, unexpected thud as the head fell off and rolled away. A gasp arose from both galleries. The King waited for a moment; and then, seeing that no one was about to retrieve the knob, stooped and picked it up himself. Cook cleared his throat and embarked, with obvious enjoyment, upon the charge.

'That he, the said Charles Stuart, being admitted King of England and therein trusted with a limited power to govern by and according to the laws of the land but not otherwise, has traitorously and maliciously levied war against the present Parliament and caused many thousands of the free people of this nation to be slain. And particularly, he has given commissions to his son the Prince and others for the continuing and renewing of war and hostility against the said people and Parliament, by which cruel and unnatural wars much innocent blood hath been spilt, many families have been undone, the public treasure exhausted, trade miserably decayed, vast damage to the nation incurred and many parts of this land spoiled – some of them even to desolation. By all which it appears that the said Charles Stuart has been the occasioner of the said unnatural, cruel and bloody wars and therein guilty of all the treasons, murders, rapines, burnings, spoils, desolations, damages and mischiefs to this nation. And I, John Cook, on behalf of the people of England do for the said treasons and crimes, impeach the said Charles Stuart as a tyrant, traitor—'

The said Charles Stuart gave a small, sardonic laugh.

Cook shot him a malevolent glance.

'As tyrant, traitor, murderer and a public enemy to the Commonwealth of England. And I pray that he may be put to answer all and every premise and that such examinations, trials, sentences and judgements may be thereupon had as shall be agreeable to justice.'

He sat down, re-rolling the indictment and placing it on the table before him next to the sword and mace.

The Lord President bent his eye upon the King.

'Sir – you have now heard your charge. The Court expects your answer.'

There was a short, uneasy silence, broken only by the shuffling of feet and a cough or two.

'I would know by what power I am called hither,' replied his Majesty coldly, at length. 'I was not long ago in the Isle of Wight. There I entered into a peace treaty with both Houses of Parliament – with as much public faith that is possible to be had of any people in the world. Now I would know by what authority I was brought from thence and carried from place to place and I know not what. Remember; I am your lawful King. And what sins you bring upon your heads and the judgement of God upon this land – think well upon it. I say, think well upon it before you go from one sin to a greater. I have a trust committed to me by God; by old and lawful descent. I will not betray it to answer to a new unlawful authority. Therefore resolve me that and you shall hear more of me.'

Bradshaw said reprovingly, 'If you had observed what was hinted to you by the Court, you would *know* by what authority. And it now requires you, in the name of the people of England of which you are elected King, to answer.'

'England was never an elective Kingdom, but an hereditary Kingdom for nearly these thousand years,' Charles retorted swiftly. 'I stand more for the liberty of my people than any here that are come to be my pretended judges. Therefore let me know by what lawful authority I am seated here and I will answer.'

'Sir, your way of answer is to interrogate the Court – which beseems you not in this condition.'

'I do not come here as submitting to the Court,' came the flat reply. 'I stand as much for the privileges of the House of Commons, rightly understood, as any man here. But I see no House of Lords that may constitute a Parliament. Let me see a legal authority and I will answer.'

Frustration darkened Bradshaw's face and he snapped, 'Sir, seeing you will not answer, the Court will consider how to proceed. In the meantime, those that brought you hither are to take charge of you back again.'

As if on a pre-arranged signal, the soldiers in the Hall began a concerted cry of 'Justice! Justice!'. The King looked round, half-amazed, half-nonplussed; and, taking advantage of this first crack in his composure, the Lord President again asked if he would answer the charge.

His Majesty looked back at him, his countenance severe.

'I desire that you give me and all the world satisfaction in this. Let me tell you it is not a slight thing you are about. I am sworn to keep the peace, and I will do it to the last breath of my body. Therefore you will do well to satisfy first God and then the country by what authority you do this. If you do it by an usurped authority, you cannot answer. I do avow it is as great a sin to withstand lawful authority as it is to submit to a tyrannical or *un*lawful authority. And therefore satisfy me and you shall receive my answer.'

'If you are not satisfied with our authority,' Bradshaw blustered, 'we are satisfied with it. This Court will adjourn until Monday 22nd when it will expect your answer.'

His Majesty did not budge. He said, 'You have shown no lawful authority to satisfy any reasonable man.'

'That is *your* apprehension. We are satisfied with it.'

'It is not my apprehension nor yours neither that ought to decide it.'

The Lord President surged to his feet.

'The Court has heard you – and you are to be disposed of as it has decided,' he responded angrily. Then, with a sweep of his arm, 'Remove the prisoner!'

The guards began to close in on the crimson velvet chair. Entirely without haste, the King stood up and gestured distastefully to the indictment. 'I do not fear *that*,' he said and, turning, allowed the guards to escort him from the Hall.

Another chorus of 'Justice!' erupted from the soldiers and was taken up by some of the spectators. Venetia leaned perilously over the rail of the gallery and, with all the force of her lungs, shouted, 'God save the King!'

The King stopped and, for a fragment of a second, stared up at her before he was hustled away. Ignoring the glaring officer below her, Venetia leaned back and grinned at Anne Fairfax. There had been no time for any sign of recognition but that did not matter. Her satisfaction lay in hearing her cry taken up by others on the public benches . . . and in knowing that his Majesty must be able to hear it, too.

The next day was Sunday and, all around the City, specially chosen texts thundered from the pulpits – from the ambiguity of 'Judge not that ye be not judged' to the glorious certainty of Hugh Peter's, 'I will bind their kings in chains'. Venetia listened to none of them and, instead, set off for the Tower and the single, niggardly hour which was all she was permitted to spend with her husband.

527

Gabriel kissed her and then sat down with his arm about her waist. He said, 'Tell me about yesterday.'

'Lady Fairfax has promised to speak to the Lord General on your behalf – in the hope that he'll over-ride Cromwell.'

'Which, since this isn't a military crisis, he won't. But I am grateful to you for trying.'

'Don't be. It's purely selfish, I assure you.' She smiled up at him. 'And I quite enjoy bearding the lions. It's what I'm good at – as you, of all people, should know.'

He laughed. 'I do. Oh I do – believe me!'

'Well, there's no need to sound so downtrodden! As I recall it, you give as good as you get.'

'Always.' His fingers strayed to the line of her neck and she tilted her face invitingly up to his. There was silence. But finally he murmured randomly, 'Sophy's a mine of surprises, isn't she? Why do you suppose she never before mentioned that she was acquainted with Anne Fairfax?'

Venetia shrugged. 'You know Sophy. Only things with four legs and fur register most of the time.'

'Mm. But it makes one wonder what other dark secrets she's harbouring. A long-standing friendship with Denzil Holles, perhaps – or a passionate, youthful affair with his Grace of Hamilton?' He paused and then, in a very different tone said, 'And that, of course, brings us back to my original question. What happened at the trial?'

'His Majesty denied the legality of the Court,' she replied and gave him a brief account of the proceedings in Westminster Hall. 'He did it well, too. All his life, he's never shown to advantage on public occasions. But yesterday he was every inch a King. He left the prosecution without a shred of credibility – and Bradshaw might as well have held up a sword and said "*Here* is our authority". It was a performance which even Lilburne might have applauded.'

'Very likely,' agreed Gabriel. 'But will it save him?'

The light faded from her face and she leaned her head against his shoulder. 'Not if they're determined to be rid of him. And I suspect . . . I very much suspect that they are.'

The following morning brought a note from Lady Gillingham suggesting that – if Venetia did not have a prior engagement with Lady Fairfax – she might care to attend that day's session of the trial with herself and Lady Newburgh. Venetia frowned at the unfamiliar name and then, shrugging, sent my Lady's servant back with a message of acceptance.

On learning that she was planning to spend a second afternoon in Westminster Hall, Sophy said anxiously, 'Is that really such a good idea? It's time you started resting more, you know. And I'm not sure you should be risking yourself amidst crowds of people in your condition.'

Venetia sighed and explained that she would again be sitting snug in one of the galleries; this time with Lady Gillingham. There was an infinitesimal silence during which Sophia's attention appeared to wander. Then she said vaguely, 'I'm sorry. Who did you say?'

'Lady Gillingham. We were at Whitehall together before the war and I met her again when Gabriel brought me to London last spring.' A gleam of humour lit the violet eyes. 'You needn't worry, Sophy. Isabel is too conscious of her dignity to go anywhere near the masses, so I'll be perfectly safe. And now I must change or I'll be late. Gallery tickets are expensive, so full plumage is obligatory.'

Lavishly attired in violet silk under a velvet cloak and wearing the gold locket which was her only remaining ornament, Venetia met Isabel, as arranged, at the head of Westminster Stairs – and immediately received a pleasant surprise. Her ladyship's vivacious companion was none other than her own friend, Kate D'Aubigny.

'You were expecting a stranger – confess it!' crowed Kate, drawing Venetia into a brief, perfumed embrace. 'Did news of my remarriage not reach the frozen north?'

Venetia shook her head. '*You* are Lady Newburgh?'

'Are you surprised?' And then, her expression clouding abruptly, 'But of course you are. And you mustn't think I've forgotten George because I haven't. But it's been six years and life has to go on. That's why you're not married to Ellis, isn't it?' The bright, slightly restless smile returned. 'Don't worry. Isabel has told me *everything!*'

Catching the coolness in Venetia's eye, Lady Gillingham said quickly, 'Is there any news of the Colonel's release?'

'None, unfortunately. But I live in hope.'

'Of course!' said Kate warmly. 'And Roundhead or not – I'm *glad* you love him. It's the only thing that counts.'

'Not quite,' said Isabel thinly. 'Not at all, in fact. Shall we go in? It's freezing out here.'

The scene inside Westminster Hall was much as it had been on Saturday. Venetia took her seat beside Isabel and noticed that Lady Fairfax was already in her accustomed place at the front of the gallery opposite. Then Kate Newburgh said sadly, 'His Majesty dined with us on his way from Hurst to Windsor, you know. James and I hoped we might help him to escape, but it came to nothing.'

Venetia smiled faintly. It was so like Kate. She and Sir William Waller's cousin, Edmund, had hatched the famous plot to seize London back in '43 – and that, too, had come to nothing. But at least no one could accuse her of not trying.

As before, the Commissioners filed in to occupy their benches – seventy of them this time, Venetia noticed – and Lord President Bradshaw took his seat. Then the proceedings opened with the announcement that anyone who created a disturbance would be instantly arrested. Lady Fairfax grinned triumphantly across at Venetia and then settled back to await Solicitor-General Cook's preamble.

His Majesty, it appeared, was waiting for it too – and when Cook continued his whispered conference with the lawyer, Isaac Dorislaus, the King awarded him a sharp jab with the point of his cane. Cook whirled round, opening his mouth on a furious objection – only to catch the Lord President's admonitory eye. Scowling, he said, 'May it please your lordship, I did at the last Court exhibit a charge of high treason against the prisoner at the bar. He was not then pleased to give an answer but did dispute the authority of this High Court. My humble motion is that the prisoner may be directed to make a positive answer. And if he shall refuse, that the charge may be taken *pro confesso* and the Court proceed according to justice.'

Lord President Bradshaw nodded to him to be seated and then, once more, invited the King to respond to the charge.

'If it were only my own particular case,' replied Charles reflectively, 'I would have satisfied myself with the protestation I made the last time I was here – that a King cannot be tried by any superior jurisdiction on earth. But it is not my case alone; it is the freedom and the liberty of the people of England. For if power without law may alter the fundamental laws of the Kingdom – I do not know what subject in England that can be sure of his life or anything that he calls his own. Therefore—'

'Sir, I must interrupt you,' snapped Bradshaw. 'You are about to dispute the authority of this Court of law before which you appear as a high Delinquent.'

'I do not know how a King can be a Delinquent,' mused Charles. 'By any law that I ever heard, all men – Delinquents or what you will – may demur against any proceeding as legal. And I do demand to be heard with my reasons. If you deny that, you deny *reason*.'

'You may *not* demur against the jurisdiction of the Court,' came the irascible reply. 'They sit here by the authority of the Commons of England – and all your predecessors and you are responsible to them. Therefore—'

'I deny that. Show me one precedent.'

'Sir, you ought not to interrupt while the Court is speaking! Clerk – read the determination of the Court.'

Andrew Broughton stood up. 'Charles Stuart – you have been accused of high treasons and other high crimes. The Court has determined that you ought to answer the same.'

'I will answer,' stated Charles, with maddening calm, 'as soon as I know by what authority you do this.'

The Lord President slammed his fist down upon the table. 'If this be all you will say, then those who brought you here may take you back again!'

The King looked back stubbornly. 'I require that I may give my reasons why I do not answer.'

'It is not for prisoners to require!'

The dark, Stuart eyes blazed with sudden anger.

'*I*, sir, am no *ordinary* prisoner. Show me that jurisdiction where reason is not be heard.'

'We show it you here – the Commons of England.'

'The Commons of England was never a Court of judicature. I would know how they came to be so.'

Already red in the face, Bradshaw hesitated and then gave up. 'Sergeant – take away the prisoner!'

The King came slowly to his feet, his gaze impaling the assembled ranks of the Commissioners. 'Remember that the King is not suffered to give his reasons – for the liberty and freedom of all his subjects.'

'How great a friend *you* have been to the laws and liberties of the people, let all England – all the world – judge!' cried Bradshaw triumphantly.

The King froze and looked back through the ring of guards closing in on him. For the first time since the trial had begun, his stammer became evident as he said, 'Sir – under favour – it was the liberty, f-freedom and laws of the subject that ever I took – d-defended myself with arms. I never took up arms against the people b-but for the laws.'

Sensing that he had the whip hand at last Bradshaw boomed, 'Clerk – record the prisoner's default in not answering the charge and his contempt of this Court of Parliament. Remove the prisoner!'

This time, the orchestrated shouts of the soldiers came as no surprise and the King's friends were ready with their reply. Then, just as Venetia was about to join in, one solitary trooper defied his orders to cry, 'God help and save your Majesty!' Colonel Axtell struck him savagely with his cane and the King paused, looking from one to the other of them. 'Poor fellow,' he said clearly. 'It is a heavy blow for a small offence.'

Outside, in the gathering dusk of New Palace Yard, Venetia said goodbye to Kate and Isabel and agreed to meet them again on the following afternoon. Then, just as she was about to descend the stairs in search of a boat, a familiar voice said, 'I don't suppose you'd like to share the cost of the journey with an impecunious scribbler, would you?' And turning, she found herself face to face with Samuel Radford.

He was dressed as shabbily as ever and clutching the inevitable sheaf of papers to his chest. Smiling a little, she said, 'I'd be happy to. Have you been reporting upon the trial for the *Moderate*?'

'Yes.' He helped her into the boat and climbed in beside her. 'My revered employer is determined not only to print a full day-to-day account but also a series of pamphlets.

Consequently, he's demanding a verbatim record. And since my stenography is better than his own, here I am.' He grinned companiably at her. 'How's the Colonel?'

'Bored – but otherwise remarkably calm,' replied Venetia. 'I'm told you tried to visit him. Why?'

'Because I owe him my forthcoming marriage to Bryony; because of what he did for Justin; because I like him,' came the straightforward response. 'And, of course, to offer him the benefit of Free-born John's vast experience in what to say and what *not* to say when he comes to trial. Speaking of which – the King's doing rather well, don't you think? John is in the wilds of County Durham at present; but I think, in certain respects, he'll be sorry to have missed such a masterly demonstration of his own tactics.'

'Quite possibly. But it's no use you expecting Gabriel to employ them. They won't work with a court-martial.'

'No. I suppose not.' There was silence for a moment and then Sam said, 'Bryony told me the whole story. Have you still no idea who laid the information?'

'None,' said Venetia flatly. 'Cromwell says the informant is no murderer, but neither Gabriel nor I can believe that. Therefore – since even Henry Ireton can't keep Gabriel under arrest forever without some kind of hard evidence – it will all start again as soon as he's released. Because after all the trouble they've gone to, I can't see whoever it is giving up now. Can you?'

Venetia visited the Tower on the following morning and then met Isabel and Lady Newburgh shortly after one o'clock in New Palace Yard. Although she would have bled to death sooner than admit it, the strain of the past few weeks was beginning to tell and she felt desperately tired. This made it difficult to respond suitably to Kate's vivacity and Isabel's subtle prying into the case against Gabriel . . . but Venetia did her best and tried to ignore the dull thudding at her temples, caused by the din arising from the public benches. Then, just as the Commissioners made their entrance, she discovered that she felt unpleasantly hot and a strange roaring invaded her ears. She swayed in her seat and the world went black.

The next thing she knew was Kate chafing her hands and Isabel waving something pungent beneath her nose. Opening her eyes, she said feebly, 'I'm sorry. How silly of me. I never fainted before in my life.'

Below in the Court, the usual roll was being called. Lady Newburgh ignored it and fanned Venetia energetically with the edge of her cloak. She murmured, 'No, love. But, at a guess, you've good reason for it now. Am I right?'

Some of Venetia's colour started to return and she managed a wry smile. Before she could speak, however, Isabel hissed sharply, 'You're *pregnant*?'

It was something which Venetia would have preferred to go on keeping to herself, but it was plainly a little late for that. She said, 'Yes. I believe so. But we can't talk about it now. The trial is starting.'

Isabel sat perfectly still, staring at her; Kate beamed and looked as though she would have liked to inquire further. Fortunately, Solicitor Cook prevented her from doing so by beginning the session with a demand that, having refused to put in a plea, the King should now be regarded as having confessed – and that sentence be passed upon him.

It seemed, however, that Lord President Bradshaw was not prepared to do this just yet. He reminded the King that justice knew no respect of persons and requested him to answer the charge in plain English. His Majesty replied that he valued the charge not a rush . . . and the afternoon wore by in much the same pattern as before. Finally, the King announced that he would never acknowledge the Court's authority till he was assured it posed no threat to the fundamental privileges of the people.

'How far *you* have preserved the privileges of the people, your actions have spoke it!' retorted Bradshaw swiftly, overjoyed by the prospect of scoring a point at last. 'Truly, Sir, you have written your meaning in bloody characters throughout the whole Kingdom. Clerk – record the default. And gentlemen, you that have charge of the prisoner, take him back again.'

'If it were only my own particular, I would not say any more nor interrupt you,' began the King. 'But—'

'You have heard the pleasure of the Court and you are –

534

notwithstanding you will not understand it – to find you are before a Court of Justice,' returned Bradshaw acidly. And then, once again, 'Remove the prisoner!'

Rising, the King stood quite still, his eyes locked with those of Oliver Cromwell. Then, with heavy emphasis, he said, 'I see I am before a *power*.' And turning, walked briskly out amidst the usual welter of conflicting cries.

Venetia had to endure a good deal more discussion on her pregnancy before she was finally able to escape and go home to tell Sophia all about it. And when she had finished talking, Sophia said thoughtfully, 'Something of the sort was bound to happen sooner or later, you know. You've been doing far too much. But it raises another question too; namely, how long you can go on keeping it from Gabriel.'

'I don't know,' sighed Venetia. 'I'd rather not tell him until he's released – because beneath the beautifully preserved *sangfroid*, I suspect he's becoming restless enough already. But if Eden doesn't work a miracle in the next month or so . . .' She stopped and shrugged wryly. 'Well, let's just say I won't be able to hide it indefinitely.'

Had she but known it, Gabriel's so-called *sangfroid* existed only when she was with him. The rest of the time, and particularly when she had just left, he was aware of a steadily increasing urge to hammer down the walls. He was unused both to life indoors and to the sheer, mindcracking boredom of enforced inactivity. His body felt caged and his mind, frustrated. Worse still, his desire for Venetia was as great as it had ever been and seeing her for one, celibate, hour each day was subtle torture.

When she visited him on the morning of Thursday 25th, it was to tell him that there had been no public session of the Court the previous afternoon and would be none again that day. 'The Commissioners are supposedly in the Painted Chamber hearing the witnesses,' she said. 'Though precisely what *sort* of witnesses, I can't imagine.'

'The sort who'll confirm the "Man of Blood" theory,' replied Gabriel, leaning against the wall on the far side of the cell and trying not to look at the curve of her mouth or the way her hair gleamed in the dull light. 'But they can't produce them until the King accepts the Court's authority.'

'I know. But what's to stop them declaring him *pro confesso* and proceeding without further ado?'

'Nothing – except that I'm sure Cromwell would prefer to complete this charade with at least the rags of respectability. And getting the King to speak is his only hope.'

'Then let's pray that he clings to it,' muttered Venetia. And then, 'Eden says Fairfax has been asking about you. That's good, isn't it? A word from him and you could be home.'

Gabriel refrained from advising her not to hold her breath and, instead, said lightly, 'It can't be too soon for me. Do you *have* to come here looking so alluring?'

She smiled at him. 'I could wear a veil, if you like.'

'Try a head-to-foot sack.'

Venetia dug her nails into her palms and sought a diversion. 'Jack has summoned us all to dinner tomorrow to discuss what else can be done. Have you any suggestions?'

'Yes,' said Gabriel. 'Tell him to make me half a dozen petards – or send me a pie with a bottle of *aqua fortis* and a rope inside it. Or, if he prefers to play safe, tell him to start digging a tunnel.'

Eden found Gabriel's suggestions funny. So, to a lesser extent, did Bryony and Sam. Jack merely scowled into a dish of eels and observed that he was glad Gabriel was still able to be flippant. Then he invited Major Maxwell to tell them how far he had progressed with his investigation.

Eden straightened out his face and accepted a slice of beef from the platter Annis was offering him. 'As far as I can. I've offered mitigating factors in defence of Gabriel's behaviour during the purge and also his absence last month. I've a statement from Venetia regarding the counterfeit coins – and ones from Baxter and Willis swearing that Justin Ambrose and Francis are a pair of ruthless fellows who escaped without help. Consequently – unless Ireton has evidence he hasn't revealed yet – I can reduce the charges to almost nil. And Cromwell knows it – as does Fairfax.'

'So Gabriel may be released soon?' asked Bryony.

'Perhaps – though not until after the King's trial.'

'And what,' said Jack single-mindedly, 'about the identity of the person who put him where he is now?'

536

Eden shook his head. 'No joy, I'm afraid. Ireton doesn't know the name of Cromwell's informant – and Old Noll takes very good care not to let me ask.'

There was a small silence while everyone thought it over. Then Sam said, 'It sounds to me as if the Lieutenant-General is protecting a friend of his.'

'That's what it sounds like to me,' agreed Venetia. 'Unfortunately, however, it doesn't help very much. He must know dozens of people who also know Gabriel. And since we can't think of anyone except Ellis who might wish Gabriel harm, it makes it difficult to know where to start.'

An arrested expression entered Eden's eyes and, seeing it, Sophia said, 'You've thought of something?'

'Not exactly. I . . . I just suddenly remembered Hugh Peter. He and Gabriel have always been at daggers-drawn – and he's close to Cromwell. But it couldn't possibly be him. He's an Army chaplain, for God's sake!'

'So?' said Jack. 'Judging by his sermons, he's also possessed of a violent and vindictive nature.'

'Very likely,' agreed Eden. 'But there's a big difference between hell-and-damnation preaching and trying to send a man to eternity just because you don't like him.'

'One would hope so,' said Venetia. 'On the other hand, it can do no harm to check the matter out. Can it?'

On the following afternoon, leaving the matter of Hugh Peter in the capable hands of Major Maxwell and Samuel Radford, Venetia joined my ladies Gillingham and Newburgh for what was strongly suspected would be the last day of the King's trial. As on the first day, sixty-eight Commissioners were present and, when the King entered the Hall, cries of 'Execution!' mingled with the usual ones of 'Justice!'. These and the fact that, for the first time, the Lord President was robed in red, told his Majesty that sentence was imminent and caused him to begin without waiting for the proper formalities.

'If it please you, Sir, I desire to be heard.'

'You shall be heard before the judgement be given,' returned Bradshaw blandly. And, to the rows of the Commissioners, 'It is well-known that the prisoner has been several times brought before the Court to make answer to a charge of treason exhibited against him in the name of the people of England. But being steadfast in his refusal to—'

'It's a lie!' shouted Venetia, before she could stop herself. 'Not a half – not a quarter of the people of England!' And, quick as a flash from the other gallery, Lady Fairfax yelled, 'Oliver Cromwell is a traitor!'

The Hall erupted into a welter of catcalls and, with rather more presence of mind than tact, Colonel Axtell barked, 'Level your muskets! Down with the whores!'

Consternation verging on panic swept through the female population of both galleries. Isabel hissed that Venetia was endangering them all and someone behind poked her angrily in the back. The ladies around Anne Fairfax, meanwhile, had succeeded in hustling her from her seat and she swept out without a backward glance. Venetia shook Isabel's hand from her arm and restored her attention to the proceedings below.

Despite the near-chaos, Bradshaw was still speaking and had announced that the Court would permit his Majesty to speak provided he used the time to defend himself rather than dispute the authority of the Court.

Charles shrugged slightly.

'Since I see you will not hear anything concerning that which I thought most material for the liberty of the subject, I shall speak nothing to it. But I must tell you that this many a day all things have been taken away from me but that which I call more dear than my life – which is my conscience and my honour. And, if I had respect for my life more than the peace of the Kingdom, I should have made a particular defence for myself – for by that, at least, I might have delayed an ugly sentence which I believe will pass upon me. Now, Sir. I conceive that a hasty sentence once passed may sooner be repented than recalled. Therefore I desire, before sentence be given, that I may be heard in the Painted Chamber before the Lords and Commons. This delay cannot be prejudicial to you whatsoever I say – though if it be reason, I am sure it is well worth the hearing. But if I cannot get this liberty, I do here protest that so fair shows of liberty and peace are *pure* shows and not otherwise since you will not hear your King.'

'This is a further declining of the jurisdiction of this Court,' observed the Lord President coldly. 'And it is not that they will not hear the King. They have patiently waited your pleasure for three Courts together. But this tends to further delay. You would offer to speak to the Lords and Commons – yet your offer there must needs be in delay of justice here. This Court be resolved for sentence.'

The shuffling and fidgeting that had been going on for some moments on the benches to Bradshaw's left suddenly exploded into full-scale commotion as one of the Commissioners shouted, 'Have we hearts of stone? Are we *men*?'

Venetia sat up straight and craned her neck to get a better look at the turbulent gentleman whose colleagues were struggling to keep him in his seat.

'No!' he panted. 'If I die for it – I must do it.'

'What ails you, Downes?' From the seat behind, Lieutenant-General Cromwell dropped a heavy hand on the younger man's shoulder and growled audibly, 'Are you mad? Can you not sit still and be quiet?'

Downes shook him off. 'Sir – no. I can't be quiet. Lord President – this Commissioner is not satisfied!'

There was a sudden confused chorus of 'Let the King be heard!' and 'Cromwell is a traitor!', punctuated with a stentorian command of 'Silence in Court!' And over it all, Downes shouted, 'I'm not satisfied to give my consent to this sentence but have reasons to offer you against it!'

Glaring irritably at him, Lord President Bradshaw snapped, 'If any member of the Court be unsatisfied, then the Court must adjourn—' His words were lost amidst a fresh outburst of catcalls and stamping.

Venetia leaned back in her seat while the King was removed and the Court below slowly cleared. Her eyes were bright and, for the first time in days, she was laughing. She said, 'A weak link on Noll Cromwell's chain? God bless him – whoever he is. He's a brave man.'

'He's a fool!' said Isabel curtly. 'That little display will make no difference whatsoever.'

'Perhaps not,' agreed Venetia, rising to go and smiling grimly at Kate. 'But there are times when the important thing is to have tried.'

It was cold outside with the promise of snow. Venetia was not sorry when Isabel announced her intention of going home rather than stand around freezing to death. For herself, nothing would have persuaded her to leave without seeing the outcome of the day; and so she clutched her cloak tightly about her and passed the next hour pacing up and down New Palace Yard with Lady Newburgh until the Sergeant-at-Arms announced that the Court was to resume its session.

Commissioner Downes had not returned with the rest. Venetia and Kate exchanged apprehensive glances . . . and the Lord President commenced his address to the King.

'Sir,' he said. 'The return I have to you from the Court is this. Notwithstanding what you have offered, they are resolved to proceed to punishment and judgement. And that is their unanimous resolution.'

A wave of mute restlessness flowed over the spectators and, for a moment, the King made no reply. Then, in a tone of arid composure, he said, 'I know it is in vain for me to dispute. I am no sceptic to deny the power that you have. I know you have power enough. I think it would have been for the Kingdom's peace if you had taken pains to show the *lawfulness* of your power.' He paused. 'I have been here now, I think, a week. But a little delay of a day or two further may give peace; whereas a hasty judgement may bring on that trouble to the Kingdom which the child that is unborn may repent of. And therefore again, I do desire that I may be heard by the Lords and Commons.'

Bradshaw dismissed him with a shrug. 'Sir, you have been already answered. The Court now requires to know whether you have any more to say for yourself before they proceed to sentence.'

'I have nothing more to say. But I desire that this may be entered – what I *have* said.'

'The Court, then, has something else to say to *you*,' responded Bradshaw, arising with the notes for his final oration clasped in one hand. 'Sir – you speak very well of a precious thing called peace. It had been much to be wished that you *had* really endeavoured the peace of the Kingdom, but your actions have been clean contrary. You have let fall such languages as if you had been no way subject to the law. The Court is very sensible that the law is your superior – that you ought to have ruled according to the law. But *you* set your single judgement against the highest Court of Justice – and that is *not* law! The end of having Kings is for enjoying justice. Now, Sir – if the King go contrary to that end, he must understand that he is but an officer in trust and he ought to *discharge* that trust. Parliaments were ordered to address the grievances of the people . . . but what the intermission of Parliaments has been in your time is very well known. Truly, Sir, your proceedings call to mind a great Roman tyrant: Caligula – who wished that the people of Rome had one head that he might at one blow cut it off!'

He paused briefly, heard a faint, disconcerting ripple of derisive laughter, and went swiftly on.

'It is a question much pressed on your side, by what precedent we proceed. It is no new thing to cite precedents where people have called their Kings to account. You know very well you are the hundred-and-ninth King of Scotland. To mention so many of them as that Kingdom has made bold to deal with would be too long. But it is not far to go for an example; your grandmother set aside and your father, an infant, crowned. And the state did it here in England. King Edward II and King Richard II were dealt with by the Parliament – and the articles charged upon them do not come near to the crimes that are laid at *your* charge.' He regarded the King forbiddingly while he turned the pages of his notes. 'Your coronation oath does plainly show that there is a contract made between the King and his people. The bond of protection is due from the sovereign as the bond of subjection is due from the subject. Sir, if this bond be once broken – farewell sovereignty!'

Grasping the momentary pause, the King said rapidly, 'These things may not be denied. But—'

'Whether you have been the protector or the destroyer of England, let all England judge!' invited Bradshaw. 'I shall not particularise the many miscarriages of your reign. They are famously known. Truly, Sir, these are your crimes. Tyranny and treason. All the bloody murders committed since division was betwixt you and your people. And if any man will ask what punishment is due a murderer, let God's law speak. As the text has it: when innocent blood has been shed whereas the land stands still defiled, it can be no way cleansed but with the shedding of the blood of he that *shed* this blood.' His voice had risen to a passionate crescendo and he took time to calm it before continuing. 'All I will say before the reading of your sentence is this. You said that you wished us to have God before our eyes. I hope all of us have so. That God with whom there is no respect of persons; that God who is the avenger of innocent blood. We have that God before us. For yourself, we do heartily wish that God would be pleased to give you a sense of your sins – that you may cry unto Him that God would deliver you from blood guiltiness.'

The silence in the great Hall as he finished speaking was so acute that Venetia could hear her own heart beating. Then the King said slowly, 'I desire only one word before you give sentence. And that is that you hear me concerning those great imputations that you have laid to my charge.'

'Truly, Sir, I would not willingly at this time interrupt you in anything you have to say. But from the first time you were pleased to disavow us, the Court needed not to have heard you one word,' announced Bradshaw, resuming his seat. 'We have given you too much liberty already. It is our duty to do what the law prescribes. What sentence the law affirms to a tyrant, traitor and murderer, you are now to hear read out to you.'

His face pale and set, Broughton rose and unrolled a scroll with fingers that were not entirely steady.

'Whereas the Commons of England in Parliament appointed us a High Court of Justice for the trying of Charles Stuart, King of England, on a charge of high treason and other crimes and misdemeanours which was read on behalf of the people of England . . . he, the said Charles Stuart was required to give his answer but he refused so to do. For all which treasons and crimes this Court does adjudge that the said Charles Stuart, as tyrant, traitor, murderer and a public enemy to the good people of this nation, shall be put to death by the severing of his head from his body.'

A strange, sighing breath arose from the Hall and a bitter chill invaded the air. Faces expressed a variety of expression

– the most common of which was a sort of shocked bewilderment. No one spoke.

Clearing his throat, Bradshaw said, 'The sentence now read is the act, judgement and resolution of the whole Court. Will the Commissioners stand to signify their assent.'

The Commissioners rose, albeit untidily, to a man. The King looked from them back to Bradshaw and said, 'Will you hear me a word, Sir?'

'You are not to be heard after sentence,' came the prompt reply. And, with almost indecent haste, 'Guard – remove the prisoner.'

Utterly disconcerted by the discovery that it could all end so abruptly, the King rose disbelievingly from his seat. 'I may speak after sentence,' he declared as the guards closed in about him. 'I may speak after sentence ever! By your favour – hold! The sentence, Sir . . . I say, I do affirm—' He stopped; surrounded, defeated and suddenly intensely bitter. 'I am not suffered to speak,' he proclaimed loudly as they started to hustle him away. 'Expect what justice other people will have.'

Already his voice was half-drowned ln the jeers of Colonel Axtell's men. Venetia and Kate Newburgh stared at each other, dry-eyed and shaking. Then, silently, they clung to each other and tried, unsuccessfully, to bear what they both knew was unbearable.

Three

Sentence had been passed on Saturday 27th and the execution was fixed for Tuesday 30th. Between the two, Eden and Sam listened to Hugh Peter preaching on the text *'Thou hast destroyed thy land and slain thy people'* but failed to find anything that might link him to Gabriel's misfortunes; and Venetia, having already endured endless lectures from Sophia and Jack, came very close to quarrelling with her husband.

'You've attended the trial – and let that be enough,' he said crisply. 'Watching the King die won't solve anything. It will be a harrowing, gruesome experience which will stay with you forever. Is that what you want?'

'No. But if it's the price I must pay, then so be it. I *have* to be there. *Not* to go would be like deserting him.'

'Rubbish! Do you think he'll see you – or even know?'

'That's not the point,' she said wearily. *'I'll* know.'

'That's the only thing we're agreed on. But what purpose will it serve?' Gabriel ran a hand through his hair and eyed her grimly. 'Have you ever seen a man butchered?'

A tiny shudder rippled through her. 'No.'

'It isn't a pretty sight. To put it bluntly, it dismantles your stomach. Are you prepared for that?'

'Probably not. But I'll manage.'

He swung away to the window swearing under his breath. Then, turning back to face her, 'And what if there's trouble? What if a riot begins amongst the crowd and the Army comes in at push of pike or worse? You could be killed.'

'I doubt that. I won't be alone, you know. I'm going with Isabel and Kate, and they'll both doubtless take a couple of servants along for protection.'

'I don't care if they take a dozen bloody eunuchs!' snapped Gabriel. 'The place will be heaving with troopers who won't have orders to be either selective or gentle. So, just for once, will you do as I ask and stay at home?'

'I can't,' said Venetia, stubbornly but with reluctance. 'I really can't. I'm sorry. But I *will* be careful.'

'Is that supposed to make me feel better?' He stared at her, as furious with his own impotence as with her obstinacy. 'If I was out of here, there'd be no question of your going. You know that, don't you?'

The merest hint of a wry smile touched her mouth.

'Not necessarily. But I admit that it would probably be more difficult.' The smile faded, leaving her face very tense. 'If I could do as you ask, I would. But I can't turn aside from this, Gabriel. Not even for you.'

Wearing her warmest cloak over a plain, dark gown, Venetia took a chair to Covent Garden on the morning of the 30th. It was bitterly cold, as it had been for days and the frost lay thick and white over roofs and trees. In the City, people went about their daily business with a sort of strained normality or stood around in huddles, talking in hushed voices. Faces expressed fear, confusion, resentment; few of them were smiling. Venetia understood how they felt. It was as if the world had spun out of control and was even now entering the void.

Gratingly self-absorbed as ever, Isabel welcomed her as though they were merely going on a shopping expedition and revealed that Lady Newburgh would not be joining them after all. Then she said, 'Sit by the fire, my dear. I've mulled some wine, and we've time for a cup before we leave.'

Venetia eyed it distastefully. 'I don't think I could.'

'I know how you feel – but you ought to try, you know. It's freezing outside and we'll probably have a long wait. This may help to keep the chill off.' The vivid blue eyes encompassed her in gentle solicitude. 'Try to drink a little, Venetia. You can't afford to risk your health now you've the baby to think of.'

Venetia took an unenthusiastic sip of the hot, spicy liquid

and then warmed her hands around the cup. She said baldly, 'I still can't believe they'll actually do it.'

'They've built a scaffold,' said Isabel. She sat down, apparently unaware of Venetia's indrawn breath. 'It's been erected outside the Banqueting House. Did you know?'

'Yes. But there must be something – or someone – capable of stopping them using it.'

'I doubt it. They say Prince Rupert's in Ireland with half-a-dozen ships, but what good's that? The Scots are against it, of course, but they won't *do* anything; and the Dutch sent envoys to the Commons but were just told to go and get their plea translated. Also, rumour has it that the Prince of Wales sent a signed sheet of blank paper, begging Parliament to name their terms for sparing the King's life. But even that won't help. Not now. It's too late.'

'It won't be too late till it's actually done!' snapped Venetia. And then, accusingly, 'How can you be so cool?'

'I'm not,' replied Isabel, without noticeable truth. 'I'm as upset as you. But one has to be realistic. His Majesty has been tried and sentenced; and, short of a miracle, he will go to the block a few hours from now.'

Venetia frowned down into her half-empty cup.

'And who,' she murmured bitterly, 'will be brave enough to sign the death warrant of a King?'

'Ah. Yes – well, that has presented difficulties, I believe. Certain of the Commissioners were unwilling to put their names to it and had to be . . . encouraged.'

'By whom? Or no. Silly question. Cromwell, no doubt?'

Her ladyship nodded and leaned forward with the air of one enjoying a confidential gossip. 'And that's not all. The document itself was incorrectly dated and ought to have been re-written – except that it was feared that some of those who'd already signed might refuse to do so again and so the mistakes were simply altered.'

The frown in Venetia's eyes intensified and she looked up. 'How do you know all this?'

'People talk. You know how it is. Nothing remains a secret for very long.' Rising, Isabel shook out the ample skirts of her bronze silk and expertly twisted one flame-red curl back into place. 'If you've finished your wine, we should go. My

547

loving mother-in-law will be down soon and I'd rather not see her just now. Also, it will be hard to find a place from which to see if we don't arrive in good time. I thought we'd walk down to Whitehall. It's not far, after all. And I've told Tom Harris to be ready to escort us. He should be sufficient protection, don't you think?'

With other things on her mind, Venetia had difficulty recalling the large young man Isabel had foisted upon her for a few weeks the previous autumn but was vaguely surprised that he was once more in her ladyship's own employ. Draining her cup and setting it aside, she said, 'I thought the Dowager wanted you to get rid of him?'

'She did, and still does, come to that.' A bright, malicious smile dawned. 'But annoying her is one of life's small pleasures. Shall we go?'

Outside, the cold took Venetia's breath away and seared her lungs. Isabel, larger than ever in an extravagant cloak lined with sable, continued to pour vitriol on the Dowager Countess all the way down the Strand and through Charing Cross – while Harris trod a respectful two paces behind, presumably listening to every word. Venetia felt her nerves start to snarl into an irritable tangle and wished she'd had the sense to realise that, on this of all days, Isabel Gillingham was probably the very last companion she wanted.

King Street was lined with soldiers, past whom people were moving in only one direction. Venetia walked grimly on, trying to batten down her emotions and prepare herself for what lay ahead. Then she caught her first glimpse of the scaffold and knew a sudden, terrible desire to turn and run.

The elegant, classical facade of Inigo Jones's Banqueting House lay at right angles to Henry VIII's red-and-black checked Holbein Gate, and, opposite to it, about forty yards away on the far side of King Street, lay the wall of the Tilt Yard. The intervening space, overlooked by a battery of guns and buildings now occupied by the Army, was the only place from which the public might watch the execution; small, relatively contained and easily guarded.

During the war, some of the windows of the Banqueting House had been bricked up. Now, however, one had been knocked through again and enlarged to form a rough doorway; and before it, about six feet high and flanked by mounted troopers, stood the black-draped platform of the scaffold.

Venetia stared at it, transfixed. Isabel shook her arm and said, 'Come along. A place near the wall will be best. Also, if we're to hear a word his Majesty says, we'll need to get nearer the front. Tom: clear a path for us.'

Scarcely aware of the complaints and buffeting of the crowd, Venetia allowed herself to be propelled forwards to a point beneath the gallery which linked the Palace to the Holbein Gate. And then, when they were no more than twenty feet from the scaffold, she stopped dead, her eyes glued to the low block. Isabel's voice droned endlessly on, attempting to persuade her to take a few more steps but Venetia ignored it. This was as close as she could bear to be; and much closer than was probably wise.

It was only then that it occurred to her to wonder why they were standing in the icy street amidst the common people instead of sitting snug in a window somewhere. It wasn't like Isabel to endure discomfort; and that sable cloak had never been intended for standing cheek-by-jowl with shopkeepers, apprentices and fishwives. Just for an instant, Venetia contemplated asking why they weren't above in the gallery with the other fur-trimmed spectators – and then changed her mind. It would only provoke another mindless monologue and she had already heard enough.

Somewhere, a church clock struck noon. The crowd was denser now and becoming tightly-packed but voices remained low and faces subdued. Isabel described, in exhaustive detail, the gown her dressmaker was currently completing. Time passed. Venetia's hands and feet grew numb with cold and her back ached with standing. The clock struck one and the crowd shuffled restlessly, amidst a sea of rumour that something had gone wrong.

Venetia's eye brightened and, cutting Isabel off in mid-sentence, she addressed the man nearest to her. 'What's that they're saying? Something about the executioner?'

'They're saying he won't do it – and that the Army's called for volunteers,' came the reply. 'Not that they'll have to look far. I reckon Nose Almighty'd be happy to oblige. Or Hugh

Hell-fire Peter, come to that. But I doubt it's true, lass, so there's no need to look so sick. Young Gregory's beheaded the Earl of Strafford and Archbishop Laud in his time. And doubtless the fee's higher for a King.'

Venetia leaned against the wall and closed her eyes. Isabel said, 'Are you all right, dearest? You're very pale.'

'Are you surprised?' Venetia forced her eyes open again. 'But don't worry. I've no intention of fainting.'

At the end of another excruciating hour, rumour said that the delay had been caused by the Commons, where the Members were rushing through an emergency bill declaring it illegal for anyone to proclaim a new king. This, Venetia acknowledged distantly, made much more sense than wildfire stories about the executioner. But, by then, she was chilled to the bone and beginning to feel decidedly unwell. Her back felt as though it was being sawn in two, she felt lightheaded and nauseous – and a dull ache was rippling spasmodically across the pit of her stomach. She wished she could sit down; she wished she might not be sick; she half-wished she had listened to Gabriel.

And then it began. Men stepped on to the black-covered scaffold. Guards holding halberds – a couple of scriveners with note-books – a clutch of anonymous Army Colonels; and then, not only masked but also bizarrely disguised by wigs and false beards, the executioner and his assistant. Her mouth dry as tinder and her nerves vibrating like plucked wires, Venetia pressed her hands hard against the wall and waited. On the ceiling of the Banqueting House beneath which his Majesty must even now be passing, Rubens had painted Justice triumphing over Rebellion. The irony of it was vaguely crippling.

Accompanied by Bishop Juxon, a slight, heavily-cloaked figure stepped out on to the platform. Charles Stuart, King of England. The crowd was silent now, its collective breath smoking on the air. Gesturing to the block, the King spoke with quiet dignity to one of the Colonels and received an apparently negative answer. Then, looking briefly at the mounted troops which were drawn up between the scaffold and the people, he drew a small piece of paper from his pocket and prepared to speak to those around him.

Isabel, meanwhile, had identified the officer as Colonel Hacker and started to give Venetia chapter and verse on his recent career as the King's chief jailer. Without turning her head, Venetia said curtly, 'For God's sake, be quiet! This is neither the time nor the place.'

The King's voice was calm and remarkably even, but his words drifted past the line of soldiers only in fragments. Straining her ears, Venetia caught some of them; most of the crowd probably heard nothing at all.

'I could hold my peace very well but I think it is my duty . . . to clear myself as an honest man,' he began. 'All the world knows that I never did begin a war first with the two Houses of Parliament . . . I do believe that ill instruments between them and me have been the chief cause of all this bloodshed.' And later, 'Those in particular that have been the chief causers of my death . . . I pray God forgive them. I wish that they may repent . . . that they may take the right way to the peace of the Kingdom.'

Venetia tried to ease the raw agony in her back – but to no avail. Her legs were like lead and, despite the fact that she was shivering, her palms were moist with sweat. She clutched her cloak about her and resolutely concentrated on the King's words about the people.

'Truly,' he said, 'I desire their liberty and freedom as much as anybody . . . it was for this that now I am come here. If I would have given way . . . to have all laws changed according to the power of the sword, I needed not . . .' His voice faded and then came back with sudden clarity, 'I am the martyr of the people.'

He spoke a little longer but Venetia could not hear what he said. Then he exchanged a few words with the grotesque figure of the executioner before putting on the cap that would hold his hair clear of his nape. The sense of nightmarish unreality which had gripped her all morning intensified abruptly and the ache in her body sharpened.

The King handed his Garter insignia to the Bishop. He said, 'I go from a corruptible to an incorruptible crown – where no disturbance can be. No disturbance in the world.'

A lump rose in Venetia's throat and tears blurred her eyes.

551

Blinking them away, she watched the King make his final preparations. He looked serene and completely unafraid as he stood for a moment in prayer. And then, with neither haste nor hesitation, he lay down and placed his neck upon the block.

Silence, heavy as a funeral pall, lay over the whole, dreadful scene and Venetia found herself struggling to breathe. A great, voiceless cry was welling up inside her, tearing her apart. Then, in the space of a single heartbeat, the King stretched out his hands and the axe commenced its slicing descent towards the block.

There was an ugly thud like distant thunder. The severed head fell – blood gushed like a conduit – and a deep, terrible groan erupted from the crowd. Her face paper-white, Venetia stood perfectly still, staring as if mesmerised while the executioner held the dripping head aloft for all to see. Then, entirely without warning, she wheeled away and vomited helplessly against the wall.

For several minutes, she was aware only of how ill she felt and of the accuracy of Gabriel's warning. '*It dismantles your stomach*,' he had said; and now she knew what he'd meant. And even though she would not look again at the blood-soaked scaffold, the horror was repeating itself over and over inside her head.

Bracing herself against the wall with her hands Venetia gazed remotely down on the mess at her feet. A little space had cleared around her and the beautiful sable cloak had been carefully moved out of harm's way. She drew a series of deep, shuddering breaths and gradually, in some far-off part of her mind, realised that Isabel was speaking to her.

'Venetia? Venetia, my dear – I had no idea it would affect you this way! We must get you to somewhere you may rest and get warm. There are soldiers coming to clear the streets – I really think we should try to go now, if you feel you can manage it.'

With extreme caution, Venetia detached herself from the wall. She said unevenly, 'I'm sorry. Of course we must go. I'll be well enough in a minute.' She paused, turning carefully so as not to see the scaffold again. 'Have – have they taken the King's body away?'

'They did it immediately. But the place is crawling with people trying to dip their kerchiefs in his blood,' reported Isabel. And then, as Venetia swayed, 'Perhaps Tom should carry you? You're not the only one to have been overcome, you know. Several persons passed out completely.'

Venetia shook her head and allowed Harris to lead her back into King Street amidst the slowly dispersing crowd. A body of tightly-packed cavalry rode smartly down towards them from Charing Cross and another could be seen approaching from Westminster. For a moment, people stared from one to the other, bewildered; then they dived into doorways and down side-turnings to avoid being trampled. Venetia found herself crushed between Isabel and a pilaster; the stone bit into her back and the breath was driven from her lungs. Then, as the horsemen swept by and Isabel was able to step back, a strange spasm convulsed her abdomen. She gasped, and Isabel said anxiously, 'You look dreadful! I doubt there's a chair to be had, but I really don't think you can walk back to Covent Garden.'

'Neither do I,' admitted Venetia shakily.

Her ladyship and her servant exchanged glances. Harris said, 'If your ladyship would be agreeable to it – we could take Mistress Brandon to my mother's house in the Axe Yard till she feels a bit better.'

'Why, of course! How clever of you!' Isabel beamed at him and then turned her attention back to Venetia. 'Tom's mother is my own old nursemaid so she'll know how best to take care of you. Also, the Axe Yard is only a few steps away. What do you think? Will you come?'

There seemed to be a fog inside Venetia's head and she wanted nothing except to lie down. With difficulty, she said, 'Yes. Yes – perhaps that would be best.'

'Good. Then Tom will carry you. No – don't argue. You're as white as a sheet. Tom?'

Venetia allowed Harris to lift her up into his arms and was conscious of instant relief. She shut her eyes and tried to force herself to breathe deeply – but all she could think of was the King's severed head, dangling by its hair in the executioner's muscular hand. Her eyes flew wide. She clasped one hand hard over her mouth and left it there.

She noticed little about the house in the Axe Yard – nor even about Harris's mother – until she had been carried up a flight of stairs and lowered gently into the depths of a leather quilt. The room around her was simply furnished and scrupulously neat and a small fire blazed in the hearth. Venetia frowned slightly. Then a thin, angular face peered down at her, a capable hand smoothed the hair back from her brow and Mistress Harris said placidly, 'Don't worry, my dear. We'll have you feeling better in no time. It's just the shock, see? Nasty things, executions – specially if you've never seen one afore. But it'll pass soon enough. All you need is a bit of a rest.'

Venetia smiled wanly. 'Thank you. You're very kind.'

'Not a bit of it.' Across the bed, the woman's eyes met those of Lady Gillingham and then returned to Venetia. 'Her ladyship tells me you're expecting a baby. Do you know how far along you are?'

'Almost three months.' Awash with sudden fear, Venetia struggled to sit up. 'What are you saying? It *is* just shock, isn't it? That and standing about in the cold for so long? I was perfectly well this morning.'

'And you will be again, dear – mark my words. There's nothing to worry about. Nothing at all.' Mistress Harris pressed her back on to the bed and smiled soothingly. 'But it does no harm to be careful, so I think I'll bring you a special potion of my own. Nothing very strong, of course. Just something to relax you. How does that sound?'

'It sounds precisely what she needs,' said Isabel firmly. And, to Venetia, 'You couldn't be in better hands, you know. Margery cared for me until the day I was married – and I trust her implicitly.'

'I always did my best for you, my lady – and always will,' came the bland reply. 'Now. Perhaps you'd be good enough to loosen Mistress Brandon's laces while I go and fetch my herb cordial? The poor dear looks quite worn out.'

The door closed softly behind her and Isabel advanced on Venetia, smiling. 'Well, shall we see about making you more comfortable? And then later, when you're feeling better, Tom shall fetch my carriage to take you home.'

The thought of Cheapside and Sophy was reassuring.

Venetia said, 'It seems I've already been enough of a nuisance. Perhaps if Tom went for the carriage now, I could—'

'Good heavens, no! I won't hear of it.' Her Ladyship removed Venetia's shoes and then sat on the bed to unfasten the laces of her gown. 'You must take Margery's potion and rest for a little while. The streets will be quite crowded still – and it would be silly to take any more risks.'

'I – yes. I suppose so.' Venetia lay back again. Her back still hurt but less than it had done and the sharp, frightening pain had once more receded into a gnawing ache. Inside her head, however, two thoughts warred persistently with one another; the first was concern for her baby . . . and the second, that the King had been dead for roughly an hour. She said vaguely, 'I suppose the Prince of Wales is King now. Charles II. It sounds so odd.'

'There *is* no King. There is only the Army – and Oliver Cromwell. But don't think of that now. It will only upset you. Tell me instead how Colonel Brandon feels about becoming a father. Doubtless he's pleased and hoping for a son?'

Venetia stared miserably up at the ceiling.

'He doesn't know I'm pregnant. I decided not to tell him until he's released from the Tower.' She paused briefly as the door opened and Mistress Harris reappeared. 'I thought it would make it harder for him – and I didn't want that.'

'Pity,' murmured Isabel. Then, as Venetia looked at her curiously, 'I was just thinking that it might have given him something to look forward to. But I'm sure you know best. And now, dearest – drink Margery's brew. Once your nerves are calm, you'll feel better in no time.'

Venetia accepted the cup from Mistress Harris and took a cautious sip. It had a slightly pungent taste but was not too unpleasant and she was half-tempted to ask what was in it. Then, deciding that it was probably little different from the potions she herself made at home, she raised the cup to her lips and quickly drained it.

Mistress Harris took it back from her and smiled.

'There, my dear. Now lie down and shut your eyes while I take her ladyship downstairs for a glass of cordial.'

Venetia did as she was bidden without argument. It sounded sensible advice; and, much as she wanted to go home, she did not think she had the energy to move. Isabel glided past her and Mistress Harris followed, shutting the door behind her. Venetia turned on to her side and concentrated on emptying her mind.

Against all expectation, she fell asleep . . . and awoke some time later, tightly curled-up and in the grip of fierce, grinding pain. For a few moments, she was utterly disorientated. Then, the pain eased a little and she heaved herself on to one elbow to discover that Isabel was watching her from a chair by the fire. The vivid eyes were bright with an expression which defied interpretation and Venetia said raggedly, 'What's happening? I feel so ill.'

There was a long silence. But finally, in tones of the purest unconcern, her ladyship said, 'You're miscarrying.'

Venetia stared at her, at first blankly and then with gathering dread. 'No,' she whispered, shaking her head; '*No*. I can't be. Help me!'

'Help you?' Smiling, Isabel rose and walked a few steps towards the bed. 'But I already have.'

Vicious claws tore at Venetia's insides. She gasped and folded her arms hard across her body, perspiration beading her brow. 'I – I know. But for God's sake get me a doctor.'

'Why?' Her ladyship looked down on her, smiling. 'It won't do any good. And you can't *really* want to bear the bastard's brat – now can you?'

At about the time Venetia was falling sleep in the Axe Yard, Major Maxwell unlocked the door of Gabriel's cell and said laconically, 'You're out.'

Gabriel's eyes narrowed and for a moment he neither moved nor spoke. Then he said, 'By whose orders?'

'Ostensibly, Ireton's. But I've a suspicion the Lord General may have given him a nudge.'

'And the charges against me?'

Eden shrugged. 'Nothing has been said. But I think you can be fairly sure they won't be resurrected.'

'Provided, of course, that I resign my command.' Smiling sardonically, Gabriel rose and set about fastening his coat. 'If that was all Henry wanted, he needn't have gone to so much trouble. I was going to do it anyway.'

Eden moved away from the door, frowning slightly.

'I suspected you were considering it. But . . .'

'But what? You know my views on what this Army has become.' Gabriel looked up, his gaze austere. 'Since you're not going to tell me, I'd better ask. Is it done?'

'Yes.' Major Maxwell stared down at his hands. 'At around half-past two. They say . . . they say he died well.'

There was a long, yawning silence. Then Gabriel said grimly, 'I daresay he did. It was the only thing left to him. The question remains, however, whether it was either necessary or desirable that he should die at all.'

Eden's mouth twisted wryly but the hazel eyes were bleak. 'I don't know. I can only say that I'd have preferred another way. But if you're asking how I can continue to serve after this . . . the answer is that I must. In the last seven years, the Army has become my life. And even though, thanks to you, I can now face up to my past and pay the occasional visit to Thorne Ash – I'll never go back to it on a permanent basis because it isn't what I want.'

'Then what is it you *do* want?'

'Mostly, to make sure that we haven't gone through all this for nothing.' Eden paused and then said, 'It's different for you. You're too much the soldier to enjoy battles fought with petitions and manifestos – and I suspect you've found something you want more than a well-fought campaign.'

A faint smile dawned. 'You may be sure of it. Does she know about my release?'

'No. I thought you'd like to surprise her.'

'I would.' With increased haste, Gabriel finished tying his sash. 'Did she go to the execution?'

'I imagine so – but she should be home by the time you get there. They cleared the streets within half an hour and there was no trouble so far as I know.'

'Thank God for that.' He crossed the room and extended his hand. 'And thank you, too. If there's any justice in the world, you'll be rewarded with my vacant shoes.'

'Well, of course.' Grinning, Eden gripped his Colonel's fingers. 'I was counting on that!'

Gabriel walked into the Cheapside house at a little after four o'clock and found the parlour occupied only by Sophia. Rising abruptly and forgetting to clutch at her shawls, she said, 'My God! They've let you *go*?'

'As you see,' he smiled. And, as she cast her substantial form against his chest, 'Careful, Sophy! Remember my weakened, half-starved state.'

She peered up at him. 'You look remarkably well to me.'

'Appearances are frequently deceptive. Where's Venetia?'

Her hands fell away from him.

'I don't know. She went to the execution and she hasn't come back yet.'

Gabriel's first reaction was one of acute disappointment. Then, frowning a little, he said, 'Perhaps she's had difficulty finding a chair or a boat to bring her home.'

'Ah yes. That's very likely, isn't it?' Her expression lightening fractionally, Sophia poured two glasses of wine and handed him one of them. 'I hadn't thought of that.'

'So what *were* you thinking of?'

'Trouble amongst the crowd, perhaps?'

'I'm told there wasn't any.'

'Oh. Well, that's a relief.' She lifted her glass and smiled at him. 'To your liberty, my dear – and a speedy return to Brandon Lacey for all of us.'

Gabriel made no move to drink. He said, 'Sophy . . . what's really worrying you?'

The smile lingered but her eyes focused themselves on a point some two feet in front of his face. 'Why, nothing. Now you are free, what could possibly—?'

'This isn't to do with me,' he said crisply. 'It's to do with Venetia, isn't it? And you can take that look off your face. I know it for what it is.'

Sophia's expression changed to one of irritable resignation. 'All right – I'm worried. I admit it. It's almost dark and she should have been home an hour ago – and watching the King die must have been particularly horrible for one who spent years in his household. There. Are you satisfied now?'

'No.' Gabriel set down his glass untouched and surveyed her with an air of mild foreboding. 'You aren't prone to needless anxiety – and you know that Venetia can take care of herself more than adequately. So there's something else, isn't there?'

He was driving her into a corner and – had it not been for the fact that she was becoming increasingly convinced that something was wrong – she would have damned his astuteness. As it was, she stared into her glass and said slowly, 'I wondered if the execution proved too much for her. She could be feeling unwell and have stayed in Covent Garden with her friend, Isabel. Perhaps you should go and see.'

'Perhaps I should,' agreed Gabriel, folding his arms. 'But not until you've told me the rest.'

Sighing, Sophia looked up at him and admitted defeat.

'It's not my business to tell you . . . and if Venetia walks in safe and sound, she'll cut my tongue out. But the truth is that she's almost three months pregnant.'

Gabriel's breath leaked away and it was a moment before he was able to speak. Then, in a voice not quite his own, he said, 'You're *sure*?'

'Perfectly.'

'But why . . . why didn't she tell me?'

'Because she thought you already had enough to worry about,' returned Sophia. And briskly, but still with faint unease, 'Now . . . are you going to Covent Garden or not?'

'Yes!' Shock had been replaced by elation, and a hint of rare colour stained his cheekbones. 'Immediately.'

'Good. Then there's something else you ought to—'

'Let me guess,' grinned Gabriel, sweeping up his hat. 'You don't want Venetia to know that you told me.'

'No. There is that, of course. But—'

'Consider it done.' He strode to the door, threw it open and directed a brief, gleaming glance at her over his shoulder. 'Don't worry, Sophy. Now I'm free, I think you'll find Venetia will have better things to do than fillet and bread you.' And he was gone.

Sophy sat down in the nearest chair and listened to the echo of his feet on the stairs. Then, gazing deep into the fire, she tried to tell herself that she was worrying over nothing.

Four

By the time Gabriel arrived in the *piazza* and found the right house, it was well after five and fully dark. He gave his name to the maidservant who admitted him, demanded to see the Countess and prowled restlessly around the hall until he was shown into the lavishly-furnished salon. Then, finding himself facing a complete stranger, he came to an abrupt halt and said uncertainly, 'I'm sorry. There seems to have been some mistake. I asked for Lady Gillingham.'

Dressed all in black, the dark-haired woman by the hearth stared motionlessly at him for what seemed a very long time. But finally she expelled a long breath and said, 'My daughter-in-law isn't here. I am Susannah Molyneux – the Dowager Countess. No one . . . mentioned me to you?'

Gabriel shook his head and advanced a few steps.

'My acquaintance with your daughter-in-law is very slight. She is actually a friend of—'

'Your wife. Yes. I know. I met her once.'

Now that he was closer, Gabriel could see how very pale she was but was still baffled by the intensity of her expression. He also had a sudden peculiar sensation of familiarity . . . as though she reminded him of someone. Since neither mattered in the slightest however, he pushed them to one side and said, 'Then perhaps you can help me. My wife attended the King's execution with her ladyship and has so far failed to come home. I hoped I might find her here – mistakenly, it seems.'

The dark gaze narrowed slightly.

'I'm afraid so. So far as I'm aware, Isabel left the house this morning with your wife and neither of them have been seen since.' She paused. 'You're anxious about her?'

'I am now,' replied Gabriel tersely. 'It's dark outside and

freezing hard – and I don't know where else to look. Also, I'm becoming increasingly afraid that the experience may have proved too much for her.'

'It was brave of her to go,' murmured the Dowager. 'I myself had less courage. But I'm sure your concern is needless. Your wife struck me as a very resilient woman.'

'She is,' he agreed. And, in response to his growing unease, 'She is. But she's also pregnant.'

The fine-boned face altered subtly and there was another long, enervating silence before Susannah said remotely, 'Does Isabel know?'

It seemed a strange question – but then, since entering this room, a good many things had seemed strange. Gabriel shrugged. 'I wouldn't have thought so – but I can't be sure. Why? Does it matter?'

'It might.' Very slowly, she sat down, gesturing for him to join her. When, with ill-concealed reluctance, he had done so, she said colourlessly, 'My daughter-in-law is ruled by a number of obsessions, Colonel. Amongst the more acceptable of them are a fixation with her dwindling looks and the desire to have a child.'

His brows contracted. 'So?'

'So she may be jealous of one who is both beautiful and soon to become a mother.'

'I daresay she may. But I don't see—' He stopped on a sharply indrawn breath. 'You're saying she may wish Venetia harm? Out of nothing more than simple *jealousy*?'

'Nothing is simple with Isabel. She takes everything to extremes. Her marriage, for example, has been an endless series of affairs. To begin with, she was reasonably discreet; then she stopped caring – both with whom she slept and how many people knew about it. At that point, my . . . my son refused to continue living with her. He's spent the last two years either on our estates in Norfolk or, as now, abroad. Isabel has remained with me. And I've had to watch her persuading her friends that George is a spineless spendthrift with a penchant for his own sex.' She paused and looked directly into his eyes. 'I am telling you this so you will understand that normal rules of behaviour do not apply to Isabel. She is fanatical, unpredictable and a very good liar.

And there have been times when – when I've wondered if she is always wholly sane.'

Gabriel stared at her, his face grim. Although he didn't doubt that she was telling him the truth as she saw it, he still wasn't convinced that Venetia could be in any danger from Isabel Molyneux. On the other hand, he wasn't prepared to take the risk. He said, 'All right. Let us assume that Isabel is jealous and that Venetia is still with her. Have you any idea where they might be?'

'I may be quite wrong – but Isabel's latest lover is the son of her old nursemaid,' supplied Susannah tensely. 'His name is Harris – your wife employed him for a short time. Isabel suggested it. I don't know why. But I *do* know that she often visits his mother – in the Axe Yard.'

Gabriel's eyes narrowed. Then, temporarily dismissing the things which didn't make sense, he said, 'Which house?'

She rose to face him. 'I'll take you there.'

'There's no need. You've been a great help and I'm grateful. But if you'll just give me the direction, I'll—'

The Dowager shook her head and moved gracefully past him towards the door. 'You may need me. And I won't delay you any longer than it takes to saddle a horse. Please wait.'

Irritably, since he plainly had little choice in the matter, Gabriel did as she asked; and less than ten minutes later they were riding side by side along the Strand. She spoke only twice.

'Does your wife love you as much as you love her?'

He glanced round sharply but saw only the pale blur of her face in the darkness. 'Yes. Why do you ask?'

'Because I imagine your union cannot always have been easy. And I wondered if . . . if you were happy.'

His brows rose and he said dryly, 'Since I can only assume that you're referring to my illegitimacy, the answer is that it has very little significance to my life in general – and none at all within my marriage. Satisfied?'

She did not reply and Gabriel, having more important matters on his mind, was glad of it. Then, when at length they turned into the Axe Yard, she pointed to a tall, narrow house on their left and said, 'There.'

Nodding curtly, Gabriel dropped from the saddle, lifted

563

his unwanted companion to the ground and secured both horses. Light showed at the upper windows of the house and, without wasting time, he rapped smartly on the door. Silence. He waited and knocked again, this time more loudly. For a few moments, there was still no response and then bolts were drawn back, the door opened a crack and Tom Harris's face peered out at them. Suspicion sharpened in Gabriel's brain and he said crisply, 'I'm looking for Lady Gillingham and my wife. Where are they?'

'Not here,' muttered Harris and tried to close the door.

Gabriel jammed his foot in the aperture and braced his arm against the oak planks. 'No? Then you won't mind if I come in and take a look, will you?'

'Yes I bloody will!' Harris paused briefly as his gaze took in the Dowager and then, recovering himself, said, 'They're not here, I tell you. And you can't—'

The words ended in a grunt as the door was rammed violently back on him, with Colonel Brandon surging over the threshold in its wake. As Harris struggled to regain his balance, a fist like a battering-ram smashed into his stomach and sent him sprawling against the foot of the stairs.

'Where's my wife?' demanded Gabriel.

'How should I know?' Harris heaved himself up and managed a sly smile. 'Maybe she's got a lover.' And he aimed a savage swipe at Gabriel's head.

Gabriel sidestepped it and brought his linked hands down hard on the back of the other man's neck. Harris bounced off the wall, collided with a crashing blow to the jaw and went down, semi-conscious.

Gabriel seized his collar in a vice-like grip and hauled him upright again. 'Mind your tongue when you speak of my wife – otherwise I'll *really* hurt you!' he snapped. And delivered one final, annihilating punch.

Harris dropped like a stone and Gabriel turned to meet the Dowager's eyes.

'He was lying,' she said. 'I'm sure of it.'

'So am I,' returned Gabriel. And, without stopping to see if she was following, stepped over Harris's recumbent form and took the narrow, worm-eaten stairs two at a time.

When he reached the turn, he found himself staring up

into the shadowed, angular face of a woman who clung to the newel-post above him and hissed, 'Get out! How dare you burst in and attack my son? You've no business here!'

A cold smile curled Gabriel's mouth and he ran swiftly up to join her on the landing. 'Convince me,' he said.

She backed away in front of him and then froze, her eyes moving past his shoulder. 'M-my lady! I didn't expect—'

'Obviously not.' Susannah's voice was hard and cold. 'And if harm comes of this day's work, I promise I'll see both you and your son behind bars for it. Now, tell me where Isabel and Mistress Brandon are.'

The woman's face crumpled. 'I only did what Mistress Isabel said, my lady! I never—'

His patience suddenly snapping, Gabriel lifted her bodily from his path and bore down upon the only door with light showing beneath it. He flung it wide . . . and stopped as suddenly as if he had walked into a wall.

The room smelled of blood and vomit. Isabel Molyneux stood by the hearth, her teeth clenched on her underlip and her eyes full of feral excitement. And before her, curled in a ball amidst the wreckage of the bed, lay Venetia. Her breath was coming in tiny, shallow sobs and beneath the wild tangle of hair, her eyes were closed and her face paper-white. A sharply-etched line of pain creased her brow, her fingers clawed at the bedcover and she was drenched with sweat.

Gabriel's stomach turned cold and his heart struggled to regain its accustomed rhythm.

'Oh my God!' breathed Susannah from behind him.

'Well, well,' purred Isabel. 'Not just the bastard – but the bitch as well. *Isn't* this a merry meeting?'

Oblivious of everything except Venetia, Gabriel reinflated his lungs and took a step towards the bed.

Isabel gave a tinkling laugh. 'She doesn't look quite so pretty now, does she? She was carrying your brat, you know – but it's dead. A pity, isn't it?'

He halted briefly as sick fear and crippling rage ripped through his body. Then he moved on across to Venetia's side and, smoothing back the matted hair from her brow, said raggedly, 'Sweetheart . . . look at me. It's all right. We'll soon have you safe.'

Isabel laughed again but he didn't hear her. Fully dilated and curiously unfocused, Venetia's eyes flickered open. 'Gabriel?' she whispered.

'Yes. I'm here. Don't worry any more.'

Her eyes closed again and tears trickled from beneath her lids. 'Not real. Nothing's real. Only Isabel.'

Susannah advanced with careful calm on her daughter-in-law. 'What have you given her?'

'What makes you think I've given her anything?'

'Because I know your fondness for herbs and potions. So which of them did you use this time?'

A malicious smile curled Isabel's mouth and for a moment there was silence. Then, shrugging, she said, 'Nothing much. Just a couple of doses of savin.'

The Dowager made a tiny, inarticulate sound. Turning his head, Gabriel said sharply, 'What the hell's savin?'

'Juniper,' came the toneless reply. 'Beloved of every old crone who makes her living ridding women of their – their unwanted pregnancies.' And, to Isabel, 'But it's not just savin, is it? What did you mix with it?'

Isabel took a couple of gliding dance-steps past her mother-in-law. 'Why are you wearing mourning? Not, surely, for the King? For we'll have another one fast enough, you know. King Noll and Queen Betty. It has a nice ring, don't you think?'

'No. But I'm sure, if it happens, you'll be the first one to profit,' replied Susannah coldly. And then, 'I'm still waiting to hear what you mixed with the savin.'

No longer smiling, Isabel pivoted in a swirl of silk. 'You shouldn't be here, bitch! And you won't stop me. You *can't*. The brat's dead, I tell you.'

Gabriel erupted to his feet in a blaze of wild anger. 'One more word and I'll kill you. I don't know why you've done this and I haven't time to find out. I'm taking Venetia out of here. And if you're wise, you'll find somewhere to hide. Because if I ever see you again, I'll—'

'Oh, no.' Isabel's hand emerged from the folds of glowing bronze silk, holding a pistol. 'You're not going anywhere. *This* time I'm going to do what Tom and those useless fools he found for me failed to do. I'm going to finish you!'

566

Gabriel froze, more in response to her words than the barrel of the pistol pointing at his chest. There was a long, cavernous silence and then, as if the words didn't make sense, he said distantly, 'It was *you*? The attacks in Moorfields and Whitehall and on the river? All you?'

'What's the matter? Haven't you worked it out yet? Or no. You probably still think it was Ellis.'

Forcing himself to concentrate, Gabriel tried to calculate his chances of reaching Isabel before she could fire. She had her back to the door and, though her voice was becoming noticeably unstable, the pistol remained steady in her hand. Shifting his position slightly so as to shield Venetia and deciding to play for time, he said, 'I know it wasn't Ellis. But I'm not convinced it was you. So why don't you let your mother-in-law take Venetia to a doctor while you tell me about it? After all, you don't want her to die too, do you?'

Her teeth gleamed. 'I don't care either way. And the saintly Susannah has to stay. Her part is yet to come. But I don't mind explaining the other things to you. Why should I? I'm in no hurry. If I'd known how much fun this would be, I'd have done it sooner.' And then, viciously, as the Dowager took a step towards her, 'Stay where you are, bitch – or I'll kill him now. And then he'll never know what we know, will he?'

Susannah stopped dead, the blood draining slowly from her skin. 'What are you talking about?'

'You know . . . But he doesn't, does he? Poor, stupid bastard, he's still waiting to hear how I nearly had him roasted alive and who killed his servant.' The venomous gaze returned to Gabriel. 'And so you shall. Since your lumbering, cretinous brain can't comprehend it without help – so you shall.' She paused, savouring the moment. Then, 'Tom overheard your pathetic scheme to free Francis Langley – and together we worked out how to use it. If Venetia hadn't come out of her room when she did, you'd have burned to death. But she saw Tom on the stairs – so he had to help save you. Don't you find that ironic?'

'Not particularly,' said Gabriel. Behind him, Venetia stirred restlessly and, forcing himself not to look at her, he said coolly, 'And the marksman by the river?'

'Tom again. He's an artist with a crossbow, you know – and he really didn't like your Mr Larkin very much. He nearly poisoned him once. But the general idea that night was that you should drown looking for him.'

Out of the tail of his eye and just out of reach, Gabriel could see Venetia's cloak lying across the foot of the bed. Keeping his eyes fixed on Isabel and making every move carefully casual, he set about edging towards it – aware that, at the same time, the Dowager was inching her way further to Isabel's right. He said, 'Then, since your friendship with Betty Cromwell robs my recent imprisonment of all its mystery, there's only one question left to be asked. Why? Why do you want to kill me? What have I done to make you hate me enough to do this to Venetia?'

Something changed in the smooth, firmly-fleshed face.

'You exist . . . and you shouldn't. So it stands to reason that your child shouldn't exist either. And now it doesn't.'

'Stop it, Isabel!' It was Susannah who spoke, thread-like from the hearth. 'Put the gun down and let Colonel Brandon take his wife home. You don't need them.'

The cornflower gaze travelled briefly towards her and Gabriel slid a few inches nearer the foot of the bed.

'But I do,' smiled Isabel. 'I want to tell him why he's here. You and I may know – but he doesn't. And I think it's time he found out.' Her eyes returned to Gabriel and with calm deliberation, she levelled the pistol at his heart. 'You want to know why I began this? I'll tell you. It's because my sanctimonious mother-in-law – the virtuous lady who has always viewed *me* as a common harlot – had a child outside her marriage bed. A child who was born at a time when her husband had been abroad for almost a year.'

A faint tremor afflicted the hand Gabriel had draped with apparent negligence against the bed-post and, for the only time – save when she had spoken of Wat – he gave Isabel his full attention. 'What are you saying?'

'How stupid are you? I'm saying she's your mother.'

There was another eviscerating silence. Then Gabriel said rigidly, 'How do you know?'

'I went looking for her will and found a bundle of love-letters instead – locked away in a cedarwood box and charmingly tied with blue ribbon. They were from a Yorkshireman called Robert . . . and they told of a son hidden away in Shoreditch. A son whose name was Gabriel.'

Gabriel drew a long unsteady breath. Then he looked across at Susannah and, in a voice that was as impervious as iron discipline could make it, said, 'Is it true?'

She had no more colour to lose and she stared down at the earthenware wine-jug whose rim lay just beneath her fingers on the table beside her. 'Yes . . . yes, it's true.'

'And you knew who I was when we met this evening?'

'Yes.'

'I see.' The grey eyes surveyed her for a moment more, before turning back to Isabel. 'And what can the facts of my parentage possibly matter to you?'

'What do you think?' Without damaging her aim, Isabel used her left hand to move the firing mechanism from half to full cock and then clamped her fingers round her right wrist. 'She has a personal fortune and I mean George to have it. I may despise him but he's still my husband and if he is rich, then so am I. But once I'd stumbled across you I knew that one day she would, too. And that was when I decided to kill you.'

'Why?' asked Gabriel. 'If all you wanted was the money, there were other ways to make sure of it.'

'Of course.' She smiled again, her eyes glittering with anticipation. 'I could have poisoned her before she changed her will or threatened to expose her secret if she didn't do as I said. I thought of both – but neither would have hurt the bitch as much as killing you. And now it's even better . . . because she can stand there and watch you die.'

Gabriel let his arm drop to his side, hoping the Dowager would use the moment to grab the jug. Then, with all the contempt he could muster, he said, 'Don't count on it. It will take more than a mad whore like you.' And, snatching up the cloak, sent it furling wildly towards her.

In the instant of confusion which followed, Gabriel launched himself across the room. Isabel stepped back, trying to deflect the cloak with her left hand and the jug flew past her head. Then there was a sudden deafening report. Red-hot pain seared the upper part of Gabriel's left arm and he checked briefly before continuing to close in on her, his expression one of cold, grim purpose.

'Just a scratch,' he said blandly. 'Too bad.'

Her eyes those of a rabid animal, she backed away on to the landing, holding the empty pistol before her like a club. Staring upwards with his mother from the foot of the stairs, Tom Harris called sharply to her . . . but Gabriel was too close for Isabel to risk turning to look. Her mouth twisted and she said, 'You think I'm finished, you bastard? I'm not!' And, with all the force at her command, she swung the butt of the pistol hard at the side of his head.

Gabriel ducked and, borne on by her own momentum, Isabel crashed awkwardly against the landing balustrade. There was an ominous sound of splintering wood and for a moment she teetered helplessly, her hands clawing at the air, her face contorted with a mixture of hatred and surprise. Then, with a final groan, the rotting wood parted beneath her weight and she fell backwards into space . . . plummeting down into the hall to hit the flagstoned floor with a sickening crack.

Margery Harris screamed and her son stared disbelievingly down on the twisted body. The smashed head lay in a dark, slowly spreading pool and the vivid blue eyes stared sightlessly upwards to where Susannah stood, frozen with shock beside Gabriel. Then, lifting his bruised face to the harsh, impenetrable one above him, Harris said unevenly, 'You'll regret that. But not for long. Come down!'

'No! No more!' His mother cast herself hysterically upon him. 'It's over. Can't you see? She's dead, and I'm sorry but she brought it on herself. So go now. Save yourself!'

He pushed her away from him so violently that she cannoned into the wall. 'This is my business! Stay out of it or it'll be the worse for you.' And again to Gabriel, 'Come down.'

A white shade bracketing his mouth and breathing rather fast, Gabriel said, 'I intend to.' And he ran swiftly down the stairs towards the long, narrow blade glimmering in Harris's hand.

Unarmed, Gabriel had only one chance. Without either slackening his pace or giving any indication of his intent, he took a sort of flying dive from the fourth step. The tip of the blade grazed his neck; then he managed to grasp the hand that held it and Harris went down like a log beneath him.

Their eyes met and Gabriel smiled coldly. Winded by the impact but otherwise unhurt, Harris clung to the knife with both hands and tried to roll over. With a subtle shift of his position, Gabriel jammed one knee into his groin and started exerting a steady, grinding pressure on his wrist.

Slowly, very slowly, the knife started to turn. And when at length Gabriel achieved precisely the angle he needed, he joined his left hand to his right and said clearly, 'This is for Wat.' Then he drove the thin blade inexorably down into the base of the other man's throat.

Harris's eyes bulged and he made a long, unpleasant gurgling sound before his head fell back, blood pumping from his open mouth. Crouched cowering by the wall, his mother relapsed into a series of tearing, hysterical sobs. Ignoring her, Gabriel came stiffly to his feet; and finally, with only the merest suggestion of a pause, turned back up the stairs towards the woman he had been told was his mother.

For a moment, he stared at her out of bitter frowning eyes. Then he said gratingly, 'Messy but effective. And now perhaps we can finally get Venetia out of this hell-hole.'

Susannah swallowed hard. 'My house is probably closest and it is at your disposal.'

He hesitated and then nodded curtly. It was not what he wanted, but Venetia was in no state to be carried all the way back to Cheapside.

The Dowager watched him wrap Venetia as warmly as he could and carry her past the bodies of Isabel and Harris as though they didn't exist. Then she helped him with the difficult business of getting up into the saddle and rode mutely beside him back to the *piazza*.

By the time they got there, Venetia was burning with fever and muttering incoherently. Opening his mouth for the first time since leaving the Axe Yard, Gabriel demanded that a doctor be sent for and then reluctantly allowed himself to be banished while the Dowager and her maid gently cleansed Venetia's body and put her to bed.

As yet incapable of proper thought but dimly aware that

Sophia must be beside herself with worry, Gabriel scribbled a brief note and told her ladyship's majordomo to have it conveyed to Cheapside. Then he prowled back and forth outside Venetia's door until he was allowed back inside.

She was tossing restlessly to and fro, her skin hot and dry and her eyes glowing with unnatural brilliance. Summoning the shreds of self-control which were all the last six, mind-numbing hours had left him, Gabriel held her hand hard between his own and tried to recall her with his voice. He had known that he loved her – but not, until now, how much. And fear that she might die was the only recognisable emotion he had left.

The physician came, confirmed that Mistress Brandon had suffered a miscarriage, shook his head over her present condition and prepared to bleed her. Promptly losing his temper, Gabriel consigned both him and his remedies to perdition and threw him out. Then, slamming the door shut, he leaned against it for a moment and, in a curiously muffled voice, said, 'Was I right or wrong? Tell me.'

'You were right,' said Susannah flatly. 'She's already weak enough. And if you're willing to let me try, I think we can do better than purges, blisters and leeches.'

He turned slowly to look at her. There were shadows around her eyes that had not been there earlier and her face was white and pinched. Drawing a long, steadying breath, he said, 'I . . . would be grateful.'

'Don't be. I owe you that much at least.' And, without waiting for his response, she walked quickly from the room.

She returned presently with a mixture of cowslip, sage and tormentil and, having sought Gabriel's help in persuading Venetia to swallow it, said prosaically, 'There will be no change for some time yet, so I'll sit with her while you go downstairs and let my maid see to your arm. It may be just a flesh wound but it ought to be cleaned. And I'm sure you'd prefer to be ministered to by someone other than myself – just as I'd prefer you not to argue.'

Gabriel stood up. Every bone and muscle in his body felt as if it had been savagely beaten. 'Argue?' he said dryly. 'I haven't the strength.'

Below in the parlour, someone had laid out food and wine

and the Dowager's maid hovered beside bowl, cloths and salve. Feeling suddenly rather sick, Gabriel told her to go away and take the damned food with her. Then he pulled off his coat, rolled up his shirt-sleeve and proceeded to deal with the powder-blackened gash in his arm.

Somewhere close by, a church clock struck eleven. Gabriel kept his mind carefully empty and worked fast. Then, having completed his handiwork, he shrugged his coat back on and was just about to go back upstairs when there was a sudden, thunderous knocking at the front door – immediately followed by Mr Morrell's voice curtly demanding his whereabouts. Swearing under his breath, Gabriel strode out into the hall intending to send his half-brother the same way as the doctor – only to discover that Jack wasn't alone. Sophia was with him. And the mere sight of her brought such indescribable relief that Gabriel heard himself saying involuntarily, 'Oh God, Sophy! I'm so glad you're here.'

'Mr Morrell was with me when your note came, so naturally we set out right away,' she responded, crossing towards him. And then stopped, paralysed by the pallor of his face and shock lingering behind his eyes.

Jack said, 'You look bloody awful. What the hell's happened? And how's Venetia?'

Gabriel frowned down at his hands.

'She . . . lost the baby. And now she has a fever.'

'Can I see her?' asked Sophia.

'Of course. I'll take you up.' He glanced vaguely at Jack. 'The parlour's there, if you want to wait. But since I don't know how long I'll be—'

'I'll wait anyway,' cut in Jack curtly.

'As you wish. Just don't count on hearing the full story. It would choke me.' And he led Sophia away upstairs.

The Dowager looked up from bathing Venetia's brow with avender water – and slowly froze.

'*Sophy?*' she said faintly.

Sophia faced her unsmilingly. 'Hello, Susannah.'

Staring blankly from one to the other of them, Gabriel said oddly, 'You *know* each other?'

'We've . . . met,' responded the Dowager. And still ooking at Sophia, 'You – you never told him. Why?'

'He never asked,' came the flat reply. 'And, truth to tell, until this moment I was never completely sure.'

There was a long, airless pause broken only by Venetia's restless murmurings. Feeling as though he was sinking deeper and deeper into a quagmire of deceit, Gabriel gazed rather desperately across at her; and then, realising that he could either get out or throw up where he stood, spun on his heel and left the room without a word.

Sophia shivered slightly and, seeing it, the Dowager said remotely, 'He will forgive you. I envy you that.'

'Why?' Sophia looked down at Venetia. 'You don't know him.'

'No. And after tonight, I never will.' A strange tremor passed over the once-beautiful face. 'He can scarcely bring himself to look at me. And who can blame him?'

Sophia reached down to clasp Venetia's hand.

'Perhaps,' she suggested reflectively, 'it might help if you told me about it?'

With his stomach once more under control, Gabriel forced himself to go back downstairs to Jack. He found him staring broodingly into an untouched glass of wine and, without giving him chance to speak, said rapidly, 'Listen carefully – for I can neither repeat nor discuss this. My would-be assassin was Isabel Molyneux – now, happily, deceased. It's thanks to her that my child will never be born and my wife is desperately ill upstairs. The so-called reason for this whole nightmare is that the Dowager Countess of Gillingham is apparently my anonymous, long-lost mother.' He paused, a pulse hammering erratically in his jaw. 'And if you ask a single question or attempt to uncover the details I will very probably hit you.'

Incredulity warring with concern, Jack said simply, 'Christ, Gabriel – if it will make you feel better, you're welcome.'

For a long moment Gabriel remained perfectly still. Then, dropping abruptly into the nearest chair, he drove his face into his hands and said, 'These last hours have been the worst of my life. At least – I hope they have. Because I'm not sure . . . I'm not sure I can take much more. If anything happens to Venetia, I don't know how I'll bear it.'

Since there was nothing he could do to help, Jack eventually took himself back through the night to Shoreditch, promising to return on the morrow; but Sophia stayed and, insisting that the Dowager got some sleep, shared the night's vigil with Gabriel. They spoke very little and only when necessary. Then, just as dawn was breaking, Gabriel said tonelessly, 'She's no better, is she?'

'No.' Across the bed, Sophia's eyes met his and held them. 'No. But I don't think she's any worse either, so there's no need to despair. She's young and strong – and there are other remedies we might try.'

'You're saying it's a matter of luck? Forgive me if I'm not comforted!' he snapped, wheeling away to the window. And then, wearily, 'Oh hell! That was unfair. I'm sorry.'

'It's all right. I understand.'

Gabriel continued staring blindly down into the deserted square. 'The Dowager told you what happened?'

'Yes,' said Sophia. And waited.

It was a long time before he spoke again and, when he did, his voice was raw with strain. 'You knew she was my mother, didn't you? You knew it all along. So why didn't you tell me? Why did you let me come here not knowing?'

Frowning slightly, Sophia smoothed back Venetia's hair and reached again for the lavender water. She said carefully, 'I tried to tell you as you were leaving – but it's not an easy thing to blurt out in a hurry. Perhaps I should have approached the subject months ago . . . but I was afraid it might do more harm than good. You never mentioned your mother, you see. And I could quite easily have been wrong.'

Gabriel turned slowly. 'But you weren't.'

'No.' She hesitated and met his eyes. 'I was too young to see Susannah often or know her well – and Robert never ever spoke of her. But she had the kind of face one always remembered and, at the age of five, you looked just like her. As, in a way, you still do.'

He frowned as if trying to make sense of it. Then he said abruptly, 'If that's really all you had to go on – I suppose I'd better acquit you, hadn't I? But I'd be grateful if you'd inform the Dowager Countess that I'm by no means ready to discuss this with her. Nor, quite possibly, will I ever be. But that shouldn't be any hardship. We've been strangers for thirty-five years, after all, so why change it now?'

Sophia's gaze grew unusually direct.

'Because of the way you found out. You have to come to terms with what happened last night so you can put it behind you. And Susannah is the only one who can help you do it – because she is suffering too.'

There was another long silence; but eventually Gabriel said indifferently, 'You may be right. But while Venetia lies there fighting for her life, you'll have to pardon me if I say I really don't give a tinker's curse.'

Five

Dawn became day and the hours dragged by on leaden feet. The Dowager re-appeared with a different potion for Venetia to swallow and Sophy bullied Gabriel into eating some bread and meat before taking herself off to lie down for an hour. Shortly after ten, Jack arrived with Annis and Bryony in tow and, a little later, Major Maxwell also turned up. The women conferred anxiously together, fed Venetia calves' foot jelly and piled the bed high with blankets. Eden and Jack exchanged a few hurried words with Sophia and then, taking the Dowager's coach, set off for the Axe Yard.

Of Margery Harris, there was no sign . . . but the bodies of Tom and Isabel still lay where Gabriel had left them. Barring a few small adjustments, Jack and Eden left the first where it was, and carried the other back to the *piazza*, wrapped in a quilt. Then Eden went off to report a possible suicide to the appropriate authorities.

While Susannah dealt with the curiosity of her servants and left Isabel's body to be prepared for burial, Gabriel remained all day at Venetia's side, talking himself hoarse out of the conviction that sooner or later she would hear him. And finally, just when the fever seemed to be at its peak and he was beginning to lose all hope, he saw the first small signs of change. For perhaps a minute he sat very still, struggling to breathe. Then, too physically and mentally drained to retain any kind of self-control, he leaned his face against his arms and wept.

A short time later Sophy entered the room and immediately saw what he had seen; the first, tiny beads of moisture which said that the fever had finally broken. By then, Venetia was sleeping peacefully – as was Gabriel. Sophia took a few minutes to master her own relief. Then she brushed the tears from her eyes and went downstairs to tell the others.

Gabriel slept for about an hour and awoke to find Annis sitting quietly by the hearth. He said, 'Did I imagine it? She *is* going to be all right, isn't she?'

'Absolutely,' replied Annis calmly, rising to bring him wine from the jug at her side. 'See for yourself. The fever's broken and her colour is returning to normal.'

'Thank God!' He pressed the heels of his hands over his bloodshot eyes. 'Thank God. Does Sophy know?'

'Everyone knows, but they'll stay away till you call. Meanwhile, there's a draught on the table for when Venetia wakes – and a slice of beef and oyster pie for yourself.' Annis smiled suddenly. 'There is also water and a razor, which I suggest you use if you want your wife to recognise you.' Then she was gone.

He shaved, drank the wine and managed to swallow a few mouthfuls of food. Then, feeling marginally better, he settled down to wait; and finally, at a little after seven, Venetia stirred and slowly opened her eyes.

'Welcome back,' said Gabriel, smiling.

A faint quiver of response touched her mouth and then was gone. Recollection awoke and the violet eyes stared back at him, stricken with voiceless anguish, until finally she whispered, 'I lost the baby, didn't I?'

A knife twisted inside his chest and his fingers tightened on hers. 'Yes, sweetheart. I'm afraid so.'

Tears drowned her eyes, gathered on her lashes and spilled down her cheeks. 'I'm sorry. I'm so sorry . . . I should have listened to you. If – if I'd stayed away from the execution, everything would still – would still—' She stopped and, turning her face into the pillow, gave way to helpless tearing sobs.

Gabriel gathered her into his arms and held her close, stroking her hair. Then, when the sobs grew quieter and he was sure of keeping his own voice level, he said, 'Sweetheart, don't. It wasn't your fault. You couldn't have known what would happen. No one could. And there's more to all this than I suspect you can remember. I'm not suggesting that it can . . . that it can make up for the baby. Nothing could do that. But you may find that it helps a little.'

Venetia drew a long shuddering breath. 'Tell me.'

'When you're stronger.' He reached for the potion Annis had left and, twining his hand in her hair, gently tilted her head back so he could look at her. 'Drink this.'

Ignoring the cup, she stared into his face and saw her own grief mirrored over and over. Then, because there were no words for what she felt, she did as he asked and drank. Gabriel set the cup down and gathered her back against his shoulder. For a time she seemed to doze and then she said shakily, 'Tell me what happened. All I remember is the pain . . . and Isabel smiling . . . and dreaming you were there. But nothing made sense. It – it still doesn't. And if you talk to me, I may manage not to think until – until I can bear it better.'

Gabriel wasn't sure he was ready for this, or, more importantly, capable of it. But because Venetia needed him and because one had to start somewhere, he summoned whatever resources he had left and used them as well as he could. Keeping his tone utterly matter-of-fact and his arms close about her, he told her everything – from the moment of his release from the Tower to Sophy's meeting with the Dowager. And, at the end of it all, he said flatly, 'So there you have it. This whole vicious mess has been brought about by . . by an accident of birth and a mad woman. And though it's hard, as yet, to find any satisfaction in the fact – we can at least be assured of one thing. It's over.'

Venetia shifted slightly so that she could look up at him. 'And . . . and your mother?'

For the first time, the grey gaze grew shuttered and opaque. Then, 'Sufficient unto the day is the evil thereof,' said Gabriel neutrally. 'But if anyone expects me to fall on her neck, they'll be disappointed.'

While Venetia slowly recovered her strength amidst a constant procession of visitors and tried to conceal the fact that the baby's loss remained like an open wound, Gabriel formally resigned his commission and continued treating the Dowager as if she was nothing more than his temporary hostess. Sophia anxiously watched all three of them, waiting for the first fissures to appear . . . and was extremely relieved when Isabel Molyneux's body left Covent Garden for discreet burial.

Outside the *piazza*, the first week of February passed in bitter cold and sullen bewilderment as ordinary men and women struggled to come to terms with the enormity of what had been done at Whitehall. And, far away across the Tweed, the Scots demonstrated both their anger and their intent by promptly proclaiming King Charles II.

On the 6th, the Commons resolved to abolish the House of Lords and Venetia came downstairs for the first time; on the 7th, the monarchy went the same way as the peers and Gabriel started making plans for returning to Brandon Lacey; and on the 8th, King Charles the Martyr was laid to rest at Windsor . . . and, with a little help from Sophia, the Dowager finally managed to isolate the frigidly courteous man who was her son.

Without giving him time to either speak or leave the room, she said baldly, 'We have to talk.'

'*We*?' asked Gabriel aridly. 'Speaking for myself, I can't think of anything I wish to say.'

'But you'll listen?'

He shrugged. 'If I must. But only up to a point.'

The warning was clear. Nodding her acceptance of it, Susannah sat down facing him and clasped her hands tight in her lap. Then she said, 'I don't know how much Robert told you . . . but I think you ought to be aware that you were not the – the consequence of a tawdry little affair. We loved each other very much. Had it been possible, we would have married; since it wasn't, we took what happiness we could.'

Gabriel surveyed her over folded arms. 'And where did your husband fit into this? Or is that a silly question?'

She flushed slightly but did not look away.

'My marriage to Gervase was an alliance of money and land . . . and when he wasn't at Court amusing the late King's father, he was discovering every vice known to Europe – and inventing a few new ones. But it wouldn't have mattered if he'd been a paragon of virtue. One can't love to order. And I loved Robert from the day we met. I still do.'

'And is that supposed to make everything all right?'

'No. Just to help you understand.' She stared down at her hands for a moment and then said, 'I know from Robert's last letter how your marriage came about. So imagine for a moment that Venetia had married Ellis – and then you had met and fallen in love. Could you have walked away from her?'

'Probably not,' came the crisp reply. 'But that's not the question at issue, is it? Surely the point is whether, in similar circumstances, I'd permit Venetia to give birth to my child in secret and then send it to be fostered so she and I could go on as if nothing had happened. And the answer to *that*, of course, is that I wouldn't.'

There was a long, suffocating silence before Susannah said haltingly, 'You have every right to be bitter. But—'

'It's generous of you to recognise it. Do I also have every right to ask why – despite both your undying passion and your pregnancy – you and Sir Robert didn't run away together? Or why, having chosen respectability rather than love, the pair of you decided that it was enough to inform me of one half my parentage but not the other?'

Her voice tight with strain, Susannah said, 'We didn't run away together because of Robert's scruples about condemning me to social leprosy in this life and hell in the hereafter. It may not sound much – but it's the way it was. As for our decision not to tell you, it was less to do with you yourself than the fact that, if you knew, the Morrells would know too. And if either my family or that of my husband ever discovered the truth, Robert's life would not have been worth a groat – nor, quite possibly, yours either.'

Gabriel's face remained utterly impervious.

'You're asking me to believe it was all done for my own good? Very well. I'll try. But what is all this supposed to lead to? Absolution?'

'No,' she sighed. 'No. That's too much to expect. But if you think we took the easy way out or that a day ever went by when I didn't think of you, you're wrong. And Robert – Robert faced other difficulties altogether. So don't think . . .

don't think we didn't care. We did. And despite all appearances to the contrary, we actually believed that we were doing our best.'

'Perhaps you did. And perhaps – at the time – you were. But it hasn't worked out very well, has it? For if I'd known the facts, it's just possible that the catalogue of disasters which finally culminated in the Axe Yard might never have happened. And my child might still be alive.'

A shiver passed over the still face. 'I know. And you can't possibly blame me any more than I blame myself.'

Gabriel opened his mouth to tell her not to be too sure . . . and then abruptly recognised the injustice of it.

She couldn't have known where her long silence would ultimately lead – any more than *he* could be sure things would have been different if she'd broken it. Neither could he honestly say that his life had been blighted by her anonymity, because the truth was that he hadn't allowed it to be. At the age of fifteen, he'd told himself that a man shaped his own destiny; that he didn't need to know who he *was* – only who he wished to *become*. And he'd spent the last twenty years proving it to be true. Consequently, there was no reason why discovery should prove any more destructive than ignorance. It was simply a matter, as Sophia had said, of facing up to it in order to put it aside.

Drawing a long, steadying breath, he said slowly, 'I'm sorry. For obvious reasons, I'm not coping with this as well as I might . . . and my last remark was less than fair. You couldn't have known what Isabel would do. And there is no guarantee that matters would have worked out any differently even if I'd known of our – our relationship. So don't blame yourself. It wasn't your fault.'

For perhaps half a minute the dark eyes, so like his own, stared frozenly back at him. Then Susannah said faintly, 'You . . . are generous.'

'Not especially. I'm just trying to regain my sense of proportion. And I don't suppose this situation is any easier for you than it is for me.'

'No. But I had one advantage. I knew who you were. And I don't think I'll ever forgive myself for allowing you to find out in – in such a way.'

'I could have done without it,' agreed Gabriel dryly. 'But what's done is done – and we are left with certain basic facts. You are my mother; but. in every sense that matters, we are strangers. And for the sake of your son, the Earl, it might be best to leave it that way.'

Susannah said carefully, 'Is that what you want?'

'I don't know. Suddenly acquiring a mother at the advanced age of thirty-five takes a little getting used to; and, as yet, the best I can manage is acceptance. I'm sorry if that sounds hard. But right now, I'm primarily concerned with Venetia's well-being – which is why I want to take her home so we can put all this behind us and begin our lives afresh.'

'I see. When will you leave?'

'As soon as she feels fit enough to make the journey.'

It was eminently reasonable but she wasn't ready to lose him again completely. She said, wistfully, 'I won't ask when we'll meet again. But . . . will you write to me sometimes?'

There was a long pause and then, for the first time, Gabriel smiled at her. 'Why not? It's probably as good a beginning as any.'

On February 10th, the Justiciary swung into action again for the trials of the Duke of Hamilton and my lords Norwich, Capel and Holland. And on the same day – in spite of Bryony's pleas that they stay to attend her wedding at the end of the month, Gabriel, Venetia and Sophia left for Brandon Lacey.

The journey took almost two weeks and was the worst that any of them could remember. Snow clogged the roads in various places, alternately slowing their progress or halting it completely and forcing Gabriel to expend a good deal of energy wielding a shovel. Sophia's joints protested vigorously against the cold and, although she was physically recovered, Venetia's spirit remained locked in some ice-bound retreat where not even Gabriel could reach it.

By the time they arrived at Brandon Lacey, all three were exhausted. As soon as they had eaten supper, Sophia took herself off, yawning, to her bed. And, looking thoughtfully at his wife's remote face, Gabriel said quietly, 'I am going to leave you to sleep alone tonight.'

The amethyst eyes widened a little. 'Why?'

'Because I suspect that – for a time, at least – it's what you want.' Each night of the journey, he had wrapped her in steady, passionless arms and tried to get her to share her grief with him, only to find himself continually shut out. 'Am I wrong?'

'I – I don't know.'

Her answer hurt but he hid it beneath a slightly crooked smile. 'Then perhaps I should give you the chance to find out. My door is always open; all you have to do is walk through it when you feel ready. But until then, and so I don't make things worse by saying something crass, I'm going to give you time to deal with this in your own way.'

Venetia's fingers whitened on the stem of her wine-cup and she said painfully, 'You are never crass. And this is my fault – not yours. But I don't know how to mend it.'

'By talking to me.'

'I *can't*. I – I don't know how.'

'Not yet, perhaps. But you will. And, in the meantime, I am quite prepared to wait.'

Over the next few days, life settled back into something approaching its usual rhythm. Gabriel visited the tenants and toured the estate with Dick Carter, discussing crop rotation, pasturage and the estate's potential yield of flax and wool for the coming year. Sophia spent hours with her beloved menagerie and found time to summon a stonemason to repair the dovecot. Venetia conducted a minute examination of the household accounts, plunged herself into an orgy of early spring-cleaning – and successfully avoided thinking.

Riding over from Ford Edge through the snow, Phoebe found her sister polite but uncommunicative. She learned the reasons for it from Gabriel, received a stern warning not to indulge her passion for probing and ended up saying doubtfully, 'Very well – if that's what you want. But I don't think it's the answer.'

'Then what would you suggest?' asked Gabriel curtly.

'Forcing her to face up to it? I can't. In the space of an afternoon, she witnessed the King's head being struck from his body, was trapped alone and in pain with a taunting she-devil and had her child murdered in her womb. I don't know how that feels – and neither do you. But since it's obvious she's been through quite enough already, I'm damned if I'm going to risk adding to it.'

Phoebe sighed. 'All right. I take your point. But perhaps you should at least try to stop her wallowing in *Eikon Basilike*.'

'I beg your pardon?'

'*Eikon Basilike*.' she repeated obligingly. 'They're calling it the King's Book – although he didn't write it. It's an account of his tribulations, mixed with prayers and meditations – and, by all accounts, it's selling quicker than it can be printed. Venetia bought a copy from the carrier. Didn't you know?'

'No,' said Gabriel wearily. 'I didn't.' He paused, frowning a little. 'Perhaps you could ask her to lend it to you?'

'My thoughts exactly,' nodded Phoebe. And then, eyeing him critically, 'You look as tense as a lute-string, you know. How long do you think you'll go on without snapping?'

He smiled wryly and took his time about answering. Then, shrugging, 'As long as I have to,' he said.

Without appearing to do so, Sophia kept a shrewd eye on Venetia's lack of progress and the effect it was beginning to have on Gabriel. And when, after they had been home for a week, she walked past the open door of the bookroom and glimpsed Gabriel sitting absolutely rigid, with his eyes pressed against the heels of his hands, she decided it was time to interfere.

She found Venetia in the linen-room and, shutting the door behind her, said quietly, 'I want you to listen to me. No one expects you to get over this easily. But it's been a month now . . . and there are a few things I think you should start considering.'

Venetia froze for an instant and then turned the page of her inventory with unsteady fingers. 'Such as?'

'Such as the fact that – terrible as your loss is – it could have been worse. You could have lost Gabriel too. Have you forgotten that?'

The stark violet eyes turned slowly towards her.

'No. Of – of course I haven't.'

'Then perhaps you might try showing it,' said Sophia. 'He's safe at your side and has every intention of remaining there. That is something to be grateful for, isn't it? And, in the fullness of time, there will be other babies.'

Venetia's breath snarled in her throat.

'I know,' she whispered. 'I *know*. But – but not *that* one. And I wanted it so much.'

Sophia hesitated briefly and came to the conclusion that there was nothing to be gained by stopping now.

'So did Gabriel . . . and he is as devastated as you are. The only difference is, being Gabriel, he will suffer in silence and go on presenting a brave face until he cracks.' She paused, watching her words sink in, and then said, 'You saw what Wat's death did to him – and you helped him cope. You were the only one who could. *Now* I don't believe you've even offered him the chance to discuss how he feels about his mother.'

Venetia swallowed and frowned down at her hands. 'No.'

'Then it's time you did. He's strong, Venetia, but he's not a machine. And he needs you to share your pain with him so he can share his with you. Think about it.'

For a long time after Sophia had gone, Venetia remained where she was, staring blindly at the closed door. At first, she merely felt dazed and empty – exactly as she had done for the last month. Then, gradually, the first dim filterings of remembrance returned . . . and, with them, anguish. Sobs tore at her throat and, folding her arms hard across her chest, she crumpled slowly amidst the sheets and bolster-slips and howled.

She cried until there were no tears left and she was exhausted. Then, almost without realising it, she began tentatively exploring the things that Sophia had said; and, in doing so, gradually found that part of herself which she had thought lost.

When Venetia's maid appeared to say that her mistress would not be coming down to supper, Sophia's heart sank. It was not the first time since their return that Venetia had chosen to take a tray in her room rather than sit at table with them, but on this particular night Sophia had hoped for better things –

586

and was also afraid she had done more harm than good. Gabriel, however, merely accepted his wife's defection without comment and addressed himself with more thoroughness than was usual to the wine-bottle.

He remained in the parlour long after Sophia had gone to bed, staring bleakly into the fire and drinking steadily. By the time he decided he'd had sufficient to stop him lying awake thinking, it was close on midnight and he was more than a little cupshot. Concentrating hard, he climbed the stairs and, as on all the other nights, made himself turn right to his own room instead of left to Venetia's. Then, throwing open his door with a sort of suppressed violence, he stepped over the threshold and stopped dead.

Standing in a pool of light by the fire, with her hair falling loose over her chamber-robe and a faintly apprehensive question in her eyes, was Venetia. Unprepared – both for her presence and what it did to him – Gabriel stood very still, holding fast to the door-latch. Finally, she said simply, 'Your door was open – and I came through it.'

With immense caution, he reinflated his lungs.

'I see,' he replied. And then, because floating somewhere inside the wine-haze was the vague idea that it mattered, 'Why?'

'To say I'm sorry it's taken me so long. And to talk . . . if that's what you still want.'

There was a long, reflective silence. Then he said carefully, 'It's what I want. But . . . there's a problem.'

She half-thought she detected the beginnings of a smile but was afraid to rely on it. 'There is?'

'Yes. You see . . . I'm not entirely sober. In fact, you might even say I'm rather drunk.'

Ludicrously, it was the very last thing she had expected. Gabriel never got drunk – or so she'd thought. She said uncertainly, 'Is that a joke?'

'No. Just lam-lamentable timing on somebody's part,' came the slightly slurred reply. Then, conversationally, 'Are you going to come over here – or what?'

Against all expectation, Venetia discovered an impulse to laugh. 'Why? Are you afraid you'll fall over?'

A glinting smile dawned. 'It's a possibility.'

This time she did laugh – and crossed the room towards him. Gabriel waited until she was within reach and then, pushing the door shut, caught her in his arms.

'About time too,' he grumbled. And, twining his fingers in her hair, sought her mouth like a man parched by thirst.

They did not talk that night – or not about the things that mattered . . . and neither did they make love. There was plenty of time, they now knew, for both; and these first hours were for nothing more than the simple, healing pleasure of being together.

They slept, eventually, and awoke slowly when the day was well advanced to lie lazily smiling at each other. Then, turning her mouth against the warm skin of his shoulder, Venetia murmured, 'I forgive you for last night. But if you now tell me you have a headache, I may not be so lenient.'

Gabriel remained perfectly still and it was a moment before he replied. 'What headache?'

A tiny gurgle of something that might have been laughter escaped her and she moved closer, her hand travelling languorously down over his ribs and beyond. His breath caught, but still he made no move to touch her and, lifting her head, she peered provocatively at him through her hair.

'There's no hurry. You can join in whenever you want.'

The grey eyes looked impenetrably back at her.

'Are you sure this is a good idea?'

'Aren't you?'

Gabriel's fingers trapped her exploring hand and stilled it. He said, expressionlessly, 'Isn't it a bit too soon?'

Her brows rose. 'You'd rather wait another month or so?'

'No. But—'

'Neither would I.' She slid her foot temptingly up his calf and waited. Then, when he neither kissed her nor released her hand, she said rapidly, 'It's all right. Do you think I'd be doing my damnedest to seduce you if it wasn't?'

'You're sure?'

'I'm sure. Why must you go on about it?'

There was a pause. Then, 'The first rule of warfare,' returned Gabriel, 'is good intelligence.' In one swift, fluid movement, he pinned her beneath him and grinned. 'The second is never to leave your flank exposed.'

'Oh. Well, judging by the scar you got at Breda, you'd know all about that, wouldn't you?'

Laughter flared in his face and then was gone. His mouth brushed hers with familiar, tantalising lightness and his hands drifted over the curves of her body. Her breathing shortened and she tried to pull him closer. As eager as she but better at concealing it, Gabriel lifted his head and looked down at her. 'Did I ever tell you about Breda?'

'No. No . . . and I'm sorry I mentioned it.'

'How sorry?'

'Very! Are you going to kiss me or not?'

'I haven't decided.' He made a small but significant shift in his position and watched her eyes darken. 'You're a wanton hussy. You know that, don't you?'

'Of course,' came the ragged reply. Then, with increased difficulty, 'But whose fault is that?'

In their own good time, they went down hand-in-hand to the parlour and found Sophia, James Bancroft and Phoebe in vociferous consultation with the stonemason.

'Oh God!' breathed Gabriel on a faint quiver of laughter. 'Don't tell me – the thrice-blasted dovecot again!'

Four pairs of eyes turned with one accord and the room fell abruptly silent. Then Phoebe grinned, Uncle James allowed his gaze to wander and Sophia said tactfully, 'My dears – I'm so glad you're here. Mr Felton was just telling us something rather intriguing about the dovecot.'

'Oh?' Gabriel slid an arm about his wife's waist and smiled blandly. 'That's nice.'

'Aren't you going to ask *what*?' demanded Phoebe.

'No. But doubtless you're going to tell me.'

Venetia laughed and leaned her head against his shoulder. 'Ignore him, Phoebe. We're fascinated. Really we are.'

'No, you're not. But you will be. Tell them, Mr Felton.'

The stonemason shrugged slightly and met the Colonel's gaze. He said, 'As you probably know, aside from the recent damage, the whole structure is in a very poor state of repair – so I've had to remove various parts of it in order to replace them. And this morning I came across what appears to be a box, wedged inside the column. I just wanted to know if I was to take it out or leave it where it is.'

'Ah!' Gabriel surveyed Phoebe with maddening calm. 'And you, of course, think it's the Garland.'

'Yes. But even if it isn't, we still have to *know*, don't we?' she demanded, almost hopping with excitement. 'And it's so obvious. The dovecot's been there forever – and it's the only place no one would ever have thought of looking. Also, who would—'

'All right – all right.' He looked back at the mason. 'Tell me. Is there any possibility that removing this box might cause the dovecot to collapse altogether?'

Mr Felton eyed him reassuringly. 'None at all, sir.'

'Pity,' said Gabriel. And then, with a grin, 'However. If I'm to get any peace at all, I suppose you'd better pull the thing out anyway.'

'I should think so too,' said Phoebe. And she hustled the stonemason, willy-nilly, to the door.

'Dear me,' said Sophia, moving to pour wine for them all. 'Dear me. I do hope it doesn't turn out to be the bones of somebody's favourite falcon.'

Ten minutes later and pink with cold, Phoebe returned clutching a small and extremely dirty lead casket.

'Pearls from India?' inquired Gabriel cheerfully.

'I don't know.' She laid it in his hands. 'It's locked.'

'And doubtless you'd like me to break it open?'

'Yes. Preferably today.'

Laughing a little, he took a cursory look at the casket, stooped to lay it on the hearth-stone and briskly struck off the rusting lock with the aid of one of the fire-irons. Then he set about trying to prise it open.

Venetia, Sophia and James Bancroft gathered with Phoebe to watch. And finally, with a protesting groan, the lid started to lift. Gabriel came slowly to his feet.

'Now?' he asked.

'Now,' said Phoebe breathlessly.

Without haste, his fingers forced the casket fully open. Inside it were no gold or jewels – or indeed anything of obvious value. Only a slender scroll of parchment, wrapped in rotting blue silk.

'Oh!' said Phoebe disappointedly. Then, brightening again, 'Perhaps it's a map.'

'God forbid!' murmured Gabriel, lifting the scroll from its bed and setting down the casket so he could unroll it. Frowning slightly, he said, 'It's not a map. I think . . . I rather think it's a poem. Venetia?'

She moved into the shelter of his arm to look down at it with him and eventually said oddly, 'Yes. Handwritten in old English and – and signed. Or so it appears.'

'Signed by whom?' asked Sophia.

Gabriel and Venetia exchanged glances. Then, Venetia said remotely, 'Geoffrey Chaucer.'

The effect was remarkable. Sophia shot out of her seat and James Bancroft stopped staring into the middle distance. In perfect unison, they said, 'Let me see it!'

Smiling, Gabriel passed it over to the erstwhile bishop and watched Sophia close in on him. For a moment, they simply stared at it, their faces expressing awed reverence; and then, drawing a slightly unsteady breath, Mr Bancroft read, '*To Rosemounde. A Balade.*'

'Who's Rosamund?' asked Phoebe.

'Philippa, probably,' said Sophia dreamily. 'Hugh's wife, you know.'

Phoebe's eyes widened. 'You mean . . . you mean you think this really *is* the Garland?'

'Well, of course, dear. It's perfect. Chaucer was employed by John of Gaunt, you know – so what would be more natural than for the Duke to commission a poem for Philippa? Read it, James. Your eyes are better than mine.'

Mr Bancroft cleared his throat.

> *Madame, ye ben of al beauty shryne*
> *As fer as cercled is the mappemounde;*
> *For as the cristal glorious ye shyne*
> *And lyke ruby ben your chekes rounde.*
> *Therewith ye ben so mery and so jocounde*
> *That at a revel whan that I see you*
> *   daunce,*
> *It is an oynement unto my wounde,*
> *Thogh ye to me ne do no daliaunce.*

He paused and Phoebe said disgustedly, 'What on earth is it supposed to mean?'

'It means,' said Venetia, 'that, contrary to popular belief, Hugh Brandon was *not* given Lacey Manor because John of Gaunt had slept with the fair Philippa.'

'Oh. How do you work that out?'

Gabriel grinned at her. *'Thogh ye to me ne do no daliaunce.* The language may be archaic – but the sense is plain enough. I know how he feels. I was having the same trouble myself until quite recently.'

'You'll have it again, too – and much sooner than you think – if you don't mind your manners,' retorted Venetia, severely. Then, to her uncle, 'Well? What do you think?'

'I think,' he said at length, his voice still a trifle dazed, 'that what we have here is an original manuscript written in Chaucer's own hand.'

There was a sudden, acute silence.

'Does that make it valuable?' asked Phoebe.

'I really couldn't say, my dear. But I imagine some scholars or collectors might be willing to pay a great deal in order to acquire it.'

'If,' said Gabriel slowly, 'we were to sell it.'

Phoebe sat down with a bump and stared at him.

'What do you mean – *if*? That piece of poetry could pay the taxes on Brandon Lacey for years!'

'Yes. I know.' He turned to Venetia and meditative dark grey eyes locked with smiling amethyst ones. 'But we can do that anyway by our own efforts. Perhaps . . . perhaps Philippa's gift is meant for something less mundane. Or am I being foolish?'

'No,' breathed Venetia. 'Or, if you are, then I am, too.'

Phoebe turned blankly to Sophia. 'Do *you* know what they're talking about?'

Sophia nodded. 'I believe so. But it's for them to say.'

'Then I wish they'd hurry up and do it!'

Without removing his eyes from Venetia, Gabriel said simply, 'We're not going to sell it, Phoebe. It hasn't waited two and a half centuries just for that – and neither, in a sense, is it ours to sell. It's part of Brandon Lacey.'

'You mean you're just going to keep it?'

'No.' It was Venetia who spoke, her voice warm and confident. 'More than that. We're going to find it a new resting-place, so that one day – just like Sophy and all the generations before her – our children will look for it. And maybe – just maybe – they'll be as lucky as we are.'

Southwark

March, 1649

'If we look upon what this House hath done since it hath voted itself the Supreme Authority and disburdened themselves of the power of the Lords – first we find a High Court of Justice erected whereby the way of trial by twelve sworn men of the neighbourhood is infringed. This is the first part of our new liberty. The next is the censuring of a Member of this House for declaring his judgement in a point of religion – which is directly opposite to the reserve in the Agreement. Then the stopping of our mouths from Printing is carefully provided for . . . and the most severe and unreasonable Ordinances of Parliament to gag us from speaking truth and discovering the tyrannies of bad men are referred to the care of the General – in searching, fining, imprisoning and other ways corporally punishing all that be guilty of unlicensed printing. They dealing with us as the Bishops of old did with the honest Puritan . . . whereby our Liberties have been more deeply wounded than since the beginning of this Parliament.'

John Lilburne
England's New Chains discovered
February, 1649

Epilogue

Despite having finally been awarded his long-awaited compensation, John Lilburne returned to London in February in a state of bitter disillusionment. He had done his utmost to secure the liberties of the people – only to have his work undone by the officers of the Army; he had been opposed to the creation of a special Court to try the King – but it had been created anyway and the King lay dead; and he had found his northern homelands being ruled by Harry Vane and Sir Arthur Haselrig in whatever manner suited them best. Nothing, it seemed, had recently gone right. And the result was a bout of wholly uncharacteristic lethargy.

'I feel like an old weather-beaten ship that would fain be in some harbour of ease and rest,' he told Sam Radford gloomily. And refused to allow himself either to be cheered up or coaxed into attending any meetings.

He moved his family to rooms in Winchester House in Southwark, settled his debts and promised Elizabeth that he'd earn his living as a coal-merchant or a soap-boiler. He looked on, without comment, while the Rump abolished the Lords and the Monarchy and set up its first Council of State without any reference to the *Agreement of the People*. And he spurned the offer of a Government post rather than be allied with a mock-Parliament, purged by force of arms.

Then just when his wife and his friends were becoming seriously alarmed, Parliament set up another High Court to try Hamilton, Holland, Norwich, Capel and Owen. At first, John merely remarked on its illegality; then he started attending the hearings; and soon he was offering to appear as a witness on behalf of the prisoners and urging them to challenge the jurisdiction of the Court.

They refused to do it. Unable to help them, John sat

through each day's proceedings with a lead weight in his chest and went back to Elizabeth in turmoil.

Then matters started to compound themselves. When the common soldiery once more petitioned Parliament for arrears of pay and an end to free quarter, their superiors declared that petitions could henceforth only be submitted through the Council of Officers – and announced that any civilian who attempted to breed discontent in the Army would be subject to martial law.

'And thus,' snapped Free-born John, sitting for the first time in two months before a blank sheet of paper, 'after these blossoms of hopeful liberty, breaks forth the vilest bondage that ever English men groaned under!'

He picked up his pen and sat for a moment, frowning at the empty page. Then, reaching for the ink, he wrote in large, savage letters, *ENGLAND'S NEW CHAINS*.

He poured vitriol on the Officers' *Agreement*, denounced current legal and religious policy and begged for a new Parliament. And four days later, with Sam Radford beside him, he presented his work at the bar of the Commons.

Sam promptly had the pamphlet printed in *The Moderate* – then went off to his wedding, secure in the knowledge that Free-born John was once more his old self. And while the Army cashiered five troopers for speaking against their officers' edict, Hamilton, Capel and Holland were beheaded outside Westminster Hall.

Lilburne bided his time. Then, when it was obvious that nothing could be expected of the Rump, he took up his pen again and set the paper alight with his opinion of the Commonwealth in general and the chief Army officers in particular. Since no other words adequately conveyed his outrage, he called the result *England's New Chains*, Part II. And on Sunday March 24th, he read it out to a hugely appreciative crowd in Southwark.

'If our hearts were not over-charged with the sense of the present miseries and approaching dangers of the nation, we would keep silent,' he began. 'But the bondage threatened is so great, imminent and apparent that – while we have breath and are not violently restrained – we cannot but cry aloud.' And cry aloud he did – maintaining that Judges were bribed and the press stifled; that the Army Grandees had forsaken their ideals and that civil authority was so crushed beneath the heel of the military that the House of Commons was now no more than 'a channel through which is conveyed all the decrees and determinations of a private Council of some few officers.'

Standing in the shelter of her new husband's arm, Bryony Radford said, 'It's true. It's all true. Why won't the Parliament *listen* to him?'

'Because he's not saying what they want to hear,' came the sardonic reply. 'And he frightens them.'

'What freedom is there left,' asked Lilburne, 'when honest soldiers are sentenced for presenting a letter in justification of their liberty? As for peace – while the officers of the Army are supreme in the Council of State – what peace can be expected?' He paused, allowing his voice to gather new power. 'We do protest against their dissolving the Council of Agitators and moulding the Army to their own designs. We protest against their bringing the Army upon the City – their breaking of the House – and their taking away of men's lives to make way for their own domination. And we do demand an *Agreement of the People* in accordance with our late desires.'

Roaring its enthusiasm, the crowd marched with him to present the petition at Westminster – where the Commons called it *'false, scandalous, seditious and destructive'* and the Council of State tried to stop its circulation by ordering the post to be searched. They were, of course, far too late. For while Bryony Radford sat alone by the hearth in Tower Street and her young husband prepared a detailed article for *The Moderate*, Leveller emissaries were already telling the men of Hertfordshire, Berkshire and Hampshire to resist all *'unnecessary rates and unreasonable taxes'*.

For four days the outcome hung in the balance. Then, before dawn on the 28th, the Army struck. A hundred or so troopers forced their way into Winchester House to arrest Free-born John. At the same time, William Walwyn, Richard Overton and Samuel Radford were likewise hauled from their respective homes. All of them were taken before the Council of State, all of them denied the said Council's power to try them . . . and all were duly committed to the Tower on suspicion of high treason.

It was not unexpected. Bryony went first to the Tower, then to see Elizabeth Lilburne and finally home to Shoreditch. Facing Jack Morrell with tears on her face and pure rebellion in her eyes, she said, 'All right. You told me so. But can you still tell me that Sam and John aren't *right*?'

For a long time Jack stared grimly back at her. Then he said curtly, 'No. I can't. And if you'll point me in the right direction, I'll sign the damned petition myself.'

Author's note

As always, I have done my best to present the historical facts as accurately as possible. The trial of Charles I is composed wholly of authentic dialogue – as, to a lesser degree, are the various debates and meetings held by the Army. The only liberty I have taken is in allowing the Duke of Hamilton to travel from Uttoxeter to Windsor via Banbury with Gabriel. As for the somewhat unlikely story of the so-called 'saddle-letter' which Cromwell and Ireton intercepted at the Blue Boar in Holborn, this comes from a biography of the Earl of Orrery – who reputedly had the tale direct from Cromwell himself.

On a fictional note – and for those readers who may be interested – the earlier adventures of Samuel Radford and Justin Ambrose are told in *A Splendid Defiance*.

Amongst the host of reference works which have helped me to write this novel, I am particularly indebted to volumes 3 and 4 of S. R. Gardiner's *History of the Great Civil War* (Windrush Press), *Free-born John* by Pauline Gregg (J. M. Dent & Sons), *The Trial of Charles I* by C. V. Wedgwood (William Collins & Son) and the Clarke MSS. as edited by A. S. P. Woodhouse in *Puritanism and Liberty* (J. M. Dent & Sons). I would also like to thank the Bodleian Library, Oxford for its help in finding various pamphlets by John Lilburne.

STELLA RILEY

A selection of bestsellers from Headline

THE GIRL FROM COTTON LANE	Harry Bowling	£5.99 ☐
MAYFIELD	Joy Chambers	£5.99 ☐
DANGEROUS LADY	Martina Cole	£4.99 ☐
DON'T CRY ALONE	Josephine Cox	£5.99 ☐
DIAMONDS IN DANBY WALK	Pamela Evans	£4.99 ☐
STARS	Kathryn Harvey	£5.99 ☐
THIS TIME NEXT YEAR	Evelyn Hood	£4.99 ☐
LOVE, COME NO MORE	Adam Kennedy	£5.99 ☐
AN IMPOSSIBLE WOMAN	James Mitchell	£5.99 ☐
FORBIDDEN FEELINGS	Una-Mary Parker	£5.99 ☐
A WOMAN POSSESSED	Malcolm Ross	£5.99 ☐
THE FEATHER AND THE STONE	Patricia Shaw	£4.99 ☐
WYCHWOOD	E V Thompson	£4.99 ☐
ADAM'S DAUGHTERS	Elizabeth Villars	£4.99 ☐

All Headline books are available at your local bookshop or newsagent, or can be ordered direct from the publisher. Just tick the titles you want and fill in the form below. Prices and availability subject to change without notice.

Headline Book Publishing PLC, Cash Sales Department, Bookpoint, 39 Milton Park, Abingdon, OXON, OX14 4TD, UK. If you have a credit card you may order by telephone — 0235 831700.

Please enclose a cheque or postal order made payable to Bookpoint Ltd to the value of the cover price and allow the following for postage and packing:
UK & BFPO: £1.00 for the first book, 50p for the second book and 30p for each additional book ordered up to a maximum charge of £3.00.
OVERSEAS & EIRE: £2.00 for the first book, £1.00 for the second book and 50p for each additional book.

Name ....

Address ....

....

....

If you would prefer to pay by credit card, please complete:
Please debit my Visa/Access/Diner's Card/American Express (delete as applicable) card no:

Signature ....Expiry Date ....